Also by Fariha Rahman

GUNS AND ROSES
A series of interconnected standalones

Billionaire's Bodyguard
Billionaire's Attraction

BILLIONAIRE'S ATTRACTION

By Fariha Rahman

Content Warning: this book contains violence which some readers may find distressing.

This is a work of fiction. Names, characters, places, and incidents either are the product of the author's imagination or are used fictitiously. Any resemblance to actual persons, living or dead, events, or locales is entirely coincidental.

BILLIONAIRE'S ATTRACTION

To my sister and Zaïdi,
and for strong women everywhere.
Fear is only a word, and power is who you are.

CONTENTS

PART 1

the day I met you,
I began to forget a life
without you

atticus

PROLOGUE

5 years ago, March.

"You look beautiful, Aria," he said with a smile, the gesture exposing the dimples that adorned his sharp facial features. Blue eyes, as deep as the ocean, twinkled when I descended the marble stairs that spiraled to the ground floor, a blush threatening to rise. "You never fail to render me speechless."

He was incredibly dashing in that black and white suit; the mere simplicity of it accentuating his godlike features. His tawny hair was neatly groomed back so it didn't shield those magnificent eyes that watched me carefully. Words failed to describe how handsome he was. Sometimes, if not often, I wondered whether he was real or not. He held his hand out and I slipped mine into his, the warmth of our skin touching sent tingles across my body like fireworks flashing across the sky. He was definitely real.

"You don't look too bad yourself," I giggled, when I noticed his bow tie looked wonky. "Although, I really wish you learnt how to do your bow ties properly."

His smile broadened whilst observing me straighten the satin bow out. His hand rested on my hip, and I swore that the heat from his touch burned through my dress and left an invisible mark on my skin. I resisted the urge to shiver – I couldn't. I wouldn't. My attraction towards him had only grown until it reached the point where it was starting to consume me. He was the drug, and I was the addict. From his sweet whispers to his sensual touches, I had loved every part of

1

it… and, yet, here I was, going to this party as his best friend. *Only* his best friend. He would never know. I wouldn't dare tell him. Not when I couldn't be sure that he felt the same. It would *risk* everything and could *change* everything. Call me a coward, but it wasn't a gamble I was willing to take.

"Aria! Nero!" The thundering sound of my father's voice broke me out of my thoughts, and I dozily glanced up, catching his azure eyes flickering away and the beautiful smile falling, marginally. I wished it didn't, praying to see it once more.

One last time.

"I guess we're late," he muttered, encasing my hand once again.

I sighed. "I don't want to go."

"This is important to our parents, Ariadne. We can't *not* go," His thumb distracted me as they drew circles against my skin absentmindedly. "Especially, when they'll be announcing your acceptance into taking the title of the Don in a couple of weeks."

My heart sank at that destined title, a reminder of the responsibilities I would bear heavily on my shoulders, the power I was *not* sure I wanted. My smile fell and I looked away with a heavy exhale. I wished it hadn't turned out this way; I wished it wasn't my destiny. But how could I disappoint my family by refusing such a prestigious and privileged title? How could I let my paranoia and fears overwhelm my duty as the heir to the Italian mafia? How could I be so selfish? So many men would kill for my position, and I was about to undesirably accept it. *What a joke.* As if he knew my worries, Nero reached out and tenderly stroke my cheek, drawing my attention to him.

"I'll always be by your side, through it all. Don't forget that," he promised. His voice was soft, yet rich and deep. "You are my Queen, Aria. I'll protect you; I promise. You'll never be alone."

"Don't make a promise you can't keep, Russo," I murmured, coldly, having heard my fair share of unfulfilled vows.

But he didn't flinch; his smile didn't drop at my glacial words; he didn't falter for a second. Instead, he wrapped his arms around me, basking me in his warmth and safety. I froze momentarily but, eventually, sunk into his hold, closing my eyes to savor every second.

"I won't betray your trust, Aria. I promise. *Sempre,*" he spoke as if he was carving the vow onto the skies of heaven. "I love you."

My body reacted before my mind. My breathing hitched. My muscles tensed. My heart stuttered. And when I finally acknowledged how platonic those words truly were, I whispered them back, swallowing my bitterness. "I love you too."

For the longest second, he held me as if he didn't want to let go. I didn't want him to let go. But something shifted and it popped the bubble we were in; he immediately removed his arms from around me. Something flickered across his face, but it disappeared before I could figure it out. He bowed playfully and I laughed, my rosy lips stretching from ear-to-ear.

Nero smirked at me, a mischievous sparkle in his cobalt eyes. "Shall we, Ariadne?"

"*Sempre,* Nero," I replied, as gentle as his touch. "Always."

*

5 years ago, December.

"I don't get this sudden change of mood," he snarled in frustration, slamming his fists onto my desk. "Who have you met, Aria? Who is causing you to act so irresponsibly?"

"I said," I hissed, through clenched teeth. "I don't want to talk about it. Now get the fuck out."

His glare could have put anyone six feet under, but they didn't affect me in the slightest. I feared no one. Not even him. *He* should be afraid. I was capable of destroying him in ways which would leave him suffering nightmares, fearing that I was hidden in the shadows, always waiting, always ready to pounce. Seeing him storm into my office in the middle of the night had irritated me, but that was overlooked by my traitorous yearning for him when I noticed he was without a shirt. A fool I was. Blinded by my love that I didn't see him for who he truly was. A narcissistic, arrogant, liar. Icily, I dismissed him so I could refocus on the task at hand. I no longer trusted him. I would never bare my fears and worries to him. I wouldn't let him hold my heart because when I did, he crushed it into pieces beyond repair. It was almost comedic, seeing him stand in front of me, demanding to know what was wrong as if he cared... as if he hadn't betrayed me.

"Why are you so interested in this group?" he interrogated. "You waste so much time and energy on them – a small, unknown organization – that you aren't even focusing on your own family, Ariadne."

3

The use of my full name had me tighten my jaw. "Are you questioning my authority?"

His brilliant blue orbs shone when he scowled. "No. I am not. I just want an explanation for your sudden change in behavior. You disappeared for months and upon returning, you suddenly aren't interested in the Italians, handing over your duties to me and Matteo as if it is not of importance."

"I'm sure you're very happy about that," I scoffed.

He frowned. "What?"

Sighing, I raised my brow. "Russo, I don't need to explain myself to anyone," My words were laced with a deadly reminder of who he was talking to. "*Especially you.*"

"And you seem to have forgotten that I'm not just anybody."

"Yes, I can see that," I said. "Shall I remind you of your place?"

He was tall, looming over my desk, his broad shoulders inked with black tattoos, covering his wounds from operations that had gone wrong. I resisted the urge to shudder when his gaze caressed my body. I had no doubt it was because I was only dressed in an illicit satin chemise, the same color as the blush that threatened to reveal itself across my cheeks. With my hair brushed back into a low ponytail, it revealed my glaring hazel eyes that were directed towards the infuriatingly handsome man in front of me.

"Amuse me, Aria."

He taunted and teased, pushing me to my limits. He wanted to see how far I could go, where my line was; he wanted the satisfaction of having power over me. I wouldn't let him win. Not even for a second. I was Aria *fucking* Moretti. And no one was more powerful than me. Gingerly, I stood up and walked around my desk to close the distance between us. He took a step back when my hands curled around his neck, tracing the intricate tattoos painted onto his sun-kissed skin. He had a few tattoos months ago but now they covered most of his upper torso, some parts of his arms, and a few on his neck. Separately, the images had their own stories, hiding the battle wounds underneath, but together, they resembled marvelous artwork… and I was the buyer. Surprise morphed across his face.

"I'm your Queen, Nero," I purred, my lips brushing his ear, earning me a shiver. "Bow down to your Queen."

Before he could fathom my order, I had him on his knees. His hands drifted up to my waist as his bewildered eyes watched in fascination like I was goddess. I bit my lip, leaning against the desk, quivering at the cool sensation of mahogany touching my exposed legs. Blue eyes darkened, dilating until I was sure they were black under the low light that came from my antique lamp. His jaw clenched, noticing how intimate this situation was. I was going to make him forget; it was a skill I had proudly perfected. Tomorrow he would not know of my plans, tomorrow he would not remember anything other than what I would give him tonight. What he had wanted the most.

Me.

Languidly, I pushed my legs apart, studying him in amusement as the shock in his eyes contorted into desire.

"Aria…" his words vanished into the air as his fingers lightly brushed my legs, trailing upwards until they disappeared underneath the chemise. I was mesmerized by the image of him on his knees like a man praying to God.

"*Sempre*, Nero," I reminded, clutching the desk whilst watching him under hooded lashes, my breathing labored. "Your Queen. *Sempre*."

"Yes," he whispered, distracted, infatuated, starved. "*Sempre*, Aria."

I'm sorry.

Words of regret would leave my lips. Soon. But not tonight. No, tonight, I was going to make sure he would never forget his place or who I was. Tonight, he was going to remember Ariadne Moretti, and then tomorrow, he would forget I ever existed.

CHAPTER 1

monsters under the lights

Lips stained a shade of blood red, sepia tendrils that tumbled down to the waist of a slender frame, vibrant hazel eyes that promised a taste of heaven and sin, and seduction laced with death running through her veins. That was how people often described me if they managed to survive long enough to tell their story. I was their favorite dream *and* their worst nightmare. Some called me death incarnate, others would say I was the devil himself. And whilst my nails were coated in the same blood red liquid that I painted across my lips; I was neither of those things. However, it *was* amusing. I could see why my mother enjoyed her job so much. It was exhilarating. I sipped on my mocktail, eyeing a man in a navy suit, his laughter contagiously spreading smiles to those around him. I tilted my head to the side, calculating every move I could potentially make and then the following moves afterwards. My brain churned as I identified all the ways I could kill him and all the ways I could make it an seem like an accident. He got up from his seat with a woman, whose face was excessively caked in layers of makeup, clinging onto his arm. She wore an overly enthusiastic smile, which only told me that his money was what triggered her happiness. Whether he knew this or not, he didn't care, as he smirked whenever she fawned over him.

That was when I decided to make my move.

I downed the rest of my drink, sliding the glass back to the bartender along with a tip, before gathering my evening gown so it wouldn't get stuck as I slipped off the stool. It was almost too easy. As soon as I walked past, I grabbed his attention. Pretending as if I had no interest in him, I purposely made sure our arms softly brushed against each other when I sauntered by. The whine from his date told me that she was deprived of his focus.

I smirked.

"Excuse me!"

I stopped, before deliberately taking my time to glance over my shoulder. The woman was no longer standing by him. My reply was as sultry and innocent as my smile. "Yes?"

His eyes drank in my appearance, from the way my fitted crimson gown hugged my chest to the scandalous slit on the side, revealing my tanned legs from the scorching sun in Thailand last weekend. His dark eyes widened, and my lips twitched.

I arched a brow. *Typical.* "Was there anything you wanted?"

As if a cold bucket of water had been tipped over him, he blinked out of his starstruck spell, and I was disappointed to see it partially disappear. Adjusting his posture, loosening his tie, he coughed awkwardly. The businessman persona returned quickly, but his eyes still looked like they were in a trance, holding the darkest of intentions.

"What is your name?" he questioned, daring to take a step forward.

"My name?"

"Yes. I want to know who you are, and possibly take you out to dinner," he smirked, his words demanding like a command. But no one told me what to do.

"How about you take me out *now*?" I suggested, alluringly, angling my body so that more skin was exposed.

He practically jumped at the offer like a lovesick puppy. Taking his hand, we slipped through the crowd, into the elevator where he pressed me against the metal wall as soon as the doors closed behind us. He claimed my lips and eagerly I responded, running my fingers through his black hair, pulling at the curled strands. He groaned and moved his hands to my hips. Everything happened so quickly. One minute we were in the elevator, the next we were on the couch in his hotel room. Ridding him of his blazer and tearing his shirt from his body; never giving him a second to catch up. I worked swiftly as I straddled him, pressing my lips on his chest, hearing the way his breath got caught in his throat when my fingers traced the curves of his muscles.

Then I found what I was looking for.

"What's this?" I asked, glancing up.

He looked at the serpent symbol inked on his hip. "A tattoo."

I wanted to roll my eyes but instead I bobbed my head and kissed him. He drew me closer to him before peppering my neck with the softest of caresses, my nails digging into his shoulders.

"I feel as if I've seen it before," I whispered breathlessly, as he unzipped my dress.

"I wouldn't be surprised. Everyone who's a part of the Serpents has one."

"What are the Serpents?" I murmured, kissing his jaw.

He sighed, stopping his actions to focus on speaking rather than my body, which gave me the advantage. My hand skimmed the side of his body until it reached behind him, finding the dagger tucked under the pillow he was laying on.

"A group that work in the Black Market, namely the Underground," Then he chuckled, his thumb gently brushing my cheek. "Selling everything from weapons to girls as beautiful as you."

When he grasped my thighs, I swallowed the bile threatening to escape and grinned, my fingers curling around the dagger. "You must make a lot of money."

My movements were cautious and slow, waiting for the opportunity to appear, like a viper hunting a mouse. He smiled, sitting up to close the distance between us. "I do, sweetheart. I make a load of fucking money."

He kissed me, fighting for dominance as he shoved his tongue into my mouth which I gave into, pressing myself close to him so I could lift the dagger out from its hidden position. A moan escaped from me, my body arching into the curves of his.

"In fact," he crooned. "There's a sale happening right now. Maybe next time you can come with me. You'd make me millions."

I was a patient woman, but my patience ended here. "You can."

He looked surprised by my answer, as if expecting anything other than a willing agreement to his suggestion. "Really?"

My smile dropped. "But, over my dead body."

Before he could comprehend what was happening, I brought the dagger to his throat and slit it open. The blood poured out as soon as the blade met his skin. He gagged, wide eyed, his hands moving from my body to his throat whilst I got off him, so my $5000 dress didn't get ruined. It *was* custom made. Zipping the dress back up, I tidied my appearance whilst his breathing became ragged, eyes painfully watching me. He only had a few short seconds left until the life was stripped away from him and as I glimpsed at the clock, I knew I only had a few short minutes until someone searched for him. Normally, I would spend time engraving my initials into the very depths of their monstrous skin, but I was low on time and, thus, was not able to enjoy this as much as I usually would. Regardless, I was proud of my artwork, basking in the way he suffered, as the blood uncontrollably poured out of him like a waterfall.

"Ar – are you – you –" he sputtered, choking on his blood, his breathing short and painful. I smiled coldly. His eyes broadened. "*Aria.*"

My name drifted into the air along with his last breath like a puff of smoke, and the sound of fireworks outside thrummed through my body. I began to disable the security locks on his hotel room doors, as a way of ensuring that it looked like he was murdered by literally anyone. Miguel had always been a disliked man amongst the Underground community so it wouldn't be a surprise to hear of his death. He was an open target and, fortunately for me, that worked to my advantage. Nevertheless, I couldn't risk anyone tracking this fatality to me, even if I was seen as a ghost in the hidden world. When I had completed my task, my heels muted by the expensive carpet of the most luxurious hotel in Brazil, I grabbed my dagger from beside the corpse, wiped the blade clean against his blazer, and sheathed it back into the holster attached to my thigh. The man was so distracted by lust that he overlooked the dagger pouch. *Foolish man.* Merrily, I returned to the party several floors below, smiling at anyone who glanced my way, acting as if I hadn't killed a man only moments ago. When I reached the bar, the hairs on my arms tingled as I asked for a glass of champagne.

"Is it done?"

I looked to the man sitting beside me. His hair was as black as the gloomiest of nights, and a scar ran down the side of his face. His eyes were shielded by thick lashes but were evidently green under the glistening chandelier hanging above us. Many would fear the sight of him, whispering crass rumors of his stoic persona, but I, on the other hand, didn't balk.

It was he who feared me.

"Well?" he waited for my response, watching as I sipped on the drink that the bartender had brought me, with a flirtatious smile that would have had girls swooning.

"In room 206," I informed. "Have someone stop the auction that is occurring right now. Be quick and try not to shed too much blood. It's always a mess to deal with afterwards."

He stood up, handing me the keys that belonged to my favorite Lamborghini. "Understood. Your plane is waiting for you."

What a perfect way to start the new year.

*

New York. It was beautiful during the day, but even more so at night. It thrived with such life and energy that I struggled to find elsewhere quite like it. It was my favorite place in the entire world. Pity that I had to leave it five years ago.

"Prepare for landing," Calix instructed.

I forced myself to tear my eyes away from the window, smiling thinly at my third-in-command when he appeared from the cockpit. His green eyes simmered with an understanding at my hesitance to return back to the city, the knife wound stretching from the top of his head, through his dark brow before ending below his ear lobe. It served as a reminder of my duty.

"Are you alright?" he asked.

"Always," I responded, looking away.

I could feel his gaze burning into the side of my face for a minute before he disappeared behind the door. Releasing a heavy sigh, I looked back to where he was standing only a few seconds ago. Calix was someone I trusted, tremendously; I would never doubt his loyalty to me. But I knew he feared what most my closest peers feared – that New York would only bring a platter of trouble that I… *we* didn't need. Although, I was truly happy to have returned home, my stomach sank at the thought of *actually* returning home. It had been too long. I had been planning this trip for months now, often delaying the journey with spontaneous visits to other countries. However, when my second-in-command demanded that I come this week, it was difficult to say no. Moreover, it *felt* like it was the right time to return. The jet landed with a slight hiccup before smoothly coming to a halt on the tarmac runway, and I began to gather my things into my Chanel bag when Calix called for me. My phone vibrated in my hand, and I sighed when I saw Melissa's name pop up on the screen. She had sent several messages, all of which I would not respond to. Tucking my phone into my bag, I stepped out of the jet, exhaling when a gush of cold city wind hit me as soon as the door lifted open, welcoming me to New York. I could hear the cars in the distance, the buzzing of life in the air, the world around me suddenly becoming much smaller to what I had gotten used to. With a dainty sun hat and shades to shield me from the scorching sun, I descended the stairs, taking Calix's hand on the last few steps so I didn't fall. Leather gloves covered my hands as I grinned at the sight of Xander, another one of my closest peers, striding towards us.

"Boss, happy to see that you landed safely. I trust your visit to Brazil was smooth sailing," he greeted, before welcoming Calix.

"As always, Xan. Did you do a sweep before my arrival?"

"Yes, ma'am."

"And?" I asked, beginning to walk to the SUV waiting for us with my men ranking my sides.

"Clear as the sky. No one has gained information about your arrival to New York," Then he added, "*Yet.*"

"Perfect. I believe this is Kira's doing?"

Xander smirked. "Of course. She's waiting for you in the car."

My lips stretched to my ears. "Thank you, Xander."

Yakira was my second-in-command, my right-hand woman, my sister. Before I decided to leave the mafia, she was the reason my life changed. And now, I sheltered girls aged as young as fourteen and raised them to become compelling, skilled warriors to protect and prevent other women (and on some occasions men) from the twisted evilness of the Underground. Her hair was a pale blonde, a few shades lighter than Xander's, but as straight as a stick, framing her small face and drawing attention to her brilliant blue eyes that looked almost like ice. She squealed at the sight of me, drawing me into a tight embrace as soon as I got into the car.

Laughing loudly, I returned the hug. "Hey, Kira."

It had been a while since I had seen her. I sent her to New York on my behalf, having her prepare the Manor and my apartment before my arrival. We hadn't had the chance to properly catch up but as she tightened her arms around me, it didn't feel as if I hadn't seen her for months, and some of the wariness within me disappeared.

"I've missed you, Aria," she murmured, pulling away. Kira didn't cry. I couldn't remember the last time I saw her upset. But, when she looked at me with those watery aquamarine orbs, I thought, for a second, that she would burst into tears. She blinked, and it disappeared.

My lips lifted. "It's been too long. How have you been holding the fort? I hope the transition went smoothly."

"It's been so stressful," she groaned. "If I knew that this position would be this demanding, I would've given the role to someone else."

I arched a brow. "Liar."

She laughed. "You know me so well."

The sound of her laugh had a tender smile take over my lips, my heart allaying at the sight of my best friend. "I've missed you, Kira."

When Kira smiled, her eyes glittered with warmth. "I've missed you too, Aria."

*

We arrived at my penthouse apartment just over an hour later, and as soon as the doors opened, my jaw dropped in astonishment. It looked exactly how I envisioned it six months ago. With accents of white, it brought a whole new meaning to modern. Most penthouse apartments had ceiling to floor windows that took over the walls, creating a panoramic view of the city, and it was important to me that mine were the highlight of the place. Daylight streamed into the living room as Calix and Xander took my things to my bedroom, situated on the floor above, thanks to Kira who had managed to get a second floor built.

In awe, I turned to her. "You did amazing."

"I know, I know," she grinned, smugly. "I'm good at my job. You can thank me later."

I rolled my eyes before admiring the delicate ornaments placed around the room. In a thirty-story building, the top floor was entirely mine and it reminded me of a place one of my uncles owned. I remembered visiting the apartment when I was a little girl, and knew I had to have one too when I grew up. Nostalgia hit me and I realized how much I truly missed home.

"Everything is set here. Is there anything left to do?" Calix questioned, returning from upstairs with Xander behind him.

"One last thing," My eyes met Kira's, and she immediately caught onto my request. Her lips tugged up. "I want to see everyone."

Unlike my penthouse, which was in the heart of the city, the Manor belonged on the outskirts of New York, completely off the grid, completely undetectable. It was a large estate, a mansion that housed over 200 women, and just over hundred men, covering acres and acres of land, hidden by soaring coniferous trees. There were four floors, separated by the east and west wing. The eastern wing was dedicated to the bedrooms; the fourth floor belonged to me and Kira, and housed my office. The third floor accommodated the women, and the second was for the men. The first floor was the library, and the ground floor was the living room and kitchen. In the west wing, it was mostly for training and education, as I strongly wanted to provide everyone in the Manor the opportunity to learn. Everyone had a story. Some were worse than others. But, they were all taken in and, with Kira's help, shaped into the powerful assassins they were today. Girls as young as fourteen sat on the couch, huddling closely together, as men who were treated like faceless servants guarded them like protective brothers. What I saw in their eyes was not fear but peace. The coldness of my heart thawed at the sight. The older women were talking, their bodies relaxed in the presence of men around despite having been once treated like rag dolls by their male assailants. I remembered when they used to flinch at the sight of a man and now they laughed amongst them. I spent five years raising this family, re-birthing them into stronger versions of themselves, giving them an opportunity to armor their past and fight back against those who stripped them of their freedom, dignity and courage. As soon as I stepped into the room, the air shifted and everyone looked my way, conversations coming to a halt.

"I'm home," I announced, breaking the silence.

A second later, cheers roared throughout the house, and I broke into a huge grin, waving my hand in the air to tell them to settle down. I greeted everyone as I made my way to the front, Kira following closely behind me. Everyone looked happier, healthier, safer, and it blossomed the pride within me to see them become the people they were destined to be. When I reached the fireplace, everyone hushed as my eyes welcomed the sight of my family.

"It's good to be home. *Finally.* I haven't stepped into New York for a while, and to see everyone settled in the Manor happily is great news.

I hope the transition went well and everyone has been looking after themselves," I glanced around the room. "I know you have suffered. I know that many of you will never be able to return to the people you once were. I know you've been hurt, betrayed, and treated like an object. You've been priced like cattle, sold as if your lives cost nothing, broken like glass. I know."

The layer of sadness in the air was suffocating, so thick and raw that I swallowed back a cry of anger. Pressing my lips together, I gave a tight smile.

"But look at who you are now. Fighters. Warriors. You chose to save those in need, and kill those who deserve the punishment, because hell isn't nearly as bad as we can be. I promised to protect you all, and you remained loyal to me, placing your trust in me. I know that was hard to do but I'm in debt to you for doing so. And we will destroy them all. They won't see us coming because they underestimated you. And you'll prove them wrong."

Everyone hailed in agreement, jumping out of their seats, punching their fists in the air, ready for the war that was looming over the mountains. A war I knew we would win.

"With that said, we have a new guest arriving, so I expect everyone to be on their best behavior. She is no less than you. Calix and Xander will be informing the men of what is to come, whilst I'll be having a meeting with the women to discuss our next steps. Girls, you'll be attending your lessons and trainings regularly and promptly, along with the boys. Work together, not against each other." Just before I left, I smiled to my warriors. "I'm happy to be home. We have much to do."

With the sound of thundering applause ending my speech, I quickly gave my thanks and dismissed them, observing them proudly as they rushed off to do what was expected of them. My smile fell when I saw the sullen look on Kira's face. She lifted my phone up, the screen blinking with Melissa's name.

"She's persistent."

I sighed. "That's Melissa for you."

"Aren't you excited to see your family soon?" Kira asked in a tone that made me wonder if she ever missed hers.

"Not at all," Tucking my phone into my coat pocket, I wrinkled my nose. "I can already hear the questions they'll be asking."

Kira laughed. "I'm betting most of them will be coming from your mother."

"Most definitely."

Her grin morphed into a smirk. "So, how about anyone else?"

My face soured. "Be quiet."

"Whatever you say, Boss," she sang, a laugh threatening to escape her coral lips. "I hope you brushed up on your Italian, since you'll be hearing a lot of it soon."

"Kira," I warned darkly but she didn't flinch, raising her brow.

"I'm just reminding you, Aria. You might have left New York to avoid your problems but now that you're back, so are your problems," I opened my mouth to argue but she continued before I could. "The moment he finds out that you're here, he's going to wonder why and that could ruin everything."

"Don't you think I know that, Kira?" I drew in a deep breath of air. "Only, this time, it's my game and I'm the controller. The role of the leader might have been given to him, but I was born to become one," I looked at my family. "It's my game and I decide who wins. And this time, it's going to be me."

"You better hope so, Aria," her voice dropped a couple of octaves, a glimmer of worry leaving me uneasy. "Because last time you lost… and he took your heart and the throne."

CHAPTER 2

pretty little promises

I woke up, refreshed and… *hungry?*

My nose crinkled at the delicious smell that wafted into my bedroom, the taste of sweetness dancing on my tastebuds, my stomach growling with eagerness. I frowned, knowing that I wasn't expecting any guests. Especially, this early. Peeping my eyes open, the sunlight blinded me as it managed to slip between the gaps of my curtains, radiating me with warmth and light. I wanted to groan in annoyance, irked that an uninvited guest had interrupted my peaceful morning. Grumbling quietly under my breath, I grabbed my gun that was tucked underneath my bedside table and carefully got out of bed, ensuring I didn't make a sound. Having learnt how to move swiftly and with agility, I managed to tiptoe down my stairs without alerting the intruder, whose chestnut hair swayed side to side as they danced in my kitchen.

My frown deepened. "Mom?"

Xena Moretti looked over her shoulder with a pretty smile, flipping a pancake into the air expertly. "Oh, good morning, sweetie."

I gaped at her. My jaw literally dropped to the floor. Speechless. Because I literally had no idea what was happening right now. My mother didn't bat an eye, waving me over.

"Close your mouth, honey. You'll catch flies."

"How – how –"

"Baby, I'm your mother. It's quite insulting how you didn't think I'd find out. Honestly, I'm hurt," She pouted, touching her chest as if her heart was actually aching. I didn't even know how to respond, watching her set the kitchen island, stacking homemade pancakes onto the China plates Kira bought me. "Come and sit. You have some explaining to do."

Wordlessly, I obeyed my mother, sitting on the stool, whilst she began to clean up like it was her own kitchen. Stabbing my pancakes, I started to munch on them as she took a seat beside me with a coffee mug in her hold. She raised her brow, silently asking the question that I knew she wanted to ask.

"What?"

"Why didn't you tell me that you were coming home?"

I stuffed a sliced piece of pancake in my mouth. "I have my reasons."

"When did you get back? Why are you back? And for goodness sake, don't eat like a starved animal!" she scolded, and I blinked at her, innocently. Mom sighed, shaking her head when she realized I wasn't going to answer her questions. "Honestly, you and your father are exactly the same. So stubborn and secretive."

The corner of my lips quirked up at the mention of my father before disappearing when I realized how much I missed him, and how much I needed him whilst I was gone. All those times when I wanted to call him for advice and guidance, but I couldn't. I couldn't risk damaging the plan I so meticulously spent the last couple of years cultivating. I couldn't let anyone foil it. *Stop me.* I couldn't. My heart sunk. Noting that I had gone very quiet, my mother looked at me, fondly, her eyes implored for mine as if they would give her all the answers. And maybe they would. She was skilled like that.

"Your father misses you a lot, Ari. You would call so rarely, and even then, it wasn't for long. We were beyond grateful for those moments, but it didn't fill the hole in our heart. You weren't home, *agapi mu.*"

Hearing the woe in her voice had me placing my hand over hers, forcing a warm smile despite the guilt that shadowed me from my sudden departure. "I had to leave, Mama. I know Dad wasn't impressed with me leaving the mafia but... but I had to go. I couldn't take the role he held, the responsibilities, the para –" I stopped myself short. I couldn't deal with my paranoias. My throat contracted and I whispered, "It was a cowardly move to make, and I hate that I disappointed you, but it wasn't my destiny. And I'm so sorry for that."

My mother was a typically cold woman. She never did approve much of my lifestyle growing up. She didn't like that I spent time partying when I should be studying, breaking the rules when I should be following them. But she wouldn't argue against them. A part of me wanted her to, but with little words, she managed to let me grow and blossom into the strong, independent woman I was today. With little words, she taught me that actions were louder than words. And whilst she never raised her voice at me, she did reprimand me for my wrongdoings. She trained me to be better than her. She trained me to love unconditionally. She trained to me to be the best. And I was, many years later. She took my hands, encasing them in her motherly warmth, and returned the smile. When her lips reached ear-to-ear, it made her look twenty years younger. She was truly beautiful. Many said that I inherited her striking features and my father's wit. We shared the same eyes, a soft umber with golden flecks, and brown hair, except mine was slightly straighter than hers with the softest of curls at the tips. A part of me wondered whether she would run away like me. But my mother wasn't afraid of anything.

"I know, honey. I'm just happy you're home."

And sometimes, I felt like I was afraid of everything.

"So am I."

*

In the afternoon, I returned to the Manor, awaiting our newest arrival. The mansion was spotless, and everyone was busily getting ready, the girls more than the men. In fact, the men were about to leave with Calix for training just as I entered the living room. From the beginning, I made sure that when a girl was to enter the Manor, all the boys disappeared from sight. Kira suggested the idea. It helped ease the girls into the environment instead of throwing them into the deep end, especially if they had spent most of their lives being tortured at the hands of a man.

"Rita," I called, and a girl with ebony hair glanced my way, stopping mid-way through setting the table. Her eyes were as dark as her hair, her skin was a stunning olive, as she was of Indian descent. "Can you check if her room is ready? I told Andrew to do it yesterday, but I can't be sure that he's done it properly, if you know what I mean."

Rita laughed. "Got it, Aria."

The sound of Kira snapping at anyone who weren't doing their tasks correctly caught my attention. I tried not to smile because I knew she was stressed out for a worthy cause, but she was starting to frighten people. These girls always worked hard to ensure the arrivals felt comfortable; it was something I took great care in. I wanted nothing to go wrong and neither did Kira.

"Kira, relax. We don't want to scare anyone, especially the younger girls," I muttered, when I walked by. She sent me an apologetic look before returning to her task with a far calmer demeanor. Heading to the youngest group of girls, who were all gathered by the display cases, I grinned when they noticed me coming.

"Girls, I thought you'd be in training today."

"We had a choice," Irina, a blonde Australian replied, the eldest of the younger girls, aged seventeen. "And we chose to help. Even if it meant suffering Kira's wrath."

Her response broadened my smile. "A brave choice. How comes?"

They shared a look amongst each other, one that I noticed in plenty of other girls after spending several months away from their previous lives. It was a fragment of healing. A look which told me they had conquered their fears and were on their journey to becoming powerful young women. Expecting Irina to respond, my eyes shot up when someone else opted to answer. Especially, as this particular girl rarely spoke.

"We wanted to assure her that she'll be okay her, and that no one can hurt her," Amira murmured, shuffling under the eyes that flickered her way.

My gaze softened at the Arabian girl who was found extremely malnourished only two years ago, hidden behind the market stalls on the streets of Qatar. I still remembered the image Xander had sent me of her frail body hooked up to IVs, that our Manor doctors set up to help replenish her body that severely lacked sustenance. Now, she was the youngest arrival at the Manor at only fourteen-years-old.

"I want her to feel how I'm feeling."

"And how is that?" I questioned, gently.

Amira's eyes were a rich gold. "Safe, secure… and happy."

Tears spiked the back of my eyes and I opened my arms, embracing the girls as they giggled. After checking if they needed any help, I left them to their tasks and joined Xander, who was by the dining table, his head stuck in front of the laptop. I had known Xander for over four years and he was quite possibly the only person I knew to be extremely talented when it came to technology *and* combat. He peered up when he caught me towering over him so I could see the screen.

"She's twelve," he said, and I inhaled, sharply. *The youngest arrival ever.* Hesitant to say any more, he waited until I was fine before proceeding. "From what I have found out so far, she lived in Arizona. They planned on selling her to a German billionaire, Viktor Von Dorson. Apparently, he's been looking for a young bride since his one ran away, and was then shot the night before their wedding. Though, I'm not sure how true that might be."

"How comes?"

"Sources told me that she knew of his illegal businesses and when she tried to escape, he killed her."

"So, why does he want another bride?"

Xander's smile was cold. "He's a wealthy man, whose legacy depends on an heir." I clenched my jaw in disgust, the fire within me bubbling as my vow replayed incessantly at the back of my mind. "She was an orphan, but she was adopted, and her foster mother had a track record of alcoholic misconduct. A nicer way of saying that she was a drinker."

"That's why she was an easy target. No one would care if she disappeared," I murmured. "Not even her foster mother. For all we know, she probably was sold to the man."

"It's a possibility. I haven't had the chance to look in depth but that is what I have managed to find so far."

Something didn't seem right. I drew my brows together, staring at the profile of our newest arrival. "But why her?"

"Sorry?"

I shook my head. "Why her, Xander? He could have any girl he wanted, but he went specifically after her. A girl in Arizona whilst he was across the ocean."

Xander frowned. "I'm not sure."

"We need to find that out. I want to know the reason he went after her."

"Understood," he answered, bobbing his head.

My heart ached for the girl. It was unfair. It was wrong. It was evil. To be stripped away of your rights as a human and treated like a puppet. I couldn't stand it and the anger seized my body. Glancing at the clock, I noticed she was going to arrive soon and ordered Xander to leave the room. I watched as he grabbed his things and disappeared down the corridor, heading to the western wing, where I assumed he would join the other men in training. With everything prepared, I exhaled quietly and ushered the girls into their places, shaking away the nerves that constantly seemed to greet me every time a new survivor would arrive. I clapped loudly, silencing the chatter in the room, and directing everyone's attention to me.

"Okay, she will be here soon. You all know the drill, so make me proud."

As soon as I finished that sentence, I heard the front door open and looked pointedly at everyone, who acted as casually as they could, speaking in low tones whilst I stood by Kira, who looked as tense as I did. It was always nerve wracking to meet our arrivals because we never knew how it would turn out. Ninety-eight percent of the time it was successful, but there was the rare occasion when the arrival would be so beaten down by their oppressors that the mere sight of other people would have them sent into a hyperventilative state. We never took the risk. A few moments later, Sophie, one of the earliest additions to the family, entered with a young girl clutching her arm, fearfully. Our newest arrival had silky ebony hair, smooth milky skin and the most striking eyes. I had never seen anything like it. In the daylight, they looked green but as she shifted her head, there was this subtle violet hue that was likely prominently visible at night. Those eyes skittered around the room, focusing on everything and anything, completely on guard. Sophie leaned down and murmured something to the young girl, succeeding in convincing her to let Sophie's arm go. The girl's response was a robotic nod, her hands dropping to her side. I drew in a breath of air before moving when Sophie sent me a look which told me to proceed with the plan. Everyone else tried hard not to stare, but the younger girls couldn't help it – curiosity had gotten the best of them.

I closed the distance, feeling the girl's startling eyes on me, and smiled. "And this is?"

Sophie was about to answer, but one glance from me told her not to. She pursed her lips and waited for the girl to respond. At first, she was hesitant to answer, confused by her surroundings, and looked at Sophie for assistance. But after receiving a slight nod of encouragement, the girl mumbled, "Violetta."

"Nice to meet you, Violetta," I knelt to her height, in awe of the color of her orbs and how fitting her name was. My smile spoke a thousand words and I knew Violetta heard every single one of them as her lips quivered. "Welcome to the Manor. You're safe now."

She burst into tears and fell straight into my arms as soon as I opened them, holding her tightly, whilst she trembled with silent sobs; the horrors from the monsters had wounded her, but from that short interaction, I knew it hadn't destroyed her. She was still a fighter. I could feel it, and I wouldn't stop fighting for her freedom until my very last breath, if that was what it would take.

"It's okay, sweetheart," I hushed, softly, peering up to find everyone staring, all most likely remembering their own arrival to the Manor. But something was different, something I knew I had wished to see in Violetta's eyes one day. *Strength.* "You're home now."

*

It had been over a week since Violetta had arrived and although her progress had been slow, it was better than most arrivals. She had slowly gotten into the swing on how things worked in the Manor and began to come out of her shell. By the fourth day, Kira suggested that it was time to allow the men to come out of hiding. I was cynical at first but agreed, proposing that we should start with a few men. Monitoring Violetta closely, we introduced her to Xander first, who warmly greeted her with his charming self. Violetta blushed and murmured a quiet acknowledgment, before returning to her drawing that she was sketching with the other younger girls. Drawing out a breath of relief, I sent a nod to Sophie, and she went to inform the other men. During the day, Violetta didn't seem to mind the large men walking around the house, even speaking to some, but she did show signs of sudden distress if they were ever about to touch her. Kira made sure all the men knew not to touch her after that. Compared to the day she had arrived, when she was skittish and constantly bursting into tears, the improvement was substantial.

Since she had arrived, she remained holed up in her bedroom, locking herself away from the outside world. But it wasn't until one evening, when the men were in their rooms, and the girls were all gathered in the living room to watch a movie, did she finally make her presence known. She had tiptoed her way into the room, surprising us all, and ended up watching the entire movie. Afterwards, without saying good night, she hurried up the stairs, flinching at the sound of any unexpected noise. It was all too familiar. I had seen similar behavior in Kira when we first met. The signs of abuse. The truth slapped me in the face and made me feel sick to my stomach. Rage blinded me and I ended up spending the rest of the night beating the living daylights out of a punching bag in the gym.

After that night, Violetta was seen out of her bedroom more often. My heart was touched at everyone's effort to ensure that she was comfortable. As the youngest to ever arrive at the Manor, everyone treated her with more care and empathy, bathing her in affection and kindness, showing her respect in ways that I knew she had never encountered in her life before. In the Manor, Violetta was given a choice, and when she realized this, I knew she was trying to make the best of it. However, it wasn't until the seventh day after her arrival that she had made the greatest progress I had seen to date. In the west wing of the Manor, found on the third floor, was the music room where we dedicated the area to different instruments to encourage everyone to pursue any passion they desired in their heart. That afternoon, I had been watching Calix as his fingers kissed the keys of a piano, a tune as dark and gloomy as his past echoing throughout the room. He knew I was watching despite my presence being hidden by the shadows of the room. He knew I was there. I taught him to always see and feel everything. Nevertheless, I was one of the very few that he allowed to see his vulnerability – his pain. He never played in front of others, no matter what, always removing himself from the antique instrument as if it had burned him whenever he was seen playing. That was why it had surprised me when I noticed Violetta poking her head into the room with curiosity. Her violet eyes lit up at the sound of the piano, and lightly, with footsteps of a kitten, she made her way to Calix. Although she tried her best to remain unheard, Calix heard everything. He stopped playing, his fingers hovering above the black and white keys, and slowly peered over his shoulders. His eyes were a luminous green when he caught Violetta's, who came to halt like a deer caught in headlights. Her eyes widened and her mouth opened and closed, unable to form words.

"I-I-I'm s-s-sorry," she stammered.

Usually I would jump in, saving her from this situation, but the slight tilt of Calix's head stopped me, and I observed the interaction. He studied her before gesturing for her to come over. She looked hesitant at first, scared by the emotionless expression on his face, or perhaps the scarred blemish that most often left people gaping. Eventually, she moved. When she was close enough, he finally spoke, "Do you play?"

She swallowed. "I used to."

"Would you like to play with me?" he questioned, and both me and Violetta gawked at Calix, stunned by his request.

Violetta struggled to speak before deciding to settle with a short nod. Calix shuffled further down the stool, giving her the space to sit beside him which she did, timidly. The silence in the room was so tense that you could hear a pin drop. Calix didn't look at Violetta as his finger pressed down a key, the note vibrating out of the instrument. Then, he pressed another, and then another, and then another, until a melodic tune sang in the air. Violetta watched in awe, but he paid no attention and continued to move down the lower notes of the piano. Suddenly, higher notes joined his music, and Calix's eyes snapped to the young girl. His gaze was piercing and yet, she didn't flinch, pressing onto the keys that deeply contrasted his. I choked back a sob, feeling the tears prick my eyes at the progress this girl was making, after all the horrors she had faced. The music was dark yet light; there was hope and then there was dismay; there was anger and then happiness; there was Calix and there was Violetta. Together, they created a story of their lives and when it finally ended, they sat back and embraced the quietness.

Then she spoke.

"You remind me of my older brother."

Calix stilled.

So did I.

Siblings were a sore subject for him, given his traumatic past which involved his younger sister being ruthlessly killed in front of him. I really thought Calix would leave the room but instead he looked down at Violetta, a girl less than half his height, and muttered, "I bet he is a great guy."

Her smile was sad yet happy, if that was even possible. "Yeah… he was."

My breath hitched.

"Do you miss him?" Calix's voice was the softest I'd ever heard it.

"I do," was her response, after a brief second. "But he's safer up there than down here. Just like I'm safer here."

"Do you remember him?"

Her black tendrils swayed when she shook her head. "I was really little when we were spilt apart. But I do remember one thing…" she paused. "He said he would always protect me, promised that he'd never let anything harm me."

Calix didn't speak at first. Then, he placed a hand on her shoulders. I waited for her to jerk away. She did not.

"If you let me, I'll protect you," he said.

Violetta's eyes shot up. "You will?"

Calix smiled, his eyes softening. "Of course."

Without any warning, she threw her arms around him, catching him by surprise. His arms stayed limp by his side, his eyes wide, but a heartbeat later, he hugged her back, drawing her small frame close to him.

"Thank you," Violetta whispered.

She didn't see it, but I did. I saw how he looked at her. There was affection in his usually cold green eyes, a new promise forming within his soul.

"Thank you."

CHAPTER 3

italian king

Nero

"What do you mean '*dead*'?" I snapped, irritated. "His body was found in an alley; it was hard to tell that it was him, but we did some analysis to double check. He was fucked up pretty bad, man. Someone got really creative with him," Matteo whistled, in admiration.

I sent him a dark look, but his grin didn't drop. "Stop acting so pleased."

"He was a dick, Nero. We all saw this coming."

"Do you know who did it? It can't have been a street gang like the feds are claiming," I sifted between the pictures of the corpse on my desk. "It's clearly been done by someone with evident and substantial skills."

Matteo's smile dropped. "There's something you need to know."

I frowned. That was not a good sign. I didn't like the tone he used; it had never meant anything good in the past. When I had taken over the Italians, Matteo was given the position as my second without a thought. Not only was he the nephew of Antonio Moretti, the former Don, but he was also my closest friend, practically my brother, as we had grown up together. We spent years training with each other, battling and heading into operations which required full trust in each other's abilities. Although, he was infuriatingly arrogant, he kept me

26

grounded when the title weighed too heavily on my shoulders. He looked a lot like his father with shaggy sable hair that kissed the dark brows on his face, and hazel eyes that always taunted me. There was a nick across his brow, a reminder of the time when we got into a brawl with the French during a bad meeting. He was tall but his frame was leaner than mine, and he constantly wore a cocky smirk that characterized his personality. Today was different. He was too somber for my liking and that always meant something bad.

"What is it?"

There was a knock on my door that halted Matteo from speaking, and both of us looked over at the culprit as they poked their head in the room with a sheepish smile. "Hi."

"Mel, what are you doing here?" Matteo demanded, as his stepsister glided into the office.

Melissa Nilsson was a stunning five-foot-six Swedish woman with hair so golden that it would have had Rumpelstiltskin fervently wanting to get his hands on it. After her mother remarried a widowed Valentino Moretti, and secured her heritage left in her grandmother's will, Melissa and Matteo had become the unlikeliest of siblings. As her older brother, Matteo often dealt with a lot of arguments due to his sister, who captured everyone and anyone's eyes, and her flirtatious tendencies which left her in trouble. Other than that, Melissa was incredibly ferocious and very gifted in archery. With many contacts, she managed to help spread the influence of the Italians and thus, she was crucial to our family. Fearlessly, Melissa ignored her brother's glare and waved at me, cheerily, before turning back to him.

"Have you told him yet?" she responded, instead of answering his question.

Matteo sulked. "I was just about to."

"*Oh*," she said. Then she took a seat in the chair opposite me and grinned up at her stepbrother. "Well, carry on then."

I looked between the two stepsiblings and rolled my eyes when Matteo sent her an annoyed look, to which Melissa stuck her tongue out like a child.

"Can someone please just tell me what's going on?" I groaned. Matteo's expression instantly morphed into something serious, and once again my stomach sunk, especially when I saw the apprehension in his sister's face.

"I received words of a sighting at the airport over a week ago," he

27

began, chewing his lip nervously, glancing at his sister. "A woman."

That piqued my curiosity, and I leaned onto my desk. "Continue."

"Sources say she got off the jet that arrived from London. She was seen getting into an SUV with two other men, both assumed to be American, and another woman. A blonde of Asian descent."

"Do you have photos?"

He drew something out from the inside of his blazer and slid it across my desk. Our mystery woman wore a blazer over her dress, and those expensive red bottom heels I had seen on women during my business meetings and *other* trips. The sun hat covered her face, along with her aviators, but under the direct sun her hair was a silky mass of fawn curls. Other than that, it was difficult to see her features in detail, and figure out who she could be. Inspecting the other three photos, I saw the two men and women Matteo mentioned.

"So, why is this relevant?" I asked.

"On the eve of Miguel's death, this woman was spotted at the hotel. She was seen with this man hours before the murder," he stated, pointing at the man with the scar on his face. "And then around twelve at night, she was seen with him at the bar. Miguel was found dead at one in the morning. Everyone had been so preoccupied with the New Year, they didn't realize he was missing until over an hour later. There was no security footage prior to the murder, except from the hallway to his hotel room. Only one tape. And he was with that woman as they entered the elevator."

"I'm surprised he wasn't killed ages ago," Melissa chirped, and I tossed her a glower that had her shrugging. "What? He was a douche."

Turning back to Matteo, I asked, "And you think she's involved in his murder?"

My frown deepened when I saw the siblings share a look.

I narrowed my eyes. "Well, is she?"

"It's a high possibility. Although the feds ruled it off as a street gang, she may be the one who killed him. But, Nero…" Matteo stopped. He hesitated, "We think it's Aria Moretti."

*

I had become the Don of the Italians five years ago, bearing the power and the many responsibilities that came with it. A title that came with losses rather than gains. When I had received the title, it was not out of choice – it was never mine in the first place. Someone else was destined for this title. Aria Moretti. The only daughter of Antonio Moretti. The sole heir to the Italians, and a descendant of the Russian mob. When she left, she took part of me with her. Disappearing into the darkness of the night, she abandoned the Italians, leaving us all stranded, unaware of the foreboding future. As I was the son of Claudio Russo, Antonio's right hand, I became the next choice. There were frantic preparations to prepare me for my new responsibilities towards all the people in the Estate. I had learned the ropes alongside Aria, but I had grown to become her second. People wouldn't think there was a significant difference between the Don and their right-hand man, but there was a huge difference and, hence, when I took over, there was almost too much pressure to handle. I had always been disappointed in how Aria left.

Without a word. Without warning. Just *poof*. Gone.

We were best friends; I knew her better than anyone else, and yet, after a couple of months of being the Don of the Italians, she had completely changed and suddenly I didn't know her at all. I was angry. I still was angry. The night she left; she had drugged me so that when I woke up my memories of her had vanished. It had messed up my thoughts that when it came to the next morning, I didn't even know she existed. With Matteo's help, I spent months trying to piece the puzzle of my memories together as they slowly began to come back to me, but even after five years, there was always one piece missing. Why did she leave?

My heart shattered at the thought of her. Aria and I were actually meant to get married when we got older. Although, we never spoke it to each other, it was a responsibility that our families whispered into the air. Our parents were best friends, and it was something that was often spoken amongst each other's families. Even then, I knew Aria was someone I would *marry*. She was passionate, strong, and God… she was beautiful. She made me laugh and she pushed me to the edge, but I could never beat her. She made sure of that. Aria Moretti. A true enigma.

With the photo in my hand of the woman coming down from the jet, I muttered to myself, "Why is she back?"

I couldn't think of a reason why she would return back to New York after five years. She never once stepped into the city during her disappearance, so why was she back now? Did she want the Italians?

Did she want revenge? What did she want? I looked at the photo. Was she the same Aria? Had she changed? Who was she now? I ran my fingers through my dark locks, staring at my reflection in the mirror that hung above the bathroom sink. Her presence made me feel uneasy. I didn't like not knowing things – especially when it came to her. Suddenly, my mind took me to the night she left. I could still remember the bewitching sound that left her red lips, and how soft her skin felt - as if I was touching the clouds. I could see the red blush painting her skin, and her hazel eyes that danced with desire. I could remember it as if it was yesterday. And it fucking pissed me off.

"Damn it!" I hissed, splashing icy water of my face, hoping the memories would leave me. But they didn't. They continued to replay in my mind, like a broken record.

I tossed the photo onto the cabinet and stormed out of the bathroom. I was angry and I refused to feel like this. The Estate, a mansion located outside of New York City, was home to everyone in the mafia and most, if not all, resided here. It was late, and I was aware some of my men still lurked around, especially knowing that Aria could potentially be home. They wanted to know what that meant, they wanted answers, but I had none to give because I didn't even know myself. All I could see was red as I marched down to the basement, several floors below ground – a cold, isolated place where we held our prisoners. It was securely guarded with a rotation of five men every six hours. Our oldest and most valuable prisoner, stayed in the deepest part of the basement, several corridors away from life. Coldness seeped in, and the fluorescent bulbs offered some light source in the darkness. I didn't shiver as I moved from corridor to corridor until I reached the furthest jail. Behind a steel door, with a small, barred hole to serve as a window, was Konstantin Romanov, a man found guilty of treason against the Italians. When I stepped foot into his jail, his head lazily lifted, and I took in the disaster he was. His lips were busted, and he was bruised in all places, dried blood sticking to his skin. He smirked, his skin lacked color, and his body was emaciated, covered in rags with his ankles chained to the wall.

Traitor.

"Back for more fun?" he snickered, coughing afterwards.

"Are you going to tell me who you were working for?" My fingers curled as I stepped closer.

In the glacial, desolate, concrete room that lacked light and warmth,

I saw the spark of amusement in his eyes as he gave me a toothy grin, yellow teeth taunting me. "Of course not."

"Then fun we shall have."

*

Blood used to disgust me. In the sense that it ruined my clothes and left stains which were a pain to deal with. It was, however, gratifying to see. Watching it spill from my enemies, along with their shrieks of pain. My knuckles were busted open, my t-shirt was blood stained and sweat dripped from my forehead. I tried to level my breathing, deciding to let Konstantin rest for the night. His head bowed as I removed a knife from his jugular, a bellowing scream escaping his lips before disappearing into thin air. I could hear it echo around me. The buildup of anger had left me spending two hours pummeling it out of him, but eventually it had disappeared. I clenched my jaw and glared at him.

"Next time, give me a better answer."

"You'll be waiting a long time, Russo," he spat out blood. "You're no ruler. The Italians will fall because of you. It won't be long until someone takes that throne away from you."

I scrutinized the old man, unflinching at his words, before slowly smirking. "Have a good night."

I could hear his shouts as I left the cell; they were my favorite tune to hear. Wasting no time to clean myself up, I hurried to my bedroom and stripped out of my clothes, discarding the blood-soaked material to the side. As soon as I stepped into the shower, my muscles relaxed when the hot water pelted me, trickling down my body, a sense of serenity cocooning me. I sighed, running my fingers through my sweaty hair. And then Aria popped into my mind. *Fuck me.* I grunted and switched the water to cold. After twenty excruciating minutes, I dried up and dressed myself in some sweats, before making my way to my office, my hair still damp, dripping water onto my white sweater. The office was quiet. It always was. The sound reminded me of the day when Antonio told me I was going to become the Don. I was worried. I didn't know if I was capable. But he wasn't concerned or scared. I could see him leaning back against the chair that now belonged to me. He had crossed his arms over his chest and had been studying me with very dark eyes.

"It's always been you, Nero," I didn't know what he meant by that.

"And you knew it."

But what did I know? I could never have seen this future. In the depths of my subconsciousness, I wondered whether I knew exactly what his vague words were saying. The lights flickered on when I pressed the switch, illuminating the black themed office. Hanging above the fireplace was a portrait of me, a tradition passed on from Don to Don; it signified leadership and power. In all honesty, it was meant to fuel our egos. My exhale was heavy as I sunk into my chair, the leather molding against my bulky frame. Then I saw it. From the corner of my eye, a note attached to my portrait. Someone had been in my office. I wasted no time to inspect the note, and when I opened it, I read the message swirled in neat italic handwriting.

Home sweet home.

CHAPTER 4

plans and plots

"Our goal is simple," I studied everyone sitting around the glass table. "We're taking down the Serpents."

Eyes of different colors, belonging to those of different nationalities, meticulously sharpened their attention on me, hanging onto every word that left my lips, like a devoted prayer. For the first time in over two years, I had gathered all those that played the most important roles in the Manor for a meeting to discuss our next step. The weather had dropped a few degrees since the other day but the sun was still vibrantly beaming outside despite it being January. Per usual, I had taken the seat at the head of the table with Kira on my right, and Calix on the left. Xander sat beside Calix, laptop out, tapping at the keyboard; he seldom spoke during these meetings, only answering with the briefest of comments but those were enough. Then, there was Sophie, sitting beside Kira, her copper hair trimmed to her shoulders, bangs slightly touching her brows as her honey eyes gleamed at her boyfriend. After Xander, Sophie had been the next person to be taken in after her brutal treatment by a wealthy Greek billionaire. Kira had been the one to save her. Their paths had crossed before me, and when Kira had the resources, she went and saved Sophie. There were things we never spoke about – Sophie's past was one of them.

Her boyfriend, on the other hand, was well known in the Manor for his history. Mark was a soldier, forced to follow the rules of his leader after his family were held captive, hunting down innocent people. But after getting severely wounded, he was left to rot until Xander found him. He was the only solider we had taken in since then. Mark was reserved as he sat beside Sophie, their fingers entwined on the table. His skin was like porcelain which made his auburn hair stand out, and when he spoke, his words were laced with a British accent. Opposite him sat Ciara, whose hair was in tight black curls, and who donned caramel eyes like the pigment of her skin. She was loving and friendly despite being sold like cattle. Originally, from Egypt, she was a long way from home, and I knew she missed it, but the fear of being caught was stronger than the desire to return home. Finally, Dom, who was the youngest amongst us, but who was also the voice for our young ones. His eyes were as deep and rich as his skin, a smooth ebony embellished with knife wounds during his time in captivity. In this room were the people I trusted the most. Each and every person here had suffered at the hands of their oppressors, but each had also courageously joined the mission to destroy these monsters. Our hatred towards them was deep-rooted, stemming from the core of our souls.

"I'm sure you all know the Serpents," I continued. No one flinched. "And I'm also sure that you've all had your fair share of spending time with them."

"Fucking bastards," Dom grunted.

My lips quirked up slightly. "They are an organization, who have been stripping away the freedom of those who are vulnerable. Their main focus is trafficking, primarily sex-trafficking. They target mostly girls, especially younger girls, but we all know how power-hungry people can be. Therefore, they didn't stop there. They turned to boys, kidnapping and training them to either become soldiers, or selling them as slaves. They target anyone, mostly the defenseless, those who don't have a dollar to their name, and sometimes," I glanced at Kira, but she didn't look at me. "They'll go after the rich too."

The tension was heavy in the room as everyone was reminded of the people we were taking on. The Serpents were an old group, dating back many, many years. At first, they stemmed from an old money Russian family, who constantly challenged my family's power. Eventually, they twisted into something darker, becoming an organization hellbent on stripping freedom from innocent people in exchange for money. Luckily, my family had managed to destroy their foundations before it all got out of hand. Except, there was only so much you could stop. And someone was continuing their legacy. It was a few years ago that the Serpents again became well known in the Underground. Everyone feared for their lives, for their money, for their power because the Serpents were everywhere. Oil trades, banks, weaponry, drugs, land. They were the backbone of the darkness that spined our world, and I intended to break that spine.

"These people don't know what mercy is. It is vital to remember that. You see a Serpent member, you kill on sight," Mark winced, but I ignored it. "There are only a few you can save, and those serving the Serpents are long gone. We can't save *everyone*, but we can stop *them*."

It was a tough pill to swallow, but Serpent soldiers were always the hardest to stop. Not because they were skilled, because most were forced to aid the organization. But most, if not all, were taken in at young ages, and indoctrinated to believe the Serpents' creed.

"In the files in front of you is the Serpents' history. In brief terms, they originate from the Petrovs, one of the largest families in Russia. The Petrovs used to be loyal to the Russian mob until they decided they wanted more. They were all eventually killed. By my aunt." I smiled, darkly. Although, in name, the Petrovs were no longer around, it did *not* mean that they were gone forever. There was always someone left. But that was speculation, and speculation remained speculation until there was evidence to prove otherwise. Turning to Kira, I passed the control to her. "Kira."

Kira, or Yakira, Adachi was of Japanese descent. Her life before captivity was very brief, and she didn't have many memories of Japan. She never spoke about her life back then. I think it reminded her of the person she could have been. As she stood up, her piercing blue eyes held everyone hostage, blonde ringlets swayed. Once upon a time, before she met me, her hair used to be as dark as onyx. That was before the Serpents. Life had changed, and so had she. The scars that haunted her were now a symbol of her past, and she wore them, proudly. Kira was an amazing woman. Strong, determined and powerful. Even when I first met her, I saw the fire that burned within. She rose from the ashes. She became untouchable.

"Viktor Von Dorson is infamous in the trade industry. A German multimillionaire, dare I say billionaire?" Kira began, pulling out an image of Von Dorson from the files and showing everyone. "He is known for his extravagant events, very high maintenance, and they regularly take place across the world."

"I'm assuming there's a reason behind these events," Sophie stated.

Kira nodded. "Yes. As we all know, the Serpents enjoy their auctions behind the scenes, and Viktor holds most of them. From what we know, he's a major shareholder in the ghost organization, if that's even possible, so he funds their entire program."

"So, this is very super-secret and like, elite?" Dom frowned.

Kira rolled her eyes, and I smiled, responding, "Yes, Dom."

As mentioned previously, Dom was the youngest in the room. Meeting him was definitely an experience that could not be forgotten. I had found him, frail and bruised, covered in torn clothes, hiding behind a dumpster in Mozambique. He was only thirteen at the time. Since he was a child, Dom was forced to work in one of the Serpents' warehouses, producing an extensive amount of weaponry. With little food, care, and practically no money, he was tortured into working long hours, where they would beat him if he even flinched. After a few months in the Manor, Dom quickly returned to his charming self.

"Oh my god! I am going to be like Batman? That would be so awesome! We should totally have undercover names!"

The kid hadn't left my side ever since.

"Anyways," Kira sighed, ignoring Dom's comment. "Luckily, Viktor is holding one in New York."

"I don't believe in luck. It must be because of Violetta," Xander murmured. Everyone looked at him, but I knew what he was talking about. Seeing that everyone was confused, he quickly filled them in about Violetta's background.

Ciara's lips curled down. "But why Violetta?"

"That's what Xander and I were wondering too. Perhaps we can get some answers," I said, flicking through the file.

"How so?"

"Viktor's event is raising money for children in need," Kira continued.

Calix rose a brow. "The irony."

"I know," she replied, her lips coiling into a twisted grin. "We are going to hit that auction."

Mark frowned, his eyes furrowing as they looked at me. "I thought we were staying low."

"Oh, we are," I smiled. "Viktor's visit to New York isn't just to see where his bride has gone, but it is also to hold his event to soften any blows the Serpents may face because they lost Violetta."

"Why would he do that? He's one of the main people, no?" Dom pointed out.

"I'm not sure. But I do know that this is an opening, and if we need to root out the Serpents, we start with their funds."

"So, what? We're killing the man?"

"No. We aren't killing Viktor."

This time, Sophie frowned. "Then, what are we doing?"

I smirked.

"We're kidnapping him."

*

When I was little, I had been taught, trained and brought up to carry the weight of a prestigious, powerful position. I was heir to the Italian mafia. At the time, I was the sole heir. My brothers were too young for the position, and my father needed to retire as he had been leading them for longer than any other Don before. I left that title five years ago. I wonder what would have happened if I had stayed, if I didn't know what I did. My father would always tell me that betrayal was the norm in the Underground – I just never expected it from my best friend. Blinded by a stupid infatuation called love, and charmed by his lies and false promises, I couldn't see the truth. It was my mistake, but it was a catalyst to something new – something revolutionary. I may have lost my inheritance that day I left, but I found a new world, a new family, a meaning that I had been desperately searching for.

"Aria," a whisper in the air, her voice faint and soft like the patters of rain against my bedroom window in the Manor. "You know that Nero will be attending?"

"I've known for some time," I answered, looking out into the distance as the grey clouds covered the night sky.

"What are we going to do?"

"The plan continues, Kira. He's nobody."

"He's the Don of the Italians. Trust me, that isn't nobody," she reminded. "It would be foolish to ignore him."

"No, it would be foolish to acknowledge him," My eyes flickered over to her, noting the look of conflict across her face. "Don't worry, Yakira."

She didn't speak for a second, her name halting her to a stop. Then, a sliver of second later, she exhaled. "I just worry for you. I'm not questioning your decision but… Aria, his influence over you –"

Holding my hand up, I cut her off. "This time is different. I'm not the same person I was five years ago."

"But, maybe, neither is he."

*

My dress was a subtle mauve that complimented the darkness of my hair and brought attention to the redness of my lips. It cinched my waist and then pooled around my feet, covering my heels. The satin material dipped down my cleavage and then disappeared at my navel. It showed enough to attract the eyes of those around me, but to also blend into the background. Moving my hair to one side, I grabbed my diamond necklace from the vanity just as Calix poked his head into the room after a short knock.

"Are you ready?" he asked, before he quickly drank me in. "You look beautiful."

"Thank you, Calix. Just got to clip this necklace, and I'm good to go," I replied, struggling to find the clasp.

My irritation was clear to Calix as he chuckled and strolled over, my eyes finally taking him in. He was dressed in a dark blue suit, a silver tie and his black hair was groomed into an undercut. Taking the necklace from me, he dropped it around my neck, his fingers brushing against my skin as he began to clip it in place.

"You clean up well," I muttered, studying his reflection in the mirror.

He smirked. "Is that a compliment I hear?"

"Appreciate it," I warned, and he held his hands up in fake surrender with a grin. Thanking him for the help, I grabbed my things, tucking my dagger into the sheath attached to my thigh.

"You look very beautiful, *vasílissa*," he suddenly said. I glanced up and grinned. His native tongue – Greek – always left butterflies in my stomach, fluttering about. Holding his hand out, I gingerly took it, ignoring how it sent tingles up my arm.

"It's been a while since we've done something like this," I whispered, in anticipation.

"Yet, it's always our favorite part."

I chuckled. "I've always known you were hiding your inner sadist,

Calix."

"How have you forgotten?" his green eyes darkened, and the corner of his lips pulled up into an impish grin. "I would've thought you'd know. Or should I refresh your memory quickly?"

I shuddered when his fingers caressed the contour of my frame, my cheeks betraying me as I blushed. "Behave."

"Of course. Can't have you flushed before the event, can we?" he teased, biting back his smile.

I smacked his arm and he laughed. "Don't push it."

His eyes twinkled. "How about after then? As a reward?"

Although he was teasing, I could hear the need in his voice, the hunger that was abundantly clear in those emerald eyes, especially as he drew me closer to him, his hand burning through the thin material of my dress. Licking my lips, his eyes followed the action, and I tilted my head to the side, arching a brow. "If you can get the job done, then we can talk about rewards."

His lips curled into a challenging smirk. "Very well then."

CHAPTER 5

red carpet royalty

The white fur shawl covered my shoulders as I made my way down the red carpet, shielded from the blast of cold New York air. Usually, I would avoid high profile events in order to be kept out of tabloids but in Viktor's case, I couldn't risk the chance of missing out. Lights flashed from all directions, blinding me, another thing I tremendously despised. My smile was mastered, my cheeks aching at how broad it was, and my head spun as I climbed up the stairs to the Mandarin Oriental Hotel in central Manhattan. My hand felt sore after how much I waved at the parasites with cameras attached to their hands, waiting to find their latest victims. Luckily for me, and by no surprise, Viktor's charity event required masks, and therefore everyone's identity was hidden behind a thin layer of dainty fabric, bedazzled in jewels and luxurious embroidery. From the corner of my eye, I caught Calix as he smiled charmingly to an interviewer, whilst Kira and Xander exited their car, arms hooked through one another's, laughing amongst themselves as if they weren't planning to shed blood this beautiful evening. Kira's porcelain skin was illuminated under her velvet black dress, and her flaxen hair caressed the exposed part of her back where her dress dipped down to just above the bottom of her spine.

Touching my earrings, I fixed the earpiece hidden underneath my hair, and saw Kira do the same. Training my warriors in field-op was essential. They learnt all the ways to communicate with or without an earpiece, reading the signals and body language of their teammates. It was one of the key skills taught at the Manor, in order to prepare them for dangerous and complex operations such as this. Unlike Kira and I, Xander and Calix went without earpieces, and had to solely rely on any actions that we made throughout the night. Calix had seen the subtle hair fix I did despite the distance, and began to separate himself from the interviewer, heading up the stairs, only a few meters behind me. The Mandarin Ballroom was one of New York's most renowned venues. Thousands of square feet of ground were festooned with golden banners and majestic fairy lights, which illuminated the balloons floating above us. Three quarters of the walls were windows, and I almost gasped at how stunning New York appeared at night, glittering with life and light. As soon as everyone entered, I could feel the room still, mesmerized by the three elliptical chandeliers that were, without a doubt, the showpiece of the venue, creating a shore of crystals that twinkled across the ceiling. If only tonight was under better circumstances, I would have enjoyed my time but alas, it was very rare that beautiful things led to good times. And I had no doubt that a lot of money was invested in this event, but all for the wrong reasons.

"Is everything set?" I asked Kira.

"Yes," her static reply came back in my earpiece.

"Do you see him?" I murmured, when Calix reached my side, his hand softly touching the small of my back as he kissed my cheek, mocking a formal greeting.

"No," he responded, his lips brushing my ear. "But I think you should check your three o'clock."

My spine stiffened when I saw a familiar mahogany-haired man, his build and voice instantly recognizable to me. There was this fleeting sharpness in my heart, but I swallowed thickly and looked away. The mere glance had given me enough time to drink in his appearance. It had been a while and yet he seemed to look more sinful than the last. I knew he caught the attention of many people tonight, especially the women, some who whispered and giggled amongst their friends when they walked by him. Calix handed me a glass of champagne and in the faint reflection of the glass, I saw *his* smile broaden when he greeted two other men, clinking *his* glass against theirs. I saw the heart-stopping dimples. I saw *him*.

41

"Kira," I muttered, sipping the champagne thirstily as I suddenly seemed parched. "Keep an eye on Nero."

"Got it. Over," was her response, before she took Xander and disappeared into the crowd.

"We need to find him soon," I said to Calix, once I knew that they had it under control.

"Already have," Calix replied, nodding to the bar. "Look over there."

Viktor was a dashing man who was incredibly well groomed. At thirty-five, he was a womanizer who lured his prey with false promises and trapped them in the dangerous work of brutality and male domination. He was a pretty man with thick, flaxen hair, strong facial features, and brilliant gray eyes. He was a liar, and a cheater, a man capable of terrible things and yet… he was our way in. It would not be easy to crack a man like Viktor but seeing as he had never needed to do the gritty work himself, it shouldn't take long for him to spill the secrets of the Serpents, which were heavily guarded underneath lavish parties and illegal trading.

"Are you okay?" Calix asked.

I hummed, deflecting the truth, and untangled myself from his arm, forcing a smile across my face. Failing was not an option. "I'll go after Viktor, just watch my back."

For the first time ever, Calix looked hesitant to let me go, but reluctantly nodded. I pursed my lips, straightened my posture, and strode towards Von Dorson with an alluring grin. He saw me almost instantly, his conversation cutting short when he locked his gaze onto me. A smirk coiled onto his lips, and I knew he was studying me, lifting a glass to his lips and drinking languidly in a way that insinuated only wicked things. After a few short words to the man he was speaking to, he closed the distance between us, taking my hand and warming my knuckles with a soft kiss.

"Good evening, mademoiselle," he spoke in a heavy German accent, his gray eyes framed by a silver mask, perilous intent swimming in the depths of his irises. "We must never have met before because I'd remember a beauty like yourself."

"I've heard many rumors about you, Mr. Von Dorson. I wonder if any are true?" I moved closer, curling my lips seductively. "I wonder if you live up to them."

"And what have you heard, beautiful? All good things I hope."

I laughed. "Some are, but it depends on what you view as good."

His smile widened until he resembled something like the Joker, daring me to take the risk, test his patience and play into his mastery of manipulation. And gladly, I would.

"Question is," I brushed my hand down his arm. "How good are you, Von Dorson?"

Like a fish taking the bait, he inched forward, his warm breath laced in champagne and cigars fanning across my cheeks. "How about we take this some place more… private, *häschen*?"

"It would be my pleasure," my red lips met my ears as he grasped my hand, ridding our drinks at the bar, and leading me through the crowd of people, who all wanted a piece of Viktor. The man was impatient, ending conversations short and curt before returning to his mission.

"Honestly, I sometimes detest holding these events," he grunted, snaking an arm around my waist to draw me closer.

I observed every corner we took and noted all the hallways we passed. "So, why continue to do so?"

"I have a business to run," he answered, finally opening a door several meters from the ballroom, a door to a room that I was familiar with. "Plus, it's for charity."

My knuckles itched to knock the living daylights out of him, but instead I opted for a less violent approach and dragged my nails down his arms. That just seemed to tempt him, as a sadistic twinkle in his gray eyes lit up the dark room.

"Feisty, aren't you?" he whispered. "And impatient."

"Of course," I purred, hearing the door close behind us.

The only source of light came from the windows behind Viktor as he pinned me up against the wall, the moonlight illuminating our frames and the way it molded against the contours of each other's bodies. With my back pressed against his chest, I let him pepper my neck with dainty kisses, and I let him touch my arms with a strong grip. In other circumstances, if I were not well trained, my anxiety would have skyrocketed out of the roof, but I knew exactly how to get myself out of this situation. I just had to play the long game. In the pitch black, I had nothing to worry about. In fact, Viktor should be worried. But the poor man had no clue what was about to occur and continued his voyage discovering all the inches of skin I concealed. I closed my eyes, inhaling sharply when his heavy cologne hit my nose, overwhelming me, but I remained sharp and attentive, arching back when his knuckles pressed my navel.

"You know what, Viktor?" the words left me like a breathless whisper.

"Yes, *häschen*?"

"You are a very bad man," I couldn't stop the moan when his lips found a particular sensitive spot on my neck.

He smiled against my skin. "Is that so?"

"And do you know what happens to bad men?"

I heard his breathing stop. For a moment no one moved. And then, in one swift and easy movement, he spun me around, cradling the side of my face as his silver eyes implored an answer from within me, trying to gauge a reaction when his grip tightened on my hips.

"What happens to them?" he smirked. "Something good?"

I tilted forward and brushed my lips against his neck. His breathing rapidly becoming erratic and labored as he waited. Waited, for my next move.

"They get hurt," I whispered, lightly kissing the side of his neck. "Really," *Kiss.* "Really," *Kiss.* My smirk touched his ear. "Badly."

I felt him still but before he could question my erratic statement, two sets of hands grabbed him by the shoulders and tore him away from me. Even in the darkness, I saw the confusion washing over his face.

"What is going on here?!" he bellowed. When the lights flickered on, I smiled at him, and then to the men beside him. Viktor blinked as he glanced at Calix and Xander, trying to refocus his eyes. "What is this fucking nonsense? Explain yourself! Who the fuck are you?"

Suddenly, the pretty man looked incredibly ugly as he glared at me, expecting me to tremble under his gaze. Instead, I angled my head to the side and lifted a brow, a wicked smile dancing on my blood-kissed lips. "It's so wonderful to meet you. Though, I am disappointed not to see the notorious and powerful man everyone claimed you to be."

His face flushed red with anger. "You better start making sense, or I swear –"

I kissed my teeth in disappointment, cutting his warning short. "You're in no position to make threats, Viktor. I don't think you realize who I am. You should be afraid of me. In fact, you're *going* to be afraid of me."

The anger morphed into bewilderment, but underneath that

bewilderment was an almost unnoticeable layer of fear, as he pinched his brows together. "Who-who are you?"

My grin was as wide as a Cheshire Cat when I slowly took off my mask, and my violent nature set ablaze when his moonlike eyes became transfixed with terror, after hearing me say, "I'm Aria. And we're going to have *so* much fun together."

*

After instructing the men to take a now unconscious Viktor out of the hotel and back to the Manor, I hid behind my mask once again to make a quick getaway before anyone noticed Von Dorson's disappearance. I could not leave without Kira, and after unsuccessfully getting no reply from the earpiece, I was starting to get worried. My eyes skimmed the venue, a frown on my lips when I was unable to see her. I started to panic, fearing she had got caught but then a flash of blonde glided through the crowd and gathered beside Sophie, who was near the exit. The two girls sent a look my way as if feeling my gaze, and even though we were far from each other, they caught the brief nod I sent in their direction. I saw the smiles on their faces before they disappeared out of the ballroom, heading off to stop the auction in a room several floors above. The tension rolled off my shoulders at the successful operation and I decided it was time to leave, no longer enjoying my time. My steps were quick and short, and my smile was brief to those who greeted me, but as soon as I reached the exit, I bumped into a very hard wall. Or, at least, I wish it had been a wall.

Stumbling back from the abrupt impact, I nearly tripped over my dress when a hand shot out and steadied me onto my feet.

"Are you alright?" The person attached to the hand asked.

I quickly rolled back my shoulders, dusting off the embarrassment burning my skin before I responded. But the words never came out. Because as soon as I lifted my eyes, the air was trapped in my throat at the sight of unique indigo eyes. The gaze was hot and intense, and my skin crawled when I noticed that a mask no longer concealed the owner's handsome features. A shade darker than his eyes, his suit outlined every crevice and the tone of his body, and my hands fisted by my side. A look of concern across his face made me realize that I had yet to reply.

"Sorry," I swallowed the panic, shoving away my forbidden feelings and mastering the great art of deception. "I'm okay. Thank you for your concern."

"I didn't see you there. I do apologize if I have hurt you."

"No!" I answered, perhaps too quickly as he looked surprised. I quickly composed myself, coughing awkwardly, unable to act the way I should have. "I mean, you haven't. You didn't hurt me."

Shit, I was messing up. I needed to get out of here.

He furrowed his thick brows, glancing me up and down, no doubt trying to figure out whether he knew me, or maybe considering if I could be the next person he would sleep with. His question revealed that it was the former.

"Have we met before?"

"I don't think we've had the pleasure," I replied, as calmly as possible. "But anyways, I'm sorry for the collision. I should leave, I don't want to keep you all evening."

A fraction of a second later, his face hardened, void of any type of emotions, as he straightened his back and tucked his hands into his pockets. "Yes, of course. Well, have a good evening."

"And you."

"I hope that the next time we meet is in better circumstances," the tone of his voice made me uncomfortable.

My heart accelerated, but I kept my composure and gave a pleasant smile. "I hope so too."

His eyes never left mine when he moved to the side, clearing my getaway path, scrutinizing my every movement. "Until next time."

"Until next time."

With one last smile in his direction, I walked away, my back stiff with anxiety and alarm, unfaltering even when I felt his gaze burn into my back.

Fuck.

He knew.

CHAPTER 6

dinner & her

Nero

"Find her," I ordered. "Now!"

"Nero –"

I slammed my fists onto the wooden desk, a force so strong that it should have splintered the furniture apart, had it not been made out of the most superior mahogany wood. Matteo gulped whatever words he was about to say, faltering as I sent him a piercing glare.

My anger didn't simmer as I repeated my command, accentuating every single word with rage, *"Find. Aria. Moretti."*

I was blinded by my wrath, my blood boiling with frustration, my heart aching with pain from the loss of the most important person in my life. I was mad at her. I was mad at myself. I was mad and I wanted answers.

"Immediately. I want to know her every movement, the people she meets, the places she's visiting, even the fucking food she's eating. Every goddamn thing," I snarled. *"Do you understand*, Matteo?"

Matteo bobbed his head, and I knew he was biting his tongue – a wise move as I wouldn't have been able to control my fury had he spoken. He left as soon as my order was given, and the room became eerily quiet, leaving me with my haunting thoughts. Sinking into the comfort of my leather chair, I tried to control myself, closing my eyes and levelling out my breathing. I didn't realize it was her when we first collided. It had taken me a long minute to even wrap my head around the fact that she was standing next to me, alive and well. But eventually, when that realization passed, the hurt settled in. I was able to confirm my suspicions when I saw the conspicuous scratch below her chin. It was undetectable to a regular person but given that I was trained to see everything in the room with a mere glance, it practically stood out to me like a sore thumb. She had gotten it when we were sparring as kids and claimed it would be one of the many scars she would bear in order to save the good people. And I promised that I would take those scars for her. She was astonishing to say the least, wearing that tempting evening gown and *Jesus*, those salacious red lips. I couldn't get the image of her staring up at me under those thick lashes out of my head ever since that night. A torturous reminder that I could never have her despite every fiber of my body craving for a taste. Frustrated, I knew it would do me no good if I didn't get the feeling under control, and I knew that I had to act before I lashed out unreasonably towards my men. Therefore, before I reached the apex of my irritation, I stormed to the basement, ignoring any stares thrown my way along with the whispers of gossip, and greeted my prey, who cowered in the dark, solitude of his cell. I saw him shiver at the sight of my presence and admired the dried bloody coating on his porcelain skin.

"Ah, he's back for more fun," he snickered, before falling into fits of coughs. Peering up, he grinned at me through blood-stained teeth. "This is pathetic, Nero. It no longer hurts."

"Yet, I'm able to stand whilst you on the other hand…" I paused, kicking his leg to reveal a gaping hole where a knife had been shoved in, the wound beginning to bleed. He hissed. I smirked. "Are barely able to sit."

He snarled, "Burn in hell, bastard."

I grinned. "Gladly."

I wasn't sure how long I spent venting my anger on the traitor. I lost track of time as I threw another bone-crushing punch into his stomach. He screamed, spatters of blood painting the ground, whilst I exhaled heavily, taking a step back. My fists ached, covered in his blood, and bruised from the amount of weight thrown behind my assaults. Blood trickled from his mouth, and he winced when he tried to clench his jaw. His face looked almost unrecognizable and a few more minutes with me would guarantee that it would never look the same again. As I crouched, the door opened abruptly and Matteo, not even sparing a look at Konstantin, grinned at me.

"We located her," he began.

My heart stopped.

Then it started again.

I stood up, taking the rag Matteo offered me, and cleaned my hands. "Where?"

"Aria has a penthouse in Manhattan. My men have been closely tracking all real estate in the Upper East and apparently, this particular building has been bought under the name of Lyra Kyrokos."

I knew that name. I knew it all too well. It was her alias. Which meant that it was Aria. I opened my mouth to speak but the words of someone else halted me, a quiver in his question, a stammer that had me question everything I knew, "Wait... Ar-Aria... sh-she-she's back?"

Matteo and I shared a look, before we frowned at the man who was glaring at me only a few short seconds ago, but now looked like a timid puppy. The fear was bright in those dark eyes of his, and his skin became pale, as if he had seen a ghost or lost ounces and ounces of blood.

"You know Aria?" I asked.

He didn't answer and instead scrambled onto his knees, clasping his hands like a prayer, ignoring the thundering pain which probably made him feel like he was on fire. "I beg you, Nero. Please, just kill me now. Please, show me mercy. If our friendship ever meant anything, please just kill me."

I was absolutely stupefied.

A man who refused to spill the secrets of his betrayal for a year and give in to my brutal beatings, was now on his knees for a woman – a very powerful woman, no doubt. Clearly, I underestimated her. I pursed my lips and narrowed my eyes as Konstantin began to mumble incoherent things under his breath. Ridiculous. As I turned away, he bolted from his place, his weak knees barely able to hold the weight of his body.

"Please, Nero!" he cried.

I ignored him and left the room.

"No! Nero! Please don't leave me here!" he screeched, like a banshee, as the steel door closed behind us. "NERO!"

Striding to my office with Matteo hot on my tail, I tried to think of all the ways I could confront her, the way I should approach her, what, even, to say. But I failed to even think. The words were lodged in my throat, and even then, I knew she wouldn't want to listen to what I had to say. Perhaps, I deserved that. However, too many years had gone by, and I still couldn't figure out what went wrong. I was an idiot for all the things I had done afterwards, reacting badly to her sudden change of behavior, but I at least deserved an answer for what happened.

"What are you going to do, Nero?" Matteo finally spoke, after the strained silence from the moment Konstantin expressed his terror.

"I don't know why she's back, or what she wants," I glanced down the hallway of the fourth floor of our Estate. Several meters from my bedroom and my office was a room that used to belong to her. I hadn't stepped foot in there for five years. That locked door mocked me.

"So, what now?"

"Now," I clenched my jaw. "I'm going to pay our Queen a visit."

*

Her home was located in the heart of the city. Skyscrapers stretched as far as possible into the clouds, as if they were all competing to see who was the tallest. As the owner of the building, Aria had the penthouse suite, very similar to the one I had bought for myself when I became the Don. It was my escape from my responsibilities, far from the Estate, from the pressure left in Aria's presence. The elevator was made of glass, rising to the thirtieth floor, my eyes remained glued to the numbers as they changed until a loud *beep* indicated that I had arrived. Matteo informed me that she wasn't home and suggested it could be a good opportunity to seek out information without her knowing. I loosened the tie around my neck, my heart racing, and stepped out of the elevator. Her floor was empty, a few couches here and there, and the most magical view of the city. The sunset of New York released a ray of colors, and the cars below looked like small bokeh of light. I could stand here forever, and I knew it was probably why Aria chose this location. Taking the keys that I swiped from the desk after masterfully flirting my way past the receptionist, I opened the white doors with the number 123 in gold attached to the oak. Immediately, a waft of delicious linguine hit my nose.

I frowned. This wasn't right. No one was supposed to be home.

My steps were tentative as I stepped into her home, heading down the hallways where her heels were neatly stacked on a golden rack beside a cabinet, where an image of her family was framed beside a vase of roses. There was a mirror, hanging above the cabinet, taking up more than a quarter of the wall, and a canvas on the opposite wall. At the end of the corridor was the living room. It was large and attached to an open plan kitchen. All I saw was white. From the couch to the walls to the frame of her glass dining table. It was completely different to mine in all aspects. Whilst hers was bright, greenery adding a splash of color, mine was dark with black accents. I heard the clatter of plates, and my eyes shot to the kitchen. Music played faintly and someone hummed along with the melody, their frame hidden behind the silver fridge door that was open. I moved closer, noticing the table was set with cutlery, champagne and a dainty flower in the middle.

"Ah!" they said, and the fridge door closed with a loud *thud*. I looked at the culprit and caught a glance in my direction, followed with a broad grin. "You've finally arrived. I was afraid the food would get cold. I wasn't sure when exactly you were coming."

"Aria."

Her name was a whisper on my tongue, breathlessly taken back by how magnificent she looked after all these years. Without the mask, I could see how she had matured but, at the same time, had not aged one bit. Her brown curls were messily tied up in a bun and yet they looked flawless. Her eyes were an accumulation of green and golden specks, creating a stunning hue of hazel. Her frame was much more slender than before, and I knew she would be swallowed in my arms. But I could see the muscles on her shoulders and legs from the way her negligee shaped her body. It was like seeing her in the evening gown again, but with less material. Every contour and curve, I noticed. She was naturally very beautiful, and her skin was a smooth olive under the rays of the golden sun that shone into the room. There was a twinkle in her eyes as she rose a brow, her coral lips moving but I paid no attention to what she was saying, gravitating towards her like the Earth moved to the sun.

"Russo?" I snapped out of my daze. She frowned. "Are you okay?"

"What are you doing here?" I managed to ask, the distance between us becoming extremely small.

"Business," was her answer, before she returned her focus on the meal she was cooking.

"How did you know I was coming?"

"I know you better than you know yourself," she sighed. "It's a shame you've forgotten, Russo."

Taunting. Teasing. She was testing the limits. My entire body tightened. Peering over her shoulders, I noticed there was a little smirk itching to expose itself.

"Don't be a grouch. Sit down and eat. We have so much to catch up on. I made linguine, your favorite," she sang cheerily.

At first, I made no movement, but she shoved the bowel of pasta into my hands and observed me reluctantly walk to the table and set the bowl of pasta down. Instinctively, I settled at one end of the table, and watched her take the seat on the opposite end. I never had someone at the other end of the table in the Estate. It surprised me to see her do that, but then I remembered this was her domain. Her kingdom. Vigilantly, I studied her plating up the homemade Italian linguine. She was quiet, her concentration focused on the plate, as she topped it off with basil and cheese, passing it to me along with a glass of champagne. Then she made a plate for herself.

"So," she started, twirling the pasta onto her fork as those almond eyes peered up. "How have you been?"

"This is such bullshit," I let out a short laugh of disbelief. "What the fuck are you doing back?"

Her eyes widened innocently. "Russo, come on."

Pushing the plate away from me, I leaned over the table. "You betrayed the family, Aria, and left us to scramble to put the broken pieces back together. Do you even care about what you did?"

Aria seemed indifferent to my sudden attack, eating her food calmly because she knew it was killing me that I couldn't get an immediate answer from her. She knew it infuriated me when I didn't get the answers I was looking for. She knew that I had no authority over her, because, at the end of the day… she was the true heir and I, simply her replacement.

"It worked out well for you in the end, didn't it?" she replied.

I drew my brows together. "What are you talking about? That's not the point –"

"Then what are you complaining about, Russo?" she sighed, rolling her eyes. "I left because I couldn't have succeeded. But you did. You were capable of doing everything I couldn't."

I whispered, "You left without a word, Ari."

Her eyes abruptly narrowed, and her fork clattered onto the plate as she stoically stared at me.

"Do not call me that," she punctuated every word with wrath. "You lost that right a long time ago."

My heart sunk. *What?* Confusion and hurt blinded my judgement. The hatred across her face pinned me in place, but I was completely lost. Unless –

With an exhale, she resumed eating. "*Sit down* and eat, Russo."

"Why did you leave that note in my office?" I responded instead.

Aria frowned. "What note?"

"At least tell me how you knew I was coming?" I was beginning to get annoyed that she wasn't answering any of my questions.

"I have my eyes around New York," she smiled, slightly, to herself. "Plus, did you really think I wouldn't have known that you were coming for me?"

"Why did you come back? If you wanted to stay away, you should have," I said, darkly. "*Forever.*"

Aria pouted. "Now, that's quite extreme." When she saw that I found this to be no laughing matter, she leaned back into her chair and squinted at me, taking a sip of her champagne. "You think I'll threaten your reign. Don't worry. I won't. I'm not back for the mafia. I don't want anything to do with it. But if you do get in my way… well then, I guess we'll have an issue, Russo."

"*Nero,*" I gritted. Her eyebrows pushed together. "My name is Nero."

"My apologies," Aria corrected herself, "Nero."

I wasn't sure how to feel. I was so utterly overwhelmed by her presence that it killed me to see our reunion become so sour. I didn't want it to be like this. I hoped we could work it out. But she was angry about something, and she wasn't going to tell me what it was. It was no use. Too much time had been lost between us. I ran my fingers through my dark hair with a heavy exhale.

"I'm so mad that you made me forget about you," I couldn't look at her. I felt like she could see right through me, and that sort of vulnerability didn't sit well with me. "I woke up the morning after and I had no memories of you. Your existence was nothing. For months, I only remembered fragments of you. Until it all came rushing back. The gaping hole in my heart suddenly made sense. I have never felt *so* betrayed."

She was silent for such a long time that it made me uncomfortable, so I looked up and saw her in deep thought. Her eyes were transfixed on me. She sat there in front of me, but for some reason she had never felt so far away.

And then, when she finally spoke, the space only grew.

"I'm glad the drug worked," her voice was taciturn and distant, like two strangers meeting for the first time. "I had to leave that place, Ru – sorry – *Nero*."

I studied her for a while, and it felt like hours had gone by. She didn't flinch under my gaze, straightening her spine, her usually warm eyes looking as cold as the Arctic. She was no longer the girl I once knew.

"You're never going to tell me anything," I stated, and her pursed lips confirmed my assumption. "This is all just a game to you."

"A game I *do* intend on winning," Then she rose her glass in the air as if she were making a toast, and her lips coiled into something wicked, as the glimmer in her eyes became shockingly clear. "I lost last time. And I won't lose again."

But what game were we playing? And how far would this go? The look in her eyes scared me. Not because I was terrified of her, but because I was terrified *for* her. Because that look told me she was seeking to spill blood. A look I was all too familiar with, and I remember how she would leave her prey. Torn. Tattered. Twisted. Until they were fragments of what they used to be. And something told me that I would be her next target if I pushed too hard. I tightened my jaw, curling my fingers until they were fisted, my knuckles going white from the force. I couldn't hold back my anger, I couldn't control my feelings, something I usually mastered, but she made me lose my mind. She made me lose control. So, I thundered away from the table, only to be halted by her icy yet tender voice.

"Do not push my limits, Russo, or I *promise* you'll regret it. You know nothing about me anymore – so, let's keep it that way."

I inhaled.

Then I exhaled.

Before glancing over my shoulder with a cold expression of my own, to match my frosty response, "*Sempre*, Ariadne."

CHAPTER 7

viole(n)t

"Oh, Viktor," I purred. Gliding the blade across his handsome face, barely touching his skin, I pouted. "You're far too valuable for me to kill."

He glared. "You're a fucking bitch. And bitches like you deserve to be broken. Someone needs to fucking train you."

"And tell me," I moved closer until our faces were inches apart. His eyes flickered down when I smirked, my tongue rolling across my pearly teeth. "Where can I go to get broken in?"

My voice was as soft as fur, as light as a feather, and as cool as snow, and it worked wondrously against Viktor Von Dorson. His body shivered, a mixture of delight and dread dancing in his moonlit eyes.

"So, that's what you want to know? Where we send our pets?" he laughed and my face darkened. "I'll never tell you."

"You want to know a secret," Standing up, I towered over his frame that was tied up to a steel chair. My fingers grabbed his hair and I pulled it back, forcing him to look up at me. "I can be very, *very*, nice to those who are nice to me. Let's be nice to each other."

"I know who you are, Aria," his face was starting to bruise from the punches Xander gave him. I didn't stop him. I was mad too. "Where did that magnificent girl who was going to become the next Don go?"

His words aimed to rattle me but sorely failed, and I was getting terribly bored of the same questions being asked. Rolling my eyes, I let my dagger touch his arm, slicing the material of his shirt.

"Don't try to piss me off," I cocked my head to the side. "If you're aware of who I am, then you know the things that I'm capable of."

"Yes, you are extremely skilled in the fine art of killing. Everyone in the Underground wants you, especially after they heard that you are no longer involved with the Italians. You have no loyalty. An assassin of your pedigree could earn plenty of money, which would leave you and three generations afterwards extremely comfortable. So, why are you getting involved in Serpent business?" Viktor rose a busted brow in curiosity.

"The same reason you are."

"Power? Or money? Is it both?"

I kissed my teeth, releasing my grip on his hair. "Ah, I guess we haven't got the same reasons."

Viktor glowered. "You are making a foolish decision, Miss Moretti."

"I prefer to be called Aria," I crouched down, my hands grasping his thighs. Viktor swallowed but kept the cool expression on his face. "And I don't think you actually mind at all. Is it foolish of me to be here, *Viktor*? Because I think you're enjoying it."

"You are a beautiful woman, no doubt, but you are fucking crazy."

My smile stretched from ear-to-ear. "They say all the best women are the craziest ones. Keeps you on your toes. But I think you prefer your women young. *Extremely young.*"

He shifted uncomfortably in his seat, arms bound behind his back and his legs chained to the steel chair. His suit was covered in grime, and he didn't look as pretty as he did only a few nights ago. Viktor was aware of what I was talking about; his eyes flickered around the cell nervously. The Manor had inbuilt cells several meters underground, but I often got rid of my prisoners before they had a chance to get familiar with their prisons. Something about keeping my enemies below us didn't sit well with me.

"Where am I?" Viktor questioned instead.

His cell was draughty, gray and sparse, with a barred gate keeping him separated from freedom. There was nothing else besides the bucket in the corner. I didn't want to give them a comfortable stay. Again, not many lasted the night.

"Somewhere," I slowly trailed a finger up his chest. "Come on, Viktor. We *can* be friends, can't we?"

He ground his teeth together. "Have you ever had friends, Aria? You're known to be a lone wolf."

"But even a lone wolf has a pack," I arched a brow, amused by the way he was drinking me in like he couldn't decide whether he should desire me or hate me. "And my pack is everywhere around this world. Including your soon-to-be-bride."

He stilled.

"You were wondering where she was, weren't you? Making the effort to travel to New York and hunt her down. The irony is that she fell right into my hands, and is safe and sound several meters above you," I brushed the tip of my thumb across his chin. "So, let's be nice to each other."

"How did you get her?" he demanded; eyes as wide as saucers.

I clicked my tongue in disappointment. "You are in no position to ask any questions, but I'll do you a trade. You answer mine, and I'll answer one of yours."

"That's not a fair trade," he scoffed, shaking his head.

"I'm not known to be fair," I shrugged.

"No, you're known for all the horrible ways you kill people," Then Viktor's orbs brightened with ghastly realization. "You killed Miguel."

"Now, that's a strong accusation. I heard it was a street gang. Poor Miguel. He'll be sorely missed," I bit my lower lip to fight back the smile, but I failed as I felt my cheeks crease my eyes. "He did have such wandering hands. I guess those are what got him into trouble."

Viktor shook in his chair, struggling against his shackles. "You're sick. You're a fucking sick woman."

"Where did they find those hands?" I asked, indifferent to the pelts of insults. "I heard they found them in a chest full of jewels that he used to gift his women. How artistic. I bet his women are relieved; he used to beat them every day with those jewels, to remind them of their place."

Suddenly, Viktor looked very pale, and sank against his chair, exhausted from the resistance against his chains. His head bowed and I smiled, trailing my fingers down his jaw until they reached his chin. I tilted his head up and met a pair of defeated eyes. The beast within me quietly waited for their moment to pounce. The taste of blood so tantalizing, I could almost smell it.

"Tell me, Viktor, those hands of yours are pretty talented, seeing as you're an incredibly wealthy man. I wonder how many people were touched by those hands. I wonder how many people would be excited to see them go," I threatened, in the sweetest voice ever, keeping a tone that sounded alluring to the ear but deadly to the heart. "So, are we going to be friends, or will we have a problem?"

His eyes betrayed him. Despite the scowl he sent and the way his jaw ticked in irritation; his eyes were as transparent as glass. And Viktor Von Dorson feared me. "What do you want to know?"

I grinned.

"Wise choice."

My finger traced the shape of his mouth before I drew his lower lip out and dug my nail into his flesh. He winced. Blood spilt. My smile dropped. And all signs of pleasantry vanished like a puff of smoke.

"Now... why do you want Violetta?"

*

"Did you know?" Xander questioned the young girl, who sat on the couch in my office, her brows pinching together in confusion.

She frowned. "What are you talking about?"

I sighed, settling into my seat behind the desk, as Violetta glanced at me, the fear evident across her face made me send a harsh look to Xander, who thankfully backed away from his interrogation. I ran my hands over my face as I tried to digest the information handed to me. Violetta swallowed, her eyes flickering to me and Xander.

"What's going on?" she asked, uneasily.

"Vi," I began, not sure how to even explain but decided that I might as well be completely honest instead of beating around the bush. "Xander has just found out that you're an heiress."

Her jaw fell. "I'm a what?"

Violetta was a pretty girl that easily stood out in the crowd. Her hair was a darker shade of brown, braided with flowers in each weave, and those startling violet eyes that contrasted her slightly ivory skin. She fingered the hems of her sleeves nervously, chewing her lip, her eyes completely in panic mode at the sudden information thrown at her. So, I went and sat beside her, taking her hand with a tender smile, despite having hammered a man many floors beneath us only a few short hours ago.

"An heiress is usually a woman from a wealthy family. Your grandfather was well known, and a very rich man. He left a lot of money in your name."

Her eyes softened as she slumped against the couch. "I-I have a family?"

"He never met you. We don't have a lot of information on your birth parents, but we know that your mother kept you hidden from your grandfather and many other people. From what we know, your grandfather never had the chance to meet you."

"Why did she hide me?"

"I'm not sure, sweetheart," I squeezed her hand. "But I promise we will find out."

Violetta bobbed her head softly. "So, my grandfather left a bunch of money to me?"

"He left everything to you. Real estate, businesses, money, everything that will help you secure your future."

"How do you know this is true?"

Glancing over at Xander, his eyes twinkled as he smiled humbly when I replied, "Because Xander is very good at his job."

And I was excellent at retrieving information from people. After spending a couple of hours with Viktor, he spilt everything he knew about Violetta. Including why the Serpents were after her. I couldn't take his word for it; I would be an idiot to trust a man like Von Dorson. So, I had Xander confirm what I heard, and within an hour, Xander pulled up the files we needed, so we could learn more about Violetta's history. It wasn't a lot given how short notice I had given him, but it was enough to verify one thing – the Serpents were after Violetta's money.

The little girl looked like she was about to faint, her shoulders slugging as she stared at me with wide, bewildered eyes. "So, basically, I'm rich?"

I chuckled. "Very, very rich. I believe that's why those men were after you."

Her shoulders tensed for a fraction of a second, and if you weren't paying close attention, you would have easily missed it. But I missed nothing. And I knew she was still suffering from everything she had been through. Recovery was a process that had no timestamp, and solely relied on strength and patience. I didn't doubt Violetta's capability. She had never once shown that she wasn't capable of getting past this. She was going to be alright. It was just a matter of time, and that was why so many people in the Manor continued to suffer from the darkness of their past.

"What now? What do we do?" she asked.

"Well now, we will protect that inheritance, making sure it goes to no one except you when you turn eighteen. Until then, it will be safely hidden away. No one knows where it is currently, but that doesn't reduce any chance of you being in danger. These people… they're not going to stop looking for you until they get what they want."

Her face paled, as she stammered, "I'm never going to be safe, am I?"

My heart shattered into tiny fragments at the sound of her broken hope and the heavy weight of horror she carried on her shoulders. I wanted to take it all away, to protect her forever, to make sure no harm ever came about. I wanted to keep the truth away from her, but I knew that would do more harm than good. Sometimes, facing the truth was the only way to get out of the nightmare. I knew it all too well. Sending Xander a look, he nodded and left the room. His presence left a detectable stillness as I caught Violetta staring out into the distance, lost in her thoughts. I didn't know what to say to her, what to tell her to help ease the worry. It was unfair that a girl her age had to suffer so much. She barely had the chance of a proper childhood. It made me so angry that I couldn't think about it without wanting to impale my dagger into someone's heart. I blew out a breath of air and placed a hand on her arm.

"I'm never going to let anyone hurt you, or even touch you," I pledged. "I swear."

She was silent, her eyes glancing around my office before they finally settled onto me. They were glassy; it was like staring at amethysts in the sunlight. Tears brimmed her lower lash line. "Why am I here, Aria?"

"Why don't you start off by telling me what happened that night? Afterwards, I'll tell you."

She seemed hesitant at first, and I couldn't blame her, but eventually she slowly moved her head and retold those horrible moments, "I was going to get married off. That's all I heard when those men came for me. Before they had come, I was home, by myself. I was waiting for Tiana, my adopted mother, to come back from work. She would usually be late, but she would never be later than twelve at night. That was when I started to get scared.

Her voice trembled so I gave her an encouraging smile, knowing this was the first time she had ever spoken about that night. "Go on."

"It happened all so quickly. They broke into my house before I could call the police. I could hear the sound of them breaking things downstairs, so I hid in the wardrobe in an empty room. I used it as a safe place when Tiana got angry," her words quietened at the end, and she blinked away her tears.

We both knew what had happened next.

"They found you in the end?"

Sometimes saying it was scarier than reliving the horror. Because you were finally accepting the truth.

Violetta smiled sadly. "I guess I'm not the best at hiding."

I didn't speak afterwards, studying her and assessing the situation. Then, I said, "This is the Manor. We save girls, sometimes boys, like yourself, from exploitation and harmful people. These people are called the Serpents. They are an evil group that kidnap people and sell them to make money. Xander and Mark found you at one of the Serpent camps that are scattered around the world. Along with a few other victims, you were also brought back here."

I allowed Violetta to digest the information and when I was sure that she was not about to freak out, I continued, "You are at the Manor, remaining safe here, until you are old enough to make your own decisions. When you reach that age, the choice is yours to stay and help me, and everyone else in this Manor… or leave, forgetting everything about the world you were brought into."

"If I stay, what will I do?"

"You'll learn the ropes behind what I do."

Violetta rose her brow, inquisitively. "And what do you do, Aria?"

"I train every woman and man in this Manor to become the most powerful version of themselves," I responded, truthfully. "Everyone here has a horrible past, and everyone was taken in by me. I gave them the freedom they thought was stripped away from them. Violetta, I give them the chance to choose for themselves. I offer a new beginning. And I train them to be skilled in combat, ready for anything."

"But why? It's so dangerous. Why would you risk putting yourself in that position?"

I exhaled. It sounded shaky but I was sure that was just me hearing things. "I come from a powerful family, Vi, and I was in line to take the throne. But I didn't."

Puzzled, she asked what everyone wanted to know, "Why not?"

I smiled lopsidedly, not really wanting to speak much on the matter. There was only so much I revealed about my life and that part of it, I wasn't ready to talk about. "Don't you worry about that."

Moving from the couch, I strode to the bookshelf and scanned the book spines until I pinpointed the one I wanted. I pulled it out from its position, brushing away the dust and opened it up. Instead of pages and pages of words, it was hollow with a brass key hidden in the hole.

"Every person has the choice of undergoing training. It's not too intense but it will be enough to allow you to defend yourself, so it's definitely not easy."

I started to make my way to the painting hanging behind my desk chair and pressed the key against the unnoticeable button on the bottom corner of the frame. The painting whirred opened, and I heard Violetta gasp behind me when she saw the hidden safe. Quickly punching the numbers into the keypad, the vault unlocked and sitting on top of files was a blue vial that reminded me of someone's eyes.

"Once you turn eighteen, you'll be asked whether you want to stay or not. Depending on your decision, you'll either undergo further training, far more intense than usual, or…" I paused, showing Violetta the capsule. "You'll drink this and forget ever being here. Some of your memories will be intact but most will either be removed or altered to ensure your safety. To give you a new beginning. I won't leave you stranded. You'll be given a home and enough money, if not more, to start your life again."

Violetta was at a loss for words and for a moment, I forgot she was only twelve and remembered she would need time to process what had been said. However, she continued to prove me wrong, as she angled her head slightly in an inquisitive manner and her eyes simmered with amazement.

"How many people have left?" she whispered, surprising me.

I smiled as I answered, "None."

*

By nightfall, I decided it was time to retire for the day after spending some time with the younger girls, however I was stopped by Calix, who looked too serious for my liking. Sophie followed soon after, and in the end, I excused myself from the girls, promising to return tomorrow, and took the pair into a quieter room.

"We need Konstantin," Calix stated gruffly. "Or we can't make our next move."

I frowned. "And why not?"

"He's a liability, Aria," Sophie explained, worried. "And he's in the hands of Nero Russo. What if he reveals to Russo what we are doing?"

"If Nero was going to find out anything, he would have found out by now. But the silence from his side, tells me he's doing a good job of keeping out of my business," I assured, slightly irked by the suggestion.

"Regardless, he's a liability and he also has answers that we need about the Inner Circle."

"I know you don't want him near K –"

Calix's words were cut off by a sharp glare as I hissed, "– No, I don't want him near *my family*. He makes me fucking sick, and I swear to God, if I lay my hands on him, he won't last a second. He should be fucking grateful Nero is holding him captive. At least he'll still be alive."

"We spoke to her," Sophie murmured. "She agreed that it's the right decision to make. She offered to get him herself."

"We are speaking about taking him out of fucking Nero Russo's hands," I laughed in disbelief. "I heard Konstantin betrayed them. So, what makes you think they'll happily hand him over to us?"

Without missing a beat, Calix said, "Because of you."

I glowered at my third, fisting my hands. "I'd be careful of what you're suggesting, Calix."

"Calix," Sophie nibbled her lip anxiously, but he ignored her, holding my gaze unflinchingly.

"You know I'm right, Aria. You are our best bet. We need Konstantin, and he's terrified of you. Nero is practically giving him a safe haven. He doesn't fucking deserve that. When he gives us the answers we need, we can get rid of him. All debts need to be paid, and he has yet to pay for his."

I weighed his advice, cursing under my breath as I turned away from them. I hated that he was right. I hated that this was a move we needed to make. Although, I incessantly had the urge that would drive me to the brink of madness, a screaming desire to tear Konstantin's heart out from his body – right now, he was better alive than dead. A situation I knew Nero would eventually realize. Therefore, after a long moment of contemplation, I glimpsed over my shoulder, gritted my teeth and grudgingly agreed.

"*Fine.* But afterwards, I'm tearing him apart."

CHAPTER 8

negotiator

Nero

Buzzzz. Buzzzz. Buzzzz.

I groaned before cursing under my breath as my phone relentlessly vibrated in urgency. I blinked, trying to adjust my eyes to the blue light of my screen, the blurriness of my sight focusing onto Matteo's name. Running my hand over my face, I answered the stupid phone with a groggy greeting.

"– You need to come down," Matteo said, before I could speak.

"Why?" I grunted, tossing the blanket off my body and staggering onto my feet. My body was starting to ache after the hardcore session I spent at the gym last night. Rolling my shoulders, I began to head into the bathroom.

"Because Aria decided to make an appearance at the Estate."

I stopped.

"What?" My mind was still working past the sleepiness, so I thought I heard him wrong. Then he repeated himself. Suddenly, I became more awake than I was thirty seconds ago. "Why?"

"She's not saying –"

"Hurry up, idiot. I'm on a tight schedule," Aria's honey-like voice chirped in the back, interrupting Matteo.

Annoyance rang through me when I heard them squabble on the other end of the line before I decided to hang up. Cursing her with every curse word under the sun, in three languages, I rushed to get ready, ignoring the burning sensation coursing through my muscles. I had spent yesterday at the Estate, sorting through a mountain of paperwork before deciding to spend my night thrusting all my energy into a punching bag and metal machines. I couldn't get rid of the frustration and eventually passed out in my bedroom, too exhausted to head back to my penthouse. Splashing my face with cold water, I closed my eyes and tried to level my emotions. I couldn't let them get the better of me, but at the same time I wasn't sure how long I could spend feeling like this - until I eventually exploded. The lack of control scared me, and Aria was an unanticipated character. I had to be ready for anything. After dressing into a new suit, ready for the meeting I had later today, I reluctantly made my way downstairs. The second I set foot on the ground floor, I noticed her by the front door, talking to one of the men in the photo Matteo showed me. The corner of her eyes creased when she smiled, a curl of her lips told me she was amused about something the man had said. She hadn't realized that I had arrived so I took a quick minute to absorb her presence. Today, she wore a cerise satin blouse, tucked into her black trousers that made her look taller than she actually was. Everything clung loosely to her frame and yet, at the same time, it showed off all the curves that left a man wanting more. Her hair was a shade lighter than my own, and like waves, gently fell past her waist, aviators pushing strands away from her face. For a second, I forgot why I had come down, utterly mesmerized. As if she could feel my gaze, she glanced up and met my eyes whilst I walked down the last few steps. Her smile fell, and then lifted into a smirk.

"Finally," she mumbled, exasperated, and the man beside her chuckled.

Before I settled my attention onto her, I glimpsed around the room to see my men gathering, whispering amongst each other when they realized who Aria was. I had yet to tell my men about Aria's arrival and confirm the rumors that were slithering throughout the Estate. Her sudden appearance did not help settle those speculations that threatened my position in the mafia. Matteo stopped talking to the men that guarded the front entrance, noticing me with a look of relief. He muttered something to the men before striding to me, stopping Aria in her tracks. His eyes sought for an answer, but I was at a loss myself.

"Why are you here?" I finally asked Aria, peering over to her.

"It's good be back at the Estate; it's been a while," she mused, her eyes sparkling with delight when she saw the apprehension flash across my face. "I'm assuming you haven't told them about me."

Referring to my men, I grumbled, "I was going to today but you obviously like making an entrance."

She rolled her eyes. "Always doing the job for you, Nero."

I didn't respond, my ears catching the whispers fluttering around us.

"Is that Aria?" someone asked, whilst another muttered, "Does she want the mafia back?"

Followed by someone commenting, "She's fucking hot."

The murmur of agreement that followed soon after made me flinch, and, without thinking, I sent my men a sharp look, silencing whatever they wanted to say next. I caught Aria's lips twitch in amusement, and I narrowed my gaze onto her.

"What do you want, Aria?"

Admiring her nails that looked as sharp as the stilettoes she was wearing and as red as the lipstick painted across her lips, she replied, "A person."

Her vague response had me tighten my jaw. "I can't help you if you don't give me a name."

She was entertained by how easily she could irritate me, retrieving a photo from the man beside her, before showing me. Matteo peeked at the image, before looking up, his eyes flickering between me and Aria with hesitance.

"Isn't that –"

"Konstantin Romanov? Yes, it is," she quipped.

"Why do you want him?" Then I corrected myself, "Actually, why do you think I'll hand him to you?"

Aria drew her dark brows together as if to say, *'why not?'* and then she actually said, "Because it's me."

The man snorted beside her, and I glowered whilst Matteo rolled his eyes in disbelief. "Excuse me?"

Her lips broadened. "I just want Konstantin. *Please.*"

I scoffed, hearing Matteo snicker beside me. It was amusing to think that I would hand the man I hated the most to the woman I trusted the least. I chuckled, shaking my head in disappointment, questioning whether she had lost her commonsense whist on her little *'finding herself'* trip. "Okay, Aria. You've proved that you're an independent woman and that no one –"

"Don't mock me, Russo," she said in a manner that took me by surprise. Her smile didn't drop but it twisted into something cold and terrifying. "You have no idea of what I am capable of. Now, I want the man, and I want him *now*. Will I have to tear him away from you, or will you just fucking hand him over? Either way is fine with me."

I gritted, "Why?"

She laughed.

She actually laughed, the anger creeping away from her eyes.

"That's for me to know and you to…" Her words disappeared into the smirk she gave me.

"I won't hand him to you. I'm not done. He's a traitor. How do I know you won't let him go?"

She examined me with those hazel eyes. "I can guarantee that I will not let him go. If he does escape, it's over my dead body. Romanov deserves nothing but pain. Something I am personally very good at giving."

Aria took a confident step towards me and, despite wearing heels, I still towered over her frame but, in that moment, she held the cards in her hands, and I was just waiting for her next move. The minimal distance between us made me dizzy when the scent of jasmine overwhelmed my senses.

"I want that man to feel every second of pain. He won't leave my hands unless he's dead."

She didn't back down, holding my gaze in a way that had me reconsider everything I thought about her. She looked so dainty and delicate, like a rose, and I was attracted by the colors of her beauty. Only, beneath it all, were thorns that pricked me, drawing out blood, reminding me that this enticing woman was someone to not mess with. With her so close, I could feel her warm breath caressing my face and her lips suddenly looked very inviting. I was tempted to run my thumb against them. I stopped myself.

"I don't trust you, Aria. Not one bit, so let's get that straight," I said, quietly enough so only she could hear me, and coldly enough that she understood the message.

Instead of being hurt, she was smiling like it meant nothing to her, and I was certain that was the case. "And I'm not saying you should. But know that we both want him to suffer, and you know how colorful my mind can be with punishments... so, what's the verdict?"

For a good minute or two, I thought against it, but my curiosity had gotten the best of me and I decided to bring Romanov down. Matteo knew immediately what my decision was and began shaking his head in disagreement, but I ignored him.

"Go grab him."

"But –"

"Matteo," I warned, and he held my gaze, as if considering ignoring my command but he knew better and sighed with great unwillingness. Gesturing for two other men to follow him, they disappeared into the west wing. My remaining men stayed on guard, shifting closer to me when Aria smiled, ominously.

"You've made the right choice," she murmured.

"Don't think you've won just yet," I scowled.

She ignored the look and turned to the man beside her, the side of his face sporting a scar that most definitely occurred during a violent fight. The way he looked at her left me deeply unsettled, green eyes awaiting her command.

"You can tell Kira we're coming soon, Calix," was all she had to say before he disappeared out of the house, another man replacing his position.

This man was the blond that greeted Aria at the airport. I wondered how many of them followed her. I wondered why they followed her. Aria was always seen as a lone wolf; people often described her as someone that worked alone. But the last two weeks had only proven otherwise. It hurt that she traded one family for another, and I swallowed the resentment that threatened to appear. The blond whispered something that made her expression shift from anticipation to annoyance in a matter of seconds. Before she could reply, we heard a grunt and the sound of struggling from behind, and our eyes moved in that direction at the same time. The last time I saw Konstantin was a few days ago and he had yet to recover from the beating I gifted him. His face was battered, dried blood stuck to his skin and clothes, and I saw him sporting new bruises. He saw me first and sneered, trying to shrug off my men that gripped his arm. In return, I smirked at his pathetic attempt to seem strong.

"I haven't been out of that shithole in months. You could've warned me before yanking me out of my cell, fucking lights blinding me," he complained angrily, in a thick Russian accent. "Are you finally done with me?"

I snorted at his naivety. "Actually the opposite. How do you know Aria?"

"Why the fuck would I tell you that? Bitch is after my head. Do you know what she would do if she —" he stopped short and then frowned. "Why are you asking?"

"If she what?" I demanded. He didn't reply, finally noticing Aria, who stood startlingly silent by the entrance. I repeated myself, "If she what, Konstantin?"

"No," he whispered, a single word laced with more fear than I had seen in over a year. His body stilled, his face went slack with horror, and his eyes widened until they looked like saucers. "Aria?"

I watched the interaction with surprise and before I could say anything, she quickly jumped in, taking a step towards the bruised traitor. The way her emotions changed stunned me. In less than a second, the warmth from her face vanished, replaced with something cool and emotionless. It was like looking at a completely different person. Her eyes thinned and the curl of her lips was anything but nice.

"Konstantin..." she paused, peering at the trembling man. "Have you paid your debt?"

It seemed like he was shocked, terrified and in disbelief all at the same time. Until Calix walked back in. Instantly, he must have connected whatever dots were missing and looked back at Aria, horrified. Aria responded with a smile that sent chills down my spine. To everyone's surprise but hers, Konstantin dropped onto his knees and clasped his hands together, his lips quivering like he was about to cry. Matteo's face was washed by shock, and I knew I must have looked the same as Aria sent me an amused glance.

"Please have mercy on me! Please, I'll do anything! I swear!" he cried out.

Aria kissed her teeth, shaking her head. "Silly man. Of course, you'll do anything for me, but mercy, I'm afraid, ends with your time with Nero."

One look from Aria was all Calix and the blond man needed to understand her instruction. Without a word, they strode towards Konstantin, who fought against his captors, stumbling back into my men. Her men were not gentle and did not entertain Konstantin, jerking him away from his old captors. He thrashed in their arms, begging to be released, shrieking with disturbing panic, before going completely limp at the touch of Aria. Her fingers gripped his chin when he hung his head and forced him to look up. Looming over him like his darkest fear, her eyes pinned him in his place and her voice was like a mixture of divinity and impiety.

"You'll repay me with a name and location, Konstantin. We'll have such an exciting evening together."

Then, as if her tone couldn't get any darker, her voice dropped a couple of octaves when she purred, digging her polished nails into his cheeks, "Your daughter also looks forward to seeing you."

My eyes couldn't help but widen at this new information and I swear I heard Matteo curse beside me. From our intel, Konstantin had no family, no wife, no child. But once again, everything I had known was a lie. A burst of rage flooded me as I shot my gaze to Matteo, but he looked equally taken back and shook his head in confusion.

"Daugh-daughter?" Konstantin stammered.

Aira looked incredibly disappointed. "Have you forgotten her, or did you choose not to remember? Because she hasn't forgotten you, or the things you did. Maybe your memory will improve when you see her face. I'm sure it won't be the father-daughter reunion that you're expecting."

She moved away before he could speak, and watched her men drag him out of the Estate, his cries fading until there was nothing but unnerving silence fanning the air. Matteo looked like he wanted to protest but Aria arched her brow, challenging him to speak against her. He was pissed off, taking a step towards her, but I grabbed his arm, stopping him. Matteo opened and closed his mouth, resembling a fish, before deciding that it wasn't worth the argument and settled with a glare towards Aria. The day hadn't even begun, and wariness hit me, Aria taking a toll on my mentality.

So, I muttered, "Take the men and leave us, Matteo. We'll reconvene in the living room."

He didn't bother to fight my request and shouted some orders in Italian, which had our bewildered men disperse after lingering for a short moment. I could hear their whispers and I knew I had to address their concerns, but first...

Aria sighed, thoughtfully. "He hasn't changed one bit."

The emptiness of the front entrance made me realize how claustrophobic it had started to become, with so many people surrounding us. My eyes fell onto the woman with the red lips, who stared in the direction of where Matteo disappeared.

"You'd think after five years but…" she didn't finish what she was saying, peering at me. "You haven't either."

"I can't say the same about you," I retorted, running my fingers through my hair, wearily. Her eyes followed the movement before looking away.

"No," she said, quietly. "No, you can't."

She grabbed her coat that I just noticed hung on the rack and slipped it on. Maybe it was my mind playing tricks on me, but her face looked almost heartbroken before a grin took place.

"But that's what makes it all the more fun." Aria winked playfully. "Don't you agree?"

I didn't know how to respond. Not when she stood in front of me, looking effortlessly beautiful, stealing my words like a thief in the night. There was something dangerously daunting about her, and yet, something sinfully spellbinding that knocked the air straight out of my lungs when she looked at me. And I knew I was screwed. As if she could see right through me, she laughed and began to walk off, her fragrance leaving me weak in the knees.

"Don't be so glum, Russo. There's so much enjoyment in life."

Before I could process what I was doing, my hand shot out and grasped her wrist, tugging her back to me. She staggered towards me, startled from the sudden action but also at how close we suddenly became. If it was even possible, I could hear her heartbeat and feel the warmth radiate off her skin. Her lips parted involuntarily with a small gasp. Every atom in my body set alight and I resisted the craving festering within, my body needing to kiss her but my mind needing to understand her. I caught her glance at my lips before looking back at me. Something pulsated through me, knowing that she wanted me as much as I wanted her. She was like the epitome of seduction, a form of sensuality that devastated me. I wanted to breathe her in, follow after her, do anything she wanted because she was a drug in my system that I couldn't survive. Toxic and irresistible, I just needed one taste. But I defied the need vibrating in my body.

I defied her.

"Why are you back, Aria?" I spoke, hoarsely, my throat tight with desire.

At first, she gave no reply, indifferent to the pull between us. Then, her hand darted out and she lightly brushed my cheek. A small pulse of heat tingled where she touched me, and I shuddered. Her hand moved away, and we both looked down, noticing the eyelash that she had just brushed off.

"You ask too many questions," she exhaled deeply. "Why don't you give up?"

"I can't. Not with you. You left without a word and returned without notice. I'm allowed to ask questions. I deserve at least that much," I delicately tucked a loose strand of hair behind her ear. "Especially if it's you."

"You need to learn that some answers won't be given to you when you want them. You might be the Don but to me that means nothing," Aria answered, curtly. Hesitantly, she stroked the side of my face before pressing her lips against my cheek. Everything set aflame within me. Brushing her hand off me, I watched it fall slack to her side.

"I hate you," I spoke a heartbeat later. "For everything you've done."

She studied me, aloofly. "They all do. But, believe me, the feeling is mutual." My jaw tensed. "I'll see you around, Nero."

For a spilt second, I was sure I felt her linger, but that second was gone before I could blink and so was she. No longer in my grasp, no longer in my sight. Like a shooting star, her stay was fleeting, and I was left with my thoughts. But not for long as deliberately slow claps broke my daze.

"Well, that was interesting," Matteo commented, snickering.

I ignored him. "I want to know where she's staying."

"We've already done that, mate," he chuckled.

"No, Matteo," I turned to him. "Where she *lives*. That penthouse was not her home."

I glanced towards the direction she had left, an icy and enigmatic presence left in her wake.

"I want to know what she's up to."

CHAPTER 9

the fire in me

He screamed and it was like music to my ears.

His eyes were large, watching the blood trickle down his leg. His skin paled as I twisted the knife that was impaled into his thigh. Nero had already done a good job at tearing Konstantin apart, but I was the expert at making them fear every breathing second.

"Konstantin, you're not that valuable to me," I crooned. "I could just kill you now, but you have something I need. Information."

Tears streamed down his face, wetting his bruised cheeks. Bloody and battered, cuts and wounds patterned his frame. He was honestly a sight to see. If only he gave in.

What a pity.

"This is only the beginning, and I promise, if you don't help, the pain will be never ending," I smiled, malevolently. "So, how about helping a girl out? There's only so much pain you can take."

Konstantin was a stubborn man, and I had to hand it to him as he threw me a sneer, even after the pain that must have been searing through his body. But pride can only take you so far and unfortunately, I didn't have much time. I wrenched my dagger out, earning a sharp cry of pain from him.

"Idiot," Discarding the knife onto the table beside me, I shrugged at Konstantin. "Well, if you aren't going to answer to me…"

He watched through teary eyes as I moved to the metal door of his cell. It opened with a groan, revealing Calix, who passed me some wipes to clean the blood stains on my hands. Simultaneously, someone else sauntered into the room, flinging their dagger from hand to hand, effortlessly. Someone whose expression was deadlier than mine, angrier than mine, bloodthirsty and vengeful. Flaxen hair tied into a ponytail, dressed in black from head to toe, and the bluest eyes I had ever seen, belonged to Kira, and she stared at the man opposite her with a malicious smirk. Their features were not similar, but one could say that they shared the same dark smile. By no surprise, I saw the way his frightful eyes, stunned with disbelief, absorbed in the woman in front of him. It had been seven years since he last saw her.

"Kira?" he spoke her name, heavy with grief. "Little bird?"

Yakira stilled, her smirk falling and her eyes dropping several degrees Fahrenheit. She needed this more than I did, so I left her to do what she did best.

Her callous words iced the entire prison sector, "Hi, Daddy."

And as soon as the metallic door slammed shut, a ferocious scream rattled in the air, belonging to the man that had betrayed Kira's heart.

*

The aroma of risotto greeted me as soon as I entered my penthouse, light spilling into the hallway from the living room. I stepped out of my heels, dropping my bag onto the cabinet, and set off to inspect my intruder. The risotto was a dead giveaway of who it could be, but I was still startled by Nero's appearance as he chopped up peppers and spring onions, dumping them into a bowl and pouring olive oil on top. The sound of sizzles and satisfying crunches made my stomach growl loudly, and Nero looked up.

I tossed my coat onto the couch. "What are you doing here?"

"Making dinner. How was your day?" he asked, as if it was completely normal for him to be in my home, unannounced.

So, I played along.

"Exhausting. You know how paperwork can be," I leaned over the counter, studying him in fascination.

He looked incredibly dashing with his sleeves rolled up past his elbows, his arms tensing in a way that had my body shiver with delight. He moved with precision, and I knew his father must have taught him how to cook – his mother never really liked cooking. I could see every flex and ripple of his muscles because that shirt *did not* hide his frame. His hair looked damp as if he had just taken a shower, so it was also shaggy, brushing against his azure eyes. I noted that he had his beard trimmed, not too much but enough that he looked ruggedly gorgeous. My heart skipped a beat and I cursed it for being so weak.

I glanced away when he looked up, and questioned, "How about you?"

"Paperwork and training," his response as vague as mine. Turning back to the stove, there was pure concentration stamped onto his face as he sampled the dish.

I pursed my lips. "Sounds like fun."

He peeked over his shoulders and lifted a brow. "You don't seem to have had that much of a better day than me."

I hesitated at first, before saying, "Actually, it got interesting near the end."

"Oh?" Nero didn't look back, stirring the pot. "How comes?"

"I got to torture Konstantin. A stress reliever, one could say," I smirked to myself, remembering the marvelous sight of his blood splattered across the concrete cell.

Nero stopped. And then looked at me. "Really?"

"Yes," I shrugged. "He wasn't giving in, so his daughter took my place. She did an excellent job at making him crack."

"His daughter tortured him?" Curiosity laced in his questioned, as he moved around the kitchen like it was his own.

"Sorry, step-daughter," I corrected, grabbing the plates and cutlery out from the cupboards.

"Why would she do that?"

"Why wouldn't she?"

Nero gave me a bewildered look. "Because she's his daughter."

"Not after what he's done."

I began to set the table, seating us closer together than at opposite ends, unlike before. Briefly, I realized how domestic this all felt but quickly shrugged the feeling off. He was silent and I knew he was lost in his thoughts; I could practically hear his thoughts churning all over the place, as his eyes burnt into my back.

"Why would anyone forgive a man like Konstantin? Don't you agree?" I glimpsed up and found him standing in the same position I had left him. "Why are you punishing Konstantin? I heard he betrayed you… But why do I feel like that's not the full story?"

Nero's gaze cooled. "He tried to hurt the one I love."

My heart stammered at how he said *'one'* and not *'ones,'* and I couldn't help but wonder if he meant me.

Stupid girl. There I go again, falling for his charm.

I knew he had plenty of lady friends; he was most likely talking about one of them. Years had gone by between us, and I was sure those feelings that sizzled in the background of our friendship had been doused by the layers of hurt and anger.

"Why are you helping her?" Nero pressed, grabbing the dish and bringing it over. I came to a halt, caught off guard before peeking at him when I felt him stand beside me. He was like a human furnace, warmth radiating off his frame as he placed the bowl onto the table. "What made you want to help her?"

I didn't know how to answer him. I wasn't sure how much I could tell him. A large part of me wanted to tell him everything, but the risks were too high and as we had nearly reached our goal, I couldn't have him stop me. I knew he would. No matter how much he hated me, Nero still cared for my safety. It was why he came over tonight. It was why he was asking these questions. But, all he wanted to do was protect me when all I wanted to do was protect others. I was capable of looking after myself and it still irritated me knowing that Nero didn't fully believe that. I understood his protective nature, but I had my limits, and I knew if he found out what I planned on doing, he would do everything to stop me.

So, I opted for, "She's my closest friend. I'd do anything for her."

Nero sat down, mutely, as I settled onto the seat beside him, plating us up the food he made. So close and yet so far apart. I wanted to know what he was thinking. I wanted to know his thoughts. The room was tense for a long moment, and it felt as if hours had gone by.

Pushing some risotto from the plate onto my fork, I decided to speak up first, "You should meet her one day. Properly."

"Properly?" he frowned.

I laughed. "Nero, you must have met her about twenty times. Someone had to ensure my security whilst I was away and she had to keep an eye on key people. I'm honestly surprised you didn't recognize her, considering how often you met."

His lips pressed together as I ate my food and, from the corner of my eye, I knew he was staring at me. Heat began to crawl up my neck and I tried to ignore his intense gaze, resisting the need to look up. But eventually, my curiosity got the best of me and I peered up under my lashes. Out of everything about him, his eyes were what stood out the most. They were a piercing blue, much darker than Kira's, resembling the ocean in Maldives.

"How did you meet her?" he said, softly.

"We met in London," I replied, my first honest answer of the evening.

I stopped eating momentarily, memories flashing back to that particular day when I met Kira. I could still remember it like it was yesterday; it haunted me, yet it was the reason I was here doing what I was today. It had been five years since we met; five years since she changed my life. I never regretted meeting her or leaving the mafia afterwards. She opened my eyes to the true dark side of the Underground, and I would always be grateful for that. She was the beginning, and the Serpents were the end.

"I'll tell you one thing," I began, solemnly. He listened. I had his attention. "She is the reason for everything I am doing."

*

5 years ago, September.

The cold nipped my fingers when I finally left the hotel in London, getting ready to have dinner with a bunch of men my father refused to meet. They were important to the mafia, so I had to take his place. Unfortunately, misogyny was a thing, and I had no doubt my irritation would eventually show at some point this evening. Waiting for my car, I hugged my fur coat tightly to shield myself from the chilly air when I noticed a girl stumbling down the road, her cheeks stained with tears, wearing far less clothes than me. She met my gaze and instantly looked away when she realized I was watching. Immediately, I frowned and knew something was not quite right. The girl was quick, but I was quicker, stopping her in her tracks.

"Are you okay?" I asked, noticing a flinch and the way she looked at me, restlessly.

"Yes," was her response, almost instantly.

I frowned, unsure whether to believe her, but the sound of my car arriving had me nod my head and slowly walk away. I kept glancing back but the girl didn't move from her place. She looked shaken up, as though she had seen a murder. My instincts were telling me to stay, to go back to her. The driver opened the door but before I disappeared inside, I stole one last look. A man stood in front of her, his arms wrapping around her. In the dark, it was hard to tell what was going on, but it seemed like she was fine, so I shoved the apprehension away and got into the car. When I finally arrived back at the hotel, it was three in the morning and the moon was beginning to hide from the sky. My heels were in my hands, my feet exhausted along with my throat after having argued with several men, who seemed to think that I was just a pretty face that would agree with whatever they said. Knowing I wasn't far from my bedroom had my eyes feel heavy and a dreamy smile crawl across my face. However, my journey halted when I heard a sound that would have had someone think they were hearing things. But I was trained well enough to recognize a scream. Following the direction of the sound, I drew out the dagger tucked away in my purse and zeroed in on the room at the far end of the hallway, secluded from anyone else. The screams became louder with every step and soon, I could hear sobs. I was afraid to see what was on the other side of the door, but I ignored the feeling and reached for the knob.

Tentatively, I entered the room and what I saw horrified me, breaking my already damaged heart into a thousands more pieces. The girl I had seen earlier was bound to the wall, restraints on her ankles and wrists. She was stripped naked, her cheeks bruised and wet with tears, her body decorated in scars, blood pooling around her feet. There were two men in the room, I noticed when slipping into the shadows silently. One man inhaled his cigar, before releasing the puff of smoke into her face. Her vision was clouded, so she did not see him brand the butt of his cigar into the side of her body. A scream ripped through her throat and the men laughed, whilst she tried to curl into a ball, hoping to protect herself. Anger raged within me, but I had to stop myself from acting impulsively or the girl could suffer for my mistakes. I pressed my body against the wall, the lack of light leaving no shadows, which worked to my advantage. There was a spotlight on the girl as if she was on some sort of display. With the men having their backs to me, they would not see me coming.

"Fresh meat?" the other man asked, chuckling.

He slipped his fingers between her legs, and she trembled in response, trying to shrivel against his intrusion.

"Fresh but not new. I received her a couple weeks ago. Her daddy got bored of her body and used her to pay off his debts."

Her eyes pleaded with the man to stop his assault, but he ignored her, acting in a way which made me think he wanted to rip out her soul. *I* wanted to rip out *his* throat. My hands itched for blood. My knife was heavy in my hands, waiting for its moment.

"What did his wife say?" the man spread her legs further apart whilst she begged him to stop, but her restraints stopped her and, in the end, there was only pain.

"Nothing. That bitch was dead the minute she stopped him fucking this whore. But Romanov is a lucky fella, you know. His wife and stepdaughter are pretty little sluts and they sure are good fucks. We can gift her to the boss. Boss likes his whores when they cry."

His words were vile and I nearly vomited, but I suppressed the urge and began to unload their guns that they stupidly left unguarded. Tossing the bullets quietly onto the carpet, I inched closer to the men.

"Really?" the second man smirked, noticing her struggling had finally stopped. "I look forward to trying her out. Perhaps get her hooked on some shit and get a couple of other guys to fuck her at the same time. Prepare her for the boss."

He grabbed her chin, forcing her to look at him, but her eyes looked lifeless. I tightened my grip on the handle of my knife, slowly steadying my breathing.

"What do you think, bitch? How does that sound? Do you want that?" When she gave no reply, he slapped her, tears spilling from the sudden pain. "Answer me, whore!"

She gave no reply.

Fury took over and he began to unbuckle his trousers. "Fine, I'll treat you the way a slut should be treated."

Unable to stand this for a second longer, I threw my dagger and watched it slice through the air, piercing the man's skull with little hassle. The girl's eyes widened as he dropped to his knees before crumpling onto the floor, blood spilling from behind.

"What the fuck?" the first man bellowed, spinning around but not quite quickly enough.

I moved swiftly and thrusted my second knife into his stomach. His cigar rolled out of his hand, hunching over in pain, staring up at me when I revealed myself from the shadows. The man pressed down on the open wound, but blood trickled between his fingers, a color so dark that it reminded me of my lipstick.

"I wonder if your boss also likes his men dead," I smiled, pulling the knife out of him and spearing his throat.

He gurgled as I shoved the knife deeper until I saw the top of the blade on the other side of his throat. The silver tip glinted under the light, red liquid pouring out of him as he collapsed onto the floor. But I wasn't done with him. Rage made me lose all sense of control. I continued my art by mutilating his body like there was no tomorrow and, by the time I was done, he looked so maimed that it was hard to tell he was human.

In all honesty, he was *never* human at all.

I sighed happily, grinning, before glancing up when I remembered that the girl had witnessed a horrific scene. She shook with fear and the anger melted away as I inched closer, slowly dropping my weapon, holding my hands up to show that I didn't want to hurt her.

"I'm not going to hurt you," I whispered, retrieving the keys from the dead man that I dismembered. "I'm here to save you."

The girl stopped fighting, studying me with extreme caution. She was mute whilst I unchained her, her body limp after the ruthless assault she had just faced. I was afraid she would fight against me but as soon as she was free, the exhaustion caught up, and she fell straight into my arms.

*

I was drinking coffee when she woke up. After being passed out for a full three days, she eventually awoke with alarm, stumbling into the adjoining room of my bedroom in the hotel. I was worried that her health had been severely compromised but after having a doctor check up on her, she assured me that the girl would be okay. However, it would be only after an extensive period of recovery, if not months, perhaps years. It didn't matter – as long as she was *going* to be okay. The girl finally exposed her scared face, her eyes feverishly taking in her surroundings, whilst I was skimming over some paperwork Melissa had e-mailed over while I was abroad.

I noticed her before she noticed me.

But when she did notice me, I could sense her backing away.

"Don't be scared," I said, breaking the silence thrumming in the lounge. As expected, she didn't reply, but she didn't move. "Come, sit."

There was no response, so I halted my actions and peered up. Her body stilled when our eyes met. In daylight, her sharp blue eyes were as pale as ice and brought startling attention to her flaxen hair. Though, I doubted blonde was her natural hair color as I could see her dark roots starting to appear from the lack of maintenance. Her cheeks were high, her jaw was sharp, and her nose was straight and hooked. Compared to me, the girl was too thin for my liking, and the loose t-shirt that she wore practically engulfed her.

"What's your name?"

"Why am I here?" she responded instead.

It surprised me, and her. A smile threatened to appear.

"I saved you. You're safe. Those men and any other men who were there are dead. Tortured. Ruined," I answered truthfully, letting the words linger in her mind. "Can you answer my question?"

Quiet. Hesitant. And then, "Yakira. My name is Yakira Adachi."

Studying her carefully, I finally broke into a smile. "Ariadne Moretti. It's nice to meet you, Yakira. Please, take a seat."

She was cautious before settling into the chair opposite me, her body sinking against the patent leather. I watched her, picking up on her small habits such as flinching at any sign of movement. She refused to meet my gaze, nervously, shifting in her seat.

"Why am I here?"

"Do you want to go back to those men, Yakira?"

She became silent and I knew she was thinking of her next reply, so I returned my focus back onto my work, scribbling my signature across treaties that I didn't wholly agree with, for men that I hated, tremendously.

"Why did you save me?" she asked, minutes later. "You don't even know me."

My eyes scanned a contract as I replied, "Is it that hard to believe that there are good people in the world?"

"Yes," her answer was without hesitation, so sure and certain of herself. It caused me to look up. Her demons would always be lurking in the background, but I saw the fire burning in her eyes and I knew she could overcome them instead of letting them take her down.

"What do you want from me?"

"Nothing," I sighed. "I'm here to help you."

"How? Everything I thought I had is gone. My entire life and freedom was stripped away from me the minute he –" she stopped mid-way, tears brimming her eyes as she sank back into the couch. "The minute he touched me."

I didn't know what to say at first; I didn't know how to make it better. She was an innocent girl, who was brought into the darkest of worlds, and who had suffered such unpleasant and horrendous things that the darkness became her reality, as well as her nightmare. She would spend the rest of her life looking over her shoulders in fear because of it. It ruined me. I glanced at the contracts on the table. There were two.

I inhaled, slowly, carefully. "Only you will be able to fight the demons that will haunt you, Yakira. But with my help, I promise to make the fight easier."

Yakira drew her brows together as I slid the two contracts in front of her. Her eyes studied them with curiosity, leaning closer to read it but then she stopped, and looked up.

"You can either take my money, a sum of five million dollars, and rebuild a new life, with a new identity, live away from the Underground and I will ensure your security for the rest of your life, as long as you promise never to look back on your past life," I began, tapping the first contract.

Yakira's jaw dropped. "Five-five million?"

I moved onto the next contract, continuing, "Or, you can help me."

Yakira's expression morphed into something that bordered between bewilderment and shock. "Wh-what?"

I leaned back into the couch, crossing one leg over the over, amused by her reaction. "Help me stop this from ever happening again."

Yakira looked like she was about to protest but I quickly cut her off, "I never understood what I was doing. I inherited a group of warriors, a family, and I don't even know if that's what is meant for me. People tell me it's what I was destined for, but it felt wrong every time I stepped into my office. I've been here for a couple of weeks, telling myself it was for business, but I knew what it truly was. *Space*. I needed space from the Estate, from my family, from…"

Swallowing the rest of my words, I looked away, running my hand through my hair. From my hotel room, you could see the Tower Bridge; it was quite a beautiful sight. It looked peaceful. I hadn't felt at peace for a very long time. Trapped in my paranoia and betrayed by the person I loved the most, I couldn't remember what peace felt like. Even after all these months. Yet I couldn't rest my heavy heart. I exhaled, unsteadily, miserably. A butterfly fluttered by the window, interrupting my thoughts. It was too cold for it to have survived this long. Something about that thought nestled a patch of warmth over my brittle heart.

"It wasn't until that night, that's when I realized that the Underground was a sickening place with disgusting creatures and innocent people being abused. I want to make it stop. The man with the cigar —"

"Tio," she whispered.

I nodded, slowly. "Yes. Tio. He mentioned something about a boss. So, I dug deeper into that information, and with some help from a few connections, I found out about the Serpents."

Standing up, I headed to the small kitchen and began to brew up some coffee for her. I could feel Yakira's gaze, following me as I moved around, dropping sugar cubes into the mug, pouring the water, stirring the ground coffee beans.

"The Serpents?" Yakira repeated, but it sounded more like a question than a statement.

I poured the milk and said, "They are an organization like a mob that steals innocent young girls, women, men and abuses them and removes their freedom. All for money and power. That's when it hit me. As females we will never be safe; men will always view us as the inferior sex and, despite all the inheritance or labels, they will never bow down to us. Because to them we are prey. That ends today."

I could hear the rage in my voice despite my attempt to control it, but I was angry and I wanted a lot of people to suffer for their crimes. Yakira inspected at me as I passed her the coffee, before taking my seat again.

"You want to take them down?" she concluded.

I could hear the worry in her voice like she didn't quite believe it would be possible. But I was capable of anything and everything, and I would spend the rest of my breathing life fighting the Serpents. You would have to be an idiot, or damn right evil to overlook their crimes. And I was neither. My lips twisted into an arrogant smile.

"I want *us* to take them down," I corrected.

"There's two of us. We can't do it by ourselves."

"And we won't have to, Yakira," I assured. "We will build a team. Our own family. Assassins. And together we will bring them down."

She looked as if she couldn't quite believe me, but at the same time like she wanted to put her full faith in me. I couldn't blame her. I had no doubt that for the most of her life she was lied to and betrayed. I could see the hundreds of thoughts running through her mind, her aquamarine eyes filled with anxiety but razed with a fiery determination. For a second, I wondered who she would have been had she not been brought into this world. I pushed the pen towards her, waiting to see what the outcome would be, what the next chapter of our lives would be.

"It's *your* choice, Yakira," I whispered, and she looked up. "Do you want to live a new, *safer* life, or do want to help me save others from this *dangerous* life?"

She held my gaze for a good minute, and I allowed her to see everything. All the truths, all the anger, all the fears. In that moment, something shifted between us. I noticed her blue eyes looked translucent when reflected by the sun streaming through the windows. I guess I had always known what her choice would be. I knew it the second I saw her. The courage and terror danced in the depth of her irises as she glimpsed back at the contracts once more, before shakily lifting up the pen.

And with a deep and sharp inhale, she sealed her fate.

CHAPTER 10

familia

"Come on, darling," Mom pouted. "It's just one lunch. What harm can that do?"

"Quite a bit, mother," I responded. "I don't think you understand how important it is that I stay under the radar, and if there is any sort of news linking me back to the Moretti family it could ruin my entire plan."

She narrowed her eyes. "You and I both know you can come without anyone finding out. Plus, your father misses you, and so do your brothers. Have you not given it one thought of the effect your disappearance had on all of us?"

My mother was a master at guilt-tripping people; it was the reason my father gave in to her so often. Regardless, I knew she spoke the truth and I instantly felt bad. Sometimes, I would go weeks, if not months, not calling my parents to ensure that no one could track me down, and I guess I had forgotten that I was also a daughter to someone. It wasn't on purpose; I just couldn't take the risk. My mother looked solemn, and my heart fractured as I sank into the leather couch.

"I didn't mean to hurt you," I whispered.

"I know, my dear. I know you didn't. But I think this disappearing act can no longer be played with your family… we deserve that, at least."

Weighing her words, I sighed as I ran my fingers through my hair, glancing out of the windows of my penthouse. It was a sunny day, with clear skies and there was little sign of it changing anytime soon, despite it being February. Mom had arrived during the early morning to convince me to attend our family dinner and, as much as I knew I shouldn't go, I gave in to her request with a slow nod. Her entire face lit up as she beamed brightly at me, jumping onto her feet, clapping her hands together in excitement.

"How great! I can't wait to tell your dad that you agreed."

I frowned. "Wait, what?"

Noticing that she messed up, her eyes widened, and her lips pressed together. My face paled as I watched her avoid eye contact with me, brushing off the specks of dust on her dress when she stood up.

"Mom?" I pressed on.

Smiling sheepishly, she answered, "Your father may or may not have known about your arrival in New York since a few weeks ago… maybe from the day you arrived."

My jaw dropped as my mother laughed nervously. I wasn't even surprised that he knew – of course, he would know. My dad knew *everything*. I was just surprised he hadn't reached out but at the same time, I was thankful that he didn't. Because he understood that he couldn't. Yet, I felt guiltier than I did a few minutes ago. My dad would risk everything for me, and I left him in the dark.

"Anyways," my mother's voice broke me from my thoughts. "It's tomorrow. Three o'clock sharp. Don't be late, Aria."

"But –"

She ignored me, grabbing her purse and sauntering down the hallway, with a little bounce in her step that told me she succeeded in her mission – as always. "Oh, and make sure to dress up nicely. The Russos will be joining us as well."

"Excuse me?" I jumped up from the couch, getting ready to refuse going but my mother was a sly woman and, with a smirk on her lips, she peered over her shoulders.

"I'll see you there, darling."

She left before I could say another word, the door slamming resonating with my heart dropping as I collapsed onto the couch with a loud groan of frustration.

*

I didn't normally dress in pink. I often avoided such a color but today was different. The tube skirt was the palest shade of pink and stopped just below my ankles, and I matched it with a white blouse. Donning some gold accessories to complete the look, I settled for a soft glow instead of my usual blood red lips. Having told Kira about my plans today, she agreed to continue preparing for our next step whilst I dealt with my family. I wasn't sure how I would be able to because the thought of seeing the Russos made my stomach sink with anxiety. Whilst my car zipped through the streets from my penthouse to the suburbs, I chanted over and over in my head to remain calm and keep my composure. The Russos were incredibly close to my family, which meant that I was incredibly important to them, so I had no doubt they would also grill me about my disappearance, especially Nero's mother.

The Russos had been the best of friends to my parents many years before I was born. I didn't want to lie but I knew I had to... I knew I was *going* to. My family lived in quite a wealthy area, miles away from the city. The neighborhood was decked out in lavish mansions with acres of land behind them. The driveway was as wide as the road itself when I pulled into it, and it looked normal enough that my parents were able to do a good job of hiding away from media scroungers. Using the rear-view mirror, I reapplied my lip gloss and fixed my hair until I felt prepared enough to enter the house. It was scary that I couldn't remember the last time I was here. After I had become the Don, I spent most of my days at the Estate and my time at home was limited. Once I left, I never returned home. My exhale was rickety and so were my feet as I walked to the front door, struggling to keep my anxiety at bay. My grip tightened on my bag, and I tried not to think too much about what would occur soon, but that was all I could think of, and it took everything in me not to run away.

I guess I hadn't changed as much as I thought I did.

"Aria!" someone yelled, and my body stilled by the entrance.

Peeking over my shoulder, I saw Nico as he strolled towards me with a bag of groceries in his hand. Now fifteen, my younger brother was taller and leaner than he used to be. His shoulders were becoming broader and it most likely was due to the training and gym, but that also meant the baby fat on his face was beginning to shape itself. My father took great pride in Nico, constantly commenting on how he looked exactly like my father when he was younger. With chestnut hair and dark eyes, I could see the similarities now more than ever before.

"Finally," he said. "You came. I've been waiting, you know. Ever since you landed."

Who didn't know I was in New York?

I narrowed my eyes. "And how did you know?"

He smirked. "I have my sources. You aren't the only person to know people. Come on; everyone is waiting for you. Didn't Mom say three o'clock sharp?"

"You've only got more annoying, Nico. I would've thought that would have changed by now."

He laughed, opening the front door. "Dear sister, you've been gone far too long."

Before I could comment on what he said, I was drawn into a very tight hug as soon I stepped foot into the house. My breath was knocked straight out of me as I wriggled in the arms of Coco Russo.

"Aria!" she shrieked. "I missed you! I can't believe it's been so long. I'm incredibly angry with you for not staying in touch."

"Can't… breathe… please…" I choked out.

Behind her, someone chuckled and helped me out of her powerful hold, pulling her off me. Gulping in air frantically to save my lungs, I staggered back and sent my aunt a glower. I had forgotten how strong she was. She didn't blink at my glare, smiling innocently whilst her husband sent me a grin, a startling spitting image of Nero, except far older.

Claudio Russo, who bore a strong likeness to his son save for the eyes, remarked, "My sincerest apologizes, Aria."

"It's fine," I murmured, shifting uncomfortably under Coco's intense scrutiny.

"Why are you apologizing? Maybe she deserves it," Coco glared at her husband.

He rolled his eyes. "How are you, princess?"

"Much better," I replied, as honestly as I could. There was a flicker in his eyes, but he didn't say anything else. He understood me and knew there was nothing else to say on the matter. "How are you? I've missed you so much."

Coco opened her mouth, getting ready to spout something fiery, but thankfully, Claudio jumped in, covering his wife's mouth before she bit my head off. "Just great. *Cordelia* opened her own store a few months ago. You should visit one day when you're free."

At the mention of her government name, Coco huffed and crossed her arms over her chest, hearing the warning Claudio sent her. I pursed my lips to fight the smile and agreed to my uncle's request. Leading me into the living room, they began to tell me about their travels since commencing their retirement whilst we waited for my father to make his presence known. The lounge was very homely, and I knew my mother must have spent her sweet time decorating the place until she was fully satisfied. With expensive art hanging on the walls and accents of light oak and brown brightening the area, it felt alien to be standing in this room. Mom strolled into the living room with a tray of potatoes and Luca followed her tail, taking plates to the table that Nico was setting. As soon as she noticed me, she quickly hugged me, once again cutting off the oxygen supply to my lungs. These women were remarkably strong.

"Oh, sweetheart, you came," she sighed.

"Of course. You would've killed me had I not," I stated, sarcastically. My mother didn't appreciate the tone, smacking my arm lightly whilst Coco snickered.

"Hey Ari," Luca grinned, roguishly.

Luca was only two years younger than Nico, but his features were strikingly similar to our mother. His hair was lighter, curlier and longer, covering his hazel eyes. He was still a child, and yet he never looked older. Something pricked my heart at the thought of not seeing my youngest brother grow up – he was only eight when I had left.

"Luca, are you following Nico's footsteps? Because that's not a good idea," I teased.

Nico's eyes thinned. "I'd have you know that I'm an amazing role model. Can't say the same for you."

Although that slightly hurt, I let him have it. I couldn't say he was wrong. Instead, I rose my brow. "Touché, little brother."

Nico seemed surprised as if expecting me to retaliate, but when I did no such thing he frowned and looked away. Coco gestured me to sit beside her on the sofa, grinning as she took my hand.

"Tell me, where have you been?" she questioned.

"I travelled everywhere. I met so many amazing people and learnt about their stories; it was such an eye-opening experience," I gushed. "I looked after myself too, so don't worry."

She smiled, sadly. "You've just grown so much. I'm sad I couldn't experience watching you turn into such a gorgeous woman."

My throat tightened and words failed me. Fortunately, my father strode into the room and everyone's attention gravitated to him. With a stiff back and a crease in his forehead as he scanned the room, his dark eyes finally settled onto me.

There he was. Antonio Moretti.

"Aria," he whispered, and I jumped onto my feet. "My beautiful daughter."

I broke into a grin as he embraced me, tenderly brushing my hair, and I curled into the security of his arms, knowing that this was the safest place I could ever be.

"I missed you, Dad," I mumbled.

He chuckled. "Not enough. You should've come here as soon as you arrived."

"I had my reasons for why I didn't."

"I know," he replied, glancing down at me with the softest of gazes and the most loving smile ever, that one would not have thought that he used to be the Don of the Italians. "That's why I didn't force you to. I heard you've been doing amazing things, and perhaps completely changing people's lives in the process."

I nodded, my tense heart suddenly blossoming with warmth when I saw the approval in my father's eyes. "I have. It's been a journey but I'm glad I decided to go down this road. I… I am sorry that I left without a word."

My father looked at me for a long minute and it was hard to tell what he was thinking. But then he pressed his lips against the crown of my head, and murmured, "I'm not. I knew it wasn't your calling. I knew you weren't happy then. But you are now, and that's all that matters to me, *principessa*."

*

Maybe I did miss my family. My stomach hurt so much as I bent over, laughing as I listened to Coco and Mom argue about who was the best during their 'prime times.' My mother and Coco had been friends since they were teenagers and began to learn the skills of becoming assassins together. It was something I knew my grandfather did not like about my mother, but it was something my mother loved about herself. She was exceptional, phenomenal, *deadly*. And I followed her footsteps. She was a powerful woman and at the end of the day, wasn't that what we were all trying to be? Like my mother, Coco was extremely talented in the art of killing. They used to work for a company who would send hired assassins to do the crimes others could not. And then it all went sour when their boss decided to betray the Russian mafia thus betraying my family. I knew my mother sometimes thought about those days, but it was her job that led her to my father, so I guess it did work out in the end.

Coco pouted whilst my mother sat in her seat with a triumphant smile, sipping her wine, when she saw that her best friend gave in to the argument. My smile broadened when my father rolled his eyes, shaking his head, whilst Claudio comforted his other half despite the smile threatening to escape. Just like my mother and Coco, my father and Claudio had also been best friends since they were children. In fact, Claudio used to be my father's second before they both stepped down. I often found myself musing over how everything worked out so brilliantly between the four of them, how easily they found their match, and then my mind would wander to a certain man and my mood would immediately sour. Shaking away that feeling, I glanced around the table, realizing how normal it felt to be sitting here with them, eating lunch, acting as if we all weren't part of the Underground and all the beautifully dark parts of it. I knew my family tried to keep themselves away from the darkest chasms of the Underground but sometimes, with business, this was not an easy thing to do.

The Underground was a fancy term to describe all the businesses that occurred underneath the noses of the world leaders, but often (if not, all the time) those leaders were usually the main source of the corruption Underground. It had been operating for as long as I had been alive and even longer still. Legal and illegal activities were hidden by exorbitant balls and auctions, where men and women would battle to be the most influential person in the community – if you could even call it that. My family had been involved in the Underground for decades now, running the Italian mafia and expanding their influence across the globe. For many years, the Italians had bad blood with the Russians, but that all changed when my mother met my father. Women in the Russian mob were feared throughout the Underground, but at the same time, they were desired by many because they were extremely talented and resourceful in their pursuits. When my mother was sent to basically murder my father, things did not quite turn out that way and they ended up falling in love – my father claimed it was his charms that caused my mother to fall for him, but I always knew it was my father who fell first. After their relationship was brought to the attention of the Underground, the Italians and Russians joined hands in partnership, and now, more than ever, they were the strongest influence in the Underground.

But having so much power meant there was a target on our backs. *Constantly.* My aunt, Gabrielle, had suffered frequent attacks prior to her accession to the Russian mafia, and even when she finally became the Pakhan, she struggled to maintain the power. As a woman, she was belittled and undermined but, like my mother, she was strong willed and determined to stake her position in the Underground. And she did a hell of a good job. Now, Gabrielle was one, if not *the* most important person in the Underground. Sometimes, it was useful to have a woman like that as your family. It reminded me of my duty, and the respect I had for my family. Normality wasn't just a gift for us – it was a miracle. It was something only a few could be blessed with. And right now, sitting with my family, I had never felt more grateful for it. I didn't have the feeling of needing to look over my shoulder every second because being here… I was safe.

"Why do you have to argue all the time?" Nico grumbled, like the moany teenager he was.

Coco glared. "Okay mister –"

"Anyway," Claudio interrupted his wife, with a smile in my direction. *Great.* "Aria, tell us everything you've been up to."

I could say I was caught off guard but that wasn't true. I knew it was coming and as I quickly tried to think of something to say, a look from my father told me not to lie to them. To my family. So, I sighed but just as I opened my mouth, the doorbell rang and my heart started racing again. My mother rushed to see who was at the door, whilst the rest of us waited, the focus shifting away from me. I could hear her laugh to whomever came before she returned with our latest guest. Once again, my cold heart stilled at the sight of Nero. And *Jesus*, he looked amazing. I would be a liar if I said that Nero Russo wasn't the most gorgeous man I had ever met, and I had met plenty of men. He adorned a simple turtleneck and chinos, and a silver chain hanging around his neck. There was something so impishly handsome about him, and yet, breathlessly provocative. Our eyes met briefly and whatever ounce of happiness was ringing throughout my body was suddenly brought to a standstill. A glimmer of shock sparked in his blue orbs before he looked away, smiling as he greeted everyone.

"You're very late," Coco complained, as he pecked her cheek.

"Sorry. I got caught up at the Estate," he answered, his voice scratchy and low, doing all kinds of things to me – I was worried that I would *not* get through this afternoon.

"Is everything alright?" my father questioned, drinking his whiskey despite my mother complaining otherwise.

Nero's expression became profoundly serious in front of my father, nodding short and sternly. "Just paperwork."

It became very tense as Nero settled into an empty seat. The empty seat, unfortunately, being beside me. I couldn't think as I drank my wine, parched, whilst Nero plated himself up. Of course, it would be tense; the role he had used to belong to me, and no one knew why I left it.

"Aria," Claudio broke the silence, slicing his chicken. "You were telling us about your trips."

"Right," I said, through a clenched smile. "Like I said, I went everywhere."

"Where were your favorite places?"

Nero's hand brushed over mine when he reached for the salt. I inhaled sharply under my breath, unnoticeably. "Tokyo."

Mom looked surprised, arching her brow. "How comes?"

"One of my closest friends used to live there when she was a little girl. You'd love her, Mom."

"Now I'm curious. You should invite her for dinner one day."

"Of course."

"Any place else?" Coco wondered.

"Why didn't you get us souvenirs?" Luca muttered, stabbing his chicken in annoyance.

I ignored him, answering Coco's question, "I visited Italy. Quite a few times."

I saw everyone peer in my direction, including Nero. Even my father stopped eating, his eyes shifting upwards as he drew his brows together in interest.

"Italy?" Mom frowned.

"Nothing interesting," I said, pretending to be interested in the meal on my plate. "Just visited a few people."

Dad looked dissatisfied with my answer, slowing drinking his whiskey. "Like whom?"

I glimpsed over at my dad, his brown eyes holding me hostage as if I was under interrogation – which I most definitely was.

"Like I said, no one of interest," I responded, refusing to give in to his intimidation.

He opened his mouth to say something, which he would have had my mother not touched his arm subtly whilst observing me carefully, a calculated smile that I knew all too well, creeping across her coral lips.

"I hope you enjoyed the scenery. It's quite beautiful," she commented, my dad sulking beside her.

"The sunsets were ethereal. Almost made me stay."

"I'm glad you came home," Claudio spoke, softly, as everyone returned back to eating. Nero still hadn't spoken one word, eating his meal with intense concentration. I began to cut my chicken when Claudio then said, "It's been too long, sweetheart. My last memory of you was when you and Nero were caught messing about in Antonio's office. Man, I've never seen him so pissed before."

Everything stopped. Or maybe it was just me. I knew I stopped. I halted my actions. I froze whilst everyone continued to move. Coco hummed, wistfully, and I could almost see Nero stiffen beside me. His jaw clenched and then unclenched, as he gripped the fork tightly. I couldn't breathe.

Suddenly, I felt claustrophobic.

Suddenly, I remembered why I left.

Suddenly, I wanted to leave again.

"You two were quite the pair," Coco mused. I held my breath as I waited for her next words, but I already knew what she was going to say. "I always thought you'd end up together."

My stomach churned. I couldn't breathe. I couldn't move. And then, I abruptly placed my cutlery down, feeling everyone's eyes move onto me. "Well, we didn't."

Coco frowned. "Aria –"

"– Please, excuse me," I murmured, leaving the table with a heavy heart and frustration lingering deep within, as I felt a particular set of eyes burning into my retreating back.

*

I silently washed the dishes as my mother cleared the kitchen whilst everyone remained in the lounge. My mind was all over the place; my thoughts didn't seem coherent, and it was difficult to figure out why. I hated the assumption of ending up with Nero. I hated it more than before. Because, before, I was a fool. I was totally and indescribably in love with him. I thought he was my future and my other half.

But I guess betrayal was common. Even with best friends.

"Nero, you know you are better suited to be the leader —"

"— Aria," I jolted out of my melancholy thoughts at the sound of my mother's voice. She placed a hand on my shoulder. I didn't look back. "I don't know what happened or why you left, or why you can't even look at Nero, but I want you to know that I'm here for you. Always, sweetheart. I'm proud of who you've become. Regardless of what happened."

I swallowed like there was something lodged in my throat, and blinked back the tears, moving away to dry my hands. I heard my mother sigh. I couldn't — no — I *wouldn't* say anything about what happened. If they knew, it would ruin everything… it would ruin Coco and Claudio. They could never know. There was a knock on the door before it opened, but I already knew who arrived. I recognized the voice as my father greeted them, and the sound of their footsteps was familiar to me as they neared the kitchen. Finally, their green eyes landed on me.

"Aria," he noted the fragile state I was in, but didn't comment any further.

I forced the smile. "Thanks for coming, Calix."

"Who's this?" Mom asked in confusion, as I grabbed my bag.

"Calix, meet my mother, Xena Moretti, and my father, who you just met, Antonio Moretti."

Calix plastered on his charming smile, capturing my mother's heart as I watched her physically swoon when he shook her hand. "A pleasure to finally meet you. I've heard such amazing stories about you."

Mom blushed. *Actually blushed.* "The pleasure is all mine."

Beside me, Dad crinkled his nose and scoffed, rolling his eyes. "I guess I need to remind your mother who she belongs to."

I choked back a laugh at my dad's possessive behavior, knowing I couldn't expect anything less. Turning to him, I pressed a kiss on his cheek and saw as he looked at me like I was the most important person in his life.

"I'll visit you soon, papa."

"I love you, Aria," he sighed, hugging me. "Stay safe. Whatever you're doing or plan on doing, just know if you need anything – *anything at all* – let me know."

Smiling at him, I eased his worries with a soft nod before speaking to Calix, "Let's go."

After Calix said his goodbyes, he waited for me to say my farewells to everyone else, leading me out the house. Nero's blue eyes tracked me before glaring at Calix, who wore a small smirk at the sight of his jealousy. So, I pinched Calix's arm, earning a small pout in return. After what felt like forever, we were finally on our way back to the Manor to prepare our next plan, but my focus was distracted. I could only see Nero.

"Was it bad?" Calix asked after a while, his voice quiet.

I sighed, watching the suburban landscape morph into the city central. "I'm not so sure anymore."

CHAPTER 11

seeing red

Nero

"What do you mean *'not found'*, Matteo?" I glared at my second as he stood in front of me, pursing his lips at my apparent frustration.

He sighed. "I don't know what else to tell you, man. I don't know at all. Viktor is nowhere to be seen, and people haven't heard from him for quite some time. Word has gotten out, and there's a lot of speculation around him being dead."

"We need to find him," I pinched the bridge of my nose. "*Soon.*"

"I have our best trackers hunting him down. I'll try and spread the news that he's safe but until there is physical evidence, no one will believe a word we say. I'm afraid, there are people thinking we might be involved in his disappearance."

"Fuck!" I bellowed, smashing a glass of whiskey against the bookshelf. It splintered into thousands of tiny pieces, liquid staining the dark carpet, bruising the oak frame. "Viktor is protected twenty-four seven. He has a guard stationed with him every second of his life. How the fuck do you lose someone like that?"

"You don't. Not unless you have someone highly skilled and intelligent enough to gain access to Viktor and ensure he is taken without leaving a trace."

I stopped.

Then I frowned.

Something Matteo had said triggered a memory shoved deep in my subconscious. A brief memory, but a memory, nevertheless. However, it occurred to me that this buried memory may have held information that was crucial to our investigation. But I had to be sure – a hundred percent sure. However, it occurred to me that this buried memory may have held information that was crucial to our investigation.

"Matteo, where did you say was the last place he was seen?"

He angled his head, drawing his brows together with a look of concentration masking his face, answering, "At his charity event. The one that happened a couple weeks back. You know, the one where you…"

He never managed to complete that sentence, eyes widening with sudden realization as everything fell into place. How Viktor was lured out. How Viktor was captured. How Viktor remained hidden. My jaw tightened and I grabbed my coat from the coach, fury raging through my bloodstream as I went to hunt down the culprit.

"You don't think –"

"I don't need to think," I replied, briskly. "I know exactly who has him."

*

She came home a little later than usual.

Her hair wasn't tied back so it fell down to her hips, brushing against her blazer dress that cinched at the waist, enhancing her lengthy, lean legs in the most artistic way possible. Like a goddess. Her suede boots reached her thighs and in the dimly lit corridor, I watched as she unzipped them, tossing them next to the shoe rack. She hummed absentmindedly, completely unaware of my presence. The redness of her lips looked tempting as the moonlight spotlighted her when she moved into the living room. Dropping her bag by the table, she switched the lights on and jumped in shock when she noticed me, sipping a glass of whiskey, on her couch. Her eyes widened, her breath hitched, and her body stilled. But a second later it morphed into her façade.

"Nero," the word left her in a breathless surprise.

The unexpected need to hear her say it again, and again, and again, was almost too hard to ignore. I wanted to hear it in the morning, in the afternoon and in the evening, when I kissed her until she lost her breath. I wanted to hear my name called from those sinful lips that told me hundreds of lies and had broken my heart into thousands of pieces. But I wasn't in the mood. At least, not entirely. I had a mission to accomplish first.

"Where is he, Aria?" I asked, downing the last drops of alcohol, suddenly very parched at the ethereal sight of her.

"I don't know who you are talking about," she answered, stepping closer to me with intense caution.

"It took me a while to figure it out, I'll admit. But, when I did, I was incredibly pissed off," I laughed in disbelief. "I mean, did it not occur to you that your fucking plan, or whatever the fuck you're doing, is disrupting my business along with many others? God, you must be fucking insane to have pulled this off. "

Her face became very stoic and unreadable, but that was enough. It gave me the truth I would never hear from her lips. "*Oh.*"

"*Oh?*" I stood up, placing the glass onto the coffee table. "That's all you have to say?"

"Nero, I don't really know what you want me to say," was her response.

I scoffed, running my hand over my face. "You don't fucking get it, Aria. You never did. Stop this fucking charade of being a hero and open your fucking eyes. Viktor is one of our supplier and the Italian's largest source of income. Trade, dealings and all that fucking shit you never liked to learn about, so I fucking did!"

My chest heaved up and down as I tried to control the anger. I wasn't sure when I closed the distance between us, but as I glared at the petite female, my rage quickly dissipated. She had that effect on people. She was calm in the face of wrath. She didn't even wince when I bellowed at her. All she did was study me, pressing her lips together.

"So, that's what this is about?" she whispered, into the tense silence. "About me leaving?"

She shook her head in disappointment. Of course, she would think it was about that. It was always about her. I was burning with fiery anger and yet... I couldn't stop the appetite blooming within me as I reveled at how beautiful she was when the moonshine touched her. She was no angel, but she had never looked so heavenly. The scent of roses emanated off her as I watched her chest rise and fall in a steady beat. I could reach out and caress her caramel skin. I wanted to trace my fingers against her body and memorize every scar and crevice. My hands ached as I held back my desire, maintaining my icy expression, but I couldn't stop the softness in my voice when I spoke.

"This is not about you, Aria. It's more than that. When word gets out that Viktor is dead, suspicions will arise amongst everyone. Who will be next? If Viktor can be murdered - a man who is more heavily guarded than the fucking president, who's to say anyone else is safe? We can't afford to have another war with a major family, Ariadne."

"It's already begun, Nero. In fact, it's been happening for years, festering underneath the betrayal and lies, covered by the drugs and weapons. It's always been there. Waiting to happen. I just made it arrive sooner."

"Your family did not build an empire for you to destroy it."

Her eyes broadened; a fester of incredulity caught in the darkness of her hazel irises. Her crimson lips parted as she faltered, taking a step back. The hurt on her face soon followed after. It broke me before I knew it. I regretted the words the second I saw her swallowing thickly and her eyes glistening when she stared at me. Tears.

Fuck.

"I'm doing this to save people, Nero. I know you don't understand that now. I get it. But I never intended on destroying my family's dynasty, nor will I," She reached out and gently placed her dainty hands above my heart, peering up at me underneath her long black lashes. "Please, put your pride to the side and try to trust me. I know I haven't given you a reason to, but just try."

My faced hardened as her touch had shivers running down my back like electricity. "Where is he?"

"I don't ˮ

"I swear to fucking God, Ariadne, if you lie to me –"

Suddenly, her eyes thinned and she pushed herself away from me, a scowl twisting on her lips. All signs of innocence and softness were now contorted into fury and frustration. There she was. My fiery Queen. Strong and stubborn. A part of me did trust her; I knew that she wasn't trying to harm anyone. Even though I hadn't seen her for so long, I knew her. She was always my Aria.

"Or what, Nero? What are you going to do?" she badgered. "Interrogate me? Lock me away? Torture me? Or better yet, kill me? What exactly are you going to fucking do?"

In that second, I saw her façade crumble.

It wasn't a lot but it wavered, and I saw her eyes glow with tears – whether it was from anger or hurt, I couldn't be sure. Her cheeks were flushed, as red as her lips. The ones I'd been dying to taste for so long. Aria was a complicated woman. I had never met anyone like her. She drove me mad and she loved it. The irony of it was that so did I.

"You aren't going to do shit," Aria snarled. "Because, Nero, no matter what you say or what you do, you will always care about me. That's what our twisted, sick relationship has come to. You will never be satisfied until you can control me, but news flash, you won't. *Ever.*"

My jaw tightened and I fisted my hands, scowling at the most stunning woman I had ever known. She rose a brow, taunting me with a smirk, triumph seething in the darkness of her glacial eyes. She knew she was pissing me off. She knew how to push my buttons until she was on a very thin line. But she was right... Aria was anything but stupid, and she was right. My words were silenced whilst I watched her burn with rage, rage that had her eyes blazing up like fire dancing in the abyss.

"So, I'll ask again, *Russo.*"

She stepped closer until her chest was pressed up against mine. I stiffened, maintaining an impassive look, refusing to be affected by the warmth of our skin touching each other. Every fiber of my body was begging to finally close the distance. Every atom was gravitating towards her. Every single fucking thing was pushing me to her.

Jesus, I hate her.

"What are you going to do?"

I should have moved back but one look at her and all inhibition slipped away.

Ah, fuck it.

"You're so frustrating, Aria," I hissed.

Her eyes widened as my arm curled around her waist, tugging her closer until she was on her toes. Her hands grasped my shoulders, steadying herself, and before she could retort something sardonic, I silenced her with a kiss, stealing her words away whilst she stole my breath.

CHAPTER 12

the aftermath

His lips moved in a hungry fashion, like a beast who had been starving, as his hands drew me closer, curling around the fabric of my dress. My mind went completely numb as I sunk into the passionate kiss between us, consumed by the scorching shock setting off within me like fireworks. All those emotions I had spent years locking away came crashing into me like a tsunami, wave after wave of feelings breaking into the barrier of the one organ I refused to let him hold. But it was undone so effortlessly. Like a knot, he pulled one string and suddenly everything unraveled. I should have moved away but instead I twisted my arms around his neck and inched into his body, wantonly. The feeling of him grasping my hair to angle our heads triggered shudders down my back. It was absolutely surreal. My fingers tingled and my heart hammered. My world unexpectedly paused as I savored his touch. He groaned against my lips, drawing out a sigh, parting them gently which only allowed him to deepen our kiss further. He was a man on a mission, and I let him do whatever he wanted. I hadn't felt anything like this in five years. Nothing could or would ever match this intoxicating feeling. Flashbacks of that night reminded me how dominant he could be, and he made sure I remembered it now. I may be resistant to his orders, but now, I fell into submission from his touches.

I heard my name when I pushed the coat off his shoulders, running my hands down his chest that flexed under my cold touch. It was like being on drugs. I was hooked. I couldn't stop, even when I knew I should. My fingers followed every ripple and flex of his back as they moved. It was just one kiss but my desire for him unraveled within me. A traitorous moan left me when he brought us to the couch. Mounted on top of him, my brown locks curtained around us, and his hands found their position on my hips. The sensation came dangerously close to seeing the moon and stars. The buzz in my body rising, as he moved his attention to my neck and then my shoulders, rocking me slowly. This was probably the stupidest thing I could have done but I didn't want it to stop. I could feel everything. The pounding of his heart against my chest, the tender movement of his fingers as they ran down my spine, the warmth of his breath when he kissed me again. It was everything and more.

I gasped, when he drew my lip between his teeth. He ignored me and continued his exploration. "*Nero…*"

I couldn't form a single sentence and that caused his lips to tug as he finally glanced up. It was like staring into blue flames.

"This is mine, Aria," he cautioned. "All mine. It's been a while so let me remind you. If another man lays his hand on you, I swear I'll show no mercy."

His promise set me off. I shouldn't have liked it as much as I did, but the vow had me swallow back a scathing remark. As he cradled my face in his hands, his frigid countenance disguising his true feelings as I moved above him, my heart thudded.

"Do you understand, Aria?"

I bit my tongue, refusing to submit.

His jaw flexed. "Words."

"You don't own me," I managed to say, but his wandering hands distracted me from speaking any further. My head tilted back when they found solace underneath my dress, my nails digging into his shoulders.

"I beg to differ," he responded, frostily.

"Oh, you'll be begging alright," I spat out, venomously, before he knocked my breath away with a kiss. Only, I needed more as he tipped me to the edge. Against his lips, I murmured, "I hate you."

"Do you, Aria?" he whispered, pulling away. I jolted, feeling his fingers curl. He smirked. "Do you really?"

"Yes," I said. My head fell onto his shoulders, biting my lip as I reached a whole other world of ecstasy. "Yes, I do."

"I hate you more," he breathed out, and I inhaled those words like it gave me life.

Opening my mouth to argue, he silenced me with a hard kiss and my body slumped into his arms. My ears were ringing with white noise, my body pulsating with euphoria and my mind felt disoriented. When he moved back, I levelled my breathing, trying to ignore him as he removed his rough hands from the torturous material covering me. My skin itched to peel it off, too hot under his gaze. I heard his lips smack together and saw his tongue dart out just I lifted my head.

His eyes twinkled. "Like I said, I beg to differ."

I exhaled, sharply. The aftermath was always the worst.

"Get the fuck out."

*

Fatigued, I returned to the Manor. I had no intention in staying at my penthouse after tonight. The mansion was quiet when I arrived; everyone was most likely asleep. Dragging my limp body into the lounge, I finally collapsed onto the sofa and ran my fingers through the knots off my hair, cursing myself for giving in to him so easily.

Stupid, stupid girl.

"Aria?" Kira's voice broke me out of my self-hating daze. She arched her brow when she entered the room, having not changed into something comfier. "Why are you back?"

"Why are you still up? It's like two in the morning," I replied, evading the question.

Thankfully, she didn't push for more and responded, "Couldn't sleep."

Settling beside me, she exhaled. Her shoulders were heavy with exhaustion and her eyes had dark circles; mascara smudged onto her lower lash line.

"I can't kill him, Aria. No matter how much I hate that man, he was still my father. I can't do it," she bowed her head. "I'm sorry for disappointing you."

My forehead creased as I drew my brows together. She thought that I would be mad, but why would I when she had overcome so much more than simply facing her stepfather? It didn't make her any less strong. Tenderly, I took her hand and squeezed it.

"You could never disappoint me, Yakira. I understand completely. I won't force you to do it. The option was yours to take because I thought this could be your closure. But sometimes closure doesn't involve killing the person who hurt you the most. Closure can always be time too."

"Can you just warn me before it happens? So, I can see him one last time?"

"No actions will be taken against him without you knowing, I promise," I replied, embracing my dearest friend. "You're so strong, Kira. Don't forget that."

I felt her body shake and I knew she was crying, but I also knew she wouldn't want me to point that out. Therefore, I kept my lips closed and comforted her. It had felt like hours until she peered up at me with swollen bloodshot eyes. Pain was a funny thing. Sometimes, like a scar, it would last for years and years until it faded, or sometimes like a wound, it would heal until there was no memory of it. Everyone suffered differently. Everyone felt pain differently. But the hardest part was the recovery. The aftermath. At first, it seemed like nothing would ever get better, that you would be stuck in the constant cycle of living but not living. Until eventually, one day, it wouldn't hurt as much and as the days would go on, the pain would turn into a pinch of the past. It was a reminder of what we lost and what we could lose. It reminded us that we were humans. I spent so much time running from my past and as I looked at Kira, I wondered whether I was only denying myself the chance to recover. How was I any better if I didn't follow the words I taught?

"What about you?" Kira murmured.

I frowned. "What do you mean?"

"I know Nero visited you. Something must've happened for you to return back to the Manor."

Shame crushed my heart as I glanced away, memories burned in my brain. "I don't want to talk about it, Kira."

"And you don't need to," Kira said, a second later. "Don't let him tear you down, Aria. Not now."

"I know," I murmured, closing my eyes to fight the tears.

"I know you loved him, Aria," Her words had my body freeze. I felt my heart in my throat. "I'm sorry that it still hurts."

"It's okay, Kira," I forced a smile across my face as I looked back at her, her concerned cerulean eyes tried to read me but no matter how skilled she was, that was the one thing she could never do. No one ever could. "It was never meant to be."

*

My phone rang three times during the morning. The first time, I ignored the call. The second time I declined the call. The third time, I finally picked up. Melissa's voice greeted me, callously.

"Oh, she actually picked up," the words were meant to be sarcastic and snarky, but I ignored it.

"Melissa."

"Don't Melissa me," she hissed. "I can't believe you, Aria. You have been in New York for how long and you're telling me you didn't think once to call me."

"I've been busy," I managed to say, but she didn't care as she laughed so bitterly that it left a sour taste on my tongue.

"You're actually ridiculous."

I ran my fingers through my locks, sighing. "I don't know what to tell you."

"Maybe begin with why you are back?" she questioned, furiously.

"I-I can't tell you," I stammered, feeling oddly intimidated by the fury in my old friend's voice.

Melissa was Matteo's stepsister, and thus my cousin by marriage. When my uncle had lost his wife during childbirth, Matteo had grown without a mother figure for many years, and my mother and Nero's mother were his only source of maternal love. My uncle Valentino grieved for a very long time and vowed to never marry again, until he met Melissa's mother. He had bumped into her during a meeting in Sweden and pretended to be her fiancé when he discovered that her parents were forcing her to marry a man she had never met before. Melissa's great-grandmother had left a huge sum of money in her mother's name but the only condition she had was to get married. The terms on who she was to get married to were never clear, but she met my uncle… and the rest was history. I had grown up with Melissa and she was incredibly loyal to me, through thick and thin – I knew when I left that I could never forgive myself for not explaining to her why.

"You can never tell me," The sadness from Melissa's voice had me sink into my leather chair. "What happened, Aria?"

"So much," I whispered, staring at the framed picture of Kira and I on my desk. We had taken it in my safe house in Italy after buying the plot of land to build the Manor.

"I've missed you."

"I've missed you too."

There was this long silence before she spoke again, her voice this time much lighter than it was a few moments ago, "Well… are there any men in your life?"

My lips tugged as she laughed, and I knew everything was going to be alright. After spending over an hour on the phone with Melissa, listening to her rants about unsuccessful *sexcapades* (as she liked to call them), and her many arguments with Matteo about said sexcapades, we eventually called it a day and I promised to reach out soon. Then she politely threatened to break my fingers if I didn't. We both knew she would never win against me, but I still giggled and vowed that I would call her again. Something about speaking to Melissa had taken the burden off my shoulders and I was glad that I had friends who trusted that I knew what I was doing and didn't question my intentions.

Feeling a large presence in the office, I greeted my visitor, "Good afternoon, Xan. What have you found for me?"

Handing me a folder which contained information crucial to building a case around Violetta, he answered, "Violetta was born in Spain. Her parents are Fredrik Rossi and Mauve Rossi, both elite members of the Serpents."

I frowned, shuffling through the folder. "What do you mean both?"

"Before Mauve married Fredrik, she was not only a member of the Serpents, but she was also to be part of the Inner Circle."

"But that's not possible."

The Serpents were extremely exclusive. Businessmen, mafia bosses, drug lords, every corrupt industry out there was involved with the Serpents, but the Inner Circle was the foundation of it all. They were who we were going to hit. If we broke them, we would break all of them. For men, it was not hard to be a part of the Serpents. It was usually inherited but corruption had a part to play as well. Women, on the other hand, often had to be married into the organization and even then, they were given minimal access. Misogyny played a part in all factors of the Serpents, so to hear that Mauve Rossi was to be a part of the Inner Circle didn't seem right.

Xander nodded in agreement. "That's what I thought, but I did some digging and discovered it was inherited."

"So, Vi's grandfather was a member of the Inner Circle?"

"It appeared so but something went wrong, and eventually the

Rossis left the Serpents."

I rose a brow at Xander. "Can you even do that? It's like a fucking cult."

Xander shrugged. "Apparently, it's possible. There are no current ties between them and the Serpents."

"It then makes sense that the Serpents are after Vi. They want revenge maybe."

"Serpents' law states that any assets owned by a former member should go to them," Xander pointed out.

I snorted. "What a ridiculous rule."

Xander's lip quirked up. "Another way they protect their secrets."

I sighed, studying the folder he had given me. Mauve and Fredrik's pictures were tucked inside and as I inspected them closely, I couldn't really see the similarities between them and their daughter. I guess she took after her grandparents.

My gaze moved to Xander. "Her grandfather hid his wealth away from them, leaving it in Violetta's name, so when the Serpents discovered this, they wanted to claim what was theirs."

"Essentially," Xander confirmed. "But there's more."

Reaching down, he flicked through the folder, taking out a specific sheet that caught my attention as it had a table filled with statistics, expect these weren't ordinary numbers. These exposed every bank or account which the Serpents had access to. Xander was extremely skilled in his field, and how he gained access, I didn't need to know. Regardless, it gave us an advantage.

"Similar to how the mafia has a Chip which holds all information about transactions and shipments, etc., this provides information of every source of income the Serpents have access to and their locations," His finger trailed down the sheet, tapping on a certain location. "And the most often place is —"

I breathed out, reading the word into existence. "Greece."

There was a moment of silence that settled over us as we allowed the information to soak in. This meant that the Serpents' main source of income came from Greece, which could only mean that Greece was their roots.

"Do you know the exact location?" I questioned, and he shook his head. "We need to find that out. It could help narrow down the people we are searching for."

"Aria, there is one other thing you should know," Xander said before he left. I looked up from the newly found information scattered across my desk. "Nero nearly signed a business contract with Enzo Rossi."

"Who is that?"

"Violetta's older brother."

Confusion lurched within me as I vaguely recalled Violetta telling Calix that her brother wasn't alive. Then again, when the memory replayed itself, realization smacked me in the face. Although implied, Violetta never actually said her brother was dead. It just sounded like he could be. Regardless, clearly Violetta and Enzo were separated when she was much younger, and I doubted she knew where he could possibly be.

"What was the contract for?"

"A hotel plan, but it never followed through," Xander stated. "If this Enzo is part of the Serpents, he's maybe our way in. I think you need to get Nero to forge a new business with Enzo. It makes sense because they were supposed to be partners before."

"Nero won't agree to help."

Xander arched a brow in skepticism. "For you, the man will do anything. He just needs a little convincing. A skill that you have mastered."

I dwelled over this plan, pinching my forehead as I began to feel a headache form. I had no intention of seeing Nero after what happened last night but now it seemed inevitable. He was always getting himself in trouble and didn't even see it. I groaned inwardly after weighing out the pros and cons. Xander immediately grinned at me with a sparkle in his eyes, as if he knew what I was about to say.

"Xander, I need you to check the name Enzo Rossi in any countries north of Spain, start with Switzerland," I ordered.

"And Nero?"

I clenched my jaw, the sound of his name giving me PTSD from last night. I could still feel his lips against my own, the invisible burn marks that his fingers left sown across my skin, the way we moved together in synchrony until I reached my blissful high. I could feel it all as if it was happening again. I crossed my legs, trying to numb the need, but I knew nothing could satisfy me like Nero.

"I'll talk to him," I muttered. "Leave that to me."

CHAPTER 13

whiskey lies

Nero

Her bony fingers ran through my hair, tugging my sweaty strands as she released a scream loud enough that I had no doubt would have caught the attention of everyone in the club. I silenced her with a kiss, grunting as I reached my high soon after. Her body went limp in my arms, her legs tightening around my hips, as she shuddered in delight. Glancing up, she gave me a languid smile on her Barbie pink lips. She ran her fingers down the side of my jaw, before leaning in for another kiss. It was smothering as she literally sucked the life out of me, to my displeasure. I cringed, untangling myself from her captivity, shuffling my trousers back on and fixing myself up whilst she whined for me to come back.

"Shut up," I muttered, exasperatedly. With a pout, she fluttered her eyes, but it only made feel more nauseous.

"Don't be such a tease, Nero."

I rolled my eyes, ignoring her as she batted her lashes that were starting to fall off. *Fucking hell.*

"Leave."

"But —"

"Get. Out," I snapped. Her eyes widened, tears brimming. "You're annoying me."

The blonde gasped whilst I poured myself a glass of whiskey.

Grumbling in annoyance, she hopped off the desk and redressed herself in whatever was left of her skimpy clothing, before returning back to the club were her friends were. The door closed with a loud *slam*. I collapsed onto the couch, recalling the number of women I had been with since I was with Aria many days ago. But none could ever match the level of passion that she elicited. It was fucking infuriating but to my dismay, all I could think about was the flushed look across her face when she gave in. I could feel her body rocking against mine in perfect synchrony, fitting in my arms, as though that was exactly where she was meant to be. Her brown hair wild as it curtained around me when she kissed me, teasing me as her tongue traced the inside of my mouth, biting against my lower lip and crying out in pleasure when she reached her apex, her eyes burning with hunger, yet she easily masked it with anger.

I was so fucking screwed.

"Shit," I grunted, feeling my entire body tense at the thought of her.

My muscles flexed as I angrily drank the last drops of whiskey which burned my throat, before grabbing my coat and fleeing this claustrophobic private room. I could hear Matteo's inebriated voice calling after me as I stormed through the club, shoving past anyone who got in my way with a scowl. I just wanted to drown myself in drinks and paperwork – it was the only way I could get her out of my head, instead of sinking deep into numerous women, whose names I couldn't even remember. Not that it mattered when Aria invaded my mind, day and night. And on top of that, my conversation with Melissa replayed on my mind, incessantly, and I couldn't stop thinking about it.

"What do you what, Mel?" I sighed, when she slipped into my office.

The blonde woman smiled, innocently, though her eyes spoke of other intentions. "I spoke to Aria." I didn't respond, so she took that as an invitation to continue. "It seems like she has a lot going on. She didn't tell me anything if that's what you're thinking. She just seemed like... not herself."

"What do you mean?" my eyes moved away from the screen on my computer to Melissa as she settled onto the couch, admiring her white nails that looked too long to be safe.

"I don't know what happened between you guys, but I know Aria and I know she loved –"

"Stop right there," I curtly gritted . Melissa blinked at me, startled. "Love and Aria do not belong in the same sentence."

For a second, Melissa said nothing and then she burst into laughter. Stunned, I watched her hunch over as if she was in pain and cackle. This went on for another five minutes, and every time she looked at me, she started laughing again. I was completely baffled that I didn't even know how to respond, staring at her with wide eyes. Eventually, her laughs turned in giggles as she grinned at me, showing off those pearly white teeth that dazzled men left, right and center.

"Oh Nero," she breathed out another laugh. "You stupid boy."

"Excuse me?" I gasped, and she arched her brow, shaking her head as if I was the most oblivious person in the entire world.

"I said you're a stupid boy. If only you knew how much she loved you. How much she cared. How much she tried. She loved you, Nero. She still loves you. You're an idiot if you can't see that," Melissa pressed her lips into a tight smile. "And you're a bigger idiot if you can't see that you still love her back."

She strode out of the room before I could get a word out, leaving me with a grenade of unfathomable realities.

When I finally returned to the Estate, quietness welcomed me. A heavy sigh echoed down the hall when I remembered that many of my men had gone out for the evening. I trudged up the stairs, browsing through the messages on my phone as I mindlessly led myself to my office, but the aroma of roses had me stopping, abruptly. A frown slipped onto my face as I drew my brows together. Slowly, lifting my eyes up, I noticed my office door was open and immediately prepared a defensive stance, tucking my phone away before proceeding with caution towards the room. Silently, I pushed the door open, my attention locked onto the stranger sitting in *my* chair, long, lean legs covered in black tights propped on top of *my* desk whilst their eyes focused on the device in their hands with minimal interest.

"Why are you here?" I stiffened my back.

Her hazel eyes blinked up, a smirk playing on her red lips that I burned with desire to kiss and taint with my name. Wearing this enticing black dress that clung to her body enhancing every curve that God blessed her with, I lost my breath at the sight of her.

Holy fucking shit. She was gorgeous.

"You're early. Was blondie not enough?" she teased, with a mischievous twinkle in her eyes which studied me momentarily, her tongue slipping out and wetting her plump lips, tempting me to take a bite. Angling her head to the side, her mahogany hair fell off her shoulders, revealing the exposed part of her neck that I remembered, painstakingly. I clenched my jaw, stepping forward, kicking the door shut behind me.

"Are you here for another round, Aria? Couldn't get enough of me?"

She laughed. It was the most angelic sound I had ever heard, knocking the air out of my lungs. Her eyes squinted together, and her cheeks broadened in amusement.

"Don't flatter yourself, Nero. It wasn't that good," she remarked, standing up and closing the distance between us. "Although, if those skinny little models weren't enough for you, I don't mind helping out. Or am I *different*?"

Her warm breath fanned my face, running her fingers down my chest, lips inviting me as they wavered above mine with false promises and potentially painful damage. I glared down at her, wanting to hate her instead of lusting after her, like a love-sick puppy. Her sadistic smile stretched ear-to-ear as she withdrew from me, her heavenly rose scent intoxicating my senses, and leaned against the desk. *Jesus*, I had never seen anyone more enticing than her.

"Sadly, I don't have time for that today," she purred. "Instead, I have a favor to ask."

"Why would I ever think of helping you?"

With a little pout, she replied in a mocking tone, "Because I'm your best friend."

I didn't reply, grinding my teeth together at the sound of her scornful laughter. The corner of her lips coiled into a dark smile when she noticed the aggravated look across my face, reaching behind her to grab what I was late to notice – a brown folder.

"The man I want is Enzo Rossi. Sound familiar?" she asked, handing me the folder.

"Perhaps," I answered, sifting through the file, knowing exactly who she was talking about, and curious to know how she even found out about his existence. Enzo was a very low-profile businessman, and from experience, I knew that I would never want to go into partnership with him.

Ever.

"Well, you are going to ask to have a partnership with Rossi."

My eyes shot up in utter astonishment, her composure completely serious yet, for some reason, I expected her to say *'psyche!'* I shoved the brown folder into her hand, glaring at the beauty with anger and infuriation. Angry because she thought she could demand things from me, and infuriated because I would still listen to her in a heartbeat.

"No."

"If you sign this deal, I'll give you anything you want," Aria vowed.

I knew better than to make a deal with the devil. Especially if the devil tasted like heaven.

"Will you tell me why you want me to do this?" She pursed her lips together and my brow rose, not even surprised. "Exactly. You can't give me everything then."

I moved around her to settle into my seat, but her hand shot out, curling around my wrist, her eyes glittering with something I hadn't seen before. Then it disappeared.

"Please, Nero," she added, softly.

"He's bad news, Aria. I would be putting people at risk if I was to get involved with Enzo."

"I promise that he won't hurt anyone, Nero."

"Your promises mean nothing, Aria," I bit back, spitefully, shoving her hand off me. "Leave."

She held my gaze for a lengthy, taut moment, before exhaling deeply and grabbing her bag from my desk. I watched her retreating back, her wavy coffee-colored hair swaying side to side, the dress she wore clinging to her like a second skin, and bit back my tongue from calling her name and submitting to her demands. I had my pride, just as she had hers. She couldn't leave me in the dark and ask me to do ridiculous favors – not when they put my family at risk. They might no longer be hers to care for, but they were now mine. Before she left, Aria glanced over her shoulder, her enthralling eyes sucking me deeper into the void of her. They held a lot of pain. I could see it no matter how much she hid it from me. There were fragments of heartbreak in the abyss of her irises, shielded by this persona who stood before me. Melissa may have claimed that Aria loved me, but I couldn't believe it because the woman in front of me looked like she was seeking revenge. Forgiving Aria would be the last thing I would do; she didn't deserve it. Not when she betrayed my trust the day she left.

Except, my heart still broke when she whispered, timidly, "Can you at least think about it, Nero?"

"Will you ever tell me the truth?" I countered, leaning over the desk with my hands clasped together.

I already knew her answer before it had left her lethal, red lips. "No."

Slouching back against the chair with my arms crossed over my chest, I replied back, icily, "Then, there's your answer."

CHAPTER 14

velvet kisses

The ambience of the room had adrenaline rushing through my body like a shot of heroin, as I swayed to the beat of the music. I allowed myself to be fully immersed in every song, sipping on a martini here and there, but never once moving away from the center of the room, as the strobe lights flashed around us in mayhem. But, despite the amount of liquor in my system, I could still feel his brooding eyes on me. He sat in the far distance, in the VIP lounge, along with three of his men – one of whom was Matteo, who seemed preoccupied with the brunette on his lap who wore practically nothing. But, hey, I wasn't judging. A girl's got to do what a girl's got to do. Well, at least that was my mindset until she turned her attention to *him*. Her breasts were basically spilling out of her top, which just looked like a thin sheet of material. I shouldn't have been so annoyed at the sight of it, but it made my blood boil, yet I didn't blink in his direction, embracing the mixture of adrenaline and alcohol, and the tingling sensation numbing my inhibitions. Kira laughed as Xander playfully danced with her, her blonde hair swaying wildly, as she flung her arms around his neck with a bright beam. Back at our table, in a more secluded area of the club, was Calix. He looked ravishing in a simple black t-shirt and jeans, doing the bare minimum but nevertheless looking like a magnificent masterpiece. Still, my eyes found themselves trailing over to where *he* was sitting. For a brief moment, I caught his eyes before quickly playing it off as if I was looking at someone behind him. I noticed the frown etched on his face as he glanced over his shoulders, but I took that second to my advantage and disappeared from sight. My cheeks were flushed as I huffed, stumbling into a seat besides Calix, who smirked at me in amusement.

"Are you alright, Boss?"

"Yeah," I answered, too quickly to fool anyone, even Calix. *Especially* Calix. "I'm good, I just need another drink."

"I think you've had plenty this evening," he commented, moving his glass out of my reach as I went to grab it.

Including a pout, I sulked. His eyes twinkled as he downed the rest of the contents of the glass, before turning his attention on me, tucking a strand of loose hair behind my ear.

"You look pretty hot, Aria," he murmured, brushing his lips against mine.

My eyes fluttered shut as he snaked his arm around my waist, dragging me onto his lap. With a squeal of surprise, I grinned at him as my arms locked around his neck.

"You don't look too bad yourself, Calix," I purred, looking up at him underneath hooded lashes, a seductive smile spreading across my red lips.

He hummed in reply, his chest rumbling, obviously liking what he heard, before pressing his lips against mine. Usually, I'd protest to public displays of affection, but I was too high on the euphoric feeling to give a shit. And God, did it feel good. I moaned, twisting closer to him as he plunged his tongue into my mouth, angling his head to taste every inch. One of his hands slipped between my thighs, pushing my dress up, as his lips peppered kisses along my neck. My breathing was ragged, my chest heaving, as he gifted me the pleasure of his lips and touch, a thrill that I had deeply enjoyed for the last three years.

"Oh God," I sighed, wanting to taste him again, and therefore turning his head so that I could be blessed with those soft lips once more, which curled into a wolfish grin as he watched me fall helplessly under his spell.

"If we don't stop, I'm going to take you right here, Aria," Calix grunted, as I shifted above him so that I straddled him. A more comfortable position. With alcohol in my system, the epinephrine pumped through me so rapidly that I wanted more. I *needed* more.

I shook my head, cupping his face as I murmured, "Don't stop."

His eyes flickered up in surprise, mostly likely due to how far I was taking this, but this quickly dissipated when I unbuckled his belt, hiking my dress up to my waist, and sinking into the chasm of pleasure in this dark, red booth where our moans were engulfed by the cacophony of sounds created by the thundering music and boisterous chatter, and the silhouette of our bodies danced beneath the rainbow beams.

*

"He was so fucking drunk that night," Kira giggled, as Xander impishly stuck his tongue out at her.

I rolled my eyes, shifting closer towards Calix as his arm draped over my shoulder, quietly sipping on his drink. Whilst Kira and Xander continued to bicker, he observed and chuckled. He didn't speak much and preferred to listen. It was something I quickly learnt about him after a few weeks of meeting. He was aware of everything, and could multitask like a pro, but when it came to conversations, his words were kept to himself, and his ears took in everything. Unlike Xander, who lit up the room regardless of who he was with, people often thought Calix was sullen, but he was reserved, and I knew that the darkest part of him wasn't even the scariest piece.

"I was not as drunk as you, blondie," Xander huffed. "You were on some other shit. I swear you were high."

"The fuck are you on about?" Kira exclaimed, incredulously. "Xander, just accept you can't hold your liquor."

"Yes," he hiccupped, his cheeks flushed with heat as he grinned lazily. "I can."

With a raised brow, Kira leaned back against the velvet sofa, sighing. "Point made."

"You guys argue way too much," I complained.

"Sorry, Aria, that not everyone is mature like you," she replied childishly, before her smile coiled into a mischievous grin. "Although, I did see a certain someone run away from the dance floor. Did you perhaps catch someone's eye?"

Xander laughed. "Probably Calix. That's why she's glowing right now."

"*Xander!*" I gasped, a red burn spreading across my face whilst Kira and Calix laughed along with him. Calix drew circles on my arms as he grinned in amusement at my dismay, his green eyes sparkling with

119

pride.

"Don't deny it, Boss. We all know you did the nasty," Xander teased, his words ending with a slur and eyes suddenly bright as he downed another drink.

I glowered. "I'm going to murder you."

"Catch me if you can," he smirked, jumping out his seat and disappearing into the crowd as I pounced over the table. But Calix held me back, wrapping his arms around me with a breathy chuckle that tickled my neck.

Kira chortled. "I swear he has a death wish."

"*It's Xander.* That's all he ever asks for," Calix stated, pressing a kiss against the side of my head so tenderly that, for a second, I forgot about cursing Xander under my breath.

Kira studied us, a smile creeping onto her lips, before she leaned over the table. "But, seriously, Aria. Who did you see?"

My mood soured, but my heartbeat doubled. It was difficult to figure out what I felt nowadays but *he* never made me feel anything good. At least that is what I had to tell myself so that I would hate him. Suddenly, remembering that he was here, I had no doubt it was because he was tracking me. He regularly kept tabs on me when we were younger – I think he was afraid that one day, I might share the same fates as my mother and her cousins. Captured, tortured and beaten. He was scared *for* me back then, and now, he was scared *of* me. I held Kira's gaze, sipping on the noxious booze which burned my throat. Challenging my gaze, she didn't give in and slanted her head to the side with pure curiosity.

"Who do you think?"

Her eyes broadened slightly. "He's here?"

I nodded slowly.

"Do you think he's tracking you?"

"Of course," I answered, coldly, untangling myself from Calix and slipping out of the booth. "I'm heading to the ladies room. I know we agreed to no work but, unfortunately, that was before I was aware of his presence. Kira, when you find Xander, I need you to both check the car for any tracking bugs or wires – *anything*. And, Calix, I want to know when he arrived and with whom."

Kira sighed, exasperatedly, before reluctantly agreeing to my orders, her drunken state vanishing as she masked her face, and ventured into the crowd to find Xander. Calix glanced at me underneath his long, dark lashes, taking his time to drink his vodka.

"Are you okay?" he asked.

"No," I didn't bother to pretend otherwise.

He didn't bat an eye at my answer, getting out the booth and pressing his lips against mine before he left to do what was expected of him. For a fraction of a minute, I stared at his retreating back, but then I forced myself to move, shoving past the crowd, heading to the restrooms. Calix and I had a complicated relationship; I mean, we kissed, we fucked, we would protect each other, but we always knew that we would never love one another. It would be messy and complicated, and a part of us – or, I guess, a part of me knew that I didn't know how to love another. The feelings between us were mutual because I knew he couldn't love me either. We were like two broken pieces of a plate, and whilst it could be repaired with a little time and glue, it would never be in the perfect condition it once was. We could never be perfect. Our pasts would always haunt us, and one day, we would crack. In the end, I was his Boss, and he was just doing what was expected of him.

In the restroom, I washed my hands after using the toilet and then reapplied the shade of red across my lips. Fixing my hair, I stopped and stared at my reflection under the spotlight from above. Makeup covered the circles under my eyes, and I was able to pretend my skin was far brighter and healthier than it actually was, but when it was all gone – when the veil came off – I couldn't really see the girl I once was. I just saw my fears. The paranoia. The looming future. I knew I was powerful; I didn't question my abilities. But, my heart was cold and heavy. They called me an Ice Queen; they said I was the devil. So, the darkness became my friend and the girl in the mirror looked dead inside. Most nights, I barely recognized her. With a hard swallow, I exhaled and exited the lavatory, ignoring the catcalls and shouts for my attention as I strode down the hallway back to the club. I didn't want to spend another second in this club, or maybe it was the alcohol finally clearing from my body, as my throat felt trapped with cries. I just kept walking. All of a sudden, someone yanked me into an empty room, pressing me against the cold wall as I yelped. Before I could fight off the culprit, I looked up and my breath hitched. Sterling blue eyes scorched me, pinning me in my position, as he held my wrists above my head.

"*Aria*," he greeted, with a soft purr.

"Nero, what the fuck?" I hollered, thrashing underneath his captivity. "What are you doing?"

"I decided to cash in that request," Nero replied, causing me to stop.

"Does that mean you're going to help?"

He smirked, and God, I would be lying if I said it didn't make my entire body prickle with delight. "Only if you promise to do whatever I want."

My brows drew in together. "What is it?"

Licking his lips, his eyes ran up and down my body, before pressing himself closer against me. I didn't back away from his gaze, ignoring how my heart pounded so loudly I swear I could feel it in my throat. Everything burned, especially where he held me. I could feel my cheeks heating up and, yet I didn't look away. I wouldn't give him the satisfaction. It wasn't like me to give in. Only, his Jack Frost gaze startled me as they simmered with blue embers. I knew this was a bad idea. I could see it. Alas, the daredevil in me wanted to play. I loved the games. I was the best at them. I wanted to push and pull, until he was like putty in my hands. I knew how easily he gave into me - how easily he *used* to give in to me. Years might have gone by, but I was sure Nero remained the same when it came to me. It was the one thing Calix couldn't completely give me. His devotion. Calix might be loyal to the bone, but Nero worshipped the ground I had walked on. Calix had never made me feel this powerful. Yet, as I stood in front of Nero, I could sense that he had closed that part of himself off from me. He wanted to be in charge. He needed to control me. He needed to tame me. But, *no one* could tame *me*. So, I had taunted the beast until he decided to show his real desire. I could see it in his eyes, his posture, the way he was pressed against me. I could *feel* it. It was wrong. So, so wrong. But, why did it feel so right? Kira would get angry. I couldn't give in to the seductive temptation that was in the form of Nero Russo.

I shouldn't.

But I did.

"Nero, what do you want?" I repeated. *Slowly.*

I was afraid to hear the answer.

Or maybe I was afraid to hear the truth.

"You," was his response.

My eyes widened as I felt myself stop breathing. I couldn't stop the rush of *want* rattle throughout my body. With a twinkle in his eyes that revealed his devilish intent, Nero wavered his lips above mine, as he repeated his truest desire and mine.

"*I want you.*"

CHAPTER 15

the deal

"*I want you.*"

I couldn't tell you how long I had been waiting to hear those words. What I wanted to know was what he truly and honestly desired. They should have made my heart burst in pure happiness, or cause a smile so bright and wide across my face, or have me crumble at his demands. They should have made me happy; I had been waiting so long to hear them.

But they didn't.

Instead, they filled me with distrust, made me defensive as I narrowed my eyes at him. "Excuse me?"

His smirk widened as he rose a brow. "I want you, Aria. That's the cost for my participation in your little plan."

"Start making sense, Nero. I have places to be other than here," I hissed, twisting my wrists in his grip.

Nero chuckled, darkly, and moved away, crossing his arms over his chest. The way he looked at me had me rapidly losing oxygen, as he responded, "You know exactly what I'm talking about, Aria. You're a smart girl. But, in case you need me to spell it out for you. Whenever I want you, I have you. That's the cost."

"What the fuck do you think I am?" I snarled, pushing him away from me, an icy glare attached to his grinning face. "A call girl? Someone who you can use whenever you want to? You're clearly drunk and not thinking straight."

"I'm thinking perfectly straight," he replied. "You said you'd do anything I want if I agree to help you. Well, this is the cost of my assistance."

"Do you have no respect for me?" I scoffed. "If you want a prostitute, trust that you can find plenty to your liking. I'm not someone you can choose when and where to fuck."

"There are plenty of other things you can do for me, but I'm not opposed to sleeping together."

"*No*," I stated, firmly, holding his gaze which housed those chilly blue eyes I once loved very much. "Never again in my fucking life."

"What about that night –"

"A mistake," I interrupted, through clenched teeth. For a second, I swear I saw a flash of hurt but it soon disappeared, a frosty shield shrouding his true emotions – something I would never have the privilege of knowing again. "It was a mistake, Nero. It won't happen again."

He stayed eerily quiet for a very long time, studying me underneath those long lashes that protected his azure eyes which had me hypnotized like a sucker. My jaw clenched as I held the emotionless façade I wore across my face. Inside, I could feel the emotions I spent years burying slowly reveal themselves, my heart clenching in this sort of agony I hadn't felt in the longest time and my throat suddenly felt very dry, as I forced the tears away. He stood there, looking wickedly beautiful, waiting for me to submit to his demands and collapse into those arms, which denied me of the truth and left me in throes of betrayal. I could see it all flash before my eyes.

We were never meant to be.

Nero inhaled deeply, before releasing a heavy sigh with a slow nod, his eyes giving nothing away, as he responded, "Ok."

I blinked, waiting for him to withdraw that statement, but he didn't. For a brief second, I wanted him to fight for me but then I immediately dismissed the idea of it. Why should he fight for me? Why did I want him to fight for me?

"Ok," I finally whispered.

We held each other's gaze, our mouths locking up the words we wanted to say but refused to do so. Eventually, I walked out of the room. I wasn't sure how far I had gotten until I felt his hand grip my wrist, tugging me into his arms, my eyes widening. I looked up at him, noticing how dark they had gotten under those thick lashes of his, a twinkle in the ocean's depth of his irises which explained enough.

He wasn't done.

"Don't think this means you can go to another man, Aria. If it's not me, then it's no one."

Stilling, I began to argue, "Nero –"

Silencing me with a punishing kiss, hot and hard, stealing my breath away and breaking those barriers I erected to defend myself against him. One hand rested on the small of my back, the other held my neck as he drove his tongue into my mouth, tainting me and reminding me of his honey-like taste. I moaned, grasping his blazer, fighting against his dominance but failing as he growled, pressing my body against his. I could remember every curve and muscle of his body as he fucked with my mind, giving me a sample of what could be expected if I accepted his request. Making sure I remembered what I was missing. God, I wanted to stop him, but I couldn't, because I wanted this as much as he did. My body felt flaccid in his hold, melting into his arms because they felt like home. His kisses gave me life, filling a void I never knew existed, branding me as his in front of strangers. It was only then that I realized that he had seen me with Calix; it explained his sudden territorial behavior. Fury succumbed the desire and I mustered up all my strength to shove him away. Stumbling back, I nearly tripped had I not steadied myself a second later. Our chests rose as we tried to fill our lungs with the oxygen we were deprived of, staring at each other in shock.

"I can't believe you," I whispered.

"What?"

"Nothing is going to happen. I can sleep with whoever I fucking want to. It is none of your business. *You are not my boyfriend.*"

Nero released a short breath of air in disbelief. "And he is?"

My jaw tightened. "My relationship with Calix has nothing to do with you. Just like how I couldn't give a shit about whether you slept with blondie, or little miss no clothes over there."

I didn't care whether I sounded jealous or not. He had no right to demand such a thing from me. These double standards had my head spinning and, in my world, they did not exist. If he wanted me to stop, he needed to stop himself. I was tired of men telling me to stop doing things that they couldn't fulfil themselves. As if he knew the thoughts I was having, Nero chuckled. It was cold and unsettling. His eyes looked past my shoulders, down the corridor, before moving onto me. His gaze held such a freezing fire that I almost shivered at the sight of it. It would leave me scorched with the reminiscence of him.

"He won't be able to give you want you need, Aria," Nero warned. "Deny it all you want, but you know that only I can give you what you want and need. It's addictive, but that's what we were. And you loved it. High on the feeling. Bad for each other, but also so fucking good. I'm not a coward, Aria. I won't lie about what I want, and that's you."

"What you want is to control me."

"Why do you think that?"

"Because you haven't shown me a reason to think otherwise."

He shook his head slowly. "You act as if you hate it. From what I recall, you enjoyed it. Quite thoroughly if I remember correctly."

"You're so confident that I haven't changed," I arched my brow, curling my hands into a fist. "You're sorely mistaken."

"Am I?" he retorted.

I continued to stare at him, shaking in anger and hatred towards this man that I wished I never loved so much, whilst I levelled out my breath. I didn't want to give him the satisfaction of knowing that he affected me *or just how profound those emotions were.*

"I won't forgive you. I hate you," I responded shakily, trying to numb the feeling that gnawed against my heart. I would not be vulnerable to him. Never. "*Sempre.*"

The corner of his lips tugged into an icy smile as he observed me. "Keep lying to yourself. Let's see how long you'll last."

I remained where I stood as he strode past. But he didn't leave. Instead, he stopped and pressed one last, firm kiss against the side of my head.

"This will be the last time I kiss you without your permission," he vowed, and my body stilled. "The next time I do it will be because you want me to."

I didn't respond. I didn't know what else to say. He lingered for a second and my eyes fluttered shut, pressing my lips together. I thought he would say something else, but when I opened my eyes, he was no longer there. Releasing the breath of air that I didn't even know I was holding, I felt the tears prick my eyes before I blinked them away. I expected to see him down the corridor when I glanced back. But he wasn't there. I ingested the silent sobs threatening to escape into the quiet hallway, as the music boomed throughout the club, drowning out the sound of my shattering heart.

*

I liked to drink away my problems. It was often my solution to every dilemma I faced. Only, I couldn't get the sight of his face out of my head. I was barely drunk. I knew how to handle my liquor, but eventually I gave up, huffing as I pushed the glass of vodka away from me. There was a short knock on my office door before Kira peeped in with a small smile across her coral pink lips.

"Are you alright? You've been really quiet since we came home last night," she asked, closing the door before heading towards me. Her eyes glanced at the empty glasses and vodka bottles. "Vi also mentioned that you've been stuck in your office all day. Has something happened?"

"No," I answered. "Nothing's wrong."

"I'm not stupid, Aria. Clearly, something must've happened," she paused, narrowing her eyes. "Did Nero do something?"

I didn't respond, earning me a heavy sigh from Kira as she settled into the seat in front of me, concern swimming in her blue eyes that were bright and filled with warmth, yet that also reminded me of Nero. I closed my eyes, holding my face in my hands as I suppressed everything I spent years burying. It was difficult. It killed me, nibbling against my heart until all that was left was broken fragments.

"Talk to me, Aria. I hate it when you shut me out."

"I asked him for a favor, something that would help us in our mission to destroy the Serpents," I began quietly, glancing up to see her full attention on me. "And he asked for a favor back. One that I don't think I can abide to, but it was his only request. What do I do?"

"Trust yourself," she responded, not even a second later, which had me frowning, causing her to smile and her eyes to crease as her cheeks lifted. "You always expect anything asked of you. When it came to negotiating terms with men you despised, you would expect and anticipate their demands and you succeeded. You can do anything because you are fearless; you are untouchable; you are *Aria*. You just need to remember that. But, if you rejected him, it's because you don't trust yourself. You don't trust *your* actions and judgements. That is what will stop you from succeeding. No demand is too much for you, Aria. The game is in your hands. Shuffle the cards and place them in the players' hands, but it's always in your control."

"What if he is demanding something that I shouldn't do?"

She chuckled, standing up. Her blue eyes sparkled, and her lips twitched. I knew what she was trying to say, and she knew what I was saying. But she trusted me, and for that reason I knew what I had to do.

"Men will always demand the impossible," she reminded, earnestly. "They forget that women always hold the power to do anything. He knew you wouldn't accept his demands. He was just testing you to see if you knew what your limits were. That's why he asked. But you have no limits, Aria," Kira shrugged. "Just show him that."

"Kira…"

My words trailed off when she shook her head, refusing to hear anymore, refusing to hear what he asked, and I knew it was because she respected mine and Nero's past. Our business was our business; she would support my decision whatever it was, even if she didn't know the full story because she trusted that I made it for the right reasons. Before she left for the night, she gave me a soft smile that creased her eyes and warmed my heart.

"Go to him, Moretti. Prove that you're no longer the same girl he knew five years ago. This time, you control the game."

*

I could remember the first time I heard of the building Nero owned. It was in the heart of the city, towering over the smaller buildings with forty-five floors, of which he lived in the penthouse. I was surprised to hear that he bought the place when he used to be so adamant about living in the Estate. Calix had revealed that Nero moved out of the Estate a couple of weeks after I had left the mafia. He never told me the reason why. He didn't need to. I stood in front of a large mahogany door as the bell rang, trying to not tremble underneath the trench coat I was wearing. It rang twice until I heard the lock click. The door opened and Nero's eyes thinned. From the looks of it, he must have arrived home a while ago since his tie was loosened and his sleeves were rolled to his elbows, sans the blazer.

"We need to talk," I said, before he could question my appearance, pushing past him and entering his home.

The interior of his home stunned me. It was very open and very clean, with a recurring noir theme from the walls to the wooden floorboards. Noting the empty wine glasses on the coffee table, I concluded that he had a guest over and immediately began rethinking my decision. What if it was a woman? God, then I would seriously look like an idiot. But, as soon as I glanced at Nero those thoughts were knocked straight out of me. He leaned against the archway of the living room, with his arms crossed over his chest. I wanted to take a picture of him. He never looked more like sin then he did there.

"What do you want to talk about?" he questioned in a gruff voice, eyes scanning me from head to toe.

"Your request."

He raised his brow in surprise. "I thought you rejected the offer."

"I reconsidered."

Suspicion immediately flooded his sky-blue eyes. "Why?"

I rolled off the nervousness and sighed, thoughtfully. A playful smile teased my cerise lips as I placed my bag onto the couch. His eyes tracked me with cynicism, yet he was interested; I saw it in how the blue hues of his eyes darkened with fiery hunger, like he was trying to hold back what he wanted. The mere thought had set my body aflame with desire and instantly made me feel more powerful.

"I'll sacrifice myself to save the people I love," I answered.

As if something switched within him, his jaw tensed and he pushed himself off the wall, striding towards me with a cold expression that had me really rethink my decision. "We are not doing this."

Stunned, my mouth fell. "Why not? Was this not what you wanted?"

"I'll do what you want, Aria. Forget what I asked," he began to head to the stairs.

"Why are you taking it back now?" I exclaimed, staring at him in confusion.

He spun around, snapping, "Because I want you to come to me willingly, not like this!"

I shook my head, incredulously. "So, why did you act like that in the first place?"

"Because I'm a dick. I was drunk and angry," he snarled. "I'd seen you with that man, with his hands all over you, and I never wanted to kill someone as much as I did then. I shouldn't have treated you the way I did, and I'm sorry for that, but I never wanted you to sell yourself for my assistance."

I released a bitter laugh, stepping away from him as I tried to reassert myself but failed to because this situation was absurd. "You're fucking ridiculous. I can't believe you."

"Well, believe it, Aria," he spat out, frostily. "We are not doing this."

Suddenly, he was walking away. Suddenly, I was panicking. Suddenly, I realized that I had wanted this as much as he did. Suddenly, I knew this was my only chance. Suddenly, I blurted out, "What if I do want this?"

He halted. Even if he was dressed, I saw all his muscles harden, before he gazed over his shoulders with his brows drawn together, dark blue eyes hidden under long lashes, hunger and anger masking his face. The look he gave me knocked my breath away; it was filled with such carnal desire, like he couldn't tell whether he wanted to kick me out his home or fuck me raw.

Lord save me. And I knew I wanted the latter.

"I promised to give you whatever you wanted if you did what I wanted you to do," I said, treading lightly, afraid to make a sudden movement in case he pounced because the way he was looking at me reminded me of a lion and a deer. And in that moment, I felt like the deer. "You can have me, for whatever you want, whenever you want, and wherever you want. That was the deal."

"Careful with what you're agreeing too, Ariadne."

His voice rumbled from the lowest part of his chest, and the way he said my name sent tremors down my spine and goosebumps across my arms like the flickering flame of a burning candle. He was trying to hold back, and I could see it in his eyes. He was right. We were bad for each other, but we were also so fucking good. And I knew that I could play this game and leave it unscathed. It was different this time. I held the cards. He was the player. I was the dealer. And I just gave him the best deck of his life. So, I stepped towards him as he slowly turned around, his eyes cloudy with searing, hot passion, dilating when my lips, painted signature red, curled into a seductive smile, hidden with dark intentions I knew he wanted to discover.

"Are you going to back out of the deal, Nero?"

"You're going to regret this."

I didn't regret anything. As I unbuttoned my coat, slipping it off my shoulders, standing in front of him with nothing on but lingerie and black heels, I knew I had him where I wanted him. I would give him what he wanted, I would submit to his demands, I would do anything to destroy my enemies. And he was going to help me do it.

"Deal?"

Because there was nothing more powerful than a woman scorned.

His eyes forced themselves to tear away from my body, scorching me with yearning, and his lips coiled into an enticing smirk as he said, "Deal."

CHAPTER 16

it's you

"Where are you hiding?" Nero said, and I pressed myself closer against the wall, hiding in the shadows of his bedroom, trying not to give away my location. "You know I'll find you in the end."

I had no doubt he would, but I bit back the laughter threatening to escape. I heard him enter the bedroom and slowly roam around, his shadow trailing behind him, brushing past my own. I could feel my heart pounding in my chest and the blood racing through my body like a shot of adrenaline. I resisted the urge to shiver when his blue eyes twinkled in the darkness of the room. He moved stealthily but not enough to hide his presence from me.

"Come on, I promise that I'll play nice," he grinned, cheekily, pearly white teeth almost blinding me when he glanced in the direction of my hiding spot. I knew he found me but I still didn't come out, trying to sink as far into the wall as I possibly could. "I'll always find you."

The words were like a vow and before I could blink, I was snatched out from the darkness. Stumbling into his arms, I glowered as he smirked down at me. His fingers brushed the hair away from my face before trailing down the length of my arm, entwining our hands together.

"Found you."

"I didn't mean to do it," I quickly said, and he arched a brow, amused. "It was an accident."

"You accidently pushed me into the pool?" I nodded, blinking innocently. Nero stared at me before laughing. The rich sound made my toes curl. "You're a terrible liar."

"It's what happened," I shrugged, stepping back. *Nero didn't let go of my hand, and I didn't want him to. "You probably drank too much to realize."*

"If you're suggesting I can't handle my liquor, you're sorely mistaken."

My lips tugged into a smirk, and I swear I saw him glance at them before meeting my eyes. The blueness of his eyes were a translucent masterpiece and it knocked the breath out of me. For a second, I forgot what I was going to say before I managed to stammer, "Now, you're a terrible liar."

Nero's smile blew me away and that was when I knew I had to leave. It was impossible to be in the same room as him without wanting a taste. Just a small taste. I spent years dying to know what it would be like to kiss him and every second alone was pure torture. I had to leave before I did something bad. I could hear the thumping music from the Christmas party below, but nothing was as loud as the sound of my heartbeat when Nero looked at me like that. Like I was the sun and the moon. Like I was everything.

"We should go back," I said, but it sounded like a breathless whisper.

"Maybe," was his response, his gaze giving nothing away. *"Or we could stay here."*

My laugh was short. "Our parents would kill us."

He inched closer, and my smile dropped. "They'll never know. How about it, Ari?"

"And do what?" I asked, almost trembling when his hand gripped mine whilst the other caressed the side of my face. His eyes were luminous in the dark and the corner of his lips pulled. He looked down to my lips. I swallowed, thickly. *"What do you want, Nero?"*

"You," he whispered. *I held my breath. He looked up and those orbs brought me back to life. "I always* want *you."*

*

Before I could blink, Nero's hands drew me towards him, his eyes dancing down the length of my body before looking back up. He seemed hesitant to kiss me and then I remembered why – he wanted my permission. His gaze searched for mine and he whispered, "Can I kiss you?"

Four simple words and yet my entire body torched at the sound. My throat bobbed and said, "Yes."

Without skipping a beat, Nero's lips found mine. The second he kissed me I saw sparklers explode in the back of my mind. He curled his arms around my body, and I clutched his shirt, tugging him closer.

Everything about him tasted like heaven and sin, reminding me of how long I spent deprived of that feeling. It reminded me of how long I spent searching for an alternative. But there was nothing that tasted as good as Nero. I bit his lower lip, drawing it out playfully, peering up with an impish grin.

"Aria, stop looking at me like that," he grunted. "There's only so much I can control."

"Make me," I retorted, like the brat I was.

Those blue eyes bubbled with wickedness and suddenly, I was brought back to that evening when we first kissed. Everything changed after that. Prompted by my challenge, Nero swooped me into his arms and brought me to the couch, having me mount on top of him. He didn't kiss me straight away like I expected him to. Instead, he brushed his thumb over my lips and smiled.

"You know I'll always want you," he swore.

"You don't need to pretend this means anything more to you," I laughed and he frowned.

"But it does," he replied, and I stopped laughing. His gaze was too serious for me to lighten the mood. His thumb idly kept tracing my lips. "This waiting to be with you, it's just a self-preservation thing… because once we go there, once we become… this intimate again, I'll never want to stop. So, for my own sake, I need you to be sure. I need you to understand that this is something *you* want, that you'll keep me, that you *want* me to keep you."

I wanted to tell him that I had wanted him for as long as I could possibly remember. I could have laid my heart out there on a platter, but I didn't. It didn't end well the last time I did. He was a drug. One taste and the intoxication was instant. Whatever he wanted to do was what we would do, and there wasn't a thing I could do to stop him – not that I would want to. His strong gust of citrus that was powerfully anchored by the Ambroxan unleashed a strong woody scent, sending me into a heady trance. One that wouldn't end until our bodies lost any inhibitions. With the door closed, every pretense fell away. The façade we showed the world melted and all we wanted to do was ruin each other's soul in the most delicious kinds of way.

"I want you, Nero," I finally murmured, kissing him softly enough that it had him yearning for more. "I'm sure about this."

He studied me under his long lashes before kissing me again. Every kiss had a raw intensity – breaths fast, heart rates faster. Then, before

I knew how it had happened, we were as bare as our souls and moving in harmony with each other. His fingertips were electric; they must have been, for wherever he touched sent tingles across my skin in a frenzy of static. As they moved over my skin, my body had a transitory paralysis; my mind unable to process the pleasure so fast. His head moved around to my ears, and he would whisper the breathtaking things he had planned for me. Suddenly, my body was off pause-mode, and I pulled back for a kiss that was both soft and hard. Both of us moving in an intoxicated dance of limbs, never making the exact same moves twice. He laid me onto the couch and my back arched to fit the curve of his frame.

He worked fast to remove any items of clothing and when he reached my heels, he said, wolfishly, "You have to keep *them* on."

I laughed and he smiled against the crook of my neck. One touch and it was over; it had always been like that with Nero. I could feel the sparks across my skin and like magic, I was hypnotized. I could have easily taken control but something about watching Nero completely taint me was captivating. From there on in, it was all passion, intense and intoxicating. It was my release, my escape, my solace. Too many of my switches were flicked for a reserve gear to be possible. If this was it, all I could do now was go along for the ride and pray my instincts were right. Then all at once, he stopped, and I sucked in a sharp breath of air as he looked down at me. His eyes as blue as the sky on a summer's day. They watched me as I writhed, wanting him to continue.

"What are you doing?" I managed to breathe out.

"Beg for me, Aria," Again, four simple words trapped the air in my lungs.

"What?"

He shifted and I seized his shoulders, curving my spine. "You heard me."

"I don't beg," It was a lie and he saw right through me like glass.

"You tasted like honey," Nero spoke in a deep voice that rumbled from his chest and had me almost give in. "No matter what I did, I couldn't forget how you tasted. It was like heaven."

"Stop," I murmured, not wanting to hear any of those compliments from his lips despite how they made my body jolt in delight.

He tilted his head. "Stop what? Praising you? Because I could do that all day."

I couldn't stop staring at him because his gaze burned as bright as a forest fire. He was taking small pieces of me until I would have nothing left. I couldn't let him take those pieces again, but I couldn't stop him. My inner dilemma had me wanting to disappear, especially when he looked at me like that. It was so intense. So starved. So heart-shattering.

"Do you hate me, Aria?"

I paused. "Yes."

"Good," Nero said but his eyes said something else. I just couldn't figure it out. "Because I hate you too." Something about those words pained me more than I expected. Our gaze clashed. Fire against ice. "Did you miss me, Aria?"

I finally drank him in. From top to bottom. For the first time that evening, I saw every flex and contour of his frame. I saw how chiseled his torso was from years of training. I saw his corded arms and the veins that tensed when he moved. I saw *him*. He could have easily swallowed me in his arms, but he held himself above me with ease, placing on hand on my hip, drawing circles, lazily. I saw his ink, although it didn't cover his entire chest, it might as well have. Beneath every tattoo was a scar. He was a ruthless soldier growing up. He trained and trained and trained until nothing hurt him. I remembered getting so mad when he would come back with another scar during training, or worse, wounds from operations my father would send us on. Most often, I would leave unscathed because he had taken the brunt of it. I hated him for it. I hated him for always protecting me. I hated him because he made me feel like I was enough. I hated him tonight for making me feel like he still loved me.

"No," I answered, pushing against his chest. He fell back, surprised, and I used that to my advantage, straddling him. "But I think you missed me."

Before he could respond, our bodies morphed into one and I silenced his question with a kiss. Everything stopped and I felt so consumed by him that I couldn't even remember why I was here in the first place. But I didn't care. I didn't care anymore. Because when he kissed me back, when he rested his hands on my waist, when he watched me, when he let me take control, nothing mattered except us in that moment. I spent too long being deprived of Nero that one taste became an addiction. My hair curtained around us when I rested my forehead against his, feeling his warm breath caress my cheeks. In his home, we forgot our responsibilities and our differences. We were drunk on each other and molded together like we were made for each other. It wasn't soft or gentle but hungry and territorial like we needed this. As if we wanted to prove something to each other. And when the moment was over and the stars in the night sky burnt as brilliantly as Nero's eyes, I sucked in a sharp breath of air and begged for more.

Because he was right. I would always want more.

And I was right. He did miss me.

But that didn't matter because we would never admit it to each other.

"I look forward to working with you," Nero hummed, stealing a final kiss.

I met his gaze. "As do I."

Not if we would never let the other win.

*

"I'll always want you."

The second he said that I found myself kissing him. I shouldn't have done it. I knew it the moment I did. When our lips met, he didn't move as if he was taken aback. My cheeks flushed in embarrassment at the blatant rejection, so I began to pull away. But then his hand found the small of my back and the other, still holding my hand, tugged me closer.

And he kissed me back.

We crossed the line and there was no way back.

But I didn't care because I had never been kissed like this before. He was like the air I didn't know I needed. He backed me against the wall, gripping my hips as I wantonly sought for more. I needed more. He was all I had ever wanted and finally, I gave in to my desires. I wasn't sure whether he felt the same, but I was too afraid to ask in case it broke the spell we were in. All those years of teasing one another came down to this. And I didn't regret a second of it.

He kissed me like he had nothing to lose, but what he didn't realize was that I had everything to lose.

I just didn't realize that everything would be him.

CHAPTER 17

a week

Kira was leaning over a corpse by the time I reached her. Having learnt of another auction, we both decided to gate crash the event. Luckily for us, it had barely begun, giving us plenty of time to snap the necks of the guards and free their captives. With Sophie and Mark's help, we gathered all of the victims, many whom where young girls, and send them back to the Manor to be rehabilitated. Since then, we've had time to make a lot of bad people suffer. Kira kicked the body and then poked his arm, as if to check whether the man was actually dead or not. I had no clue as to who he was, but I knew he had no chance up against her. She was ruthlessly callous with her methods, taking pleasure in inflicting pain. The thought made me proud. With the man's arm bent awkwardly, a leg broken, and blood gushing out from a wound in his stomach, he should've been on the brink of death. Only to my amazement, the man groaned and staggered back onto his feet, anguish clear across his face. Kira sighed, almost as if she was disappointed. Spitting out blood, he glared at her, reaching for his gun, but she knocked him down, her heel crushing his kneecap. I heard bones shatter and I shook my head, fascinated. Yelling out, the man collapsed into a sack of flesh and bones. Kira grasped the sweaty strands of his hair, lifting his face, and I could see all the bloody wounds and bruises that she inflicted.

"You just don't give up," she hummed, cocking her head. "I kind of respect that."

"Kira, stop playing with your food," I muttered, stepping over another corpse, blood dripping off my blade.

"But, it's so fun," Like a child, she grinned at me, toothily. "Go finish up. I'll have my fun out here."

After sending her victim a pitiful look, I disappeared out from the back and appeared onto the stage, my eyes savouring the chaos we havocked. Bodies. So many dead bodies. Bloody. Broken. Battered. It was a glorious battlefield of death. Someone wept, quietly, by the podium and I caught a body trying to hide themselves from me. *Too late.* I didn't bother being quiet, allowing them to hear the loud taps of my heels. Why should I hide myself from my prey? The fear of knowing you were about to die was far stronger than the fear of being caught. I could see their quivering body behind the dais, failing miserably to hide, a gravel rolling back and forth beside them. My lips tugged to my ears.

"Come out, come out," I sang. "Wherever you are."

A choked sob was my response.

"Hiding will only prolong the pain."

"Wh-who are you?" the person stammered out. A man.

I dragged the blade across the podium, leaning over just as they peered up. I smirked. "I'm Aria."

"P-please," he begged, his silver eyes imploring me for mercy. I knelt beside him, my fingers ran through his hair, softly, earning a small whimper, eyes watery and bloodshot with fear.

"*Shh…*" I hushed, like a mother soothing their baby.

"What are you going to do?"

"*Ah,*" I clicked my tongue, bring the sharp knife to their throat. "Where do I begin?"

*

"Nero," I hissed, when he moved from behind me. "*Fuck.*"

Hiking up my skirt to my hips, his fingers stroked my waist as he pressed me against the side of his desk. He chuckled at the sound of my curse, angling my head to the side where he captured my lips with a hard and punishing kiss. Devastating me, I collapsed with novae exploding at the back of my mind. A rush of fatigue followed afterwards, and I sighed, tilting my head to the side to allow him access to the sensitive part of my neck. I shouldn't have enjoyed this as much as I did, but who was I to deny myself of pleasure?

"How comes you came so quickly?" he murmured, his words tickling my skin. "Missed me?"

"Don't get too cocky, Nero," I responded, turning around, and hooking my arms around his neck. "I was already on my way here."

He raised a brow, lifting me onto the desk before settling between my legs, my back arching as I bit back a moan. My body was recovering from the earth-shattering experiences that Nero had consistently put me through during the last hour, and here he was heading in for another. When I arrived with new information, he demanded that I fulfil his request before we talked business. Usually, I would have put up more of a fight but before I could, he had already stifled me with a toe-curling kiss, and then nothing else really mattered afterwards. He was slowly overwhelming me with this powerful, heated passion that left me craving for more. I didn't beg; I would never ask, but it wouldn't matter because the second he looked at me, all sense of right collapsed like dominoes.

"How comes?"

"Enzo..." I gasped, falling apart again underneath his hypnotic ocean-like eyes. He arched his brow, waiting for me to finish. "...has an appointment with you two days from now, at noon."

Nero bent down to kiss me, tenderly, tucking my torn underwear into his back pocket, before he fixed himself up whilst I sat, heaving, trying to catch my breath. I was going to hell. I was sure of it. I mean, I already knew this, given that I had so much blood on my hands that repentance was a long-gone possibility. But now, I was one hundred percent sure, because if I couldn't stop myself from *wanting* Nero, soon I wouldn't be able to stop myself from *needing* Nero. And that was far more dangerous. My mind felt dazed, and I scolded myself for getting so distracted, but I couldn't help it. He was like heroin in my bloodstream, and I couldn't survive without having a taste of him.

"I see," he said, my attention snapping back to him.

Pouring himself a glass of whiskey, he drank it very quickly, his Adam's apple bobbing, which had me clenching my thighs as a sudden burst of need flourished once again. I should have hoped that he didn't notice, but nothing got past him. He saw everything. His eyes twinkled and a smirk coiled onto his lips as he settled into his seat whilst I jumped off his desk, tidying up my skirt and buttoning my blouse that he had annoyingly ripped opened.

"Don't be late, Nero. This partnership will only work if you do what I say. You are offering him a deal, make sure he doesn't refuse. I don't care what you have to say for him to agree, but you need to get him to sign this." Taking the contract out from my bag, I slid it across his desk where he scanned it, thoroughly. "I'm relying on you."

"I haven't heard you say that in a long time," he quipped, playfully. I wasn't amused. "Don't make me take it back then."

Blue eyes implored me, his tongue wetting his pink lips swollen from my kisses, before he lifted up a brow. I didn't back down from his gaze, but my body burned at the force of it. The room became silent as I waited for him to say something, but all I heard was the sound of his men outside in the training grounds. The sound reminded me of when we were younger, and the hours we would spend battling one another. Yet, the years had gone by, and we were faced in another battle. A battle of dominance. He sat there, staring. A smirk grew on his lips, and I began to wonder if I had succumbed to a spell, a curse of sorts. Because the longer he stared, the weaker my knees became. Nero seemed amused when he realized I wouldn't submit, masking his true expression, as he pushed the contract to the side, and leaned back against his chair.

"Come here, Aria," he ordered, his voice dropping a few octaves.

I sighed, feeling sore yet an appetite raged within me, not that I would ever let him know that. "Nero, are you even listening to me?"

"I have listened to you. Now it's your turn to listen to me," Nero responded, firmly. "I won't repeat myself a third time. Come here."

I weighed the rights and wrongs, before reluctantly surrendering. I knew if I wanted Nero to be like putty in my hands, I had a game to play and only I could play the game. However, that didn't mean I couldn't enjoy myself. I sauntered over – well, more like limped, which had him fighting back a smile. As soon as I reached him, he brought me onto his lap, one hand at the bottom of my spine, and the other disappearing under my skirt.

"I'm glad you wore a skirt today," he muttered, more to himself than me, but it had the corner of my lips lifting before they dropped as a cry escaped from my mouth. "Christ, I won't ever get used to this. I won't ever get used to you. You truly are magnificent, *amore*."

I rested my head against his, my chest pressing against his body as my grip tightened on his arms. Unbridled, I forgot why I had come to see him and instead focused on our movements, which reminded me of the waves crashing against the shoreline in Italy.

"Who's the boss, Aria?" he questioned. His aquamarine orbs heatedly watching me fall under his control.

"*Nero…*"

"Answer me, Aria," Nero all but purred, his lips brushing against mine. "Who's the boss?"

We both knew it was me, but there was something so bewitching about letting him control me. Something that possessed me to say, "You." I found myself locking onto his gaze and I breathed out, "Always you."

Nero smirked, but it was hard to tell whether it was because he didn't believe me, or because he loved my answer. It didn't matter. He removed his hand from its escapade, much to my dismay, but not even a minute later, he replaced the feeling with something far better. I knocked my head back when I felt him reach the very depth of me, stealing a piece of my heart whilst he was there, and with every motion, he took another piece. I wasn't sure how much was left of my frozen heart, but I was sure that by the time he was done, he would hold all the pieces and I would have nothing left to separate me from human and sin. Surely, I should be upset about it, but for some twisted reason, I couldn't care less. He could take everything from me, and I would still be at the top because power didn't come from having a heart; it came from knowing when and how to use your heart. The sensation was overwhelming when we moved together in a hungry fashion, but I welcomed it with open arms. He clutched my hair and kissed me as if I was the reason he could breathe. Whilst he was taking parts of me, I was taking parts of him. I would be the reason he wanted to breathe. It was only fair. I wouldn't lose. I couldn't.

"After we are done here," he snarled against my lips, my fingers grasping his hair tightly whilst his rested on my waist to help me move above him at a crazy consistent yet fast pace. "I'm taking you against every other surface in this room."

"Yes," I panted, holding his searing blue eyes. "Do as you please."

"*Sempre*, my Queen."

*

Enzo Rossi was an extremely well-kept and quiet man. He had disturbing, green eyes and black hair that fell to his shoulders in small swells. He was dressed in a beige suit, wearing thin silver rims over his eyes, and a watch with glittering diamonds around the bezel. Inhaling his cigar, he studied me, carefully, before greeting me with a simper.

"I didn't realize we had a guest joining us," he stated, studying me from head to toe. His accent was distinctively Spanish, but it sounded like he had been far from home for too long.

"Unfortunately, I won't be able to join you," I replied, with a saccharine smile. "I have a meeting to attend to, so I'll have to say my goodbyes."

"*How unfortunate*. It's not every day I get meet such a beautiful lady."

From the corner of my eye, I noticed Nero clenching his jaw before he glanced up with a tight smile, squeezing my hand. "I'll pick you up for dinner at eight."

I resisted the urge to roll my eyes at his possessive behavior and bobbed my head in agreement, pressing my lips against his, playing the role of a dutiful girlfriend. I had arrived two hours early, wanting to prep Nero, but ended up spending at least one of those hours fucking him in his bedroom. That insatiable man and his insane appetite. Fortunately, I managed to satisfy both our needs before I gave him a rundown of what to expect from Enzo Rossi. Though, I was marginally surprised when he told me that he had already done his homework and was thoroughly prepared without my help. So, naturally, I rewarded him for good behavior. I wasn't a goddess, but *holy fuck*, he knew how to make me feel like one.

"I'll call you when I'm done," I murmured, before sending one last look to Enzo, who was staring enviously, as I left Nero's office.

I felt Enzo's gaze until the door closed behind me. Finally, I exhaled, pressing my back against the door, managing to regain my composure. A moment after, I noticed Matteo striding towards my direction and took that as my cue to leave. I straightened out my dress that Nero successfully managed to leave intact and veiled any worry I had. I had to trust Nero, but that thought left a plummeting feeling in my stomach. I had no choice and swallowed my anxieties, before smiling brightly at Matteo.

He didn't notice my concern and said, "They've prepared the room for you, Aria."

"Thank you, Matteo," I responded.

I followed his lead as he took us into an empty room where I could carefully monitor the interaction between Nero and Enzo. The room was fitted with the most advanced surveillance technology and gear, along with Kira and Xander, who were concentrating on setting everything up. Having arrived with me this morning, they managed to set up a temporary camera system in Nero's office whilst I was occupied with him in his bedroom. I didn't think Nero liked the idea of having cameras in his office, but after I assured him that it was only for this meeting and promised him some other questionable things, he gave in. When I left his bedroom, Kira didn't waste any time to tease me, but more importantly, she reminded me that Nero was completely in my control. Control. The word had me pause for a second. But I ignored the guilt and continued with the plan. Nero was just using me like I was using him, and that was all there was to it.

"*I'll always want you.*"

"Aria?" My eyes flickered to Matteo, who studied me with concern. "You okay?"

I nodded and proceeded to move towards Kira and Xander. Having heard me, Kira glanced up with a smile before looking at Matteo. Her smile only broadened until it reminded me of something vaguely familiar to the Cheshire cat in *Alice in Wonderland*.

"You must be Matteo?" she asked, and he frowned as if realizing something.

"Weren't you at —"

"The club? The restaurant? Your house?" she interrupted, a twinkle in the paleness of her azure irises.

"Wait, his house?" I raised my brow and she shot me a grin.

"I'd rate his hospitality five stars."

Glimpsing at Matteo, I noticed his ears beginning to burn as he glared at the Japanese girl. I wanted to know more, but something told me that these two had a lot of history and I would need more than a few minutes to hear it all.

Shaking my head, I chuckled, amused. "Kira, what happened to *not* mixing business with pleasure?"

"That was before Matteo," she chirped, sending him a wink. "We should hook up again if you're free."

"You little —"

"*Anyways,*" Xander thankfully interjected, with a warning look at Kira, who playfully put her hands up in surrender, pursing her smile. "Aria, would you like to see what's happening?"

Bobbing my head, I slipped into the empty seat besides Xander and concentrated on the screens set up in front of me. There were cameras stationed in all corners of the room so we had the optimum angles and could study Enzo carefully without missing a beat. I heard Kira shuffle to stand beside me, whilst Matteo leaned over Xander's shoulder. On the screens, we watched Enzo lean forward as Nero poured them whiskey into heavy tumbler glasses. His jade eyes tracked Nero's movements before narrowing as the corner of his lips lifted.

"She's a beauty. What is her name?" Enzo asked, indifferently but I heard the curiosity in his voice. Which meant, so did Nero.

But he didn't flinch as he continued to pour. "Lyra."

"Have you been together for long?"

I prayed Nero had grown out of the temperamental attitude that he used to show as a teenager and could easily conform to the ambience that Enzo brought to the room. I held my breath when I noticed Nero tense before relaxing less than a second later, a lazy smirk gracing his lips as he gave Enzo the glass.

"You could say that," he answered, settling into the seat opposite him.

Enzo chuckled. "Well, you're a truly lucky man. She looks like something special."

"Thanks, man," he clinked his glass against Enzo's.

"So, what prompted this meeting? I thought last time we spoke you didn't want to accept my proposal."

Nero shrugged, unbothered by Enzo's clipped tone. "People change, and so does circumstances."

Enzo rose a brow. "Why are we meeting, Russo?"

Pushing the contract that I drafted up in front of Enzo, Nero stated, "I want to expand my business. I realize that to stay at the top I need to make some sacrifices. The Italian mafia, alongside the Russians, are one of the largest organizations in the world, and I intend to protect that title."

"Why does this include me?" he questioned.

"You and I both know that you have extremely valuable resources which could be of vast help to the mafia."

Enzo chuckled, ominously. "I've had my fair share of experiences with the mafia, Russo. And let's just say, they are *not* experiences that I'd like to have again."

"What can I do to get you to agree?"

Nero slouched back against his couch, one leg crossed over the other as he downed the rest of his drink, not looking worried by Enzo's refusal. Enzo narrowed his eyes, cocking his head to the side as a brow raised in fascination.

"Now thinking about it, there's something I do want."

"What is it?"

A sinister smile twisted onto the green-eyed man's lips. "I have a younger sister."

Instantly, warning bells sounded off in the back of my head and I clenched my jaw as Xander sent me a careful look. Nero didn't know about Violetta, let alone that she was in my custody. His eyes narrowed as he urged Enzo to continue. I stilled as I waited.

"Her name is Violetta. I haven't been in touch with her since our parents passed away. She was adopted, and unfortunately I was too young to care for her, so we got separated," *Liar.* These were all lies. His parents were alive. And Violetta wasn't orphaned but hidden. These were all lies. "Anyway, I can't find her, and I fear that she's in the wrong hands. If you promise to find her, I'll sign this proposal."

I saw Nero ponder over the idea, not understanding what was actually at stake. Enzo didn't care for Violetta; he cared for her value. And once he got hold of her, who was to say that she would be safe. I jumped out of my seat, digging out my phone from my pocket as I noticed Nero opening his mouth to speak, instantly dialing his number. Before he could say a word, his phone rang, the tension thick in both his office and the room I was in. Xander and Kira both gave me worried looks as Matteo seemed confused at my sudden outburst. Nero halted, grabbing his phone from the inside of his blazer, his face not making a single movement when he noticed my name blinking on the screen.

"Is it important?" Enzo queried, sipping his drink.

"Sorry, please excuse me," Nero muttered, getting out his seat and leaving the room.

"Aria, what are you doing?" I heard Kira say, as I hung up to meet Nero outside in the foyer.

"I'm not letting him sell Vi for our golden ticket in," I hissed, storming out of the room where I met with a confused blue-eyed Italian halfway down.

"What is going on?" he said, in hushed tones.

"Don't agree to it," I ordered.

"Why not?" Nero frowned. "You said at any cost."

"Not a young girl's life."

"It's his sister."

"His sister who is worth *fifty-five million* dollars," I snapped.

Nero's face changed instantly. "*What?*"

"Can you trust me, Nero?" I pleaded, feeling desperate in fear of Violetta's safety. "Just don't agree to his terms."

He was silent for a long time, studying me carefully, his eyes gave away nothing as his jaw clenched and then unclenched.

"Do you have her?" he asked, catching me off guard. "That's why you're adamant about not accepting this deal. She's in your care."

"She's twelve, Nero. Abandoned and abused. She doesn't deserve anymore pain," I murmured, bowing my head as I remembered the fear in Violetta's eyes. So clear, like the morning sky during the winter.

It was the reason I gave myself to Nero. I made a deal with the devil and Violetta was one of the many people that I did it for. Perhaps, my desires changed at some point, but the reason stayed the same. I needed to protect them. No matter what. My tormented thoughts were broken when I felt his hand cradle the side of my face, surprising me as I glanced up to see him wearing a tender expression.

"I wish you told me what happened. What changed you because I'm scared that whatever you have going on will end up hurting you."

I wanted to tell him everything. But I couldn't. I didn't know where to start and where to end. So, I closed my eyes, savored his touch, before stepping back. His hand fell to his side and made no action to touch me again.

"Perhaps, one day," I replied, quietly. "But that day isn't today."

Nero didn't say anything before releasing a heavy sigh, kissing my forehead. Then, he turned around on his heel and strode back into his office, rolling the tension off his shoulders. With one last glimpse at me, I saw how troubled his cerulean eyes were before he closed the door. I stood there for a long second before darting back to the monitor room, ignoring everyone's imploring gaze, as I sought the screens.

"What happened?" Xander asked, as I sat back in my seat but I hushed him, leaning forward to hear Nero's verdict.

"I'm sorry about that," Nero said, pretending to tuck his phone back into his blazer.

Enzo shook his head. "No problem. Care to share?"

"Just a brawl at one of my clubs. Some of the men don't know how

148

to fight without using their guns," Nero chuckled.

Enzo returned the laughter, except it was colder and uncaring, bobbing his head in agreement, fully convinced with Nero's story. "I agree. Men are passionate though, wouldn't you say?"

Nero's response was somewhat calm and calculated, along with the dark smile that looked disconcertingly different from the tender expression he had given me. "A hundred percent. Now, your request. Do you have a picture of this girl?"

Shaking his head, Enzo sighed, pitifully. "Sadly not. But I do know her last whereabouts was in Arizona. I'd start there if I was you."

"So, she's a ghost?"

"I didn't say that." With thinned eyes, Enzo asked, "Are you rejecting my deal?"

"Can I ask why you want my assistance when I'm sure there are plenty of others you could ask?"

"Everyone knows you are the best at finding things. A specialty that would work well in my case."

Nero didn't seem to be flattered by the compliment and angled his head to the side with a mocking smile. "No offense, Rossi, but how can I search for a girl who may no longer exist?"

Enzo's jaw tightened. "Then, I guess we haven't got a deal."

"Don't be so rash," Nero laughed, frostily and dismissively. "I'll look for the girl, but if I can't find her in a week, then I'm calling the search off. That's all I'm offering. My time is limited and, as you said yourself, I do track down plenty of things. Do try to understand."

Enzo's expression darkened before it morphed into a lazy smirk, taking place where that scowl was only a few seconds ago. "Fair enough. One week."

"Aria?" Kira whispered, but I shook my head, informing her silently that I was not listening.

"We'll have to host a banquet in celebration of our partnership," Enzo suggested, with a wry grin.

"If that is what you desire."

"And as soon as it's over, you will search for her," Enzo said it like a question, but it sounded like a statement.

Nero nodded. "As soon as the banquet is over."

The two men stood up as Enzo crooned, "This is the beginning of a brilliant partnership."

"I guess we got ourselves a deal," Nero smiled, holding his hand out which Enzo clasped a second later with a rather icy smile himself.

"I believe we do."

I released a heavy breath that sounded shaky, slugging against my chair as I glanced at Kira and Xander, who had worry etched on their faces. Matteo still looked baffled about what was going on, but I overlooked it and tried to rack up reasons why Nero would blatantly ignore my request. Was he trying to piss me off? That didn't make sense. Something about his tone didn't suggest so, and I knew there was something I was missing. I just couldn't see the bigger picture.

"Aria…" Xander started but couldn't finish his sentence, his words disappearing into the tension filled air.

"What about Vi?" Kira murmured, a second later.

My mind halted as I tried to understand Nero's plan, but I failed to see where he was coming from. I wanted to run into his office and demand to know what he was doing. A week was enough to find anyone if Nero had anything to do with it; he was one of the best trackers in the world. He wouldn't even be able to lie to Enzo. Not with Enzo tracking his every movement. There was no loophole out of this situation. But it just didn't seem right, and the more I pondered over *'a week,'* the more I noticed why it was so familiar to me.

"I'll give you a week, Ariadne," Nero laughed, as I huffed in annoyance, pouting at the sixteen-year-old boy, who stupidly wanted my favorite gun.

"What?"

"A week," he smirked, crossing his arms over his chest. "I'll always give you a week to hide whatever I want or need. After that week, I won't search anymore. Sempre.*"*

"A week," I gasped. Kira frowned in confusion as she glanced at Xander in hope to make sense of what I said

"Sorry?" she looked at me as if I was mad.

I glanced at the pair, wide-eyed filled with understanding. "A week."

Xander laughed nervously, stretching the back of his neck as his eyes flickered between myself and Kira. "Yeah, I know, Boss. I heard what Russo said."

*"*You don't get it. He's giving us a week," I stated, trying to show them that Nero was giving us a chance.

"Okay, now I'm so confused," Matteo chimed in from behind.

I shook my head, noting that there was no time to waste, and I turned to Kira with vital orders, "Violetta will be staying with my family for the time being. Prepare her visit and inform my parents about her arrival tonight. She is not to return home until the week after the banquet."

"Is that a good idea? She'll be too much of a risk outside of the Manor." Xander questioned.

"In the house of the ex-mafia boss and assassin?" I rose a brow, almost laughing at the notion. "Nothing gets through Antonio and Xena Moretti."

"A week?" Kira repeated, her words were still laced with hesitance and doubt.

I ignored the look she shared with Xander and nodded slowly, turning my gaze onto the screens, where I observed Nero as he clinked his glass against Enzo's, celebrating the beginning of a new partnership. As the two men drank the whiskey, his eyes peered up at one of the cameras whilst Enzo was distracted, and a small – almost unnoticeable – smirk made its way onto his face.

Game. Set. And match.

"Yes," I responded, with my own twisted smile. "A week."

CHAPTER 18

games of us

I arched a brow. *"A week?"*

His smirk didn't waver as he gave a sharp nod. "A week."

"What the hell is that meant to mean?"

"It means, Ariadne, that if I ever want or need something that you have, I'll give you a week to hide it. Like a game of hide and seek. I'll do my best to find it, don't you worry. I won't go easy on you. But after a week, if I haven't found it then I'll stop looking for it forever."

The gun rested heavily in my hand as I looked at him, apprehensively. "This applies to anything from here on out?"

"Yes."

"How do you know you'll find it?"

He chuckled, running his fingers through his thick, dark locks. "Because I'm the best tracker."

"And if you don't?"

His eyebrow rose and a wolfish grin beamed on his face. "Then, you're the best hider."

"A week?" I arched a brow, feeling the coldness of my favorite gun strapped onto my thigh. The metal kissed my skin as I crossed one leg over the over. "Are you serious?"

He shrugged, sipping on the glass of red wine. "Deadly."

"What are we? Fifteen?" I sighed, tossing my hair over my shoulder. "A game of hide and seek. Honestly, Nero, out of everything you could've said."

"This is going to be fun, Aria. Don't try denying it. You *always* loved me chasing after you," he stated, mimicking my arched brow.

I glowered. "You're not funny."

"I beg to differ. I think I'm hilarious," Nero mused, grinning. When he noticed that I wasn't laughing, he sighed and rolled his eyes. "Come on, Aria. It will be fun."

I kissed my teeth, unable to reply as the waiter brought our meal to the table, causing the tension to disperse for a short moment. I thanked the waiter, to which he sent a small smirk and wink, dismissing Nero's presence entirely, as he strode away confidently. Nero knit his brows together, frowning as he threw daggers into the poor boy's back.

"*He's a kid*," I exhaled, annoyed, slicing my steak up, when I noticed his glare not faltering. "Stop looking at him as if you want to kill him."

"Perhaps I will. Does he have no manners?" Nero scowled. "I ought to teach him a lesson or two."

Rolling my eyes, I ignored his comments. "I'm surprised he didn't read the fine print."

"Of course, Enzo wouldn't. Not when I just practically offered him a plate of gold. Greedy men don't care about the loss," Nero explained, in a matter-of-fact manner.

I stopped eating midway, glancing up at him underneath hooded lashes. "What about you?"

What about me?" he asked, taking a bite of the juicy steak on his plate.

"Do you care about the losses?"

Nero halted, steel blue eyes flickering away from his plate to hold my interrogating gaze. "I'm not greedy."

"I didn't say you were."

"You're insinuating it."

With our gazes locked, we silently battled one another – questioning who would back down first. It was a competition, no matter what we did. But that was what made it fun. The challenge – *oh, how we loved the challenge.*

"How about we make a bet?" he proposed. "If I find Violetta, you're mine for a whole day. To do whatever I want. But if I don't, I'm yours to play with."

"Are we actually betting on little girl's life?" I scoffed, leaning back in my seat.

Nero chuckled, darkly. "Don't pretend to be the better person, Aria. Me and you, both know you'll never back down from a bet. You love the thrill of it, the high and the glory of winning. Like sex. The feeling of your legs wrapped around my waist, your nails leaving scratch marks on my back as I pound into you. *Quick and rough.* That's how these games make you feel."

"Do you have to be so crude?" I hissed under my breath, ignoring the burning of my cheeks at the thought of someone hearing him.

"I think you rather like it when I am."

My breath become chopped and heavy, as I tried to feign how unaffected I was by his errant words.

"I'm not like that anymore," I gritted.

Lifting a brow, amused, he said, "Oh?"

"These games are childish. We're not fifteen anymore."

"So, why have we made this deal then?"

I scowled. "That's different."

"How?" Nero asked, pouring himself another glass of wine. "It was the only way you could make me agree. It's in our nature to play games. Like always, from the beginning till the end. *Sempre.*"

"I'm not agreeing to this bet, Nero. You're not going to find Vi," I declared, causing him to lean across the table.

"Then let's bet on it if you're so confident. I am the best tracker, Aria, and I don't think you realize how polished my skills have gotten since you left."

"Clearly not well enough, if you were still unable to find me," I smirked, when I noticed his eyes flash with annoyance and his jaw tighten. Something else, though, caught his attention. It almost threw me off my game. I couldn't tell what it was, so I ignored it.

"Taunt me all you want, Aria," he replied in a low, almost inaudible tone, laced with dominance and desire. "But tonight, I promise you won't be able to walk tomorrow."

Taken aback, my breath hitched, and the longing disrupted my senses; I squeezed my legs together, burning up underneath his intense heated look. Utterly lost in Nero's deep, oceanic eyes, I didn't even realize the waiter from before standing by our table with a flirty glance directed at me.

"Is there anything else I can get for you?" he asked, but the words completely washed over me.

"No," Nero responded, his gaze unwavering.

"Is there anything else I can get for you?" The waiter repeated, and it wasn't until Nero's eyes snapped up to the boy, did I comprehend how the waiter was only focused on me - waiting for a response. *Well, fuck.*

Nero's eyes narrowed into thin shards as he countered, menacingly, "We don't need anything else. Or do you not understand basic English. In fact, do you even have any manners?"

The waiter's eyes widened; his face burned in chagrin as everyone in the restaurant glanced in our direction to see what the commotion was. "I'm sorry, Sir –"

Nero abruptly stood up, throwing his napkin onto his barely touched plate. "No need. We're done here. Place the bill under my name."

Before the waiter could respond, Nero strode past him, his fingers curling around my wrist as he tugged me out of my seat, shock glazing my face when he pulled me behind him as we left the restaurant. I could barely keep up with his large strides having worn my red bottom stilettos. As soon as we were outside, I felt the frosty winter air hit my face, cooling the redness building across my skin.

"Nero!" I exclaimed, shaking his hold off me when we were in front of his car. "What the fuck is wrong with you?"

Dark cobalt eyes scrutinized me. "I hate the way he was looking at you."

I exhaled sharply. "He's a little boy!"

"I don't fucking care. You do not deserve to be stared at or talked about as if you're some sort of toy."

"Oh, that's rich coming from you after you fucking yanked me out of that restaurant," I scoffed, curling my lips in anger.

Nero ran his fingers through his hair, his eyes closing momentarily – something he did to contain his frustration and anger. A second later, he sighed, "Get in the car, Aria."

"No," I spat out.

"Don't piss me off," he warned, impatiently.

I folded my arms over my chest, challenging him as I rose a brow. "Or what?"

His entire face darkened, taking two steps until he was towering over me, warm and minty breath fanning over my face as he leaned down, whispering, forebodingly, "Do you want me to fuck you in public?"

Mortified by how much those words affected me, I opened my mouth and then closed it like a fish, absolutely speechless. When I didn't reply, he moved back with a triumphant look, opening the door to his car. I bit back a caustic retort, grudgingly getting inside. I grumbled as I sulked in the seat of his beautiful Benz, whilst he paid the concierge before slipping into the driver's seat. With a growl from his expensive car with a leather interior, we shot off onto the road back home. The silence thickly encased us with tension, his eyes flickering in my direction every now and then, but I stubbornly looked ahead, not wanting to give him the satisfaction of my attention. I knew he was feeling bad about his actions; I knew him better than he knew himself.

With one hand on the steering wheel, the other rested on my thigh, squeezing it slightly as he exhaled heavily. "I'm sorry. I didn't mean to act the way I did, Aria. It was wrong of me."

I rolled my eyes, avoiding his stare as I looked out of the window, trying to admire the magnificent city and its sparkling lights alongside the crowds of people. I didn't want to forgive him just yet and angled my body away from him. I heard him release another sigh, moving his hand away from my thigh and onto the steering wheel, when he made a sudden U-turn. A squeal of surprise escaped my lips as I held onto my bag that nearly fell off my lap. Confusion filled me as I noticed him parking into a desolate street, cutting the engine short before he directed his full attention onto me.

"What are you doing?" I frowned.

"Did I mention how beautiful you look in that black dress?" he answered instead, catching me off guard.

I narrowed my eyes in cynicism. "What are you trying to do, Nero?"

He didn't respond and instead leaned over my lap where he unbuckled my seatbelt, the strap snapping back to its holster. He didn't give me time to blink and pulled me onto his lap so I that I mounted him, my hands gripping onto his shoulders for balance, shocking me. The warmth of his azure eyes steadily held my gaze despite the surprise shrouding my face. He reached out to tuck a strand of hair behind my ear, before trailing his fingers down from my jawline to my collarbone. His hot breath blew across my face, causing my eyes to flutter shut, involuntarily.

"So beautiful," he murmured, continuing his journey with his hands down to arch of my chest to the crevasse between my legs. "Forgive me, Aria."

"Do you even know what you did wrong?" I managed to say, as he drew circles against the skin that my dress didn't cover. I only had Kira to blame since she pushed me to wear this short, black dress.

"I shouldn't try to control you."

"No, you shouldn't," I swallowed when his lips met my throat.

"And I shouldn't have acted so rashly."

"No, you shouldn't," the words sounded like a faint whisper.

"But, Aria," he began, brushing his nose against my collarbone before moving his lips above mine. All I needed to do was bend forward and steal that kiss he was keeping away from me. I hummed and he looked up at me under those long lashes. "You shouldn't look so enthralling in public. It doesn't help my case."

"You're not fair, Nero," I breathed out, seeing the appetite swimming in his dusky, blue eyes.

"Forgive me," Finally, locating his hand between my thighs with a tender graze from his thumb. "*Please*, Aria."

Before I could even react, I gasped in shock, jolting forward with a tight grasp on his shoulders as his fingers found their final destination. He watched me, expectantly, arching a brow as he awaited my answer. I swallowed again, shoving the feelings away, bobbing my head, which had him breaking into a devastating, provocative smile before he proceeded to wreak havoc within – leaving me in rubble for a *very* long time.

*

"Now that Enzo signed the contract yesterday, we can move onto Phase Two," I commenced, my eyes scouting the people sitting around the meeting table, attentively focused on my words. "Operation Locksmith. Kira, if you may."

She slipped out of her seat beside me, settling in front of the projected screen which revealed detailed plans about our way into the Serpents' lair. Her blonde hair was effortlessly groomed back, a red dress perfectly suiting her slim frame, and the silver accessories complimented her porcelain complexion, as her blue eyes examined us with so much power that they could easily intimidate people. It was one of the reasons she was my right-hand woman.

"Operation Locksmith is a series of steps that will ensure us access into the Serpents' lair," she clarified, gesturing to the large estate that was barricaded with tall, spiked gates and from one look, maybe a hundred or so armed men. "This estate is found on the outskirts of New York. It's far up north, just before the borders of Canada."

"This estate is home to the key players of their Inner Circle," I added, everyone glancing in my direction. "Viktor, who is currently in our captivity, and Enzo are only two of six men that control the Serpents. The aim is to root them out and watch the foundations crumble."

"How are we going to get in?" Sophie asked with a frown. "That looks virtually impossible to even enter."

I gave her a leveled gaze. "Nothing's impossible, Sophie."

She looked uneasy but bobbed her head in understanding. Impossible wasn't in our dictionary, not when they had all been to hell and back. Betrayed, abused, and lied to. Nothing was impossible in a world filled with monsters. And I created the best of them. I trusted that their experiences would empower them, and they did. You gave a girl a gun and instead of running away, she would put a bullet through your heart. I never wanted anyone to do anything they didn't want to do, but they also acknowledged that some things meant having blood on their hands. My eyes found Kira. I recalled the day she killed her first victim. It had been over a year since I found her, and I trained her from what little knowledge she had before. And when it was time, we hunted down our first victim. Her abuser. I could still remember it like it was yesterday. When she held the gun against the temple of his head, and when she pulled the trigger, and the sound of the bullet slicing through his skull. Her hand didn't tremble, and she didn't look away as he collapsed onto his knees in front of her, and the blood pooled around her Jimmy Choo's. I knew that day haunted her, but the relief superseded the fear, because killing her abuser meant that we got to save Sophie.

"Enzo signed the contract but didn't read the small print, which now means all of his bank transfers can be routed to us. We'll know exactly where the money is going and to whom it's going. Moreover, his so-called partnership with Nero means that the other members of the Inner Circle will be forced to crawl out of their dens and intervene," Kira said, and I blinked out of my daze.

Dom's head tilted in confusion, pressing his brows together. "Why would they intervene?"

"Nero Russo is the Don of the Italian mafia," I responded, crossing my arms over my chest. "That means competition. If I remember correctly, with Viktor thought to be dead, and Enzo partnering with Nero, it means their main two links to resources have been cut off."

"They'll come to make sure Enzo doesn't go through with the partnership," Xander murmured, filling in the gaps.

"Essentially."

"It doesn't matter who or how many appear, even if it's just one – it's enough," Kira revealed, turning back to the projected screen which displayed the entrance to the estate. "All we need is a fingerprint."

"Why don't we use Enzo's or Viktor's if they're also part of the Inner Circle?" Mark questioned, breaking his silence, his arm over his girlfriend's shoulders.

"We've tried," I sighed. "It didn't work hence why we are on a slightly tighter schedule."

"I visited the place as soon as I got their fingerprints," Calix shook his head. "Nothing. Maybe they aren't as important as we think they are."

"Perhaps, but we can't risk letting them disappear from our sight. The second the Serpents are aware of us; our plans will be for nothing. This mission requires complete invisibility. We don't exist. We need to stay like that."

Sophie frowned. "So, we're holding Viktor captive for no reason?"

"He may have failed to do his part, but he's a resourceful man, and now he's in my control," I said, darkly. "He's a liability if we let him go."

"So, we just have to pray that one of the four other men that come will have access to this estate," Dom sighed, running his fingers through his hair with a scoff of disbelief.

"Not just any man," Calix dropped a file onto the table, and I took the liberty to be the first to inspect it. "Just Barak Doukas."

Skimming my eyes over what seemed like a guest list, I spotted the name 'Barak Doukas' just as it left Calix's lip. I saw Kira still beside me.

"Who's Barka Dow…" Dom trailed off, struggling to remember the name, pouting when he failed to complete his question.

"Barak Doukas," Kira gnashed, before rolling her eyes. "Idiot."

Dom glared at her. Kira glared back. I ignored their childish behavior and proceeded to answer Dom's question to help bring everyone up to date, "A very old and very rich man. He went into retirement after being in the travel industry for over fifty years. Last year, he declared that he was finally retiring, handing the company to his son, Darius Doukas." After this explanation, I turned to Calix with a small frown. "How comes he's coming?"

Calix shrugged. "Matteo sent this to me before our meeting. It's the finalized guest list to the dinner party Nero and Enzo are holding in celebration of their partnership. Enzo must have added him in thinking that people wouldn't notice."

"He's our man," I muttered, thoughtfully.

"So, what's the plan, Boss?" Xander grinned. Everyone else mimicked the same action, anticipation swimming in their eyes, alongside the hint of sadistic need to bring down these sick bastards.

I smirked, standing up. "Operation Locksmith starts today. And step one is to get a fingerprint from Barak Doukas."

*

I moaned gently, rolling onto my side as a wave of serenity and bliss rushed over me. My eyes fluttered shut when I felt his hot breath against my neck, before he peppered me with small kisses, his finger drawing circles on my shoulder.

"I missed you," he murmured, huskily.

"You literally saw me a couple hours ago," I retorted, cheekily, turning to face him, his emerald eyes burnt brightly but he wasn't amused.

"Hilarious," he grunted.

He lifted one of my legs over his so he could nestle deeply in between me, knocking my breath away, my back arching as I closed my eyes. Hissing underneath his breath, he moved on top where he captured a fervent kiss from me, greedily devouring me and distracting me from my rational thoughts. Blue eyes flashed in the back of my mind and my eyes shot open in surprise, a gasp escaping my lips when I saw green eyes instead. Calix grunted, one hand resting underneath my back to lift me up to his demanding thrusts. My heart hammered, as we collapsed into thousands of splintering novae. My body tingled as he groaned before rolling off me and onto the bed with a sated sigh. But I was still stunned. Guilt chomped at my stomach. How could I be thinking of another guy whilst in bed with someone else? Christ, I was a terrible person.

Why was I thinking about Nero? No, I couldn't. I wasn't.

"Aria," he whispered. I hummed in reply, idly. "Are you okay?"

Nodding tiredly, I hid the bewilderment painted evidently across my face and sent him a broad smile, leaning forward to kiss him gently to distract him of my guilt. He matched the pace of my kiss, never demanding for more. Not like Nero would – *wait, what?* The thought had me stop and I pinched my eyes closed, hoping that Nero would vanish from my mind, but alas, he haunted me there too.

"Aria?" Calix called out when I moved away, sitting up on my bed, running my fingers through my disheveled hair. "What's wrong?"

"Nothing. I'm just stressed," I murmured.

"Are you sure?"

Bobbing my head slowly, I exhaled. "I'm going to get a drink."

I didn't wait for his reply as I slipped out of my bed, grabbing my silk gown that was discarded onto the floor besides Calix's clothes. I wrapped it around my body before trekking down to my kitchen. I searched for a glass and a bottle of wine, immediately pouring myself a glass which I drank in one gulp. Then I wiped my mouth before pouring myself another glass. There was this dull ache in my chest, causing me to draw my brows together as I rubbed against where I felt the pain. My heart never hurt like that, as if someone had wrenched it out of my body. I didn't understand what was going on. But a part of me wasn't sure if I wanted to. I was afraid of what it could mean. Suddenly, my doorbell rang, breaking me out of my muddled spell. Puzzled, I placed the wine down, heading over to see who was visiting me so late at night. The bell rang again just as I opened the door, and my breath was taken away with a loud *whoosh* when I was greeted by steel blue eyes.

"*Nero*," I said, breathlessly.

Shock masked my face as I blinked at the domineering Italian man, who stood before me, scrutinizing me with icy eyes. They ran up and down my body before darkening like the pitch-black night; his jaw clamping just as I realized the current state I was in. There was this sudden burst of anger which caused his cobalt irises to dance with flames, as his lips coiled into a dark scowl.

"Aria."

Fuck.

CHAPTER 19

rivals

"Nero," I whispered, stunned.

"Aria," My name left his lips bitterly, as he stepped into my home, his eyes searching my corridor before settling on the pair of shoes that didn't belong to me. "You didn't pick up my calls."

"I was busy," I replied, closing the door behind me, hesitantly. My eyes flittered around, refusing to meet his piercing gaze.

"Clearly," he said, coldly, striding towards my living room.

I quickly followed him, biting my lower lip nervously. "Why are you here?"

He didn't respond, inspecting the area, before he glanced over his shoulder, blue eyes darkening as they scrutinized me.

"Where's your guest?"

"What do you want?"

"Answer my question, Aria."

"Answer mine, Nero."

We glared at each other, holding one another's glare, unwilling to back down in submission and answer the other person's question. I clenched my jaw, crossing my arms over my chest as I arched a brow.

"Are we really going to argue right now? I'm busy, so let's reschedule," I scoffed, pettily.

Before he could speak, someone else got there first; my eyes widened and my heart stopped as we both looked towards my stairs where Calix strolled down the stairs, running his fingers through his hair with a frown, his trousers loosely hung around his waist and his torso exposed with jagged scars running diagonally across his tanned skin.

"What's going on –"

His words were cut short when he caught Nero's icy glower which burned with fury. I sucked in a sharp breath of air when I noticed Nero's jaw tightening and his fingers curling into a fist, paling as he dug his nails into his palms. His spine stiffened as he pushed his shoulders back, sizing his opponent up. Calix glimpsed briefly at me, his green eyes sparkling with sudden interest, before they resettled on Nero, along with the slight smirk teasing his lips that were stained with my lipstick.

"Russo, what brings you here?" he asked, condescendingly.

"I would ask the same but I'm sure I already know the answer," Nero bit back.

Calix's smirk grew. "I didn't realize you'd be coming, otherwise I would have been dressed more *appropriately*."

Nero took a step forward, anger flaring across his face, before I quickly interjected, sending a sharp look towards the Greek, "Calix, *please*."

Calix refocused his attention onto me, merriment twinkling in his eyes as he playfully held his hands up in surrender, knowing his place.

"I'll be off then," he muttered, heading upstairs to grab his belongings.

Nero was eerily quiet, fuming with anger as he remained frozen in his spot even when Calix returned back downstairs, fully dressed, his disheveled black hair covering his emerald orbs that stared at Nero with annoyance. Sending me one hard look, Calix ignored Nero's scowls that could have put someone six feet under, and left my penthouse, the door slamming behind him. Nero waited until he could no longer see the green-eyed man anymore to then spin on his heels, glaring at me with abrupt fury that knocked the breath right out of me.

"Why was he here? Is this what you guys do?" he questioned.

"You can't tell me who I can or can't fuck, Nero," I almost laughed at how ridiculous he sounded in that moment. "I am my own woman. Find someone else to control."

"Yes, I can, if the man you're sleeping with looks at you as if he loves you!"

I scoffed in disbelief, rolling my eyes. "Calix doesn't love me. You're just being fucking jealous for no reason."

He sighed, exasperated, running his hand through his thick brown locks that had me begging to pull it. "Look, if we are going to do this, it means that me and you are exclusive. Do you understand?"

My face fell, my eyes widening as his request felt like a slap in the face. "*What?* When the fuck did we agree to that?"

His lips twisted into a smirk, as if amused that I would assume otherwise. Then he took a large step towards me, looming over my petite frame; the raw power and dominance emitting off him would have had anyone who was not me looking away submissively, but I held my ground as I glared up at him.

"It means if you need someone to *appease* you, it's going to be me. Anytime, anywhere. *Only me.* Do you understand, Aria?"

His words were like sin and, yet, I could have gone down on my knees, and I would have loved it. I was at a loss for words, trying to form something coherent to say but I failed miserably when the rough pads of his fingers trailed up my legs and continued to follow the shape of my body until they reached my lips. My breathing became chopped and labored as if I had been running for hours. I may as well have been at this point, since the way he looked at me reminded me of someone who would destroy the planet purely to be happy. I anticipated his next move even when I didn't want to – I couldn't help it. It was Nero.

"I don't want him touching you anymore, Ariadne. And if he does," Nero murmured, frostily, mesmerized by my lips. "I promise I'll break him into pieces. You know my capability so don't test me."

"This isn't fair. You have all these double standards and only expect me to uphold them," I said, through clenched teeth. He looked up, and something darkened in those opium eyes of his.

"I haven't been with another woman since we made that deal." My eyes widened at the declaration, and I didn't doubt the sincerity in his voice. "I'm a man of my word. *And you're mine, Aria.*"

I felt my body tremble from the rush of emotions, but I managed to retort back, bravely, "Since when?"

The inferno in his eyes burned brighter, his entire persona shifting to something more animalistic. I swallowed, stepping away from the beast in front of me that appeared as if he would burn the universe just to have me. The look in his eyes made my heart stammer because no one had ever looked at me like that before.

I directed the conversation away, not wanting to hear the answer to my question because if I did, I knew nothing would stop me from making sure he was mine for good. "Why did you come, Nero?"

"You're going to be my date to the banquet on Saturday, so I'll pick you up at seven o'clock," he informed, tucking his hand into his pocket.

"You could've just texted me – I would've seen it."

"I wanted to see you," was his response.

Once again, he managed to make me mute, my soul leaving my body and my mind drawing a blank. His steel gaze observed me, attentively, and the urge to shift was overwhelming but I wasn't someone who would quiver in the face of adversity. Especially if it was Nero.

"I'll leave you to enjoy the rest of your evening," he said finally, and it broke the tension that suffocated as.

Without waiting for a reply, he strode past me, tucking his hands into his pockets. His entire aura reeked of power and in this battle of dominance, he seemed to win. So, I let him. Sometimes, losing one battle meant winning two more. The cards were dealt, and he just made his move. Just as he reached the door, he glanced over his shoulder.

"And Aria?" I stilled when those oceanic eyes crashed into me, and I fell into a never-ending gulf of desire. The corner of his lips tugged up and my breath hitched. "You have always belonged to me."

*

After Nero informed me of the dress code, the gown I chose was a dazzling silver. It girded around my waist and then pooled over my heels like someone had poured moonlight onto me. The thin straps arched over my shoulders and then plunged down my back, leaving my spine exposed to the bitter cold. My honey skin was flattered by the argent mermaid gown, and it appraised the frame of my body by accentuating the curves. The décolletage arced over my breasts and dipped between the cleavage in a way that guaranteed several eyes on me. I was making my debut into Nero's world, or at least that was what people would believe. My brown curls tumbled past my shoulders but was tied back with a rhinestone pin and I quickly painted my lips a lustrous red. Taking a good look in the mirror, I grinned at how beautiful I looked – how beautiful I felt. I was glowing, my cheeks colored with soft carmine, but my eyes were framed with warm brown hues, black liner creating a feline eye shape. As the doorbell rang, I shoved my things into a purse, including my pocketknife, and made my way downstairs. Unexpectedly, I became very nervous; I could feel my heartbeat accelerate at the thought of seeing Nero. I felt like a high school girl with a silly little crush again and scowled at myself, shaking away the feeling. The bell rang again, and I knew he was getting impatient. My reflection in the corridor mirror greeted me when I walked by, and something about it had reasserted the power I knew I had. Opening the door, striking aquamarines welcomed me, and I was surprised by how good Nero looked in a black suit and a satin, hoary tie that matched my dress. His dark tawny hair was trimmed and combed back into an undercut, displaying the tattoos on the back of his neck. I barely had the time to admire the ink as his eyes absorbed me. They widened after a quick skim, before creasing when he smiled, revealing those dimples I adored.

"You look beautiful," he said.

"You don't look too bad either," I replied, closing the door behind me.

"Although, I wish you only wore this for me," he chirped, cheekily. My cheeks flushed as I looked at him, noticing how he was avoiding my gaze and biting back his smirk. "At least, I'll be the one to tear it off you tonight."

My jaw slacked and I came to a halt, burning holes into his back when he strolled ahead, whistling to himself with a hand tucked into his pocket as if nothing happened. It took me a long minute to finally register what had just been said before my brain decided to work again. My heart suddenly hiccupped as I scowled.

"Excuse me, who said you can rip this dress?" I exclaimed, mortified. "Do you know how expensive this dress was?"

He didn't reply but I knew he heard me as his shoulders shook, indicating that he was laughing to himself, whilst he continued to walk ahead despite the fact that I remained frozen in my spot.

"Nero!"

*

"Where is Matteo?" I asked, squinting at Nero.

I tried to ignore the way my skin burned with his arm wrapped around my waist, tightly, as he drew me closer to his side whilst we navigated through the crowd. With no time to waste, as Enzo eagerly wanted the pursuit for his sister to begin, he requested for the banquet to be held within five days after Nero and himself signed their faux partnership. Although time was limited, Matteo and Kira – to their dismay – teamed up to arrange the event. I was absolutely astounded that they managed to pull it off and at such a high standard, nonetheless. The banquet was hosted at the grandest riverfront venue in Manhattan. It was situated on the docks that encircled the bustling Chelsea district, with breathtaking views of the Hudson River dazzled by the light reflected by the bridge. Pier Sixty was renowned for its floor-to-ceiling windows, which immaculately framed the river. Over 10,000 square feet of magnificent column-free space was effortlessly transformed and decked out in exquisite silver decorations that made me glance down at my attire for tonight's event. It was then that I saw that Nero purposefully ensured only I wore silver tonight. Everyone else was wearing an array of bright colors, whilst I stood out in platinum sparkles on Nero's arm.

"…Greeting some investors. He'll join us later," he said, breaking my thoughts. And then a moment later, he mumbled, "I'm assuming your men are somewhere around the venue."

I ignored the slight narrowing of his eyes and the curt tone he used, bobbing my head. "Calix and Kira are in the venue, but Xander is upstairs, watching the security cameras. I also have four additional individuals on standby. We can never be too sure."

He hummed, his attention turning to the couple that greeted us as we walked by. The smile on his face would have dazzled anyone and by the looks of the lady's face, it did its job perfectly. I hated that about him. No matter where we went, everyone gawked at him, the girls flocked around him, and he relished in the undivided attention. His smile was a rarity, considering he always wore an impassive expression in public. His eyes twinkled with merriment, a small cleft exposed, looking a hundred times more attractive. It bothered me that he smiled at others. It was too beautiful for them to see. I swallowed my jealousy.

"Will you start the search after tonight?" I wondered, apathetically. Tearing his eyes away from the group of girls that adored him in the distance, he slanted his head to the side, arching a brow.

"Started as soon as the sun set." I didn't expect anything less.

"You've gotten better at hiding. Is our bet still on?"

"I never agreed to it."

He chuckled. "Okay, Aria."

Just as I was about to riposte, Nero rudely cut me off, welcoming Enzo as he sauntered in our direction with a cute redhead attached to his arm. I frowned, noticing how she sent a flirty smile in Nero's direction, completely dismissing my presence. Now, that wasn't very nice. There was this uncomfortable feeling in my stomach that made me want to tear her pretty little head off her model-like body. She was thin and tall, and I could easily snap her in numerous places. The thought settled the beast prowling in me. Sparing me a short glance, I saw how her lips coiled in distaste and immediately, I glared. Then, I remembered where I was, and my glare warmed into a dark smile as I pressed myself closer to Nero. Surprised, he looked down briefly before glancing back at Enzo.

"Nero, it's so wonderful to see you," Enzo greeted, with a charming grin as he shook Nero's hand. Then, his eyes fell onto me, and like magic, the charming façade contorted into want. "Lyra, I must say you look *absolutely* breathless."

Tucking a strand of hair behind my ear, I beamed, decorously. "Enzo, it's nice to see you again."

"How are enjoying yourself this evening?"

"The venue is stunning. You truly outdid yourself," I praised, his smile widening as I fed his ego.

"You flatter me," he chuckled. His words were anything but friendly when he said, "She's definitely a keeper, Russo."

Nero didn't like the sound of that, and I knew it in the way his grip tautened my waist, as he smirked through clenched teeth. "When did you arrive?"

"Just now. There was a slight issue along the way but nothing that couldn't be solved," he commented. "Will you start the search for our little bird after tonight?"

My throat constricted at the mention of Violetta. I hated the words he used; it was as if she wasn't his blood but a prized possession. I forced the smile to remain on my face and from the way Nero's fingers dug slightly into my skin, I knew he was holding me back from pouncing onto Enzo and beating the living shit out of him.

"My men are already on the hunt. Nothing so far. The lead we had came to a dead end. I'm beginning to believe she's no longer alive,

Rossi," Nero responded, curtly.

Enzo didn't flinch. "She's alive. I have no doubt. Just hiding. You know how much girls *love* hiding."

I wanted to throttle him right there and then; I didn't care who was watching. I just wanted to break all 206 bones in his body and make him suffer as his blood stained the slate tiles. But I couldn't. I bit my tongue and pretended as if his words didn't matter to me. I couldn't risk Violetta's chance of surviving; my stupid outburst could be the cause of her losing her life, and that was not a gamble I was willing to take.

"Shall we take our seats at the table? I believe they'll be serving the food now," Nero quickly diverted the conversation elsewhere, spotting how I was fuming besides him. Enzo directed him and his date to their designated table whilst Nero and I went to ours – I silently thanked Matteo for placing Enzo on a different table to us. If I spent a second longer near him, I was going to rip his head off his scheming body.

"I'm going to kill him," I muttered, more to myself, menacingly. "Once this is over, I'm going to shove a dagger in his eye and tear his arms off his body."

"*So violent*," Nero laughed, under his breath before blowing out a heavy exhale. "You'll get your opportunity, but for now play the dutiful girlfriend, Aria."

"Fucking kill me now," I grumbled, settling into my seat once Nero pulled it out. His lips quirked up at the sound of my complaints as he sat beside me, taking my hand into his.

"Just a few more hours," he promised, pressing his lips against the side of my head. I pouted, my heart warming up at the sight of his blue orbs which glittered in blithe. "If it helps, you do look *absolutely breathless*, Aria."

The color of my cheeks were already red, but they darkened at his sensual purr of words, I scoffed, playing off my shyness in the face of his praise, and shoved his hand off me, glancing away with my arms crossed over my chest. "Just eat your food, Russo."

The sound of his laughter caused butterflies to erupt in my stomach and, despite my best efforts, I couldn't stop the smile sneaking its way onto my lips.

CHAPTER 20

silver starlet

Nero

"Who is Barak Doukas?" I frowned at Aria, as she sipped silently on her wine, her eyes searching the banquet hall.

"A very, *very* old businessman," she replied, and then glanced my way. "I'm surprised you haven't heard of him."

I shook my head in reply. "Not at all."

"His son is Darius Doukas. Does that sound familiar?"

The name was familiar, but I couldn't quite remember where from. As Aria went back to scouting the room, I tried to search my memories to figure out how I knew that name. Then it hit me. I had met Darius at a club several months ago. He owned a successful airline and was infamous for having several girlfriends at the same time, not like they cared. He would shower them with gifts, and they would keep their complaints tucked away behind their synthetic little lips. I also remembered that he tried to create a partnership with me to expand his influence, but with his short-temper and reputation, I thought against it. I didn't care whether he was a playboy, some would call me the same thing, but I *did* care about his attitude towards women and I hadn't heard the best of things.

"I did meet Darius," I clarified. "Barak is his father?"

"Surely, you must have met Barak before."

"I didn't know the man existed."

"Well, he did step down from his position last year for Darius to it take over," Then she drew her brows together as if something didn't quite make sense. "I am surprised that you didn't know."

"I'm surprised too," I murmured.

Aria didn't reply and mumbled something which I assumed must have been for her team. Her hair covered the comms that Xander set up, brushing her shoulders when she looked around. Her forehead creased as her lips coiled into a scowl, her eyes flitting over to me very briefly before she murmured a reply too quietly for me to hear.

"Everything alright?" I questioned, after she calmed down, but it was difficult to be able to tell as she did such a great job at hiding her true feelings behind her cold, hazel eyes.

"Calix was just informed that Barak may not be attending tonight's banquet," she replied, and then exhaled. I could feel the stress radiate off her. "I needed him to come. This could ruin everything."

"Don't worry, Aria," I comforted, placing my hand onto her thigh when I noticed it shaking underneath the table, agitatedly. "He'll come."

She didn't look fully convinced but said nothing else as she nodded, staring off into the distance and clenching her jaw. I knew she would continue to be tense for the entire night if things didn't work out; it was just like her to, but like always, we had to be patient. Patience was never our strongest trait, but here it would be our biggest advantage. Throughout the rest of the dinner, Aria remained still beside me, curtly making conversation, though people didn't see that as she was brilliant at acting like everything was fine. She donned a bright smile that said she was interested, and her gaze was warm like she actually cared about what people were saying. She was a master at disguise, and it stunned me. I studied her carefully when she wasn't looking, as she beamed when one of the guests lionized about how gorgeous she was. The red color of her cheeks indicated that she was startled by the comment. Her crimson smile didn't entirely reach her eyes, but it brought out her sharp features astonishingly, nevertheless. They were the shape of almonds and stared tenderly as she bobbed her head obediently when someone was speaking to her. Then, there was the dress she wore. I deliberately made sure she was the only one to wear silver. I wanted her to stand out. And in the sea filled with colors, she looked like moonlight. I itched to rip it off and leave no part of her golden skin untouched. Aria had me captivated with the slightest of movements – I was consumed by her presence. She set a flame within me, and it burnt brighter and brighter whenever she was around. I felt like a little kid with a huge crush when I was around her. The world stopped and she was the center of all things beautiful.

Like the goddess she was.

As if she felt my stare, she glanced up, tilting her head to the side, and arching her brow, curiously. Silently asking me a question, I responded with a smile, shaking my head. I took her head and gently pressed my lips against her knuckles. She didn't say anything. She just mirrored my smile as her gaze softened. Once we had finished our dinner, Aria and I made our final rounds, greeting those we didn't have a chance to see beforehand, taking our time to enjoy the rest of the night. I couldn't remember anyone we had spoken to. My attention would always turn to Aria; whether it was due to her melodic laughter or her honey-glazed voice, I could only see her.

"Nero," she said, gently, her brows pinching together. "Are you okay? You've been awfully quiet."

I hummed in reply, thoughtfully, as I focused on the titian hues of her eyes which twinkled underneath the glittering chandelier above.

"Are you sure? You seem distracted."

I smirked. "Only by you, *cara*."

She glowered, unable to fight the blush on her cheeks. "Shut up."

Chuckling, I kissed the crown of her head, my heart melting at the sound of the delicate sigh that escaped from her red lips. "How about we go for a dance?"

"*Dance?*" she raised a brow in amusement. "When was the last time you waltzed, Nero?"

"I'll have you know that I am an incredible dancer," I huffed at the accusation.

Aria smiled to herself, shaking her head, whilst I led her to the middle of the venue. We weren't the only people swaying to the sound of the melody, but for some reason it felt like we were. When we moved it was in sync, the tempo mimicking the sound of my pounding heart, her eyes remaining steadily on mine. I could feel every arc of her body as she pressed closely against me. Her warm breath caressed my face when she peered up with doe eyes, hidden underneath hooded lashes. I bent down to rest my forehead against hers whilst keeping our gaze locked, entranced with one another.

Then, I asked for something that I had been dying to do all night. "Can I kiss you?"

She looked slightly surprised but nodded timidly, nonetheless, giving me complete permission to kiss her wicked red lips. They tasted like wine and honey, lightly moving against mine as I angled my head to the side ever-so-slightly to gain deeper access. I wanted to remember every inch of her; I couldn't get enough of how she tasted.

Like heaven.

She moaned quietly, her mouth opening slightly which I took full advantage of, plunging my tongue in and drawing out a small whimper. Her fingers ran through my hair, grasping onto the locks and tugging them softly whilst my arms snaked around her waist. We were each other's destruction and salvation. Time stopped when she was in my arms; it was as if the universe had blessed me with a universe of my own and it was called Aria. I felt the fireworks – the ones she would joke about wanting to feel when we were little kids, the ones she saw in her Disney films – and I felt it in my veins. Shivers running down my spine, adrenaline rushing through my bloodstream, my body naturally responding to the temptress in my hold. This high could drive me to insanity but I would gladly go there because as long as I had Aria, I had everything. I would do anything for her. We finally broke away when we could no longer breathe, her lips swollen and more flushed than her blush, her eyes dilated as she tried to level out her breathing.

"I never want you to be with another man ever again, Ariadne," I whispered, gruffly, with desire. "This is it. You and me. *Sempre.*"

"*Nero,*" she gasped, when I stole another kiss. What she didn't know was that she was stealing pieces of me.

"You drive me insane. Always have and always will. You can't run away from me, Aria. Not anymore. I won't let you," I cradled her face in my hands, daintily. "Wherever you go, I will find you."

She swallowed hard, bobbing her head as she glanced away. "I'm sorry. For everything. But you know it's more difficult than that."

"I know," I responded, letting her go. The spell cast over me faded as I returned to my stoic, impassive expression, but my eyes greedily devoured her. "But you'll always be mine. My Queen. *No matter what.*"

Before she could reply, her hand reached for the little earpiece in her ear, and she listened to whoever was speaking. I looked away, noticing Darius Doukas greeting Enzo with a charming grin, shaking his hand before he introduced Enzo to the man beside him.

"That's Barak," Aria muttered, breaking my daze, as my eyes flicked over to her. The thick cloud of licentiousness hanging above us began to dispel. "Barak Doukas."

"No, that's not Barak," I answered, wondering if Aria had identified the right man. "That's Kal Doukas, Darius' uncle."

Aria frowned, shaking her head. "Are you sure?"

"Yes."

Her frown deepened further before she reached for her earpiece again. "Kira, was Kal a twin?" There was a pause before Aria looked back at the Doukas.' "He was?"

"What?" I mused, and she puckered her lips, debating whether to tell me.

"Kal was killed years ago. I have a feeling that man over there is Barak and if I'm right, he may be pretending to be his brother," she answered me, before returning to Kira. The crease between her brows relaxed as a smirk lazily drew itself onto her lips. "Thanks, Kira."

"What is it?"

Aria chuckled. "It's a case of mistaken identity."

This time, I frowned. "Are you saying that man is Barak and not Kal?"

"Like I said, Kal was killed years ago. Kira had told me that Kal had a brother, but she wasn't aware they were twins. Barak must have taken Kal's identity after he died. It wasn't public knowledge that Kal had a twin, so when Barak was in danger, he must have taken the opportunity to pretend to be his dead brother. It would completely throw people off his scent."

"So, why would he be in danger?"

"It might be the same reason why I want him," Aria replied, mysteriously. She entwined her fingers with mine, tossing me a grin as she arched her brow. "Let's go greet our guests, Russo."

She tugged me through the crowd, smiling so politely at the guests that she had them enchanted by her beauty and grace. Moving her hand from mine onto my arm instead, she gave me a slight squeeze that had me glancing down at her. Her head made this almost unnoticeable gesture to my left which had me glancing in that direction. My eyes narrowed onto the five men, all dressed in black suits, standing tall and aloof by the entrance of the venue. I knew those were not any of my men or hers.

"I need Barak's handprint," she murmured quietly, through a plastered smile.

"How are you going to get it?" I questioned, daubing on an ascetic expression when Enzo noticed us walking in his direction. From the corner of my eye, I noticed a smirk on Aria's red lips as she thinned her hazel eyes at the men.

"Don't underestimate me, Nero," she replied, with a cheeky grin. "I'm Aria Moretti."

Before I could press any further, Enzo greeted us warmly despite the coldness lingering in his dark eyes. "Nero and Lyra, I would like you to meet a close friend of mine, Kal Doukas, former owner of Aeras, an airline famously known across the world, and his nephew, the current CEO, Darius Doukas."

"It's nice to see you again," I shook Darius's hand, a man who I loomed over just slightly, with blonde hair that looked almost golden and dark brown eyes before shaking the Kal-imposter's hand. He was an old man with silvery hair that matched the knob on his ebony walking stick.

"Likewise, Nero. It's been a while," Darius responded, his eyes glimpsing at Aria, who stood dutifully beside me. "And you must be Nero's girlfriend."

She blushed - an actress that would put others to shame - tucking her hair behind her ear, modestly. "Yes, that is me. It's a pleasure to meet you, Darius and Mr. Doukas – I've heard so much about your airline."

The older Doukas man looked caught off guard but then his gaze became molten into a heated stare as he took Aria's hand, kissing her knuckles. "It's a pleasure to meet you too, Lyra."

Her smile broadened, eyes gleaming in a way that mesmerized the men around her. Underestimating Aria was the last thing I would do because she had consistently proven that underestimating her was most unwise; her skills had clearly sharpened and strengthened since she left. Seeing her on the field actually using everything she had learnt from all those training sessions whilst adding her own seductive twist was another thing. The men around her seemed to be enthralled as they all gave her lascivious glances. Aria had previously managed to get incredibly powerful men to go weak at their knees, so I how could I underestimate her? She batted her lashes, gently, hiding her smile as she feigned being shy, her red lips promised angelic wishes, but I knew they held devilish intentions. It was what she wanted them to see and, *Jesus,* she did a good job at it. Something boiled deep within me at the knowledge that I would be the only man to see her darkest side.

"You are truly a lucky man," Darius grinned at me. "She's absolutely stunning."

They spoke about her like she was a prize to be won, and if I heard it, I was sure Aria did too. However, she made no indication of caring. "Thank you, Darius."

"I'll have to steal her off you, Nero," he joked, sending her a sultry wink.

Aria laughed and it sounded like the angels were singing. "I'll have to apologize because that won't be possible."

Both brows raised as he said, "How come?"

"Because I'm *madly* in love with this man," she answered, peering at me with a soft smile that knocked the air right out of me. Her words meant nothing to her as they left her lips, and I knew that, but my heart still stuttered and the fire within me burned brighter as I mirrored her smile.

"*How adorable,*" Enzo chuckled with a sneer in his tone, breaking the spell between us two. "I'm incredibly jealous."

Aria's smile didn't drop but something had darkened in her eyes. No one had taken notice as they shifted the conversation elsewhere, but I squeezed Aria's hand and in return, I had gotten a small smile that told me she was okay... for now.

"Did you hear about Miguel's untimely death? And Viktor's?" Darius said suddenly and my attention snapped back onto the men in front of us. Aria, once again, didn't flinch. Darius shook his head, sadly. "What a pity. They were good men. I heard that it was that assassin again."

"What assassin?" Barak questioned, grabbing a glass of champagne from the waiter that strode by.

"You know," then Darius looked around before whispering, "*Aria.*"

I visibly stiffened, and I was fortunate that no one noticed as everyone else was too interested in what Darius was saying, as if it was taboo. Aria's head angled and I knew she was amused, her face still wearing this look of innocence and naivety. Barak frowned and Enzo rolled his eyes.

"Who is Aria?" the older Doukas asked his son, and I wondered if

Darius knew of his father's deceitful identity.

"Have you not heard of her? She is very well known in the Underground. People claim she's the best mercenary out there. Though, if it's a woman, I have my doubts," Darius laughed, and the other men followed. I forced a chuckle, but it sounded terse, whilst Aria giggled, two pitches higher than should be allowed.

"Sounds like someone we should have in our service," Barak grinned. "Would do me a great deal of peace."

"Unfortunately," I began, eyes snapping in my direction. "I heard that she's a lone wolf. Doesn't work for anyone, doesn't exist. I'm sure this 'Aria' is just a ghost story, seeing as no one has ever seen her."

The corner of Aria's lips tugged, inconspicuously, whilst both Doukas men looked slightly upset by the notion and Enzo seemed like he couldn't care less. I mused over how amusing it would be if these men knew that Aria stood in front of them right now and intended on making them her next victims. My bloodthirsty Queen. As if Barak finally remembered Aria's presence, his eyes widened in regret.

"We shouldn't be talking about such topics in the presence of a lady," he apologized, and Aria brushed it off with a dainty wave.

"Please, it's okay. I know how these talks can be," her laughter was as saccharine as her smile, but all the men melted like butter at the sound of it. "I'll just leave you men to your business talks."

"Where are you off to?" Darius asked, charmingly.

"To grab a drink," Aria giggled, as if she was an air-headed heiress. "I'm not fit to understand all those technical talks when it comes to business."

"May I join you?" Barak asked, shocking me but Aria didn't look surprised, as she raised a brow questioningly. "I am no longer in charge of Aeras, so I can finally avoid those technical talks too."

Aria bobbed her head eagerly, pressing her lips against my jaw before taking Barak's outstretched hand, sending him a dazzling smile, then tossing one back to me attached with a look that said everything – *keep them distracted.* I watched them walk off; Aria laughed when Barak spoke, her hand flirtatiously touching his arm, so subtly and delicately, her eyes trained on him with full concentration. I bit back a smirk at Aria's antics and turned to Enzo and Darius as they began to speak about expanding Aeras.

"Cargo planes are our best source of income," Darius pointed out. "Uncle mentioned that it would be worth looking into."

"Depending on what sort of cargo you're bringing," Enzo replied, suggestively.

"I agree with your uncle," I chimed, and they both glanced at me. "Cargo is definitely my best source of income. People trying to find a way to transport their goods in or out of the country. I have men docked at every port, airport and motorway monitoring everything that enters America and Italy."

"That seems like a lot of supervision. How do you make sure no one is bringing in things that aren't approved?" Darius asked.

"Besides being a businessman, I am the Don of the Italians. I also have extremely close connections with the Russian Mafia," I answered with a smirk. "No one is going to cross me."

Enzo studied me, sedulously, before he gestured to Aria, who was sitting by the bar with Barak Doukas, a beam across her face as she spoke to him, her eyes as bright as her gown.

"Not even those dressed in pearls and diamonds?"

As if she could feel our gaze on her, Aria glanced in our direction and our eyes met. For a moment, my thoughts evaporated into thin air, and I was left, gawking at this glorious beauty. For a second, I saw the perplexity lingering in the chasm of her dark orbs, before she gave me a warm smile that rendered me breathless. She owned my heart; there was no doubt about that, and I gladly let her. But a small sliver of doubt lingered in the back of my mind, and the distrust seeped in. She arched a brow, her eyes squinted, and her cherry lips twisted. I remained impassive but a part of me wondered whether or not Aria would betray me. And by the looks of it, she knew *exactly* what I was thinking.

"*No*," I responded, coolly, as her hazelnut eyes that were once filled with such warmth hardened, yet her infamous smirk never dropped. "Not even them."

CHAPTER 21

he (lies)

Nero

Of course, I knew my feelings for Aria were based off something more than just lust. It was as if I was a tree and she was the fire burning me down, wreaking havoc in the peace of the forest. The journey back to her house was strangely quiet; only the humming of the music broke the silence between us, but it didn't ease the tension. Something in the air had shifted and I knew she felt it too. But she was Aria, and she would never speak up first. Instead, she was deeply involved in a conversation with Calix on the phone. Her eyes were creased when she frowned, causing her nose to wrinkle like a bunny. It made me smile a little when I snuck a look. Finally, she hung up with a sigh, rubbing her forehead, wearily.

"Everything okay?" I asked.

"Just a little bit of family drama," she answered, distractedly, her fingers typing away on her phone.

"Anything I can do to help?"

She shook her head and that was all I needed to know. I didn't bombard her with questions, peering at her whenever possible, studying the pure concentration masked across her face. The frustration on her face didn't disappear during our journey, and I couldn't help but notice how adorable she looked when she was annoyed. It was at times like this that I was surprised she was the same woman who could easily break a man's neck and wouldn't blink twice. Once again, a smile teased on my lips as I appreciated the beautiful girl besides me.

So beautiful.

"Did you manage to get the handprint?" I asked, after a moment.

As if remembering I was still there, she glanced up with pursed lips and bobbed her head. Smirking, Aria revealed a napkin that was hidden in a plastic bag inside her purse.

I lifted a brow, dubiously. "That's the handprint?"

"It would've been easier to slice his hand off, but this will suffice for now," Aria sighed, sadly, and I sent her a look which said I was anything but amused. Rolling her eyes, she tucked the napkin back into her purse. "Once you add powder, it will stick to the oils released from the handprint. That's Xander's field. He deals with all the technical and scientific stuff. Have I mentioned how big of a nerd he is?"

Although she was joking, I heard the light-heartedness in her voice suggesting she adored Xander very much. I should have been worried, but something told me he wasn't the guy I had to keep my eye on.

"You guys must be pretty close," I pointed out.

"Like I said before, we're a family," she smiled. "Xander, Calix and Yakira have been with me from the start. They have guided me and helped me, whether it was strengthening my skills or giving me advice – I wouldn't be where I am without them."

"So, how did you meet Xander?"

Aria had this faraway look lingering in her eyes, sinking into the leather seat with a short inhale that she blew out before she began, "I met Xander when I was Cairo. He was seventeen at the time and had been traveling from country to country serving terrible men. He was living on the streets, having to do… *favors*, one could call it, in order to get by. He had skills unlike any other when it came to technology, and in the wrong hands, he managed to destroy hundreds of lives."

"And you forgave him?"

She looked at me as if she couldn't believe that I would suggest otherwise. "Of course, I did."

"What happened when you found him?"

"Xander was an orphan and this made him an easy target. They found him when he was maybe ten or eleven. At first, he did whatever they wanted because they sheltered him and he earned money, and I guess it was better than the life he had before. But the older he got, the more he realized that something wasn't quite right. They started asking him to track down girls and find out information that shouldn't be in another person's hands. So, he refused. But refusing isn't something you can do so easily."

Her inhale was short and sharp as if she had remembered something horrifying, and I had no doubt that she did. The pale look across her face sent icy tremors down my spine. I had never seen that look before. It was unnerving. Fisting her hands, she scowled to her reflection in the window.

"They *hurt* him. In ways I never thought was possible. Branded him a coward for three years and even then, he didn't obey their orders. The way he lived was much worse than being on the streets. Scars remained on his skin and wounds left scars in his heart."

There was a moment of silence, dark and taciturn that left a deafening strain between us. Her eyes were sub-zero and inexpressive, scarlet lips thinning as she stared out of the window, watching the cars drive and the buildings flicker by as we zipped through Manhattan.

"One day, he managed to escape," she whispered, her tone detached like the look in her eyes. "I was walking through the streets of Cairo with Kira, and he was running with blood trickling down his head, his arms and his legs, soaking the dirty rags he wore. He bumped into us, apologizing at first, before begging us to save him."

"What did you do?"

"Kira was hesitant to offer our assistance, especially as she still wasn't strong in combat – in fairness, there would be only one of me and six of them."

My grip on the steering wheel tightened. "What did you do?"

"I led them into an abandoned home and killed them," she stated, like it was nothing. "Kira took Xander away whilst I torn them limb by limb. Without mercy, I made sure that their leader had my name engraved into his forehead so that people would remember my name. So, that they would remember who was responsible. A warning that they weren't safe, not if I had anything to do with it."

"Aria…"

"Think what you must but I don't ever regret that day. I don't regret putting my life on the line. I saved Xander and he saved hundreds of girls that could've been kidnapped, raped or mutilated. His refusal may have nearly cost his life, but it was the bravest thing he had ever done because it saved hundreds of others."

"I-I didn't realize the danger you put yourself in," I muttered, after a pregnant moment.

Aria tore her eyes away from the window, burning her gaze into the side of my face. "I did it because no one else would."

"Then, let me help you. Just tell me who these people are, Aria," I pleaded, desperately because the thought of her in danger again only made me want to rip my heart out from my body. Her face relaxed, but I could see the worry in her eyes. Alas, eventually, she shook her head and glanced out of the window.

"In time, Nero, but not now."

Once again, the car became silent and all I could hear was the purr of the engine as we drove. It wasn't uncomfortable because it made me see everything more clearly. Many years had passed between us, and Aria had changed – there was no doubt about it. Except, she had changed for the better. She had always been so resilient and determined, but she was tormented by the sins of others and in turn, she became the judge, jury, and executioner. Suddenly, I could see how she changed. She wasn't afraid of her own shadow. She wasn't afraid of the darkness. Instead, she became the darkness. Recalling what Enzo suggested, the small seed of doubt he tried to plant, I immediately weeded out, because the girl in the moonshine gown was anything but a traitor. I was blinded by my need to protect her, but I failed to see that she needed to protect others. She nurtured those in need and raised warriors that were completely loyal to her. She may have left one family, but she went to save another. The icy, bitterness from her disappearance began to thaw and my heart warmed at the thought of her standing up for this family, because she was standing up for something she believed in. Aria was brave yet shielded, hidden underneath layers of a frosty exterior, but that was one of the many reasons why I had fallen so deeply into her world. Even as teenagers, she stole my breath away with her courage and passion – a true leader – but she was never destined to guide soldiers. She was fated to lead warriors into a battle that she knew she would win. Was this the reason why my heart stumbled back to her? Nonetheless, the realization made me question my next move and I concluded that this time I wouldn't leave it too long. A part of me was hesitant because my pride told me she didn't feel the same. She ran her fingers through her hair as I finally parked in front of her block, switching the engine off – the only sound that disturbed the silence between us. We sat quietly, waiting for the other to speak first but no one did – we didn't know what to say.

Tossing me a lax smile, she grabbed her purse as she finally spoke, "Thanks for tonight, Nero. I didn't mean for it get so depressing."

I shook my head, noticing the stiffness in her light words "You didn't. You were honest with me. That's all I asked for."

Her smile expanded but only marginally, and her eyes thinned when doing so. "I'll catch you later, Russo."

As she went to leave, my hand impulsively snaked out, grabbing her arm and bringing her to halt. Aria looked puzzled as I inclined my head to the side and lifted a brow with a small smirk.

"Will you invite me inside, Aria?" I blurted; tone laced with a need that was burning within me. A flame that was ignited and wouldn't calm until it consumed the very person who started it.

She studied me momentarily as if she knew my intentions, but nodded, causing me to break into a full-blown grin. Throughout the journey to her penthouse, I scrutinized her with famished eyes, rapt by the goddess in front of me. She nibbled on her lower lip, impatiently, fiddling with her bracelet as if she could feel my gaze on her. I held back the urge to touch her.

Until the doors opened.

She gasped when I pressed her against the wall, her purse dropping onto the floor, her eyes wild with surprise. I held her hands above her head and ran my tongue down the side of her neck, drawing out a deep moan that left me ravenous for more. I wanted to devour her pretty cries and her sated sighs. I wanted to bottle up all the sounds she made when I kissed her and listen to it on repeat. I wanted her more than anything in the world, and frustration overcame me when I knew she would never fully comprehend how much I wanted her. Because wanting her was like needing to breathe. She was the sun and I gravitated towards her. She was life *and* death, and I would be reincarnated just to live in her world again. She was absolute and I never loved the idea more. I was completely mad for this woman, and she didn't even know.

"*Nero*," she said, but it came out hoarse. "What are you doing?"

"You are the most amazing woman I have ever met."

I released her hands and unzipped her dress, pushing the straps down her shoulders and watching in awe as the material puddled around her feet. Her chest raised unevenly, as she kicked off her heels and ran her hands down my arms. I unclipped the pin that held her hair back, and watched brown tendrils bounce onto her shoulders. *Christ*, I had never met anyone else more beautiful.

"I once told you that I would give you the world and I am sure I will, because Aria," I whispered, cradling her face, affectionately. "You deserve the world. Let me worship you, every inch of your body because you deserve to be worshipped like the Queen you are."

The words left my lips like a prayer. Her gaze was so intense that I felt like I couldn't breathe. Her fingers lightly brushed my jawline before she silenced me with a zealous kiss that had my entire being possessed by her and only her. She ran her hands through my hair as I deepened the kiss, wanting to taste the honey lingering on her red lips. Running my hands down her body, I lifted her up against the wall, her legs curling around my waist, before moving us to the living room. I was drunk by her company, grunting as she drew my lower lip out with a sultry glance at me that nearly had me combust. Her couch was large enough for me to lay her down on, and I swiftly removed my clothes whilst she stared, propping herself up on her elbows.

"You're mine. *Sempre*, Ariadne," Everything slowed down as I rose on top of her, her hands clasping my arms as she stared in anticipation. "Body, heart, and soul. You give me life just like you did five years ago. You're the fire that burns within me and you know I'll happily let you do so. I'll break down walls for you, kill people for you; I'll do anything, because Aria, you're mine."

"Nero, please," she whimpered, tormented. She looked at me as if she couldn't tell whether she should hate me or not, but I saw the tears brim her docile eyes. "Don't say things you don't mean."

"Listen to me, Moretti," I wavered my lips above hers, curling my fingers into her hair. Aria lifted her head up for more, whining when I tugged her hair gently, creating that torturous distance. "You're mine in this lifetime and the next, and the one after. *Forever*. Remember that."

She gasped but I paid little attention to it, knowing full well that she was stubborn and would never give in first. I kissed her arguments away, arching her body into mine, gripping her hair. Everything I felt I gave to her. And she melted into my arms, allowing me to dominate her body. My head spun as I acted impulsively on my emotions and briefly wondered whether I would regret it. If I would regret giving her my heart.

But when I heard her soft words, I knew I wouldn't. "Don't lie to me, Nero."

Five words that sounded as broken as they made my heart feel; it was then that I understood that we still had a long way to go, and I knew there were still bridges to repair. I wasn't worried. I would spend eternity begging for her forgiveness, if it meant that she was in my arms at the end of the night. But, for now, I would start here.

"I'll spend forever trying to convince you, Aria."

Then, I kissed her so softly that it made our bodies shudder.

Her eyes were closed, armoring her emotions. She swept her lips against mine, a catalyst for the destruction soon to come. Then, the gentle whisper of a single word brought me back to reality.

"*Liar.*"

*

I wept in my pretty pink dress, ruining the hairdo my mother had spent hours perfecting as I hid my face in my arms, tucking my legs into my chest. Blood smeared the poufy material as it trickled down from my arm, the injury causing me to hiss in pain whenever I moved even the slightest bit. Hidden in the bathroom of a fancy hotel, I knew I should return to the party honoring my father's latest partnership, but how could I show my face when I was so weak upon facing those rich girls. I was furious, wanting to prove them wrong, but they were older and stronger, pushing me about because they knew that I wouldn't react in front of a crowd. I trembled, blinded by the red wrath when a soft knock had me stiffen, halting my sobs.

"Ari?" Nero's voice resonated from the other side, drenched in concern. "Are you alright? Can I come in?"

"Go away, Nero," I choked out, biting back my cries so that he wouldn't come bursting in, demanding to name the culprit to my sorrow. "It's the girls' bathroom!"

"I know you've been crying, Moretti," he responded. "I can hear it in your voice." I cursed under my breath. "I'm coming in."

Before I could refuse, the door swept open and a six-year-old Nero zeroed onto me. His eyes widened before he rushed over, kneeling beside me, his hands moving to the gash on my elbow. I rarely saw Nero angry; he was often good at leveling his temper unlike myself, so I was completely surprised to see his blue eyes thin into icicles.

"Who did this?" He pulled out a napkin and began to dab the open wound. "Why did you not come to me?"

"It wouldn't have helped," I stammered.

"Was it those girls again?" Nero demanded. "I knew we should've told Mom."

"If we told them then it would prove those bullies right," I argued. "They just like to pick on me because I'm little and weak."

Nero frowned. "You're not little or weak, Aria."

I scoffed, removing my arm from his grip. "Tell them that."

"You're not weak, Ariadne," he repeated, his words forcing me to look at him. Blue eyes were as bright as the stones my mother wore on her neck. "You are the daughter of Antonio Moretti. You are his heir. You are not weak. They are scared of you and that's why they hurt you."

I twiddled my finger, my cheeks flushed and damp with tears. "Do you think so?"

For a second, he didn't say anything until he reached out and brushed my tears away. Smiling at me, Nero said, "I'll spend forever trying to convince you."

I giggled as my best friend helped me stand back onto my own two feet. "Don't lie to me."

His gaze softened. "I would never lie to you."

PART 2

I've lived only for you;
I have dedicated myself to you.
Your faith has held me together,
and taken away all my sorrows.
My destiny is tied with you,
and with you, I have become complete.

tum hi ho

CHAPTER 22

saint & sinners

Perhaps, it was his smile. Or maybe it was his words. Was it the warmth in his deep, blue eyes when he kissed me or the gentle graze of his fingertips against my cold skin after he had taken me to another galaxy? What made me fall for Nero Russo? I asked myself that question for years. It was baffling and left me in a lake of emotions. Why did I like him so much? Who was that girl that fell so mercilessly in his presence? She was a traitor to her heart, and he was the betrayer. Five years. Five years it had taken me to finally comprehend the reason why I liked Nero – or *dare I say, loved*. Five years to understand that it was simply everything. Everything about him plagued my thoughts and left me begging for more. His loving smile and his teasing smirk. The glitter of amusement in his oceanic eyes whenever he would whisper his sinful words and promises. The tenderest touch of his fingers as they ran down my body, causing goosebumps to scatter across my skin. It was everything.

But there was one thing that completely ruined me.

And it was the way he looked at me which scared me the most. Like I was his solace. The way he looked at me was like crying in the rain, because he saw the darkest parts of me and never expected me to change.

And that would be my downfall.

*

"Aria," Kira said, as she strolled into my office during a humid day, the heat causing my cheeks to flush. The abrupt change in temperature was the one thing I didn't miss in New York. "I have something for you to look at."

She slid what looked like the results of Barak's handprint analysis across my desk. I frowned, pinching my brows together as I studied it, carefully.

"He hasn't been taken off the database?" I questioned. "I thought he was registered dead."

"Apparently not. I had to double-check with our friends in the force and Barak came in the other day, without being disguised as his brother Kal, to visit one of the convicts."

"Why would he do that? He's supposed to be dead."

"Perhaps he's dead to the public, but to the Underground he's not."

"That defeats the point of his death."

Kira shook her head whilst I read her report. "Not entirely. It means that there is no way of tracking him if he was to ever get caught by the feds."

"That doesn't answer why he'd go into a prison, knowing full well that he's a wanted man."

"That's what I was wondering, until I dug deeper and found out the person he was visiting was Tristan Piers."

"Who's Tristan Piers?" Puzzled, I looked at Kira for an answer.

"I don't know," she shrugged, before raising her brow. "But I'm pretty sure Beau St. Clair does."

Beau lived in a large house located on the outskirts of New York's suburban streets. It was similar to the neighborhood my parents lived in, except there were a few major differences – one being that the next house was acres and acres of land away. The mansion was heavily guarded with at least fifteen men docked somewhere outside, three snipers hidden in towers that pillared the iron picketed gate, which only opened for authorized personnel, and two more stationed at the end of the road. It was practically impossible to enter.

Luckily for me, Beau was my uncle.

My car drove past the opened iron gates, parking up in front of the marble stairs that lead to large white doors, beautiful Grecian style pillars ranking each side. I pushed my shades onto my head as I slipped out of the car, handing my keys to the valet that welcomed me, with such a bright smile that could have fooled anyone into thinking he wasn't armed. But if you paid attention to details, you would have seen the two guns tucked under the waistband of his pants, hidden from view by his blazer. I didn't doubt that he had a knife pocketed in his shirt. I mean, I had one attached to my thigh. The mansion itself was larger than most and had a recurrent Grecian theme, with its cream and white accents donning the agate and concrete pillars, specifically designed to look like those in Athens. Inside the mansion, it was far more modern with a beautiful diamond chandelier hanging in the middle of the foyer and marble stairs that ascended upwards on both sides of the room, adjoining in the middle where it mimicked a balcony. The decor was elegant with blue, gold and white accents that vaguely reminded me of Tiffany and Co. Although, I wouldn't expect anything less from my aunt.

Speaking of the devil – she came down the stairs with a luminous smile across her face, alluring jade eyes that my uncle loved so dearly beamed as she embraced me. She was the youngest of the cousins, and like the rest of my family, absolutely stunning. Men fell on their knees at the sight of her. Woman sneered with envy when she walked by. She was one of the most powerful women in the world.

She was the Pakhan of the Russian mafia.

"Aria, it's been so long. Oh, look how you've grown!" she cried out. "When did you come back to New York? I can't believe your mother didn't tell us!"

"Thanks, Gabrielle. You don't look bad yourself. You haven't aged at all," I grinned. "I arrived in New York over two months ago. You have to forgive me – I didn't want anyone to know I was back."

Gabrielle St. Clair rolled her eyes at me, but that didn't stop the smile stretching across her face as she basked in the compliment. As the leader of the Russian mob, ultimately, the position had landed in her hands. When my aunt Chantelle and my mother respectfully backed down, it gave Gabrielle the opportunity to show just how powerful she could be. She was strong, smart, and so incredibly skillful that I was pretty sure, a fight against her would not end well. She was tall and stunning, with a childish personality that immediately switched to a dominant leader when commanding her people. Her hair was darker than my own, tendrils cascaded past her shoulders, framing the shape of her face perfectly. Green eyes that reminded me of emerald stones peered curiously at me, a small smirk playing on her coral lips as she cocked her head to the side.

"Why did you surprise us with this visit?" she asked, hooking her arm through mine as she led us to the living room. "Is something wrong?"

"I needed to talk to Beau actually."

Gabrielle's brows rose in surprise. "Beau?"

"Yeah, apparently he knows this person that I'm looking into," I explained, choosing my words carefully. Gabrielle hummed, thoughtfully, but didn't say anything else. I quickly steered the conversation elsewhere, glancing around to see if I could catch my two younger cousins. "Where's Anzhela and Zariyah?"

Gabrielle's eyes instantly lit up at the mention of her two girls, flailing her hands dismissively. "The girls are somewhere. They've been getting on my nerves today – the troublesome two."

"That sounds like them," I responded, with a laugh.

Gabrielle chuckled and was about to say something else before the loud bickering echoing throughout the house stopped her. With a sigh, she shook her head and pointed at the door nearby the fireplace in the living room.

"He's in there. When you are done, why don't you join us for dinner? We have so much to catch up on."

"Will do."

I mirrored her smile and watched her stride away with this powerful aura lingering trailing after her. The way she walked was with elegance and strength; as a younger girl, I could remember how rebellious my aunt was but, as she grew up and started becoming more in control of the mob, maturity welcomed her. That didn't stop the moments of defiance which would appear from time to time. I didn't question the flicker of hesitancy that I saw in her moss green orbs when she sent me a quick glance back before disappearing out of the room. Gabrielle had secrets, many of them, and I had no doubt so did Beau. The pair were made for each other. As her bodyguard, Beau had fallen for Gabrielle's charms, and she had fallen for the man who swore to take a bullet for her. The pair were extremely powerful and ran the Russian mafia with an iron fist. Moreover, the pair were extremely secretive and reclusive about their operations. It made it impossible to infiltrate the mob. I knocked on the wooden door twice before opening it, peeking into the room, cautiously. I saw him before he noticed me, engrossed with whoever he was on the phone to as he paced around the room with irritation curled on his lips.

"Don't fucking piss me off, Tian," he snarled, a tone that was heavy with anger and ice-cold irritation. "Get it done. Gabrielle said this needed to be sorted a week ago, so why are you late? You don't want to push me to my limits. I won't ask again. Do your fucking job."

He hung up, tossed the phone onto the couch and hunched over his desk, his body stiff with aggravation. I nibbled on my lower lip, not sure what I wanted to say as I had caught him at a bad time, but before I managed to figure out a plan, gray stormy eyes glimpsed over in my direction. Beau St. Clair was a very large man, easily soaring over me. He had the broadest shoulders I had ever seen, which held a considerable amount of power. Black ink appeared when he tugged the collar of his shirt, disappearing over his shoulders and down his torso. Lush, ebony hair was groomed back to have a rippling quality and stunning silver eyes, that my aunt adored so tenderly, held me in my spot. Like my aunt, he lifted his brows in surprise and his face softened, the lingering anger dispersing.

I smiled.

"Aria," he welcomed, turning to me with a less strained frame. "It's been a while."

"How have you been?" I embraced my uncle when he opened his arms, noting how he still swallowed me in his hold just like he did when I was a little girl.

He sighed, releasing me, and shrugged. "Busy. As you can see. It's been too long, and you've grown so much."

"Gabrielle said the same thing," I laughed. "Five years is a long time and I'm not a baby girl anymore."

His gaze became tender. "No. No, you're not. Should I ask why you left?"

"You can, but you won't get the answer you desire."

He chuckled, gesturing for me to take a seat on the sofa by his bookcase that was ornamented with pictures of his family. The irony of seeing a man who could effortlessly kill someone with one action, and then seeing the same man who adored his family so ferociously that he decorated his office with their pictures, was unreal. I guess, you could have the best of both worlds.

"So, what is it you need?" he pressed.

"A man I'm currently tracking was reported to visit a criminal," I replied, getting straight to the point. "A criminal that you are familiar with. Have you heard of Tristan Piers?"

Beau's face hardened. Gray eyes soured into thin daggers.

"Do *not* associate yourself with Piers, Ariadne," he warned, in a tone that almost made me not want to ask for more information. "Why are you asking?"

"Because the man who visited Piers is dead to the world publicly, yet he managed to visit this criminal under his true name. I want to know the relevance of Piers."

He didn't say anything for a long second, but the anguished look in his eyes made me glance away. It was only then that I saw the framed picture of his family on the desk, besides another picture of him and Gabrielle on their wedding day. You could see the small bump she had when she wore a beautiful, white gown. Beau stood beside her, staring at her with love clearly glittering in his eyes, whilst she stared at the camera, unaware of his gaze with a full-blown grin across her face. I could still remember that day despite me being a young girl; she was so happy. It made me dream of having a love as strong as theirs.

"I see," he responded, uneasily. Sighing, his fingers ran through his dark curls, and I forced my attention back onto him. "Back during my war days, Piers and I were comrades. Honor, blood and glory. That was all we knew. But those leave haunted images and sometimes you can't be cured from the trauma. Piers never got better. He wanted more, he needed more. He loved the screams of his victims and the thrill of killing. He was merciless. Killing became addictive. So, when we finally left, he walked down a dark path. He became involved in a group called the Serpents. A dangerous group of men that threatened the peace of the Underground. Before I became Gabrielle's bodyguard, he managed to get me involved with the Serpents."

I frowned, having never heard of any of this before. "You worked with the Serpents?"

"I didn't work with them personally. I didn't even know who they were, but I was a veteran, and I did their dirty work when I was called. Easy money. When I failed to do my job, they'd punish me. Torture me until I knew my purpose."

I hesitated. "Does —"

"I told Gabrielle years ago. It wasn't a secret I took pride in. I was ashamed, but I was young and foolish. These people had managed to get into the head of my friend, and somehow worked their manipulative ways into mine. It wasn't easy leaving, but when I left, I decided to be better. When I left, the Serpents weren't as well-known as they are now, hence why it was far easier to walk away."

Or in other words: *there was less risk of losing his life.*

There was a thick layer of tension suffocating us. The silence was excruciating. I tried to figure out what to say, except I couldn't. My own uncle had been involved with the Serpents; I wondered who else they dragged into their twisted games.

"How did Tristan end up in jail?" I questioned, instead of pressing to know more about Beau's history.

"He got caught. A man called Barak Doukas was Piers' next target from what I had heard. Barak had a brother, and when his brother died, he took his identity and wiped himself from existence. Piers couldn't find a man who hadn't been heard of before in public — essentially, he was a ghost. No one knows who Barak was. And just as Piers managed to find him, the feds got there first."

I frowned, trying to piece the information I had found out together. Why would the Serpents want to kill Barak if he was one of the Inner Circles? Betrayal, back-stabbing or purely to get money? It was difficult to tell. As the days went on, the reasons to seek vengeance became more blurred. I realized the Serpents were much more significant and ruthless than a normal organized crime group. There was more to them than the people they enslaved and the money they used to gain power. Something else was happening that I couldn't quite see.

"Does that answer all your questions?" Beau wondered, seeing as I hadn't spoken for a while.

I forced a smile, bobbing my head. "Thank you, Beau. I appreciate it."

"I'll have you know, Aria, that the Serpents are a bloodthirsty and callous people. Trust me. I already know who you're involving yourself with, and I'm telling you to think about the situation more carefully. How many people need to die for you to understand that you can't destroy the Serpents?" His eyes became very cold and aloof as they glanced away. "I lost too many people because I wanted to get revenge for the way they had used and abused me. But they harmed those I loved. Tell me, Aria, are you willing to risk the safety of your loved ones to get justice?"

I stood up, pondering over the question my uncle had asked. How many people would I need to lose to get justice? I had underestimated the Serpents and their abilities. My uncle was an exceptionally strong man but even he was a victim to the Serpents. Who were these people? What was their end goal? Every fiber of my body refused to look away from this injustice, from the reason I left my birthright. I knew that there would be consequences to my actions, to the answers I was seeking, but I knew no one else would look. People were selfish. We lived in a world where we couldn't trust one another, where we couldn't trust ourselves. We lived in a world where ignorance was better than fighting, but that made us no different to those bringing harm to others. I spent years searching for an answer and I was not going to turn away now. The Serpents were going to die. And I would be the one to do it.

So, how many people have to be in danger for me to go out and get justice?

"*None*," I answered, punctuating every word with confidence. "Because I'm Aria Moretti and nothing is as dangerous as me."

CHAPTER 23

(t)his world

I paced around my office, trying to figure out the missing piece of the puzzle. Something didn't fit quite right. It was as if I knew what the missing puzzle piece was, yet it was on the tip of my tongue, and I couldn't bring myself to say the words. Beau had known that Barak was alive, which meant so did the Serpents. However, if they were so adamant about wanting him dead, why was he still alive and why was Barak pretending to be Kal? It was all so confusing. And that was frustrating. I didn't like it when things made no sense to me. Just like my own stupid emotions. My phone buzzed and I glanced at the lit-up screen. Nero's name illuminated the room as the phone trilled, and I sighed, switching it off. I wasn't sure how to face him. It wasn't often that I would meet someone who would leave me speechless. I knew exactly how to retort back to those who challenged me, but with Nero, I failed – I really sucked at it. God, I blamed him and his intense cerulean eyes. They were too piercing for me to even stop to catch a breath. My mind flashed back to a couple of nights ago.

"I'll spend forever trying to convince you, Aria."

Yeah, fucking right – and wait for the perfect opportunity to stab me in the back. I trusted Nero as far as I could throw him, which meant I didn't trust him at all because he weighed like an elephant, and I knew I was strong, but not that strong. Growling to myself in frustration, I ran my fingers through my hair and peeked back at my silent phone. I knew exactly what he was saying, and I hated that he was saying it now. Where was that energy five years ago when I needed someone to tell

197

me that I wasn't going crazy? When I needed him to tell me that what I heard what just a lie? No. He didn't say anything. He allowed the distance to grow between us. He allowed my paranoia to feast off my plate of distrust. He *allowed* me to walk away. *And* he never came after me.

"You're not even denying it, Nero. You know what I am saying is true. Pretend if you must, but you know that Aria could never lead —"

I hissed at the memory and poured myself another glass of whiskey, before returning my attention to the files spread across my desk. There was no point pondering over the past whilst the Serpents were still around. Barak's picture taunted me, a stupid smirk on his face as he stood beside a beautiful Columbian girl. *Wait*. I frowned, reaching out to the photo that was laid besides Barak's file. The girl looked like she was eighteen or nineteen, her hair black, long and wavy, and pretty brown eyes that looked golden when the sunlight spotlighted her. Barak had his arm around her waist, leering at the camera, whereas she wore no facial expression. Her eyes were pretty, but dull and lifeless. The attire she wore – a dress that covered every inch of her body, leaving no skin exposed – tightly clung to her body but it was enough to show me one thing. She was pregnant. I felt disgusted, scowling when I gathered Barak must have held this girl against her free will. My second thought was Darius, but I immediately dismissed that idea as he was a few years older than this girl, and the picture was taken three years ago as suggested by the date sprawled on the back of the image.

Which could only mean one thing, Barak had another child.

Settling into my seat, I pursed my lips, trying to see if I had missed anything else. The coldness of the room didn't bother me as I poured yet another glass of whiskey. The golden liquid immediately soothed my sudden thirst, an exhale leaving me just as my office door opened. Calix peered in, his green eyes rose, amused, when he saw the state of my office. I was usually a clean freak but with my thoughts all over the place, so were my files as they began to pile up on the bookshelf, the fireplace, the couch and basically, the entire room.

"Well," he drawled, closing the door behind him. "You've been busy."

"You could say that," I grunted. "Except all I've been getting is dead ends."

"Can I be of any help?" He inched forward, leaning over the desk, his body brushing past the pile of files, and grazing his lips slightly against mine.

The temptation to kiss him was unbelievably strong but all I could hear was the deathly threat Nero left ringing in my ears, "*I don't want him touching you anymore, Ariadne. And if he does, I promise I'll break him into pieces.*"

A glimpse of brilliant blue hues flashed behind my eyes, and I sighed, shoving Calix away with a shake of my head. *Damn it, Nero.* If he was dedicated to keeping us exclusive, despite my stupor at this clause, then I had to honor it too. Avoiding Calix's stare, I bit the inside of my cheeks. "I'm good here. Can you send Kira up, if that's alright?"

Calix didn't question my actions; he didn't have to because he already knew the answer. We both did. Although Kira was the only one who knew of my deal with Nero, I had no doubt that Calix was aware that I was sleeping with him. I didn't try to soothe the burn I left in my presence. We both knew that one day this would come to an end, and if he expected anything more then something was obviously miscommunicated at some point during our relationship. He pursed his lips and narrowed his gaze, glancing back at me one last time before he disappeared out of the room. A part of me was irritated by my actions. When had I ever left a man dictate my life? Regardless, I couldn't bring myself to be with him. It wasn't the same. It didn't make my toes curl with deep delight or my body hum in pleasure. It didn't feel like anything. Nero was right about one thing – I wouldn't be able to lay with another. Not after being with Nero. I was a fucking wreck. Moments later, Kira entered the room with two cups of coffee in her hands, mirroring the same expression Calix wore when she saw the state of the room.

"You need to clean this room," her nose wrinkled, as she passed me a cup before settling into the seat opposite me.

Unlike most days, she wore looser clothing because I had sent her on a short mission to hunt down Piers whilst I investigated Barak. Having arrived back at the Manor at noon, she told me that Piers refused to cooperate until she suggested alternative methods. From the black jumper and the dark jeans, I had no doubt she mentioned gorier consequences. Her Jimmy Choo's were black stilettoes and my lips tugged at the memory of us buying them. They had been the first item to belong to her after I saved her from captivity. I wasn't surprised by her choice. I believed the heels chose the person, and naturally these were the ones that chose her. It was befitting. Her flaxen hair was damp which suggested she must have had a shower before meeting me, and her porcelain skin glimmered due to the lotion she used.

I passed her the photo of Barak and the woman. "He had another child. Why wasn't I aware of this?"

She frowned. "He did? How did you get to that conclusion?"

I tapped the girl and where Barak placed his hand. "Look at her. The dress she is wearing is almost skin-tight but if you focus on her frame, you can see the bump. She's probably a couple of weeks pregnant. Her hands are on her stomach and her body is angled in a protective manner whilst his posture states territory. It's like she's protecting the child from him."

"And you got this," Kira's eyes flickered up in awe. "From one picture?"

"You would too if you paid attention. You are usually the first to spot these things," I noted, lifting my brow at my second, suggestively. "You haven't been very focused as of late. Where's your mind at?"

"I could ask the same thing," she bit back, and I knew she was talking about Nero. I didn't even flinch, waiting for her answer. Kira sighed. "He knows more than he's letting on."

"You've been too focused on Konstantin, Kira. He's getting to your head. You're letting him get to you."

"I know, I know," she said, tossing her hair over her shoulder. "I just need more time."

I held my hand up, not needing to hear anymore. "He's your father."

"My step-father," she corrected.

I leveled my gaze. "Your *father*. He's the closest thing you had to a paternal figure. He was all you knew growing up. I understand it's hard but you're letting him consume you. He's a liability in our home."

"He's not doing anything to me," was her defense.

"What is it that has you so caught up in him? Is it the rage? Or the hurt?"

"Stop it, Aria," she whispered. Her eyes became glassy, and she swallowed inaudibly. Then, she closed her eyes and said, despondently, "I just need closure."

I took her hand and when she opened her eyes, I saw how exhausted she was. The blueness of her gaze was far too cool, tormented by her past and it killed me. I wanted to destroy Konstantin and every man that laid their hands on her. I wanted to tear their fingers off and force them to watch as I shoved them into their mouths. I wanted to rain my fury down on them. But she looked so tired, and those feelings were not mine to act on. Some nights, I would find her standing in front of the mirror in a loose nightdress, her eyes tracking the scars on her body. They were everywhere. The ones on her arms had faded over time, but the ones on her torso darkened with age. When she would peer in the mirror, she had an indistinguishable expression. She would stare blankly and her fingers would trace the wounds. It terrified me how desensitized she had become to the sight, and this enraged the monster within me. She would never admit it, but Konstantin stole the one thing she had left – her strength – and with one look, he stole it from her again like a thief in the night. The Yakira Adachi that sat opposite me wasn't the same as the one who had brought numerous men to their doom. She was beginning to return to the old shell of her past self, and God forbid, I would ever allow that to happen. Her strength was my courage, and her courage was my strength. We were two flames of the same inferno and without her, I would lose myself.

"Have you ever considered that it might just be time for closure?" I brushed my thumb against the scar on her wrist. "You're asking all these questions but how can you move forward when you're seeking answers to the past?"

"He loved me."

"Yes, he did," I confirmed. "But the man downstairs isn't the same man who took you under his wing."

She didn't say anything else. Konstantin would be punished eventually. Taking a deep breath of air, I released it as I let go of her.

"He needs to pay for him crimes," I vowed, darkly. I eyed the scar on her shoulder that the jumper didn't cover. It was a knife wound from someone who pierced her flesh. That man was dead, as would the rest of them be. "Justice will be served."

*

It was pitch black by the time I arrived back home, and the main roads were still, not a person in sight. The temperature had dropped, dramatically, causing me to shudder as the freezing wind nipped against my skin that wasn't covered by the coat. As soon as I stepped into the penthouse, warmth washed over me and I exhaled in relief, kicking my heels off that were beginning to give me cramps in my legs. After spending the day holed up in my office, I managed to phone my parents to get an update on Violetta. They absolutely adored her, and my mother couldn't stop fawning about how pretty she was. Pleased that Violetta was still safe, I made a mental note that Nero had only four days left to find her. So far, I had nothing to be worried about, but with Nero, anything could happen and I wasn't letting my guard down just yet. He was the best at finding things, though I seriously questioned how good he could be if he didn't manage to find me... or perhaps, he just never looked. I stumbled towards my empty living room, collapsing onto the couch, the exhaustion that I had been avoiding finally greeted me with open arms. So, I closed my eyes, rubbing my forehead when I noticed a headache raging. I could lay here forever, but my stomach gurgled, and I groaned. Despite the fatigue, I forced myself to get up from the comfort of my couch and cook myself a meal – I couldn't remember the last time I had eaten. However, to my surprise, I saw a meal already precooked for me on the countertop. I frowned and glanced behind me, suddenly noticing a dull light coming from upstairs. I overlooked the plate of food even though my stomach was growling in hunger, and began to run upstairs, getting ready to confront my intruder.

I pushed my bedroom door open and found, to my surprise, a sleeping Nero, curled underneath my silk duvet. Quietly, I inched closer, admiring how he looked like an innocent child, his long lashes caressing his cheeks, and a smile gracing his lips for a small second, as if he was dreaming of something sweet. I contemplated whether I should wake him up but thought against it, recognizing the lethargy that his body donned. Leaving Nero where he was, I began to undress, changing into something comfier and loosening my hair from the tight ponytail it was in. I would stop moving whenever I heard him make a sound, afraid to wake him up, but eventually I managed to clean myself up before I went back to the kitchen. After warming up the meal he had prepared for me, I settled onto the couch and switched the television on, wanting to divert my mind from the chaos that surrounded me, the screen illuminating the semi-dark room. I wasn't sure how long I spent downstairs but at some point, Nero woke up, rubbing his eyes like a baby, as he trekked down the stairs, sluggishly. Despite having just woken up, he still managed to look effortlessly captivating; his bed hair was unkempt, covering his blue eyes as they searched the entire room until they found me.

"When did you come back?" he asked, hoarsely, as he sank into the seat next to me. Even his bed voice was attractive.

"A while back. I didn't want to disturb you, although next time I'd prefer you to sleep in your own bed, or at least, take the guest room," I replied, with a twinge of irritation. "But the meal made up for that."

He managed to give me lazy smirk. "Italian food always wins the heart."

I didn't respond, staring blankly at the screen to distract myself from Nero's presence. However, it didn't work. From the corner of my eye, I spotted Nero running his fingers through his sepia mane, straightening out his white sweatshirt and then rolling up his sleeves. My heart pounded at every single action he made, and I cursed myself for being so easily swayed by his carnal presence.

"Why have you been ignoring my calls?" he asked. When my answer was silence, he snatched the remote out my hands, earning a cry of complaint, and switched the television off. I sulked beside him, pouting as I sent him a murderous glare. He wasn't deterred. "It's been three days, Aria."

"I've been preoccupied," I lied, biting back my tongue. Before he could press on any further, I quickly diverted the conversation elsewhere. "I just discovered Barak had another child with a woman who wasn't his wife."

He followed behind me a moment later, after I got up to grab myself something to drink. Leaning over the marble island, he studied me as I poured myself some wine. I really should be careful with my alcohol intake, seeing as I drank nearly a whole bottle of whiskey today, but it was the only way to ease the tension off my body. I didn't have time to relax or step back and just breathe. There were people out there who would never get the opportunity to relax, as they were being brutalized by the Serpents. I was constantly working, and the only way to unwind was to drink. The look in his eyes told me that he was aware of this, and that he didn't approve of my methods.

"So, Darius isn't an only child?" he opted, to say instead.

I shook my head. "It seems so."

"What does that mean?"

"It means out there in the world are his child and mistress, heavily guarded, and if my suspicions are right, I think they believe Barak is dead."

Nero frowned. "Everyone thinks Barak is dead."

"Apparently not everyone," I slid a poured glass of red liquor across to him. "It seems that those who wanted Barak dead actually know that he's alive, yet Barak continues to use his brother's identity. Complicated, I know."

"Surely, there's a reason for him to pretend to be Kal."

"At first, I thought it was because he was hiding from assassination attempts, but recent news has told me that's not the case. Barak is dead to the public but to the Underground, he is very much alive."

"And you think that child and mistress may be the reason why," he grasped. I pursed my lips, nodding, sourly. "So, where are they now?"

"Fuck knows," I chugged down another glass of alcohol, feeling it burn my throat but relishing the sensation. "I'm waiting for updates but they have all been dead ends. All very frustrating."

"You've always been impatient," he chortled.

I shrugged, indifferently, gazing away as my mind began to wander. My head buzzed, and I reminded myself to take some aspirin before I went to sleep, or I would wake up with a migraine in the morning. There was a pregnant pause before I heard Nero's sigh, his footsteps shuffling on the wooden flooring indicating that he was moving around. By the time I looked in his direction, he was standing right in front of me.

"Now that we've spoken about what's on your mind right now, let's discuss what's been on your mind the last few days."

My jaw clicked. "If you haven't already realized, I'm always busy which means I don't have time to deal with your childish superstitions or frequent messages to know how I am."

"No," he spoke in a low and dark tone, which mirrored his crystal eyes that looked bottomless when they stared at me. "Not then. But now, you can deal with it. You *have* to deal with it.

"I think it's time for you to leave," Holding my ground, I turned away from him.

"No."

I opened my mouth to object, but he stopped me by pressing his lips against mine. The second they touched the tension rolled off me in waves, as I evaporated into his arms when they wrapped around me. His kiss sent chills at a hundred miles an hour throughout my body, easily stealing my breath. I hooked my arms around his neck, tiptoeing so I could reach for more. Groaning into my mouth, he lifted me onto the counter and settled himself between my legs. In that moment of the kiss, our chemistry became an ever-bright flame. The way he kissed me wasn't the same as those seen in movies, but one that was steeped in a passion that ignited a firecracker of emotions. It was the promise of realness, of primal desire which lived in us. And with it, he told me that he was awake and connected within – that he embraced himself rather than hid himself as a copy of those romantic ideologies. It was carnal and feral, so wild and hot, that all my worries scrambled at the thrill. All I could think of was how warm my body felt pressed against his. It broke me and healed me all at the same time. I was a coward for not confronting him. I should ask him about that night five years ago. Still, those words were trapped in my throat, and his kiss allowed me to swallow my fears. Because kissing him was like jumping off a cliff and loving the fall. *And Lord save me,* I loved the fall. Pulling away, he pecked the tip of my nose as I tried to steady my breathing, aware of my thundering heartbeat.

It was quiet for a while, before he spoke, "Do you remember when we were kids and there was that old tire swing in the backyard of my parents' house? We'd swing on it whenever we could."

"Hardly," I lied, slightly shocked that he remembered such a specific memory. "Why?"

"You used to ask me to push you harder so you could see past the evergreens," he chuckled to himself, and the sound thawed my callous exterior. "Well, ten years have gone by and now I'm asking you to stop trying so hard to push me away."

I had never seen Nero so vulnerable until tonight. My brows pinched together as I stared at him in melancholy. His ice blue eyes heated when he caressed my cheek, gifting me a smile that told me he was okay. But I wasn't. I wasn't okay at all.

"I can't get distracted anymore. There are people depending on me – people I need to save," I swallowed back a sob, closing my eyes to hold the tears caused by the way he looked at me, so heartbroken and exhausted. "I have to protect those fighting for their lives in this world.

"You still don't you get it," he responded, in a tone so soft that it felt like a feather being swept against my skin. "The world is you, Aria."

My eyes shot open as I stared at him in shock, my heart stuttering at his words. His eyes sparkled as he rested his forehead against mine.

"My world starts with you."

CHAPTER 24

challenges and pledges

Nero

She was the sun and I was a planet, orbiting around her, enthralled by her gravitational pull. She was the moon, and I was a mere star, envious of her luminous beauty. She was the ocean, and I was a tiny fish, drowning in her bottomless eyes. She was the universe, and I was a worshipper, praying to be blessed with her presence. I remembered every detail of her. From the color of her nails to the exact scars found on her body. I could remember the scent and taste of her; it made me an addict and on her, I would happily overdose. She smiled, and the world lit up. Sitting in my office, I wondered why I stopped searching for her. Why did I not keep looking all those years? Granted, all recollection of her had disappeared the morning she left, but over time bits and pieces of memories started to come back to me until I retrieved the full memory of the night of her birthday. After months and months of lingering outside her locked bedroom door, I finally mustered the courage to open it and seek beyond what I already knew. Despite being gone for half a year, the scent of her perfume was still in the air, heavy and thick – a mixture of fruits, laced with freesia and coffee fusion alongside the sliver of rose and Amberwood. Her satin bedsheets were untouched from the crumpled state they were left, a reminder of the night we had shared together. Not a single piece of clothing was left littered on the floor or hanging in her extremely large closet. Her vanity table didn't leave a single trace of her presence, except for the polaroid tucked in the frame of her mirror – an image of us on her sixteenth birthday. With my arm around her waist, her lips teemed with joy as she squinted her eyes whilst I got distracted by her, glancing down just as the camera flashed. It was then that my memories came rushing back and I was left with a banging headache, which took me days to recover from, and a broken heart that I, still to this day, was healing from. Every day I spent trying to remember a part of her. Every second I spent trying to understand why she left. And then I stopped.

I could still remember that night, vividly, like a movie. It haunted me like a ghost but what tormented me the most was the way she had looked at me. God, I loved her eyes. They held the whole fucking galaxy. When she was happy, they were clear, radiant and bright amber. They were usually slightly crinkled around the corners as she laughed or even when she smiled. There was never a trace of a storm. But when she was angry? Oh, that was a completely different matter. They were dark and murky, and they blazed with rage. Those eyes could burn a hole in your soul. And when she was sad? They turned frosty, cold, and totally unlike her. There were a few clouds but mostly it was ice. That usually hurt me the most. So, the night before she left, they were an odd mix of the three. Those eyes swallowed me whole, and I was still trying to get out of them. There was a faint knock on my door and my ears strained at the sound as the door opened. Matteo came in with the usual crease between his brows and slid a brown envelope across my desk that always held good or bad news – often it was the latter. I arched a brow as I examined the envelope, waiting for an explanation for his sudden appearance.

"I looked into anything that would link Barak to his secret mistress and child, as you asked, but like Aria already said, I've only reached dead ends. Whoever his secret family is, Barak is doing an incredibly good job at hiding them or if anything, making sure they don't exist. Anywhere," Matteo informed.

I seized the files in the envelope, skimming my eyes over every piece of communication and all bank transactions that Barak had been involved in within the last three years. "What about the years before?"

"Sorry?"

Glancing up, I pointed at the first date. "You've only searched the last three years, but Barak must've known the girl for a much longer time than that. Search at least six years back and then let me know what you find."

"Nero, if you just thought of this that means that surely, Aria has already done it," Matteo stated, knowing how Aria was always five steps ahead.

"She might have missed something. She's been distracted lately, even though she doesn't show it, so her mind hasn't been focused on the task. Plus, there's no harm in double-checking."

Matteo thought to argue but one look from me told him otherwise. Tucking the files back into the envelope, he gave me a wary look before retreating out of the room. Silence. It greeted me, welcoming me with open arms. I closed my eyes, leaned back against the chair, and sighed, wanting to be left alone with my thoughts.

Then my phone shrilled.

Squeezing my lips together in annoyance, I considered whether I should respond or leave it but after several incessant rings, I answered, vexation leaking into my greeting, "What?"

"How rude," The feminine voice kissed her teeth. Surprised, I glanced at my caller ID to see Aria's name blink. "Do you always respond to your calls so rudely?"

I pinched the bridge of my nose. "How can I help you, Miss Moretti?"

"Pack your bags. We're going on a little trip."

*

Aria never ceased to amaze me. From her secretive smiles to her unexpected excursions, she was an enigma that I was never able to solve. As she stood at the end of the steps leading to the private jet, dressed in a raven-colored bandeau dress that left little to the imagination, red soled heels high enough to pierce a man's heart, a fur shawl shielding her from the April weather, and gold-rimmed shades, I wondered what was going through her wonderfully exquisite mind. With her phone pressed against her ear, she chewed her gum as she spoke and then she stopped, her lips curved into something which imitated displeasure, and then she spoke again. Even from the distance as my car drove onto the runway, I knew she was scolding whoever was on the other end of the line. One hand reached out to take her glasses off whilst the other gently patted the sides of her nose, her eyes rolling as she cursed before she hung up. I puckered my lips together, fighting back a smile, as I parked up beside the silver Audi on the runway. Aria squinted in my direction and all signs of irritation vanished. A cagey smile toyed on her lips as she waved me over, whilst I grabbed my bags from the trunk.

"You came," she grinned. No surprise could be detected in her tone, as if she knew I would come. Like I had a choice when it came to her.

"I'm starting to question why," I grunted, handing my belongings to the baggage handlers.

Aria didn't bat an eye at my brash tone and slipped her shades back on. "Ever been to Greece, Nero?"

"A few times. Why –" Realization dawned over me whilst Aria's smile broadened. I scolded, "Do you know how reckless this is? Barak will know you're onto him."

"Not necessarily," she chirped, vaguely, heading up the stairs.

"What does that mean?" I frowned.

She halted, glancing over her shoulder with a little smirk. "How does a pre-honeymoon holiday sound, fiancé?"

*

I always envisioned that one day I would marry Aria. Even before I knew how deep my feelings truly were towards her, I knew she would be the woman that I would marry. Not because our families wanted us to, but because she was probably the fiercest woman I had ever met, and I instantly knew she would be the one I would want to spend the rest of my life with. Only, I knew this was not what I had expected. Then again, she had continued to debunk my expectations. So, honestly and truly, I was at fault to expect otherwise.

"*Fiancé?*" I questioned, for the nth time since we got on the plane.

Aria sighed, exasperatedly, rolling her eyes as she placed her magazine down and turned to a stewardess who walked by. "How long until we land?"

"Eight and a half hours, more or less," she replied with a bright smile that eventually faded as Aria glared at her.

"We've only been flying for less than three hours?" she asked, appalled, but it was more of a rhetorical question. However, the stewardess wasn't sure whether to answer her or not, stammering as

209

she glanced between Aria and me, before Aria finally got annoyed and dismissed her with a wave of her hand as if she was a pesky fly. The stewardess quickly bowed her head before darting out of the cabin, fleeing Aria's wrath.

"Aria," I grated. She glanced at me with a raised brow, nonchalantly. "You can't just say I'm your fiancé without explaining why on earth we are getting married?"

"*Uh-uh*," she held a finger up. "Only until we get back to New York."

I wasn't amused, and she clearly knew that, but still the corner of her lips quirked into a cheeky smile before she rolled her eyes.

"Barak's wife, or widower, is hosting a society for soon-to-be-married couples at the Doukas estate, where Barak used to live and where that photograph of him and his mistress was taken," she explained, after a moment. "If anyone is going to know about this dead man's dirty secrets, it's going to be a scorned wife – or widower, in this case. Especially if it's about a mistress."

"And how do you know his wife is going to have the information required?" I questioned as she got up, heading to the minibar to pour two glasses of champagne.

Handing me one, she answered, "My mother can be very useful when it comes to her relatives in Greece and let's also just call it intuition."

"So, you want to base this entire plan on intuition?" I cocked a brow, incredulously, up at her as she peered down.

She smirked. And that told me everything.

"Exactly," she held her glass out, a mischievous twinkle in her eyes had me wanting to tempt my luck. "A toast. To a happy couple like us."

I mirrored her smirk, clinking my glass against hers, and downing the liquor at once. By the time I was finished, she had barely drunk half the glass but I was impatient, wanting to see how far she would go. My hands trailed up her legs and then to her waist, where I drew her closer. Her eyes briefly went wide as I pinched the glass out of her hand and placed it on the table beside me, before dragging her onto my lap, a soft squeal escaping her lips before the glare.

"So, fiancé, how about we celebrate this joyous news more appropriately? We have eight hours to spare," I alluded, huskily, touching my lips against the side of her neck. I smirked when I heard her breathing quicken before she shoved me away.

"I'd rather not. Sex on the plane doesn't sound flattering to me."

"I never said it would be sex," I chuckled, both at her lie and her broad eyes, her mouth failing to react with a snarky comeback. "But I do like that idea much better."

"Nero," she warned, but it didn't have the effect she wanted. Instead, my name left her lips like a prayer, her eyes dilated with longing as my lips wavered over hers. She was in a trance and, unconsciously, her hands grabbed my shoulders as mine pushed the shawl off her shoulders so I could pepper her skin in dainty kisses.

"One day, you're going to have a ring on your finger. And I'm going to be the one to put it there," I promised, her head tilting at an angle as my lips reached the crook of her neck, marking her as mine.

But, despite the pleasure that placed her in a daze, she still managed to whisper, "Never."

As I reached her lips, moving away from her jaw, her remarkable amber eyes never looked darker than they did right then. "Is that a challenge?"

Aria reached out, cupping the side of my face, her eyes dazzlingly icy and taciturn, and brushed her lips against mine, seducing me with the faintest of touches and enticing me with her honey-like taste. Yet, even then, as I was distracted by her temptress-like behavior, I heard her say, "It's a promise."

*

5 years ago, November.

She smiled. A Cheshire cat smile. A smile which gave me tremors down my spine and goosebumps across my arms. Her fingers reached out and almost like a feather, she caressed my cheeks, following a trail to the junction between my neck and shoulder. I held my breath. Closed my eyes. Fought the urge to grab her by the waist and throw her onto the bed behind me. My nails dug into the palms of my hand, as my jaw clenched when I felt her lips press against my jaw.

"Do you love me, Nero?" she whispered, but it was so sensual I could feel my eyes roll back at the sound of it. It was like listening to a siren sing.

"Do you want me to?" I answered, stilling.

Despite my eyes being closed, I could picture the corner of her lips tugging into an amused smirk when I felt a breathy laugh fan across my face. She grabbed my jaw, her nails digging into my cheeks, which caused my eyes to flutter open and narrow into thin daggers.

"Tell me, Nero, have you ever loved me?" her red lips moved, patronizingly, waiting for an answer, but her cold eyes told me enough. They told me this was more than a conversation between two former best friends – it was an interrogation.

"Tell me, Aria," I murmured, noticing the flame from the candle lit on the bedside table behind us dancing in her icy eyes. "Have you ever loved anyone before?"

Her smile widened, unscathed by my words. The way her lips pursed as she smirked, or the slight lift of her eyebrow as her eyes twinkled, indifferently yet frostily, showed how callous she was. My hands itched to reach out and claim her, despite the sadistic nature of our relationship, despite me knowing how cruel and twisted she was, deep down underneath her seductive smile and flirtatious words. The beautiful gowns she would wear, the expensive jewelry that she would adorn, or the lavish cars that she would drive, all spoke volumes when you truly understood the nature of Aria Moretti.

She was just a girl seeking a way out.

And she found it in the battlefield of blood and glory.

"I'll only love you if you say please," she sang, as she crossed her arms over her chest. Her words were taunting, mocking me.

This time, my lips twitched into a smile. "I'll never beg."

"Then, I'll never love you."

Leaning forward, I finally allowed my hands to capture what belonged to me – her. Gripping her waist as I settled on the bed behind me, I pulled her onto my lap, ever-so-softly brushing my lips against hers, my tongue darting out and gently wetting her lower lip, drinking in her enticing, venomous kiss.

"Is that a challenge?" I breathed.

She moved forward, pressing her searing hot lips against mine as she whispered, "It's a promise."

CHAPTER 25

(w)ringed heart

Greece was absolutely picturesque. The ocean was so incredibly blue and transparent that I could see the fish swimming in a school, and the beautiful corals that were dotted around giving a burst of color to the water. The sand glimmered like specks of diamonds as it shimmered under the scorching sunlight. The grass sported flowers of all types and the trees were a lush green, housing chirping birds as they sang a soft melody when we drove by. The car curved through the contours of the Grecian cliffs, my eyes never leaving the stunning sights outside the window. Beside me, Nero was on the phone, most likely talking to Matteo to inform him of our arrival, but I was too lost in the scenery and wondered whether I should discover my Greek heritage – the heritage that my mother would never talk about. I had never met my grandparents but from what my mother had told me, I didn't think I wanted to. They had abandoned her when her little sister, Vera, had passed away, because they didn't approve of her job, because they blamed Vera's death on the lifestyle we were born into. But none of it was my mother's fault – Vera was terminally ill and that was not a fact my grandparents were willing to accept so easily. Despite it all, I always wondered about this side of my life that I was yet to discover. I knew my grandparents had migrated to Athens a few years back to rest during their retirement; it was information I had Kira look into after I had left, when I didn't know whether I wanted to turn away from the world I was born into or put my foot down and change it. The latter was my calling.

If my mother ever knew that I searched for my grandparents, I had no doubt she would kill me. She was the only person in this world I would never win against. My eyes moved to Nero who I noticed was muttering in Italian, the frustration on his face as clear as the frustration in his voice. Something wasn't right. Before I could question him, the car stopped, and we finally arrived at the villa we would be staying at for the next few days. Located on the far south of Athens, you could see the ocean pulsating against the shoreline in a steady, rhythmic beat. Similar to most Grecian architecture, the villa was white, and built from conglomerate stones. The flat roof featured swells of red, clay tiles and the window frames were painted a blue that echoed the sea and sky. There were already a few guards stationed around the complex; two were patrolling the premises, guns in their hands and two knives tucked in their cargo pants. I counted four snipers at the two towers parallel to one another, guarding the iron gates that led to the villa which opened once our identities were confirmed.

"I see you spared no expense," Nero commented, taking in the location but I knew he was memorizing every face that we saw. I smiled as I slipped my sunglasses on, the sun beating down on my face when we stepped out of the car.

"Of course not," I replied, his eyes flickering over to me, catching the teasing grin. "It's our pre-honeymoon."

Maybe ten hours ago he would have argued at the idea but now he nodded, staying silent on the matter, and focusing his attention elsewhere. I frowned, hoping to evoke a reaction from him, but whatever was said on the phone must have stayed with him. When we finally got out of the car, two maids came to collect our luggage and, to Nero's surprise, Kira walked out of the villa in a beautiful white sundress, her blonde hair loosely braided and rose gold sunglasses perched on her head, revealing her eyes that were as blue as the Greek flag, which twinkled when they caught sight of us.

"Finally," she exhaled, impatiently. "I was wondering when you two were going to arrive."

I saw Nero frown, his eyes scanning Kira before they moved over to me. "Who is this?"

"Nero meet Yakira Adachi, my second-in-command," I introduced. Kira waved with a cheery grin. "Kira, Nero Russo."

"It's a pleasure to finally meet you, Nero," I scoffed, when I heard the formality in her voice as she held her hand out which Nero cautiously took. "I've heard great things about you."

"You must be Konstantin's daughter?" he questioned, putting the pieces together.

Kira's perfect smile stiffened. "*Step-daughter.*"

Nero squinted his eyes at her curt correction. "No wonder we weren't able to find any traces of her existence. Although, I'm surprised that I wasn't aware Konstantin remarried."

"That's because he didn't," she explained. "Konstantin was my father by force. He never legally married my mother and bought us from my biological father, since he owed Konstantin a lot of money. Please, follow me; I'll show you the rooms that you'll be staying in for the week."

I knew Nero was curious to learn more about Yakira – most men were. She was an enigma and barely let out a slip of her past life. It was like nothing had ever happened. However, whilst he was intrigued, he also recognized the friction in her voice and kept any further questions to himself. I had no doubt those questions would be targeted at me when we were alone.

"How long have you known Aria?" he asked, as we entered the villa.

I smiled appreciatively at Kira, admiring her fancy work in picking out such spectacular place to stay in. The ceilings were painted a glossy azure, and the floor was a white marble. It was so clean one could imagine them being hosed down and dried by the sea breeze.

"Five years," Kira said, and my attention returned onto them.

Nero glanced at me. "I'm assuming that Kira was the reason for your disappearance."

"Not necessarily. Meeting her changed my entire perception of the Underground, but I finally understood what I wanted for the first time in my life," I declared, noticing the small smile Kira had directed towards me.

"And what did you want?" his eyes studied me as he spoke the question that I finally had the answer to.

"To protect people," I replied, earnestly. "The Underground is a dark place, stripping the freedom of the innocent by the hands of the corrupt and powerful. It needs to be put to an end or no one will be safe. Including you."

For the longest time he said nothing, his eyes never left mine and for the first time, I couldn't tell what he was thinking. Then, he exhaled, running his fingers through his hair as he broke his gaze away. I glanced at Kira, who silently watched Nero, waiting for his next question which we both already knew would be.

"How did you save Kira?"

"She saved me from the hands of men who used my body as a toy," Kira response was so honest and blunt that it caught me off guard as I didn't know that she would be so truthful about her uncanny history. "She saved me from Konstantin."

Nero's eyes momentarily widened before he nodded mutely, walking ahead of us. Kira and I glanced at each other, wondering what was going through his mind, but we followed him half a beat later. I wasn't sure how to fill the silence between us as we walked through the villa, familiarizing ourselves with our surroundings, but thankfully Kira was an expert of such situations and began informing me about everything that was occurring back in New York. Whilst she was giving me a verbal report, I couldn't tear my eyes away from Nero's back, waiting for him to turn around, to say something, anything. Then, when she mentioned Mykonos, an island further south to Athens, Nero halted.

"I guess you found the location of Barak's last bank transaction," he muttered. My eyes widened and I turned to Kira to confirm this information to which she nodded, solemnly. "I'm surprised you didn't check further than three years, Aria."

"I thought I did," I frowned and knitted my brows. "I guess I was too –"

"Distracted?" Nero interrupted, peering over his shoulder. I didn't say anything and just clicked my tongue. After, he eyed Kira. "We've met before, haven't we?"

Finally, I understood why he had been so quiet. Kira smiled in a reticent manner. "I was wondering when you'd recall. Only several times, but I was wearing different disguises, a new woman each time so I'm not surprised that you didn't catch on."

"Someone had to keep an eye on everything in New York whilst I was gone, recruiting new people," I reminded, taking the attention away from Kira.

He laughed but it sounded condescending. "You mean, someone had to keep an eye on me."

I didn't confirm nor deny his statement, propping my shades onto my head. "Whatever helps you sleep at night."

Before he could reply, Kira quickly cut him off, "I'd like to inform you that Althaia Doukas' society party is tomorrow night. Your window of opportunity will decrease every second you two spend arguing with one another. I understand you have history that neither of you can seem to let go, but for the sake of the mission, tomorrow night I want you both to be the most loved-up couple in that room. Can you do that?"

For the longest minute, neither of us said anything and I was so tempted to be petty and say 'no,' until I heard Nero utter a stiff, "Yes."

"Aria?" Kira pressed.

I swallowed my pride and glimpsed over my shoulder, forcing the biggest, sugary smile I could muster. "Let me show you our rings, honey."

Nero frowned and Kira bit back her smile, as he glanced at her in confusion before turning back to me. "Our rings?"

Kira's amused wrinkled eyes infuriated me as she gently patted Nero's arm and murmured, "I'll leave you two to settle in," before walking away, leaving a perplexed Italian man staring at me as if I had two heads in the corridor.

*

The sun began to set by the time I was finally done unpacking and prepping Nero with all the information required for tomorrow's society gala. I yawned, closing my laptop, and pushing it onto the bed, then stretching my body as I began to feel my muscles stiffening - I hated when that would lead to cramps. Groaning, I managed to push myself off the comfort of my bed and wandered towards the full-length windows that encompassed three-quarters of the bedroom walls, light spilling in, whether it was from the searing sun or the magnificent moon. Dusk looked more magical in Greece than it did in New York – a part of me speculated whether my mother would have left her life in Russia, New York or even Italy to live inconspicuously in Greece. I think a part of her always wanted to. Sometimes though, the past was just too much to bear. My thoughts were briefly cut off when I caught a glimpse of Nero's silhouette, staring out into the distance, looking over the striking panoramic view of Greece. My favorite feature of the villa was that it was on a precipice and from the back of the villa you were able to get the most scenic landscape of the country. I didn't waste any time, my body moving faster than my mind, and before I knew it, I had a silk frock on protecting me from the salty breeze as I stood behind Nero.

"Do you remember when we would pretend to be someone else when we'd be sent on black ops by Alexei?" he asked, without glancing behind him to know it was me. He had gotten changed out of his suit and wore some comfy sweats, his fingers tracing the metal barrier along the cliff. I smiled, reminiscing about those days.

"Our first mission was when we had both turned sixteen and we begged Uncle Alexei to send us on a mission. Any mission – we were both too eager to get a taste of the world we had been preparing for since we were kids," I replied, my voice so timid that I was worried he didn't hear me. Then, he released a breathy chuckle.

"We were competitive. We wanted to see who the best would be."

I hesitated, before stepping next to him. "We were fools."

"Yes, we were," he glanced down as I looked up. Despite the fact that the temperature was not particularly cold, I couldn't help but shudder as a chill raced down my spine when I saw the darkness in his eyes. It mirrored my soul. "Because back then we were too competitive to accept our mistakes."

My eyes drifted back to the glittering lights in the distance that reminded me of the stars. "Nothing has changed."

"We have," his steel blue eyes unnerved me when I peered up, trying to pace my pounding heart that I was sure he could hear.

"Have we?" Although my words were quiet, they spoke volumes as if I had screamed it.

Nero didn't say anything, and his eyes gave nothing away. They say the eyes are the window to the soul, but his looked like the hollow shell of someone he used to be. I wondered if that was how he perceived me. The unspoken betrayal and the lies between us were bound to spill out one day, but neither of us were willing to speak first. In that moment, I had felt like I was sixteen again, on a black op, trying to get the million dollars hidden in the bank safe before Nero did. I was going to win. Except this time, standing in front of him, I debated whether my silence only cost my win.

Ba-dump.

There it was again. A monotonous pain in my heart. I held back five years' worth of tears and pursed my lips, sealing five years' worth of heartache. His eyes never looked away as if they were imploring for answers in mine, and when he failed to find them, his impassive face turned away, he held his hands behind his back as he straightened his spine.

"After tomorrow, half of Europe will know that I'm engaged and by the end of the week, the rest of the world. You do understand the risk, because for someone who wanted to remain non-existent, you'll be under the watchful scrutiny of every publication and media outlet, plus our enemies and families."

"I understand."

"And if your plan fails tomorrow, years of preparation could be ruined."

I smirked when he turned to me, squinting as he waited for an answer to what sounded like impending doom. Alas, I was never one to back down from a challenge. "Well, it better not fail."

"Why did you decide to wear rings?" Nero questioned, after a brief moment of silence, tilting his head to the side. There was this insipid glimmer in his eyes which had me inhale.

"Kira said we can't be engaged without wearing them. I couldn't convince her out of it," I explained, my voice void of emotion.

"I didn't think it would be that easy to convince you."

"It isn't, but I know that my feelings mean little compared to how much is at stake when it comes to the mission."

"The mission," he murmured, more to himself than to me, and he looked away. "Of course."

I wasn't sure how to respond and held back the words that threatened to spill from the tip of my tongue, in fear that I would say something wrong. Nero blew out a breath of air before placing his hands onto the steel railing, thrumming his fingers in a rhythmic beat. My eyes caught the shine of the silver band on his left hand by the moonlight. Beautiful diamonds embellished his platinum ring, looking tiny compared to the Harry Winston on mine.

"Are you scared, Nero?" I whispered, second guessing whether I was asking the question to myself instead.

"Terrified," was his answer after a pregnant moment. "Are you?"

"Incredibly."

The golden sun had finally set, and the beautiful, rosy sky blackened; we said nothing else as we stared out into the expanse, wallowing in the loud silence of our obscure fate, and wearing the weight of our glittering diamonds which sealed the unknown future.

CHAPTER 26

mistress mystery

My gown was unlike anything I had ever worn before. Kira suggested I wear something different, but I didn't realize how different she meant. Instead of the usual dark colors, she chose a shade that reminded me of buttercup flowers. Designed by Teuta Matoshi, the dress was made to measure my frame perfectly. Compared to the women in my family, my thighs were slightly on the thicker side, and I often found some dresses unflattering as they created this amorphous image of me. However, this A-line silhouette brought attention to my bust and waist, spilling past my hips in a way that stunned me. It was created by yellow mesh net fabric, and the corset had built-in pads and boning. There was a small v-opening in the front, dripping between my cleavage, but it looked supremely sophisticated instead of illicitly irresistible. The bodice had beautiful, netted floral designs similar to the pleated skirt, which was separated by a decorative green belt that toned down the vibrant yellow of the dress. What I loved the most, however, was the straps that were embellished with embroidered ivy daisies and green leaves which slinked down the side of the dress, stopping just past my hips. On my neck, was a simple diamond choker to match the stones in my ears, which glistened under the moonlight whilst I waited for Nero. Sighing, impatiently, I fiddled with the exquisite Harry Winston rock on my left hand that felt far colder than the holster attached to my thigh. The ring suffocated me, so I distracted myself by admiring the view outside the villa. With my hair donned in a low, messy bun, a diamond clip attached against the side of my head, I began to worry that Nero wouldn't show.

The plan was pretty simple in theory: infiltrate Barak's office. Luckily for us, Althaia decided to host the gala in the comfort of her own home. It was a mansion large enough to fit over 200 people, and still have space. Unluckily for us, however, the event being held at her home meant that security would be much stricter, and it could be almost impossible to break into his office. The fate of the mission rested on the success of tonight, and right now, it didn't look so likely since Nero was running late. My jaw clenched as I waited outside the villa like Nero had instructed me to do. I wasn't sure where he had gone but I hadn't seen him all day. I was slightly concerned that he had backed out of helping me. Could he not handle the pressure, or was it because he was now engaged to me? A fake engagement, but an engagement, nonetheless. I guess I should have been considerate of his feelings, seeing as betrothals were not something I looked forward to as much as I used to. I was stupid to think that he would be happy to set his principles aside for the time being – until I took down the Serpents.

My heels tapped rhythmically as I glanced at my phone, noticing how we were getting dangerously close to being late. My patience was running thin, and I blew out a breath of annoyance, concluding that Nero wasn't going to show up. Scolding myself, I didn't notice the limousine pulling up in front of me until I heard someone call my name. My eyes widened at the sight of Nero when he got out of the vehicle, wearing his signature smirk that looked twice as seductive as soon as my gaze fell onto his attire. I always knew Nero looked gorgeous in suits, but this evening, he looked extra ravishing in a black three-piece suit with a yellow tie to match my gown. His hair was primed into a faded undercut which must have been freshly done as it hadn't looked like that last night. Under the night sky, I saw how his blue eyes twinkled like the ocean, but my stare thinned when I saw the bandage on his neck peeking out from under his collar. Again, it must have been done today, as I was sure I hadn't seen it before.

"Are you coming?" he asked, but he was soaking me in, and something darkened in his lingering gaze.

"When did you get a new tattoo?" I finally questioned.

Subconsciously, his hand reached for the back of his neck. He shrugged and outstretched his hand to help me into the limo. "I got it done this morning. I can show you after tonight if that's what you want?"

Of course, I wanted that. I narrowed my eyes, rejecting his hand, and slipped into the car. "In your dreams."

He chuckled and followed me. "I'm sorry I was late. I had some errands to run before tonight's event."

"This is cutting it close, Nero," I glowered, as the limousine began to move. "What on earth could you have been doing to be this late?"

That stupid smirk he wore didn't falter even when I glared menacingly at him. Instead, he reached into his blazer and pulled out a Cartier box that had my eyes widening as it revealed a stunning diamond bracelet. I was speechless as he took my hand and clasped the bracelet on.

"Happy anniversary, Aria," he murmured. My breath hitched as I stared incredulously at him. I tried to remember what today was but came up blank. As if he knew I wouldn't, he smiled. "You became the Don of the Italians five years ago."

My heart stuttered as that moment vividly replayed in my mind. The moment when my father headed the reigns to me. The moment when hundreds of men and women stood in front of me and kneeled, promising their loyalty to me. The moment when Nero and I finally gave into our desires. The moment when everything changed. April had never felt as cold as it did right then.

"Nero, I-I don't know what to say," I stammered, holding back the sudden urge to cry.

"Don't say anything. I don't understand what happened, but it looks as if you're in a much happier position right now, and that's all I want for you. That's all I *ever* wanted for you," he responded, rubbing his thumb against my hand. "I wish you could forgive me for the past, for whatever I did to hurt you. I hate that I don't know what it is, but when you are ready, I'll know then. For now, all I want is for you to be happy, Aria."

I swallowed, thickly, feeling the sobs trapped in my throat. "You didn't bug this?"

He laughed at my attempt to lighten the heavy mood, and I smiled. "No, but you can have Xander double check."

I released a short breathy laugh. "It's okay. I'll take your word for it."

It felt like hours had gone by without either of us saying anything.

We were just lost in each other's eyes, trying to find the right words but failing. The things we wanted to say, the unspoken truth that rested between us struggled to leave our tongues. I stared at the man with the mesmeric blue eyes, the man that I used to love so dearly, the man who was managing to weasel his way back into my cold, barricaded heart. And I wondered whether what happened five years ago was nothing but a nightmare I had been living in for too long, or the unsettling truth that I couldn't accept. I knew the only way I would get my answer was to ask him, but the fear of finding out the truth was too powerful, and I sealed the question away behind my red lips. I didn't know when we had arrived, but I finally snapped out of my daze the second I felt his hand against my cheek, a burning sensation causing my body to feel like it was on fire. His eyes were so tender and warm that they mimicked the smile on his lips.

"I didn't get to say this earlier, but you look radiant, like the sun, *fiancé*," he muttered, before closing the distance between us. He then kissed me so gently that I almost didn't feel it but the goosebumps scattering across my arms told me it had happened. His tongue swept out and caressed my lower lips, stealing my breath away too. My heart hammered like the music I could hear outside, and the world stilled, because being here with Nero was like being at home. When we finally broke apart, I tried to steady my labored breathing and calm my racing heart.

"You look pretty good too, Russo."

Nero smiled.

And I smiled back.

*

Althaia Doukas was a very vibrant woman with stunning red hair that looked like actual flames under the luminous chandeliers which hung in the marquee set out in her backyard. She had extraordinary sea green eyes and a smile that triggered people to gravitate to her. Despite being nearly 50 years old, Althaia showed no signs of aging and I questioned why someone like Barak would have a mistress when his wife was honestly model material. Unless the problem was internal.

"Are you thinking what I'm thinking?" I whispered to Nero as he handed me a glass of champagne. His eyes followed mine and his brow rose, trying to figure out what was running through my mind.

"Why would Barak have an affair?"

"No," I shook my head, slowly. "See, the difference between a man and a boy is that a boy would find any reason to cheat. They are afraid of being inferior and a woman like Althaia would certainly make any boy feel inferior. But only a man would have an affair if the problem were internal rather than feeling inferior."

"So, what are you proposing?"

"It's all about perspective, Nero. The first thing you noticed about Althaia was her appearance. She's gorgeous, no doubt, but a boy would only take notice of her appearance. Tell me, Nero, are you a boy or a man?" I challenged, glancing up at him. He narrowed his eyes at my blatant mockery, but it sparked his interest. I smirked. "Good. What else did you notice about her?"

He glanced back at Althaia, studying her attentively, whilst she greeted her guests, gushing and laughing with them. Knitting his brows, his nose crinkled adorably as he stated, "I guess she has this sort of energy. It's very spirited – I can't describe it. She looks like a woman any man would want to marry. Someone for the long run."

"Exactly," I snapped my fingers as he was spot-on. "Men think of women like fish. You hook them in, take a bite and throw it out when you're done. As Steve Harvey once stated, *'if a man isn't ready for a serious relationship, he's going to treat you like a sport fish.'* Can you see where I'm going with this?"

"Aria, I'm struggling to find the correlation here," he sighed.

"Althaia isn't a sport fish and if Barak married her, it was for one of four reasons: status, money, love or..." I explained, my body buzzing at my discovery.

"What's the fourth reason?"

My eyes drifted back to Althaia as I sipped my champagne, the cogs in my brain spinning as I concluded what I had failed to see all this time. "From past research, Barak married her because he loved her. They were high school sweethearts apparently. Barak had everything – the money, the status, even love. But an affair – there's only one reason why he would have one, and that's reason number four," Nero frowned when I turned to him, my lips quirking up into an elated smirk. *"An heir."*

His eyes expanded as he glued together all the fragments of evidence I laid out in front of him. If I was right – *and I was certain that I was* – that meant Barak didn't have a mistress. The woman was their surrogate, carrying Althaia and Barak's child. In the Underground, nothing was more powerful than having an heir to your legacy because it ensured that your name would live on, and the older the legacy, the more power you had.

"Let's say you're right," Nero responded, after a minute. "It doesn't explain why Barak hid their surrogate."

"No, it doesn't," I agreed. And then as if the answer to my prayer was revealed, Althaia's voice boomed from the speaker as she beamed at the crowd. A devious grin twisted my lips. "But I know someone who does."

*

"You can't just ask her," Nero hissed, as we glided through the sea of people.

"Why not?" I frowned, when he grabbed my arm, bringing us to a halt.

"Because you're going to blow our cover, Aria. We are meant to be engaged. Storming up to Althaia and asking questions about her supposedly dead husband when we came to celebrate our engagement is going to raise questions that I'm pretty sure you don't want to be answering."

I pursed my lips, mulling over what he was saying, and begrudgingly accepted defeat. Sighing, I crossed my arms over my chest. "What do you advise we do then?"

Grinning, his arm snaked around my waist, and he drew me closer. "Smile and celebrate, *wifey*."

Before I could protest, he slithered us through the crowd, effortlessly greeting people he had never met before and catching the eye of many soon-to-be-married women. I scowled to myself when I noticed a group of girls swooning over him and sent them a dangerous glare that immediately shut them up. Noticing my abhorrence, Nero chuckled to himself despite the dirty look I gave him.

"This is your plan?" I grunted, in annoyance. "Greeting people and having those shameless girls fawning over you?"

His lips transformed into a secretive smile, but he never once glanced in my direction. "Not necessarily."

I frowned and followed his train of sight, noticing Althaia moving towards us with a warm smile that knocked my breath away. God,

Nero called me the sun, but this woman was like the whole damn universe.

"It's such a pleasure to meet you. I'm Althaia Doukas, the hostess for tonight's event," she welcomed, reaching to give me a kiss on my cheeks before she glanced at Nero. "You must be Nero Russo. I've heard so much about you."

"Thank you for extending the invitation, Althaia. This is my fiancé, Lyra Kyrokos," Nero introduced, gesturing to me with a loving smile that I mirrored a beat later.

Althaia crooned, pure and genuine awe across her face, "You are such a perfect pair. Lyra, you're absolutely stunning and I love that gown you are wearing. I don't think I've heard of your family before."

"Most of my family have migrated to the US, but originally we used to live in Santorini," I lied, smoothly. Thankfully, she didn't doubt my story and quickly moved onto how Nero and I met.

We didn't have enough time to discuss our background and panic flooded me. I glanced at Nero for help, but he didn't look the slightest bit worried as he said, "Lyra and I were childhood friends. I'm sure you've heard of Xenia Moretti."

"Of course!" Althaia exclaimed before turning to me, wide-eyed. "Are you her daughter? I heard she has one."

I shook my head with a smile that spoke innocence and suddenly I understood Kira's intentions with this gown. "No, no. She's very close friends with my mother. Nero and I had grown up together but drifted onto different paths as we grew older. It was only recently that we managed to gravitate back to one another."

Glancing up, my breath was lodged in my throat when I saw Nero already staring at me, affection lingering in his icy orbs, but there was also something else that I couldn't quite put my finger on. Unable to form coherent thoughts, the words got stuck because of the intensity of his eyes. Nero managed to fill in the silence, his lips tugging into a heart-breaking smile.

"And I asked for her hand in marriage. I didn't want to spend any longer away from her," he finished off. Something in his tone suggested authentic truth but I couldn't bring myself to believe it.

"How romantic," Althaia gushed, pouting at us like a little girl reading her favorite fairy-tale. "It's so beautiful seeing young lovers find their happiness."

I blushed when Nero pressed his lips against my forehead.

"Happiness is one of the many feelings that she brings me."

Althaia placed her hand above her heart and sighed. "I hope you enjoy the rest of your evening and best wishes on your marriage."

After thanking her, Althaia disappeared into the large crowd, as did her balmy spellbinding aura. I wasn't sure what to say to break the awkwardness between us and fidgeted in Nero's arm. Eventually, his grip loosened, and I muttered an excuse before slipping into the crowd, trying to find a restroom to catch my breath. Stumbling into a stall, I pressed my back against the door and heaved heavily, trying to stabilize my breathing and collect my emotions. I pressed my lips together and blinked back the tears that I had been holding in since the start of the night, burying my feelings deep within me. Once, I felt confident that I wouldn't break down, I unlocked the door only to then lock it when I heard two women enter the restroom – one of them being Althaia.

"All these lovesick fools," she all but snarled, her warm persona completely disappearing and indeed, left a woman scorned.

"Only a few more hours, Althaia. This is an annual event and for you to cancel it will raise questions. Unless you want people to find out that your dead husband cheated on you, you need to continue playing the role of a romantic," her friend sighed, as if she was getting bored of repeating herself.

"Remind me again why I'm doing this."

"Because your pathetic husband didn't leave any money to you in his will and the only way you'll be able to maintain the reputation you've upheld is to pretend that the money you're raising tonight will be going to charity."

"I still can't believe that whore managed to wrap her unpolished hands around my husband. The gold digger was meant to carry my child only but then she got my husband, my money and my child. How did my fortune become so terrible?" Althaia sneered, smacking her lips together which suggested she had reapplied her lipstick.

"As if you care about the child," her friend laughed, spitefully. "You only agreed to have it because you knew Barak would put you as the sole owner of his shares until the child is eighteen."

"The only thing I didn't know was that he'd fall in love with that peasant. If I wasn't as invested in saving myself, I'd kill the bitch," she squawked, and I cringed. After a brief minute or two, she exhaled and morphed back into that quirky persona of hers. "I guess the show must go on."

I counted to thirty after they had left. When I was sure that they weren't going to return, I slipped out of the restroom, swiftly reapplying my red lipstick , before heading off to find Nero. It didn't take me long to find him – I just had to follow the trail of giggling women. He was at the bar, drinking alone despite the endless number of girls who greeted him, but he rejected their advances. On any other occasion, this would have made me grin proudly, but after my latest discovery, I didn't think much of it. As if feeling my gaze, Nero glanced in my direction and the tired appearance he wore suddenly disappeared, replaced with this bright energy that illuminated him once again. It didn't take him long to realize that something wasn't quite right.

"Is everything okay?" he asked, as soon as he closed the distance between us.

"Change of plans," I muttered, my eyes scouring the crowd to find Althaia. "I was partially wrong."

"What?" His voice laced in confusion and shock as he responded.

"Althaia and Barak had a surrogate, but Barak fell in love with the surrogate. Althaia didn't care about having a child and she knew that she would be in control of Barak's assets if he was to ever die, only until the child was eighteen. Except, it must've backfired because not only did Barak fall in love with the surrogate, he also didn't leave anything in Althaia's name – including the child's inheritance."

"That doesn't make sense. Someone would have to hold onto those assets until the child is eighteen."

As soon as I spotted Althaia, watching her smile as if she wasn't robbing people of their money, I glanced back at Nero, who was waiting for me to fill in the gaps he failed to fill. "Exactly, and who else could it be except the surrogate? Which could only mean that Barak knew Althaia's true intentions and hid the child and surrogate from her, but as a safety measure also left her absolutely nothing, and thus continuing to hide himself from public eye –"

"– Because if Althaia was to find out he was alive, she could either plot to kill him again or change his will entirely," Nero completed in disbelief. I bobbed my head and he peeked at Althaia, his eyes thinning into a dark glare which only made me excited to hear what he had to say next. "How does blackmail sound?"

I smirked. Great minds think alike. "I thought you'd never ask."

Entwining our fingers, he led us through the crowd, until we were standing directly in front of Althaia, who was taken aback at first, before warmth masked her skepticism. "Is something wrong?"

"We need to speak," I ordered, removing any ounce of the familiarity I had early on. "*Privately.*"

Althaia examined us momentarily, before nodding slowly, motioning for us to follow her. When we were finally alone in a room several meters away from the marquee, her friendliness disappeared, and her eyes glowered at us in annoyance. "*What do you want?*"

"The location of your surrogate," I stated, curtly. Stunned, Althaia fumbled with her words as she struggled to form an excuse, glancing at Nero as if he could save her from my interrogation. Rolling my eyes, I scoffed. "I'd suggest you tell us because a rumor like that could ruin the precious reputation you hold so dearly. I find it humorous that a woman like you is conning people in order to protect your reputation with all those invites to high society galas. But I'm not surprised, I mean, you were once a peasant girl."

Her jaw clenched and the green emeralds that men would fall onto their knees for glowered at me. "You don't know what you're talking about."

"I must admit, at first, I fell for your little act. A peasant girl catching the eye of a bigshot billionaire. I mean, how cliché. Except, you didn't catch his eye, I mean, not entirely. '*Highschool sweethearts*' – what a pathetic story to sell. It took me a while to figure it out, but when I heard that you didn't have a cent to your name, I knew why," I smirked, angling my head. "Men are foolish when it comes to love but even a billionaire like Barak would choose not do a prenup. Which brings me to my next two questions: how you did you actually meet him and where's the child?"

"What are you? A fucking detective?" she snarled, taking a threatening step towards me, as if that would scare me.

From the corner of my eye, I saw Nero react, but immediately stopped his hand. He gave me a confused look as I shook my head, slowly, hoping he could read my mind and back off. As if he heard my silent order, he moved away but kept his eyes trained onto Althaia, watching out for any sudden movement. I moved my gaze away from Althaia, ensuring she was still in my periphery, and turned to Nero, who knew what I was going to ask before I had said it. He frowned, disapproving of my request, but I knew Althaia wasn't going to speak with him in the room. I wasn't stupid; even without seeing the mirror behind her, I knew she was armed. I could see the small knife in her grasp, and it glinted when the light reflected off the blade. I had to make her believe the fight wouldn't be fair or she wouldn't speak. But, again, people were fools. Nero clenched his jaw when he noticed I wasn't going to budge. So, sending one last deathly glare to Althaia, he left the room but the intimidating presence he had only doubled as I sized Althaia up.

"You're going to wish I was once I'm done with you," I chuckled, crossing my arms over my chest, as I turned back to her. "Answer the damn questions."

She leered. "He came to my town in Epirus in order to find someone to marry to carry his heir. The stupid man was so dead set on getting a child, that the second he saw me, he wanted to marry me. Except, he didn't want to take the risk and needed to make sure I could carry a child. Thus, we slept together."

"Darius was born out of wedlock," I whispered, more to myself, but Althaia heard me and scowled.

"Unfortunately, I wasn't able to carry another child and went through several miscarriages. Barak got frustrated and wanted us to go through with surrogation. I listened to all his orders because I knew the second he was dead… everything would go to me. At least, that's what I thought. I was under false pretenses that Barak and I did not have a prenup and spent nearly thirty years of my life believing that. That sneaky bastard must've had me sign one without my knowledge."

I raised a brow, unsurprised. "And the second you found out he was in love with the surrogate, you plotted to kill him, believing you would gain full ownership of his assets when in fact you didn't get anything."

"I didn't waste my life to end up poor again!" she screeched, before a maniacal expression took over her face. Poor woman. "And now that you know the truth, I'm afraid you'll be buried with it."

The thing about people who were not trained to act before your instincts kicked in meant they were at more risk of being killed. Althaia reacted very rapidly for a girl who was a peasant as she grew up and then had everything handed to her during her adult life. Which meant, she learnt the art of killing young in order to protect herself. When the knife was above me, I leaned to the left swiftly, which caused her to miss and stumble. Floundering gave me a five second window and I contemplated whether I should end the game now or play a little longer. The evening was getting so boring, therefore, I decided the latter. Five seconds later, she found her footing and charged at me, targeting the knife directly towards my heart. Before it pierced my skin, I grabbed her wrist and broke it, causing the knife to drop onto the ground with a loud clatter. Althaia shrieked in pain and collapsed to her knees. The sight of her kneeling had me smirking. If she thought she could beat me then she had another thing coming, because I was capable of killing her and making sure my dress didn't get ruined in the process. I didn't give her any time to react and shattered her kneecap with my stiletto, releasing another cry from her lips. A part of me wondered whether she would give up, but I saw the fire in her eyes and knew she was far from defeated. Her intact hand moved to grab the knife beside her and tried to slice my legs, except she missed as I twisted to the side and kicked the left side of her body, hearing her ribs crack at the force. The sound had me on a high as I knocked the knife out of her hand and stooped down to her height, watching her sob as blood spewed out of her mouth. I played with her knife, humming a sweet tune which had her quieten, her cries turning into short hiccups.

"See, this would've been so easy and painless if you just told me where the child is. It's not like you *want* to protect them –" I stopped speaking and cocked my head to the side, studying her reaction with beady eyes. "Unless, you have to. You don't know which Doukas twin died, and if it wasn't Barak, he'll be coming after you because you're holding his lover and child hostage," she gurgled as my hand went to her throat, holding the knife directly above her heart, singing, "*And the plot thickens.*"

She struggled in my grasp, clawing at my hand on her neck, her whimpers silenced as she began to whiten, gradually losing the ability to breath. Though, I couldn't let her go too easily. A child was in danger and she still hadn't given me their location. Loosening my grip, marginally, she sucked in oxygen, her chest rising and falling, the color returning to her face. She no longer looked as pretty as I thought she once was. In fact, she reminded me of a tomato.

"I'll ask again, Althaia, where is the child?" I probed, glaring at her. She didn't respond at first, the words failing to leave her glossy lips until my grip tightened and she hammered at my hand, silently weeping.

"Canada," she choked out. I loosened my hold, allowing her to breathe. Hunching over, she took short breaths of air. "Canada.

They're in a remote area called Yukon in Canada."

I smirked, triumphantly, removing my hand from her throat, tucking her pocket blade into the corset of my dress. "Now, that wasn't hard, was it?"

With the little strength she had left, she looked up at me, not looking as beautiful or warm as I had first perceived her to be. "Who," *breathe*, "the fuck," *breathe*, "are you?"

I chuckled, darkly. "Are you sure you want to know?"

She didn't reply. Not taking it as a yes or a no, I leaned down until there was little distance between us and answered for her, "*Aria*,"

Her eyes widened as panic set in, and I knew she had heard of me. Good. That meant she knew what came next. She shuffled back frantically but I dug my nails into her thighs, causing her cry out in pain, unable to move as blood spilt onto the white rug. The smile on my lips was wicked and audacious, taunting and crazed, but it only broadened when I noticed her finally resigning to her fate.

"They know me as Aria."

Before she could react, my hands reached for her neck and snapped it in one fluid motion. Her body crumpled onto the expensive rug and blood stained around her, darkening the color of her dress. Standing up, I straightened my back and admired my handwork. It had been a while since I killed someone. I didn't spend too long loitering around Althaia, knowing someone would be looking for her soon, and thus swiftly removed any trace of my presence in the room, before slipping out, closing the door quietly behind me. Nero was pacing up and down the corridor but stopped abruptly when he saw me. Noticing that I was alone, his eyes flickered back to the closed room. I wondered whether he would yell or lecture me. But when he did neither, I was surprised – more by the concern which glassed over his eyes.

"What happened?" he asked, the words leaving his lips like a whisper as if he was afraid to even ask.

"Canada. We're travelling to Canada."

CHAPTER 27

(don't) leave me

Nero was quiet on the journey home. I wasn't sure how to fill the empty stillness between us. It made me uncomfortable and there was an aggravating nausea in my stomach that I had never felt before, especially after killing someone. Usually, I would be on this euphoric high but the holster on my thigh and the knife in my corset were beginning to dig into my flesh, and I was too worried about making any movement which could slice this silence apart. I fiddled with the ring on my finger, admiring how gorgeous it was, and the way it perfectly fit my finger, when I glanced up and caught Nero staring at me. His face was void of any emotion, eyes blank, even the corner of his lips were pursed into a straight line – it startled me.

"What?" I pried, bothered by how he was staring at me.

"Why did you kill her?" he questioned, coldly.

Fleetingly, my eyes expanded at his question, but then I clamped my jaw and looked away, my voice as cold as his. "Better to die at my hands than anyone else's."

"You don't get to decide that."

"So, you'd rather she wasn't killed?" I scoffed, glancing back at him in disbelief. "Even though she's conning people out of their money, and holding a child hostage?"

"You can't go through your entire life killing every human who's done something wrong. That's not always a decision for you to make,

233

especially if you don't know the full story. You're basing your actions off one side of the story," Nero stated, with a firmness in his tone that made me feel inferior, like a child being scolded for doing something wrong. Except, what I had done would have been the same thing he would have done if given the opportunity. Hypocrisy was laced in his words and that irritated me. My eyes narrowed, sharply, unwavering even as he looked away with a heavy sigh of exasperation and ran his hand over his face.

"Yet, if you were to kill her, you'd be praised. The same rules apply to you too, Nero," I declared, candidly. When he didn't reply, I exhaled, my fingers running through my hair in frustration. "So what? Do you want me to apologize? Is that what you need to hear? Will that make you feel better? I'm not sorry about what I did and if you can't handle it, then why are you here?"

Nero's eyes frosted as he peered over. He was furious, there was no doubt about it, but even then, despite the iciness that glassed his blue orbs, there was also this splinter of trepidation. Worry. Fear. Time stilled and within the blink of an eye, we had arrived back at the villa, but I was lost in the abyss of those cerulean eyes that belonged to the man beside me.

"You can never see it, Aria," he whispered. I heard his voice crack and a second later, I felt my heart throb in pain. A pain that I tried to numb whenever I was around Nero. He looked at me as if he couldn't tell whether he wanted to kiss me or fight me. Maybe it was both. But either option would hurt him. They would hurt us. "I have watched the world bend its knee to you, have seen the fear that resides in the eyes of the people who look upon you. You terrify them, haunt their nightmares with that charming smirk and those amber eyes that bore into their skulls like you are digging through their thoughts for something you can't seem to find. But, one day, all of this will catch up to you and you might find yourself in a situation where even I can't save you."

I swallowed, before responding nonchalantly, trying to conceal what he was causing me to feel. Guilt. "I'm not asking to be saved, Nero. I'm not a princess."

He reached out and cradled my face, his thumb gently tracing my jaw. "No, you're not. But you're Aria Moretti and that's a hell of a lot worthier a title."

Before I could savor in his touch, it was gone and the cold greeted me. I never thought Nero would fear something. Growing up with him, he never feared anything – it was one of the qualities I loved about him. Yet, as he moved away, taking his warmth with him, he also carried the dread that struck his heart.

Before he got out, I finally mustered up the courage to ask the question I needed to ask, the one I feared the answer to, "What are you so afraid of?"

He halted. A minute went by and there was no movement. For a second, I thought he would ridicule me for even suggesting he was scared about something. Then, ever so slowly, he looked over his shoulder and replied, "That one day you'll never come home back to me."

My breath hitched. We were all frightened of something, but he was still scared of losing me. After all these years, that was still his biggest fear. I had lived a long tiring life where fear was something I was constantly battling. I would fight the overwhelming feeling and, just when it almost consumed me, I would emerge victorious. However, for the first time ever, I couldn't stop the fear from swallowing me. I felt it coursing through my veins. I felt my heart pounding like a caged animal, roaring to be released from its cell. I felt my stomach sink in terror. I was afraid. I couldn't stop it from devouring me and it was because I was scared of losing him too.

"I'll always come back," I murmured, uselessly, looking away.

"You can't promise that," Nero responded. "You left once. Who's to say next time around you'll come back?"

"Nero…" I trailed off, not knowing what else to say because he was right.

"The day you left, I thought that I had lost you for good," he laughed, breathily, as his hand ran through his dark locks, his eyes steeling their focus on me. "When you left, you took a part of me with you. You're my world, always have been. My best friend, the other half of me. The only person who understands me better than I understand myself. Tell me, Aria, did it hurt when you left?"

"Of course!" I cried, trying to blink away the tears that had formed at the sight of him lowering his guards and realizing what truly laid in his heart. Because his heart was a mirror of my own.

"Then why didn't you come back? Why didn't you come back to me, Aria? Why did you leave?" he insisted, anger and anguish laced in his voice.

"I had to!" The words created a thick silence that settled between us until I whispered, closing my eyes, "I had to leave."

"Why?"

"I couldn't stay. Not after what I had heard what you'd done," his eyes widened and it finally confirmed my assumptions, the ones I didn't ever want to confirm. "I left because I needed a fresh start."

"Aria," he inched closer to me, but I flinched, causing him to think twice and move away. The distance between us may have only been short but I never felt as far away from him as I did then. "I don't know what you heard but I swear I wouldn't do anything to intentionally hurt you."

"I don't really want to hear it. The past is the past," I opened the door, finally stepping out of the limo, but before I disappeared from his sight, I squinted back at the man I had loved so much that it obliterated me. "You're the Don and I'm Aria. Nothing more, nothing less."

*

Canada was cold. I couldn't tell whether it was due to the falling snow or because Nero wasn't by my side. Maybe it was both. At the runway, I stared into the distance, watching the plane disappear until it was a speck in the sky. Just before I had left, Nero informed me that he was to return to New York as he had business to attend to. I wanted to ask him what was wrong when I noticed how stressed he looked, but I was too worried to hear that the reason was me. I wondered whether Nero was thinking about me like I was thinking about him. I wondered whether we would ever have a happy ending or if we were just doomed to a miserable life. We were magnetic, unable to stay apart, but the toxicity that poisoned us was too strong to ignore. The weather was freezing to my dismay, and I rubbed my arms, trying to warm myself up but, despite wearing a fluffy coat, the chilling air still managed to bite against my skin.

"Are you cold?" Nero asked, his arms wrapping around me in an attempt to heat me up.

"I hate being cold," I complained.

"I know you do, but we have a job to complete in Canada. So, suck it up," he grinned, tapping my red nose before unwrapping his arms from around me.

I glared at him. "Your existence annoys me."

He chuckled, wearing a smug smirk, as he tucked his hands into his pockets, indifferent to the freezing winter weather. "Please, you wouldn't be able to survive without me."

"Wanna make a bet?" I challenged and raised my brow. He narrowed his eyes, tempted to agree, but before he could reply, Uncle Alexei called us over. I grumbled under my breath, causing Nero to glance back at me with an amused twinkle in his blue eyes.

"Sorry, sweetheart," Nero replied, unapologetically. "Duty calls."

"Fuck you, Nero," I grunted at the endearment, ignoring how it warmed me up from the inside.

His lip curled into a seductive smirk as he leaned down, his lips almost touching mine. "That can be arranged."

"Aria!" I snapped out of my daze and glanced over to Kira, whose eyes creased in concern, as she waited at the car. "Aren't you coming?"

I bobbed my head, walking away from my memories that always managed to linger. My memories which would haunt me, the ones I had spent a lifetime running away from. But it was useless, and despite me knowing this fact, I still ran away, but he always caught up to me – no matter where I was or who I was with, there was this constant reminder that he would always find me. Before I slipped into the car, I looked over my shoulder and saw the girl I was many years ago, wondering when everything got so fucked up.

"Aria!" he called out from the distance; my mind distracted by the beauty of the world around me. Turning to his direction, I watched his brow raise as he asked, "Aren't you coming?"

"You guys go ahead. There's somewhere I want to visit," I shouted back, trying my best to ignore the bitter wind.

His nose crinkled as if he didn't like that idea, but he sighed and conceded, nevertheless. "Don't disappear for too long. I'll always find you."

Rolling my eyes, I couldn't help but smile as my heart swooned, unwittingly. "I wouldn't except anything less."

Yukon was a desolate area, hidden by the vast number of evergreens soaring over the cabins all situated miles and miles apart from one another. I could see why Althaia decided to hide Barak's lover and child here. As the car maneuvered through the long, winding roads, my eyes instantly fell in love with the landscape and serenity that the location emitted – an ambience that almost made me forget the reason why I had come. Kira, who sat beside me, scowled as she scolded whoever the unfortunate soul was on the other end of the phone. Perhaps she thought that I was so distracted by my thoughts that I wouldn't notice the side glance she gave me briefly and how she angled her body away from me, muttering down the phone, before she hung up.

"Who was that?" I pried, breaking the silence. From the corner of my eye, I noticed her jump in surprise, her hand resting above her heart.

She responded a minute later, "No one."

"Don't lie," I replied, glancing at my second–in–command. "Was it Nero?"

Her gaze never wavered, and her face gave no expressions away. Even the best trained assassin wouldn't be able to read her. But I could. She was nervous. Worried. Distressed.

"Yes. He wanted to know if we had landed safely."

"Since when did Nero become your superior?" I asked, with an arch of my brow. The question was rhetorical, and she knew that, but still chose to answer. I didn't bother hearing what she wanted to say and interrupted her, "I'm assuming you informed him of our current status."

"Aria, he wants to apologize and is asking for you to answer your calls or messages," she sighed. "What even happened the other night?"

I didn't respond, holding her arctic eyes that were significantly colder than Nero's.

"You know, you said he betrayed you," she paused, and I stilled. "Yet, I've never seen a man more in love."

I stared at Kira for a long minute, before looking away and appreciating the picturesque site. "How long until we arrive?"

"Another ten minutes," she replied, before muttering shortly after, "Make sure the kid stays away from me."

I cracked a smile. "Why?"

Glaring at me, she grumbled, "I'm not good with babies, you know that."

The cabin was slightly larger than the rest, but it still looked tired and archaic. Built completely out of wood, snow blanketed the red roof and porch. It would have looked completely deserted if there wasn't a white car parked out front, tires hidden beneath six inches of snow. I inwardly patted myself on the back for wearing my winter boots as soon as I got out of the car, my feet sinking into the white blanket of ice crystals. Tremors sprinted throughout my body, shuddering when a gush of frosty gale breezed by. Kira seemed impassive to the frigid conditions as her blue eyes scouted the area like an eagle, before gesturing to the cars behind us to cover the perimeter. Seeing as we were heading into uncharted territory, I had Xander send out a few of our people as back up in case Althaia attempted to send us to our doom. They wasted no time and disappeared into the forest, leaving Kira and I alone in the bitter environment that immediately put me in a bad mood. With a heavy sigh, I double-checked my gun was inside my coat pocket and my knife was hidden up my sleeve, before trekking through the deep snow with significant effort until we reached the front door. Kira had my back, her eyes unwavering from the endless evergreens as if someone would suddenly ambush us. After knocking on the oak door, I dusted off the snow which encased my beautiful black boots, frowning when I saw the snow had soaked the leather and left my toes feeling so incredibly cold that I momentarily questioned whether I got frostbite.

My internal struggle was interrupted when the door opened slightly and this beautiful Columbian woman poked her head out, suspicion lingering in her murky eyes. "Who are you?"

Hostility laced her heavily accented voice. She had barely opened the door, but it was enough to grasp an idea of her features under natural lighting. Dark brown hair framed her long face, brown eyes shaped like ovals narrowed cautiously at me, and her rosy lips pursed that they almost looked like she was scowling. She didn't look afraid or worried but rather dubious as she should be of strangers. Though, the skepticism wasn't a result caused by the dangers she had experienced in her life but because of the child she hid inside. Her maternal instincts kicked in and I knew we had the right woman.

My eyes creased as the corner of my lips curled into a saccharine smile, looking at the answer to all my prayers, as I responded, "It's a pleasure to finally meet you. I'm Aria Moretti."

CHAPTER 28

fears for freedom

"Barak was the only man I'd ever been with," she spoke, gently; there was no sense of gravity or sorrow hidden behind her words. They were *just* words. "I was only eighteen when he first picked me out of a group of girls."

There was no tremor in her voice, despite her hand shaking, whilst holding her cup of tea. A brief look at Kira told me she noticed this too. After introducing ourselves, Salome welcomed us, hesitantly, into her home. She had only just turned twenty-one, but the deep circles under her eyes and the hollowness of her cheeks could make one think she was in her early thirties. Her home was cozy and warm in contrast to the weather outside. The fireplace was lit, the smell of burning wood and white cotton suffused the rather tiny living room, and two couches circled around a glass coffee table. From one glance, this cabin consisted of maybe three rooms, excluding the living room, but it was still quite condensed and lacked any sort of space. Two rooms upstairs and another one downstairs which led to the kitchen. The living room was decorated with picture frames on the walls, a few of a young boy and others of who I assumed were Salome's family. There were succulent plants on the windowsill and beside the fireplace. Candles were ignited to make up for the lack of light as the sun barely shone through the frosted windows, but, nevertheless, the cabin still felt homey and welcoming. Sipping on the cup of tea Salome had brewed, my entire body instantly warmed, the feeling returning back to my fingertips and toes.

"We were living in a town that you wouldn't find on any of the maps, held hostage by a bunch of men for several years. I was fourteen when they had taken me from my family or, to be more precise, when my family sold me off. It was only a matter of time before I'd be sold off again like cattle."

"Did you have a choice?" I asked, knowing full well that she was a victim of the Serpents' tyranny.

Salome smiled, sadly. "When you can barely stand up and then have to face an incredibly rich and powerful man, does *a choice* even exist?"

I said nothing but that was all she needed to hear. Her sigh was unsteady as she gazed away, a faraway look in her rust-colored eyes reminded me of Kira, even months after I had saved her from the Serpents' captivity. No amount of time could rid the pain which loitered in her heart, and I had no doubt that Salome had suffered since the day she was born. Used, abused, and thrown to the side. Like a doll.

"Surrogation didn't work," she continued to say. "Althaia wasn't healthy; she wasn't capable of producing fertile eggs and so every time I tried to carry their fetus, it wouldn't survive. Eventually, Barak got frustrated and decided that he wanted the child with me, at any cost. But even after he got what he wanted…he didn't stop hurting me."

This new information has me realizing that Althaia and Salome had similar backgrounds. A poor girl that was taken advantage of by a rich billionaire. Except, Althaia continued to abuse the power she had because she was entranced by money and greed. She didn't realize that she and Salome were living the same unfortunate life. She believed that Salome chose to be a surrogate, not that she was forced. And when Salome had done her job, Barak continued to take advantage of her. I could feel the bile crawling up my throat.

"So, the child is yours and Barak's?" Salome's terse nod confirmed my question. "Even though you didn't marry him?"

She pressed her lips together. "He led everyone to believe that my baby was Althaia's, and that the surrogation had worked."

"But he fell in love with you," Kira spoke, delicately, catching Salome's attention. "That's why Althaia wanted to get rid of you. She wanted the money, but the money was in the hands of the woman he loved, and that wasn't her."

"Barak loved the idea of me. Docile, obedient, young, and free. Except I wasn't free, not when he was around," she clarified, looking down at her hands or more specifically the ring attached to her finger – her shackle. "My body was covered by a black dress; I wore a veil over my face as if I was a bride, I couldn't smile at other men nor could I talk to them. The only people I was allowed to be around were my maids and him, or Althaia. Except, Althaia stopped talking to me, my maids were too afraid to speak around me and he… he was too invested in having an heir that he didn't have the patience to hear my words."

Languidly, she peeked up, dark lashes hiding her striking eyes which looked almost golden when the candlelight hit them. "Althaia may have entrapped me in this cabin, but I have never felt freer in my life."

"Salome…" My lips failed to speak the words she needed to hear, but that didn't bother her as she lightly shook her head, dismissing them into the crisp air. Instead, I reached out and took her hands into mine. My words could never express how I felt, the anger and the heartache that struck me, but my actions promised to bring her justice, to right the wrongs in her world, to bring her the freedom she needed.

"I'm okay," she said, honestly, with a smile that caused her cheeks to crease her eyes. "I'm with Matias, the person you really wanted to meet."

She took me by surprise, raising her brows knowingly. Glancing at Kira, who also seemed shocked, I couldn't help but release a breathy laugh which dispersed the tension that laid densely in the air.

"He's upstairs."

"Is that alright with you?" I asked, and she bobbed her head.

"Of course. Let me get him."

As she disappeared upstairs, I turned to Kira, who sighed, ruefully, her fingers running through her blonde hair in frustration. She looked at me with those big blue eyes that reminded me of Nero's, but they were too icy to be his. Despite the cold aura she radiated, I saw the apprehension, the worry for the future of this young girl and her child. Like me, she wanted to save her but how could we save someone who was far too gone drowning?

"What do we do?" she whispered, anxiously.

"First, let's get her somewhere safe. If my suspicion is correct, she is the only person who can help us take down Barak. Being stuck by his side 24/7 would only mean she has some knowledge of his business partners and any involvement with the Serpents. She was held captive by them, and he knew where to find her."

"But we know Barak is part of the Serpents. In fact, we know he is involved with the Inner Circle."

"Which means that his handprint *has* to work if we want to get into that Manor. Viktor's handprint didn't work, and he was part of the Inner Circle – neither did Enzo's. This could mean that the Inner Circle were selective with who had access to what."

"There's only one other person who could give us answers since Viktor is being incredibly unresponsive," Kira said, icily. Then under her breath, she cursed in Japanese. "Might as well just kill him."

I studied her very carefully. "Set up an interrogation with Konstantin as soon as we land in New York."

She didn't say anything else and nodded, understanding the order I had given her despite the task involving her stepfather, the man who practically raised her since her biological father sold her and her mother off. I sighed, pinching my nose as I felt a headache brimming due to the thoughts screaming in my mind. But I was quickly distracted when I noticed a tiny three-year-old boy hopping down the stairs with a toothy grin, Salome following closely behind him like a guardian angel.

"Matias, these are my friends, Aria and Yakira," Salome explained when the boy finally noticed our unfamiliar presence. He recoiled when he reached the last step, shying behind his mother with cautious eyes flickering in our direction. "Don't be shy. They won't hurt you."

I took the initiative to meet the young boy with a friendly smile as I neared him, kneeling to his height. "It's lovely to meet you, Matias. You don't have to be afraid; I promise."

The little boy looked skeptical but nevertheless came out from hiding and lifted his lips into a tiny smile that melted my heart easily. He looked like the spitting image of his mother with murky brown hair that tousled over his eyes that had beautiful golden specks.

"My friend, Kira, brought some sweets. Would you like some?" I offered.

Matias immediately brightened up, nodding his head, fervently, which made me laugh. His smile was like sunlight itself, brightening the entire room. I even saw Kira's resolute dissolve at the young boy as he rushed over to her, suddenly settling himself onto her lap. Her eyes widened as he became extremely comfortable and waited patiently for the sweets that were promised. Salome cracked a smile, tearing up at the sight of her son which caused the smile on my lips to slowly fade away as I stood up.

"Can we go talk someplace private?" I said, her eyes flickering away from the very love of her life to me. "Kira will take good care of him." Kira's eyes shot in my direction with pure panic across her face. I smiled tightly at her despite the glares she shot my way. "Won't you, Kira?"

Kira protested under her breath, probably muttering how she wanted to kill me or something, but I didn't let it get to me, smiling in amusement as she tried to create some distance between her and the three-year-old, who just wouldn't stay away and pouted whenever Kira took him off her lap. Salome looked reluctant but eventually led us into the kitchen which had a pretty view of the evergreen forest which surrounded the cabin, coated in white sheets of snow.

"I'll get straight to the point," I began, as soon as the door closed. "You're in danger. Not from Althaia – you no longer need to worry about her."

Salome's eyes widened. "Why? What's happened to her?"

I clenched my jaw and looked away, her eyes reminding me of how Nero looked at me the other night. Fear. "She got what was coming."

Salome didn't say anything else, her eyes softened to a somber look which made me confused when Althaia treated her like a slave. A captive. A doll. She looked upset, worried and yet there was never a point when I saw a wave of relief.

"Is everything okay?" I questioned, raising my brows, inquisitively.

"Yes," she replied, quietly. "I just can't believe she's gone."

I frowned, pinching my brows together. "Aren't you happy? You're no longer bound by her. You're free."

"I guess, but Althaia was my friend before everything got so messed up. I know at some point our friendship turned into a competition for her, but it was a friendship at the beginning after she realized how similar we both were," Salome explained, leaning against the counter with a sigh. "At first, she hated me, hated the idea of surrogation, then one night when she came to visit me, she saw that I was in immense pain. That night we lost the baby. I'm not sure what had happened, but she remained constantly by my side, and we grew closer. I guess she felt that I was the closest thing to her baby."

Salome's eyes trailed to the window, a faraway look glimmered in her dark eyes and, suddenly I felt something that I didn't know I was capable of feeling. Shame.

"I don't blame her for hating me. Barak loving me meant that her life was in danger. It meant one day he would toss her to the side to be torn apart by the next ruthless man," Salome disclosed with remorse laying thickly in her voice. "Though, I suppose dying is better than living in the captivity of your mind."

I wasn't sure what to say at first or even how to feel. My mind flashed back to Nero, his words screaming in my head but also rightfully stinging my heart.

"You can't go through your entire life killing every human who's done something wrong. That's not always a decision for you to make, especially if you don't know the full story. You're basing your actions off one side of the story."

It irritated me to no end, but even I knew when to take responsibility for my mistakes. I thoughtfully stared at Salome, noting the sad smile playing on her lips and her eyes glistening from unshed tears which only doubled the guilt that gnawed at my stomach. I sighed, running my fingers through my dark locks, closing my eyes to calm the screaming in my head, urgently needing to silence the demons in my mind which caused my loss of focus. With my eyes closed, I shut out the sounds, ignored the scents which wafted in the air, and paid little attention to the bitter taste on my tongue. *One. Two. Three. Four. Five.* I counted. Incessantly. Until the screaming stopped, and I could think rationally again.

My eyes fluttered open, and I caught Salome staring curiously at me, the words leaving my red lips were thick with regret, "I'm sorry for your loss."

"I'm not. At least, Althaia is safe where she is in now," Salome stated with a knowing look sent my way. "I think you forget you're human sometimes, Aria. It's okay to feel guilty. I'm sure you had your reasons, ones that I don't need to be explained to me. Just tell me, how are you going to keep Matias safe?"

Before I could speak, I heard another car park outside and my lips curled into a smile, forcing the guilt to be buried deep within me, resolution replacing the remorse which lingered in my voice as I declared, "I promise I'm going to keep you and Matias safe. On my life. My third-in-command, Calix, will take you and your son to another location off the grid. You won't be alone, and Matias can grow up in the presence of people other than you. The plane will leave in four hours, so you'll have enough time to pack. Unfortunately, Kira and I will not be travelling with you, but I can assure you'll be perfectly safe with my colleagues."

"Who are we running away from this time?" Salome blew out a breath of air, digesting the information I had sprung on her.

"Barak," I answered, gloomily, after hesitating for a short second. "He's alive and there's a possibility he'll come after you, Salome. Not only do you have his heir, but you are the only person other than him who knows about his role in the Serpents. Althaia kept you alive because she knew that if Barak is alive, he would come after her first to get his revenge, so holding you for ransom should keep her safe. But Barak will come after you to ensure there are no loose ends."

"Right," she nibbled on her lower lip, anxiously.

I reached out, ignoring the slight flinch when my hand rested on her arm, and looked at her with determination on my face. "You are vital to us, Salome. If we want the Serpents to end, we need every bit of information you can provide. Will you help us? Help us raise your son in a safer world?"

Her eyes hardened as they found mine and I knew the answer before she even said it. My smile stretched as I brought her into a tight hug, her body slacking against mine, tired from the fear that continued to follow no matter where she went. Eventually, we tore apart and went back into the living room, my eyes enlarging with sheer surprise when I saw Kira laughing as she played with Matias. The little boy jumped onto Kira's back, a grin on her face as he laughed with his entire heart. I envied the innocence of young children, the joy and happiness they brought into the dark world was the reason why it was bright every day. There was a warmth in my heart when I saw Matias, a reminder of the reason why I was taking down the Serpents.

"Do you have any children, Aria?" Salome whispered, not wanting to disrupt Kira and Matias, who were still unaware of our presence. I shook my head, softly, and followed the way her lips curled as she watched her son, fondly. "One day, when you do, I hope it is with someone who loves you very much because there is no greater joy in life than holding the child you created with the person you love dearly."

*

On the plane, I watched the stars twinkle in the night sky and remembered the delicate diamond on my finger. I admired it, feeling the emptiness in my heart which I had been trying to ignore the past few days. The thought of having my own child strangely created this warm sensation throughout my body and it took me a few minutes to realize that it was happiness that I was feeling. I never once thought about starting a family; it wasn't something that had ever crossed my mind. Yet, Salome's words replayed in my mind like a broken record and rather than them haunting me, they only made me wonder about the future. A scenario I had spent next to no time thinking about. What was my future after the Serpents? Perhaps it was a subconscious thought, as I instantly recalled Nero; my heart stuttered when I envisioned starting a family with him. He was my best friend. The only person who knew me better than I knew myself. That was when I knew I wanted to be with him for the rest of my life. I was an idiot for denying the feelings I had for him. Whether it was be five years or fifty, I knew that no amount of time would help me get over how I felt for Nero. I had been spending so much time ignoring how I actually felt that it began making me lose focus again. I couldn't lose focus, not when we were so close to achieving our goal.

But I wasn't that stupid, head over heels girl that I was five years ago. I was undeniably stronger, smarter and more self-sufficient. I knew that my feelings were so complicated that how I felt for Nero could never be explained to other people, and at times, even to myself. All I knew for sure was that I wanted him around me, I needed him around me. He was a reminder that I couldn't always put myself at risk because there was always someone waiting for me to come home. I wasn't sure where exactly my mind was at, but it wasn't on Kira when she told me that Violetta had returned to the Manor, or when the stewardess asked me again if I was going to eat, or when the pilot informed us that we had landed back in New York. I couldn't remember the feeling of the tepid air that greeted us, or when I got into the town car, or when I arrived in front of a penthouse door which didn't belong to me. I couldn't remember if I knocked on the door or not, but all my thoughts – irrational and rational – disappeared the second it opened, and a pair of magnetic blue eyes welcomed me.

"I'm sorry," The words slipped out of my mouth effortlessly, his eyes widening in surprise. "I missed you."

He inhaled, sharply, the hues of his blue eyes darkened as they drank me in. Then his expression softened, and his lips turned into a tender smile, which created butterflies in my stomach and my heart to suddenly feel whole again. With an outstretched hand, he grasped my fingers and tugged me towards him, closing the unnecessary distance between us with the sealing of our lips. My body melted like chocolate in his embrace; the screaming in my head finally stopped and I savored the silence. He was my solace. He was home.

Eventually, Nero rested his forehead against mine, murmuring, breathlessly, "I missed you too."

And with that, I was gone.

CHAPTER 29

before Aria

Nero
13 hours earlier

I Pinched the bridge of my nose, sighing in annoyance, whilst Matteo explained to the Board of Directors the next business plan. Alongside the mafia, I inherited several businesses as a way to cover up any dealings that could be seen as 'illegal' in the eyes of the law. Though, the law itself was often as corrupt as the Underground. It was normal for those parts of the hidden world to have side-businesses because it kept the feds off our tracks. Most often, however, the main people in these businesses were also involved in the Underground. Just like my Board of Directors, I could handpick a few men who knew about the Underground and my true position as the Don. Sometimes, though, it meant that they got a bit arrogant and brave. These meetings were becoming tedious, and they irritated me to no end, but one look from Matteo told me that I was to suck it up. I was too consumed with my thoughts about Aria to even be paying any attention to what was being said. All I could think about was whether Aria was safe, and the fact that she was ignoring my calls and messages didn't help assuage any of my worries. My sigh must have been pretty loud because about thirty pairs of eyes flickered in my direction, a sliver of worry and fear flashing within them, as if they were waiting for me to scream at them. Fortunately for them, I had no energy today.

"Is everything okay?" Director Park asked, the only person who looked bothered by my disruption. The old man had been waiting for the day I screwed up to jump at the opportunity to kick me off the board. Bastard forgot that I own him and lately, he had been getting on my last nerves.

"Yes," I responded, curtly, standing up and straightening my blazer. "Matteo will send you the diagnostics behind this plan. If there are no further questions, this meeting is adjourned."

"President Ru —" I walked off before he could finish his sentence, hearing a stream of complaints as I stormed out of the meeting room. Matteo followed closely behind with an irritated look across his face. I tugged the collar of my shirt, feeling very claustrophobic but getting some relief as soon as the button tore off, and discarded my blazer onto the couch after I arrived in my office. The door slammed behind me and I regretted looking over my shoulder, wincing when I saw the irritation across Matteo's face as he sent me a glare.

"What was that? Nero, you might own this company but those people in that room are the reason it's still running," he exclaimed, before groaning exaggeratively and collapsing onto the sofa. "I don't even know why I bother talking to you. I'm resigning."

I hummed, disapprovingly. "That would be an issue if you do. Would a raise be sufficient enough for you to stay?"

Immediately, Matteo got up from his seat and shot me a dazzling smile. "I live only to serve you."

Laughing, I rolled my eyes at my second's antics and rolled up the sleeves of my shirt, before skimming through the paperwork piled on my desk. Ever since news got out that I was engaged, business proposals had been coming in incessantly, and the media outlets exploded, trending number one everywhere I looked. I couldn't escape the numerous photographs of Aria and me holding hands and smiling at each other on social media and in the press, as if we were happy to be engaged to each other. Besides being constantly hounded by bloodthirsty reporters, people were more than willing to be in partnership with me as my reputation of a 'playboy' began to diminish until it was old news. Amidst of all the paperwork, I saw a magazine that Matteo must have failed to hide tucked underneath. Swallowing drily, my fingers traced over the image of Aria and me from Althaia's gala. Her arm was hooked through mine, a bright smile on her face that was breathlessly exquisite, unaware of me looking down at her with my own tender smile. She was picture perfect, waving at the crowd, but I was too entranced by her to notice the reporter who managed to capture this moment. She looked so radiant, I felt like I was staring at the sun.

"Have you heard from her?" Matteo asked, and I shook my head, unable to tear my eyes away from the deceiving image. "I'm sure she'll call back. She needs space, just like when we were younger."

"I wish she told me what was actually on her mind. I know she's holding stuff back but I don't understand why she isn't telling me the truth – it's unlike her to hold her feelings back," I muttered, dumping the magazine into the bottom drawer of my desk.

"She isn't the same girl anymore. We can't base our assumptions off the person we knew five years ago. It's illogical," he stated with a tight smile, tucking his hands into his pockets. "I looked into Yakira Adachi like you asked, and do you know what is said?"

I arched a brow in question.

"It's whispered amongst the Underground about her methods of torture. How it is so twisted and deranged... How it is so similar to Aria's. They are both extremely feared and, yet, desired by everyone. It seems the pair have built an impenetrable empire."

"Why is that important?" I grunted.

"Aria is not that girl we grew up with. Maybe some parts are, but, for the most, she has grown into an entirely different woman. And, perhaps that's a good thing," he reasoned.

"Doesn't that worry you? That you can no longer recognize her?"

Matteo's lips expanded into a smile that I couldn't quite decipher. "Not at all. In fact, it makes it all the more exciting." There was a long stretch of silence before he spoke again, "You have a lunch meeting. The car will be waiting outside in fifteen minutes."

The meeting at lunch was tiresome, only furthering the headache I had, but I forced a smile on my face as I spent two hours nodding my head to an agreement I had no intention of continuing. My patience finally snapped when the old man – God knows what his name was – mentioned Aria, his lips coiling into a perverted smirk that had my eyes thinning into sharp daggers.

"She is quite the beauty," he began, suggestively. "I wonder where you found her and if I can have one for myself."

I raised a brow. "I'm not sure I understand what you're suggesting, *Frank*."

"It's Francis," he corrected, but I paid little attention to him. The old man scoffed, leaning back in his seat with a mocking grin. "Don't lie to me, Nero. We've been business partners for so long. I've practically watched you grow up. A beautiful lady like Lyra doesn't just turn up out of nowhere. It's alright, you can tell me. I'll keep your secret."

"Are you calling my fiancé a *prostitute*?" I gritted.

Francis laughed. "I mean, that's not the word I'd use. It's beneath me – I prefer escort."

Anger boiled my blood and all I felt was the urge to pummel the man until his bones were broken and his sight was blinded, the ignorance in his voice pissing me off. But I swallowed back the fury and clicked my jaw, counting to ten in my head which helped soothe the need to tear the old man apart. He looked amused, sipping on his wine languidly and I cursed myself for not poisoning that drink.

"I wonder who else is beneath you, *Finn*," I responded, my words laced with venom. His eyes widened, quick to jump in and defend himself when he saw the look of death targeted his way, but I didn't miss a beat, smirking maliciously. "Does your wife know about the many *'escorts'* you have coming in and out your house whilst she's out of the country?"

"Wh-what are you talking about?" the old man sputtered, pathetically.

Crossing my arms over my chest, I drawled out lazily, "You know the *'prostitutes'* you buy. The ones who are working for me."

His eyes widened in pure shock, face whitening when he realized his mistake. "I don't understand."

"You don't need to understand, *Fred*," I replied, coolly, taking out a wad of dollar bills and throwing it onto the table as I stood up. "Consider this bill paid. You can use the extra cash to pay for your little girly friends that I'm sure your wife will look forward to meeting."

"Nero, wait!" he called out as I stormed off, curling my fingers into a tight fist, the need to punch something was overwhelming and I knew if I stayed even for a second later, he would have ended up in hospital on a ventilator. "It's Francis!"

Fucking bastard.

*

6 hours earlier

"*Nero!*" she shrilled, as I strode by, cursing under my breath when I knew she caught sight of me.

Her hand shot out, grasping my arm, and forcing me to look at her. Her makeup was ruined, mascara stains on her cheeks as she sobbed very unattractively, her red hair looking disheveled as if she was just freshly fucked, which I didn't doubt was true. I knew my past would bite me in the back. I cast her a glance, raising my eyebrow as I waited to hear what she wanted to say. I knew the second I stepped into my club it would be a mistake from the glare she sent me. After doing a quick check up on my staff and the club itself, I made a fast getaway except that was pointless, as I failed to notice her before I managed to leave. I gave her a tight smile that she did not find amusing, waiting for my response and I swore at myself for sleeping with her more than once. I was a man of my word and when I told Aria that I wouldn't be with anyone, I had meant it. Not like it mattered because no one could compare to her. I was doomed the second she let me have a taste.

"Is it true?" she hissed, gnashing out her words with venom.

"What?" I asked, obliviously.

"That you're engaged!" she screeched. "Is it true?"

"Ah," was my reply, pursing my lips.

She glowered at me, her green eyes filled with pure anger and hatred. "*Ah? Ah!* What the fuck does that mean?!"

"It means it's true. I am engaged."

"But you were going to marry me," she bawled, her cries causing me to wince and tug her hand off me.

"I never said that," I corrected. "I'm not sure who fed you false information, but we weren't ever getting married, Mia."

Her sobs turned into hiccups as she looked up at me with wide eyes that reminded me of a puppy. "Did our time together not mean anything?"

"Mia, I have no idea what you are talking about," I grunted in irritation, looking over her shoulder where I shot a glare at my security guards, who immediately rushed over when Mia fell into my arms, weeping her eyes out. They yanked her away from me, but her nails dug into my blazer, tearing the fabric when she was finally taken away.

Aw, not the suit.

"Nero! No! What does that bitch have that I don't?" she roared in anger. "She's a *whore*! She'll never be able to satisfy you like I do! NERO!"

I groaned, running my hands over my face, before turning to Matteo, who was watching the entire predicament from a distance, an amused smirk on his face. "You could've at least helped."

He shrugged. "How would that be any fun?"

I scowled, taking off my blazer and threw it at Matteo. "I don't want her working at this club anymore, send her someplace else. Preferably far away because I don't need this situation to happen again."

"You mean, you don't want Aria to find out about this situation," A deadly glare from me confirmed his suspicion, a burst of laughter leaving his lips as he held his hands up in surrender. "Got it, Boss."

*

30 minutes earlier

I let out a deep and prolonged sigh as I sunk into the comfort of my couch with a glass of vodka in my hand and the picturesque scene of the New York skyline as a view. The last two days had been extremely tiring as I had to catch up on everything I had missed whilst being in Greece. I knew that there would be more to do than usual after the public found out about my engagement – an engagement with a woman they had never seen me with before, nevertheless. When Matteo called me on the night of Althaia's party, he informed me about how the media were creating all these rumors and trying to dig into Aria's – or, Lyra's, in their case – history. I immediately knew that I had to return to New York to sort this mess out. Unfortunately, that meant I was not able to go to Canada with Aria and Kira, but I knew I had to create a less hectic environment for Aria when she was to return. Not only did I have to deal with the media by holding a press conference the morning after I arrived in New York, but I also had to tell my parents about my unforeseen engagement.

Although I didn't explain to them the truth behind my engagement, they couldn't care less about why I was engaged and were too invested in the fact that I was marrying Aria. Which then meant I had to speak to Aria's parents. I have never feared Antonio Moretti, but the way he looked at me when I told him and Xena of my engagement with Aria had me holding my breath, fearing that if I even breathed, he would kill me. Unlike my parents, Xenia and Antonio listened to the reason behind our engagement, and despite not liking the situation we were in, they were very supportive – they, being Xena. Antonio pulled me to the side whilst his wife was in the kitchen, preparing lunch, and warned me not to hurt Aria or he would kill me in ways I had not imagined before. Needless to say, I had no intention of hurting Aria again. Finally, all that was left to sort out were my business partnerships, many of whom responded with a mixture of feelings. Some were supportive, viewing my engagement as a way to portray a brighter image of my company, but others viewed this as a negative thing, suggesting that it would make me less appealing and therefore, inadvertently affecting our stocks. Nevertheless, I managed to silence everyone's opinions. For now.

As soon as I got home, I took a quick shower, hoping it would ease my muscle pains, exhaling heavily when I relished in the hot water while lathering my body. Suddenly, my mind was taken to Aria and my entire body strained as I imagined her red lips coiling into that seductive smirk I loved so much, begging me to taste her, taint her, make her mine. I grunted, pressing my head against the tiles of the bathroom and switched the water to cold. When I eventually got out of the shower, I slipped into my jogging bottoms and trekked downstairs, where I attempted to make something edible, but the pounding headache wouldn't go, so I opted for some aspirin and alcohol instead. The headache faded away until it was a dreary ache in the back of my skull, which was bearable. I cherished the silence, closing my eyes and rested my head against the sofa. But my misery was not over yet as memories of the other night with Aria interrupted the peace. The sadness was overwhelming, and my heart ached a pain I had not felt before. The urge to travel to Canada just to see her was overpowering my rational thoughts. I missed her. Her smile. Her laugh. Her warmth.

Her.

I had spent five years trying to move on past her and even then, I failed. I failed every time. Wherever I went, whoever I was with, she was always there, reminding me how much I missed her. She was my best friend. The only person who knew me better than I knew myself. That's how I knew I wanted to spend the rest of my life with her.

She looked beautiful in the gown she wore. A shimmery red that hugged her figure for the world to see how perfectly created she was. Her dark hair was elegantly tousled back in curls, a diamond pin attached on the side of her head, matching the jewelry she wore. She wasn't smiling when people greeted her; the smile she did give them lacked any sort of emotion or authenticity. As if she could feel my gaze on her, she looked up, her beautiful hazel eyes scouring the room until they settled on me.

Then, slowly, she smiled. My breath was caught in my throat, and it wasn't until Matteo poked me, did I finally snap out of my daze. Aria looked amused, biting her lip to fight back a smile, but the crease of her eyes told me she was silently laughing. I may have acted a fool but for her, I didn't care. We moved towards each other like magnets and when I finally stood in front of her, I was incapable of forming any clear thoughts. She was beautiful. I had never seen anyone like her.

She was perfect.

"You look handsome," she murmured. "But your tie isn't done properly."

I didn't reply as she straightened my tie out, my eyes watching her movements as if I was hypnotized. I noticed her cheeks start to darken when she caught my stare, but she played her embarrassment off with a cheeky smile as her hands trailed down my chest.

"Aren't you just a heartthrob? All the girls are going to have a hard time keeping their hands off you."

"I don't want all the girls," I muttered, her eyes widening, stunned. "I only want you."

I heard her breath hitch, and I knew then I never wanted to spend a second away from her. I knew she was mine for life. My hand reached out and cupped the side of her face, doe eyes watched me so carefully as if I would suddenly disappear. But I had no intention of going anywhere. I wanted to savor every touch of her, relishing in the rose scent that emitted off her. She held her breath as I leaned closer until our lips were almost touching.

"Happy birthday, Nero."

My thoughts were cut short when I heard a knock on the door, causing to me to frown as I noticed how late it had gotten. With an exasperated exhale, I forced myself up from the comfort of my sofa and strode towards the door, opening my mouth to yell at whoever had interrupted my serenity. But the words failed to come out when I was welcomed by a pair of hypnotic hazel eyes.

"I'm sorry," she blurted, before I managed to say anything. My eyes widened, stunned by her words. "I missed you."

Taken aback, I inhaled sharply, trying to gather my thoughts. But all I could think about was the woman standing in front of me. My mind shifted to wicked places when I saw how stunning she was in just a simple jumper and jeans. My eyes moved to her lips that were pouty and filled with color, pleading me to kiss them until they were swollen from my attack. Finally, I met her eyes and my heart melted at how docile they looked, as if she was afraid I would turn her away. How could I ever refuse my Queen? I smiled gently, grasping her hand, and tugging her towards me where I captured her mouth with mine. Her body melted in my arms, her hand resting against my bare chest, fitting perfectly in my hold. She tasted sweet, her lips were so soft they felt like the skin of a newborn baby, as I angled my head, plunging my tongue into her mouth in desperation to taste more of her ecstasy. She moaned, pressing herself closer to me until I could feel every curve of her body. At some point, I managed to tear myself away from her despite not wanting to, but the lack of oxygen was getting to the both of us.

"I missed you too," I muttered, resting my forehead against hers. She smiled dreamily at me, our breathing heavy as we became lost in one another's gaze. "When did you get back?"

"Just now," she whispered, licking her lips which immediately had me wanting to taste them again. She was addictive, I couldn't get enough of her. She was going to ruin me, but I would gladly let her do so. She was my beginning and end. She was my all and holding her in my arms only solidified the fact that I had no intention of letting her go again.

"Aren't you tired?" I asked, trying to distract myself away from the fact that she was pressed right up against me.

Shaking her head softly, Aria leaned up and said, "I wanted to see you," before kissing me again.

I couldn't hold back my lust for her and swooped her into my arms, causing her to squeal and laugh as I slammed the door shut. I was a man on a mission, and I had full intentions of making sure she didn't get any sleep tonight. As soon as I got to my bedroom, I dropped her onto the bed, her smile disappearing and the lust causing her eyes to darken as I towered over her.

"How much did you miss me, Aria?" I purred, rolling my hips against hers, her head falling back as she released a breathy moan that I wanted to hear over and over, and over again. "Answer me."

"So much," she panted, her dark eyes finding mine, begging me to take her. "I missed you so much."

My lips curled into a seductive smile as my fingers grasped the waistband of her jeans, tingling to tear them off her. "Let me show you how much I missed you."

Biting her lip, she failed to fight off her smile. "I'm yours."

Once again, she took me by surprise and my eyes broadened, my breath hitching. *This woman was going to be the death of me.* My heart stammered as I kissed her again. This time slowly, purposefully, gently. I couldn't pinpoint the feeling blossoming deep within me, but I welcomed it with open arms, completely captivated by Aria.

"Say that again," I ordered, hungrily, because I needed to hear those words again – because they brought me back to life.

I felt the smile on her lips as she complied with my order, uttering, "I'm yours."

"Yes, you are," I avowed, possessively, proceeding to show her, for the rest of the night, to whom she belonged.

She was mine; body and soul. And I was hers. Every inch of me was hers. God, if she wanted me to jump, I would jump because I needed nothing more than her. I didn't give her a moment to breathe or a second to act, as I removed every item of clothing that separated us from each other. It was too much to even bear and the thought of having her close to me set my body alight. Everywhere she touched made me tingle and I found succor in her adoration. She traced every scar and tattoo, she kissed every muscle and wound, she loved every part of me and, *fuck*, I would be a liar if I pretended that I didn't want to get on my knees for her. We were like animals, hungry for each other, but something was different tonight. Something shifted. So carnal. So powerful. And when we finally became one, our heartbeats synchronized, and our souls danced to the symphony of our love. Then, she reached out and stroked her finger across my lips as I stared down at her, watching her chest rise and fall in slow succession.

"I'm not perfect," she whispered. "But I want to be your idea of perfect."

My gaze softened. "You've always been perfect."

She rolled her eyes, but her lips tugged, and I knew she was fighting back a grin. However, I wanted to see that smile. I wanted to always see that smile. She was the most beautiful when she smiled. So, I brought my body into the contours of her small frame, feeling her nails scratch my back, as she arched her body then I kissed her so deeply that it made her toes curl in pleasure. Afterwards, she laid in my arms and the magic formed by our souls blanketed us with bliss. Sated, she smiled at me, drawing circles on my chest just where my heart thumped, whilst I wrapped an arm around her waist, sparks in my fingertips every time they kissed her skin.

"I want you to be happy because you deserve it," I murmured, and she looked at me in surprise. "I want you to be happy because it makes me happy, to see you the way you were always meant to be."

Before she could reply, I took her hand away from my chest and moved it to my neck. Her eyes flickered to the ink that I had done the morning before the gala. Knitting her brows, she went to ask a question before stopping herself short. I watched as realization finally dawned on her. Her gaze was wild as it shot back to me then it thronged with tears, her cheeks flushed.

"*Nero*," was all she said. It was as breathless as she made me feel.

I smiled at my goddess, loving the feeling of her finger outlining the tattoo of a cloud with musical notes dangling down from it like a crib mobile. I knew what I wanted the moment I had seen the ring on her finger, because I knew she belonged to me forever.

"You're my aria," I kissed her quivering lips, brushing away the loose tears. "You are *mine*, Aria."

CHAPTER 30

seeking secrets

For the first time in forever, I woke up and I smiled. Stretching my body, my muscles ached but I didn't mind it one bit. I sighed, softly, blinking as the sunlight shone through the window and shed light on the ruffled sheets which barely covered me, and illuminating the pillows scattered across the bedroom carpet. An amused grin continued to tug the corner of my lips as I sat up, clutching the white blanket against my naked body, blushing when I remembered what happened last night. I must admit, I was surprised, myself, by my actions of turning up at Nero's door at one in the morning. I was even more surprised when he didn't turn me away but welcomed me with the softest kiss that caused my heart to stammer until it found the beat of his. I always knew Nero had a tender side to him but last night, despite his moments of being feral, was a side I had never imagined I would see. He was so gentle, as if he were worshipping me, wanting to remember every inch and taste of my body. He never hurried me, instead taking his time to give me the most intense pleasure I had ever known. I had been with Nero multiple times, but I could say for sure, that last night was probably the best night of my life. I pursed my lips, trying to fight the ridiculous grin that was threatening to escape, and shook myself out of the spell I was under. Finally, noticing that Nero was not sleeping beside me, I frowned and got out of the bed, covering myself with the blanket as I went to search for him. What I didn't expect to see was him in the kitchen, a frustrated pouty look across his face as he attempted to make a smoothie whilst shirtless. He didn't hear me as I tiptoed, the wooden flooring causing me to shiver from the cold sensation and leaned against the archway. His blue eyes narrowed into a glare as if the machine would suddenly start working after being intensely stared at by the mafia boss.

"So, this is where you disappeared to?" I said, grinning as his eyes quickly flickered in my direction.

His cheeks darkened, as he scratched the back of his neck. "I thought you'd still be sleeping."

Clutching the blanket tighter around my body when his eyes languidly scanned me up and down, I shrugged. "I would've if you were still there, but the bed was cold and empty. I never thought you'd be the type of guy to leave a girl alone in the morning."

"Oh, trust me, I'm not," he murmured, with dark eyes that had my throat contract. "But I imagined you'd be hungry after the long and tiring night we've had."

The smirk on his face annoyed me, my eyes rolling at how proud and arrogant he sounded, but I couldn't help but press my legs together when I remembered the rush of pleasure that I relished in last night, in a way that took my breath away. Nero seemed to know exactly how I was feeling, shoving the blender to the side and stalking over to where I was, his arms entrapping me against the chilly wall; a shudder ran down my spine but I couldn't differentiate whether it was due to the coldness of the room or his warm breath fanning against my neck, as he lightly pressed his lips against my shoulder.

"Do you want a reminder?" he whispered; the air caught in my throat – I forgot how to breathe.

Shaking my head, I managed to say, meekly, "I'm good."

He chuckled and gave me one last delicate kiss on the crook of my neck before pulling away, amusement dancing in his oceanic eyes that I could easily get lost in. Before he could say anything, my stomach rumbled and ruined the moment, causing my cheeks to darken in embarrassment.

Nero grinned. "Let's feed that stomach of yours."

I didn't protest when I saw the stacks of pancakes laid beside a range of berries and syrups in the living room. My mouth watered as I sat on the sofa, watching Nero drizzle maple syrup onto the homemade pancakes, my stomach crying to be fed. I greedily ate the food, savoring the sweet honey taste and the softness of the pancakes which made me question whether they were made of air.

"God, these are amazing," I moaned. "You made this?"

"Of course," he stated, looking slightly offended that I would think otherwise.

"Aren't you going to eat?" My words muffled, as I took another bite of my third pancake. He had seen me naked, at my best and worst, so I was now indifferent to him seeing how I was eating right now – the food was too good to be bothered by his reaction. Nero laughed, shaking his head as he sipped on his coffee.

"Seeing you eat makes me full," he wiped the syrup on my mouth and licked it off his fingers, my heart stopping momentarily as I became so entranced by that single action. "Plus, you taste much better."

"Stop it. I'm trying to eat," I grumbled, ducking my head to hide how red and flustered I was getting.

His laugh was hoarse and deep. "I'm curious about something."

"What?"

"Where did you hide Enzo's little sister?" he asked, my eyes widening. "The week is over and as part of our deal, I'll search no further. Enzo wasn't exactly happy with my decision, but he didn't have a choice especially after that contract he signed."

I shoved another bite into my mouth. "At my mother's house."

Nero blinked in shock. "You're joking? You're telling me when I went to visit your parents, she was there?"

This time, I stared at him in surprise. "Wait, you visited my parents?"

He dismissed the question with a single, "Your father would've killed me horribly if I didn't explain to him why we were getting married. Anyway, back to Enzo's sister — Violetta, wasn't it?"

A ghost of a smile played on my lips at the mention of my father, but I didn't push any further about what was discussed, answering Nero's question, "She returned to the Manor yesterday morning, really early so no one would have seen her. Xander is pretty good at sneaking people out, so you must have missed her."

Nero's jaw slacked. "You're telling me that I could have I found her if I visited your parents earlier?"

Giggling, I bobbed my head as I took another pancake. *Goddamn it, these were too good – now, I definitely couldn't let him go.* Nero sulked, sinking into the sofa, displeasure flickering in his eyes which told me that he hated losing. A long moment went by where neither of us spoke, enjoying the comfortable silence. The air was still thick with uncertainty, and I knew Nero had questions he wanted to ask but he held them back, drinking his coffee whilst his azure eyes stared out of the floor-length windows that gave a panoramic view of the city skyline. When I felt full, I curled back into the sofa, bringing the blanket closer around my naked body and sighed softly in blissful peace.

"I'm guessing you have questions," I broke the silence first, and he glanced over. "I won't run away."

"It's not you if you don't," he joked, trying to ease the seriousness between us – the 'what now?'

"I'm sorry for how I behaved. You were right – I can't go about playing God and getting rid of every person that has done something bad. Not if I don't know the full story behind their intentions. Althaia was only looking out for herself; she was an innocent victim in Barak's twisted hands and if someone needed to die, it was Barak," I said with earnest. "I can't take back what I did, but I can promise to never act rashly again."

Nero placed his mug onto the table, turning his full attention to me. "I'm sorry too. You're right. There were these double standards and I failed to see how hypocritical I was being. I also kept treating you like a doll when you had proven to me multiple times how capable you were at looking after yourself. But I still treated you like an object that I needed to protect. I can't promise to never feel the need to protect you, but I can promise to trust you more."

My shoulders eased as I gave him a gentle smile. "I know you want to protect me; you've been doing that since we were young but I'm glad you can see that I don't need to be looked after all the time. I've changed, Nero."

"So have I. I think we both just failed to see how we aren't the same people we were five years ago," Nero sighed, thoughtfully. "I can't believe it's taken us this long to see that."

"Well, we are pretty dense when it comes to us," I laughed.

He stared at me with a smile that had me stop grinning. I couldn't pinpoint how exactly he was looking at me, but it made me feel like the luckiest woman on this planet. He tucked a strand of hair behind my ear, indifferent to how disheveled I must have looked but continued to stare at me as if I was the most beautiful person he had ever seen. My eyes flickered to the tattoo on his neck – the aria that he imprinted forevermore onto his skin. God, he was just asking me to fall in love with him again.

"I may have changed, but my feelings for you remain the same, Aria," he murmured, surprising me. "They have never changed. Not when you left. Not when you came back. And not now."

"*Nero*," His name left my lips very shakily, as I struggled to breathe.

"We were fools to think we could sleep with each other and ignore those feelings. But I don't want to run away anymore, Aria. I was stupid to not run to you five years ago, but I won't make the same mistake now," he declared, solemnly. "You are special to me. You are the only one I wouldn't mind losing sleep for, the only one who I could never get tired of talking to, and the only one who crosses my mind constantly throughout the day. You are the only one who can make me smile without trying."

My lips quivered and I felt like a dam waiting to explode. Nero, having sensed this, smiled so gently that I couldn't image him being the Don of the Italians, I couldn't see him as this bloodthirsty boss who would kill anyone in his way, I couldn't see him as the monster I wanted to see. He just looked at me as if he couldn't breathe without me.

"I can't explain with just words how much you mean to me, but you're the only one I'm afraid of losing and the only one I want to keep in my life."

His thumb brushed my trembling lips before wiping away the traitorous tears that splashed onto my cheeks. It was like I could no longer mask my emotions and I didn't want to. I sat there and honestly, I wanted to tell him that I felt the same way, but words failed me.

Nero said, his voice as soft as his caresses down my arm, "You're my best friend, always have been, always will be. But I don't think I can just be your best friend anymore."

His hand grasped the blanket, tugging it softly that I let it go and allowed it to pool around my feet. Blue eyes that reminded me of aquamarines darkened lustfully, as he closed the distance between us, putting an end to the painful carnal tension we were both overlooking. I wanted to hate him, I wish I could hate him but instead, I hated myself because I was weak against his charms. I needed to know the truth, I needed him to tell me what I heard five years ago wasn't true, that he wasn't going to betray me, that he did love me. However, I couldn't form the words I wanted to say, the words I *needed* to say. So, as he pulled me onto his lap, I spoke with my actions instead. Like a wildfire, every touch set me alight, burning with desire and need. I cradled his face in my hands, angling my lips as we kissed, deeply. His hands traced the curve of my back until they rested on my hips, moving me above him in a hungry fashion that caused me to lose my breath. With every touch, I became submissive to his powerful aura and could feel that hate which nestled deep within me disappear until I forgot why I was angry in the first place.

"You're mine, Ariadne," he promised, in a wild tone that I could not disagree with. "*Sempre.*"

*

"Did you speak to him?" Kira asked, as she strolled into my office, not bothering to knock.

"Sorry?" I responded, my brows pinching together.

"You never returned to your penthouse last night so I'm assuming you were with him. Therefore, did you finally speak to him?" When I didn't reply, she got the answer she wanted and sighed, shaking her head in disappointment. "How long are you going to live like this, Aria? What are you afraid to hear?"

"I'm not afraid of anything," I protested, adamantly.

"You are if you still haven't spoken to him. Are you planning on being with him and not knowing the truth? *His truth?*"

I looked away from her piercing blue eyes that said everything I did not want to hear. Running my fingers through my hair, I blew out a breath of air. "What if what I heard was the truth? How could I ever forgive him?"

"Aria," Kira's voice held such gravity that I couldn't help but look at her. With complete earnestness, she said, "You love him, and I know you won't admit it now but that's the truth. And he loves you, any fool can see that. But you will ruin your second chance of happiness with him unless you finally open up to him. Nero doesn't look like the type of person to betray you, Aria. Ever. He's too head over heels for you."

"That's now. Back then, anyone would have died for my position. Especially him – my right-hand man," I reminded, gravely. "Being the

Don meant I couldn't trust anyone, and it killed me when I found out I couldn't trust him; he was my best friend. My better half. I felt like I was dying when I had to walk away from him, but I also couldn't stay 'cause I'd be dying and he'd see right through my agony. I didn't know what was worse."

"Love is painful, hard and a fucking mess but, if you want to be with him, maybe you need to open up to the idea that what you thought you heard, or saw, wasn't the full truth. I've only known him for a brief time, but even during those brief encounters with him, I never saw him as someone who'd betray the person he loves."

"And if he is?" I whispered those sinful words which haunted me at night.

"*Was*. If he was. You just need to ask yourself if he's the same person he was when you left," Kira advised softly, understanding the pain I had gone through. Before she left, she looked over her shoulder with those icy eyes that were filled with concern for me, fear for me, heartbreak for me. "It's strange, isn't it?"

"What is?"

"How you can be desperately in love with someone even when you haven't spoken to or seen them for years. Frankly, it's incredible how despite the distance between two people, you'll never stop loving them," my heart ached at her words and Kira glanced at the ring on my finger – the one I still hadn't taken off. "That's just how love works, I suppose. You either love them forever or you never loved them to begin with. Love doesn't leave just because the person does."

My voice sounded so feeble, as I whispered, "How can you be so sure?"

Her eyes shifted and held me hostage. They were the type of blue Nero's could never be, because in her gaze were not a thousand words or the burst of adoration that he welcomed me with. In her gaze, was the truth, the shadows of the past and the hopes of the future. In her gaze was a hotel of life.

"Because I've never seen a man look at me the way Nero's looked at you," she answered. "Talk to him or you'll never be able to move on. You teach us how to battle our demons, so why don't you?"

She left me with my confused thoughts and feelings that I struggled to work out. I held my face in my hands, trying to decide what to do, when from my peripheral view I saw a magazine that Kira had failed to get rid of hidden under my stack of paperwork. Gingerly, taking it out, I could hear my heart pound like an untamed animal, when I saw the picture of Nero and I plastered on the front cover.

Except, I had not seen this particular picture.

I was smiling stiffly out to the crowd, waving, but one could mistake it as a genuine smile. Whilst Nero was staring down at me with the same look in his eyes that I noticed this morning. I didn't think he realized a reporter was taking the picture as he smiled, subtly, melting my heart with how pure and loving it looked. *'Match made in heaven'* – the title said in bold, black words. I skimmed over the article, unable to stop myself reading as the reporter went on to talk about how perfectly we were made for each other. He spoke about how we were the best-dressed couple, admiring how in sync we were, whether it was shown in our actions or how we were dressed. Was I fooling myself by believing I could be happy with Nero, if I never chose to confront him about what I saw?

"You're not even denying it, Nero," There was a deep chuckle which soon followed. "You know what I am saying is true. Pretend if you must, but you know that Aria could never lead... She's a woman; men will never bow down to the weaker gender."

My phone rang, disrupting my thoughts, and I tore my eyes away from the article, picking it up when I saw Calix's name blinking on the screen. "Yes?"

"We got into the Inner Circle's safe house. Alpha team is ready, waiting for your command," he explained, quickly, briefing me on what I had missed during the last few days. "After tracking Enzo's transactions, we noticed that they consistently go to a bank, specifically in Greece."

"Barak," I murmured, leaning back in my seat.

"I believe so. Aria, I was thinking, isn't it strange how Enzo hasn't ended his partnership with Nero. We thought that Barak would stop Enzo or maybe one of the other Inner Circle members if Barak failed to do so."

"People are greedy. Perhaps. Barak did try but Enzo's agreement with Nero was that he had to find his younger sister. Enzo didn't end the partnership as he wanted to see if Nero was capable of finding Violetta."

"Are you saying that Enzo will end the partnership soon?"

"Nero isn't looking for Violetta anymore, which means Enzo no longer needs him," I stated, trying to wrap my brain around everything happening. "Keep an eye on Enzo's transactions, money and communications. I want to know where he is going, what he is doing, and who he is with every single second of the day."

"And Barak?"

"I have my suspicions about him. For now, let's prepare the Alpha team for infiltration of the safe house. I need to speak with Konstantin and Salome," I ordered, knowing that something was missing, but I was unsure what it was. Something just did not add up.

"And Nero?" Calix asked.

"What about him?" I frowned, narrowing my eyes.

Calix sighed, profoundly, and I could almost see him shaking his head, dismissing it. "Nothing. I'll connect you to Salome in ten minutes."

He hung up before I could say anything else, but I was too baffled and blankly looked at my phone, trying to figure out what had just happened. There was an uneasy feeling in my stomach that I knew I should not have ignored, but I did because I knew dwelling on it would cause problems I did not have time to deal with right now. True to his word, Calix managed to connect me to Salome ten minutes later, her cheery voice greeting me on the phone, free of the fear that I noticed when I first spoke to her.

"Aria," Salome spoke, warmly, her voice sounded like honey, thick in a Columbian accent. "How have you been?"

"Busy and incredibly stressed," I laughed, causing her to giggle on the phone. "How are you and Matias? I hope you relocated safely."

"We did, thanks to you. Matias loves it here. It's much warmer than Canada. It reminds me of home," she replied, wistfully. "Why did you choose Singapore?"

"It's the safest place on Earth. The people are incredibly friendly, and I have a few connections down there who will help keep you protected, whilst also allowing you to live the normal life you were robbed of. I hope your house is also to your liking."

I could almost hear the grin in her voice, as she said, "Yes. Very much. Though, it's more like a mansion than a house."

"I think the term is a condo," I smiled.

"I can't thank you enough. So, why did you call?" she asked, my smile broadening when I heard Matias in the background, laughing.

"It's about Barak. I need to know everything you can remember whilst being with Barak. Something suspicious is going on, and I need to confirm my doubts. Have you ever met any of Barak's colleagues or friends?"

"Barak never brought people over – he didn't like the idea of other men seeing me, and Althaia didn't want anyone finding out about my existence," Althaia's name left a bitter taste on my tongue, but I ignored it, trying to focus on what Salome was saying. "There were these occasions where Barak would leave every month to travel to London. He was always accompanied by someone else, but I never met them."

I got up from my seat, wandering around my office, when I began to feel my legs turn numb, pins and needles prickling my feet. Something was off and the pieces that had begun to join together started to fall apart. I couldn't pinpoint exactly what I was looking for, or what it was, but the Serpents would never make finding the Inner Circle members this easy. Furthermore, why was Enzo only sending money to Greece and no other locations? Could this mean that Barak was the main leader of the Serpents? Viktor was no help, his lips were tightly sealed, and despite the tremendous, tormenting pain we put him through, he never spoke any more than what we already knew. If I was not so annoyed by his lack of help, I would be impressed by his loyalty. Nevertheless, it seemed that the Serpents were not too concerned about saving Viktor, therefore, did this mean he was not as important as I thought he was?

As if she could see my inner turmoil, Salome murmured, hesitantly, "There was one thing which might be of help."

"What is it?" I pressed on, pressing the phone against my ear in fear that I would miss a vital piece of information.

"I once attended this exclusive dinner by someone called Enzo."

"Enzo Rossi," I concluded. "What about him?"

"During the dinner, only two other men were there. Enzo was one of them. I heard that someone else was meant to attend but he wasn't able to. Enzo and the other man – I can't remember his name – were arguing about shipments, and Barak laughed, assuring them that as the Inner Circle, they were practically untouchable. The only females that attended were some strippers, so I never understood why Barak took me. Perhaps he wanted to show me off."

"Four men?" I murmured to myself, collapsing onto the couch with a furrow between my brows. "If you're right, that means the Inner Circle only consists of four men and not seven, as many believe."

"But why would they want people to believe that there was more than four of them?"

"My thoughts exactly," I responded, quietly. There was a long moment of silence that went by as I tried to wrap my mind around this new information, before I said my thanks and goodbyes to Salome. As soon as I hung up, I rushed down to find Kira, but it was no surprise when I saw her with Konstantin, watching him in the shadows of his cell. He knew she was there even if he could not see her, but his head hung down, pitifully, and neither of them spoke. Konstantin's dark eyes looked up when he heard the steel door open, widening when he caught a glimpse of me before a sluggish smirk twisted his lips.

"Another round of torture already? My daughter already had her fun," he joked, his head jerking towards where she was hidden. I did not need to look in Kira's direction to know that she revealed herself from the shadows; her polar eyes narrowed into daggers filled with intense hatred mixed with sorrow. "How can I be of assistance, Miss Aria?"

Crossing my arms over my chest, I settled into the wooden chair opposite Konstantin, my eyes scanning his shackles, before descending upon him. He was kneeling on the floor, arms outstretched and chained to the side, feet handcuffed, bruised, and decorated in grime and blood. One eye was black and blue, barely able to open whilst the other was untouched, scrutinizing me with caution. I crossed one leg over the other, mimicking the smirk on his face that had his eyes narrowing.

"Recent sources have told me that the Inner Circle consists of four leaders rather than seven. Is this true?" I ordered, not beating around the bush.

He drawled, "I don't know. Is it?"

My eyes never tore away from him but, as if she read my mind, Kira dislocated his shoulder, swiftly, before he could even blink. He shrieked in agony, tears beginning to form before laughing manically.

"The pain is only temporary. I'm becoming numb to your advances," he cackled, crazily, despite the blood pouring out of a fresh wound.

"I have my ways to make sure that doesn't happen," I replied, coldly, moving away as he reached out to grab me but failing miserably, crying in pain, pathetically.

"You are already using my daughter against me. What else could hurt me?" he snarled, the illusion of being fearless slowly slipping away and revealing his innermost thoughts. I raised a brow, amused, when Kira broke his knee, her boots crushing the bone by keeping the pressure until it was excruciating, and all he could was plead for her to stop. Konstantin wept, trying to curl into a ball but his chained arms prevented him from doing so.

"Don't call me your daughter. *Ever.* You are nothing to me," she hissed, venomously. I gave her a stern look when I noticed a familiar murderous glint in her eyes – a look which told me that she was at her breaking point. Any longer, and she would have killed him. She looked like she wanted to argue, but instead she stepped away from her stepfather, clenching and then unclenching her fists as her jaw clamped, tightly, biting back her words.

"Just answer the question and we can finally end this transaction," I promised, sweetly, but my intentions were anything but.

"A transaction means both parties are benefitted. I'm failing to see what benefits I get out of this," he spat, resentfully.

I beamed, maliciously. "Aren't you smart? For one, you get to see your daughter, although I don't think that's worked in your favor. Was this the type of father-daughter reunion you were hoping for, or would you have preferred to see her on her knees?"

He growled at me, blood splattering across the floor. "*Fuck you.*"

I kissed my teeth. "Always so predictable."

"There's a special place in Hell for people like you," Konstantin snarled, the chains rattling as he lurched forward.

"Yes, there is, and I'm the fucking Queen of it," I laughed, before peering down at him as if he was dirt on my expensive Louboutin's. "Are you going to answer the question? You're wasting my time and I no longer have any patience."

Konstantin was weighing his options; I could see it in his eyes. He and I both knew that he could prolong this, but it would just result in intense pain. Fortunately for me, he was a coward and wanted this to be over. He hung his head in shame, my eyes flickering over victoriously to Kira who wore no sort of expression, blue eyes watching the man who practically raised her.

"I may have heard that there were four men that showed up during an auction who were claiming to be the leaders of the Serpents," he murmured, reluctantly. "I believe they hold the illusion that there is more of them to throw people off."

I did not give him a response, nodding my head, as he confirmed what Salome had told me. Knowing that there was no longer any use talking to him, Kira stormed out of the room without sparing another glance in his direction. Konstantin slowly looked in the direction she had left and sighed solemnly, something unrecognizable glistening in his eyes, which had me taken back.

"She won't ever forgive me," he stated, before peeking at me with those swollen eyes that haunted Kira's thoughts. "Will she?"

"You damaged her life by leaving scars that she could never forget. Tell me, would you forgive someone who did that to you?" I responded, steadily.

I knew what he was feeling. I could see it in his eyes. In the way his body held itself. In the way he looked at her even when she had pummeled all her resentment into him. *Guilt.* Only, guilt could not make up for the time she had spent trying to save herself from men who used her body like a sheet of paper. Guilt would not stop her from reliving her nightmares in her sleep. Guilt could not take away the torture she suffered. And no amount of pain inflicted on him would ever be enough for her.

"How long do I have left until you finally kill me?" he then asked, emotionlessly.

"Anytime soon," I answered, honestly, seeing no point of hiding this fact from him, but I carefully left out the fact that I was waiting for Kira.

Konstantin bobbed his head, swallowing, inaudibly. "Do I have enough time to finally get her to forgive me?"

I studied him for the longest moment, before turning away, callously. "You've gone far past the point of asking for forgiveness."

CHAPTER 31

fight or flight

Who are you?

That was a question everyone spent most of their lives chasing an answer for. Hell, I had spent too many sleepless nights wondering who the fuck I was. After I had left New York, the first place I flew to was London, where I met up with Kira again and we began hatching our plan to destroy the Serpents. I was hesitant about leaving Kira in London, but she was adamant that she would be alright and, although she didn't necessarily understand why I had chosen to leave New York, she never asked any questions. Kira was quiet and kept to herself. She spoke only when spoken to, and there were days when I would find her standing by the window in the apartment, watching the world go by. Her eyes were blank, and her lips failed to mimic the smile I greeted her with. I never touched her, I never disturbed her personal space; I worked from afar and watched her silently every now and then, wondering if she would ever recover. She would always wear a jumper, even when the winter snow began to melt, and the blossoming flowers grew from their buds. I knew they were to cover the scars on her arms. She thought I didn't hear her when she spent all night crying but what she didn't know was that I cried alongside her. I cried for her pain and her loss, but I also cried for my pain and my loss. It wasn't until one day, when the new year came about and the wintry breeze in London finally warmed up, that she had walked up to me and surprised me by wrapping her arms around me.

"Don't cry. For me or for yourself," Kira whispered, sadly, *my eyes wide and my body stiff in shock, afraid that if I moved, she would let go. "The pain will lessen until one day it's just a sharp sting."*

I vowed to never cry again but that vow was broken when Nero whispered his truth to me, and I would break it again when I caught sight of her outside on the porch, a blanket shielding her from the bitter wind. I felt myself shed a single tear. The backyard of the Manor was incredibly big, almost looking like a golf field, with flowers planted by the younger girls and a pool and bar built the older men. The moon was bright, our only source of light in the pitch-black darkness which shrouded us. Her pale hair gently swayed as the wind swept by, unflinching at the cold which bit against our skin. I made no sound, so she did not know I was there, but she stared ahead, blankly, and said nothing. For the longest while, we basked in each other's grief and silence. The biggest lesson I had learnt during the last five years was that everyone's pain was the same. It did not matter what history you had, the pain within you remained the same. Some suffered far worse than others, some suffered far greater than others. People lost their loves ones; people lost their love for themselves. Every time they stared in the mirror, all that greeted them was a vacant look – eyes void of emotions and lips failing to smile. The pain was immeasurable. When would we finally be free of that pain and hatred we felt towards ourselves? When could we finally forgive ourselves? When would the guilt finally end? Everything was so wrong with humanity. How do we find the happiness we need to get rid of the pain within us?

"I'm sorry," she spoke, solemnly. "I hate him with every fiber of my being, but why can't I bring myself to look him in the eye and tell him that?"

I smiled, woefully, as I settled beside her, training my eyes on the empty backyard. "Because no amount of hatred can reverse the fact that at some point during your life, you loved him. He raised you and, perhaps in a better world, he would have loved you properly."

"How do you know?"

"I don't," I replied, earnestly, squinting as she looked in my direction with watery blue eyes. "But, Kira, look at yourself. Look at the person you have become – how strong and brave you are. Who wouldn't love you?" I took her shaky hands into mine, wondering whether it was due to the cold or because she was holding back her sorrow. "I am so sorry you had to experience all that pain in your life. I wish I saved you earlier because I know those demons haven't left you. But I promise you, you're going to be alright. That pain within you will lessen until it's just a sharp sting."

She pressed her wobbly lips together, her tears falling shamelessly on her porcelain cheeks that I was afraid would crack from the frosty air. "I just wished I was enough."

"You are more than enough. To me, to everyone in the Manor and to your mother," I murmured, wiping her tears away. "She's proud of you, Yakira."

There was so much she wanted to say but she didn't, as she fell into my embrace, crying her sorrow away until she felt numb. Her body trembled in my arms as I forced myself not to cry, wanting to be strong for her.

"It's going to be okay," My voice was a huge contrast to the cold, caressing her hair. "I promise."

*

The sun slipped through the cracks of my curtains, waking me up with its warm heat and blinding light. I begrudgingly got out of bed, rubbing my eyes, when I noticed I had overslept. Scattered across the bed was the paperwork I had been meaning to catch up on, and numerous different files with information about the Serpents covering the last few years. I kept feeling as if I wasn't seeing the full picture; I could feel it in my gut. The entire night I had spent rummaging through these brown files, one after another, trying to see if something would stand out. Except, the Serpents were extremely meticulous in ensuring they left no trace of their presence – especially if it had something to do with the Inner Circle. Viktor, Enzo and Barak all had one thing in common – they were easy to discover. Which could only mean the fourth member must have been the actual leader of the Serpents and discovering him was worth more than finding them. I sighed, tiredly, pushing the papers off me, and slipped out of bed with a disinclination to open the curtains that shed streams of lights into the dark room. My routine remained the same every morning; no matter what time I woke up, I always checked my phone and replied to any messages or emails that needed to be answered. As soon as I was done, I had a warm shower to help relax all my tense muscles that ached throughout the night after a long day at work, and then an extra-long night at the gym. I was so exhausted that I could barely manage returning back to my penthouse, and thus opted to stay at the Manor for the night.

Changing into pinstripe trousers and a white blouse, I quickly texted Kira to gather everyone in the meeting room for a quick conference to see where everyone was at - whether it was to do with the Serpents or the Manor in general. Kira was an early riser which meant by eight she would be up and running the entire Manor. Her reply was almost immediate, a quick '*done*' was sufficient to let me know everything was already prepared and completed. I would not be where I was today if it wasn't for Kira; she was honestly the foundation of the Manor that housed our family. Slipping into black pointed heels, I made my way down to the meeting room on the ground floor, greeting the younger girls as they scurried past me with pretty smiles. As I made my way around the corner of the first floor, where all the boys and men stayed, I saw a cluster of boys, who were speaking amongst each other with cold expressions on their faces that would usually scare any newcomers but hidden under those emotionless faces were warm smiles and amusing words. I saw them before they noticed my presence but in due time, they would master the skill of noticing everything every second of the day.

"Boys," I greeted, with a smile which they reciprocated.

"Aria, I haven't seen you in a while," Andrew, a tall blonde boy who joined us over a year ago, responded. "How have you been?"

"Busy. Very busy. How are your classes? I hope everything has been running smoothly," I questioned, and they all bobbed their heads in agreement. My smile stretched before becoming small when I saw one of the boys shift on their feet, avoiding my gaze. "Who's this?"

Travis followed my train of sight, a boy with beautiful dark hair and melanin skin, answered, "Oh, this is Peter. He's new. Joined us a few days ago. We've taken him under our wing since the older guys are too scary."

Quickly recalling Kira's briefing on our newest arrival, I said, softly, "Peter, I hope the boys have been nice to you. If they aren't, let me know and I'll kick their ass."

Peter's lips quirked in a timid smile as the boys around him exclaimed their disagreement. Andrew slung his arm around Peter's shoulder with a broad grin. "Don't worry, Aria. I have a feeling Peter is going to excel in all his classes."

"The quiet ones usually do," I chuckled, before remembering a crucially important, quiet resident in the Manor. "Speaking of quiet, has anyone see Violetta?"

The boys shook their heads, my eyes narrowing, as I quickly said my goodbyes and set off on my journey to find the heiress. Worry flooded me as I searched room after room, unable to find her until one of the girls mentioned they had just seen her in the labs only a couple of minutes ago. After telling Kira that I would be slightly late to the meeting, I raced off to the labs that were built in the east wing of the Manor. I found her perched against the desk with her nose wrinkled, as she glared at the light microscope with a scowl. I sighed in relief, my tense shoulders relaxing as I pushed open the glass door, catching her attention.

She looked at me, startled, before a cute smile replaced her scowl. "Oh, hi Aria."

"What are you doing in here, Vi?" I pried, observing the scene in front of me. Test tubes filled with different color liquids and books with biological findings were spread around her, entrapping her in this circle of knowledge.

"Mark said that I have a real talent for mixing chemicals so young. Usually, it takes years to master the skill, but he said that I'm a natural," she replied, gleefully, before glaring at the microscope again. "If only I wasn't struggling to solve this task he set for me."

I grinned in amusement when she sighed, before shuffling toward the microscope with her goggles on and a lab coat to prevent anything splashing onto her. Mark was in charge of teaching the younger girls and boys Biology, Chemistry and Physics – lessons which could be put to good use as they got older. Throughout the years, we had more people joining our forces, but it was their choice whether they wanted to leave. Regardless, we ensured everyone had a chance at education and pushed them to their limits, fueling them with the knowledge that they could take out into the world, conquering all different types of fields.

"Have you been settling in fine? I know it's been a few months since your arrival, but I hope the Manor has been kind to you."

Violetta grinned. "It's been great, Aria. Everyone is so nice and friendly – I don't think I ever want to leave," My eyes widened in surprise and a sense of happiness greeted me. "This is my family now."

Slowly but surely, a warm smile curled onto my lips, as I reached out and gently caressed Violetta's hair. "I'm glad. I'll leave you alone now so you can go back to being a genius."

Violetta giggled. "Maybe one day, I'll save you instead."

"I'm holding you to that promise," I joked, my smile creased my eyes as she burst into fits of laughter.

After ensuring that she was okay, I rushed to the meeting to which I was incredibly late. Fortunately, Kira was able to lead whilst I was absent; once again, I was eternally thankful for her presence. I thought I was discreet as I slipped into the meeting room, but I had seemingly forgotten that I personally trained all the individuals who sat around the oval table, their eyes darting in my direction.

I smiled sheepishly, waving. "What have I missed?"

Kira glowered. "Why are you *so* late?"

"I got distracted. What did I miss?"

Kira sent one last glare before returning to the task at hand, whilst I settled into my seat, grinning innocently, as everyone chuckled under their breath, causing her to scowl in annoyance, silencing everyone. While Kira continued the meeting, my phone buzzed in my pocket which earned me another glare. I pursed my lips, pointing to the door which caused her to sigh with a roll of her blue eyes. Everyone shot me a smirk, knowing that I was going to get scolded by her later, but I ignored the looks and quickly left the room before I could cause any further disruptions. My phone shrilled, relentlessly, and I muttered under my breath as I fished it out of my pocket, eyes widening when Nero's name blinked on my screen.

I picked up the phone whilst looking for an empty room, murmuring, quietly, "Yes?"

His deep, husky voice greeted me with a warm chuckle that had shivers running down my spine. "What's with the annoyed tone?"

"I was in a meeting," I responded, and then panic surged through me. "What's wrong? Is everything okay?"

"Slow down, sweetheart," he laughed, heartily. "I just called to check up on you. You haven't called me in a while and late replies are quite bothersome I've noticed."

"Check-up?" I frowned, unaware of such a concept, as I closed the door behind me when I finally found a vacant room further down the hallway.

"Yes, *stupida*," he replied, teasingly, before his voice dropped a few octaves. "Is everything okay?"

"I'm sorry that I haven't called. It's been really busy and there are a lot of preparations for tomorrow's mission."

"What's happening tomorrow?"

I was hesitant to reply at first, before I answered, honestly, "We've found the location to where Barak, Enzo and Viktor are based."

"So, you did have Viktor?" he muttered, more to himself than to me, my lips quirking into an amused smile.

"Is that all you care about?"

I could almost imagine him rolling his eyes as he grumbled, "Not at all. I knew you had him all this time. Is he dead?"

"Unfortunately, not yet. He's valuable but so far has proven himself useless," I sighed, glancing out of the window when I heard a burst of laughter. The tension on my shoulders eased when I saw some of the older girls and boys hanging about in the courtyard area, where we had built a place to sharpen their skills in archery and shooting. "Kira said to just get rid of him."

"I like Kira," Nero suddenly confessed.

My eyes narrowed suspiciously as I pressed my lips together. "What's that meant to mean?"

"She's clever, brave and..." he trailed off, becoming silent as I waited on edge to hear the end of that sentence. Before I could say anything, his laughter echoed through the phone, taking me by surprise. When he finally settled down, his words laced with humor, he asked, "Aria, are you jealous?"

Even more shocked, I gaped at his bold statement, spluttering, "Wh-what on earth are you talking about? Why would I be jealous?"

I could hear the stupid smirk in his voice as he sang, *"Aria is jealous."*

"I'm not!" I exclaimed, resolutely. "Stop being a douchebag and finish that sentence off."

He chuckled to himself, releasing a deep sigh on purpose because he knew that I was getting annoyed. "And she reminds me of someone I like very much."

I scrunched my nose like a bunny. "Who?"

"You."

And just like that, I felt the butterflies erupt in my stomach as if I was sixteen all over again.

*

"We're in – Calix was right; Barak's handprint worked. Alpha team on standby," Dom reported on the comms. "Waiting for Raven. Over."

"Roger that, Teddy," I replied, in the walkie talkie.

A second later, I heard a groan laced in the static noise. "Why did that have to be my code name?"

A smile quirked on my lips in amusement but before I could reply, Kira walked into the office, dressed in black from head to toe. A cap covered her blonde hair and she had gun holster attached to her thigh alongside the knives hidden under her protective gear. After last night, she insisted on being alone and I complied with her request, knowing that was what she needed before she set off on today's black ops mission. It was like she was a completely different girl, her blue eyes ready and fueled with a fiery passion to succeed at today's mission rather than red and swollen from the crying.

"Ready?" I checked, and she nodded firmly as she pulled her leather gloves on. "Dom is waiting for you. Everyone is in position, so when you arrive, you're the leader. Split everyone into two groups – Calix will lead the second group into the east wing of the estate, so you take yours into the west. Do not engage unless you have to. No matter what. Understand?"

"Yes, boss," she replied, jocularly, before the playfulness disappeared and left something much more serious in its place. "Are you sure you don't want to go?"

I shook my head, feeling guilty. "I can't. It's too big of a risk, especially now that my face is plastered on every form of media."

"Don't worry," she smiled slightly, noticing the guilt on my face. And then she said the words I needed to hear, but didn't ask for, "We'll come home safe."

Stiffly, I bobbed my head, twiddling my fingers, nervously, behind my back. Kira smiled one last time before she turned away to leave.

"Ah, right," she said, suddenly halting. My eyes furrowed in confusion as she peeked over. "I forgot to tell you that Xander discovered Enzo is hosting a private party and we noticed Nero has been invited. Has he mentioned anything to you?"

My eyes further narrowed, as I replied, "No, he hasn't."

"Well, the invites went out last night. It's men only but it's open to wives," she responded, squeezing her lips, as my eyes broadened in surprise, realizing what this meant. "If you wanted to attend, you need to marry Nero."

"I have no choice, but to go," I murmured, running my hand over my face, stressed. "A fake certificate won't get past them and I'm assuming they are going to want proof."

Kira nodded dejectedly, before forcing a soft smile despite the uncertainty in her eyes, as she said, "Talk to Nero. The dinner is in three weeks so I'm sure you guys can work something out."

I looked out of the window, an uneasy feeling gnawing my stomach, as I murmured, "I'm not too sure about that."

CHAPTER 32

gone girl

Kira

"Beta team on standby," Calix's voice crackled on the comms in my ear. "Heading into the west wing. Over."

"Copy that. Alpha team has successfully infiltrated the east wing. Keep me updated, Areas. Over," I responded, trying to not wince at the static.

"Copy."

After receiving Calix's transmission, I assigned a group of twenty people to different corridors in the west wing with clear instructions not to engage and not to be seen. After double-checking that those orders had been received, my group of trained assassins slipped down their designated halls so quietly that you would think you were seeing ghosts. The journey from our Manor to the estate situated just outside the Canadian borders was a little over twenty-four hours, but I managed to take a flight straight to Detroit and drive the rest of the way there. It was tedious but it gave me enough time to figure out my game plan, so that by the time I arrived at our base near the estate, I was able to quickly assign everyone to their positions. Calix was in charge of the Beta team which would investigate the east wing of the estate whilst I took over for Dom, who was the temporary leader for the Alpha team, and organized our route through the west wing after receiving the blueprints of the mansion by Sophie. Everyone was nervous; I could see it clearly, but they pushed past the nerves and focused on the task at hand, listening carefully as I repeated the three main rules: do not get caught, do not engage and do not die. Today's mission was just to scope out our target's home. With the two people at my side, we headed towards the hallway leading uphill to the estate's main office and library, after I confirmed that everyone had gone the correct way. As we cautiously navigated the passageways, ensuring that we didn't set off any traps put in place, I felt as if I wasn't allowed to take a breath. The estate was incredibly old and ancient, the corners of the walls beginning to crumble, as it was left neglected and not subject to any form of repair. Paintings in large gold frames hung on the walls of the corridor, so much so that I felt like I was in a museum.

"Beta team, anything? Over," I muttered, quietly, as my eyes fixated on everything I passed with intense caution, afraid that something would suddenly appear. My gut was telling me that something was incredibly wrong; this was all too easy, and nothing was ever this easy.

I heard a crackle before Calix responded, "Nothing. How about you? Over."

"Same here. Keep me updated, over," I replied, before turning to the two men who had accompanied me – Liam and Noah. "Liam, head back and keep an eye on the entrance we came in. Something isn't right and I have a feeling we'll be facing difficulty soon. I need you to go back and make sure our escape route is still available."

Liam looked hesitant to leave me but didn't question my orders, dashing down the hallway so quietly I thought he was gliding in the air. Noah remained by my side whilst I finally found what I assumed was the entrance to the library. Remaining stationed at the entrance, I left Noah and ventured into the library, being aware of the security cameras in the corners of the room. The library itself was almost as large as the one in the Manor. Three floors of books and in the center of it, on the ground floor, was a table that had blueprints spread out.

I clenched my jaw, touching the comms on my ear as I whispered, "Dom, cameras in the library need disabling."

"On it," he answered, a heartbeat later.

It only took him a couple of seconds to shut down the cameras but, even then, I double checked they weren't on, ensuring the red light attached to the side was no longer blinking. When I was satisfied, I moved out of the shadows, towards the table, and studied the blueprints that looked very familiar. My eyes widened in recognition.

Of course.

I would be disappointed if I did not recognize these blueprints especially as I spent five years of my adulthood planning the building of it. It was the Manor. Suddenly, terror overwhelmed me when I realized that the Serpents had the entire blueprints to the Manor; every acre of land was visible to them and this only raised the question of 'how'?

How did they gain access to this?

"Dom, who has access to the blueprints of the Manor?" I muttered.

"Not many people but then again, most of us are trained to remember every corner and crevice of the Manor so a blueprint could be easily recreated by anyone of us," Dom replied. A moment later, "Why?"

I didn't bother answering as my eyes drifted to the brown file beside it, my hands automatically reaching for it before I could fully comprehend the situation. The silence of the library was too still and, briefly, I wondered if Noah was okay, but my eyes were too focused on the words I was seeing – *Operation Quetzalcoatl.* I was dumbfounded as I read the file, discovering the Serpents plans to tear down the Russian and Italian Mafia families apart. I was dumb because I momentarily was not focusing on my surroundings. But that moment was all that was needed for everything to go wrong. My sharp ears heard the sound of struggling, like someone was choking in the background, but my brain failed to register it as danger until I heard the sound of someone messing up – the *thud* of an ornament falling. My heart pounded, yet I could not tear my eyes away from what I was reading. There, on the sheet of paper, that I failed to acknowledge, was a trap waiting for me to take the bait, was the four names of the Inner Circle members – Viktor, Enzo, Barak and – *No.*

I felt my heart plummet in dread as my eyes broadened when I read the name of the final member. No. I refused to believe it; I didn't want to. How was this possible? I didn't want to look over my shoulder; I suddenly felt the fear that only the men in my past managed to inflict on me. My hands trembled but I forced myself to remain calm as I touched the comms in my ear and whispered, "Noah? Dom? Anyone?"

But I got was no answer.

I was alone.

The comms piece in my ears made a static noise which told me that my communication was down – I truly had no one. Ever so slowly, I placed the file down, aware of the deep breathing behind me and knew instantly who it was. I swallowed and weighed my chances of survival, but I knew it was slim to none – especially if it was against a skilled assassin. I silently prayed that someone would save me before I succumbed to my unfortunate fate, spinning around so quickly that it would have taken other people off guard – except they anticipated my move before I had even made it – and suddenly the world went black as a heavy object collided with the back of my head.

And my last thought was –

Aria.

*

Aria

Kira.

My stomach sank at the sudden thought of her, a feeling I knew that did not bring any good news. I anxiously paced up and down the living room, causing a few people to wake up, but I quickly dismissed them with a reassuring smile and sent them on their way back upstairs. It was just past 3 a.m. and I hadn't received any news all day, which only caused the unease within me to escalate. Something wasn't right. Fiddling with my fingers, nervously, I kept glancing at my phone on the coffee table, just waiting for a call or a message – something which could tell me that I was worrying over nothing. Abruptly, my thoughts were interrupted, as the front door opened, my eyes darting to the entrance, as I watched everyone spill into the house with somber expressions that confirmed my suspicions. No one wanted to meet my desperate gaze; no one wanted to tell me what happened. I swallowed, thickly, as I did a quick scan to ensure everyone had come back safely but as Calix and Dom appeared out from the crowd, all I could focus on was the severely injured Noah. His eyes black and blue, his lips busted, and blood painted across his head. His neck was red and bruised as if someone had choked him, his entire body limp as he failed to stay conscious.

"Take him to the infirmary," I commanded. When no one moved, I glared at the crowd. "*Now.*"

Four people slipped out and moved towards Noah, taking him out of Calix and Dom's hands, and swiftly moving him to the infirmary down the corridor. I clenched my jaw and straightened my back, finally asking the question I did not want to ask – the one I feared the answer to.

"Where is Yakira?" The words left my mouth coldly, but they were laced with fear, fear for my best friend's life.

Glancing at everyone to tell me something, no one replied. Dom avoided my gaze, his face for the first time so solemn, as he trained his eyes onto the ground, rigid posture despite the injuries I saw on his hands which only meant they had to fight their way out of the estate. Finally, my gaze settled onto Calix, who didn't look away. Green eyes welcomed me with the answers I needed his mouth to say.

Face expressionless, void of any emotions, he answered, "Yakira was captured."

*

I wanted to cry. I wanted to bawl my fucking eyes out. The feeling was so strong that it was overwhelmingly distracting. My body shook as I drove the car through the empty streets of New York. The car zipped past others, not waiting for the green lights, swerving around the corners like a manic, before it finally stopped when I reached my destination. My body was working but my mind was frozen from shock, my feet moving slowly until they reached outside the door of a familiar penthouse. Knocking incessantly on the oak door, I wasn't worried about the neighbors; I just needed to be held. The door opened, revealing a sleepy Nero with disheveled hair that made him look incredibly sexy, especially as he only wore trousers. However, my focus was on everything but him. All I could think of was Kira. All I wanted was Kira. He rubbed his eyes, frowning when he noticed the state I was in.

"Ari – *humph*," he grunted, as I fell into his arms, tears falling down my cheeks and my body shaking. His arms wasted no seconds as they wrapped around me, embracing me in this warm and secure bubble.

"They have her," I sobbed. "They have Yakira."

He inhaled sharply and tightened his hold around me as if I would disappear if he let go. I faintly remembered the door closing and us moving from the hallway to his living room except, at the same time I didn't, too consumed in the comfort of his hold. He held me, allowing me to cry for God knows how long, but he never once spoke. Maybe he didn't know what to say or maybe he knew I didn't want to hear anything. He just hugged me as if he would never let go. I wasn't sure at what point I did finally let go and sink into the sofa, whilst Nero brought me a cup of water which I took in my shaky hands, my tear-stained eyes trained on the ground. There was a deep sigh released, before he kneeled to my height in front of me, worry swarming his beautiful eyes that reminded me of Kira, his fingers gently touching my face as if I was glass and a single touch would break me. I didn't doubt it. I felt as fragile as I must have looked.

"What happened?" he whispered, a moment later.

"I'm not sure," I answered, after a brief second. "Calix seemed so out of it and Dom was in so much shock that they couldn't explain what on earth went wrong. I've never seen them like that before."

"Was there anyone with her before she was caught?"

"Noah," I replied, shaking. My eyes closed as I tried to force the image of Noah's severely injured body out of my head. "He's been so badly hurt. I don't-I don't know if he's going to be alright."

The words that left my lips were laced with sobs, my body trembling as I looked at Nero. The expression on his face looked so jaded that I couldn't tell what on earth he was feeling.

"It's going to be okay. Kira is a strong woman, Aria. She's going to be okay," Nero assured, confidently, as if that was the only thing that could happen. "And Noah, he's going to get better. It's going to be difficult at first, but he will recover."

"I think Kira found something," I breathed out. "Dom mentioned she was in the library by herself and asked about the blueprints to the Manor. He didn't get the chance to find out why she wanted to know, but I have a strange feeling Kira saw something she wasn't supposed to see."

"How do you know for sure?"

"Because Noah was the only person who was injured, and Kira was the only person captured."

Nero's brows drew together; I wanted to know what he was thinking, what was going on in that mind of his, but before I could ask, his expression changed drastically, and he gifted me a smile that caused the anxiety within me to diminish like a flame.

"It's been a long night and I'm sure you're very tired. Come, sleep next to me tonight," Nero spoke softly, tugging my hand as he stood up. "We can figure things out in the morning."

I wanted to argue and tell him that we had to save Kira right now, but my body refused to protest to his orders. Weak and frail, I almost lost my footing as we began walking but, luckily, Nero's quick reflexes kicked in and his arms swooped under me, cradling me in his arms. My eyes failed to remain open despite my best efforts, my body slack in his arms. The second my head touched the pillow, I knocked out, my energy drained from the crying, grieving and guilt. I should have gone with her.

Would things have turned out differently?

Perhaps those thoughts lulled me to a state of deep sleep where dreams or nightmares did not greet me. Or maybe it was Nero's arms wrapped around my body as he drew me close, my head tucked into his chest, and the sound of his heartbeat that helped me sleep. I couldn't say for sure but that night, I was grateful that he was there.

If I was alone, I would have burned the entire city down just to save Kira.

And no one would have survived my wrath.

CHAPTER 33

somewhere north of New York

His eyes studied her bruised body from a distance, hidden in the shadows, as he admired the work of his men on the girl in the caged cell. The room was a hollow cube of concrete, one way in, no windows. In there, you had no idea how much time had passed or even if it was night or day. It was disorientating by design. Given enough time a person could forget their own name in there. The isolation was total, and the stimulation was zero. No sound, no light, no furniture, or cloth of any kind. Fit for the girl trapped inside. Bound and bloody, she slumped in the corner of the cold chamber, unconscious, as the energy was beaten out of her.

Good.

"She knows," Barak said, making himself seen, as he entered the basement, a cigar in his mouth. The basement was more like a bunker – all concrete, and no personality. He exhaled a puff of smoke, drawling, lazily, "Our plans will be ruined if she tells Aria."

"Then we make sure that doesn't happen," he replied, coldly. "Aria will come back for her. We make sure we don't miss this time."

"We didn't expect her *not* to come. I thought you said she was going to," Barak growled in annoyance, as if he should have known better than to trust *his* word.

"She would have," he responded, calmly. Too calmly. "But then she got engaged."

"To Nero *fucking* Russo," Barak spat out, spitefully. "How does this help us?"

"Aria will be too preoccupied with Kira's retrieval and her engagement to even notice what's happening behind the scenes," Inhaling sharply, he held his hands behind his back, trying to ignore the pain in his wrist. His gaze moved over to Barak, narrowing as he ordered, "We proceed with our plans as we intended to. We need to stay on schedule. Any more delays can risk full exposure."

"Where do we start?"

"The Italians. We hit them first."

There was a long silence in the cold basement, and, for a moment, he expected Barak to refute, seeing as that was never the plan, but instead he was interrupted by a low groan. Barak's eyes drifted over to the girl who began to gain consciousness, her head heavily lifting as she struggled to figure out what was going on.

"What of the girl?" Barak asked.

He knew he should just kill her. She was a liability, a danger to his plan. But he didn't. For some unsettling reason, he couldn't.

Clenching his jaw, he sent one last look at the girl before muttering, "She stays alive."

Kira's head lifted but her sight was slightly blurry from either the beating she had taken earlier or the lack of light – she couldn't tell. But then, she saw Barak and heard him speaking before the words were replaced with retreating footsteps. With the meagre amount of energy she had left, she glanced in the direction of the exit and noticed a tall figure striding away with a hand tucked in his trousers. Her head suddenly became heavy, but before she slipped back into unconsciousness, she saw the tall figure peer over his shoulders, and all she could remember was how his hazel eyes looked startling green in the dim incandescent light.

CHAPTER 34

i love you

When I woke up, my first thought was Yakira. My heart sunk and tears threatened to spill, but I quickly blinked them away, glancing to the side where I found Nero sleeping beside me like an angel. I couldn't help but prop my head up with my hands, as I turned to the side to study his beautiful features. My fingers reached out and softly caressed his cheeks, admiring his long lashes and plump lips that I desperately wanted to kiss. I followed his jawline to his neck, unable to fathom the fact that this man was sleeping beside me. I pressed my lips, gently, against his chest before curling closer to him, drawing the blanket around us, as his arms tightened around me.

"Why did you stop?" he murmured, sleepily. My eyes widened, glimpsing up to see sterling blue eyes watching me in amusement.

"You were awake?" When his lips coiled into a teasing smirk, it immediately confirmed my suspicions. My cheeks warmed up as I glowered at him. "Why didn't you say anything?"

"And stop your little journey?" he chuckled. "No way. Although, I wish your hands went lower."

I smacked his chest which earned me a mixture of a groan and laughter as I pushed myself away from him before he could pull me back into his captivity. His piercing gaze followed me as I grabbed one of his shirts, changing out of the clothes I wore yesterday, and covering myself with the linen material that felt like a second skin against my body. Quickly, tying my hair into a messy bun, I glanced over my shoulder to see him getting out of bed, his torso shamelessly on display as if he was a model. Chiseled chest, corded arms – every inch of him was sin and *Jesus*, I loved it. I forced myself to tear my eyes away, but one tug of my hand had me facing him, oceanic eyes looking down at me.

"I'm going to wash up. How about you make some coffee for us so we can talk?" he muttered, tucking a strand of hair behind my ear. "Sound good?"

I swallowed thickly, bobbing my head. My answer rewarded me a small smile as he pressed his lips against my forehead, before he disappeared into the bathroom, his back muscles rippling as he rolled his shoulders back. I didn't notice that I had been holding my breath until the door closed, and I exhaled heavily, my body relaxing from the tension that braced me. After brewing some coffee for him and myself, I settled in front of the windows which gave me a panorama of the entire city in its naked daylight form. I lost myself in this magnetic view that I didn't realize when Nero sat beside me, dressed in smart wear. It was only when he released a breath of air that I noticed his presence, glancing at the man whom I called my best friend.

"I want to go save her," I stated, frankly. "Now."

Nero didn't bat an eye in my direction, as he responded, "What a stupid thing to do."

"It's not stupid."

"Yes, it is," he retorted, flickering those dark blue orbs over at me. "And you know it is. You'll put everyone's lives at risk – even Kira's. Do you even know where she is?"

I sighed shakily, closing my eyes as I forced myself not to cry, "What do I do? I can't just sit here. I… I feel so useless."

"We plan, like we have trained to do since birth. If you rush into saving her, you might ultimately place her further in harm's way. Kira is going to be okay – have faith in her, Aria. She is relying on you to save her but not in a foolish way."

I didn't respond because I knew he was right, and I grudgingly decided not to take any drastic action. I had to have faith in Kira and if we were to save her, we had to do it carefully. The Serpents were smarter than I had given them credit for, and this was the consequence of me underestimating them. Kira had found something – something the Serpents did not want anyone to know about – and it had to do with the Manor. The only conclusion I was able to come to was that there was a traitor amongst us, but that was a possibility I prayed perpetually not to be true. I just hoped when we saved Kira, she could settle the doubts in my head.

The silence settled between us until I finally broke it, turning to Nero as I blurted, "Kira informed me of Enzo's party."

Nero's nod was slow. Hesitant. "I was going to tell you."

"I want to go."

He raised a brow, choosing his words carefully, "Women aren't allowed to go."

"I know. But wives are."

At first, he couldn't figure out what I was saying but when he did, his eyes widened and he shook his head fervently, surprising me as he stood up and said, "No. We are not getting married. Not like this."

My jaw fell slack as he walked away, my brain temporarily stopping until it rebooted a second later. I stumbled onto my feet, striding after him, as he disappeared into the kitchen, anger bubbling within me.

"What do you mean? Why not? Isn't this what you wanted?" I shot question after question, trying to change his mind, but Nero was stubborn and glared in my direction.

"*Not like this*," he repeated.

"Like how then, Nero? My best friend's life is on the line and you're telling me now is the time you choose to be gracious?" I scoffed. "Enzo is hosting the party, and I have a feeling that's where they'll be keeping Kira. If I go, I can save Kira. *We* can save Kira."

Nero ran his fingers through his hair, sighing, remorsefully, "Aria, the only way you can go is if we get married."

"Then, let's get married," I pleaded, desperately, taking his hands into mine. He shook his head, eyes filled with so much sadness that it hurt my heart, painfully.

"Not like this," he countered, as if his heart was breaking, his words turning into whispers. He swallowed, prying my hands off his, before he said, "Marriage might not mean anything to you, but it is an important and sacred part of my life. A vow that I have no intention of breaking. Tell me, after we get married, Aria, would you want to stay with me? Can you even marry me?"

My throat felt dry as I failed to respond with the words he needed to hear but I couldn't say them. I was too caught up in my own selfish needs that I forgot how much I had been putting him through. He constantly put me above himself and this was his last straw. This was something I could not negotiate. Suddenly, Kira's bruised face popped into my mind and the fear of her safety outweighed the guilt I felt towards Nero.

I had to save her, by any means necessary.

"I'm willing to sacrifice *everything*, Nero. Please, let me save her," I begged, tearfully.

His eyes steeled when he replied, "I'm sorry."

My jaw tightened as I narrowed my eyes at him, knowing there was no way I could win. Everything that I was feeling overwhelmed me, so I settled on the rage. I didn't care that it was misdirected. I didn't care because I was a fool to believe he would help me, that I could turn to him. I stepped back, scoffing in disbelief, as I tried to come to terms with what was happening. My eyes finally settled on his – those stunning blue eyes, the ones I wished I could hate.

"I hate you," I whispered, hoping that my words could hurt him as much he hurt me. "I shouldn't have relied on you again. I was a fool to rely on you."

Nero didn't flinch at my harsh words; his brows raised as if he was amused, and his arms crossed over his chest when he leaned against the countertop. "Is that so? Do you really hate me, Aria? Because I don't think you ever did."

"Trusting you was the worst decision I have ever made," I spat out, spinning on my heels to storm away, which I would have if his hand had not snaked out and grasped my wrist. He tugged me back into his traitorous arms that I hated myself for loving so much. I tried to twist myself out of his hold, but he was too strong, pressing me against him whilst he caressed the side of my face. My body froze as his fingers, lightly, kissed my skin, leaving small sparks of heat in their trail.

"You're the worst liar," he murmured, his warm breath fanning against my skin, little sparks fizzling within me. "Be angry with me, Aria, but you can't hate me."

"Want to bet on that?" I seethed, spitefully.

His lips lifted in delight. "I'll always win."

"Are you serious right now?"

But he didn't even look marginally affected, as if I was nothing but a pesky fly. "You seem to think that I'd be hurt by your reaction."

"I hate you," I hissed, pushing him away to create some desperately needed distance between us.

He smirked and my breath hitched when his blue eyes twinkled in wild delight. *Damn it.*

"Didn't you know, sweetheart?" He chuckled, huskily, and my body shuddered at how delicious it sounded. "Hate is just the beginning of a love story."

*

"Are you okay, Aria?" Violetta questioned, when she entered my office.

Her eyes glossed over the trail of destruction I had left before settling on me with concern. After leaving Nero's penthouse, I drove back to the Manor and tried to silence my thoughts with the alcohol I had left hidden in my cabinets. Though it was a failed attempt, as I could not find any and cursed Kira silently for hiding them. She was always too concerned that I was drinking too recklessly; I forgot to pry the location of my bottles out of her before she left. In a fit of rage, all I could see was red and everything I touched ended up being thrown across the room, sheets of paper scattered across the floor, shards of glass stuck in the carpet, broken ornaments, and my desk cleared of all stationery, which ended up on the floor. Eventually, when I finally sank into my seat behind my desk, I noticed how exhausted I was and wept for the loss of my friend. It wasn't until there was a timid knock ten minutes later that I finally wiped away my tears before anyone could bear witness to the mess I was. The state of the room clearly showed that instead.

"What are you doing here, Vi?" I grunted, my throat hoarse from the sobs.

"Are you going to come to eat dinner?" she shuffled towards me whilst being careful not to step on all pieces of glass or paperwork.

"I'm not hungry. Why aren't you in bed? It's past your bedtime."

Violetta giggled. "It's only seven o'clock, Aria."

I looked away, knowing that my mind had been on everything but the time. "Still."

"Do you want to talk?" The younger girl asked, as she sat opposite me with a warm smile that lessened some of the pain within me. Violetta was only twelve yet speaking to her sometimes made me forget that. "How did things go with Mr.. Russo? Sophie mentioned that you stayed with him last night."

"I see you girls like to gossip," I uttered.

Violetta shook her head. "It's not gossip, more like concern. We were all worried about where you disappeared to last night. I hoped you hadn't headed off to save Kira yourself."

I studied her carefully, tilting my head to the side. "And if I did?"

"I would be very worried and sad," Violetta frowned. "You're strong, Aria. But sometimes you're too strong. I think sometimes you forget that it's okay to rely on others for help. You won't have all the answers or solutions – no one is expecting you to. We're a team."

I didn't reply, my gaze moving away from the girl in front of me to the small box on my desk, which encased the ring I had worn to Althaia's party. My heart pained as I remembered how bare my hands felt without it, but I couldn't bring myself to wear it, undeserving of such a beautiful stone, undeserving of the promise it represented, undeserving of him. Because he was right – how could I expect him to break such a holy sacrament? But… what if I didn't want him to?

"Can I ask you something, Vi?" The little girl bobbed her head, eagerly, perching herself closer to me. "I need Nero's help, but he won't help me because the favor is too big to ask of him. I don't know what to do."

"Be honest with him," I frowned, confused as to what was so easy about that. Violetta rolled her eyes in amusement. "Aria, it's really clear that Mr. Russo doesn't have the slightest idea why you are doing what you are doing. There is only so much someone will help with very little information but if you open up to him, maybe he'll open up to you. We spend so much of our lives hiding away the full truth in fear of betrayal, but if he has proven his loyalty to you, surely you can reciprocate by giving something back to him. My brother used to tell me that all relationships are like transactions – we give, and we get. Except, what does Mr. Russo get?"

My jaw slacked. *What…* Trying to fathom what Violetta just said, I stammered, "Where do I even begin?"

The girl with the vibrant, violet eyes shrugged. "Maybe start with your true feelings."

Violetta's words left a deep impression on me for the rest of the evening. Perhaps she was right. Nero had sacrificed a lot for me, knowing very little about what was truly going on behind the scenes. Why would he agree to marry me? Especially, if all I did was keep secrets from him. I could not respect him enough to tell him the truth about anything, so what gave me the right to ask for his hand in marriage? I sighed, pushing open my penthouse door and basking in the silence. I had not been home in a very long time and craved to feel the comfort of my silk sheets, and the warmth beneath my feet from the underfloor heating. I dropped my bag and coat on the couch, heading to the glass cabinet, where I grabbed myself the glass of wine that I desperately needed. As I poured myself another glass, I saw movement in the reflection of the window, which I knew did not belong to me. I gripped the bottle, tightly, to use as a weapon, whilst stiffly sipping on the wine, keeping my eyes trained on the window. The figure was standing behind me and unfortunately, due to the lack of light, I was unable to tell who it was. My anxiety heightened as they neared me and I inhaled, sharply yet quietly, readying myself to act as I straightened my spine. Just before they could reach me, I spun around bringing the bottle to the infiltrator's head, though they were quicker and grabbed my wrist before it could collide against their skull. My eyes widened when I noticed their bright cobalt eyes and amused smirk.

"Well, what kind of greeting is this?" Nero muttered, disappointedly.

"You fucking idiot," I snapped, tearing my hand away from his hold. "Why would you sneak up on me like that?"

He shrugged, dismissively. "Just checking if your reflexes are as good as they were when we were younger."

I glowered. "What do you want?"

He settled on the stool in front of the kitchen island, all signs of amusement disappearing, as he replied, sincerely, "I wanted to apologize."

"What?" I blinked, startled. "Why?"

"Because I was harsh with my words. I forget the gravity of your situation and I wasn't being considerate enough."

There is always a moment in a person's life when they are in a relationship and they realize this person was their forever, their soulmate. For me, it was this moment. His words were honest and genuine; there was not an ounce of false candor. The way he looked at me was something I had never experienced before – as if he were more afraid of losing me than keeping his promise. His shoulders were shifted in my direction, eyes solely looking at me, as he gave me all his attention. I had met a lot of people in my life but only one person could cause my heart to stutter and race so rapidly.

And that was Nero Russo.

I didn't think twice as I placed my glass to the side and pressed my lips against his. I kissed him with every fiber in my body, which all solicited for his touch. He was shocked at first, but responded a second later, angling his head to kiss me deeper. Like we were both thirsty and we were each other's water. We could not breathe yet air filled my lungs when he touched me. Eventually, we tore ourselves away from each other, to my despair, but the look in Nero's eyes promised I would soon be gifted with the taste of his lips once more.

"As much as I want to kiss you, Aria," he chuckled, rubbing his thumb across my swollen lip, distractedly. "We need to talk. *Properly.*"

"Why do you apologize?" I asked, rhetorically. Before he could reply, I continued, "When it's my fault," His eyes widened in surprise, but I didn't let it stop me as I rambled, "It's usually my fault and you always say sorry first. I push you away, lie to you, hide things from you and you still say sorry first. Why?"

He smiled, moving his hands to my hips as he spread his legs apart, allowing me to stand between them. "Aria, I'll say sorry a thousand times if it makes you happy. I know you're terrified to open up and let me in – I understand. Don't ever feel guilty for that. I'll always wait for you."

My eyes watered up as my trembling hands moved to his shoulders, trying to steady myself in this daze which he has encased me in as I shakily said, "Nero, I'm sorry for everything I put you through. I never want to hurt you but that's all I seem to do."

"You don't hurt me," he denied, softly.

"Yes, I do," I protested, shifting away from him to create some distance, but he didn't let me go, pulling me closer until there was barely any space between us.

His warm gaze stole my breath like a thief at night, so effortlessly. He reached out and gently wiped the few traitorous tears that managed to escape with a breathy chuckle, "Aria, you drive me insane more than anyone else, but I want you to. My body, heart and soul are yours to play with. Tell me to walk until the edge of the Earth, and I'll do it without complaints because you are the world."

The air was trapped in my throat, unable to comprehend the words he was saying, but at the same time, I felt like I could breathe for the first time in my life. His gaze was hypnotic, and I could not tear my eyes away from him. I was falling but I didn't care. I didn't care how badly I would get hurt as long as I was with him. It was as if there was this magnetic pull between us that we tried to ignore, but every time we did, it just got stronger until I found myself pushed up against him, craving for his love.

Tearily, I whispered, "Why?"

"Because Aria, you are the only woman I ever want to marry. The only woman I will ever love."

My heart raced, pounding like a feral animal pleading to be freed. Everything in the world was messed up but standing in front of him, I forgot it all. He was my peace, my haven, the broken part of me that made me whole. I spent years chasing that feeling away but as I stared at him with teary eyes, I knew nothing would be better than the love he would be giving me. I could not stop the tears, letting them run freely down my cheeks, shamelessly, as he stood up, taking my hands into his. I spent years wondering how this moment would happen, but as he knelt on one knee, blue orbs glistening when he looked up at me with a heart-breaking smile, I could not stop the look of surprise that traversed my face. I found myself covering my mouth, stunned, crying, as I watched him bring out a beautiful navy satin box that I knew belonged to Harry Winston. But I couldn't tear my eyes away as he opened it up, revealing a stunning ring that outshone the one I had worn at Althaia's party. Perhaps it was because this time it was different. Although, the situation we were in was undesirable, I had never experienced more perfect timing then I did right now. The universe stopped, and all I knew was him. He was my universe and I wanted to spend forever discovering everything I needed to know until I could not learn anymore.

"Ariadne Moretti, I have loved you since the day you were born and I will love you until the day I die," he proclaimed with all his heart, his watery eyes that looked like the ocean, reminding me that even he could be vulnerable. "So, will you do me the greatest honor of becoming my wife?"

I could not stop the smile that stretched across my face. My cheeks ached, wet from tears stains but I was distracted by the intensity of his gaze as he waited for my reply. The words I wanted to say, the feelings I could not express, I wondered if he knew of their existence. There was this magnetic pull between us that we couldn't stay away from, and I wondered if he felt it too. But as I stared at him with wonderstruck eyes, I knew he did.

Question after question ran through my mind, one after another: would we finally get our happily ever after? Did I want to spend the rest of my life with him? Did I love him?

Finally, I found the answer I was searching for –

"Yes."

CHAPTER 35

the middle of the night

I yelled in frustration, throwing all my weight into Sophie as she attacked me. Her hands went for my waist, but I swiveled to the side, lifting my leg and colliding it into the side of her body. She collapsed onto the ground, hair sprawled out on the mat, and for a second, I thought she wasn't going to get up, but I heard a breathy laugh laced with pain as she looked up.

"You've gotten quicker," she commented. "Stronger."

"I would hope so," I responded, my chest heaving as I tried to level my breathing. "I've been training every day and night for the last two weeks to strengthen my skills."

She drew her eyebrows together. "Aria, please stop pushing yourself to the limit."

"I need to!" I exclaimed, with frantic eyes. Sophie flinched and I recoiled, glancing away from her, shamefully. "I need to. For Kira." Sophie didn't say anything, and I did not expect nor did I want her to. Clenching my jaw, I said, "Let's go again. One more time."

"Soph," The voice of someone else that didn't belong to either of us diverted our attention. Xander stood by the doorway of the lower gym, arms crossed over his chest, as he watched us under his dark hooded lashes. It was difficult to see exactly how he was feeling but the tick in his jaw was enough to tell me he was annoyed. "You're needed in the kitchen. A few boys and girls are waiting for you down there."

Sophie opened her mouth to argue, but one stern look told her otherwise. She shot me a sheepish smile before I sighed, rolling my eyes as I helped her onto her feet. She didn't leave immediately, muttering something quietly to Xander, before disappearing, but whatever it was, Xander didn't look the smallest bit bothered as he strolled over, tugging his tank top over his head, and discarding it to the side. Xander was more brains than brawn compared to the rest of the people in the Manor but that didn't mean he wasn't an experienced fighter – especially, as I had personally trained him. An American heartthrob with blonde hair and golden eyes, he was almost the same build as Nero, perhaps a bit smaller. Broad shoulders, ripped muscles that were inked with intricate artwork to hide the scars underneath, he stalked over, rolling his shoulders as he positioned himself in a defensive stance.

"Come at me," he dared.

And who was I to back down from a fight?

I roared as I sprinted with all my power, spinning to the side as he tried to grab me, similar to Sophie's technique, except he had anticipated my leg rise and for me to collide into the side of his body. Before it could make the collision, he grasped my leg and threw me onto the ground, but I quickly flipped in the air and landed perfectly onto my feet, wiggling my brows with a triumphant smirk on my face which had him laugh before mimicking my expression as if to say, 'challenge accepted.' He didn't let me breathe as he dashed towards me, throwing his right arm into the air but, narrowly, missing as I ducked, sliding in between his legs and catching him off guard as I jumped onto his back, my legs curling around his waist with a deathly grip, and my arms around his neck in a position where one quick action could result in a broken trachea.

"Don't underestimate your opponent," I whispered, before pressing my lips onto his head. "You'll end up dead, dumbass."

He chuckled breathily as I hopped off his back. "I never win against you."

"Of course. It's me," I answered, cockily. He rolled his eyes, throwing me a bottle of water, as I collapsed onto the mat, completely and utterly shattered. Taking a large gulp of water, thirstily, I shot him a quick look as I asked, "How are the plans coming along?"

"We have orders of hydrangeas that have gone through today. A four-tiered cake matching your description has been sent to that cake shop you love in New Jersey. Dresses and suits have yet to be finalized but the boys' suits have been chosen out by yours truly," he grinned, and I chuckled, sending him a small smile. "In terms of venue, I believe Nero has completely sorted that out."

My brows shot up in surprise. "Oh?"

Nero and I hadn't spoken about wedding plans over the last two weeks in a great amount of detail and decided to leave in the hands of the Xander, Sophie, and Matteo. So, to hear that he had already picked out a venue took me off guard, especially as I had not mentioned any places before.

"Yes," Xander nodded. "I was told that this was a venue you've had your eyes on since you were a little girl. The William Vale, I think it's called."

My jaw went slack as I stared at Xander, flabbergasted, expecting him to tell me it was a joke, but a minute went by, and he didn't say anything. I hadn't even realized Nero had known of my dream wedding venue; I didn't remember ever telling him but the fact that he managed to get that right stole my breath away.

"How – how did he know?" I managed to sputter out, astonished.

Xander laughed. "I mean you're marrying him. I'd hope he knows you very well."

I couldn't believe what I was hearing and let out a breathy laugh in disbelief, shaking my head as I muttered, "He's insane."

"This is quite possibly true," Xander stated, before becoming very solemn as he glanced down at me. "I'm really happy for you, Aria. I never asked what had happened between you and Nero nor have you ever told me, but I'm glad you've been able to work out your differences. I hadn't seen you happy in a long time until he came about."

Shyly, I fiddled with my fingers. "Thanks, Xander."

"Tomorrow, Soph and the girls plan on going bridesmaids shopping. You should get out of the house and have a breath of fresh air, so go with them and maybe find a dress for yourself," he instructed, standing up, before pulling me onto my feet.

"It doesn't feel right," I murmured. "Planning a wedding and I don't have my maid of honor by my side. I don't know if I can do it."

"You should talk to Nero. I know you've been distant with him lately and he doesn't want to push you, but he calls me or Sophie every day to ask about you," Xander revealed with a wry smile. I was stunned, realizing how foolish I had been acting, and how considerate he had been. Arching a brow, Xander suggested, "He arrived at his penthouse just about half an hour ago. Maybe you should catch him and spend the night there."

I didn't waste another second as I shot off to leave but quickly halted when Xander called out my name.

I peered over my shoulder, and he said, "Aren't you forgetting what day it is?"

I frowned at first, confused about what Xander was talking about, before my eyes widened in pure horror that I had forgotten it was Nero's birthday. I couldn't believe myself and didn't waste another second as I rushed off to get ready. I cursed under my breath every step along the way, rapidly having a shower to get rid of the stench of sweat and changing into a beautiful champagne satin slip dress that fell a little below my knee. How I managed to do a quick glam look in under fifteen minutes, I couldn't answer but as soon as I was done, I grabbed my things, shoving them into my purse and searched for the gift which I, thankfully, bought a little while back, before finally slipping into my nude stilettos and rushing down to the town car that Xander had called for me. I gave directions to a cake shop nearby and picked up a small cake which the owner managed to ice his name onto, before finally arriving at his home just as it had turned ten o'clock. Releasing a deep sigh, I knocked on his door twice, my body bouncing with anxiety as I nibbled on my lower lip, hoping that he would open the door quickly. Fortunately, he did, and relief swarmed my body and I smiled at him. He was still dressed in his suit, a brow raised in surprise when he caught sight of me before a heart-shattering smile made its way onto his face.

"Aria," he spoke, affectionately, taking my hand and pressing his lips against my skin. "You look exquisite."

"I apologize for being so distracted. My mind has been on everything but you," I pouted, playfully. "Forgive me?"

Chuckling, he bent down to kiss me, murmuring. "Always."

Kissing him was probably my favorite thing to do. His hand moved to my hips, jerking me closer whilst I did my best not to drop the bags in my hands. I giggled as he moved his attention to my neck, peppering me with small kisses that tickled me.

"Okay, okay," I laughed, pushing him off me. "Let me in. I have something to give you."

Arching his brow, attractively, he smirked as his eyes scanned me up and down. "Oh? Does it involve taking this dress off?"

I pressed my lips together to fight back a peal of laughter as I sauntered past him, glancing back with a sultry smile. "Only if you're good."

Instantly, his eyes darkened. "Yes, ma'am."

Whilst I dropped my things in the living room, Nero poured us a glass of wine as I moved my attention to the beautiful city landscape. I couldn't help but sigh in awe at how magical the city looked tonight. It twinkled with lights of all colors. I saw red, yellow, blue and then I saw the bokeh of cars below, zipping through the streets. The moon looked radiant in the sky, so huge that I thought I could touch it, but the stars looked like they were dancing in the night. It was magnificently spectacular, and I felt at peace with the view.

"It's stunning," I whispered, when I felt a shift of air, knowing Nero was standing beside me. "It's unreal. The world looks so small from this view but down there, it's like you're an ant in a field of sunflowers."

"You always loved New York," he stated, handing me a glass. "You said it was the most beautiful place in the world. Do you still believe that?"

Glancing at him, I smiled. "Yes."

He mirrored my smile, gingerly. "What brought you here?"

"Two things," I replied. "Firstly, I understand if it's a lot to ask but I've been feeling so unsettled the last two weeks whenever someone mentioned the wedding."

He frowned, worry masking his face. "Are you second-guessing your decision?"

My eyes widened as I shook my head, adamantly. "No, not at all," Relief replaced the temporary panic, his eyes softened as he nodded. "I just don't like the idea of planning a wedding without Kira being there. She should be there by my side. How can I celebrate this occasion if my sister isn't with me?"

"What would you like to do?"

"Well, the party is next week. I was hoping if we could just register our marriage and celebrate once Kira is home," I alluded, nervously, anticipating his response. He knitted his brows, pensively, and for a second, I thought he would disagree but, instead, he smiled, understandingly, bobbing his head to my suggestion.

"I think that's fair. Kira is important to you, and I want to celebrate our marriage happily with all our loved ones there," he answered. "Once this is all over, I promise you that we will hold the grandest wedding New York has ever seen."

I broke out into a large smile, kissing him as I murmured, "Thank you so much."

He chuckled. "Now, what is the second thing?"

I couldn't contain my grin as I swapped my glass of wine for the small, boxed gift hidden in my purse. He looked surprised as I handed it over to him, his blue eyes flickering to the gift in his hold before settling on me.

I beamed, enthusiastically, "Happy Birthday!"

At first, sheer shock masked his face before it distorted into something unrecognizable. It left me troubled, my smile slipping off my face along with the happiness bubbling within. He didn't say anything, blankly looking at my gift.

"Is something wrong?"

"What is this?" he questioned; his cold tone had me flinching.

"Your birthday gift," I explained, taking the box from his unmoving hands and revealing the chain tucked inside. It was a silver locket with a photo from when we were younger, his arm around my waist as we grinned at each other, unaware of the camera that managed to snap a picture of that moment. "Do you like it?"

"I don't celebrate my birthday, Aria," he muttered, flippantly. "I haven't in a long while."

I frowned. "Why not?"

"Because I don't. Can you just drop it?" he snapped, prompting me to recoil. The second he noticed his irritability, he sighed regretfully, scratching his beard. "I'm sorry. I didn't mean to shout."

I clenched my jaw, irritated. "Clearly you did."

He didn't bother hiding the flicker of infuriation across his face when he reached out to embrace me, but I turned away, creating a considerable amount of distance between us. "Don't be such a child."

"Excuse me," I sneered. "I'm not the one who started this."

"Aria, can we just move on?"

"No," I responded, defiantly. "Not until you explain to me what's going on."

"How can you not remember?" he said, exasperatedly.

"What? Your birthday? Are you upset that I forgot? I'm sorry but it wasn't as if I did it intentionally. I was busy, you know that."

Nero growled. "No, Aria. It's not that you forgot about my birthday. It's that you changed on my birthday."

My eyes widened and for the longest while, it was silent as his words settled over us. No one spoke; what could we say? He exhaled heavily, gazing out of the window.

"We had spent that night together and I had never been so happy in my life. But I only left for a few minutes and when I came back, you were gone. Afterwards, you iced me out. You never spoke properly to me, nor did you ever approach me for anything. It was like you became this completely different person. I spent endless nights and days wondering what I had done wrong, but every time I came to you, you turned me away. And then one day, you left and never came back."

I inhaled sharply, remembering, exactly what he was talking about. It was still painful whenever I thought about it, even for a brief second, like someone had twisted a knife in an open wound. Swallowing thickly, I couldn't find the words I had wanted to say. There was this heavy blanket of friction that smothered us, holding the words we wanted to say hostage… what do we do now?

"I don't know what to say," I revealed, twiddling with my hands. "I don't know how to fix this."

"I'm not expecting you to. All I ever wanted was the truth. That's all I ask for," he replied, gravely. "Can you give me that, Aria?"

"I…" I trailed off, my mouth failing to speak the words he wanted to hear.

"Answer me this, Aria," Nero began, steel blue eyes scrutinizing me. "I asked you before if it hurt when you left and you said it did. So why did you still go? Perhaps you were lying to me."

"Don't think for a second that it didn't hurt me to leave you," I urged. "Because it was the most painful thing that I have ever had to do. It was so, so difficult. It took every bit of strength that I had to not turn around and apologize for everything, because I knew I was hurting you. But I was so mad and blinded that I let my pride and my feelings control me," I didn't look at his reaction at my sudden proclamation and took a deep breath of air. "So, don't tell yourself that I wanted to. I didn't, not at all. But leaving you was the only way I could save myself."

"From what?" he exclaimed with wide eyes. "What did you have to save yourself from?"

"You!" I yelled, tearily. "I felt like I was drowning and, Nero, if I spent any longer in that house… God, I don't think I could've done it. My heart was bleeding in agony that I felt suffocated whenever I saw you."

I saw the anguish in his eyes, the vivid heartbreak that only caused my heart to shatter into fragments. He took a step towards me, and I told myself to move away but my body refused to listen, stilling as his hands ran down my arms until they entwined their fingers with mine.

"Why, Aria? What did I do to cause you this pain?" he asked, beseechingly. "What changed your mind about us? About the mafia? Where did you go?"

His melancholy cerulean eyes made me realize that Kira was right. This would always be a barrier in our relationship and the only way for us to finally move past it, was if I revealed everything to him. Although, I feared for the truth, I would never be happy with him until I learnt it. His eyes implored me to reveal the answer to the question that had resulted in sleepless nights. His touch had me quivering, my sobs held back as the tears ran down my face unwittingly. No amount of training or missions had prepared me for this day. Nothing could amount to how scared I was to reveal my deepest and innermost thoughts, all the secrets that I didn't share with him.

"Ariadne," he whispered, caressing the side of my face, tenderly, as a single tear ran down his cheek. "Why did my love leave me?"

I was scared.

I exhaled shakily as I spoke, praying that I wouldn't regret it, "It began when I woke up in the middle of the night alone…"

CHAPTER 36

always?

5 years ago
April

"Look, here she comes."
　　　"Oh, she looks just like her mother."
　　　"*Che Bella.*"
"Truly, a queen."

Don't trip. Look up. That's it. Now, smile. No, that smile looked stupid. Smile better. Well done. Don't forget to breathe. Okay, try not to breathe so weirdly. Relax. You are officially the Don of the Italian mafia.

"May I present Aria Moretti of the Moretti family."

My name vibrated out of the speakers, booming across the beautiful Plaza as I made my grand entrance, dressed in the most stunning champagne gown that glittered under the lights which illuminated the room. I wasn't used to receiving special treatment, but as I wandered throughout the venue, I heard waves of praises. Nero had clearly outdone himself with his preparations and meticulous attention to detail. An ethereal accent of gold adorned every inch of the venue, tables decorated with large bouquets of white roses entwined in gold-painted leaves. I was mindful of the hundreds of eyes following me, giving me their total attention as I passed. I, for one, relished this dream-inducing occasion and the scrutiny of my esteemed guests. I easily pinpointed all the guests, successfully separating the Yakuza from the Triads, and the Russian mob, where my aunt and uncle where seated, to the wealthiest people in the world, to the Italian mafia, where Nero was. I saw my mother amidst the crowd, beaming at me as she clutched onto my father's arm. My father looked stoic as ever except I could easily read him, and behind that cold exterior, he was holding back tears. I sent a small smile in his direction which he mirrored. Finally, my gaze settled on Nero, who waited at the front. His eyes were wide as he took me in, stealing my breath away. I couldn't fight the smile taking over my face when he took my hand softly, helping me onto the stage.

"You look beautiful, Ari," he murmured, then took a few steps back.

I shot him a grin before turning to the crowd, indifferent to how many people were here for me. I couldn't believe the time had come. I was to become the Don to the one of the most powerful mafias in the entire world. Before my aunt, a woman running the mafia was virtually unimaginable, but she had proven that she was capable of doing what men could do and better. Here I stood, the gaze of the unknown danger and opportunities scrutinizing me, as I made myself known to the world that had I spent years training for. Yet, despite the years of training, I couldn't help but feel anxious and unsure of my capability as a leader. I was afraid, constantly wondering who I could trust, and who I couldn't. As I stared into the crowd, I felt suffocated by my fears.

"I can't express my gratitude enough for everyone who has taken their time to celebrate with me. I vow my life to the *familia*, to my family, and all my friends, to uphold all the necessities which allow me to stand on this stage in front of many great leaders like yourselves," I tried not to flinch when my voice boomed out of the speakers, smiling prettily to the crowd.

"A toast," Nero bellowed, my eyes shifting to him, as he raised a glass of bubbly in my direction. The fears within me silenced but only temporarily as I found myself lost in his deep blue eyes. His lips coiled into a smirk, blue eyes twinkling as he said, "To Ariadne."

"To Ariadne!" Everyone cheered, before clinking their glasses.

But I was too entranced by Nero, as he shot me a wink, downing the drink all at once. Eventually, the worst part of these events came about, the rounds you had to make, the fake conversations and smiles to people who would probably stab you in the back in a second. I would need more than two hands to count the amount of people who wouldn't even blink as they put a bullet in my head.

"It's so great to see you, Mr. Ito," I greeted, shaking his hand. The Japanese man wore this expression that would have had people running for the hills before it transformed into a smile.

"Oh, Aria. It's my greatest pleasure," he replied, eagerly. "You've grown into a very fine woman indeed. Antonio must be incredibly proud."

I chuckled. "I do hope so or I'd have no idea why he finally passed the reigns over to me."

Mr. Ito laughed, gleefully, holding his stomach which briefly reminded me of Santa Claus. After speaking with him for a while, I began to make my way through the crowd, welcoming all my guests. The Triads were infamous for never attending these events, but dad must have pulled a few strings to get some of them to attend, which was no easy feat. They watched me from a distance, their glares burning holes in my back, but I refused to allow them to affect me, greeting them last.

"Aria," Mr... Zhao greeted, a smaller frame compared to most, but I knew underneath his neatly pressed suit were knives and guns, which he could skillfully employ in a matter of seconds. "Thank you for inviting us."

"Of course, Mr... Zhao."

"I apologize on behalf of Sir Wang. He, unfortunately, was too caught up with work that he was unable to attend tonight's event."

The apology was insincere, but I smiled, politely, shaking my head as I responded, "Please, it's an honor that you were able to attend. How is your daughter? I hope she is well."

Mr. Zhao stiffened. "Yes. She is fine indeed. Her travels have been going well, thankfully, and I do hope it remains that way."

"Of course," I smiled, coyly. Noticing Nero's piercing gaze from afar, I quickly said, "Excuse me. I hope you enjoy the rest of your evening."

"You too, dear."

I made my way through the crowd, slipping in between people, sending a smile whenever someone called my name until I reached my destination – until I stood in front of him. He brought the champagne to his lips which curled into a haughty smirk as he settled his searing hot gaze onto me.

"Are you trying to escape already?" he joked.

I was not amused, taking his champagne glass and finishing it off before he could even complain. I was feeling extra confident, knowing what I wanted and when. I had no intention of delaying this fiery need nestled within me. And from the look in his eyes, neither did he.

I spun on my heels, shooting him a smirk, my words laced with sultry intent, "Follow me."

It wasn't a question. It was an order. And who was he to refuse an order? Like an obedient solider, he chased after me, hot on my heels as we strode down the empty corridors until the sound of music disappeared and all that was left was our heavy breathing. I wasn't oblivious to the signs; I knew he wanted me too, but I was fed up waiting for him to act on it. The urge to have him was overwhelming to the point I felt like I would explode if I continued to bury it deep down inside of me. After months of playing cat and mouse, I needed to have more than a playful kiss here and there. I knew the Plaza like the back of my hand, having been here for several important occasions, so I already had a room booked for me. I planned tonight out carefully whilst Nero was busy with the event. In the elevator, up to the top floor, I laughed as he pressed me against the metal walls, his lips finding their path from my shoulders to my neck until they wavered over my lips – *hesitantly*.

"Are you sure?" he whispered, cerulean eyes finding mine. Lovingly, he reached out, cradling my head. "I want you to be sure."

I wasn't sure how strong my feelings were towards him, but I knew I wanted him. And that was enough. Unzipping my dress from the side, I answered, "If I want anyone to be my first, Nero, I want it to be you."

He inhaled sharply as the dress pooled around my feet, revealing the beautiful lingerie hidden underneath. His eyes mesmerized, and memorized me as if I was a piece of art, hands tracing down the contours of my body, not leaving a single curve untouched. Then he looked up.

"God, you're so fucking beautiful," he murmured, before colliding his lips against mine.

I always wondered what he tasted like but at that moment, my coherent thoughts disappeared as I immersed myself in his touch, relishing in the warmth and the sparks that set off throughout my body as if it was the fourth of July. I moaned against his skillful lips; my breath was stolen like a successful heist. My fingers playing with his hair whilst his hands skimmed down my body, drawing me closer until there was no space between us. The elevator door opened but we didn't realize, lost in our heated passion. He broke away first, giving me a rueful smile, before swooping me into his arms, a gasp of surprise leaving my lips. I erupted into fits of giggles as he impatiently stormed through the empty suite like a man on a mission. When he found the bedroom, I didn't have time to bask in the beauty of the decor as he dropped me onto the soft cloud-like bed, towering over me as he was shedding his shirt and blazer.

My breath hitched, my hands trailing down his painted, chiseled chest, tracing the outline of the scars hidden under black ink. "Why do you hide them?"

"They aren't hidden," he responded, his blue eyes darkening when they met mine. "They're embraced."

Before I could question him any further, he kissed me once more and stole my last thought, as I blissfully submitted to his dominance.

*

May

"Happy birthday," I giggled, waking up a sleepy Nero with a broad smile and a cake in hand. His eyes groggily peered open, settling onto me as he acknowledged what was happening. Then he smiled.

"Come here," he murmured, gruffly, his bed voice doing things to me that I never thought possible. I carefully placed the cake onto the side and crawled over to him, straddling his lap. "Give me a kiss."

"No, we'll end up in this room all day, knowing you. And your party is tonight."

"Just one kiss."

I shook my head. "I haven't brushed my teeth."

"Who fucking cares?" he grumbled, shifting into a seated position. "I'm the birthday boy," When I didn't cave, he pouted. "Please, baby."

Damn it.

I sighed, pecking his lips but he took quick advantage of that, one hand resting on the back of my head and the other on the curve of my back, pressing me right up against him, as his tongue darted into my mouth, drawing out a loud moan. He grunted, moving his hand in

313

between my legs until they found their location, nestled warmly within me. I couldn't resist him, allowing him to play with my body like a doll. I was always startled by how readily I surrendered to him, his dominance consuming me in ways I never imagined. He was addictive; I wanted him night and day. He worshipped me like a temple, carefully tending to my needs and wants whilst mercilessly bringing me to the highest amount of pleasure attainable.

And just like that, I was putty in his hands.

We spent all morning together, under the bedsheets, in the bathroom, leaving no corner of the room untainted by our love. And when we were done, he stared at me affectionately, tucking a strand of hair behind my ear, as he whispered, "*Sempre*, Aria. I am yours."

I smiled. "*Sempre*, Nero."

I knew at some point we would have to leave the room and when we eventually did, I managed to hurry back and quickly dress up for his party. I was so excited, adrenaline coursed through me, as I changed into a blue evening gown, embellished in delicate flowers and sapphires that reminded me of his eyes. After touching up my makeup, there was a knock on my door and I grinned, opening it to see Nero, handsomely wearing a navy suit that brought out those astonishing eyes of his.

He couldn't look away, mouth wide open as words failed to leave his lips. Amused, I entwined our fingers together, trying to ignore the shot of heat which electrocuted me. "Hey, birthday boy."

"Fuck, Aria. Let's just stay home tonight," he pleaded, like a man begging to God.

I laughed, gleefully. "Shut up. It's your birthday and we are going to celebrate it properly."

He didn't agree, sulking as I dragged him downstairs where everyone was waiting. The place was decorated exactly how I envisioned it, colors of blue and silver taking over the Estate with festive joy. Nero stopped sulking as everyone cheered when we descended the stairs, his eyes broad in surprise before softening when they fell onto me.

"You did this?" he asked, quietly.

"Happy birthday, *amore*," I replied, answering his question with a simple smile.

Lost in each other's gaze, canisters filled with confetti exploded, silver streamers cascading their way onto the floor as everyone cheered Nero's name. It was like a movie and the only person I could see was him. His blue eyes sparkled with blithe as he gently pressed his lips against my knuckles. I almost gave in to his offer but thought against that decision, allowing him to spend the rest of the night with the people we called our family. The entire night felt surreal to me. The music pounded out of the speakers, causing the ground to vibrate but no one cared as they drank and danced to their heart's content. Nero surprised me as he took me into the middle of the living room, spinning me around, before twirling me into his arms. He rocked me, our eyes never separating as we danced with our hearts. Then, he gently kissed my forehead, and I savored the sensation. He was forever mine, and I was his. We didn't need to say the words, we just knew. Everyone was lost in the sound of the music that no one focused on us, no one saw how our bodies moved in sync, as if we were making love, or how he mouthed *'tonight,'* his promise causing my body to buzz in excitement. When the night was over and after we had said our goodbyes, we disappeared upstairs, but everyone knew where we were going and what we were going to do. We couldn't hide the sexual tension that blanketed over us, nor did we want to.

He wasted no time in shedding the dress off my body and leaving love bites against my skin that I would, sooner or later, want to be rid of. He spoke promises that I would later find out were false. He made love to me, that I later saw as a betrayal. He stole my heart and I never saw it again. When I woke up, it was 3 a.m. and the space beside me was empty. I frowned, wondering where he had disappeared to when I heard low whispering outside of the room. I should not have listened, I should have stayed in bed, but my curiosity got the best of me and before I knew it, I pressed my body against the wall, the door slightly cracked open, allowing me to see the two men standing underneath the dim lights.

"Nero, you know you are better suited to be the leader," someone said, a voice I recognised that belonged to Konstantin, a member on the Board of Directors. My heart sunk and I knew I should have walked away but I couldn't.

"This is ridiculous," Nero grunted. "You could get your tongue cut off for that."

"You're not even denying it, Nero," he chuckled. "You know what I am saying is true. Pretend if you must, but you know that Aria could never lead."

"You're wasting my time, Konstantin. What did you come for?"

"You, good sir. You are the future of the Italian mafia. Not her. She's a woman; men will never bow down to the weaker gender. But you... You could lead the Italian mafia. Don't you agree?"

"My patience is running thin," Nero replied, coldly, but that was not the answer I wanted to hear.

Konstantin laughed and I could almost hear the smirk in his voice when he spoke, "Are you telling me all those plans you made with me weren't to overtake her?"

"You need to leave," Nero responded, but I heard the hesitance, an indication that he did not want me to find out about this conversation.

"Aria is afraid and it's showing in her lack of leadership, Nero. She thinks too much with her heart; she will never be capable of leading because she cares too much. This family is going to fall apart under her reign, I promise. You are the only light in this tunnel of darkness. Isn't that what you told me a few months ago? I was surprised when you didn't go through with your plans to overthrow her on the day she became the Don, but then again, it clearly seems your feelings have gotten... *confused*," Konstantin snickered, gesturing to the bedroom. "I said it then and I'll say it again, I will only support you, Nero Russo, as the boss for the Italians."

"The amount of faith you have in me is flattering but misdirected," Nero said, frostily.

"Please, you know you're only with her for the title," Konstantin scoffed. I waited for Nero to say something, dispute against such a seditious statement but when he didn't, my heart halted. Betrayal tasted bitter on my tongue. "I'm saying this as a friend. I've known you and Aria for a very long time, watching you grow up from young pups. Aria is indeed a strong woman, but her heart is too soft, too weak – she'll never survive if thrown to a pack of wolves. If I can see that you're a better fit for the Italian mafia, how long will it take for *your* men to as well?"

"That is enough, Konstantin."

But he didn't stop there and took a step towards Nero, arching his brow, throwing one last dagger at my heart, "Must I remind you that you are engaged to my daughter? Or is that another plan you choose to ignore in order to continue living in this fantasy world with Aria?"

My heart sunk.

I didn't want to listen anymore; I couldn't bear it. My heart broke into unmendable shards, and I felt like I couldn't breathe. I felt betrayed, angry, but most importantly, heartbroken. Was it true? Was he only with me to take away my title? Was everything a lie? My body worked before my mind, gathering my clothes, and disappearing out of his room through a passage that only I knew of. I felt suffocated, needing to get out of this Estate as quickly as possible. All my fears and the constant state of paranoia I experienced, came true and all I wanted to do was to run as far away as possible. Everything began to collapse and the world looked extremely bleak. I wasn't sure when I started crying but I couldn't stop, pouring my broken heart out. I just saw red, running down corridor after corridor, until I found myself outside of the mansion, the cold air greeting me despite it being the middle of spring. Like pathetic fallacy, the sky groaned before the rain poured down, drowning out my sobs of pain. I must have been outside for a while. Soaked from head to toe. But I had stopped crying. And all that was left, was a girl without a heart. Blankly staring out into the distance, I promised I would never give my heart away.

Ever again.

*

June

"What is wrong with you?" Nero hissed, as he stormed after me. "Aria."

I sighed, tiredly, slipping into my bedroom before beginning to discard the clothing I had worn last night. I couldn't remember the events of last night, but I was sore between my legs and that was all the answers I needed. Nero fumed, slamming the door behind him with so much force that it shook the room. I wish I was bothered enough to deal with him, but I couldn't care less, staring indifferently at him as I threw a shirt over my naked body.

"What?" I asked.

"*What?* Is that all you have to say?" he sneered, coldly.

"What do you want me to say?"

"Maybe begin with what has happened because I haven't seen you properly over the last month and when I do, you're entwined with some other guy or in a random hotel room."

"I'm a big girl, Nero. I can take care of myself," I chuckled, icily. "Can you leave or are you enjoying this strip show?"

"If I wanted to see a strip show, I'd go to a club," he spat back. I didn't blink, cocking a brow and shrugging at his answer. He exhaled, infuriated, running his fingers through those thick locks which I craved to touch. I resisted. He was a liar. Then he glanced over at me, tired eyes pleading me. "What happened? This isn't like you."

"You're not my boyfriend, Nero. Stop acting like it, it's unbefitting of you," I responded, frostily.

I saw the hurt in his eyes; he didn't bother hiding it. My heart pained at the sight of them until I reminded myself what had happened, what he had done. He was going to betray me, steal my heritage, break my heart. Not if I got there first. I was not going to be vulnerable. Never again. For the longest time, no one said anything as we stared in each other's eyes, as if we were hoping they would give the answers we wanted to hear. Only, how could I ask him when my heart was exposed under his control? Then, he straightened his back, rolling his shoulders before masking on a look of indifference.

"I promise, Aria, if you keep acting like this, you're going to lose me," he vowed before he left, abandoning me with the empty silence that reminded me what I could not trust anyone – not even my best friend.

The day I turned nineteen was lonelier than I had hoped for. I drowned the feelings that haunted me with all forms of alcohol and drugs. Sex became like nothing to me. My body was abused until I felt numb. Yet, I couldn't help but hope that he didn't forget. That he would come back to me one more time but when he didn't, my last piece of hope disappeared down the drain. Instead, I found him in the club, tangled with two other girls in skimpy outfits. He had the biggest smile on his face as they peppered him with kisses whilst he snorted another line of coke off another girl's stomach. My lips curled in disgust; I had the urge to tear off their pretty little heads from their bodies, and then break Nero into small pieces of nothing. However, I ignored that dull weight in my stomach and curled my fingers into a fist until my knuckles went white. Turning away from the scene, I stormed out of the club, barging past people but they all moved out of my way, noticing the fury that was emanating off me. I was sure if anyone stopped me, they would not have lived. Except, there was only one person who would take the risk; he called my name as I escaped out of the smothering club, tears threatening to fall despite my best attempts at prevention. I was out on the busy streets when a hand curled around my wrist, holding me captive which forced me to glance back. Oceanic eyes as warm as the summer air held me hostage with such an intense gaze that I found them difficult to look away from.

"*Ari*," he blew out, his chest heaving as he tried to catch his breath. "Aria, please."

"Let go of me," I said, emotionlessly, but my eyes betrayed me.

"No," he shook his head. "I'm not letting you go."

His words meant more than just the act of releasing me. He was desperate, I saw it in his eyes. He wanted to save me, but I was too far gone, drowning in a pit of misery that I carried on my shoulders like heavyweights.

I swallowed, prying his hand off me. "Let me go. I have a plane to catch."

"Aria, please," he begged, his voice cracking. "I'm sorry. I'm sorry. Whatever I did, I'm so sorry. Just stop running away!"

"You have no idea!" I snapped before pausing, trying to pull myself together before I spoke again but more calmly, "You have no idea how hard it is to see the face of someone you once cared so much about every single day," Before he could speak, I wiped away the tears that had managed to escape. "But you know what's even harder?"

I waited for a moment, wanting this to hurt him as much as this hurt me. He didn't reply, his blue eyes were watery with unshed tears.

"Seeing a stranger where you once had a home," I continued, even though my heart was crying to be held in his arms. The town car parked up in front of the club and my driver waited patiently for me to enter but for some reason, I couldn't move.

"Aria don't leave me. I'm begging you. Please, don't go," he cried, practically falling onto his knees as he reached out for me, but I stepped back, pursing my lips and steeling my heart.

"Goodbye, Nero," I replied, before disappearing into the car.

He didn't chase after me.

*

September

"What the fuck did you say?" I growled down the phone to Melissa, as she informed me that one of the cargos had been stolen.

"Last night. There was a hit during the transport," she repeated; the shakiness in her voice bothered me.

"What did they take?"

She replied, a minute later, "Weapons."

"For fuck's sake!" I exclaimed, slamming my fist onto the desk with pure rage. I inhaled sharply, pinching my nose as I tried to calm myself. "Who did it?"

"We aren't sure who did it; they were very meticulous and left no trace, but we are working our best to find out."

"Clearly not fucking enough," I snarled. "This is the third time this month. *This month*. I want names, Melissa. Give me fucking names."
I cut the phone before she could reply and grabbed the closest object next to me, throwing it against the wall in frustration. The ornament shattered as it collided with the wall, causing some of the plaster to break, pieces of rubble left on my carpet which I knew I would have to inform housekeeping about. I knew I had to manage my temper before my dinner meeting but as I prepared myself, I could not help but get random outbursts of irritation, which would result in another broken object in my hotel room. By the time I was ready, the room was in a state of mayhem, and I made a mental note to notify the front desk to send housekeeping to clear up the mess and pay for any damages I had created. The coldness bit against my skin when I left the hotel in London. A fur coat shielded me from the chilly autumn air whilst I waited for the car to arrive. Unfortunately, for both me and the guests I was entertaining, I had little patience today. I knew my irritation would be further irked when I remember that the men I was meeting were a bunch of misogynistic pieces of shit that my father refused to meet. I had a duty as his daughter to take his place, but I didn't like that. Nevertheless, I buried any complaints I had and practiced the fake smile that would be my mask for tonight's event.

Then I saw her. A girl, no younger than me, with bloodshot eyes filled with terror as she stumbled down the road, barely dressed suitably for the icy weather. She caught glimpse of me and turned away, but I was quicker, closing the distance.

"Are you okay?" I asked. She flinched; whether it was from the cold or the sound of my voice, I couldn't tell.

"Yes," her answer was abrupt and certain.

I knew I shouldn't have believed her, but I was late and, against my better judgement, I bobbed my head in disbelief before heading towards my car as it arrived. I glanced back, memorizing her features, noting that she looked battered and bruised as she stumbled into a man's arms a few minutes later. I should have stayed with her, but I didn't. How was I supposed to know that she would change my life forever? During dinner, I could not tear my focus away from the girl with the big blue eyes that lit up under the moonlight. She briefly reminded me of Nero and after that, I did not think of her again. The men around the table smoked their cigars after finishing their meal, whilst I patiently sipped on my wine. Every time I reached for the wine to refill my glass, someone would stop me and pour it for me.

"A lady shouldn't pour her own drink," Mr. Sullivan stated. I said my thanks through clenched teeth, praying for this nightmare to be over.

"Thank you once again for spending tonight with us, Aria," Mr. Bradford chuckled. "It's been an absolute delight."

"It's been a pleasure. But I must thank you for tonight," I lied right through my pearly white teeth.

They would be stupid if they couldn't tell. This entire night pissed me off; three hours of sitting with them whilst they spoke about the many women they had slept with, or the clubs with the newest strippers they had attained, or their wives, who many saw as dolls. I felt sick and had the itching urge to blow their brains out.

"Although I am surprised by your attendance, especially after last night's escapade," Mr. De Loughery commented.

My eyes iced as they flickered over to him. "I'm sorry?"

He inhaled the thick cigar, blowing out a large puff of smoke before responding, the smirk clearly hidden in his voice, "I heard that one of your cargos on the way to Greece was stolen. Any idea who was behind it?"

I replied, tentatively, "Unfortunately not."

"What a pity. I hope it wasn't a lot," Mr. Hawthorne frowned.

"Thankfully, nothing of much worth and easy expendable. Just like some humans. Wouldn't you agree, Mr. De Loughery?" I levelled my gaze at him, taking him back for a split second, before he simpered, nodding in agreement.

"Of course, dear."

"I'd be eternally grateful if anyone has any information on these attacks," I smiled, prettily.

Mr. Grimaldi leaned forward, drawing his brows together, as he spoke in his thick French accent, "I'm not sure if this is of any help but I have heard rumors about this new group forming. The Serpents, I believe they call themselves. Ruthless men who are involved in the drug and trafficking business. I, for one, would never find myself tangled with such men but perhaps that's where you should start your hunt."

I knew Mr. Grimaldi was threatened by this group rather than disagreeing with their forms of business. He just wanted me to do his dirty work. The men on the table began to chatter amongst themselves after hearing this report, but I leaned back in my chair, crossing my arms over my chest, as I leisurely sipped on my wine, basking in this newfound information. Suddenly, my mind flashed back to the girl I had seen earlier on this evening and for a second, I wondered whether the answer was closer to me than I had actually thought.

Some days, I pondered whether stumbling into Yakira was fate. Was it destiny calling me out? Or was it purely coincidental? Whatever it was, one thing was for sure: saving Kira was the beginning of a new start. For the Underground. For myself.

*

November

I didn't like the idea of leaving Kira in London, but she was adamant and practically forced me to return home to gather more information, whilst she stayed back and gathered the last few pieces of her life. After some time, I finally booked my ticket back to New York but the second I arrived, I instantly regretted it. I was not ready to see him. I was never going to be ready. The car took me through the busy city streets whilst the sky poured down, my head resting against the window, watching the buildings go by until we finally pulled up in front of an exceptionally large mansion that I knew was the Estate. It had been months since I last was here; I wondered how much must have changed during my disappearance. I could see security had been tightened by the additional snipers pinpointed at various locations around the Estate, until every acre of the land was guarded. It looked like a fortress built to keep someone in. I wondered if they intended for that someone to be me.

The front door opened and the man with cobalt eyes walked out.

He looked older, more mature, having grown a beard that made him look incredibly sexy. Dressed in a neatly pressed suit, he tucked one hand into his pocket whilst the other held a cigar. Inhaling, he blew out a puff of smoke as his eyes scrutinized me when I got out of the car. There were no signs of acknowledgement or happiness, something I desperately wanted him to have, instead he sent me a brief nod, frostily, dismissing my appearance. There was this stinging pain in my heart which concealed something else that I was struggling to pinpoint. My throat contracted and I pasted on the best indifferent expression that I could muster. Taking a few steps up those marble stairs had me hold my breath. It felt like hours had gone by until I finally stood in front of him.

He loomed over me, arching a dark brow, as he said, "Aria."

"How have you been, Nero?" I asked, ignoring his unfriendly tone. I moved past him, entering the Estate, trying to resist the urge to run into his traitorous arms. "I've been getting reports monthly from Melissa and Matteo. I'm glad you've been able to hold the fort so naturally. It's almost as if you were born to be a leader."

If he heard the double meaning, he didn't show it. "Someone had to," I wanted him to shout, scream, fight but he responded passively, his eyes staring blankly at me. "Why are you back?"

"I'm the Don of this *familia*."

"Are you?" his question threw me off guard, my eyes widening in surprise.

I quickly recovered, scoffing as I rolled my eyes. "What kind of question is that? I'll be in my office. I don't want to be disturbed."

"Of course. Whatever you want, Ariadne," he answered, satirically. I clenched my jaw, holding his icy gaze for the longest time before I finally looked away, swallowing the words I wanted to say. "I'm sure you know where the office is."

"Yes."

"I think it's best we end it here," he suddenly declared. I arched a brow in confusion, waiting for him to continue. "A person can only love someone for so long."

Giving one short nod, he strode away. I stood there, impassive, and expressionless, but I swear my heart shattered. A few seconds later, I marched in the opposite direction. Walking away, I felt the distance between us enlarge until there was no point of return. I wanted him to do something, waiting for him to take back what he said but he was done loving me, and I realized that I had only just begun.

"How is London?" I asked Yakira, one evening whilst I was in my office, solitude suffocating me to the point where I was desperate for companionship. But my only friend was 3,500 miles away from me.

"Lonely," Yakira sighed.

"Same here."

There was a long minute of silence. Neither one of us spoke, savoring the comfort of each other's tranquility.

"When are you returning home?" she asked. *Home.* One single word with thousands of meanings attached to it. It was then that I realized the Estate was no longer my home.

I placed my pen down and sunk back in the chair, staring at the ceiling, absentmindedly. "Hopefully, before the end of the year. I have a lot to do here before I return. I didn't realize how much the mafia would be affected due to my lack of presence."

"What about that Nero dude?" she muttered.

"What about him?"

"Did he not fill in the gap you created?"

I sighed. "Yes. And he did a good job at it."

"Perhaps you can leave it in his hands," she suggested.

"Perhaps I can."

My short answers were beginning to bother her, and I could tell as she exhaled, heavily, an indication of her irritation. "Aria, what's wrong?"

"Nothing. I'm just really lonely here and I don't know who to trust anymore," I replied, honestly.

"Neither do I, but I'm willing to trust you, so you should do the same."

I didn't respond to her words and decided to switch the conversation, questioning, "When you were younger, what were your parents like?"

Kira chuckled. A bitter chuckle. "My parents. That's a question indeed."

"I'm sorry," I frowned. "Are they dead?"

"No," then she corrected herself, "At least, not my stepfather,"

"And your mother?"

"She died. Committed suicide a couple of months after my stepfather decided to sell her to the highest bidder. He claimed that she was so madly in love with him, when in fact, she saw the monster he truly was. I don't blame her; my actual father sold us to him to repay his debt."

"Is your stepfather the same person who gave you to those men I saved you from a few months ago?" I murmured, after a moment.

"Yes," she responded, after a pregnant pause. "My stepfather intended on marrying me to this man weeks before you had found me."

"Marry? You were going to be forced into a marriage? Do you know who?" I asked, curiously, noting that this was the most Kira had ever revealed to me in one conversation.

"Some man, apparently he was very wealthy and powerful," Kira's voice lacked emotions and my heart faltered, knowing that she had suffered so much. "Konstantin used me like a doll."

Then my breathing stopped. My eyes widened and the world silenced. My silence must have concerned Kira, as she said, "Aria, are you still there?"

"Did you say Konstantin?" I whispered the question I wasn't sure I wanted the answer to.

"Yes, my stepfather was called Konstantin Romanov."

I had considered that Kira's past could not get any worse, until it suddenly did. I was a fool not to dig deeper into Konstantin's past, to search for the girl who was engaged to the only man I would ever love. And here she was, a hostage to these men's cruel games and gambles. But what I feared the most was that Nero was also one of those men.

*

December

The Serpents were more fucked up than I thought. I had arrived in New York over a month ago and drowned my feelings out by investing my time in discovering every little thing there was to know about the Serpents. My office was a mess, sheets of paper scattered across the room, files stacked on top of one another, my responsibilities for the mafia discarded to one side. I knew I was being foolish to ignore my duties as the Don, but I couldn't help but question whether being the Don was my calling. The more I learnt about the Serpents, the more I found myself distancing away from my roots. I failed to see how dark and twisted the Underground really was and I nearly allowed myself to ignore it just like every other person of power. It was 4 a.m., and the Estate was tranquil. I had ended my call with Kira, who was still in London, building up a reliable source of networking, whilst I addressed my duties in New York. Except, during my time here, I couldn't tear my focus away from the Serpents and finally realized the decision I had to make. It was either the mafia or the Serpents. Though, how could I turn away from my birthright? The responsibility I had been brought up to take. But how could I turn a blind eye to the disgusting actions of the Serpents that would only continue to grow if no one put a stop to them? Who was to say they wouldn't come after the mafia next? The decision was clear, and I made it without thinking twice. I had booked a one-way ticket to London in secret, but I knew there was one last obstacle I had to face before I could leave this part of my life behind. And it wore striking aquamarine eyes.

I heard his thundering footsteps before they even reached outside my office door. The door flung open, and he strode in with a glare that could put anyone six feet under. I wasn't the slightest bit affected, staring at him, impassively, as he slammed the door behind him before closing the distance between us.

"I don't get this sudden change of mood," he snarled in frustration, slamming his fists onto my desk. "Who have you met, Aria? Who is causing you to act so irresponsibly?"

"I said," I responded, coldly, clenching my jaw. "I don't want to talk about it. Now get the fuck out."

He wore nothing but a pair of sweatpants, standing in front of me in all his glory, with a glower that would have had people running for their lives. Once upon a time, that look would have made me fall to my knees and submit to his inner desires. For a split second, I wanted to do so. Only, I remembered how blinded I once was that I couldn't see the betrayal festering behind my back, and all those longing feelings vanished, along with my patience. I wanted to break him into the pieces that created his chiseled body and though my hand itched for blood, I swallowed the anger and knew I had to play this game carefully. I almost laughed when I realized his wishes of becoming the Don would come true as soon as I left – what a cruel twist of fate. Coolly, dismissing him, I refocused on the situation at hand, finally pinpointing out the main leaders of the Serpents – men who called themselves the Inner Circle. They were going to be their own destruction.

"Why are you so interested in this group?" he interrogated. ""You waste so much time and energy on them – a small, unknown organization – that you aren't even focusing on your own family, Ariadne."

"Are you questioning my authority?" I arched a brow, questioningly, but the use of my government name had me wanting to reach for my dagger and shove it into his eye.

I was violent, but he made me volatile.

The blueness of his eyes shone, vibrantly, as his lips coiled into a dark scowl. "No. I am not. I just want an explanation for your sudden change in behavior. You disappear for months and upon returning, you suddenly aren't interested in the Italians, handing over your duties to me and Matteo as if they are not of importance."

"I'm sure you're very happy about that," I wanted to laugh.

He frowned. "What?"

Not wanting to speak to him any further, I exhaled. "Russo, I don't need to explain myself to anyone," My words were laced with a deadly reminder of who he was talking to. "*Especially, you.*"

"And you seem to have forgotten that I'm not just anybody."

"Yes, I can see that," I murmured, more to myself than to him. My lips curled into a wicked smirk as I asked, rhetorically, "Shall I remind you of your place?"

I glanced up seductively at him, under my dark lashes, as he towered over my desk, his blue eyes wavered slightly, mesmerized by my appearance, seeing as I was only wearing a satin chemise that revealed much of the skin that it covered. The blush rising from my cheeks and threatening to spread to my neck, as I tossed my low ponytail over my shoulder.

Then he surprised me as he responded, daring me, "Amuse me, Aria."

There was a taunt in his words, a tease in his sentence, and I knew he was trying to push me to my limits. Except, I had no limits, and he would never win in a game with me. No one was more powerful than me. So, I moved around my desk and closed the distance between us. I caught the surprise in his eyes before it disappeared when my fingers crawled behind his neck and played with his dark hair. He had taken a step back but stopped when my hands wandered to his tattoos. I caught a glimpse of new ink during our little drunken escapade a few weeks ago. I shouldn't have allowed myself to get so tipsy but upon returning to the Estate, I found Nero in the same state. I found him in his bedroom and asked whether he loved me or not. Granted, I was disappointed when he didn't beg for me to love him, though I shouldn't have expected anything else. So, I vowed to never love him again.

Brushing my icy lips against his ear, I felt him shudder when I purred, "I'm your Queen, Nero. Bow down to your Queen."

I didn't give him a moment to comprehend my words, bringing him to his knees in a matter of seconds. No matter how much he tried to resist my influence, it was never enough. I controlled him easily, his bewildered eyes watching me in fascination as if I was the goddess of love. Then I bit my lower lip and leaned my frame against the desk as his hand wandered up my legs until they reached my waist. Cerulean eyes blackened and I saw his jaw clamp, heeding the intimacy of the situation. Yet… he didn't stop. I wondered how far I could push him, how far I could go, but I remembered not to underestimate him, because he knew all my inner desires and, despite my best attempts, even I couldn't help but want him for one more night.

Tonight, I would give him everything he wanted, what he needed – *Me*. But, tomorrow, he would forget I ever existed.

Deliberately slowly, I pushed my legs apart, the shock in his eyes was comical but the lust that soon followed was more so. Like putty in my hands, he carelessly submitted to my silent requests.

"Aria…" Words faded into the air, as his strong hands discovered the curves of my body, disappearing underneath the thin piece of material that was begging to be torn off by this beast.

"*Sempre*, Nero," I reminded him, clutching onto the desk whilst watching him under hooded eyes. I couldn't slow my breathing when his fingers found their destination, moving in a sluggish and torturous rhythm. "Your Queen, *sempre*."

"Yes," he grunted, infatuated by my soft cries of pleasure. "*Sempre*, Ariadne."

I'm sorry – I wanted to say, but the words never left my lips. One day they would. But not tonight. Tonight, I was going to make sure he would never forget his place or who I was. Tonight, he was going to remember Ariadne Moretti, and then tomorrow, he would forget I ever existed.

*

Nero

I woke up. Alone. In a bedroom that wasn't mine. I frowned, trying to figure out where I was and how I got there. Except, I couldn't remember last night. I sat up, furrowing my brows, as I frantically tried to remember anything – a name, a feature, a touch – but I couldn't remember anything. My body was heavy as if I had been drugged, and I knew for sure, the second I stood up, stumbling with a heavy head, that whoever stole my memories was very selective as I could only remember bits of the last few months. There were moments of my life that were unreachable, frustrating me as I tried my best to remember. I noticed I was barely clothed and quickly gathered my things in the partially empty room before coming to a halt when I saw a note stuck on the door.

I'm sorry.

– A

The handwriting looked familiar, the way the *'A'* had been written was something I had seen before, but I couldn't pinpoint where it was from. My heart sunk and this wave of sadness hit me as if I was missing something important in my life. Though, I didn't know what it was. Or potentially who it was. Sending one last longing glance at the master bedroom, I closed the door behind me and ventured through the corridor until I found my room. While showering, I noticed scratches and love bites across my body which could only mean that I was with someone last night. But I couldn't put a face to the person. I growled, punching the wall in frustration, which ultimately resulted in a bloody fist. Sighing, blearily, I cleaned the wound without flinching, dressing it up in bandages as soon as I got out of the shower. Whilst I changed, I tried to put together the pieces but there was always something missing. I hated that I couldn't remember anything. Finally, I made my way downstairs, wondering if Matteo could be of any help but he looked stressed himself, surrounded by a group of our men as they all spoke in a heated discussion. One of them saw me first, gesturing in my direction, which caused the rest of the guys to gaze over. Matteo's furrowed brows relaxed but only marginally as he rushed over to me, urgency laced in his voice when he spoke.

"Nero, fuck. Thank God you're here," he sighed in relief. I looked between him and the group of men in confusion, wondering what the uproar was about.

"What happened?" Matteo looked hesitant to speak at first, glancing back to the group of men who avoided my piercing gaze while I sought the answer I wanted. "Matteo?"

He swallowed before answering me, his voice carefully measured as if I would suddenly see red. "Aria is gone. She left early in the morning. Her stuff is all gone."

"Who?" I whispered, unfamiliar with the name.

However, I knew I heard it from somewhere. My head began to ache as I tried to remember something, anything which could explain the emptiness I was feeling. And then, all at once, my memories of last night came rushing back. Her smile, her touch, her lips, and her words. She had left, taking my memories of her with her. I couldn't remember everything, but I could remember last night. I could *only* remember last night.

Our last night.

My eyes widened as I finally figured out why my heart felt like a bullet had gone through it. But the only thing I could say was –

"Aria."

CHAPTER 37

so do i

We sat in silence. It hung in the air like the suspended moment before a falling glass shatters on the ground into thousands of splinters. It became a gaping void that needed to be filled with sounds, words, *anything*. It was poisonous in its nothingness, cruelly underscoring how melancholy our conversation had become. It was eerily unnatural, like dawn devoid of birdsong. Silence clung to us like a noxious cloud that at any moment could choke the life from us. Silence seeped into our pores, like a poison slowly paralyzing us from either speech or movement. The silence was the most terrifying part. And, yet we allowed the silence to suffocate us. The sun cracked over the skyline, reminding us of how much time we had spent talking, but also, at the same time, not talking. I had told him everything. From the beginning to the end. From the day I was crowned Don, to the day I heard of his betrayal to the night I saved Kira, and finally, the moment I discovered the Serpents and their horrendous crimes. Whilst I was speaking, he sat there, silently, and digested the information. I studied him, carefully, noting the way his eyes lit up, or dulled when I mentioned the night of his birthday. I had seen his brows draw together before relaxing in realization when he pieced together my intentions with the Serpents. It felt like a huge weight had lifted off my shoulders. To speak about everything that had happened in the last five years to someone other than Kira was somewhat freeing. I had explained my mission to end the Serpents, why they had to be stopped and why I had chosen this life over the one I should have had. He still didn't speak. And when I was finally done, I exhaled, shakily, and waited for him to finally say what was on his mind. Nero sat on the couch opposite me, the distance between us was vast and unbearable, but no one moved to try and close the gap. His eyes trained on the ground; hands clasped together as he hunched forward with a deep sigh, finally breaking the silence. I wanted to hear his words, but I feared that if they were the ones I ran away from, I would lose him forever. Then, slowly, he looked up.

"Aria, I never betrayed you," he began, calmly. "I would never betray you."

"What I heard, Nero –"

" – What you had heard was only part of the lie I had to set up for Konstantin."

I frowned, confusion cloaking my face. Nero's expression never changed as he gazed at me with numerous types of emotions, as if he couldn't figure out how he should feel. Eventually, they dispersed, and he chose heartbreak. His cobalt eyes glistened.

"Do you know why I had tracked Konstantin down and kept him imprisoned for so long?" he asked. When I didn't reply, he continued, "It was because he was going to betray you. Konstantin was on the Board of Directors, and he had full intentions of overthrowing you. When I heard about this, I falsely made claims to him about taking over your position. By gaining his trust, I was able to discover all the traps he had laid for you to fall into. Eventually, he discovered that I had no intention of becoming the Don and disappeared off the map, going into hiding. I spent months foiling his plans until he finally came out and approached me that night. Everything you heard happened, but what you didn't see was that we finally caught him. Before he could escape, we managed to capture him."

My eyes widened. "Why – why didn't you tell me?"

"Aria, you had so much on your plate after becoming the boss; I know I should have told you, but I kept it away from you because I knew how badly this would have affected you. I never wanted you to find out. You were so scared, and I wanted to do whatever I could to protect you."

"And your engagement?" My voice shook when I spoke. "Your arranged marriage to Yakira?"

"A farce. A trick. Misdirection," he explained. "I had never even met Kira until only recently. Konstantin spoke so much about her, but I had no intentions of marrying her. I only ever wanted to marry you."

"So, it was all a lie?" The truth was sour on my tongue.

He nodded, shamefully. I sucked in a deep breath of air.

"Why do you keep doing this?" My words sounded broken, as my heart began to swell and my tears began to well, as I stared at him. "Why do you keep hiding things from me?"

"I was trying to look out for you," he assured. "I'm sorry, Aria."

"You had no right to hide this from me. I was the Don – I *had* to know. You had no right."

I was angry and blinded by the years of pain I had to face all because of miscommunication… all because he wanted to protect me. I stepped back because I couldn't breathe, because I couldn't believe what I was hearing. He didn't tell because he didn't think I could handle it. So, he lied.

"You keep doing this to me," and then my voice started increasing in volume, until I was screaming, "You keep needing to protect me, to control me, but what you don't understand is that you can't always do that. And if you continue doing so, you'll risk putting all of us in danger. You don't ever just trust me!"

He stumbled onto his feet as he looked at me like he couldn't even believe I would suggest such a thing. "I do trust you!"

"Then, why did you hide this from me, Nero? Why are we in this position right now?"

"Because I was afraid!" he bellowed; I swear the entire building quaked at the sound of his roaring voice and the room fell silent. The air was lodged in my throat as he breathed, unevenly. Much more timidly, he repeated, "I was afraid that if I did, you would walk out of the door, and I wouldn't know if you would come back home."

"We spent our entire lives growing up learning to protect ourselves. Why can everyone but you trust that I can look after myself?"

"Because not everyone can see you like I do," was his response. The color of his eyes glistened with tears and staring at them felt like I was standing on the edge of the shoreline, watching the ocean crash against the sand. "I saw the frightened version of you – the one who wanted to run away and escape this life. I saw the truth and I saw the darkest parts of you – the ones you'd never admit to anyone, including yourself. I saw that girl. And it was that girl that I was trying to protect."

I didn't say anything for the longest second. "That girl is gone. She's been gone for a very long time."

"I know," he whispered, woefully. "I can see that now."

"Can you, Nero?" My lips quivered. "Because you're still trying to protect me from the truth."

"I…"

"You didn't trust me back then."

"Neither did you," he suddenly spat back, and I recoiled at the harshness. Nero laughed, bitterly. "Your immediate assumption was that I betrayed you, despite the fact that I continuously proved my loyalty. You never once confronted me. And when you ran away, you proved I was right in keeping this from you. So, I guess, both of us were wrong."

The truth slapped me in the face, and I found myself staggering back, unable to stand in front of him, knowing what I had known. He was right. I never confronted him. I chose to run away instead. I chose to cut him out. I chose to leave. There was this sudden wave of wrath that followed, but it didn't last when a rush of contriteness surged over me moments later. I had spent so many years running away from the truth, running away from him when all along he was just trying to protect me. My heart sunk. Whilst he had hurt me, I had hurt him for something that wasn't even happening. I pressed my eyes closed; my throat bobbed as I sunk into the seat with guilt heavy on my shoulders.

"Nero…" My words failed me, unable to leave my lips, but I needed to say something, anything. I needed to ask for his forgiveness, beg until he accepted it, but I couldn't. I didn't know how.

"I know, Aria," he murmured, a second later. I opened my eyes, finding his azure orbs watching me before they drifted elsewhere. "It's okay."

His face betrayed him. I knew it wasn't okay. How could it be? The way I had treated him was because I was a coward. It was unforgivable. There were times where my brain was completely fried. It was no excuse I know; I owned my behavior. My emotions had turned cold, fearful, anxious… I backed away, fled, and struck out at someone who loved me. I became someone who coldly isolated the one person who loved me the most. With my eyes trained on Nero, the fears I foolishly allowed to control me for so many years, that I chose to ignore, that I no longer could, came flooding back to me.

Remorseful. Guilty.

That was how I felt at that very moment. I wished for a time machine so I could go back and rectify the mistakes I had made. However, I couldn't. It was impossible. I had to live with it. Shame etched at my heart. Guilt gnawed like a worm at the core of an apple.

My voice cracked as I whispered, disjointedly, "I'm sorry too."

His eyes shifted over to me. "Aria…"

"*I am so sorry.* There are not enough words for me to describe how sorry I am. I was an idiot for not talking to you. I allowed my fears to get the best of me and I ran away. You were right. I was just so lost, and scared, that the mere thought of you betraying me had me spiraling out of control. And, God, Nero, I can't even express how sorry I am," I blurted out, before he managed to say anything else.

Catching him by surprise, Nero's eyes widened as my words settled over him. I wasn't sure if we would ever move past this – or, more importantly, if we ever could. I felt like a fool. I spent five years running away from him instead of seeking the truth. I allowed my paranoia and distrust to consume me until I questioned even the loyalty of my closest friend. My eyes watered and my heart pained, as if someone had torn it out my body when his blue eyes glowed with unshed tears.

"Ariadne, it's okay," he replied, a moment later.

"Is it, Nero?" I questioned, dubiously. I knew he was lying for my sake. The anger returned but I didn't know who it was directed towards. I couldn't hold it back as I exclaimed, "Please, just for once, stop lying. Stop protecting my feelings! It's not okay. Everything I did was not okay!"

"What do you want me to say?!" he shouted back, finally exploding as he stared at me with large cerulean eyes that couldn't decide whether they loved or hated me. My heart crumbled at the thought of it being the latter. "I know it's not okay, Aria! But what can we do now?!"

His chest rose and fell as he spoke what was truly on his mind. I didn't know how to respond, surprised by his outburst. I just stared at what I had created and wondered if he could ever love me the same again. Nero clenched his jaw, running his fingers through his thick locks in frustration, as his gaze flittered around the room before eventually settling back onto me. His jaw relaxed, shoulders drooping as he sighed, erratically, closing his eyes.

"I love you, Aria. More than you will ever know," he revealed, dejectedly. At that moment, he looked like a little boy, who was afraid of loss, who was afraid of being alone. "Loving you consumes me."

His voice cracking had me finally closing this torturous space between us. My trembling hands touched the side of his face as I gazed up at him with teary eyes. I felt the sparks between us the second I touched him and when he opened his eyes, I knew he felt it too. Everything I wanted stood right in front of me. I didn't need anything else. I accepted this control he had over me; the power of our love was all-consuming, all-powerful.

"I know, Nero. And I was a fool to not see that before and question your love for me," I whispered, with an unsteady smile. He delicately took my hands into his, his gaze searching for mine until it was locked, unable to tear away.

"I love you, Aria," he repeated, before inhaling sharply. "But I think… I think we need some time to figure this out."

The air was knocked right out of me. My heart stopped. The world came to a halt. I knew what he was saying, and rightfully so, but I couldn't help the heartbroken look which covered my face. We stared at one another, unable to speak when we should have. I wanted to apologize, beg for his forgiveness, ask him to rethink, but I knew this was the least I could do. After the pain I had caused, it was only right for him to ask for some time apart.

"Okay," I whispered, allowing our entwined fingers to separate. "*Okay.*"

I grabbed my things without looking in his direction and walked away. Every step I took broke my heart, but I didn't look back, even when I felt his gaze burning holes into my back. I walked until I was no longer in the same building as him. I walked away and didn't look back.

*

The days went by quickly, looking bleak and cynical. With the loss of my best friend and the man who owned my heart, everything was pointless. Enzo's party was just around the corner, yet I couldn't focus as everyone prepared for the mission. Matteo and Xander worked quickly on officiating my marriage to Nero with the city hall. I was surprised when there were no objections from Nero about proceeding with the registry, fully excepting him to back out. It was the only piece of hope that told me our relationship wasn't entirely dead. But as the days went by, my thoughts shifted and I drowned myself in guilt, wondering whether my decision to marry Nero would be the right thing to do. He deserved better. We had suffered so much; was there any hope in our relationship or was I fooling myself?

"Aria," Calix said, breaking me out of my spell. My eyes shifted away from the rainy weather outside of the Manor to the Greek man who had just walked into my office. "I have some thoughts about the men we're training right now. Have you got some time?"

Absentmindedly, I nodded. Calix didn't take notice of my state, settling into the seat opposite me, with his brows drawn together as he began to point out the men who still needed to train and the men who were ready for a field operation. I didn't speak, mindlessly nodding and agreeing to whatever he was saying when in fact my attention was elsewhere. I kept looking at the clock, wondering if I could finally go home and pour out the tears I had been holding back. At some point, Calix must have noticed that I wasn't paying any attention and he frowned, waving his hands in front of my dazed eyes.

I blinked, forcing a quick smile, "Yes?"

"Are you even listening?"

"Of course," I responded, defensively. "Tell the men that we can train some other day – "

"– You mean, the girls," he corrected. "We were talking about the girls now."

"*Ah*," I smiled, sheepishly. "Yes, the girls."

Calix sighed, tucking the files away into the folder. "What are we doing about Kira?"

"Enzo is holding his party at his mansion. Seeing as she wasn't at the Inner Circle's estate, I'm assuming she's being held captive there," I informed, causing Calix to arch his brow.

"How do you know they haven't moved her somewhere else?"

"Because they want me to come after her."

Calix frowned. "You?"

I collapsed back against my chair, crossing my arms over my chest as I revealed to him what I had concluded over the last two weeks. "They wanted me to be on that operation – it was me they wanted to capture. I'm not sure how they figured out that Nero's finance, Lyra, was actually me, Aria, though I'm not that surprised that they did. It means they aren't completely stupid. Nonetheless, when that plan had failed, they knew the only way to draw me in was to use Kira. Enzo is holding the event because he knows I'll come."

"So, why are you going if you risk being caught?"

"Because Kira would've done the same for me."

Calix propped himself forward as concern flickered in his green eyes. "I don't know if this is a good idea, Aria."

"You don't need to. You just have to trust me," I commanded, collecting my things and stuffing them into my bag. "I'll be taking ten people with me, excluding you and Sophie. You'll be staying here at the Manor."

I began to leave when Calix protested, "Wait, why am I not coming with you?"

I halted, glancing over my shoulder with an arched brow. "I have full intentions on weeding out whoever has been betraying me. You'll stay here and see that through. Do you understand?"

My tone left no room for argument and Calix knew that. He held my gaze for the longest second as if he wanted to argue but thought twice about it, before submitting to my order, nodding as he looked away. "Understood."

I studied him for a short minute before making my way down the corridor, where I greeted Sophie as she gave me a quick update on the wedding plans that we had temporarily placed a pause on. The Manor was as lively as ever but even then, there was no hiding the fact that there was a hole in our family. A hole which only Kira could fill. Everyone was in a state of anxiety, wondering how she was doing or how we would get her back, but I couldn't brush off the fact that someone was betraying us. Calix was next in line if anything were to happen to Kira, so having him at the Manor would be essential in capturing the traitor. There was already so much on my mind, yet I couldn't forget my conversation with Nero. I was waiting for a call or even a message, but when I got nothing, it worried me that nothing was what I would be left with. As I said my goodbyes to everyone in the living room, I wearily made my way to the car waiting outside, and slipped inside, watching the Manor turn into a speck in the distance. The roads changed quickly from residential to urban streets with skyscrapers towering over them, as the car moved through the traffic until we arrived at my penthouse, where I glanced at my phone for the nth time. I don't know why I was disappointed to see no notifications, I should have expected it, but as terrible as it was, I couldn't stop praying for Nero to give me something, anything, to ease the worry within me. I muttered my thanks to the driver, hearing a low rumble from the sky before the rain soon followed. I cursed under my breath, using my bag as a pathetic attempt to shield myself from the dark sky's tears, hurrying into the building. Fortunately, I managed to get in before the rain got worse but one look at my beautiful Prada heels had my mood further souring. I grumbled in annoyance on the way to my penthouse, flickering the lights on to the empty floor.

Except, that was what I thought I would see.

My eyes widened and my bag slipped out of my grip in shock as I noticed a trail of rose petals on the wooden floor with candles laid out on the side, creating a pathway towards my living room. At first, I was hesitant, thousands of different scenarios flickering through my mind like a film camera, but eventually, I followed the trail which brought me to a beautiful sight. Rose petals scattered across my living room floor, illuminated by small candles that scared the darkness away. And, in the center of it was Nero. One hand tucked in his trouser pocket, the other held a rose. In awe, I couldn't help but gravitate towards him like a magnet, trying to figure out what was happening.

"Wh-What's going on?" I stuttered, astonished.

The corner of his lips lifted in a tender smile as he handed me the rose. "Forgive me, Aria. I've been so distant lately."

"Rightfully so," I murmured, but I couldn't stop the smile as I marveled over the spectacle he created in my living room. Daintily, holding the rose as if it were glass, I glanced at him with a small frown. "Is everything okay?"

"More than okay," he answered.

With a sigh, his eyes moved to the small, framed picture of us on my bookshelf. It was a picture of when we were little kids, laughing over the mess we had created in the kitchen after attempting to bake. My mother had snapped a photo of that moment and sent it to me for my twenty-first birthday. Despite the cold feeling I had towards Nero, I couldn't tear myself away from that image and ended up placing it on my bookshelf. I should have known that I was screwed from then on.

"I have spent the last few days trying to figure out what I needed to do to stop this hollow feeling in my stomach after finding out everything that had happened. I thought some space would give me time to find out what I needed but then I realized, what I needed... was you," he revealed, intently, as his blue eyes peered over at me. "When you walked away, I didn't realize how terrified I was at the thought of you leaving me but then the days turned into nights, and I noticed that my life would always feel empty if you weren't part of it."

"Nero…" I trailed off, unable to complete my sentence.

"I realized that you leaving five years ago was the best thing to ever happen," he continued, surprising me. With a tender smile, he reached out and gently caressed my cheek. "Because if you didn't, who would stand up for all those people who needed saving?"

I didn't know what to say. I was so caught up with the *'what ifs'* of our relationship, that I had forgotten how I told him a vital part of my journey away from the mafia. I just wanted to know if he still loved me. Nothing else mattered to me as much as that.

"I never got to say everything that day. My mind was everywhere so I never got to tell you how proud I am of you. Maybe the way you left was undesirable, but the fact is you left, and you gained something better from it. Look at the person you are, Aria. I know for a fact that if you did stay, you wouldn't have been happy. You needed a reason to escape, and you found one," Nero resumed saying. "The way things had ended between us was horrible, but we can only move forward and learn from those mistakes. I was so caught up trying to protect you from every little thing that I didn't realize that it was making you feel suffocated and alone. Meeting Kira was fate, and you followed the destiny you were given."

There was this long stillness as his startling blue eyes held me hostage. Under this hypnotic gaze, his voice laced with remorse and heartache, "I'm sorry, Aria. For not running after you that night. I should've fought harder for you. I should've cleared the misunderstanding, but I was so caught up with my own pride that I chose to abandon you when you needed me the most. I chose to let you wallow in paranoia and distrust all because I was mad at you. I'm sorry for ever letting you slip out of my hands so easily."

"You had the right to be mad," was my response.

"That may be true but if I had truly loved you back then, I would have done anything to keep you by my side. Just as I'm trying to do now."

I was speechless. Everything that had brought us to this moment seemed pointless. We both let our pride get in the way and it ruined our friendship in the process. There was a small tremor when Nero exhaled, and I knew he was trying to hold back his tears. My heart felt constricted at the thought of making him cry.

"I should've stayed, Nero. Instead, I ran away like a coward at the first sign of betrayal," I argued, feeling the tears well up in my eyes. "I left the mafia; I ran away from my birth right."

He shook his head. "Staying would have destroyed you. It was never your calling, Aria. Yes, your heritage, but it was never your destiny. You had a bigger role to play in the world. Without you, those people you saved would have remained trapped, abused, and broken by the Serpents. I was wrong to blame you and question your loyalty to the mafia. I should have taken a step back and looked at the bigger picture, but I was so close-minded, I didn't notice how you were saving all of us from the Serpents."

Everything he was saying was so genuine, but I was unable to accept it. He was only telling me what I had wanted to hear, who was to say it was the truth? I ran away when things got difficult, and I was ashamed of the decision I had made. Regardless of the outcome, it couldn't hide the fact that I left one family to start another. Like a dam, I exploded, and all my feelings rushed out of me like a tsunami.

"Nero, I'm sorry but this is all so wrong," I whispered, somberly. "I betrayed my family, you, my parents, and I chose to hunt down a group when my loyalty was to the mafia first. I had sworn my loyalty and I broke that oath. That's unforgivable. You can't even see that. Even now, I cloud your judgement – I'm hurting you right now. Nero, I'm no good for you!"

Nero adamantly shook his head. "That's not true, Aria. My judgement is not clouded right now. For the first time in a long while, I'm finally seeing things clearly, and that is, you didn't betray us, Aria. When you left, you cut all ties with us, but you never betrayed us. Never once did you come back seeking power or trying to harm the mafia. You may have left but that was all you did."

"Nero, how I treated you can't be forgiven," I argued, incapable of stopping the tears. "I was a coward! Konstantin was right – I was weak, stupid and my heart was not strong enough."

"No," he snapped, furiously. "Konstantin was wrong. You were young, Aria, and that was not your fault. You had and you have the biggest heart, and that is not a weakness, because you cared about the *familia* so much; I never questioned your loyalty. I knew you would sacrifice yourself to save the mafia, even to this day. You are the strongest woman I have ever known."

"No, I'm not. I'm weak. I couldn't even protect Kira!"

"That was not your fault, Aria!"

"Yes, it was!" I yelled back, trying not to let his watery eyes affect me. "This is all my fault," I whimpered, stumbling back to create some distance. "The Serpents are still out there, and now they have Kira. They want me, and Kira's capture is a clear sign of that. Until they are finally killed, no one will be safe. I have failed to complete that mission. I came back to New York and all I have done is drag you into this war and placed Kira in danger. All I've done is put the people I care about the most in danger so, Nero, tell me why I shouldn't leave you right now if it means keeping you safe?"

"Aria, please," he begged, tears spilling down his face, as he reached out, but I stepped away, my lips trembling as I shook with anger, fear, and guilt.

"Tell me why I shouldn't walk away!" I cried, my cheeks stained with wet tears, my grip around the rose tightening to the point where the thorns began to impale into my palm and blood spilt down my wrist. But I couldn't feel the pain as I demanded to hear an answer, "Why shouldn't I leave you, Nero? After everything I have done, give me a reason to stay!"

He grasped my hands, his eyes imploring me as he responded, "Because I love you." My heart stopped and my sobs were silenced as I stared at him with wide eyes, tears spilling onto my face, that he gently wiped away, cupping the side of my face as he whispered sincerely, "Because I love you, Aria."

It was like those three words immobilized me. I couldn't move away even though I wanted to. I just couldn't tear myself from his intense gaze that pinned me to my spot. I couldn't look away because the emotions that glistened in his eyes were too powerful to even ignore.

"Why?" I whispered. Nero smiled as he gently caressed the side of my face, his fingers trailing to my lips before brushing away the tears.

"I want you in every way possible. I want you when you're sick. I want you when you're sad, and I want you when you're happy. I want you in the morning and at night. I want you when I make breakfast or hell, when I'm baking cupcakes. I want your hands in mine. I want you in my arms and next to me in bed. I want your lips against mine because there is no other place they belong. I want to fall asleep pressed up against you. I want to kiss your cheeks and I want to make you smile. I want you, and only you."

My cheeks were stained with wet patches, mascara trailing down my face, but he still looked at me as if I were the most beautiful person in the world. Then, he pressed his lips on the crown of my head, causing my eyes to flutter shut as I basked in the warmth of his touch. Because in his arms, I was home.

"I love you so much, Aria. That's why you have to stay," he declared. My grip around the rose loosened until it fell from my grasp, descending onto the ground, and he lifted my hand to his lips, kissing the parts where the thorns pricked me. "And I know you love me too. That's why you care so much. I'll wait forever for you because there is no one else in this universe that I could ever love as much as I love you. I know there is a long way to go before we can fully mend what has been broken, but I will spend eternity trying if it means I am with you."

"I left you."

His smile never fell. "But you're here now, and that's all that matters."

"How can you forgive me?"

He pressed his lips on the tip of my red nose. "Because I love you." I savored the sensation because it brought me back to life. He gave me life. His thumb softly stroked my cheek as he whispered, "I know you're scared, Aria, but we will get past this. I promise. So, I understand if you need some space to decide if this is still what you want."

My cries were silent, and I shuddered when he kissed me as if it was his last time doing so. It was so soft that I barely felt it, and yet my toes curled at the euphoric buzz that shot through my body. Then he let me go. He tucked a strand of hair behind my ear and then began to leave. But I had finally realized how much time I had spent allowing the things I loved to slip out of my hands; and as he walked away, I realized how I couldn't lose him again, how I would spend forever begging for his forgiveness, begging him to have me and I wouldn't care. Because there was only one person I had ever loved.

And that was him.

Just as he reached the door, I said softly, "I want you too."

He halted, his hand wavering over the handle, before his eyes peered over his shoulders, brows drawn together in confusion. "I'm sorry?"

"I said I want you too," I repeated, but more firmly. Confidently. As if those were my last words on earth and I needed him to hear them.

He angled his body towards me, cocking his head to the side which made me smile timidly as I wiped the tears from my face. "I want all of it. I want the pointless bickering, the long walks, the late-night phone calls, and the good morning texts. I want cute pictures with you, to hold your hand, to call you baby. The joking, the fighting, the love. I want to be so inseparable that people are like, *'you're still together?'*" Nero released a short, breathy laugh, and my lips tugged into a smile. "That's what I want. I want you."

I took a step forward and swallowed my fears. I took a step away from the past and into the future. I took that step because there was no life without him. So, I finally said, "I love you, Nero."

It took a minute for Nero's brain to register what I breathed into existence, but when it did, his eyes enlarged until they looked like saucers as a stunned expression took over his face. His oceanic eyes, which were brimming with tears eventually spilled, as he uttered, "Say that again."

"I love you, Nero. With all my heart."

Slowly, he began to walk closer, lessening this unbearable distance between us. "Again."

"I love you."

And closer.

"Again."

And closer.

"I love you."

There he was, standing before me. The blueness of his eyes reminded me of the sky as they implored for mine and I didn't shy away from the intensity of them, grinning widely when he brought his hands to my cheeks.

"Please, one last time," he pleaded, every word accentuated with need like he couldn't live without hearing me say them again. Tears splashed his cheeks and my heart stuttered at the sight of one of the most powerful men in the world cry, simply because of those three words.

Therefore, I pressed my hands against his chest, feeling how rapidly his heart was pounding just like mine, and tiptoed to his height. Our lips brushed against each other's as I murmured, for the final time, "I love you, Nero Russo. *Sempre.*"

"I love you too, Ariadne Moretti," he responded, with a smile that had no intentions of disappearing any time soon. "*Sempre.*"

344

When his lips touched mine, it was as if this weight chained to me had finally unshackled. Happiness consumed me, engulfing the guilt and fear I had allowed to control me for so long. And I decided I never wanted it to go away because if happiness was being with Nero, I would want this for the rest of my life.

CHAPTER 38

all the king's horses

The cell was colder today as the temperature had dropped outside. Kira found herself slipping in and out of consciousness, unable to remain awake for long, as they would inject another anesthetic in her or sometimes beat her until she could no longer fight. That was if she ever tried to get up to fight. The drugs made her weak to the point where she could open her eyes for a few minutes before passing out again. There were a few occasions where she recognized Enzo and Barak as they came to check up on her, but only rarely did she see the other man. She was too drowsy to remember his features besides the fact that he had these astonishing hazel eyes which looked emerald under the dim lighting of the basement, if that was even possible. Besides that, she couldn't figure out who this man was but quickly concluded that he was the leader of the Serpents. Her suspicions were confirmed one evening when Enzo paid her a visit, kneeling as he peered through the barred gates to take a better look at her. She pretended to be asleep but knew it was pointless as in a matter of minutes, she would pass out once again. Therefore, she tried not to move, using as little energy as possible. Having trained for situations such as this, Kira remained still on the concrete floor. Enzo pondered if she was dead. She looked too still for his liking. Of course, her condition didn't matter to him. In fact, she was a liability to their entire plan, but he wasn't in charge, unfortunately. If he was in charge, she would have been dead the moment she entered this basement. Perhaps he would amuse her for a few days, play with that pretty body of hers, before tearing her heart out of her chest. Alas, he wasn't in charge. He couldn't even touch her, or he risked having his fingers cut off. Sometimes, Enzo wondered if his leader had a soft spot for this girl despite his incessant claims otherwise.

"What are you doing?" Enzo jumped before glancing over his shoulders.

Barak arched a brow, inhaling his cigar, as he waited for an answer. Enzo never liked the old man as he was too high profile, but for the sake of the Serpents, he kept his complaints to himself. He also didn't want to risk losing his tongue if he ever uttered his thoughts to his leader.

Enzo stood up and smiled, thinly. "Studying our prized possession."

"He told you to leave her alone," Barak noted. "Or do you need to be reminded some other way?"

Enzo chuckled, holding his hands up in surrender, playfully. "I'm innocent. I swear. I was just making sure she was still alive. Boss wouldn't be too happy if she ends up dying."

Barak didn't say anything, his eyes flickering over to the girl in the corner of the cell. Her body was colored in bruises, bloodstains on her clothes, her hair disheveled as her body curled into a defensive position. He had seen that plenty of times, with his wife and mistress, after a few good beatings.

"Do you ever think that he's becoming slightly blindsided?" Barak asked, releasing a puff of smoke into the air.

"What do you mean?"

"He is too invested in Aria. I'm beginning to question whether he has intentions on actually killing her as planned," Barak explained. "And this plan of his, I'm not sure whether it will be successful."

Enzo hummed. "He has been distracted lately. The other day, I caught him staring at the wall in the library, speaking to himself. I must say, I also question the success of this plan. Aria is a brilliant woman, and I have a feeling that during the party tomorrow night, she's going to slip right through our fingers."

"Do you think?" Barak shifted his gaze towards Enzo in curiosity.

Enzo studied Kira's unmoving body and inhaled deeply, nodding his head. "All powerful leaders eventually lose their sanity. It just seems that ours has lost it to Aria Moretti."

CHAPTER 39

gentlemen's club

Nero

I waited at Aria's penthouse, fixing my cufflinks and the black bow I opted for instead of a tie. Taking a glance in the mirror, I brushed off the specks of dust on my tuxedo, pulling my blazer over my satin shirt to complete the black-on-black look. Aria had personally chosen the tux, commenting on how it would match perfectly with her gown; although, I had yet to see her attire for the evening.

"I got you something," a soft voice purred from behind me.

With a smirk on my lips, I peered over my shoulder and caught sight of Aria in the most beautiful wine-colored ballgown I had ever seen. It had a satin finish, and diamonds were scattered across the material, so it looked as if she was wearing the stars which twinkled outside. Strapless, the gown cinched at the waist before expanding out and pooling around her like crimson ink with gentle pleats. It arched over the curves of her breasts like butterfly wings, with a scandalously low décolletage that had me wanting to tear the dress off her. Her mahogany hair was tied into a low bun, and she wore a burgundy choker and diamond earrings to complete the look.

Her dark eyes raised when my smirk slipped off my face, a look of awe replacing the arrogance I was wearing a second before. "Aria, you look… *breathless.*"

"Don't I?" she giggled, unapologetically arrogant, but her cheeks turned as rosy as her lips. Her eyes glittered when she passed me a box. "Here. This is for you. Consider it a wedding gift."

Surprised, I gingerly took the box from her hands, giving her a quick confused look which she only smirked at before opening it. Admiring the silver watch, I couldn't help but break into a large grin as my eyes turned back to the love of my life. I saw her wedding ring sparkle on her finger, a reminder that I was officially married to this woman.

"I love it."

She grinned, pressing her lips softly against mine, "I thought you would."

"But I love you more," I murmured, grasping her waist and drawing her closer. "Mrs. Aria Russo."

Her smile stretched ear-to-ear and, *my goodness*, it was the most ethereal thing I had ever witnessed. She pecked the tip of my nose as her hands curled around my waist. "I love you too."

*

Enzo's home was as heavily guarded as Aria had informed me. Snipers hid at every point, men walking in pairs, around the acres of land armed with large guns, knives hidden in their boots, black hats and glasses masking their faces from curious onlookers. Aria was right; they were expecting her arrival and more importantly, Kira's retrieval. Before we entered the building, after they had checked our marriage certificate, she gave me a quick kiss for good luck and a smile, assuring me that she knew what she was doing. I trusted her. The mansion was almost as large as the Estate. People gathered on the ground floor; the front entrance swarmed by men I had met before, along with their wives. The women glanced at Aria, their eyes thinning but a sharp look from me had them turning away. Aria was not blindsided by what had just occurred, as her eyes trained to what was in front of her, but her lips curved into a smile and that told me enough.

She outshone them all. *A fucking goddess.*

Enzo found us first, his green eyes creasing, as he smirked. "Ah, my favorite couple. I'm so glad you were able to attend, although I must say I'm surprised that Lyra joined us. When did you two get married?"

"Last week," Aria lied, as smooth as honey. "It was a private ceremony. My closest friend is currently out of town, and we felt it wasn't right to hold a wedding in her absence."

If Enzo knew who she was referring to, he didn't show it, and arched a brow as he looked at her, sympathetically. "I admire your loyalty, Mrs. Russo."

"It's one of my finer traits," she mused, before turning to me, her hands snaking around my arm. "Isn't it, *sweetheart?*"

I smirked. "Yes, *dear.*"

"How adorable," he sneered, not even attempting to hide the distaste that lingered in his eyes, before turning to me with a tight lip. "Nero, I just wanted to inform you about the small gathering the men will be having in about twenty minutes. I'm sure that you can tear yourself away from your beautiful wife and meet us in the cigar room."

"Of course. That won't be a problem at all."

Enzo gave one last smile, his eyes momentarily wavering on Aria as she challenged his gaze, before they moved elsewhere, and he slipped into the crowd like the snake he was. Aria's smile fell and she turned to me with a pout, as annoyance flickered in her eyes, her clutch on my hands tightening.

"Be careful. I don't know what tricks they have up their sleeves and I sure as hell don't want anything happening to you. So, stay on guard," she murmured, softly, stroking my cheek.

I took her hand and kissed it. "I promise I'll stay aware. Don't worry – I can look after myself. I am the Don after all."

That didn't seem to ease her worries as she looked away. "That's what I'm worried about."

I wanted to question her, figure out what was going on in that complex mind of hers, but knew better and gave her hand a quick squeeze of reassurance. Aria's eyes refused to meet mine as she glanced at the room with a hidden agenda. I was worried but I had to trust her, especially if Kira's life was on the line. In a crowd filled with people that would happily stab us in the back whilst smiling, I had to be careful and shifted closer to Aria. That caught her attention. Her beautiful eyes peered up as she tilted her head to the side. The words didn't need to leave her red lips for me to know what she was trying to say. I bobbed my head and she smiled as radiantly as the moon.

"I love you," she murmured.

There it was. My heart stopped. And so did the world.

A simple three words sentence had me wanting to drop to my knees. I would worship her forever if it meant that I could hear those words again.

"I love you," I echoed, pressing my lips against hers.

It was magic whenever I kissed her. Like everything I had lost finally returned to me. She responded with urgency despite the curious onlookers who whispered amongst each other. She didn't care and neither did I. I savored her taste, knowing this woman was my soulmate and if kissing her felt like I was exploring the universe, I would do it over and over again. Her hands laid on my chest when we finally tore apart and mirrored each other's smile.

"Ready?" she muttered, the question was directed to the people stationed outside the large estate, waiting for her order, but I knew she was asking me too when her gaze steadily held mine.

I pecked her lips. "Ready."

Then I let her go.

I watched her retreating back as she disappeared into the crowd, giving me one last look over her shoulder before she was gone from my view. Blowing out a quiet breath of air, I fixed my suit and moved towards the cigar room where Enzo and his snakes awaited. I itched to check on Aria, but she was busy and I couldn't ruin this plan. I had to keep walking. A few women flashed sultry smiles and purred offers I would accept only from Aria as I strode down the hallway. I declined their advances because there was only one woman who could drive me to insanity and that was Aria Moretti.

No – Aria Russo.

A ghost of a smile played on my lips when I remembered heading into the town hall to officially register our marriage. Her hazel eyes were wide with excitement and her cheeks flushed from the morning when I sunk deeply into her piece of heaven several times. We were almost late had it not been for Xander who broke us from our love spell with a thundering knock upon Aria's door. Aria was mortified but I, on the other hand, couldn't stop laughing as she threw my clothes at my face, ordering me to get dressed despite the look of frustration. I listened only after I showered with her, where I took her to the stars for the nth time that day.

"Russo," Enzo's voice broke me from thoughts. He arched his brow as he waited by the door. "Aren't you coming in?"

It was only then did I realize that I had been standing in the middle of the hallway. Smiling rigidly, I slipped into the room and pushed my distracted thoughts of Aria to the back of my mind. The room was decorated with mahogany wood walls, a fireplace with a portrait of a family I had never seen before hanging above, a second door adjoined beside it. Dark red curtains slightly covered the door, but I caught sight of it, the luminosity from the chandeliers illuminating the darkened room. Enzo closed the door as I settled into an empty seat around the circular table. I examined the men in the room, many of whom I had known through other events but a few whom I had never even seen or met before. Enzo took his seat at the head of the table as the second door, the one hidden by the curtain, opened and two girls dressed in rags that were as red as Aria's lips, and black laced masks that hid their faces from the hungry looks directed at them. Disgust grew in my throat, but I forced the bile down as I thanked the girl who handed me a cigar before moving to the man beside me, whose eyes drank her in, his hands caressing the part of her thigh the skimpy dress failed to cover. The girl didn't balk, and I knew she had grown accustomed to the unwanted attention. My jaw clenched when I concluded she and her friend must be part of the Serpents' sex trafficking business. I glared at the man beside me, and he cowered under my fierce gaze, retracting his hand from the girl as if she had burnt him. Although the girl did not look at me, I noticed her shoulders relax and knew it was the 'thank you' I would receive. I expected the girls to leave but was deeply mistaken as they moved to Enzo, flanking his sides.

And then they kneeled. Heads bowed; eyes trained on the ground as if they were pets. I felt Enzo's intense gaze on me, and I knew he was trying to get a rise out of me, so I forced the anger to simmer down, ensuring the beast within me did not act impulsively, thus endangering these girls and the others hidden in this prison.

A smirk coiled his lips when he spoke, "It's a pleasure to be surrounded by the most powerful men on this planet."

"I must say," someone said, eyes flickering in their direction. An older man sipped on the whiskey, and I knew it was Barak. "This is quite a party you're hosting, Enzo."

Enzo's smirk didn't waver. "Thank you, Doukas. You could say it was a special occasion."

The hidden meaning was laced in his words, and I tried not to react, sipping on the liquor one of the girls had poured. I wondered for a second whether the other men in this room were aware that Barak Doukas was alive, and not Kal. I didn't have time to muse on the thought for too long before I saw the girls. I couldn't tear my eyes away from them, noticing trembles overtaking their bodies, their dresses barely covering them, let alone keeping them warm. They were thin. Too thin, and I wondered when the last time was that they had eaten.

"These girls," I spoke, unflinching to the twenty pairs of eyes shifting in my direction. "Who are they?"

Enzo peered at them darkly, before drawling, "Pets. I'm sure you're familiar with that term, Russo?"

I frowned. "I'm not sure what you're trying to suggest."

Enzo chuckled, drinking the yellow liquid in his cup, leisurely. "That wife of yours. You seem to have her on a leash. You must teach me your tricks."

The room erupted into wicked laughter. I wanted to tear his arms off. Cut his body into chunky pieces and feed them to the wolves that were hidden in the mountains that surrounded this estate. But I didn't.

Instead, I smirked, arching a brow. "There are no tricks, Enzo. Perhaps if you found a woman, you'd understand what it would mean to be in a relationship."

Enzo's nostrils flared. "I assure you; I have no trouble finding women. Look at these two kneeling beside me."

"But as you said," my smirk deepened, "They're just pets."

"They are women, are they not?" Enzo pressed, and I didn't respond, cocking my head to the side. A man's ego would be his downfall. This irritated him and I tried to fight the amused look across my face as his jaw tightened. "So, what classifies someone as a woman?"

"My wife," was my response. "Holding these women captive proves you are incapable of finding someone without forcing dominance."

Enzo looked like he was out for blood. My blood. His hands fisted until they were turning white when he leaned over the table, glowering at me, but he had little effect on me. It was like a kitten standing in front of a lion. The tension was thick, suffocating us, as the men in the room shifted their eyes between Enzo and I like a game of ping pong. We all knew I had won. In the end, Barak chuckled, trying to reduce the tension.

"As always," he drawled out, exhaling a puff of smoke. "You continue to surprise us, Nero."

I replied smugly, crossing my arms over my chest. "It's what I do best."

Barak's eyes sparkled with malicious intent despite the friendly smile he wore. "Many congratulations to you and your wife."

I didn't respond, my smile tautening when I noticed the venom laced in his voice when he said '*wife.*' My lack of response caused the conversation to change, despite Enzo fuming at the end of the table. I ignored his scorching glare and sipped my whiskey, studying the room we were in, absentmindedly. The static noise in my ear informed me that the process to extract Kira was beginning which meant I had to keep these men in this room. So, I partook in their conversation, chiding in my opinions on the current state of the economy, business ventures and whatever bullshit they were talking about to hide the fact that they were involved with the Serpents' trafficking business. Xander threw commands, my ears listening carefully as I waited for Aria's response. When she didn't speak, I wondered whether she was alright. She was to join Xander, but I wondered if she managed to successfully break away from the eagle-eyed women. Glancing at the watch she had given me, I hoped she did, but her lack of words had me questioning otherwise. A part of me worried that she got caught trying to sneak around. In my seat, I shifted restlessly, pouring another glass of whiskey and quickly drinking it as if I hadn't drunk for days. Suddenly, something caught my attention. My eyes flickered away from the men who sat around the table and glanced at the semi-closed doors. It was faint but I still heard it; a sweet, melodic voice echoing down the corridors. It was something I hadn't heard before, yet in my heart it felt like I knew who it belonged to. Curious to who the owner of the angelic voice was, I excused myself from the table and ventured down the corridors, the singer becoming louder the closer I got.

"*He said if you dare come a little closer.*"

I turned the corner, entering the hall where I noticed the guests listening intently to the singer who played the grand piano. The soft voice complimented the tune flowing out of it.

"*Round and round, and around and around, we go,*" she sang, as I walked closer, excusing myself as I pushed through the crowd until I was right in front of her. "*Now, tell me, now, tell me, now, tell me, now you know.*"

My breath got caught in my throat when I saw the beauty in the red ball gown, her fingers playing the piano as she sang, flawlessly. Her eyes never left the piano but as if she knew I was there, they flickered up, twinkling.

"*Not really sure how to feel about it, something in the way you move,*" The corner of her lips lifted up slightly, my eyes unable to leave her. "*Makes me feel like I can't live without you, and it takes me all the way.*"

She was one with the melody, her soul pouring into the song as she sang, skillfully, playing the piano, so invested with her feelings and the song. At the same time, Xander spoke into my ear, but his words flew right over my head as I was completely hypnotized by Aria. I could hear him barking orders, but my attention was on the love of my life.

"*I want you to stay,*" she held the note for a long second before breaking, claps scattering around room. The piano tune was consistent, yet as she continued the song, it felt as if the feeling got deeper and deeper. "*It's not much of a life you're living. It's not just something you take, it's given.*"

For some reason, it felt as if she was sending me a message, her fingers running down the piano as her voice got stronger. Her eyes broke away from me, peering down as she watched herself play the melody that had everyone enthralled and amazed by her.

"*Round and round, and around, and around we go. O-oh, now, tell me, now, tell me, now, tell me, now you know,*" My heart clenched with an unrecognizable feeling, but it sunk deep in my chest that I could feel it being engraved. "*Not really how to feel about it, something in the way you move. Makes me feel like I can't live without you, and it takes me all the way.*"

She was magnificent.

"*I want you to stay...*" I was astonished by the way she naturally pulled out a high note as if it was nothing. She continued to surprise me, and I knew there would not be a minute that would be boring if I remained by her side. "*Stay.*"

Her breathing was steady, and she didn't look the slightest bit out of breath as she continued to sing. When she finally reached the end, she glanced up, her beautiful eyes sparkling as they locked with mine, filled with so many emotions that it was hard to distinguish what was what, but somewhere within me, I knew we were both feeling exactly the same things. Our pride got in the way, just like it did five years ago. I let her slip away from me last time, and as I watched her sing with her whole heart poured into the melody and the glitter of her wedding ring, I vowed this time would be different.

"*I want you to stay,*" Aria whispered, the tune fading out at the same time, the last cord echoing throughout the hall.

Momentarily, no one did anything before raucous applause spread throughout the entire hall, amazement and enjoyment shown clearly across people's face as Aria smiled, quite coyly, and curtseyed when she stood up. It took me a moment to fathom what had just occurred before making my way towards her, that timid expression still on her face when she noticed me closing the distance. I took her hands in mine, lifting them up to press my lips against her knuckles, her eyes unwavering as they watched my every movement. Not once did my own break away from her.

"You never fail to amaze me, *amore*," I murmured, for only her to hear.

Her smile expanded and her eyes softened as they glanced down, shyly, surprising me by how petite she looked right now. Usually, she was so sure of herself, holding her head high with a confident smirk but this beautiful woman in front of me, dressed in a red dress, lips coated in red and cheeks blushing pink, was a completely different person. She looked so docile. Yet, it made me want her even more. As we moved past the crowd, I fought the burning desire to steal her breath away just as she had done to me. Only, I stopped myself when I noticed the glimmer of worry that sparked her hazel eyes. I wanted to question her, but I noticed a few eyes flickering in our direction and decided to take her far from the unwanted attention. When we were finally in a quiet corner, she embraced me. Taken aback, I responded a second later and curled my arms around her small frame, as she laid her head on my chest, exhaling heavily.

"Is everything okay?" I asked, drawing my brows together as I peered down at her.

Aria nodded. "I found her."

My lips broadened into a smile at the good news, wondering why she didn't seem happier at the plan being a success. Her eyes refused to meet mine, her fingers clutching onto my shirt for dear life as if I would disappear.

"That's amazing. I was so worried when you made no indication of finding her."

"No, Nero," she then said, her words thick with something I couldn't quite pinpoint, "*I found her.*"

My smile fell.

"Is she alright?" Aria didn't say anything, her lips pressed together as if she was trying to hold something back. Every second she didn't speak triggered me to think of the worst. I placed my hands on her shoulders, shaking her slightly to break her from the daze she was in. "Aria?"

Aria swallowed, and when she looked up, I saw her glassy eyes and my heart sunk. "She can't remember anything. Not even me."

CHAPTER 40

lucid dreams

"Hey babe," I murmured, as I knelt beside Yakira's bed. She fluttered her eyes open. Took in her surroundings. And then closed her eyes again. I shoved down the sobs when I took a glimpse at her wounds, bandages wrapped around the bruises on her legs, arms and torso. "You need to get up, Kira. You've been in bed for days and the doctor said you need to start walking or your muscles are going to get stiff."

"Who are you?" she asked, abruptly.

My heart faltered. Her baby blue eyes searched for mine as I slowly stood up, admiring how her bedroom was the literal embodiment of Kira. Her room was farther down the hall than mine, furnished with a large closet, a desk where she had left her plans to destroy the Serpents, her weapons neatly polished and hanging on the wall in a glass cabinet. Perhaps I should put a lock on that as Calix suggested. At the same time, I couldn't. I knew that underneath the guard she had created in her mind that Kira was still there. The doctor gave no promising news about her mental recovery – it could be ages until she remembered, because it would mean that she had allowed herself to remember what she had suffered in that bunker. Xander's voice broke when he had informed me that he found her and, whilst Nero was busying himself with the men, I took the opportunity to see her myself. Instead of getting that warm and tearful reunion, the Japanese girl clutched onto the blanket Xander gave her and asked who I was. The doctor confirmed what Xander had told me as I stared at the helpless Kira with teary eyes.

PTSD. She was trying to protect herself because no one else could.

"Aria," was my reply. I forced a smile as I turned to her. "Come on. Let's have a tour of the Manor, it might jog a memory."

Kira was hesitant, I saw it in her eyes but there was this spark, and I knew she was still there. Her hands gingerly took mine and together we walked through the Manor. The younger girls attempted to cheer her up with get well soon gifts and the boys kept their distance until Kira was confident enough in their presence. It was like bringing a new girl into the family again. Baby steps. I knew I would wait eternally for her to recover. I would never give up on my sister. She wore loose clothing compared to the tight attire she usually dressed herself up in before the kidnapping. Her hair was braided loosely, and her face was bare of makeup. She looked like the girl I had seen in my hotel room in London. I was afraid I had lost her forever. And it was my fault.

"It's not your fault," Nero sighed, over the phone one afternoon, when I could no longer hold my emotions inside. Kira was in the kitchen with Violetta, preparing lunch, when Nero surprised me with a call. I left the girls and quietly slipped into an empty study further down the hall, answering his call with tears. "You can't blame anyone but the Serpents for what happened. All you can do is help her recover and stay by her side."

"I can't let this happen to anyone else," I sniffled, leaning against the wall as my eyes turned to the window when the sound of laughter caught my attention. "I can't, Nero."

"Then don't," he replied. "Stop the Serpents once and for all."

In the evening, the girls settled around the television to watch a film – Kira's choice. She blinked in surprise as we waited for her response as if she couldn't believe she had an option, a choice. Her swollen lips, scarred with cuts, curled into a smile as she said Mulan like it was an instinct. And maybe it was. Although, she wasn't sure of her answer, I knew why. It was the film her mother played for Kira when she wanted to mute the arguments with her husband, so her daughter wouldn't hear those hurtful words which tore her mother apart. It silenced the demons.

It silenced the demons to this day.

The movie played as we all huddled on the couch or on the carpet, with blankets to shield us from the cold, passing around the popcorn and brownies. Everything was fine at first, everyone was invested in the Disney film, until we had reached halfway, and Kira screamed, jolting everyone from their seats. I quickly rushed to her aid, Sophie heading to the kitchen to grab some medicine as Kira clutched her head, whilst the younger girls fearfully stared at the strongest women they had ever known.

"Kira," I yelled, over her shrieks.

But my attempts were futile as her screams were laced with sobs, tears running down her face just as the boys rushed to see the commotion. Xander hastily moved to Kira, concern evident all over his face, whilst Calix swiftly had everyone evacuate the living room and head to their respective rooms.

Then Xander looked at me and I knew what was happening.

Her memories were returning.

"We should take her to her room," Xander ordered, and I listened, complying to his rushed commands, whilst he scooped the shaking Kira into his arms and hurriedly strode upstairs with Sophie hot on his tail with medical care.

Fumbling for my phone in my pocket, I called the doctor who informed me he would be on his way, before calling Nero, who picked up before the second ring.

"Aria, is everything okay? I thought you were busy tonight," he said anxiously, and I could hear shuffling which told me he was still in his office. My heart stuttered and I knew I needed support, someone by my side whilst I tried to be strong for Kira – I needed someone to be strong for me.

"You need to come," was my response.

"Where?" was his answer. I didn't think twice as I gave him the address, knowing there was no going back now that he knew the Manor's location. At first, he was confused but quickly pieced together where he was heading and hung up with a quick, "I love you."

Kira was no longer screaming by the time I reached her bedroom, and I concluded that Sophie must have given her something to numb the pain and calm her down. She sat on the bed, clasping her hands and training her blank eyes at the wall in front of her where a picture of us hung. I carefully walked into the room, hesitant with my steps, but I knew everyone heard me despite how quiet I was. Xander's eyes peeked at me before he muttered something to Sophie, which had her standing up from where she had knelt beside Kira, grabbing her things, and following Xander out of the room. Timidly, I settled beside Kira on the bed. We didn't speak. Neither of us. Just the sound of our breathing broke the silence.

Then she whispered, "I'm sorry."

"Why?" I frowned.

"That it took me so long to remember," she answered, brokenly. "And even then, I still can't remember everything."

"It's okay, Kira. Stop forcing yourself to remember everything straight away and start focusing on getting better."

"But you need to know someone is betraying us in this Manor."

I inhaled, sharply. "I'm aware."

"I saw their face, Aria. So why can't I remember?" she cried, so I embraced her in my arms, her shoulders shaking as she sobbed, staining my jumper with her frustrated tears.

"We will find them, Kira. I promise," I vowed. "I'll kill them for you. I swear it."

Her glassy eyes peered up as she choked on the sobs. "I'm sorry I forgot you."

I chuckled, brushing the tears away from her rosy cheeks that brought out the paleness of her skin. "It's okay. It's a job requirement of mine – no one is allowed to remember me."

That earned me a smile – no matter how small it was, she had smiled, and I knew everything was going to be okay.

*

"Nero is here," Calix notified me, as soon as he walked into my office, disrupting me from my papers. I glanced at him, tucking my sheets into their brown folders, and locking them up in the drawer. "I can't believe you told him our location. How reckless is that?"

"I trust him," I said, curtly, not appreciating his tone.

"He could be working for the Serpents for all we know, and you just gave him the fucking golden egg," Calix snarled.

I recoiled at his harsh tone as if he had slapped me, because he had never spoken to me like that before. I was aware that Calix didn't like Nero, but I had hoped that he would have been mature enough to set his personal feelings aside. I guess, I was wrong. My mood only further soured when Calix didn't even apologize like he normally would have.

I narrowed my eyes, pursing my lips in annoyance. "What I do is not your business, Calix. I understand your concern, but I trust Nero with my life, and you should too, because not only is he my *husband*, but he is also the only other person who I can rely on as much as I rely on Kira."

"So, what does that mean for me?" he whispered, his green eyes softening with an emotion that I had never seen before.

My throat felt tight with guilt before I shoved it deep down because I knew that regardless of my past history with Calix, we were adult enough to move forward without damaging our friendship in the process. I thought Calix was on the same page as me, but his jaded eyes told me a different story. Suddenly, I wanted Nero here with me.

"Calix… don't think you are inferior to Nero. You just need to remember your position," I assured, closing the distance, with a smile in hopes that I could ease whatever worries were flitting in his mind. "You have been by my side from the beginning, almost as long as Kira. But I promise you, don't worry about Nero."

His jaw clamped tight as he looked away, stepping back.

"You're losing your focus," he scoffed, and my smile fell. "Maybe this marriage wasn't a good idea after all."

Before I could respond, he stormed out of the room, leaving me utterly speechless.

*

Nero's eyes were wide with awe when he took in the Manor, Xander had informed me with amusement. He admired the wooden walls, gold accents in the decor, and the people who welcomed him, warmly, despite him being a stranger. To them, he was as important as me. I descended the stairs where I found him laughing with Xander and Dom in the living room, chatting as if they had known each other for years and were old friends catching up. The bitter words of Calix faded into nothing when I saw how easily Nero got along with everyone else. I didn't let my bad mood ruin this moment. Eventually, he saw me, and he failed to complete his sentence, which had Xander and Dom turn in my direction before they sent a smirk to each other.

"Aria," Nero stood up, pressing his lips against my cheek before scrutinizing me with apprehension. "Are you okay?"

I wanted to tell him, but I was afraid that I would be making a big deal out of nothing – plus, nothing good would come out of telling Nero about Calix. So, instead I replied, "Yes. Did you get here alright?"

Nero studied me before finally saying, "It was a bit of a journey, but it was fine. How is Kira?"

"Resting. It's been a long day," I responded, with a smile which alleviated Nero's tension, ignoring the way his eyes searched for mine. "How do you like the Manor?"

He smiled, proudly. "I must say, how you managed to stay off-grid is beyond my imagination but honestly, I can't help but admire you for that," then he chuckled, taking my hands into his, "You truly have built a haven. I'm so proud."

His words replaced the restlessness with the warmth I needed during these tough times. I caressed his cheek lovingly, before kissing him, murmuring, "I love you."

He smiled in the kiss before tearing himself away from me when giggles erupted behind me. Nero's cheeks darkened, as I looked over my shoulder to see Violetta and a few other girls huddling by the stairs with dreamy grins. I guess, I wasn't the only one to fall for Nero.

I bit back my laughter. "Girls, this is Nero Russo."

"So, you're the man Aria is madly in love with," Violetta stated, bluntly, shocking me but amusing Nero, who threw me an arrogant smirk. Dom and Xander cackled from behind but a glare from me had them quieten their laughter, though it was useless as I could hear them stifling it. "You are pretty handsome, so I can see why."

"Oh god, Vi," I covered my face in embarrassment, causing everyone to laugh.

"Thank you, sweetheart," Nero chuckled, pressing his lips on the crown of my forehead, as he drew me into his chest. "But I'm the lucky one."

My cheeks reddened as I refused to meet his piercing gaze, muttering, "Do you want to see Kira?"

Nero held back his teases and nodded, saying his farewells to everyone, before following me up the stairs where he bombarded me with questions regarding the Manor. I answered his burning enquiries with laughs, entertained when he sulked because he had failed to locate the Manor himself. A comment about him losing his touch earned me a growl and a promise that I would be losing myself to him very soon. That caused me to become very flustered and smack his arm, pathetically, as a desperate attempt to hide my mortification. He laughed and I pouted at him. Nero's grin never fell as he kissed me back to peace. Amidst our kiss, we didn't realize someone had seen us until there was a loud cough. I instantly moved back and saw Calix by Kira's door with his arms crossed over his chest, eyes showing his displeasure as he nodded stiffly at Nero, a half-assed greeting. Nero's smile didn't fall but he did curl his arm around my waist and responded with a terse nod of his own.

Men.

"Aria, I need you to look through some of these plans," Calix said, his green eyes holding hostility towards Nero, who didn't flinch under the glower.

I opened my mouth to refute but Nero spoke first, smiling reassuringly at me, "It's okay, babe. Maybe it might be good for me to speak with Kira alone."

I crinkled my nose to which he kissed, before agreeing with heavy reluctance and following Calix to my office. The bubble of solace popped as I disappeared down the corridor, glancing over my shoulder to see Nero vanishing into Kira's bedroom.

CHAPTER 41

pills & potions

Nero

I *found Aria throwing punches with all her might into a boxing bag larger than her. She huffed and puffed with every assault, swirling around, using her foot to attack. Sweat dripping down her face, her t-shirt stuck to her skin as she wiped her forehead. Focus stamped her face, her brows furrowed together, her lips puckered, her cheeks rosy against her softly tanned skin. I leaned against the wall, observing how invested she was in every maneuver. She was an adaptive learner. After four lessons, she managed to master moves that men much older than us struggled to perfect. She was her mother's daughter indeed.*

"Stop staring," she grunted. Her eyes glanced over her shoulders. "I hate it when you stare."

"You shouldn't spend so much time in here," I remarked, coolly. "A normal eight-year-old would prefer being outside during the summer."

"I'm not a normal eight-year-old," was her reply, as she took a swig from her bottle.

"I can see that," I strolled towards her, scooping up the dagger that had been tossed by the gym mat. "Shall we?"

That earned me a smile. And what a beautiful smile it was.

As she readied herself, straightening her posture, I circled her like a vulture. Then, before I could blink, she charged at me. I threw my arm out in defense, the dagger narrowly missing her arm as she swiveled to the right. She kicked her feet, knocking me down. I managed to recover before she could grab the weapon, striking her shin with my heel. She yelped, landing on one knee, annoyance flickering across her face when I shot her an arrogant smirk.

"Give in?" I taunted.

Aria grinned. "Never."

And then, she pounced.

*

Kira was by the window when I found her. Her knees were brought up against her chest, arms hugging them tightly, as she rested her head against the glass pane. She didn't spare me a glance and sighed, unevenly, mist forming on the window, where she then drew a broken heart. Despite gaining her memories back, I knew it would be a long while until she returned to her usual self – if that was even possible.

"I was wondering when you would finally see our home," she spoke without the confidence I was used to.

She didn't need to look to know that I had entered the room, and a part of me took that as a good sign, because it meant she was tapping into the skills Aria had taught her – it meant she was reaching into herself and remembering the Kira she became with Aria. I pressed my lips together as I nodded, answering her question that was more of a statement.

"How's your head?" I sat on the bed, my eyes trying to search for hers.

Then, she looked up and I saw the same blue eyes I had. Except, she didn't have any sort of emotions that could brighten them. Icy and indifferent, she shrugged. "No '*how are you?*'"

I smiled at her response. "I'm sure you've been asked that plenty of times recently."

"One more time and I'll tear someone's head off," she joked… then again, I was not entirely sure she was actually joking. She exhaled once more, watching her warm breath fog up the glass pane, as she faintly touched her head. There were no bruises on her forehead but there was a bruise within, one that would take more than a simple few days of recovery before it disappeared. "My head is fine. I guess I'm shocked by how many traumatic experiences I've been through and I'm only twenty-two. Must be some sort of world record?"

"I could double-check that for you," I suggested, feigning seriousness, and there was a tug of her lips.

Her mouth had stitches just like the ones on her brow bone. The bruises on her eyes were colors of blue and green, a stark contrast to her white skin. Bandages were wrapped around her hands, and her fingers looked swollen with cuts. I saw the purple bruise on her neck that she attempted to cover with a hoodie, and I knew they must have tried to choke her at some point during their torture. She didn't look like a girl they wanted to kill. No. She looked like a girl they tried to break. But her smile told me that they had not achieved that goal.

"How much do you remember?" I mused, leaning forward, as she shifted her body so that she was facing me, resting her back against the cold window. Perchance, she found comfort in that cold. The only consistent thing.

"Everything up until they knocked me out in the library. I faintly remember the bunker, when they beat me, and their lack of food but other than that, I'm drawing a blank," she blew out air, irritated. "All because I found out who the boss is."

"Do you have any idea?"

She shook her head, a frown curling her lips. "Not the faintest clue."

There was a long silence between us. We didn't know what to say. Because the girl who sat in front of me was a girl I could have saved, had I known Konstantin's business. We were bound by words of marriage, and broken by my love for Aria, yet, at the same time, here we sat because of Aria. I studied Kira and wondered what my life would have been like had I married her as Konstantin intended – what would her life have been like? Would she have become the woman she was today?

"Do you ever think what a coincidence that I met Aria," she began as if she had read my mind, breaking the stillness that enveloped her bedroom. "When I was to be engaged to you?"

"I think it was fate," I replied.

"How so?"

"Because, despite everything Aria and I had gone through, it was something that needed to happen. She needed to leave the mafia and she needed to save those people who didn't have a hero. She needed to save you… She… She *needed* you. I think at some point, had I actually married you, Aria still would have left the mafia after learning about you, and she would still be on this journey to take down the Serpents."

"Would you have still loved her if you were married to me?" Kira questioned, quietly.

"Yes, but I would never have acted on it. It would always be an underlying feeling, and I respect you enough as a human to never betray your trust, no matter how much I loved Aria."

She didn't respond but looked satisfied with my answer and I took that as my blessing to be with Aria. It was a wonder how interconnected everything was and, despite learning Kira's relationship with Konstantin several months ago, I had completely forgotten about my engagement to her until Aria brought it up. It never once crossed my mind. Kira was a good friend to me, to Aria, and I knew even if I had married her, it would still be the same.

"We will find him, Kira, and make him pay for everything he has done to you, to Xander, to everyone in this Manor," I promised, lacing my words with sincerity. A twinkle in her eyes told me something had amused her which had me arching a brow. "What?"

"Nothing," she laughed softly. "I forgot how similar you are to Aria."

Her laughter drew a small smile from me. "She's really worried about you, you know."

Kira's laughter died away slowly as she nodded, the grin on her lips colored in sadness. "I know. I just wish I could do something."

"All you can do is recover," I answered, standing up to go and search for Aria. "She needs you."

Kira didn't say anything, tearing her eyes away from me and onto the darkness outside and I wondered if that was the only thing she could see, so I moved to the door before I was stopped with a quiet, "Nero."

I peered over my shoulder and found her brows pulled together; her cobalt eyes conflicted with the hundred different things racing through her mind.

"There was one thing that's been bugging me," she revealed. "I haven't told anyone else because I don't want to create false hope."

"What is it?"

"Their eyes," was her answer. I frowned in confusion, and she ran her fingers through her blonde locks that didn't look in the pristine condition she would usually style it in. Then, she continued, "Their eyes. I know I've seen them before."

"Do you remember what color they were ?" I inched closer, worried

I might miss her response if I didn't listen closely.

Kira looked at me. Her blue eyes glowed under the moonlight. "Hazel, but I swear, they could have been green."

*

At the same time

Aria huffed and slacked against her chair, as the pair finally completed work that had been put aside for many days. Calix, who sat on the opposite side of her desk, chuckled at her reaction, and ran his fingers through his hair.

"How about a drink?" he suggested, heading to Aria's cabinet of alcohol that ranged from the weakest to the strongest. He pulled out one of the strongest and Aria arched a brow in surprise at his choice. "To celebrate Kira's recovery and completing all this fucking work."

Aria laughed. Her laugh was soft, and it had Calix smiling, affectionately, as her nod indicated her answer. The stress rolled right off her shoulders as she sighed, knowing that everything was going to be okay. Calix poured two glasses of whiskey whilst Aria was distracted by her glittering diamond ring that twinkled beautifully under the light. Everything was going to be alright, she just knew it, and she anticipated the days when they finally brought the Circle and their entire operation down. Her hands itched to spill blood, especially after what had happened to Kira, and she hummed, thoughtfully, picturing all the different types of ways she could make the Inner Circle squirm. Perhaps tearing their rib cages out, rib by rib or cutting their tongues out. Maybe she would carve their eyes out from their faces and etch her name across their skin using her favorite knife. That reminded her to sharpen her knife.

Her thoughts were interrupted by Calix abruptly placing her glass on the desk, her eyes creasing when she grinned. "Thank you."

His eyes were dark and mysterious; Aria often wondered what he was thinking, though he would never reveal the answers. Settling in his seat, he drank leisurely before exhaling, whilst Aria took the heavy glass in her hands and admired the yellow liquid, knowing it was her favorite whiskey that she had received. A gift from her father for the occasion of her twenty-first birthday when Aria was in Rome, and after months of tracking her, Antonio managed to find his daughter. She was amazed but didn't expect anything less as he had left the bottle on the table and disappeared before she returned home. She knew it was from him because that was also his favorite whiskey. In their own ways, Aria and her father knew they were more similar than most people thought.

"Do you remember when we first met?" Aria asked, swirling the whiskey in her hand.

"Yes," Calix's lips teased a smile. "I bumped into Kira, and you nearly beat the shit out of me."

Aria laughed. "Did I? Oops, my mistake."

Calix grinned. "Despite being twice your size, you managed to kick my butt."

"That was so long ago," Aria sighed, sadness flickering through her eyes which disappeared as quickly as it had come. "It was just over a year after I had met Kira and then we found you in Greece. You know, you've never revealed the full extent of what happened to you before us."

He looked away and Aria noticed a dangerous look in his eyes, speculating whether she may have pushed him too far again. Aria knew the basics of Calix's life pre-Aria: his family had shunned him, left him on the streets where he was saved by another family, who were killed by the Circle when they refused to give Calix into their possession, as a way to repay their debt. Calix watched his family die; he watched his sister get killed right in front of his eyes.

And then they broke him.

"Some things are better left in the past, Aria," he replied, words he continued to answer with whenever this topic came about. So, Aria respected his wishes and decided it was time to change the conversation.

"There is an auction coming up soon," she informed. "That's when we will hit them."

"All of them?"

"Yes. *All of them.*"

Calix frowned. "How do you know the leader will be there?"

"Because I'll be there," her reply was vague, just like her plans and Calix knew he couldn't talk her out of it, despite how reckless it was. This was Aria and she was as stubborn as a mule. "We'll take the fight to them."

"Whatever you say, Aria," Then he tilted his head to the side, noting she didn't once touch her drink and arched his brow in confusion.

"Aren't you going to take a sip?"

"*Oh!*" Surprise masked her face when she realized that she hadn't drunk any of the whiskey because she was lost in her thoughts, and grinned sheepishly as her cheeks blushed red. "How about a toast?"

"To whom?" Calix mused, lifting his glass as she did the same.

Aria's red lips curled into a smirk. Deadly and seductive. Like her.

"To us," she answered. "To taking down the Serpents."

Calix mirrored her smirk. "To taking down the Serpents."

The pair clinked their glasses; the incandescent light above illuminated the whiskey's rich color. A deep copper that looked like it was caramelized. Except, only one of them was dark yellow. The other looked slightly lighter, fizzing at the top. Aria didn't notice how strange it was, grinning at her most trusted friend, as she drank the alcohol, ignoring the burn in her throat as she swallowed it all, greedily, consuming the expensive drink and the tiny little pill that swam underneath the bubbles. Calix drank, deliberately taking his time, relishing in the taste whilst his eyes admired Aria, wondering why on Earth this beautiful woman was not his. But that was life, and all was fair in love and war. Possibly, that was why he continued to pour her drink, basking in the attention she gave him. From her laugh to the twinkle in her eyes, he was enchanted. It pained him to think he would never be with her.

And all whilst that was happening, Aria found herself lost in the richness of his eyes and wondered, whether it was due to the drinks or the lighting in her office, that Calix's eyes had always looked a startling hazel despite being emerald since the day she met him five years ago.

CHAPTER 42

in his arms

"Good morning," Nero purred, lightly, into my ear as I rolled over, curling closer into his arms. "*Wife.*"

"Good morning," I smiled, glancing up at the love of my life.

His electric blue eyes gleamed vividly; shaggy brown hair tousled over his brows as he leant down to kiss me. Our lips touched and my entire body set alight, my fingers reaching out to grasp his locks as I shifted my body onto his. His hands quickly found their destination and there, we were lost in each other until the sun reached its apex. When we finally managed to disentangle ourselves from each other, I hopped into the shower whilst Nero called Matteo to get updates on the conditions of the mafia. Something had been worrying him for some time and I knew he was holding something back, but I trusted that he would eventually tell me. As the water pelted against my skin and soothed my aching muscles, I savored in the warmth, running my fingers through my brown hair, before my eyes shifted as the bathroom door opened. Nero sighed, his distracted eyes flickering away from me to the cabinet, where he had left a few of his things from when he had stayed over mine. His entire body was rigid, and I knew the call with Matteo had not contained any good news. Frowning, I switched off the shower and grabbed my towel to wrap around my body, ignoring the water dripping from my hair as I moved towards Nero. He gripped the marble sink, his knuckles whitening, as he glared at the tap.

"Nero?" I called out, softly. It broke him from his thoughts, his cerulean eyes moved to me where they suddenly darkened. The breath was knocked right of me, and I knew what he was going to do.

"*No.*"

He ignored me and took three large strides, then he captured my lips, silencing my curiosity. He was avoiding the conversation, knocking the air out of me, until I was so lightheaded that I couldn't ask what was wrong. But he was angry; I felt it in his hard kiss. Needing him to open up, I shoved him away from me with a glare.

"What's wrong?" I asked.

His jaw clenched. "Nothing."

"Nero."

"Aria."

We held each other's gaze in a deadlock, neither of us wanting to be the first to look away. But I knew him and I knew he would eventually break. With a groan, he ran his fingers through his hair, and I smirked, crossing my arms over my chest with an arch of my brow.

"Someone hijacked our cargo with weapons. They had all the latest technology, billions gone down the fucking drain and we don't know who took it," Nero explained, leaning against the doorway.

I sucked in a sharp breath of air, knowing this was incredibly serious. "When did this happen?"

"Last night," was his response. There was a long moment of silence, neither of us knowing what to say, before I reached out and took his hands into mine, rubbing my thumb against his skin. He looked away; his blue eyes darkening with something I couldn't quite pinpoint, but it looked like anger. "I should get to Matteo."

"I understand," I murmured, before pressing my lips against his jaw. "I'll see you for dinner."

He nodded rigidly before leaving. Watching his retreating back, I knew what we were both thinking. This attack was no coincidence. It was the Serpents, and they were getting their revenge. This was only the beginning, and I couldn't help but feel guilty for what had happened. I knew I shouldn't have gotten Nero involved in my mess. With a heavy sigh, I forced myself to move from the bathroom and towards my closet, where I began to prepare my attire for the day. I had a long day, involving the paperwork of newcomers that Xander and Calix had retrieved over the last few weeks. Grabbing a brown blazer, some leather pants, and a black ribbed top, I quickly began to change when a sudden urge to double up came over me. My stomach shrieked in pain, and I rushed to the bathroom where I threw up. I knew one thing for sure and that was that I *never* threw up, even when I was drunk. So, I was thoroughly astonished when I clutched the toilet, and spilt my guts out. Groaning in pain, my stomach cried, and I swallowed thickly as I noticed blood mixed with the yellow liquid. I staggered onto my feet, flushing the toilet, before cleaning myself up, trying to think of valid reasons why I had thrown up. There was no way in hell that I was pregnant; it really would not even be a possibility considering how safe we always were. Especially, given the circumstances we were in.

It must be something I ate, I speculated to myself, whilst pulling my blazer on and zipping up my boots. I thought about whether I should inform Nero of this incident but decided against it since he already had too much on his plate. It was probably nothing anyways. Regardless, I didn't want to take the risk of throwing up again whilst at the Manor, knowing it would probably set off alarm bells and Kira or Xander would send me home before I could defend myself. Therefore, I swallowed some pills and thought against eating breakfast. I guess it will be just water today. On the way to the Manor, my stomach continued to ache, and I concluded it must be cramps, seeing as I was to start my period next week. I didn't think about it for the rest of the day. The Manor was lively as I entered the mansion, little girls giggling and laughing as they settled around the large television with the men who were playing a round of Call of Duty. The men swore at each other which had the girls bursting into fits of laughter, and I smiled to myself. They were safe. All of them. I found the younger boys in the kitchen – it was their day to prepare lunch – and I laughed when I saw the mess they created. Knowing they would get an earful from Sophie, I sent them a grin before heading to my office. Kira was already in the room, looking more like herself as she was wearing blue jeans, a white shirt tucked in, and stilettos to complete the outfit. Her blonde hair tossed over her shoulders when she got up from the seat as soon as she saw me, folder and a phone in hand that was buzzing with messages.

"You should be resting, Kira," I lamented, settling my bag onto the desk, and sitting down. My second shrugged, her blue eyes following my hands, as I switched the laptop on and gestured for her to hand me the folder she was holding. "What's this?"

"Something Xander prepared for you, he wanted me to give it to you," Kira explained, before taking a seat in the chair opposite me. "And I couldn't rest. It's been a few days, Aria, and all I've been doing is resting. I wanted to get back to doing what I usually did."

"Did the doctor give you the green light?" I looked up at her under my lashes, arching a brow.

She shrugged again. "Would it even matter?"

I knew it would be pointless to argue with her and returned my attention to what was tucked into the folder. Xander had pulled up a list of companies that were supplying the Serpents after Viktor let it slip, during one interrogation, that the Serpents had people supporting them. Sifting through the pieces of paper, I noticed that several of these companies were Spanish and wondered if that had any correlation to the Serpents.

"Has anything suspicious been happening in Spain?" I wondered, glancing at Kira, who was scrolling on her phone.

"Not to my knowledge," she responded, before frowning at her phone. "Though, it seems the King will be stepping down and his son will have a coronation in a few months, but I'm not too sure why it would connect with the Serpents."

"You never know. Keep an eye on Spain for now," I ordered, and she bobbed her head. Another pain struck my stomach, and I bit my lip back to hold the groan threatening to escape.

Unfortunately, nothing passed Kira's eyes, and she narrowed them at me. "What's wrong?"

"Nothing," I squeaked.

"You look like you're about pass out. Are you not feeling well? Why did you come in?" she scolded, reaching over to press the back of her hand against my forehead. Her eyes widened as she blinked at me. "Aria, you're burning up."

"I'm fine," I coughed, pushing her hand away from me. Shoving everything back into the folder, I tucked it into the drawer of my desk and ignored Kira's piercing gaze, as I returned to the paperwork I didn't manage to finish off last night.

"*Aria.*"

"I'm fine, Yakira," I said.

I knew she was concerned about my wellbeing, but this was nothing except something that could backtrack my duties. She pressed her lips into a thin line and nodded stiffly before leaving my office, an indication that she was now mad. I stopped what I was doing and watched her walk away, disappearing at the end of the hallway as she entered the elevator. I nibbled on my lower lip before reaching out and touching my forehead. My skin burnt at the touch, and I frowned, wondering what on earth was going on. Knowing that Kira would probably tell Xander or Calix, I dialed the Manor doctor before any of them did and informed him of what was occurring. After discussing my symptoms, he notified me that he would be on his way but assured me that it might seem like I was coming down with a severe case of flu, but it could also be food poisoning. I knew that was the most reasonable explanation, but something nagged me. I ignored the feeling and decided to continue working until the doctor came. My body burned whilst I was working so I opened my windows, hoping the cold air would cool the heat rushing throughout my body. Worry left me with a sinking feeling in my stomach, and I forced myself to think nothing but positive thoughts. Eventually, the doctor came an hour later with his briefcase filled with equipment he used to do a quick check-up. Xander, unfortunately, walked in at the same time with a frown, narrowing his eyes as he leaned against the doorway and watched the doctor press the stethoscope against my chest before getting all my readings, jotting it down in his notebook. I didn't meet Xander's gaze and waited for the doctor's verdict, pressing my lips together.

"I'm sure it's nothing serious," he said with a warm smile. It didn't ease my tension as I nodded stiffly. "But to be on the safe side, I'll need to do a quick blood test."

I swallowed thickly and looked away as he pushed my sleeve up, inserting a cold thin needle into my arm where he gathered three test tubes of blood. It was then that I finally looked up at Xander, who had concern dancing in his eyes, nibbling on his lower lip despite his attempt to remain impassive. Like glass, I saw right through him. He watched the doctor draw out the blood from my arm before shifting his gaze upon me. Our eyes met. I smiled. A minute later, so did he. Finally, the doctor was done, tucking his things back into the briefcase whilst I pushed my sleeve down over the band-aid on my arm. He turned to me with a friendly grin, but I didn't return it.

"You should get your test result by the end of the week. For now, it would be best for you to return home and rest. You need to drink a lot of fluids, especially if you're feeling sick as you're losing minerals every time you vomit," the doctor ordered, clicking the briefcase shut.

"Thank you for coming on such short notice," I said, and he chuckled.

"Anything for you, Aria. I'll be off and I'll get back to you as soon as possible," With a small bow and a nod in Xander's direction, he left the room.

Xander didn't say anything and for once I didn't know what he was thinking. His dark eyes were trained on the ground as I sighed and forced myself to return to my desk, where I began to shuffle through my paperwork.

"I'll have one of the men take you home," he suddenly spoke, my eyes flickering up to where I met his.

"Xander –"

" – No," he held his hand up, cutting my protest short. "You will head home, Aria. It's not a suggestion."

"And who said you were the boss of me?"

"I'm not," Xander responded, coolly, ignoring my glare. "I'm your friend. Gather the things you want to take back with you; the car will be ready in ten."

I wanted to argue, claim that I was okay, but the last time I had felt this unwell was several years ago. I thankfully had a robust immune system so I wouldn't easily fall ill, so I knew this could be something serious. And so did Xander. I bobbed my head and looked away, running my fingers through my hair in frustration. He clenched his jaw and strode off, his large frame disappearing into the elevator that opened up and revealed Kira. After a few short words with her, the two disappeared but I didn't miss the look they sent in my direction. On the journey back home, I flicked through the messages on my phone and noticed how Nero hadn't messaged me once today. I was worried. I debated on whether I should call him but quickly thought against it, knowing I didn't want to bother him any further. With the help of two of my men, we brought my stacks of paperwork into my penthouse and dropped them off on the glass dining table. The men made sure that I would be alright by myself, before they reluctantly left me. I had grumbled my complaints and shoved them out of my home, saluting them, playfully. I knew they weren't at ease with leaving me alone, but they didn't voice their concerns after the glare I shot in their direction and they obeyed my commands. My penthouse was quiet without Nero or someone else keeping me company, but the ringing in my head was thankful for that as I forced myself to change into something far cozier. Pulling on some joggers and a loose t-shirt, I tied my hair back into a messy bun whilst heading downstairs to brew myself some herbal tea.

My mother was a huge fan of herbal medicines, and I was skeptical but desperate times called for desperate measures. Humming, I stirred in some sugar into the spice tea, before heading to my couch after grabbing an armful of paperwork. I hated it but to support everyone in the Manor, I had to go through several different forms of paperwork. I pulled my legs up onto the couch where I crossed one over the other and then reached out to sort through the first amount of work. Time passed quickly as I managed to finish my work off late in the evening. I groaned, stretching my aching muscles, and glanced at the clock, noticing how late it had gotten. Nero hadn't returned home yet. I nibbled on my lower lip, worriedly, glimpsing at my phone and itching to call him. It wasn't like him not to call all day, but I knew he had good reason not to. I tried to weigh the pros and cons before opting otherwise, hearing the sound of my stomach grumble. Famished, I stumbled into my kitchen and made myself soup, seeing as I couldn't stomach anything else. I watched the city's liveliness from my windows whilst eating, admiring how pretty the skyline was under the twinkling stars and illuminating moon. I pondered over how much my life had changed this year. To think I hated Nero when I first arrived in New York and now I was married to him.

It amused me thoroughly and I found myself smiling, shaking my head with a soft chuckle. We were so close to finally taking the Serpents down, the beast within me was bloodthirsty for revenge. She wanted me to tear these men apart until they were nothing but pieces of who they used to be. I wanted to break them, as they had broken all those people, that they had held captive against their free will. A dark feeling shrouded me and I soothed the monster, quietly promising that I would satisfy her demands. My thoughts were broken by the sound of footsteps, that I knew belonged to the love of my life. Dropping my bowl into the kitchen sink, I rushed to see Nero as he entered the living room, looking incredibly tired with deep sunken circles under his eyes and his hair disheveled, as if he had run his fingers through his dark locks several times.

Yet, he still looked gorgeous.

He fell against the couch, leaning his head back whilst I quietly shifted to his side, unsure of what to say or do. I wasn't good at comforting people; that was something he did. Hesitantly, I moved to him before freezing as blue orbs snapped in my direction. My eyes widened and my breath hitched under his electric gaze.

"Aria," he murmured, in his deep voice that had shivers running down my spine. "I thought you'd be asleep."

"I couldn't sleep. You weren't there," was my response.

My words were too quiet for him to hear but I knew he did as he outstretched his hand, waiting for me to take it. Gingerly, I slipped my hand into his and staggered as he tugged me towards him until I was settled in between his legs. He glanced up, his hands moving to my hips and drew me closer, causing me to reach out and grab his shoulders for support. My cheeks burned under his gaze and anticipation overwhelmed me, a burning need that only he could satisfy flamed within me. His fingers brushed my hips as they scrunched up the hems of my t-shirt, gripping them tightly.

"Did you manage to sort everything out?" I forced myself to say, almost choking at my words when his blue eyes darkened as they skimmed down the length of my body.

"No," he replied. "Our only option is to track down whoever hijacked our cargo."

"Do you have any idea who it could be?" I questioned, candidly.

Aquamarines shone. "Do you?"

Yes. "No."

Then he smiled. He saw right through my lie. Yet, he smiled for the first time today and that warmed my heart.

"We'll stop them. Don't you worry," he murmured, before glancing at my lips. "Can I kiss you?"

I wanted to say yes but I didn't know what was wrong with me and, in fear of Nero catching it too, I shook my head. "Not today."

He frowned as I tore myself away from his arms and began to tidy the mess I had created with my stacks of paperwork. I felt his hot gaze as I moved around the room, cleaning up, before halting when the tingling sensation of warm breath skimmed my neck. My body froze and I knew he was right behind me. His lips wavered above my neck as his arms curled around my body, pressing me right up against his own.

"What's wrong?" he muttered.

"Nothing, I'm just not feeling well," I replied, dismissively, and that earned me a frown as I glanced over my shoulder. Nero's brows were drawn together as he took in this information before he reached out and gently touched my forehead like Kira did this afternoon.

"You're burning up," he stated, before narrowing his eyes. "Why didn't you call me? Did you call the doctor? Why aren't you resting? When did you get home?"

He shot question after question in my direction, and I knew this was why I didn't want to tell him. I sighed, pushing his hand away from me. "I'm fine, Nero. The doctor said it's just a cold and I came home a couple of hours ago, but there was a lot of work to finish up, so I brought most of it home with me."

He crinkled his nose. "Why didn't you call me?"

"I didn't want to worry you. You were already busy, and this was nothing for you to get too concerned over," I explained, gently rubbing my thumb against his cheek, his beard brushing against my skin. "I swear I'm okay."

His jaw flexed which meant he didn't believe me. Before I could process what was happening, he swept me into his arms and strode upstairs, towards our bedroom. In a blink of an eye, I was in bed, and he was pulling the blanket over my body before discarding his blazer to the side and rolling his sleeves up to his elbows. If I weren't so enthralled in the mere action, I would have voiced my complaints, but Nero was startling godly, therefore the words remained trapped in my throat. He disappeared into the bathroom before coming out a few minutes later with a damp cloth and settling beside me on the bed, surprising me as he pressed the cold fabric against my forehead and then, my neck. With full concentration, he lightly tended to me. I watched him, silently, my heart stuttering at how compassionate he was as he took care of me. The depth and vibrancy of his cobalt eyes were a sight I could unwittingly get lost in, twinkling when the moonlight hit them. Despite how tired he was, he continued to look after me. I wanted him to stop but I couldn't help relish in the warm touch that not only caused butterflies in my stomach, but also made me fall deeper in love with him. So, under the twilight sky, I fell asleep at the soothing caress of my love.

When I woke up, the sun broke through the curtains that had been drawn together and the rays of light brightened the room thus forcing me to open my eyes. I yawned, feeling slightly better than yesterday, and glanced at the space beside me which I found to be empty. My lips turned down and I speculated as to where Nero could have disappeared off to as I slipped out of bed, pulling a gown over my body. While dressing, I noticed I had been changed into a negligee instead of the items of clothing I remember wearing last night. At that, I narrowed my eyes and concluded Nero must have changed me whilst I was passed out which meant he had gone through my closet and seen everything. And I mean *everything.* I ignored the heat threatening to color my cheeks and continued my journey to find a certain Italian man. As I stepped down the stairs, I wondered if he had gone to work but seeing his shoes by mine in the hallway quickly dispelled that thought. My eyes scouted the living room before the kitchen, where I found him hunched over the stove, and halted. I greedily relished at his beautifully chiseled body, from the pair of PJ bottoms he was wearing loosely around his hips, to the apron thrown over his very exposed chest. His back muscles flexed as he stirred the pan with those corded arms, and I wondered if I had died and gone to heaven. The scene was almost something out of a movie and I was afraid that any sudden movement would break this moment. As he pushed his shoulders back, straightening his spine, every contour of his delicious muscles rippled, and my eyes widened. My cheeks burned but I couldn't tell whether it was from the cold or the sight of Nero. As if he could feel my lewd gaze, he peered over his shoulder and then raised a brow at the sight of me. I didn't care to move. Then, he gave me a lopsided grin and moved slightly, revealing a homemade omelet.

"I made breakfast," he said, adorably. I hummed in appreciation, and forced my legs to move towards him as he finished off cooking. Sitting at the kitchen island, I watched as he plated our meals and poured us orange juice, ignorant to my longing eyes. "I was going to bring it upstairs."

I didn't answer, completely consumed by his presence. Noting my lack of reply, he glanced up, where he caught me in the act. His lips teased an amused smile, as he chuckled.

"Aria, your cheeks are incredibly red," he pointed out.

"Your fault," was my reply. "Can we go upstairs?"

"You need to eat."

"I want to eat you," My retort took him off guard, his eyes widened and his cheeks reddening at how candidly I was speaking. Smirking, I leaned forward and blinked at him innocently. "What do you say,

Russo?"

His jaw tightened and he shook his head with such remarkable restraint. "No. You need to eat and then rest."

I rolled my eyes. "How comes you're still here?"

"I took the day off," he responded, sliding my plate over to me.

I narrowed my eyes. "Nero."

"No arguing. I'll be taking care of you until you get better."

He left no room to argue, as he turned away from me and began to make himself a coffee. I threw daggers into his back before reluctantly giving into his stubbornness. I knew he was worried; he didn't even bother hiding it in his eyes, but I wasn't sure what I could do to make it go away. Thus, I allowed him to take care of me without any further complaints for the rest of the day. At lunch, he prepared carbonara and I studied him, dreamily, as he expertly took over the kitchen. With ease, he cooked the dish despite my scrutinizing gaze. I wasn't the best in the kitchen, so I was glad he could easily fulfil the role. After scoffing down the meal, satisfying my famished stomach, he forced me to head upstairs and rest when he caught me sniffling and clutching the cardigan tighter around my body. My body was ice cold, so I happily complied to his order, seeking the warmth of my blanket, whilst he finished eating. Just as I had managed to doze off, my phone rang, and I saw Calix's name blink on the lit screen. I contemplated answering but before I could, the ringing stopped, and I shrugged. I would get back to him later. I must have been exhausted because when I woke up the sun was beginning to set, and the sky was a beautiful shade of pink and purple inked with orange and yellow. My body was crying in pain, but I pushed myself out of the comfort of my bed to find Nero, seeing as he was not in the room. Treading lightly down the stairs, I pulled the hoodie I grabbed before leaving my room over my body. I found Nero by the couch, hunched over as he flicked through the file on the coffee table, a glass of half-drunken whiskey in his hand and the shirt he was wearing tightly clinging onto his broad torso, accentuating his muscles.

Although my steps were practically mute, he heard me and looked up with a frown. "You're awake."

"How long was I out for?" I murmured, curling beside him on the couch.

"A few hours," he replied, and touched my cheeks. "You're still hot. Let me grab some aspirin."

I watched him disappear into the adjoining kitchen before glancing at his files. My eyes skimmed the sheets of paper and I frowned when I saw the damage the Serpents had caused the Italians. The cargo, which was being sent to New York, was filled with the latest weaponry and technology from Austria, an alliance I remember my father had made with them when he was in charge. However, the hijacking had now caused tension and from these files, it seemed the Austrians were not happy that their exports weren't protected and that they had to send another batch to the Italians - more than they agreed to. Another sheet had the agreement between the Italians and Russians, and I instantly recognized my aunt Gabrielle's signature scrawled across the bottom.

"Here," Nero said, my eyes flickering over to him as he passed me a glass of water and aspirin.

"What are you doing?" I asked, gulping the medicine.

Nero sat back beside me with a heavy sigh. "Trying to sort out this mess."

There was a thick silence between us, and I couldn't ignore the guilty feeling gnawing at my stomach as I bit my lip, clutching the empty glass in my hand whilst Nero drank the remaining liquid in his.

"I feel like this is my fault," I blurted. He looked at me in confusion. With a sigh, I placed the glass on the table and shrugged my shoulders. "I mean, I know it's my fault. If I didn't get you involved with my plot, then the Serpents wouldn't have attacked you, and now the Italians are practically defenseless."

A deep chuckle surprised me; my eyes widened as Nero ran a hand over his face, a smile teasing his lips before he looked at me. "Aria, you can't possibly blame yourself for this. It's not like you told them to hijack the cargo," then he arched his brow, "Unless you did?"

I scowled. "Of course not."

He grinned. "Then this is no one's fault but theirs."

"You don't seriously believe that?"

"Of course, I do. I must admit I was mad at first but at myself, because I've been forgetting my responsibilities lately but only to spend time with you, and for that, I don't regret it all," he took my hands, and I watched how they disappeared in his large hands. "This is their fault and as I said, we will stop them."

I exhaled, nodding my head to which he responded by pressing his lips on my forehead. Then, he returned to his work, and I shifted closer, placing my chin onto his shoulder to peer at the files. "Is there anything I can do to help?"

"All you can do for me is get better," he replied, glimpsing back and his blue eyes found mine. "Are you hungry?"

"Only a little a bit," I admitted, quietly.

"I'll go prepare dinner," he kissed me before I could move away, and my cheeks burnt as he smirked when he pulled back. The surprise across my face amused him, my jaw-dropping, and he chuckled to himself, shoulders shaking as his chest reverberated. "Close your mouth unless you want to put it to good use."

Flustered, I sputtered out, "Excuse me, I-I am ill."

He raised a brow. "So?"

I didn't know what to say when I saw the dark spark in his azure orbs, a seductive promise that I knew he would certainly fulfil. They stole my breath away and the words right out of my mouth. He knew he was gorgeous and grinned at my dumbfounded reaction, shaking his head at my speechless antics. But what could I say when I wanted him as much as he wanted me? Coughing, awkwardly, I broke myself from the spell he placed on me and scratched my head as I looked away.

"Why don't you take a break? You shouldn't work too hard," I muttered.

"What do you have in mind?" he mused, a ghost of a smile on his lips and twinkle in his eyes.

I thinned my eyes. "Get your mind out of the gutter."

Smiling innocently, he shrugged. "I'm not sure what you're thinking but I thought we could watch a film," Nero narrowed his eyes teasingly. "Maybe, it's you who needs to get their mind out of the gutter."

I sulked as he laughed, drawing me into his arms despite my attempts to shrug him off me. He kissed the side of my head and brought me onto his lap whilst I crossed my arms over my chest and refused to look at him, childishly.

"How about we take a nap?" he suggested, kissing my neck, fondly.

"I already napped," I grumbled, ignoring the tingling sensation on my neck.

"Well, I haven't, and I want you beside me," he retorted, and I struggled to wriggle out of his arms as he laid us on the couch, using his arm as my pillow, and turning me around so I was facing him. I wrinkled my nose as he smiled wolfishly, running his hand down my arm before entwining our fingers.

"I don't consent to this," I muttered.

He rolled his eyes before closing them. "Shut up, Aria, and go to sleep."

His lashes fanned across his cheek, hiding those magnetic blue eyes from me as he rested. He must have been tired because, after a few minutes, all I heard was the sound of his steady breathing as his chest rose and fell. I wasn't tired, having already taken my nap, but I wanted to cherish being in his arms, so I snuggled up closer to his body, fitting in the contours of his frame perfectly, and tucked my head under his chin. Instinctively, his arms wrapped around me and held me in that comfortable position. Within minutes, I was lulled back to sleep by Nero's soft breathing and the warmth of his body against mine.

CHAPTER 43

traitor

Kira

"So, what's the plan?" Dom asked, as he settled into his designated seat whilst the rest of us poured into the room. Aria stood at the front; she looked far healthier and there was a glow to her skin that I knew was a result of Nero.

"Phase 3," she stated. "We're taking down the Serpents."

There was a long silence which soon followed her words. This was it. This was what we had spent the last five years preparing for. Everything up until now was to gather enough information on the Serpents so we knew exactly how to root them out in a way which would prevent them from ever forming again. My eyes took stock of the room. Each one of us had been taken under Aria's wing when we were broken pieces of someone we used to be, but now we were stronger than anyone could have imagined.

Than *we* once could have imagined.

Xander was the first to speak, "How?"

A simple question but the most important one.

"We have enough information on the Serpents; from where they keep their weapons, to their bank information, and finally the locations of the people they're holding hostage. Most importantly, we have the three names of the Inner Circle."

"We still don't know who the boss is," Sophie pointed out. For some reason, her words made me flinch. If Aria saw it, she didn't show it.

She nodded. "This is true but after their attack on the Italians, I decided we have wasted enough time gathering more information, when we have more than enough to attack."

"And how do you propose we do this?" Calix asked, leaning forward, as his green eyes narrowed. "To go blindly into Enzo's estate and shoot everyone?"

I saw the tick in Aria's jaw and almost frowned. She had never acted this way before. Especially with Calix. My eyes moved to him and for the first time in a long while, I noticed that he looked as if he hadn't slept for days, with dark rings creating a shadow under his emerald eyes. Those eyes that used to be so innocent and playful were now hostile and defiant. And if I had seen it, so did Aria. She arched her brow at him, the corner of her lips curling into a smile.

"Exactly," were her words. He looked a bit stunned and by the sound of whispers which followed, so was everyone else. Aria ignored the bewildered looks, tossing her brown tendrils over her shoulders, her hazel eyes scanning the room. "I want them dead. Every single one of them. So, as Calix said, we will be storming Enzo's estate."

"Aria, this is suicidal," Xander frowned.

"Certainly, but Operation Quetzalcoatl, as Kira discovered, involves the destruction of the mafias, which means that the hijacking of the Italian weaponry was no revenge act but the beginning of their final plan. We need to stop them before they hit their next target," she explained.

"And where's that?" Ciara speculated, pushing her framed rims onto her nose.

"My aunt has informed me about their latest shipment arriving in New York at the end of this week," Aria said. Having never met Aria's family, it still surprised me to know that she was a descendent of both the Russian and the Italian mafias. She could have everything and anything she wanted with a snap of her fingers, but here she stood helping take down the worst criminals on this planet and save the less fortunate. I was immensely proud of her. "I suspect that's their next target."

"How can you be sure?" Mark frowned, as he entwined his fingers with Sophie's, his girlfriend, curling closer to his side.

I smiled. They were cute. When Sophie first arrived at the Manor,

Mark was the only man she was comfortable around. After being surrounded by men who abused her body like she was a doll, Mark helped her overcome those fears and the two naturally gravitated to each other. Likewise, Sophie stopped all the nightmares Mark suffered after being forced to kill children whenever the Serpents raided small towns. He was tortured after every attack until he couldn't feel anything. Then, he met Sophie. They found peace in each other; many of us would envy that privilege, because not all of us would ever experience it.

"The Serpents are getting lazy. They're too predictable. I had a feeling they'd go after the Italians, knowing that Nero was currently occupied with me, which means he wouldn't be paying attention to the mafia. They'd go after the Russians next because they have enough resources to take on a stronger opponent. The next shipment contains the Russian's batch of weaponry from Austria, which means that is what the Serpents are after."

"Why?" I spoke, for the first time since we started this meeting.

Aria's eyes flickered to me. "I'm not entirely sure. I can't say for certain but with the amount of weaponry they are gathering, I have a feeling they're planning something big. I suspect Operation Quetzalcoatl is more than robbing the Italians and Russians.

"Why haven't they attacked the other mobs like the Triads?" Xander mused.

"I think they have. After speaking to my aunt, it seems there are rumors going around that the Triads and Yakuza shared similar fates to the Italians. They didn't want to be vocal about it because they're a proud bunch," Aria replied with a sigh. Xander kissed his teeth in response. We were all thinking the same thing – if they had spoken up, we could have stopped the attack on the Italians before it had happened. She continued, "These armaments from Austria are extremely valuable, powerful and limited. If the Serpents get a hold of these, there is no way we can stop them. We need to hit the estate when they least expect it."

"When do you plan on doing that?" Calix questioned.

"I haven't finalized the details yet, but I wanted you all to be aware," Aria answered, settling into her seat with an unreadable look in her eyes. I saw her wince when she sat down and knew she was far from recovered – that was why she couldn't give us a date.

"Aria –" I went to speak but her dark eyes silenced me.

They couldn't know.

I saw the message and pressed my lips together. *Why?* I wanted to ask. I wanted to know why she wouldn't disclose that tiny piece of information to the rest of the group. But if I knew Aria, I knew she didn't do things without a good reason. For the rest of the meeting, whether we were discussing the status of our training system or the new arrivals we had, I remained quiet and carefully studied my closest friend. Something was troubling her. I just knew it, but I couldn't pinpoint what it was. She leaned back in her chair, one leg crossed over the other, her finger tapping her lip thoughtfully, as Calix informed her about expanding the Manor since we were gaining more people or otherwise, we should temporarily pause our retrieval of Serpent victims. At that notion, Aria's eyes chilled. It was a mixture of disbelief and irritation like she couldn't fathom why he would suggest such a thing. I almost voiced my opinion, but the way Calix cowered at her intense gaze had me staying quiet. I could see that he wanted to fight but Aria's word was final.

"That shouldn't even be an option," she said, in a frosty tone that dropped the temperature of the room. Everyone stilled whilst she kept her cold eyes on the Greek man, who clenched his jaw. "Don't ever suggest something like that again."

Calix sighed. "It was a thought."

"A thought that shouldn't have ever crossed your mind. Where is your mind at lately, Calix?" she leaned forward, narrowing her eyes. "You've been distracted lately. Everyone can see it. Want to explain?"

"It's just that we are so close, I don't want us to screw this up," he answered, but we all knew it was a lie. That was the con of living together for so long. Nonetheless, no one voiced the obvious, including Aria. She nodded her head and relaxed back into her seat, clasping her hands together.

"You've been given your orders. That will be all," As soon as those words left her lips, everyone scattered out of the room in fear that they would be the next to suffer her wrath. I was the last to leave, gathering the agenda for today's meeting along with extra files, but just as I stood up, a quiet call of my name stopped me in my position. My eyes flickered to Aria, who absentmindedly played with her wedding ring. "Konstantin will be killed tomorrow."

My heart stopped. I had forgotten about him. Months of delaying his death and tomorrow he would finally be gone. I should have been relieved, but I wasn't because I still didn't get the closure I deserved. I knew Aria had plans to kill him, no matter what, and I didn't want to stop her, but I also wanted closure. Maybe, the sick part of all this was that I would never get the closure I deserved, and all I was doing was delaying the punishment of the man responsible for all my demons.

"I'm telling you this because I need to know if I can do this."

"Right," I muttered. A beat later, "When?"

"In the morning. Xander will be completing the task," she stated, her eyes trained on the windows which were covered in raindrops. "But, only if you're okay with it."

I inhaled a deep breath of air. I knew what she was asking me between the lines – was I finally ready to move on? I didn't know if I ever would be, but I did know that the longer I spent with Konstantin, the more I remained connected with the girl from the past.

"Okay."

"Okay," There was a long silence and neither of us knew what else to say until Aria broke it, "You can ask now."

"Sorry?" I furrowed my brows.

She looked up. "Ask me why."

At first, I was still lost as to what she was suggesting before realization dawned on me. "Why didn't you tell them that you're still not feeling well?"

"Because there's a traitor amongst us."

Those words knocked the air right out of me. A traitor. I knew there was one in the Manor, but to claim that it was within the close group of people that helped form this family we were part of today… that was another thing. I couldn't imagine why anyone would choose to betray us, especially if we had saved them from the Serpents. It made no logical sense. Only, to Aria, it did.

"Who?" I managed to say.

She shook her head. "I don't know the answer to that yet, but I'm sure we will find out soon."

"How can you be so sure?"

"Call it a gut feeling," she stood up, fixed her blazer, and walked out. It took me a few seconds to process what she had told me before I hurried after her. "If they find out that I'm not feeling well, they'll use it to their advantage. We need to keep up the facade that I am healthy. Okay?"

"But are you okay?" I whispered.

She didn't respond.

*

That evening, I was in the library, east of the main section of the Manor, thus, far from the noise. I couldn't work with all the sounds resonating off the walls. Ever since I had gotten my memories back, fragments of my time in captivity returned back to me, yet I never told anyone in fear that I would only give them incorrect information for something I conceivably never saw. The doctor didn't want to say it but we both knew that it was a possibility that I would never know the truth of those days. The mind was a complex structure – it tried to protect me at my weakest. But it was still protecting me now. Small flashbacks of those nights would come to me in my nightmares, haunting me like a ghost in an abandoned building. I remembered the whips slashing my back, the wounds that were now covered in bandages that were once bleeding profusely. Blood spilt onto the ground as they pelted punches into my stomach until they broke my ribs. My body was thrown around like a rag doll until I got pretty scars across my arms and bruises on my face. I could see Barak's indifferent expression and Enzo's sadistic smile as they watched me get beaten to the point of death, hearing the word '*stop*' just before they could take my last breath. I remembered wanting to die, begging them to just kill me but they never did. They just brought me to the edge, and they stripped away the liberty of death.

At one point, Enzo had come down with his men and after beating me, he tilted his head to the side and smirked. I saw the look in his eyes, and I knew what it meant. I saw it in those men who Konstantin sold me to. A scream had torn through my throat as two men held me down whilst the third unbuckled his trousers. All whilst Enzo watched. However, before the man could touch me, he froze. My screaming stopped and I felt something drip onto my cheek. Then, I looked up and saw blood. He had been shot. In the head. I couldn't breathe as the man crumpled onto the floor, his body narrowly missing me, whilst the other two men stumbled to their feet in shock at the sight of their comrade dying. Enzo's smile fell and he looked behind him, so I followed his gaze and that was when I saw the other man – the boss – holding a gun. I couldn't remember his face, no matter how much I tried. All I could remember was those eyes.

Hazel eyes.

They swirled with such irritation as they glared at Enzo, who looked visibly afraid. Without saying a word, Enzo and his men left the room whilst I curled into the corner as the unknown man strolled leisurely to the bar. The lighting missed him by a long shot, his face hidden by the shadows, but the fluorescent light hit his eyes and illuminated them to be a startling hazel – a mixture of green and gold. He didn't say anything as he stared, taking in my naked body that was raw with the wounds inflicted by his men, then he left.

There was a dull sensation in the back of my mind as I tried to finish my work, hunched over the desk as I scribbled my signature across agreements which would allow us free passage in states and countries that were heavily guarded and secured. We needed these agreements if we intended on expanding our mission worldwide. After we would take down the Serpents, the next steps would be to establish homes across the world where victims under the Serpents' reigns could reside until they could manage to be on their own in the world.

We wanted to provide a safe haven; it was the very word Aria had used to describe her mission when she first met me.

"I want to create a safe haven for those who have fallen, been forgotten or can never fight their demons alone. I want to bring peace," Aria said, with resolute.

"How will you do that?" I murmured, quietly.

She smiled.

And here we were. Finally bringing the Serpents' reign to an end and starting a new chapter of our lives. For five years, all I had known was the destruction of the Serpents, the burning need to destroy what had destroyed me. Yet here I was preparing for the aftermath – the rehabilitation. I couldn't help but smile. We were nearly there. Just one last hurdle.

"What you doing?" a voice disrupted my thoughts, and I saw Calix leaning against the bookshelves, his eyes on the sheets of paper chaotically scattered across the desk.

I sighed. "Just some work I couldn't do before."

His green eyes softened. "How are you feeling?"

I shrugged in response. We didn't say anything for a while, basking in the silence of each other's company. When I first met Calix, he was a boy who had stumbled into us on the streets. He was covered in wounds, with some deeper than others. I often speculated if he had ever recovered from them. Unlike the majority of us, Calix had always been reserved, lost in his thoughts, but he was charismatic and many of the girls loved that. Aria loved that. Albeit she *used* to love that. Calix and Aria had been the strongest pair for as long as I had known them both. They worked perfectly and in harmony with one another. Their constant bickering had turned into something else as we grew up, something that needed to be satisfied. Curiosity. I wasn't blind to their sexual affairs but, despite my words of warning, it wasn't my position to have a say in what they decided to do. Sometimes, I wondered if, at one point, they ever loved each other.

"Do you want to explain what's happened between you and Aria?" I speculated.

Calix frowned. "What do you mean?"

"Why haven't you been on the same page as Aria? You always backed her and now it seems you're always against her."

I saw the tick in his jaw which meant that I was right. He looked away with a dark expression that I couldn't read. "She's just making decisions that I don't think will ultimately benefit us."

"Like what?" Then, I arched my brow. "Like marrying Nero?"

He didn't reply at first, but that slight hesitance before his reply gave me my answer. "No."

I exhaled disappointedly, shaking my head as I placed my pen down. "Oh, Calix."

"What?"

"You went and caught feelings for her," I stated, frankly. He didn't wince. "You love her."

"And what about it?"

"She's married. She's happy. So, don't ruin it."

My words came out harsher than I intended, but I knew I got my message across when he looked down at the floor, a somber expression crossing his face, lashes hiding his green orbs. He didn't say anything for the longest time, training his eyes onto the ground as if there was something interesting about it, but I knew it was because he knew that if I saw his eyes, I would be able to tell exactly what he was feeling.

"I won't," was his response.

"Good," I bobbed my head and returned to my work.

"Have you remembered anything?" he questioned, diverting the attention to me as he settled in the seat opposite me.

"Nothing," I mumbled, chewing on my lower lip as I contemplated telling him about the brief memories of me in that basement. Calix's unfocused eyes scanned the paper on the table, so I decided against the idea and quickly masked an indifferent expression before he caught me in the lie.

"I'm sure it will eventually come back to you," he reassured. "Just don't force yourself. We'll find the traitor soon enough."

"I hope so. Aria just isn't herself nowadays and I'm worried."

"Once this is all over, everything is going to be okay."

I didn't reply because I didn't want to be a pessimist. Something told me this was far from over and it was all because I couldn't remember who the traitor was. It was frustrating, like a hole that I couldn't fill no matter what I did. I sighed heavily and leaned back in the chair, running my fingers through my blonde locks as I glanced at Calix, who, once again, was in deep thought. There was something on his mind, but I knew he would never speak it because he was always closed off.

"Can I ask something?" he murmured; his voice low as if he was afraid others would hear, despite the fact that we were the only people in the library. I nodded and he drew in a terse breath of air. "What did they do to you? Whilst, you know, you were held captive?"

I suspected he had been wanting to know so I wasn't thrown off guard, and I crossed my arms over my chest as my eyes flickered to the painting on the wall. It had been the first one we got after building the Manor. A portrait of Aria and me. It took in the softness of her brown hair and the harshness of her hazel eyes as she sat on the leather wingback chair, her legs crossed by the ankles and her hands on the arm rests. At the same time, it brightened the complexion of my pale skin and drew attention to my flaxen hair which I had dyed several months beforehand during captivity. I was shy at first, wanting to stand behind her because Aria was radiantly gorgeous, and I looked plain in comparison. However, she was adamant that I station myself beside her because we were equals. I could remember her smile as she brought me to her side and placed my hand onto her shoulder, whilst the other rested on my hip. Afterwards, we smiled at the painter and laughed about how ridiculous this would look in the years to come. I was still surprised by how easily she managed to convince me that this would be a good idea. Remembering that Calix was waiting for my answer, I held onto the good memories to remind me that the bad times were long gone.

"They hurt me. A lot. It wouldn't stop. Twenty-four hours.

Everyday. Until I was saved. Xander found me just before I passed out," The darkness in his eyes frightened me as he clenched his jaw. "I'm okay *now*."

"They will pay. I promise."

I smiled and took his hand. "I know."

He gave me quick squeeze and we got lost in the depth of the eyes of each other. As the corner of his lips quirked up, his eyes creased and the dim light above us hit them. There, those green stones shone brilliantly, and I found myself envious of their rarity.

That was until the green began to look slightly gold.

I squinted, trying to check if I was looking at him properly. Had his eyes always been hazel? He raised a brow and I quickly beamed, shuddering this bad feeling away.

"Is everything okay?" he queried, and I shook my head, recoiling my hand as if something had burnt me.

"Yeah, I'm just tired," I lied, and he frowned, dubiously, as he nodded. There was a long silence as I resumed my work before I stopped and looked at Calix, whose eyes flickered around the room. "Curious question, but what was your surname again?"

He tilted his head to the side. "Zervas. You know this."

I laughed. "Just double checking. I had forgotten."

Whether he believed me or not, I couldn't tell because this nagging feeling had turned into something darker, and I felt my entire body go cold. *No. No. No. This couldn't be possible*. Everything stilled. His jade orbs glittered with specks of gold and that was when I realized the color I had seen was green – they had *always* been green. But under the caliginous lights in the basement, it became hazel because the greenness of his iris was too dark to make clear, whilst the gold appeared vibrantly.

How was this possible?

It was that mere question that triggered my memories, and like a tsunami they crashed over me to the point where I nearly winced, had I not discreetly pinched my thigh and smiled tightly at the confused man in front of me. I remembered it all. I remembered seeing his name.

Calix Zervas.

It was written in bold with his signature scrawled underneath.

No.

He was the traitor.

"Kira?" he called out, narrowed eyes scrutinizing me, as he waved a hand in front of my face.

I nearly flinched but managed to stop as I blinked at him, trying to force the fear away. "Sorry, my mind is everywhere lately, ever since Aria told me Konstantin will be killed tomorrow."

Pity swam in Calix's eyes. Wrong move – Calix never felt pity, no matter who it was for. He knew something was up – he knew I was lying – which meant I had to leave. I had to tell Aria before he could stop me. "I'm sorry."

"I'm not. It's about time," I responded, coolly, as I stood up, gathering my things calmly despite the urgency spiking the adrenaline within me. "I should visit him before I get to bed."

Calix nodded, standing up and shoving his hands into his pockets. "Are you sure you're okay?"

No, never again.

I smiled, lightly. "Perfect."

CHAPTER 44

sacrifice

Kira

I had to find Aria. I had to find her. I rushed down the corridors frantically, wild eyes searching the rooms until I found her. Xander crossed paths with me, concern swimming in his eyes as he grabbed my arms, stopping me in my pursuit.

"Kira, what's wrong?"

"I need to find Aria," I stammered. "I have to tell her."

"Tell her what?" I struggled in Xander's hold, wanting to be let go, his words going right over my head, as I tried to move past him. *I need to get to Aria.* He shook me, becoming anxious as he called my name, "Kira?"

"I need Aria. Where is Aria?" I couldn't tell Xander, not until I had told Aria. I couldn't. It would break him. Calix was practically a brother to him. Through thick and thin. I couldn't do it. His dark eyes implored me to tell him the answer, but it was one I couldn't give him, not until Aria knew first. Accentuating every word with urgency, I demanded, "Xander, where is Aria?"

"She's just gone home. She wasn't feeling well so Nero picked her up. They just left. What's wrong?"

"You need to call Aria. She needs to come back."

"Kira, you're scaring me," his words shook, laced in fear and panic.

"Xander, you need to call Aria," I forced myself to say, calmly, my

396

body turning rigid when I caught sight of Calix strolling down the hallway, one hand tucked in his pocket and the other scrolling on his phone, idly. Swallowing thickly, I dropped my voice a couple of octaves so only Xander could hear, "Do not tell anyone what you're doing. No one. *Go.*"

He knitted his brows, and I knew he fought the urge to question me even more, but he heard the gravity of my words, and, like a loyal soldier, he finally let me go just as Calix looked up. Surprise flickered in his eyes when he caught sight of us, a frown teasing his lips, whilst I plastered on an indifferent expression which Xander mirrored. Yet, I saw the confusion at my sudden change of emotions.

"Why are you still here? I thought you were going to visit Konstantin?" Calix asked, eyes flitting between Xander and I.

"Bumped into Xander," I smiled, sheepishly. "I'm heading there now."

"Do you want company?" Calix offered, but I shook my head.

"I'll be good," I lied, straight through my teeth, and Calix suspiciously bobbed his head, whilst Xander watched this interaction, worriedly. "I'll catch you boys later."

Before they could say another word, I disappeared down the hallway with my heart in my throat. My thoughts were everywhere but I had to wait for Aria to arrive back at the Manor, so I pushed myself towards the basement despite every step I took being one I wish I didn't. The basement was cold when I finally arrived. It was void of any source of light similar to the place I was held captive but as you walked down doors ranked each side. Not every room was filled; we didn't often allow our captives to be alive for so long. It would only be a matter of time until Aria asked for them to be removed. Konstantin was an exception along with Viktor. Just as I reached my stepfather's jail, I stopped by Viktor's cell and caught him sleeping in the empty room, chained against the wall. He would be killed next. Aria had kept him alive for too long that he was becoming a liability, and now that I knew Calix was the traitor, it meant we were not safe with Viktor in the Manor. So, I knew his time would come soon. I itched to enter the room but decided against it, knowing I was only delaying the inevitable. Konstantin was dozing off when I slipped into the room, hidden in the shadows of his cell. But the corner of his lips quirked up and I knew he sensed me. With his back against the wall and legs outstretched on the cold floor, chained with metal shackles, his eyes flickered open and settled on me.

Despite the darkness shrouding me, he *still* saw me.

"I was wondering when you'd finally pay a visit," he whispered, a scratchy and raspy voice filled the silence. I didn't reply and kept my eyes on him. "I guess that means I'll be dead soon. It's about time."

"It's been delayed for too long," I said.

"Only because you wanted it to be," was his response. His chuckle that followed had my lips coiling into a scowl. "So, who's my executioner? You?"

I looked away and he saw it.

"Of course not. You couldn't bring yourself to do it," he sighed, almost in disappointment. "You never could."

"Do you wish I could?"

"Yes."

His answer surprised me. There was a long silence before I moved out of the shadows and into the obscured section of the room. The bulb hanging above us swayed slowly, flickering every now and then, and I felt the air chill as it wafted into the room from the cracks in the ceiling. I saw the wounds inflicted on his skin and pondered how many of them were from me. No matter how much I tortured him, the anger never died. It would keep on eating me until it consumed me. This pain, this heartbreak, this betrayal – I wondered if it would ever go.

"Did you ever love me?" the words left my lips without a second thought.

I knew I took him off guard as he blinked at me, mouth gaping slightly, before he quickly concealed the humanity and trained his eyes onto the ground. His brows drew together, and his mouth opened then closed, like a fish, as if he couldn't figure out what he wanted to say. I waited for him to speak, keeping my eyes tracked on the man who I was sold to, and who then later sold me off again. Like I was nothing. Only I couldn't help but speculate whether he felt anything for me in those years we spent together. Was *everything* a lie? My biological father had sold me and my mother to Konstantin when I was a little girl, so I had spent most of my childhood in his household until I was sixteen. He brought me up, trained me, educated me, made me his prized possession and yet... he still sold me off. Like cattle. I didn't want to believe that he never cared for me. He must have, at least once during that period, right?.

"Yes. Very much so," were his words. I didn't question the sincerity of it – I could hear it in the way they trembled, brokenly. "I thought of you as my own daughter. Although you weren't my blood, I brought you up as my own."

"So why did you let me go?"

"Because I was a selfish bastard. I thought of my survival only. Your mother was never happy, and she never would be – rightfully so. But it was you who grounded me, reminded me of my morals."

"Your questionable morals," I scoffed, almost laughing. He didn't speak. "Kal Doukas thought I wasn't a virgin, but he was the first man to break me – so, naturally, I was the only woman to kill him."

Konstantin dark eyes enlarged at the statement, fumbling with words to say but I didn't give him a second to speak – not when I had so much to say.

"Why did you lie to Kal? Why did Tio and Idris believe that you stripped my purity away? You never touched me once, but you told them you did; they thought my body was used, and that you had killed my mother when she actually committed suicide. She killed herself but you chose to withhold that information from them. Why?"

"If they knew you were a virgin, they would have ruined you in ways you couldn't imagine."

"They still ruined me!" I bellowed, unable to hold back my pain, and the room quaked at the roaring rage. "They broke me! They raped me, and raped me, and raped me until I couldn't breathe. I didn't know my mother had committed suicide when I was sold off. You let me believe that she suffered the same fate as me. It wasn't until I joined Aria, I found out the truth. You took everything from me. She was all I had left and... I couldn't save her."

Tears loosely streamed down my cheeks and Konstantin gritted his jaw at the sight, agony lingering in his brown eyes. "I'm sorry."

"They destroyed me. I didn't deserve that," I whispered, his futile words passing over my head. "I didn't deserve any of this, but the second you took me from my real father was the moment everything fell apart. I lost my mother, my dignity, my purity, *myself* to men. Monsters who still haunt me. And it was because of you."

"Yakira, I don't know what to say," he muttered, pathetically.

I shook my head, limply, wiping away those traitorous tears, and spoke in a calm yet cold tone that had him shiver when the words kissed his skin, "You don't need to say anything. There is nothing you can say. I just want you to know that you killed the little girl you loved so much. You killed the girl I could have been. You *killed* me. And now you'll kill yourself. All because you were selfish."

"I did what I could to survive."

"Clearly not well enough," I spat out in incredulity, and he ducked his head in shame. "I was lucky Aria found me before I was completely gone. Some girls aren't as lucky as I am. Some girls suffer in the hands of many men. Some girls *don't survive*. I was raped, and destroyed, and mutilated, and tortured until I barely hung by a thread, until I wanted to tighten the leash around my throat just for it to all go away. And to this day, I still can't move past this. So, imagine the girls out there who are suffering from far worse. Girls who are being passed around as if they're dolls. Girls who just wanted to live a normal life. You said you loved me, but love isn't what you did. Love is protecting your family no matter what."

I paused, before continuing to speak from the bottom of my heart, words that he needed to hear. "You didn't love me. You loved the idea of a perfect family and that was why you robbed me from the chance of having one. Because you never had that opportunity. And I'm sorry for that."

His blinked at me, stuttering, "Wh-what?"

"I know what your parents did to you. I know they abused you badly and although that doesn't excuse you for the pain you've caused upon me, I'm sorry that you suffered as a child."

He was completely shell-shocked at my words and the heaviness in my heart lightened slightly. After I was taken under Aria's wing, my first mission was to find my mother but when I found out she had died, my world crashed down on me. The strongest woman in my life was gone because she couldn't handle the pain being inflicted on her. I was mad, I was bloodthirsty, I wanted revenge. So, I dug deep into Konstantin's past. I wanted to know where the worst place would be to hit him. Granted, it was difficult to find anything because he did a good job at burying it so deep, but everyone has skeletons in their closet that were bound to come out one day. Eventually, I found his.

"How…"

"How do I know this?" I finished off his sentence with an arch of my brow. A potent sensation surged over me. "I'm a powerful woman, Konstantin. I can find *anything*."

Standing in front of him, I felt like the most powerful woman in the world. His swollen eyes refused to find mine and fixated on the dull concrete wall. Then he swallowed *hard*, his bruised throat bobbing.

"Yakira, I know what I did can never be forgiven but I pray one day, you'll forget them," he whispered, remorsefully, glancing at me.

I smiled, bitterly. "I won't ever forget, nor will I ever forgive you. I realize now that was not what I needed to gain closure. What I need is for you to know how sorry I am for the way you were brought up. I'm sorry your parents forced you to watch your sister die in front of you, just so you could learn to be cold-hearted. I'm sorry for all the times they raised their hands on you. I'm sorry for you losing them in a tragic fire, which we both know you caused. I'm sorry that they were monsters who stripped you of your freedom, as you did to me. I'm sorry you grew up alone and isolated. I'm sorry your greed and selfishness had gotten the best of you. I'm sorry you became the same monsters as your parents. I'm sorry that you aren't any different to them."

Grief struck his eyes and although I was surprised, I didn't show it. All those months of being tortured, I never once saw pain so twisted and heart-wrenching than the pain I could see right now. That was how I knew he was finally broken. I felt something shift in the air and my heart suddenly felt a thousand times lighter, as if the weight which was chained to me had finally been stripped away and the shackles I wore just disappeared.

Closure.

Konstantin would never understand the magnitude of his actions, despite how horrendous his past was, but the way his eyes looked so fractured and penitent, I knew he finally saw the damage he had caused. And that was enough for me.

"I'm sorry," he repeated the words again, and this time I knew he meant it.

"I know you are," I stared at him, pitifully. "Not because you ruined my life, but because you are no less evil than your parents. And you probably spent half your life trying not to be."

He hung his head, ashamed, and I found myself exhaling heavily, shakily, freely. For the first time ever, I was liberated from the scars I had thought would never disappear. A smile appeared on my face as I tossed my blonde hair over my shoulders and peered at the old man who looked helpless, bound by chains. Money could not save him now. It was a pity because I knew he could have been a good father despite stripping me of my real one – he could have been a good substitute and one day, maybe I would have forgiven him. However, men were all the same. They loved, they hated, and they would do anything to ensure that they would never be blamed. They would never accept responsibility for the actions they had taken, and the consequences of them. This didn't mean all men were bad people, but most of them were and the minority wouldn't do anything to stop them for reasons beyond me. But it was these reasons that allowed injustices to continue.

"I don't know what else to say," he mumbled, quietly.

I shrugged. "You don't have to say anything. I just pray one day, if we ever meet again – in another life – you'll know what love means and what it means to be loved."

"Will we ever meet again?" he whispered, hope lingering in his voice. Hope that he could win me back one day.

I studied him, meticulously, and then rolled my shoulders back. I held my head high as I uttered, "For your sake, I hope to God not."

He stared at me like he wanted to cry, but I didn't let it affect me – it wouldn't affect me – instead, I moved to the chains on the walls and, using the key I grabbed on my way down, I unshackled him. At first, he was stunned, wide eyes watching me as the metal chains produced a hard, sharp non-resonant sound when they fell to the floor. Despite his scrutinizing gaze, I didn't stop and unlocked the final chain before taking a step back.

"What are you doing?" he questioned, dubiously. "I thought it was tomorrow."

"It is," My voice as cold as the temperature of the prison. "But I wanted to give you one last taste of freedom, even if it's in this cell."

At first, he seemed hesitant, cautious, distrustful of my words but when he noticed I wasn't going to do anything, he forced himself onto his feet. Staggering up, I took in his lanky frame that was covered by the torn, grimy clothing that barely covered him. He was skinny, hollow cheeks and pale skin, void from any nutrition. He reminded me of the girl I once was. Konstantin ran his nimble fingers through his brown hair with grey strands and blew out a breath of disbelief.

"You will still show me mercy?" he whispered. "Despite everything I have done."

"Yes," was my response. "Because I wish someone had done the same for me."

He reached out for me, and I allowed him to, surprising myself when I didn't flinch as his glacial hand rested on my arm, shivers slithering down my spine like snakes. I forced myself to remain still and stoic, watching tears well up in his eyes. Torment, animosity, shame, resentment. It was all there. But I didn't wince once. I stared at the old man as he cried. For whom? I couldn't tell.

"I'm sorry, Kira. I'm so sorry. Please forgive me. *Please*," he pleaded, knees trembling as if they wanted to fall into a position of prayer. "I can't die knowing you haven't forgiven me."

"It's not forgiveness you seek, it's retribution and liberation," I pushed his hands off me and watched them swing in defeat by his side. "You can die knowing, despite this all, I *am* and *will* be happy."

"No matter what you think, I have always loved you," Konstantin confessed, with resolute.

"Thank you, but that isn't enough."

I turned to walk off when his arms wrapped around me and before I could react, he spun me around and shoved me across the cell. My body hurtled onto the floor as I scrambled to gain balance, and my eyes became huge at the sudden strength that I couldn't recover quickly enough, giving him time to escape.

Except... he didn't.

Looking up, I found Konstantin staring at me with a sad smile, tears brimming his dark eyes. Then, sluggishly, like everything was in slow-motion, his eyes fell down and so did mine. There, piercing his heart, was a silver knife. A deafening cry ripped from my throat as Konstantin finally fell to his knees and his body crumpled onto the ground, revealing the culprit behind the act.

Calix.

His green or brown or whatever eyes swam with dissatisfaction, before they fell onto me. "Sorry."

"How could you?" I breathed out, suddenly aware of the tear stains on my cheeks.

Calix smirked. "He was going to die anyway. Why delay the inevitable?"

"You won't get away with this," I snarled.

"I already did," he laughed, wickedly. "You were always just two steps behind."

That was when it hit me. Aria. Calix saw me put the final pieces together and his lips coiled into a malicious grin.

"Aria isn't looking too peachy. Send her my regards."

Before I could react, he had vanished. Before I had the opportunity to blink, the shadows swallowed him. Somewhere in the darkness, he was lurking, but I couldn't think about that. Not while Konstantin began to choke on the dark blood spilling from his mouth. I crawled to him, lifting his head onto my lap, and pursed my lips to hold back this sudden urge to break into sobs. His eyes widened as he gagged, violently, blood spurting everywhere.

"Why did you save me?" I gasped, in disbelief.

"Because I loved you. Once upon a time," he coughed again, and I ignored the red stains on my hands and clothes. "You were right. I tried to save myself and, in the end, I'm just going to die."

"Konstantin…"

"He's going to kill her," he whispered, winded. I drew my brows together and he finished off, "Aria."

"What about you?" I choked out, blinking back the tears.

"All I've been is selfish. This was the least I could do," The blood didn't stop gushing, his face paled, and I knew in a matter of seconds he would be dead. He coughed, vehemently, and blood spilt from his nose and mouth. His dark eyes softened as his quivering hand found mine. "You were right, little bird; I am a monster."

And he took his final breath.

For the longest time, I didn't move. I couldn't move as I watched the only father figure I could remember die in my arms. He was gone. That part of my life had finally ended. Everything, including the girl he had brought up, died in this room. All the memories, all those nights in his office where he taught me Russian, all those early mornings when he trained me in combat, all those silent conversations that told me he cared… all of it, it was gone. My hands trembled as I laid Konstantin onto the ground and released his grip from mine, letting go of that girl who once belonged to me. My fingers trembled as I closed his dark eyes, and I whispered a silent prayer for the death of my past. The blood stains on my hands forced me to move into action and this rush of urgency emerged within me, as I forced myself onto my feet and dial Aria's number. She picked up within a heartbeat.

"Kira, what's going on?" she demanded. I could hear the panic in her voice. "I'm still at the penthouse but I'm getting ready to come back."

"Aria, Konstantin's dead."

There was a long silence.

"I'm sorry," she finally said. "How?"

"Calix."

"*What?!*" Alarm ricocheted through the phone, and my brain began to work on auto-drive, my bloody heels moving away from the basement floor, my senses overly aware that Calix could be anywhere. "Kira, what is going on? Why would he do that?"

"Aria, you need to stay where you are."

"No, I'm coming back," she said, stubbornly, which soon followed with a cough that had my heart stop. "Kira, why would he do that?"

"Aria, just listen. You are in danger. Stay there," I commanded, now beginning to run, ignoring the looks thrown my way at the sight of me. I pushed myself to Calix's room despite my entire body crying with pain. "Do you understand? *Stay there.*"

"Kira..." she coughed again, and her voice was so frail, "...why would he do that?"

"Aria," my reply was a whisper, but it gave her the answer and, despite being miles away from each other, I sensed her heart dropping when she replied, because my heart fell too.

"No."

Xander saw me but I didn't stop, hearing his footsteps thundering behind me before we halted in front of Calix's bedroom. Swallowing, apprehensively, I pushed the door open, as I said, "Calix is the traitor."

Xander sucked in a sharp breath of air from behind me as we took in the sight of the empty bedroom, completely stripped from all the things that were once here. He was gone. Everything we thought we knew was a lie. Aria cried out before she coughed again, more brutally than the last time, almost choking as if she couldn't inhale any more oxygen. I heard Nero call her name in the background, but she kept coughing, louder and harsher.

"Aria?" I called out, worriedly. Turning to Xander, we both held our breath. "*Aria?*"

But she couldn't respond; the coughs were not stopping, and they began to be laced with sobs of pain, until I finally heard a loud *thud*, followed with Nero's voice bellowing, "*ARIA!*"

CHAPTER 45

VOWS

"Hey, Aria," a little boy with dark shaggy brown hair that tousled over his ocean eyes said, as the girl, slightly shorter than him but twice as confident, glided into the room. Her hair was a lighter shade of brown and her eyes were hazel, golden specks dancing with the green, tantalizingly. She wore a cute little white dress that made her look so angelic and pure, a smile teasing her lips when she caught sight of her best friend.

"Nero," she replied, softly. Her voice made shivers run down his spine and he mirrored the smile. "Why aren't you downstairs?"

He crinkled his nose. "They're talking about business again."

She rolled her eyes. "You're going to have to get used to it because that will be us one day."

The ten-year-olds found themselves grinning at each other. One day, the throne would be passed to them, and they would rule with an iron fist. They spoke no more about their futures and began to inform one another about the things that had occurred over the last few days whilst they were apart. They never usually spent so long away from each other, but Nero's family had to visit his mother's parents back in Russia for an annual family gathering. Aria knew Nero didn't like going. As he was the youngest, he didn't get along with his relatives in Russia, especially as his mother only had an older brother, which meant he had cousins many years older than him. Nero ranted about everything he had suffered the last few days, and Aria listened. She found herself getting lost in his world and wondered why she would ever need anyone else when she could spend the rest of her life with Nero. She didn't trust *anyone else more than she trusted him. Whilst Aria listened, chiming in her opinion now and then, Nero couldn't help but smile to himself and found himself asking why he would want to be with anyone else if he already had Aria. He didn't love anyone else more than he loved her. Perhaps that was when their relationship had shifted. When their friendship began to grow into something deeper – something more meaningful. Something dangerous. They were scared.*

Who should make the first move? Could there be two winners to this dangerous game? What if they both lost?

As they stared at one another, speaking words that neither of them was listening to, focusing on the intensity that glistened in each other's gaze, unaware of what the other was feeling, they both silently prayed for the same thing – that no matter what they would remain in each other's lives. Forever.

For better, for worse. For richer, for poorer. In sickness and in health. To love and to cherish. Their friendship could withstand it all.

Till death do them part.

*

Nero

She stirred as she woke up.

Her breathing was unsteady, and her heart rate was unstable. An IV bag hung from a stand beside her, administrating saline through her veins. Her skin was pale, as white as paper. Her cheeks were hollow, and there was a lack of color – the usual redness that I loved so much was absent. Her eyes were dazed, the hazel intensity replaced with an unfamiliar dullness, as she settled her gaze onto me. Her nimble hands weakly reached out for me, and I shifted closer, dragging my chair closer to her bed.

"How are you feeling?" I asked, taking her trembling hands.

She coughed before replying, "Like shit."

Even then, she managed to crack a smile. Despite the need to break into tears, I forced a smile on my face. There was so much we wanted to say, words that needed to be said, but neither of us spoke because if we did, I feared we would never stop. So, we held each other's gaze, comforting one another with soft caresses against our hands, and a smile that was filled with uncertainty. After she had passed out, I immediately took her to the hospital and informed Kira while we were on our journey there. Kira and Xander met up with us at the hospital, their faces paling at the sight of Aria laying still on a hospital bed, as they rushed her off to do tests and figure out what had happened. Xander had informed me that she already had a visit from the doctor earlier this week, and I speculated whether she would have ever told me this information but gathered that she didn't want to worry me. Anxiously, we waited for the verdict and that was when Kira told me about Calix. The heartbreak in her eyes was an unbearable sight, but it was enough to stop me from leaving the hospital and pummeling Calix until he was nothing but a bag of bashed bones. Nonetheless, I made a silent promise that once Aria was strong enough, I would hunt Calix down and feed him to the wolves. All those thoughts disappeared as soon as the doctor made his presence known. Unlike regular doctors, this one was specifically for those in the Manor, and as he had already tended to Aria earlier this week, he had already performed some tests on her. After explaining that Aria's vitals were unstable right now, he proceeded to tell us that her blood test results were showing symptoms of poisoning, but they were unsure what type. Furthermore, they were unsure how far the poison had spread. My heart halted at those words.

Poison.

Aria was still asleep, hooked up to all these wires, lashes fanned over her pale cheeks, when Kira, Xander and I had trickled back into the room. Kira had sucked in a sharp breath of air whilst Xander cursed quietly. I couldn't say anything and had forced myself to settle into the seat beside her. And I remained there ever since. After spending some time with Aria, Kira and Xander left to return to the Manor as they didn't know what Calix would do next now that Aria was injured. We were all thinking the same thing. This was a distraction. A major diversion for something bigger. My thoughts were interrupted as the door to Aria's hospital room opened and her parents rushed in; Xena's face looked wet with tears and Antonio was stoic as ever, but I could see the fear in his eyes as he took in the fragility of his daughter.

"Aria," Xena cried, moving to her daughter's side. "Oh, my sweet girl. How are you feeling?"

"I'm okay, mama," Aria responded, weakly, before glancing at her dad. "I promise."

Antonio's jaw tightened. "Who's behind this?"

"Dad, I'm okay" she repeated, but he ignored her words and turned to me.

Dark eyes dimmed further as they narrowed. "Nero, who is behind this?"

I was caught between answering and remaining quiet. The look that both Aria and Antonio sent in my direction had me freeze in my position, the words trapped in my throat and I nearly shrunk from their heated scrutinization. Xena sighed and smacked her husband's arm, earning a scowl from him as the attention finally moved off me. I exhaled a breath of relief, my shoulders relaxing but I knew this was far from over.

"Dad, leave him alone," Aria answered for me. Antonio's eyes thinned before he backed down, allowing his daughter to win this round. For now. "I need a favor."

Xena's eyes widened as she nodded fervently, leaning closer to her daughter as if those were the only words she needed to hear. "Of course, anything"

"I need men stationed around the Manor temporarily. Until Kira has moved them to the safe house."

"And where's the Manor?" Antonio asked.

"Kira will send you the location," Aria replied.

"Is this the girl you met in London?" Xena questioned, and Aria bobbed her head. Sharing a look with her husband, Xena sighed. "We can do that for you. I'm sure Nero wouldn't mind sparing a few of his men."

"No, I don't need Nero's men," Aria said suddenly, catching us all by surprise. "I need Dad's men."

Xena and I both frowned in confusion, but Antonio didn't flinch, understanding his daughter's request. In his cool, calm tone, he said, "This is a large demand you are asking of me, Aria."

"I understand but this is important. I wouldn't ask if I didn't think it was necessary."

Antonio held his daughter's piercing gaze and I realized how similar they looked. Despite sharing most of her mother's features, Aria looked very much like her father from their high cheekbones to their jawlines. The similarity was uncanny.

Xena's frown deepened. "Can someone explain to me what is going on?"

Antonio sighed. "It seems my dear daughter has found out about the group of highly qualified men that I keep on the side in case of extreme circumstances."

"How skilled?" I managed to say, unaware of this information yet not even the tad bit surprised.

"*Remarkably*. We're talking stronger and faster than assassins. Faceless mercenaries, whose loyalties lie with me," Antonio explained, crossing his arms over his chest, arrogantly.

Xena didn't look too happy with his vague response. "We'll talk about this when we get home."

There was a ghost of a smile on Antonio's lips, as he said, "Yes, dear."

She paid little attention to him and looked back at her daughter. "Why do you want these specific men?"

"Because the people in the Manor will be in danger during the transition. I need to know they'll be protected if I ever…" her words trailed off, but we all knew what she was saying.

The dark reality. Those words were enough for her father to accept her request and her mother to remain eerily silent about any complaints she had. Once again, her parents shared a look before Xena smiled at her daughter, a smile that I knew gave Aria strength, from the way her eyes lit up only momentarily.

"We'll get right on it. You focus on getting better," she kissed the top of her daughter's head and allowed Antonio to do the same, before her hazel eyes flickered to me. "We'll give you guys some space. Let us know if you need anything else."

"Thank you," I managed to smile, and Xena reached out to embrace me, her warm hug easing some of the tension which held my body hostage.

Afterwards, I shook Antonio's hand, his steel gaze reminding me of my place before he took his wife's arm and led her out of the room. There was a long silence after they had left which Aria finally broke with a sigh.

"So, what have I missed?" her voice had my attention moving back to her. Noticing that she was trying to sit up, I quickly aided her before settling back into my seat, running my fingers through my dark hair whilst Aria pushed her copper locks over her shoulders.

"Not much."

Her eyes thinned. "What did the doctor say?"

"Nothing you should be worried around."

Aria sighed, frustratedly. "Nero, I know it's poisoning. Calix must have done it when we were having drinks. It's probably a slow-moving poison. It's the oldest trick in the book. From my calculations, it might be too late to save me."

"Aria."

"Kira will have to transition into my position. She'll struggle for a bit but she's a natural leader and in time, she'll be able to fill the role better than I ever did."

"Aria."

"And the Manor needs to be protected. Kira knows where they can go for the time being whilst Xander finds a new location if they can't stop the Serpents."

"Aria."

"Calix knows too much. I don't think you'll be able to stop him but the safety of everyone in the Manor comes first."

"Aria!" I yelled, breaking her rambling. Her eyes widened as she blinked at me, stunned, before she meekly nodded whilst I exhaled, heavily, running a hand over my face. "Just stop. *Please*."

"Nero, I can't," she whispered, morosely. "I can't *not* think about the aftermath."

My heart shattered at her words, but I knew that I had to try and understand the position she was in. Everything was uncertain, even her life, but Aria still couldn't help but worry about everyone other than herself. She was scared for everyone else whilst everyone was scared for her. The love of my life looked feeble and frail in the bed, yet her eyes burned with a fire I knew would never burn out. I entwined our fingers together, warming her cold hand, and smiled.

"Everything will be sorted out," I promised.

Her smile didn't reach her eyes, as she joked, "You always said one day you won't be able to save me."

I rolled my eyes as she laughed. "You shouldn't joke about that."

Grinning cheekily, she pressed her lips on my hand. "Lighten up, love."

Once again, we descended into a comfortable silence, basking in each other's comfort. The sun appeared from behind the clouds, and I wondered what time it was; perhaps it was noon. I was still impatiently waiting for the doctor's results, but I withheld that information from Aria. For now. My thumb gently stroked her hand before I spoke again.

"I'll get revenge for what they have done, I promise you this," I murmured, darkly. She didn't respond straight away but I knew she

411

heard me because she inhaled so lengthily that she had my eyes flickering up. Aria bobbed her head slowly, a slight smile playing on her lips.

"I don't want revenge, Nero," I was about to disagree, but she continued, her gaze holding me hostage, "I want justice."

With our eyes locked on one another, I knew what had to be done. I knew what she was asking for. I knew that she wanted to destroy the Serpents and everything they built. But I feared that it wouldn't be me who would complete this demand, or maybe it was not my duty to do so, even though I desperately wanted to. She knew it too. I saw it in her eyes. I didn't reply as I gently squeezed her hand and bent forward, where I kissed her, gently, her warm breath caressing my skin. Before tearing myself away from her, I lightly pressed my lips on her forehead, noticing how her eyes fluttered shut and a gentle smile teased her lips. Sometimes, the fear would make us stronger. Other times, it tore us down until we were fragments of the person we used to be. I knew if anything happened to Aria, the latter would happen to me. She took my heart, and there was no way I would ever get it back.

*

Aria eventually fell back to sleep after a while, so I took the opportunity to call Matteo for updates on the mafia and tracking down Calix. But like the other seven, all I got was that Calix was nowhere to be found. It infuriated me to no end but eventually, I allowed this to sit on the back burner whilst Aria recovered. Her recovery was the most important thing right now. At some point, Xander returned with some of Aria's belongings and mentioned that it could help her feel more at ease if she saw familiar things. I watched him quietly scatter little plants and ornaments that he collected from her bedroom when my eyes caught sight of a framed picture of Aria and me during our wedding registry. She had worn this short white dress, which was made from the finest lace material, embroidered with diamonds around the hem.

She looked like an angel.

Xander noticed my gaze and handed the frame to me without a sound. Wordlessly, I took it and brushed my finger across the image. I had worn a black suit, a white rose pinned on my blazer, with my arm around Aria's waist and her head slightly tilted in my direction as she smiled. I smiled back at her and without us knowing, Sophie must have snapped a photo.

"Nero," Xander said, quietly enough for me to hear, but not to wake Aria up. "Whatever happens next, thank you for everything you have done."

"I haven't done anything," I responded, but he smiled, knowingly.

"Aria saved me and all those other people in the Manor. I didn't used to believe in a God, but Aria showed me that although fate can be cruel, it will always bring you the justice you deserve," his eyes flickered to her. "We're going to be okay. I know we will."

Whether he was talking about himself or not, I would never know, but as my eyes moved to Aria, I didn't ask and knew whatever happened next, Aria would never be forgotten. Later that evening, the spring air wafted into the room from the slight crack of the open window and Aria shivered in her sleep as it kissed her cold skin. It was pretty warm, but I still got up and closed it, silently, afraid to wake Aria from her deep slumber. Xander had left to bring Kira, who was preparing for the aftermath, despite her protests. Aria managed to get the last word. Her chestnut hair fanned across the pillow, her body curled under the blankets, and she slept, soundlessly. My eyes never left her as I settled back into the chair, frightened that if I blinked, she would disappear. I couldn't remember how long I had spent sitting there but finally, I fell asleep, drifting into silent dreams that taunted me with memories of Aria and I, when we were kids. I couldn't imagine a world without her, but the more I thought about it, the more that nightmare became a reality. No one wanted to say it, but we all feared that the poisoning had dug its roots too deeply within her and that she would not survive. We didn't know how long she had left. When the morning came about, my slumber was rudely broken by Kira's loud voice and Xander's boisterous laughter. Blinking, I shielded my sensitive eyes from the searing sunlight that broke from the blinds, before I finally focused my sight onto Aria, who was sitting up with a bright beam on her face.

She saw me first and grinned. "Good morning, hubby."

"When did these two come in?" I asked, groggily, fixing the clothes that I had been wearing for over a day.

"Like an hour ago," Aria shrugged. "When was the last time you got changed?"

Her crinkled nose had me shoot her an annoyed glare, which she dismissed with an innocent smile. Kira chuckled and Xander threw me a bag that I inspected carefully, discovering a set of fresh clothes.

"What a sweet bunch," I grumbled, staggering to my feet, and heading to the bathroom whilst ignoring the laughter erupting from behind me.

I stripped out of my clothes and discarded them into the bag after pulling on the jeans and sweatshirt Xander bought me. I noted Matteo must have given it to them as these were items he had seen in my wardrobe and I marveled at when they had time to retrieve it. When I returned into the room, Xander had taken my spot whilst Kira sat on the end of the bed, giggling with Aria as they whispered to one another like schoolgirls. I threw Xander a scowl, but he only smirked in response and continued scrolling on his phone, whilst I dumped my bag beside Aria's bags in the corner of the room.

"What are you girls giggling about?" I muttered, brushing my disheveled hair back with my fingers. Aria watched me and her eyes darkened to my amusement, which had Kira roll her eyes and answer the question.

"Your old baby photos."

I blinked. Once. Then twice.

"What?"

Aria laughed as Kira grinned, cheekily, and Xander coughed back his chuckle. The mischievous glint in Aria's eyes and rosy, flushed cheeks from the laughter would make one think she was healthy and, despite knowing that she was anything but, I couldn't stop my heart from warming at the sight.

"It seems my mother took a liking to Kira, and sent her my baby pictures along with yours," Aria explained, and my jaw fell. "I never knew you wore Superman nappies."

"Aria," I growled, and reached for the phone that she mercilessly kept out of my grasp, laughing alongside Kira.

As I tried to grab the phone and delete the humiliation of my childhood thanks to my father's love for Superman, the doctor strolled in before stopping short and squinted at what was occurring. Immediately, I stopped, which caught everyone's attention, their gaze following mine. The light air iced instantly, and Aria's smile dropped, dramatically.

The doctor noticed the abrupt change of mood and shifted on his feet, uneasily. "Should I come back later?"

He was asking because Aria was awake. We all knew it. Before I could respond, Aria spoke first, "No. What's the verdict, doc?"

"As I'm sure you already know, you were poisoned which was seen in your blood samples from earlier this week," he began, and I couldn't stop breathing erratically because the news still hadn't settled with me. Aria remained apathetic, prompting the doctor to continue with a clipped nod. "We weren't sure how far the poison had spread but from the results of the blood tests we took yesterday, it seems that in less than forty-eight hours it will reach your main organs."

Kira's eyes widened. "What does that mean?"

"That by tomorrow evening, all of Aria's organs will shut down and the poison will effectively kill her," the doctor answered, gravely.

The news that the doctor gave us had left us in a sorrowful mood for the rest of the day and, even with Aria's attempts to lighten the cold atmosphere, no one could forget the inevitable. Including Aria. Knowing her attempts were fruitless, she asked for a moment with each of us. Xander went first, so Kira and I respectfully left the room to give them space. Silently, we waited in the hallway, unsure what to say, unsure what to do.

"I always thought if anyone could survive anything, it would be Aria," Kira said suddenly, causing me to glance at her. She chuckled, like there was something sour on her tongue. "How wrong was I?"

"We all shared the same thought," I whispered.

She didn't respond for a long moment before turning to me. "It's scary, isn't it?"

"What?"

"That everything you loved could be taken away in the blink of an eye."

"*Love*," I corrected, and she frowned. "That everything I love. Not, loved. Even after, I will still love her. I can never *not* love her. That doesn't exist."

Kira thinned her eyes before cracking a smile. "Of course."

Xander exited the room and broke the brief moment Kira and I shared. His eyes were wet, and I knew he had shed tears from the damp patches on his cheeks, but no one mentioned it as he strode towards us, gruffly saying, "You can go, Kira."

Kira stared at him for a loaded second, before nodding stiffly and disappearing into Aria's room. I watched Kira's retreating back as I asked Xander, "What did she say?"

"Everything I knew she would say," was his response and I found myself studying him. Xander was a large man, who could properly scare people with his impassive expression, but the man in front of me looked like someone had torn out his heart, and I knew that Aria would forever leave that impression on him. "I'll inform her parents."

I swallowed hard and watched him walk away, rolling his shoulders back, and brushing the wetness off his cheeks. However, before he disappeared around the corner, he stopped and glanced at me. Something sparked in his eyes, something so brilliant but so dark. Something that looked a lot like heartbreak. Then, his eyes shifted to Aria's closed door, and they softened. He wasn't a man of many words but there, I swear, that was the most he had ever spoken, even if the words didn't leave his lips. Regret. It was a familiar feeling, and I knew he was regretful. Of what? I would never know but I knew it was enough to break him apart because I had never seen a man as broken as him. Finally, he left, and I was alone in the corridor with my back against the cold wall; my head leaned back and I sighed. Kira finally left the room with red eyes and silent tears rolling down her cheeks, which she tried to get rid of before I saw her, but she was a few seconds too late. The blonde Japanese woman stepped slowly like she was carrying weights on her shoulders before she paused in front of me.

It was my time.

"What did she say?" I asked, again.

Kira smiled, ruefully. "Everything I knew she wouldn't say." Like Xander, her ambiguous answer had me frowning but I didn't press on any further as Kira gestured to the room. "She's asking for you."

"Where are you going?" I questioned, when she began to walk.

Kira paused. "Home. I need to inform everyone."

The question was on the tip of my tongue, but she strode off before I could ask. When she finally disappeared, I took a deep breath of air and moved into Aria's room, where I caught her staring out of the room, wistfully. I knew she was aware of my presence, but she didn't make any move to look, but sighed, her shoulders relaxing until they were as light as the smile on her face.

"What did you say to them?" I asked.

"That's for you to never know," was her response. Then she looked at me and I felt the air knock right out of my lungs. She was beautiful. "You know I love you."

"And I love you," I replied, without hesitating. My answer earned me a dazzling grin that could knock anyone off their feet. "So, what do you want to tell me?"

"I used to believe in fairy tales. The prince. The princess. The trapped tower. The fiery dragon. Everything. But with you, life wasn't a fairy tale. Yet, I couldn't help but fall madly and uncontrollably in love with you," she began. "It's been hard. For both of us and I'm sorry that it couldn't end happily. I prayed that it would end happily."

"Aria, just knowing that you love me is all the happiness I would ever need," I took her hands, engulfing them in mine and I peered at her teary eyes. "You are my happiness."

"I'm sorry for everything that happened."

"So am I, but that's the past and if we keep bringing it up, we will never have a future."

"It's a bit too late for that, isn't it?" she snorted, bitterly.

I smiled, sadly. "It's never too late."

"So many years," she murmured, nibbling on her lower lip that was teasing me. "We wasted so much time."

"Time we needed to grow from the kids we once were," I assured, and kissed her. She melted against my touch, grasping my shoulders as my hands rested on her waist. I ignored the fact that I could feel her bones and relished in the intoxicating sensation that rushed throughout my body.

She was my heart. Forever.

"You always know what to say, don't you?" she laughed breathlessly but it was mixed with a layer of sadness that one could not notice if you didn't listen hard enough.

"I'll spend the rest of my life proving that we belong together," I grinned, and although she rolled her eyes, there was a ghost of a smile on her pink lips that were swollen from my kiss. "Are you going to be alright?"

Aria's response didn't come until a few moments later, followed with a heavy exhale as her hazel eyes softened, "Take care of my family, especially my brothers. I wasn't the best figurehead so maybe you could guide them."

"Of course," I agreed, without a second thought. "Mind if I sit beside you?"

She answered by shuffling across the bed, allowing some space for me. I kicked my shoes off and slipped into the space beside her, curling an arm over her body, and drew her against me whilst my hand reached out and entwined our fingers. She fiddled with the silver bracelet on my wrist, absent-mindedly, as we savored each other's presence.

"I'm not afraid to die," she said, quietly. I didn't respond but I looked at her. "If that's what you're asking, then that's my answer."

"Why?" It was a simple question.

"Because it was written for me."

"So, what are you afraid of?"

Her shaky hands caressed my cheek. "That once I go, you won't learn to love again."

I blinked the tears away. "There's no one like you."

"Of course not," then she smiled, "But there's always someone else who can love you too."

I didn't speak and I didn't think she wanted me to because we both knew that those words hurt her more than they hurt me. So, instead, I kissed her again and brought her closer to me, terrified to let her go. There, we sat silently for the rest of the night, with the diamonds on our fingers reminding us that nothing was forever.

*

Aria

The look in Nero's eyes haunted me and I struggled to fall asleep that night even though I was in his arms. However, he slept soundly beside me, steadily breathing in contrast to my labored and erratic breathing, , dark lashes caressing his cheeks. I knew he was exhausted; I could see how dark the circles were under his eyes and the hollowness of his cheeks from the lack of nutrition. I knew he was worried. So was I. I rolled over at the same time as his arm tightened around my body, and rested my head on his chest, peeking at our interwoven hands. His platinum ring glittered under the moonlight which broke through the blinds. His diamonds looked like the stars in the night sky. My eyes flickered to my own ring, and I smiled. I had both a wedding band and engagement ring, both with diamonds molten on the bands. They were truly beautiful. What made them more beautiful was the fact that Nero had bought them without guidance. It was more than memorable. I peeked at him, my heart melting at how serene he looked without the stress on his face. The future was certain for me but uncertain for him; I just hoped whoever he ended up spending the rest of his life with treated him much better than I ever could. My heart pained at the thought, but I knew it would be selfish of me if I didn't let him go. I winced at the sudden sharp stab of pain in my stomach and had to force myself not to curl into a ball. The last few days had been hell on my body, but I tried my best to hide how much pain I was actually in.

In short, my body felt like it was on fire. Everywhere burned and the slightest movement killed me in excruciating torment. There were moments where I silently begged for the torture to end but other times, I felt like I was numb. Yet, those moments were sadly short-lived as the pain would increase tenfold, as if it realized that I was getting used to it. I exhaled erratically. My lungs felt constricted, and my heart felt as if someone was squeezing it. I knew the poison had finally reached its final destination. I tried to not think about it – about anything – because if I did, I feared I wouldn't stop crying and I had to be strong. I had to be strong enough to let Nero go. At some point, my agonizing thoughts lulled me to sleep. No dreams visited me that night. And I was silently thankful for it. I knew that I couldn't have false hope, I had to accept the reality. It would be easier that way. Yet, why did this feel like the hardest thing I had ever done?

"Is she still asleep?" someone muttered. Someone young.

"Yeah, she's been out for a couple of hours," another replied. Someone older.

Someone else asked, "Where are her parents?"

"Outside talking to the doctors."

"How long has she got left?"

There was a long silence before a dark, "Not long enough."

No one else spoke afterwards. I took that as my cue to wake up. The morning sun blinded me, causing me to squint, before I forced myself to open my eyes and face the reality. Blinking to adjust my focus, I saw Kira by the windows, her arms crossed over her chest as she leaned against the wall with a solemn expression, and Xander beside Violetta who sat at the end of my bed, clutching onto a bunch of handpicked flowers. Nero had moved from the space beside me and settled into the seat that had been his home for the last three days. They didn't notice I was awake until I began to move, turning my shoulders back as I slowly sat up. Nero came to my aid, but I swatted his hand away and sent him a small glare.

"I can do it myself. I'm not made of glass," I scowled.

He narrowed his eyes. "How are you feeling?"

"Like death," my words left my lips before I could think, and they cut through the air like glass, shocking everyone. Even myself. With wide eyes, I blinked before rubbing my face. "I'm sorry, that was insensitive."

"As expected," Kira muttered, cutting me off before I could argue with a simple, "Your parents are here."

"When did they arrive?" I gestured for Nero to hand me a glass of water and he obeyed, silently.

"Over an hour ago. They couldn't come earlier because –" Kira stopped suddenly, and I frowned in confusion as she shared a look with Nero, who wore an unreadable expression.

"What happened?" I demanded. Once again, they shared a look and that began to annoy me. "Hello?"

Nero sighed, tiredly. "It seems that outside your family home there were people stationed there, basically keeping your family hostage. All communications with them had been cut off, so Kira went to see what was happening. After I received the news, I sent some of my men and Kira took some of yours. We managed to outnumber them and escort your family to the hospital safely whilst capturing those who failed to get away."

Shock washed over me before I laughed in disbelief. "So, not only did Calix poison me, but he also tried to prevent my family from seeing me by endangering them?"

"It's okay. Your family is here now and that's all that matters," Kira assured. "I'll deal with everything else."

I saw the deadly promise in her eyes and stiffly nodded before I finally acknowledged Violetta, who nervously swung her legs, and softened my gaze. "Why are you here, Vi?"

She nibbled on her lip as she gave me the flowers. I couldn't help but break into a smile as I admired how beautiful they were before looking at Violetta who seemed apprehensive. "I wanted to see you before... you know."

Those words pained my heart, so I placed the flowers to the side and outstretched my arms which she quickly rushed into, her little body shaking which indicated that she was crying.

"It's going to be okay. Kira will look after you and Xander will make sure that you'll grow up to be the strongest and smartest girl in the Manor."

"That was meant to be your job, Aria," she sobbed. "You can't go.

You can't leave me."

"Vi —" I silenced Xander with a look, causing him to halt in his position, and with a shake of my head, he recoiled his arms back to his side.

"I wish I didn't have to, sweetheart," I murmured, as I pulled back and brushed the tears from her cheeks, her beautiful violet eyes sparkling like they were made from glass. "But, if I had to do this all again, I wouldn't change anything."

"I love you, Aria," Violetta sniffled.

"I love you too, Violetta," I smiled tenderly, which she mirrored before I glanced at Xander. "Xan, how about you guys grab something to eat whilst I talk to my family?"

Xander nodded and, after one more hug, Violetta took his hand and left the room but not before sparing me one last longing look. That look which I knew would kill me more than the poison in my veins. Kira murmured something about getting my family and left the room after them, my eyes watching her disappear out of the door before they finally rested on the silent Italian man beside me.

"Nero, stop it," I sighed.

He frowned. "What?"

"Stop thinking, please," I leaned forward and kissed him. "I love you, okay?"

"I love you too, Aria," was his reply, and I swear I heard his voice crack. But before I could question it, my family rushed in and he quickly stood up, muttering, "I'll give you some space."

I didn't want him to leave but as my family surrounded me, I lost sight of him. Ignoring the burning feeling of my heart shattering, I smiled weakly as everyone threw questions in my direction. My mother cried into my father's arms, as my younger brothers showed me what had been happening whilst I was gone. Nico mentioned a girl he had been talking to and after a few short words with him, he promised to treat her right. Whilst Luca talked about how his skills in knife combat had improved and Dad commented that it was because he was training with the best. My mother laughed weakly, and I cracked a smile as the boys tried to lift the mood. But moments later, it dampened as my mother settled beside me on the bed and shakily took my hands.

"My baby girl," she sniffled. "I love you so much, sweetheart, and you can't even fathom how proud I am of you."

My eyes pricked with tears. "You don't need to cry, mama. I know you are."

She embraced me tightly and I silently sobbed in her arms whilst she cried in mine. Eventually, she let go and I turned to my father. Antonio Moretti always wore a stone-cold exterior, but I saw the cracks in his eyes and knew he was broken inside. All my life, my father had brought me up to withstand everything and strengthen me to become the strongest person to have ever lived. I wondered if I had failed him.

"I'm sorry, daddy," I whispered, and his eyes softened. "I'm not as strong as you think I am."

"Oh baby," my father murmured and gathered me into his arms. "You are the strongest person I have ever known. The bravest, the kindest, the fiercest. And I'm so proud of you. For everything you have achieved without anyone's help."

"I love you," I choked back my cry. The strong front that I tried desperately to keep up began to crumble right in front of my eyes and for the first time, I didn't care one bit.

"I love you too, angel," he responded, brokenly. When we finally tore apart, he wiped my tears away and smiled tenderly, caressing my cheek with his thumb. "We called everyone and they're on their way, but we don't think they'll be able to make it before…"

I swallowed thickly. "I understand. Just give them my love if it's too late."

He nodded stiffly before turning to my mother, who kissed the crown of his head and placed her hand on his shoulder as my brothers inched closer. I used to be scared that when I died, I wouldn't see my family for the last time, but as they all stood around me wearing smiles that mirrored bravery and sorrow, I had never felt so lucky.

"I take back what I said," Nico muttered suddenly, and I lifted a brow. "You're an amazing role model."

I chuckled through my sobs as he cracked a grin whilst Luca rolled his eyes with a snarky response, "It's about time."

For the rest of the afternoon, I spent time with my family, and we spoke about anything and everything. No one mentioned what would happen afterwards, no one wanted to. We only spoke about what was happening right at this moment and the memories we had. We shed tears and shared laughter. We ignored the inevitable and I was grateful for that because having my family here gave me the most strength I had felt in the longest time. Eventually, they allowed me to get some rest whilst they all ate and I reluctantly agreed, especially when I noticed how exhausted I was becoming.

Laying alone on my bed, I stared out the window, aimlessly, when my door opened, and Kira slipped inside.

"I thought you'd be asleep by now," she mused.

"I couldn't. If I close my eyes, I'm scared I won't open them again," I admitted and she nodded, mutely. As our eyes focused on the sunset outside with the sky colored in rays of pink, purple and orange, I savored in this silence and reminisced about the day we first met. "I love you, Kira. More than you could ever know and you're going to be alright."

"Perhaps," she replied. "But it will be only after a long time."

I tried to smile to ease the sorrow, but my lips quivered. "Thank you for agreeing to join me when you could've chosen the better and easier life."

Kira shook her head. "This *is* the better life. I have never once regretted the decision I made five years ago."

"Neither do I."

We shared a grin.

"What about Nero?" Kira asked, after a moment.

I sighed. "I don't know."

"I'll keep an eye on him," she offered, but I shook my head.

"No. I need to let him go," I pressed my lips together to prevent the cry that was threatening to escape, but Kira wasn't oblivious to my attempts and her eyes brimmed with molten blue grief. "He needs to be happy."

As much as it shattered me inside to think of Nero with someone else, I knew it would kill me more to see him alone for the rest of his life. He deserved to be happy even if happy didn't mean with me.

I thought she would protest but instead Kira responded, "I understand."

"Where is he?" I finally asked the question I had been wanting to know the answer to ever since he left.

"Outside. He's been sitting there ever since. I'll send him in," Kira said, and I bobbed my head. As she stood up, her glassy topaz eyes settled on me, and her lips pursed; she did her best to fight her tears. "It was my greatest honor to work alongside you, and become your sister, Aria."

The tears rolled down my cheeks before I knew it, as I exhaled shakily. "No, Kira. It was *my* greatest honor to work with the woman who changed my entire life."

Kira didn't hold back as she hugged me, and I embraced her tightly with tears wetting our cheeks and each other's shoulders when they fell. My body shook in her arms, and I never wanted to let go. I couldn't but we both knew we had to. We just had to. So, with great reluctance, we entangled ourselves from each other's arms and smiled bravely at one another before she left the room without another word. I cried silently in my hands, my heart constricted with pain that I willed to disappear, but my time was short, and I knew there was nothing left I could do. I brushed my tears away and sniffled as Nero finally came back into the room, closing the door behind him. Electric blue eyes held me hostage, knocking the air right out of me as soon as we made eye contact. I always wondered what it meant to see your life flash before your eyes, and at that moment, I experienced just that. Except I saw what our future could have been. I saw the house we would have bought. The children we would have raised. The way we would have grown old.

Together.

I saw it all. I saw the world in his oceanic eyes. The world which would no longer include me.

"Hi baby, he said, fondly, and I burst into tears again. Without another thought, he gathered me into his arms, hugging me like he never wanted me to go. Hushing me softly, he soothed my pain and eventually, my cries turned into short hiccups as I wiped the tears away. "It's going to be okay."

"I love you, Nero. More than you'll ever know," I confessed, and he kissed the tip of my nose, smiling down at me tenderly. There was something so brilliant about his eyes that I knew I would never forget – that I knew I *couldn't* forget.

"I love you, Aria. *Sempre.*"

I forced a smile, but an abrupt cough left me, breaking our moment. I hunched over in pain, but the tormented look in Nero's eyes caused me more anguish than the poison. We knew I didn't have long left. I could feel my body deteriorating by the second as my main organs began to shut down. I glanced at the heart monitor and watched how my heart rate began to decrease.

"You need to let me go," I whispered. "You need to move on."

"No, Aria. I won't ever let you go," Nero's eyes watered as he fervently shook his head.

"It's not a request, Nero. It's an order," I forced myself to say, despite the desire to tell him to stay with me forever. I couldn't do it to him. He deserved the entire world and more. "*Please.*"

He didn't want to hear any of it, but I knew he had to as I noticed that it was getting harder to breathe. The fire in my body scorched me everywhere that I had to pull his arms away from me in case he could feel it too. But it was too late. His azure eyes widened, and the tears spilt from them, splattering against the hospital bedsheets as he gathered my hands, holding onto me as tightly as possible.

"Please, Aria," he begged, with tears streaming down his face shamelessly as he seized my hands crushingly. "Please, don't leave me, baby. You can fight it. Let me go get the doctor; we'll get past this."

I smiled weakly, an unsteady hand reaching out to touch his face one last time. Devastating blue stones glistened with heartbreak and agony, the intensity making my heart ache.

"Shh," I whispered. "Don't cry, baby. Everything is going to be okay."

"I need you, Aria. I *need* you," he said heartbrokenly, my smile faltering. "You're my reason to breathe, always have been, always will be. I fucked up, there are not enough words which I could use to take back the last five years without you. But loving you was the best thing I have ever done. I don't regret once second of it. So, please don't leave me. *Please.*"

His voice cracked. I swallowed my sobs and blinked my tears away as I tried to be brave, as I forced my lips to lift up, as I ignored the way my heart smashed into thousands of pieces.

"You're going to be alright, Nero," I murmured, my thumb slowly touching his lip. Those beautiful soft lips. The ones which loved me beyond words. "I promise."

Ba-dump…

Ba-dump…

Ba… dump…

Ba… dum…p…

His eyes widened.

I wondered if they were always so blue.

He looked like peace.

He looked like home.

He looked like the man I love.

"Please, stay with me, Aria," he pleaded, desperately. Taking my frail hands again, he did nothing to stop the tears from falling. The ruthless mafia boss cried for me. The grief in his eyes would haunt me perpetually but I knew I could not do anything. I just wished I could do something. Then he whispered the words I could spend forever hearing, "I love you."

Although my heartbeat had completely slowed down, I felt a blip and it raced for a short moment. Somewhere, I felt the sparks shooting through my body. Somewhere, I felt my soul finally rest in peace. Somewhere, I felt happiness. True and pure happiness.

"Kiss me, Russo."

He didn't waste another second and bent down, pressing his lips against mine delicately, stealing my last breath away.

Sempre.

Till death do us part.

PART 3

she wears strength and
darkness equally well,
that girl has always been
half goddess, half hell.

nikita gill

CHAPTER 46

rain

It was the first day of June and it rained.

The sky wouldn't settle as if it was mourning the loss of a great warrior.

And maybe it was.

The Japanese woman couldn't tell whether her cheeks were stained from the raindrops or her tears, as she emotionlessly stared out into the distance from the rooftop of the hospital. The city looked startling silent tonight. The moonlit streets were void of people, who quickly tried to find shelter from the sudden showers. The clouds concealed the stars and blackened the mournful night. The abrupt change of weather from the painting-like sunset to monsoon showers amused her. The irony of how something so bright and beautiful could be stripped away within a matter of seconds. The lack of outerwear would result in many days of being sick as her body was drenched, yet she didn't flinch, as the chilling air lightly kissed her. She couldn't feel anything.

It was like a void. A dark void. A never-ending dark void that consumed everything, that left her feeling nothing. The clouds that engulfed the sun which appeared this morning mirrored the loss that engulfed her ability to feeling something. Anything.

She was numb.

She had lost her best friend. *Her sister.* It had only been a few hours since she died and yet it felt as if it had been years. Something had shifted within the blonde, something mixed with grief and anger. It was like she had lost the meaning of her life. The reason why she continued to fight to be alive. She wanted to cry – sometimes, she did. But the tears were indistinguishable from the rain. And for the first time in her life, all she heard was silence. Until the silence was disrupted by the sound of footsteps, treading on the flooded ground of the rooftop. An umbrella shielded over her, preventing the rain from soaking her any further. Kira didn't need to look to see who it was – there was only one person it could be.

"She's gone," Kira stated, matter-of-factly. Even the sound of the thundering rain couldn't quell the truth that everyone feared to hear.

"Yes, she is," he replied, the lack of emotions in his voice worried her.

"What now?"

He exhaled heavily as the raindrops pelted onto the umbrella. "Well, the doctors will do a quick check before confirming her time of death. Her family will probably hold a private memorial –"

" – No, Nero," she interrupted sharply, her icy eyes peering up at the Italian mafia boss. "What do *we* do now?"

He studied her under hooded lashes before gazing away. He said nothing immediately, as though he didn't have an answer, and his response a minute later confirmed that. "I don't know."

Below them, the streets began to fill up with cars of people who desired to get home to their loved ones. Kira didn't know who she was going home to anymore. Without Aria, Kira was lost like a little lamb, and she felt as if she had been thrown to a pack of wolves. It was the stillness that hovered above them as the sky cried which reminded her that she could not and would never revert back to the person she was before Aria. She remembered what Aria had told her – *stay alive*. Two simple words but they told Kira enough. She knew what she had to do.

Kira inhaled and then released a shaky breath of air. "Do you know the first thing Aria said to me?" Nero didn't answer. "She asked if I wanted to help stop others from being hurt like I was. She might not have completed her mission, but I intend to carry it out to the end."

"Kira," he whispered. "No matter what you do, the grief will catch up to you. Let yourself grieve before you throw yourself down this road."

"I'm not trying to run away from the grief. I've lived a long, tiring life full of it. But I am going to kill every last one of the Inner Circle. I am going to destroy the Serpents. *No matter what,*" Kira declared. As if the sky agreed, it boomed. She turned to the blue-eyed man and raised her brow. "Will you help me, Nero?"

The Italian stared at her. He finally understood why Aria had kept Kira by her side all these years. His heart was heavily filled with grief, but bloodthirst lingered in his veins – he wanted justice. He knew he could spend years and years chasing the Serpents to avenge Aria. He knew he would spend the rest of his life avenging her. Then, he tucked one hand into his pocket as the other steadily held the umbrella over them. It covered most of Kira's slender frame, however he was much larger which meant the left side of his body was completely exposed to the rain's merciless tears. He didn't care.

"I wish you the best, Yakira," he replied, coolly, and that was all she needed. "If you need anything – *anything at all* – let me know and I'll do my best to provide it."

Kira's lips quirked up. "Perhaps we'll bump into each other again. I look forward to that day."

"Take care of yourself. Those assassins need a new leader."

"No. There will *never* be a leader like Aria," Kira responded. "But I will protect them until the day I die. I will try and do her justice."

He didn't say anything else. There was nothing left to say. Kira and Nero had two different paths, and the one set in front of him meant that he was to leave the past in the past. As much as he wanted to stop the Serpents, Nero could not stray away from his responsibility of being the Don – *she* would not want him to do that; you *always* protect your own first. The Italians were practically defenseless with their lack of weaponry and to throw themselves into a war they were not prepared for would be suicidal. Kira understood that, and as she stared at him, she respected his decision. So, after one last smile, she walked away, her red bottom heels tapping against the helipad where they were standing.

She wasn't sure when she would meet Nero again, but something told her it would be very soon.

CHAPTER 47

ghost of you

Nero
3 weeks later

Exhaustion washed over me as I pushed open the door to Aria's penthouse, stumbling into the silent home of ours. Coldness nipped my skin, reminding me that it had been a couple of days since any other sort of life form was present here. I had been spending my days and nights at the Estate, burying myself under mountains of paperwork, drowning my thoughts with whiskey and gin, numbing every inch of me until I could feel nothing, Matteo finally ordered me back home. Despite my attempts to argue, he didn't listen to one word and shoved me out of the Estate. I should have gone straight to my own building, but I couldn't. I knew Matteo didn't believe me, but I was getting better – and the days were becoming easier. Yet, there in the back of my mind was a lingering thought which refused to leave me, like a stain on white fabric. It inundated me. Some days, I swear I felt her presence, as if she was watching over me, but like many of my days, those were just my dark thoughts taunting me. I shuffled down the corridor, flicking all the lights on with a heavy sigh as I watched the incandescent spotlights irradiate my gloomy surroundings. I dumped my things on the kitchen table before grabbing a beer from the fridge, chugging it down as soon as I managed to open it. The silence was unnerving, but it strangely became my best friend, substituting the presence of Aria. I languidly made my way back into the living room whilst scrolling through my phones, wondering if I had gotten any messages from Kira or anyone else. I didn't know why I was disappointed when I saw nothing – Kira had disappeared off the face of this planet, along with Xander and everyone else in the Manor. I knew they were following Aria's last orders, but I couldn't help but hope that someone would be at the Manor when I had visited a week after Aria's death, unbeknownst to Matteo.

The mansion was completely abandoned; any traces of human activity were erased, and they left no sort of trail behind that I could use to find them. It was then that I decided to start moving forwards. I was too busy chasing the past and the way I was going, I knew I would soon endanger all the people in the mafia, including my family. So, I picked myself up, rebuilt the broken pieces that were filled by Aria, and started again. To lose her a second time was heart–shattering, world-changing, terrifying. But I couldn't bring her back and I knew I would forever feel guilty for not protecting her enough. Despite my best efforts, I was unable to track Calix down, and there were numerous days where we would find the slightest lead that would ultimately result in a dead-end. He was trained well. Of course, he would be. He was trained by the best. He was trained by Aria. And she knew how to disappear better than the rest of us. I exhaled deeply and collapsed onto the sofa, watching my phone bounce as I threw it against the pillow, before tilting my head back to take another chug of the cold beer. The refreshing feeling was interrupted when I glanced in the direction of the window, noticing a figure standing there with their arms crossed over their chest, beady eyes watching the city below. I didn't flinch at the sight and drank again.

"Here to haunt me again?" I asked, coldly. The figure didn't move. "I thought so."

"When will you stop drinking?" It asked a second later, following with the action of looking over their shoulder. Brown waves tousled past the slender frame as hazel eyes narrowed in disappointment.

I hummed as if I was actually thinking of a response, before slyly grinning, "Never?"

It shook its head. "You shouldn't do this to yourself. It's going to kill you."

"You can't kill what was never alive."

"You are very much alive, Nero," the figure hissed, before striding towards me. With steeled eyes, it ordered, "Stop it."

"Come back," was my response, as I challenged its gaze.

Blinking in astonishment, it recoiled as it looked away and then responded, brokenly, almost guiltily, "You know I can't do that."

"Then I won't stop because the only way I can see you is if I'm completely wasted."

"Nero," the voice was soft and angelic, but it held so much gravity that it made me stop, look up, and wait for the next words to leave its coral lips. Hazel eyes downturned, training their focus on the ground as if something was interesting about the grey rug. "Please stop hurting yourself. I'm never going to come back; let me go and live your life properly. You deserve better than this."

"I deserve you," I swallowed my sob, placing the beer onto the coffee table and reaching out to take the slender figure's hands. Frail and nimble in my hold, coldness ran up my arms at the touch like a colony of ants. The mere action caused the hazel eyes to look at me, lost and sorrowful, laced with pain. "I need only you. You were my purpose, my reason to breathe and live, and now… now I don't know what I'm doing anymore."

"I'm sorry," it sniffled, glassy eyes breaking my heart. "I wish… I wish that this didn't happen."

I smiled, woefully. "So do I."

"You know I love you," it began a moment later, as I rubbed my thumbs against their glacial hands, soothingly. "So much."

"I love you too," I replied, trying to hold back my tears and maintain my smile despite the dire need to break down like my fragmented heart. "So much."

It smiled, pensively, slowly withdrawing its hands from my hold. "But you have to let me go."

I frowned, as the figure that looked so much like the love of my life bent down and pressed its icy lips against my forehead. My eyes, by their own command, fluttered shut and embraced the tingling sensation, savoring it with all my might because I never wanted to forget it. But as soon as I opened my eyes, I regretted ever closing them. Where the figure stood only a few seconds ago was a simple stream of moonlight that spilt into the room. And just like, it was as if nothing had happened. I breathed shakily and reached for the beer bottle, only to be stopped as a certain glimmer hit the corner of my eyes. In a marble pot filled with little knickknacks, I saw something that I had not seen in nearly a month. Aria's ring.

My heart stuttered before it began to race madly as I trembled when reaching for the piece of silver that shimmered under the moonshine. I was sure that Aria had been buried with this ring; I had seen it on her before she was taken to her coffin. Her parents insisted on having a closed-casket funeral with only her very close relatives, mainly because the rest of the world did not even know that Aria still existed. Many assumed she was already dead. Instead, she was a ghost. She had always been one since she left five years ago. Confusion impelled me to study the band, check that it was hers but from the small marking on the silver with the letter 'N' engraved, I knew it could only belong to her. But how did it get here? *How* – My mind stopped. *Kira.* She was here.

"I can't believe we're married!" Aria beamed, her eyes adoring the wedding band next to her engagement ring.

She looked like a vision in a white dress, and although this was not the fairy tale wedding she once dreamed of, this had felt much better. Because it was just us two and no one else mattered. I chuckled, kissing the crown of her head, and she glanced up at me, affectionately, as we left the town hall.

"You're stuck with me for life now," she warned.

I grinned. "I've been stuck with you since the day you were born. I'm not going anywhere. We're meant to be, Aria. Do you not agree?"

Her eyes softened and she stroked my cheek, as she said, "If we are meant to be together, then I will always find my way back to you, no matter what life we're in."

"And what if you get lost along the way?" I arched my brow, amused.

"Then you'll find me," she spoke with so much confidence, as if there was no other answer that could be given – as if she trusted me that much. My heart swelled and she kissed me. "I know you will."

Holding the ring between my hands, I sank back into the sofa as shock followed with grief waved over me. I pursed my lips, blinked back the tears, and choked back my sobs. However, the second I looked up, and my eyes settled on the frame of us during our wedding reception, I cried. And I cried, and cried for the rest of the night, doubting if I could ever survive without Aria.

*

Buzz.
Buzz.
Buzz.

What the fuck was that sound?

I groaned as I lifted my head from my pillow, blinking in discomfort when the sunlight hit my eyes seeing as I didn't close my curtains last night before I passed out. The incessant buzzing didn't stop as my phone rattled on the bedside table until I grumpily reached out to answer the call. Matteo's name blinded me and with an exasperated sigh, I answered the call with a groan.

"Good morning to you, too," he muttered back. "Did you drink again?"

I heard Melissa's scold in the background, "He's still drinking?!"

"Perhaps," I pushed myself up, running my fingers through my disheveled hair. "Have you called to yell, or has something happened?"

Melissa shouted, "Both!"

Matteo answered in his own sardonic tone, "Get your ass to the Estate – I think we've found Calix."

He didn't need to say anymore as I jumped out of bed, hanging up the phone, and rushing straight to the bathroom. I tried not to enjoy the sensation of the warm pelts of water against my tense and sore muscles, knowing that if I did, I would be in here all morning, and quickly cleaned the grime and sweat from my body and hair before jumping out. As soon as I was done in the bathroom, I grabbed a fresh suit from Aria's wardrobe, where I had left some of my belongings from those nights when I would stay over. After we had gotten married, she suggested for me to move in and, despite the fact that I adored my own penthouse, I didn't think twice when I had agreed. However, I had not managed to bring all my things to hers, but I had most of my stuff - although, it was nowhere near the amount that Aria owned. *Like, who needs two closets just filled with shoes?* The thought tugged my lips when I walked by said closets before disappearing at how unsullied they were.

Buttoning up my pressed white shirt, I took in my reflection in the full-length mirror I stood in front of. The man I saw was overwhelmed with grief; he looked as if he had not slept peacefully for days with tell-tale dark circles under his eyes, hollow cheeks and the lack of light within his blue eyes, which were red and puffy. I sighed and shrugged on a grey blazer over my shirt, fixing my lilac tie before drawing on some socks and slipping into a pair of dress shoes. My phone rang again as I cuffed my links and one glance at the screen told me it was my father. I sighed when I answered it, immediately placing him on speaker so that I could finish getting ready.

"Nero," my father greeted, in his usual deep and disconnected voice.

"Father," was my response, in the same tone, combing my hair back with gel. "How can I help?"

"Your mother has been pestering me about when you'll visit. You haven't called in days, and she's been growing concerned," he explained. "Give her a call when you are free."

"I will do ."

There was a long silence and for a second, I thought he hung up until I saw that the call was still connected. Then, he sighed. "How are you?"

Thrown off by his question, I blinked before quickly recovering, muttering a quiet, "I'm fine."

"It's okay, *figlio*, to not be okay. I know you and Aria were close and intended on getting married this summer."

"We actually did get married," I admitted.

"When?" my father asked, surprise laced in his word.

"Over a month ago."

"Why weren't we informed of this?" he questioned. "Do Xena and Antonio know?"

"Aria didn't want to tell anyone. She knew it wasn't traditional like you guys would have wanted. Our marriage was essential for a task she needed to complete, and we couldn't wait any longer. We planned to hold a ceremony later on with our friends and family," I answered, whilst heading to the kitchen to prepare myself a coffee. Once again, he did not reply for the longest time and I questioned whether he had finally hung up because he was pissed off that I had kept this away from him, until he drew in a slow breath of air.

"Nero, I love you and I trust your judgement, but I hope you aren't acting without thinking."

My father was a cold yet compassionate man. As the right-hand to Antonio Moretti, my mother often said that I acquired many of his characteristics. Claudio Russo was a man of few words; but he was charismatic, brave and merciful. He understood pain in ways I could never and growing up, I knew he was who I wanted to become. I knew I had a long way to go before I achieved that goal, but hearing him say that he trusted my judgement, set alight a confidence booster I did not realize I needed. For the first time since Aria's death, my heart seemed lighter.

"I am, father. I promise. I love Aria," I stated, assertively. "I would have married her either way. She was who I wanted to spend the rest of my life with."

"I know, son. I know."

And I didn't doubt his words for one second.

*

"Enzo is holding a masquerade party," Matteo informed, as we settled in my office. I pulled off my blazer, hanging it behind my chair, before I sat down, rolling up my sleeves to my elbows. "I think Calix might be there."

"How sure are you?" I asked, with narrowed eyes as Matteo passed me Enzo's beautifully decorated invitation. I didn't bother asking how he acquired this ticket, knowing that Enzo had not sent me one.

"Maybe eighty per cent sure?" he grinned, but I was not amused. With a roll of his eyes, he handed me a photograph and I quickly noticed the man in the image was Calix. As I inspected it carefully, Matteo explained, "Melissa discovered this. It was taken at the airport just a few days ago. After some digging, we found out that he was taking a plane to Canada. Enzo's event will be taking place at the Ellington Grand," I arched my brow, and he concluded with, "*Toronto*."

"So, you think Calix will be attending?"

"It's a possibility."

I mused over the idea before sliding the image back to Matteo. "Prepare the jet for Toronto this evening, and have Melissa send me something to wear. It seems as if there's a ball for me to attend."

Toronto was as beautiful as it was two years ago when I last visited for a friend's wedding. I was familiar with Ellington Grand, a stunning venue that reminded me very much of old movie theaters. It was perfect for the masquerade ball Enzo was holding. Although I was not entirely sure of his intention behind this event, I knew it would not be anything good and most importantly, like all events in the Underground, it was a façade for the truth. I inhaled my cigar as I leaned against a lamppost across the street, a few meters away from the location, scouting my environs. Having arrived in Toronto the same evening I had left, I used some of my time to do a little recon before the actual day, so that I knew what I could potentially be dealing with. A grey flat cap shielded my face from any onlookers, and a long trench coat shielded my body from the bitter air. As puffs of smoke surrounded me, I watched a few men enter and leave the venue with boxes bound in white tape which said 'fragile.' I could not hear what the men were saying as they spoke amongst each other, but with my training, I could read their lips, easily.

"Careful," one said, as he smacked the other for recklessly handling the box. He was clearly in charge of them with dark eyes and a bald head inked in tattoos. Scars painted his neck that the t-shirt failed to hide, and his large build made him look threatening to his men. "Boss will kill us if these break."

"What's inside them?" someone else asked, as his friend placed another box in his arms as soon as he arrived back. He was skinny and frail, and I swear I could snap him in half. He wore a baseball cap over his shaggy black hair, and I noticed his gold teeth when the moonlight hit them.

"Dunno, but I'm not risking getting my eyes gouged out just to satisfy my curiosity," the bald one grumbled, a frown on his lips.

The skinny one laughed but the bald one did not. Neither did the other men. Noticing that his friends were not amused, the skinny one's laughter died out before he drew his brows together. "You aren't serious, are you?"

The bald man didn't answer but another one did with a simple, "You're new, mate. You haven't seen what we have. Here, take this."

The scrawny man fumbled as he nodded with fear, stumbling into the venue with the boxes in his twig-like arms. As I exhaled the fumes from the cigar, my attention suddenly shifted from the group of men to the shadowy, slender figure that appeared from the side of the venue, hidden by the darkness so that no one caught sight of them. I frowned, unable to deduce who the figure was as they wore a cloak over their frame, a hood covering their face from curious eyes. But I caught sight of their red bottom heels that tapped against the pavement, the lamppost irradiating the soles of their shoes as they strolled away from the venue.

From the short glimpse of the cloaked being, I quickly assumed it was a woman. My only question was who?

CHAPTER 48

phantom hope

Nero

"**S**urely, you can't be serious," I crinkled my nose at the tub in her hand. "Why would I ever put that on my face? It looks like... gunk."

She sighed; her body fatigued from the hours we had spent dueling each other. "It's good for your skin."

I wasn't convinced. I examined the skincare product, suspiciously. "It's charcoal. Why would that be good for my skin?"

"Nero, can you just trust me?" Hopping onto the countertop beside the sink, she uncapped the tub and scooped out a large swad of charcoal with what looked like a small plastic spatula. "Now, c'mere."

Wiggling her fingers, Aria beamed at me but I couldn't take her seriously with the green mask slathered across her face. It was beginning to harden so her smile was scarily similar to the Joker. I wanted to fight against this but she had been persistent about me 'detoxing' my skin, whatever that meant. Therefore, after much internalized debating, I stepped between her legs and allowed her to smear the cool substance across my skin. I wanted to shiver as her fingers brushed over my stubble, then over my nose and my forehead, but instead I grasped the granite counter until my knuckles went white. Her warm breath fanned against my face, smelling of fresh mint, as concentration etched her brows. Hazel eyes warmed with childish delight as she inspected her masterpiece before continuing. Losing my initial wariness, all I could think about was how easy it would be to kiss her if I just leaned forward. She occupied my thoughts most of the time, and tonight was no different. I got lost in *her, unaware of how much time had passed until she clicked her tongue, bopping in her seat, gleefully.*

Her happiness made me smile.

"What?" I asked, but it sounded breathless.

Thankfully, she didn't notice as she responded, "Seventeen looks good on you, Russo, but tomorrow you'll look even better."

I stole a glance in the mirror and my smile fell. I looked like a swamp monster. Voicing my thoughts, Aria exploded into a fit of laughter.

*

On the evening of the masquerade ball, as I waited for my car to arrive, I studied Enzo's intricate invitation with black swirls and gold inked writing. He had a troubling fascination with masquerade balls, I pondered. Remembering the time I attended that private event at his mansion with Aria, I wondered whether these masquerades meant something. Unlike last time, I wore a red three-piece suit that reminded me of Aria's gown from that night. My waistcoat over my white shirt was red and black, with an embroidered design to compliment the satin red blazer with black lapels, and the tie that had the same design as the waistcoat with a napkin tucked into my chest pocket. I had gotten my beard and dark brown hair trimmed for tonight's event, seeing as it had grown over the last couple of weeks due to my lack of care. My hair was tidily groomed back into an undercut with a rippling quality and made it comfortable to wear a black mask over my eyes. A knock on my door told me that my transport had arrived, so, after checking that I had my gun tucked into the waistband of my carmine trousers, and a pocketknife tucked into my white socks, I slipped my dress shoes on, attached a silver tie clip, and left the hotel room that Matteo had booked for me.

The town car travelled down the large roads of Toronto, my eyes admiring the view as I promised myself to return here one day for a vacation. The buzzing of my phone drew my attention down to my lap, and I saw Matteo's messages informing me that three of our men would also be at the venue pretending to be security in case anything happened. I texted him my thanks before tucking my phone into my blazer as the car pulled up in front of the venue. Unlike the other night, the historic movie theater venue was lit up by beams as if it was presenting a film screening. A red carpet ran down the middle with

441

reporters flanking either side, red velvet ropes preventing them from stampeding the guests. My door opened with help from the driver, and I slipped out as soon as I straightened my blazer. Sticking my hands into my trouser pockets, I strolled down the red carpet, ignoring the questions thrown in my direction, unblinking to the incessant flashes of light from the large cameras that attacked me from all directions. I handed the bouncer my invitation and entered the venue, my eyes absorbing the interior of the location. Instead of rows of seats, the hall was large with a platform at the far back, and an enormous screen behind it. Circles of tables lined either side of the room and a huge space in the middle that was crammed with guests. A table filled with snacks and an ice sculpture had grabbed the fascination of many of the guests as they gushed over it, but I was interested in the group of men huddled together near the stage. I immediately recognized Enzo as one of the men in that group from the way he smirked wickedly at them, but I couldn't see Calix. I wondered if Matteo was mistaken.

Then, something caught the corner of my eye.

A woman in a beautiful black satin gown with diamonds scattered across the material and tulle sleeves that covered the lengths of her arms and neck. The ballgown cinched around her waist before expanding outwards and covered much of the mass of the floor, glittering as if she was wearing literal stars. Her silver mask covered the entirety of her face, but her eyes were vibrant with black and red eyeshadow. She moved through the room with confidence and gravity, like she was sure of herself.

My heart stopped. Aria.

But it couldn't be her.

Before I could make my way to her, a group of people blocked my path and by the time they moved, she was gone. My heart stuttered and I swallowed hard before shaking my head. I had to focus. I had to. I could not allow myself to be distracted. I grabbed a glass of champagne from the waiter that walked past and drank it greedily, as if I hadn't drunk for days, before I set off on my mission. Weaving in and out of the crowd, I tried to find Calix, but people wore masks, and I couldn't tell who was who. Frustration was getting the best of me, and after three more glasses of champagnes, I decided to stop and reassess my plan. I drank the champagne slowly, scrutinizing the crowd, especially where Enzo was. Until a girl in an emerald gown glided towards me, a black mask failing to cover her lips which coiled into a seductive smirk.

"Care to dance, sir?" she asked, holding her hand out.

I narrowed my eyes and began to refuse but she grasped my hand and dragged me to the middle of the room before I could complain. I didn't want to create a fuss and gain unwanted attention, so I sucked it up and allowed her to twirl her arms around my neck, placing my hands on her waist, loosely. My eyes flicked over her shoulders, and I caught sight of the woman in the black dress again. Wanting to separate myself from the girl, I began to detach myself but her hold around my neck only had me stagger closer. I sent her a glare, which she quickly dismissed, before looking up to see that the woman had once again disappeared, and I considered whether I was imagining things.

"Have I seen you around before?" the girl in the emerald dress purred, her dark blonde hair caressing her skin as we swayed.

"I'm wearing a mask; you have no idea who I am," I replied, curtly, hoping my rude tone would turn her off but it had the opposite effect.

She didn't flinch, and her smirk broadened. "Is that a challenge?"

The question threw me off because it was something Aria would say. Suddenly, my throat contracted as I held back the grief threatening to rise because this woman was not Aria. She would never *be* Aria.

Stiffy, I retorted, "It's a fact."

She laughed, throwing her head back in a way that exposed the skin of her neck, baring it to me, where it would have once tempted me to taste it, but now it made me feel uncomfortable and irritated. Her eyes had a wicked glint as she pressed herself closer to me.

"You are funny. I'm sure we can get to know each other better," her lips grazed my ear, and I stilled. "Somewhere private."

I didn't have a chance to respond as someone bumped into us, separating the woman from my arms. I stumbled back before glancing at the culprit, stopping short when I noticed it was the woman in the night sky dress. The girl I had been dancing with glared at her, a scowl set on her lips.

"Excuse me, don't you have something to say?" she demanded, but the woman didn't reply.

I could not even tell what she was thinking as her mask covered her entire face, leaving only her eyes exposed. The lighting of the room was too dark to tell what the color of her eyes was, but I knew they thinned as they stared at the scowling girl.

I quickly jumped in when I noticed a few eyes shifting in our direction and held my hand out to the mysterious woman. "A dance, my lady?"

She didn't say anything, but I saw her hesitance before she slipped her gloved hand into mine. As I drew her body against mine, I faintly heard a frustrated huff and watched the blonde disappear into the crowd. My shoulders finally relaxed as I moved to place one of my hands on the woman's waist, whilst she placed one on my upper arm.

"Thank you for saving me," I muttered, her eyes flickering up. They were dark and cryptic, and her only response was a short nod of acknowledgement. "Do you have a name?"

She shook her head.

I rose my brows in surprise. "You don't have a name?"

She shook her head again.

"So, are you a ghost?"

Her eyes softened and I took that as a yes.

"Surely you can't be real then?" I mused.

Her eyes twinkled with amusement as she continued to tease me, and she spun around before swiftly returning into my arms. Her dark hair followed her in gentle waves, dancing as we moved around the venue, in sync and as one. For the first time in weeks, my heart felt at peace, but I had the dying need to know who this stranger was. Thick lashes alluringly batted as I continued to ask her questions, mirth glinting in her eyes and I wondered if she was smiling under her mask. The music began to quieten, and I knew I didn't have long left. She knew, too. Her eyes moved over my shoulders where they iced and as I followed her gaze, I caught sight of those boxes I had seen the other day hiding behind the curtains draped from the ceiling.

I glanced back at her. "Do you know what's inside them?"

She didn't respond.

"Were you here the other night when they were bringing these boxes into the venue?" I questioned, with narrowed eyes.

She didn't respond.

Her eyes remained on mine, unmoving, unflinching.

Yet, there was something so familiar about them; I just could not pinpoint what it was.

Breathlessly, I whispered, "Who are you?"

This time, she tilted her head to the side and her cold eyes melted, the frosty exterior revealing the only thing she had shared tonight. Her compassion. As soon as the music ended, she broke free from my grasp and disappeared into the crowd. My feet were frozen to the ground by the sudden action. I immediately broke myself from my shock and shot off in her direction, pushing through the drunken bodies that staggered in my way. I caught sight of her glittering black dress and knew I was nearly there. I could almost touch her. Then, a group of men blocked my path as they raucously laughed, their drinks sloshing as they staggered around me. I growled, shoving through them, but she was gone by the time I reached the other side. My shoulders slugged as I halted, angry that I had lost the mysterious woman, angry that this night has been a total failure, angry that, once again, I was alone. My jaw tightened and I turned to walk back to where I was originally when I collided into another woman. She stumbled back, nearly tripping over her dress, but I swiftly grabbed her arm and drew her onto her feet.

"Thanks," she muttered, dusting her navy gown off, and tossing her blonde hair over her shoulders so it was not in the way of her gold mask.

"Sorry, I didn't see you…" my words trailed off, as I recognized her voice. Eyes wide, my heart stuttered, and the blonde woman looked at me in confusion. But I would recognize those blue eyes anywhere, and before I could stop myself, I whispered, "Kira?"

*

Outside of the main hall was a quiet, isolated hallway that allowed us to speak freely with no fear of anyone listening. Kira leaned against the wall, her arms crossed over her chest, head tilting back as she sighed. Without her mask, I could see how sunken the circles were under her eyes and the cavities of her cheeks which told me she had lost weight. She looked exhausted and I did not doubt that she was.

I pulled my mask off, running a hand over my face, as I asked, "Why are you here?"

Her cool blue eyes peered at me. "Same reason as you. I'm assuming you thought you'd find Calix here?"

"Did you find him?" She shook her head with a press of her lips. I didn't know what I could say. For weeks, I had been wanting to see her but now that she was finally in front of me, the words were trapped in my throat.

Kira thankfully filled in the silence, her voice as aloof as her gaze,

"How have you been?"

I did not meet her intense stare, fearing that if I did I would break down into tears and admit that I had not been doing as well as I thought I was. Instead, I answered, "Fine. How are you?"

"Struggling," was her response. She continued to inspect me, and I knew she did not believe me. Instead of pressing me to know more, Kira inhaled, sharply, pushed herself off the wall, and tied the mask back on. "I've failed to capture Calix, and I knew he wouldn't be here, yet I came anyway. Because I've been struggling to let go of the idea that maybe Aria was right, that I need to stop."

My throat bobbed. "Is that what she told you at the hospital?"

With a nod of her head, Kira said, "Yes. She said I'd die trying, and risk taking everyone down with me if I wasn't careful."

"She was looking out for you. Even on her death bed."

There was this chill in the air as if someone had left a window open, but it was refreshing and, for some reason, much needed. In this narrow hallway, I was beginning to feel claustrophobic like the walls were closing in on me and I was trapped. Kira shifted on her feet; her navy gown sparkled as the candlelit chandelier above us spotlighted her.

"I wasn't going to listen," Kira spoke with assertion, something I missed, and the corner of my lips twitched.

"I know," Tucking my hands into my pockets, I straightened my spine and arched a brow. "How about we work to find Calix together? Maybe we'll find something."

She squinted, dubiously. "I thought you didn't want to help."

"Didn't and couldn't are two different words," I looked down the hallway where the dull sound of music echoed from, bouncing off the walls until they were a soft hum when they reached our ears. "I don't think I can move on until Calix is in my grasp."

"Fair enough," she shrugged. For the first time this evening, I smiled, and Kira mirrored it. "Shall we head back?"

I held my hand out which she took, hooking her arm through mine before we walked back with a new profound sense of confidence. We slipped back into the darkened room undetected, and as we glided through the crowd, we attempted to keep a sharp look out for Calix. Bodies pressed against ours, and if the dance floor could speak it would be a tale of enlivened souls who were unwittingly selling their lives to the devil. Speaking of the devil, I brought Kira to a halt when I caught sight of Enzo heading up onto the large platform, standing behind a podium with the screen behind him enlightened, large pictures plastered for all to see. I recognized a few from Enzo's questionable partnerships and speculated as to what he had planned. Kira and I shared a look, and I knew she was thinking the same thing. Before I could say anything, his voice boomed out of the speakers when he leaned towards the microphone with a smirk.

"Good evening, and thank you for attending tonight's event," Thundering applause followed soon after those words, to which he bowed respectfully, yet arrogantly. When the room became silent again, he continued, "It is my greatest pleasure to announce that I will be expanding my business from America to the rest of the world."

"Expanding?" Kira whispered, with her brows drawn together. I didn't respond.

"After many discussions behind the scenes with my partners, we have decided it was time to take the enterprise that generations of families failed to succeed in, and finally accomplish their lifelong goal."

As Enzo spoke, the screen behind him changed to pictures of young boys and girls looking as if they were being given shelter and food, when in fact their freedom was being stripped away from them. My heart stammered as I examined the photos, realizing how manipulative Enzo was being regarding this 'enterprise.' To those who were unaware about the Serpents' activities, this looked like a foundation created to support those in need.

"Do you think the family he's talking about are the Petrovs?" Kira murmured, and I looked down at her in surprise.

"Aria told you about the Petrovs?" She nodded in response, waiting for an answer. I weighed out the chances before concluding, "I don't think it would be possible. Gabrielle had ensured that the Petrovs were all killed and she left no trace of their existence. I'm sure Aria told you about the war her family had with them."

Kira once again nodded. Years before either Aria or I were born, her family were in a continuous battle with the Petrovs as they tried to control the Russian mafia. First, they came after Xena and tried to have her kill Antonio, but when that plot failed, Nikolay, the eldest son of the Petrovs, kidnapped Xena to weed out Antonio. Thankfully, Antonio managed to save Xena and the two killed Nikolay before he succeeded in destroying both the Russian and Italian mafias. Then there was Chantelle Kolsov. Her father had been the boss of the

Russians before he handed the throne to his niece, Gabrielle. But before that had happened, the sacred Chip, a device that had all sorts of information from business transactions, to agreements, to government treaties, had been stolen. Chantelle had to search for the Chip, which was in the possession of Coal Black. That was the beginning of their story. However, once again, the Petrovs attacked and managed to bring the Chip into their custody. Fortunately, with help of Coal, Chantelle was able to retrieve the device and put a stop to the Petrov's plan by sending Dimitri, the father, to jail. Finally, they attacked Gabrielle. Using the burning need for revenge from Gabrielle's ex-bodyguard and his best friend, the Petrovs plotted to kidnap Gabrielle and sell her off. That was at the height of their business in sex trafficking. Once again, the Kolsovs foiled their plans and this time ensured they were all killed, wiping out their entire bloodline and destroying their enterprise. The Petrovs had not been heard of since. At least, I had hoped that was the case.

"But, Russo," Kira said lowly. "What if they missed someone?"

I didn't know how to reply because, despite my knowledge that the Kolsovs were very thorough in their hunt, there was always a slight chance that they missed someone. I chose not to say anything else on the matter, afraid that if I did there was a possibility Kira could be right. And she knew that too from the way her blue eyes darkened, looking askance at Enzo.

"I'd like to invite you all to the grand opening, which will occur in a couple of weeks after our special guest arrives," Enzo's lips twisted into a wickedly malicious grin. "It will be the event of the century."

After those final words, another round of raucous applause followed as Enzo waved whilst descending the stairs and walking to the group of men waiting for him at the front. Kira stiffened beside me, and I knew we had to get out of here before someone caught sight of us. So, I grasped her hand and pulled us through the mass of people who wore fancy feathered masks and expensive, luxurious clothing that were paid for by their involvement in dangerous industries and nefarious operations. I was not a saint and being involved in the mafia meant there were often times where the business I would conduct was questionable and immoral, but I knew where to draw the line and at the end of the day, that would always mean I would stop those who threatened the safety and peace of the existence of others. Especially those who had no connection with or clue about the Underground. As soon as we were out of the venue, my car was already waiting upfront, so I swiftly led us to the safety of my transport and away from the ruthless eyes of the tabloids, who snapped pictures of us, throwing questions regarding our identity. I knew tomorrow Matteo would have a lot of damage control to do to ensure Enzo had no idea that I ever attended the event.

"Who do you think he is talking about?" Kira asked after a while, her eyes trained on the buildings we passed, driving further and further away from the venue, away from the darkest parts of the Underground. She gnawed on her lip, anxiously, glancing at me and I tore the mask away from my face.

"I'm not sure. But we need to find out and put an end to his plans," I responded, in determination. Then I held her gaze, watching the apprehension melt away and something else settled in its place as I said, "For Aria."

"For Aria," she repeated. We held each other's gaze, an understanding forming between us until she broke it, untying the mask on her face and leaning her head back against the black leather seat of the town car. A playful smirk washed the worry away, curling her rosy lips. "I suppose that means it's time to bring you to our safe house again."

I furrowed my brows in confusion. "It's located in Canada?"

"It's near Whiteface Mountain, back in New York," she replied, before arching her dark brow as her ultramarine eyes glittered, an unspoken question being asked within its icy depths. "Aria said it was her favorite place in the world."

I wrenched my gaze away from Kira, moving it towards the window as I watched the streets merge into the highways, until there was nothing but cars and trees surrounding us. The stars above us sparkled like diamonds. The moon was radiant in its occult presence which took over a large part of the night-sky.

Beneath the moonlight, I remembered the mysterious woman with the stunning silver mask, and said, "It's where I first fell in love with her."

CHAPTER 49

the devil's nightmare

Tap. Tap. Tap.

The sound echoed throughout the cold chamber with walls that were half rock and half polished steel. A substantial portion of the room was taken up by the boxing ring situated in the center with people crowding around as they watched two enormous men covered in scars and tattoos pummel each other until one was nearly dead. The spectators held their breath, unaware of the woman in the black cloak, shielding her face and frame from their eyes. One of the fighters smashed his fist into the other's face, causing his opponent to topple back with blood splattering onto the rubber of the arena, a vibrant ruby, like the sole of her stilettos. His opponent did not get up from the ground. He was most likely dead. The winner roared, and the bystanders echoed his animalistic cheer of triumph with bloodlust rushing throughout their bodies, adrenaline having them chant for more, as they threw their cash at him. More fights. More blood. More death.

The Underground's famous fighting rink smelled like death and sin.

And bloodshed was the devil's ink.

Arc lights beamed from above, illuminating the semi–dark subterranean location. Armed guards, dressed in black tactical uniforms and wearing helmets that obscured their faces, waited at each doorway, patrolling the mass of criminals, gang members, hitmen, and the unfortunate, making sure no one harmed each other. This place was a haven, and everyone must abide by the unspoken rules. Here, no one was allowed to know anyone else's identity; if you asked, your tongue would be sliced. The cartel, the mob, the most emotionally indifferent monsters the money-nexus ever birthed, all retired here to spend the evenings away from their responsibilities, fueling their bloodlust but also to search for recruits – hence, the fighters in the ring. There were only two things you could gain here: information, and people.

She was looking for information.

There would now be a short intermission in which people scattered away from the boxing ring and returned to their booked tables, bubbling with adrenaline. During that time, it was much easier to see people's faces. She saw many that she recognized. Men she wanted to kill. Wives of men she had killed. Hitmen who had tried to find and kill her. Mistresses she had killed for. Yet, they would never recognize her. She was a ghost. Always had been, always would be.

As she walked, some people tried to get a glimpse of her hidden features, but it was difficult to deduce her appearance as the hood cloaked her face. But when she was briefly under the dim lighting above, people caught an impression of her looks and began to whisper amongst themselves, unaware that she could hear them. They spoke about her appearance as if God took the time to build her, yet there was a devilish aura that polished her presence. Her lips were red. Blood red. And the way she smirked would have had men fall to their knees to beg for mercy and her affection at the same time. Her eyes danced with a haunting secret and twinkled like the full moon. Her fingers were stained, painted, and coated in scarlet liquid, but no one questioned who they belonged to. No one dared to. For they knew that this woman could kill them before they could even blink. And, yet they all were asking the same question – *who was she?*

When she finally found the table that held the answers she needed, she stopped and waited for the man, who was shuffling a deck of cards, calmly, to acknowledge her presence. He was bald but his head was covered in black ink. He was broad, large and if he stood up, she knew he would be taller than her. Though he wore a black t-shirt, it was apparent that the tattoos on both arms crawled up to his neck. There was one large scar from the end of his right brow to the bottom of his jaw. Another began at his neck and disappeared behind his t-shirt. He looked frightening, but she knew she could kill him within seconds.

"And what can I do for you?" he asked, in a guttural voice.

"I'm looking for someone and I heard you're the man to come to," she responded silkily, which immediately had the men closest to the table shiver as if she had spewed out ice and caused the temperature to drop.

The man saw this, pouring a bottle of liquor into two glasses, before sliding one across the table. Her fingers were painted the same color as the wine, dark carmine like her lips, and as they curled around the glass, the drink sloshed on contact. She sipped the drink, her hood covering her eyes that the man was curious to see.

"You attract a lot of attention," the man mused, setting cards in front of her before dealing himself some, then sorting the black and red chips.

"It's inherited," she gathered her cards and the corner of her lips twitched, then they began to play.

"Who is it that you are looking for?" he placed three cards down from the deck beside him.

She drawled, pushing her chip towards him, "Calix Zervas."

"Popular man," was his response, thrusting his chips into the middle before revealing the fourth card from the deck. He saw her smile under the hood. "What will I get for this information?"

"I'll let you live," she pushed more chips into the middle.

"Is that a challenge?" He rolled his shoulders back, as a lion would tower over their competitor to show their dominance. He did not believe her, and that would be his downfall.

She did not flinch, mildly amused by the question. "No, a fact."

He chuckled deeply, with mirth. "Sounds like you're making a threat rather than asking for a favor."

"It can be both. I'm good at keeping my word," she watched him like he was her prey, as he pushed some more chips into the middle. "So, will you give me what I want?"

"I like you," the man smirked, before placing the final card from the deck down. She did not respond or act, waiting for his decision.

The place and its atmosphere were bitter and icy; perhaps it was *her* presence that caused the temperature to drop. She tapped her manicured nails, the ones covered in what was most definitely dry blood, against the wooden table, rhythmically. It reminded the man of something from a horror film. He briefly wondered if she actually had a face under that cloak, or whether it so ugly that it would be horrifying to see. She showed no signs of leaving; steely, silently, and staunchly waiting for the answer. The tapping continued – it unnerved him, as he could almost feel the sensation of her nails digging into his neck and tearing his spine from his body. The image had him rubbing his neck, unwittingly, and he weighed out whether he should take heed of her threat or not.

Eventually, he exhaled, leaning back sluggishly, and tilted his head to the side, inquisitively. "He was last seen in Toronto; many say that he was attending Enzo's masquerade ball, but my sources tell me they didn't catch sight of him."

"So, where is he now?"

He shrugged. "Can't say for sure."

"Where is he?"

He narrowed his eyes. "I'm not sure."

"I won't ask again."

"What makes you think I'll have the answer?"

"You used to be Enzo's right-hand man."

The man blinked. For the first time ever, he was taken by surprise.

"I'm sure you don't want anyone finding out, especially since working with Enzo means you've collected a fine list of enemies, many of whom are in this room right now," she remarked, lazily admiring her blood-coated nails. "Now, where is he?"

He drew in a long breath of air. "Staying at Enzo's condo on St. Thomas."

"I don't understand why I must always resort to blackmail to finally get an answer," her jaw clenched in irritation, but she noted the location he had mentioned. "When will he return to New York?"

The man began to fiddle with his cards; he was intimidated, and she relished in it. "Not sure, but it will be soon."

"Why?"

"Enzo is hosting another event in the upcoming weeks to celebrate the expansion of his business."

"Sex trafficking?" she probed, candidly. "Forced labor? Or both?"

This caused the man's jaw to clench. He answered, stiffly, "Yes."

She hummed in reply, gazing around the building, from its concrete ceilings, to the stoned walls, to the lack of light, to the criminals it harbored. She could kill everyone here and they still would not know how she looked. The thought amused her, and for a second, there was a ghost of a smile teasing her lips.

"You should be scared. Terrified of what I'm going to do to you," she sighed.

He smirked. "What's a pretty woman like you going to do?"

She arched her brow, as a wicked smile teased her lips filled with the darkest of intentions. "I'm going to rip your heart out."

Then, the woman leaned forward, allowing the man to catch a glimpse of her cleavage as the cloak around her body loosened only slightly at the movement. He didn't hide the fact that he took a glimpse before arching his brow, his dark eyes studying her lips as they were the only feature he could see under the hood.

She knew he was curious. She just wondered how much.

"One last question," she whispered, her tone sultry, frosty, and dark. "Who is Enzo's special guest?"

The man didn't respond immediately, before saying, "Violetta Rossi." This caught her by surprise, although she did a brilliant job at not showing it. "He knows where she is. He's after Violetta Rossi."

After a long tense minute, the woman with the red lips leaned back and revealed her cards. "Thank you for your cooperation."

She didn't wait to see his cards, knowing she had won the game. She didn't wait to hear his response, as she stood up and began to walk away. Then he yelled, "Who the hell are you?"

She halted, aware of the eyes that shifted in her direction, all of them belonging to owners who were holding their breath in anticipation, curiosity and desire. Then they shifted to the bald man, who realized his mistake.

The cardinal rule: *Never ask for someone's identity.*

His eyes widened, his face paled, and he smacked his hand over his mouth, but he was too late. The words had already left his lips. The armed guards pounced into action before anyone could bat an eye, moving as swiftly as a coalition of cheetahs, and seized the man, who put up a fight and thrashed in their iron grasp. She inhaled slowly before glancing over her shoulder, and even then, her hood never came off. Yet, under the dim lighting of the Underground's worst fighting rink, the spectators caught sight of her cerise lips that were as dark as the blood of the fighter who lost, and her luminous gold eyes that sparkled with the darkest of intentions, promises of death, and a seductive vow that had people needing more. The man began to weep as he was dragged out of the room to meet his sinister fate, the armed guards showing no remorse as he cried. She supposed she should have felt pity but this was not her fault. Curiosity could get you killed. And if that did not kill you, she would.

Instead, in a low voice, laced in allurement, she purred, "I'm your worst nightmare."

CHAPTER 50

mountains apart

Nero

Blood gushed out of my opponent when the bullet went straight through their head. A single silver bullet was all it took to take someone's life away, and I had ten rounds of them. I didn't stop there, stepping over the corpse and moving onto the next man, whilst Yakira danced through the men that circled her, two daggers in each hand that cleaved through their bodies with such ease that it reminded me of tearing up paper. Like water, she weaved past the soldiers in combat black uniform, her movements as graceful as a ballerina. She looked like she was dancing, and the smile on her face told me she was enjoying it. I fought back a smile, amused by her sadistic nature, and turned my attention to my own fight. They failed as they tried to attack me. One man pulled his gun on me, but before he managed to shoot, I grabbed his weapon, twisted it from his hand, and stabbed my gun into his abdomen. He hunched over, loosening the grip on his gun, which allowed me to grasp it in my free hands. I shot him before he got back onto his feet. Then I moved onto the next man. This went on for about twenty men until the building was bleeding red from all floors. I ignored the bodies that Kira left in her path, stepping over them, my shoes soaked in crimson liquid, but my suit managed to survive the battle with minimal red stains. I chose a good day to avoid wearing white.

I found Kira knelt over a man in the hallway; she drew one dagger out of his eye and another out of his stomach, before looking up in my direction. "Are we good?"

"You could've at least warned me that we were going straight into the lion's den" I sighed.

She shrugged, wiping her dagger clean on the dead man's blazer. "That would take the fun out of it. Plus, I thought it would help improve your mood. You've been such a Debbie downer lately."

"I'm sorry that my wife died," I stated, bluntly.

Her eyes softened. "You know that's not what I meant." I didn't respond but instead held out a hand to help her onto her feet. Kira pulled herself up, and then dusted the dirt off her leather jacket, frowning when she caught sight of the sticky blood on her sleeve. "Aw, this was my favorite jacket."

"We didn't find what we came for anyway," Ignoring her childish pout, I looked around the corridor. "All we found were Serpent lackeys."

"I say this is good enough."

"*Kira.*"

She exhaled, shaking her head, her blonde ponytail swayed from side to side. "Nero, I'm feeling much better for killing them. Don't you?" I didn't answer, and she rolled her eyes. "If anything, it means fewer men for the Serpents which is good for us. Stop being such a pessimist."

"We haven't found Calix yet, and not a single man was able to disclose his location," I grunted, frustratedly kicking a corpse.

Kira didn't balk, arching her dark brow. "You clearly didn't kill enough men. Lucky for you, I left one just in case this happened."

She did not let me get a word in as she kicked down the closed office door to her right, and entered, where I heard shouts of resistance, before returning a few moments later with a man three times her size. She dragged him by the arm, his leg crippled by the dagger in his thigh. His nose was smashed, blood spilling onto the carpet, and both eyes began to bruise in colors of purple and blue. I was in awe of her strength as she dropped the man by my feet and tilted her head to the side.

"Ta-da!" she sang, merrily.

I crinkled my nose, trying not to show how much I needed to kill someone, as I mused, "You're a fucking psycho."

Kira grinned. "I am, aren't I?"

*

It was early morning when Kira asked, "What's our next move?" as soon as she entered the room.

Xander and I were hunched over the large table, blueprints and sheets of information scattered across it. We were in the middle of a conversation in the office that would have belonged to Aria had she been alive. The sun barely appeared over the horizon, the sky picturesque hues of blue, orange and yellow, streaks across the sky as if someone had used a paintbrush to create the image. After Kira had shown me their safe house the other night, one that *only* Kira and Aria knew of, I had visited everyone regularly and even stayed a few nights, before returning to the Estate to update Matteo on our progress. Whilst Matteo took control over the Italians temporarily, I aided Kira and everyone else from the Manor. It was what Aria would have wanted me to do. I brought supplies, food, and the armory they needed whilst hiding out in the snowy mountains. Surprisingly, although the safe house could be mistaken for a large estate, it managed to blend in with nature and stay hidden from tourists who visited to go skiing and take part in other winter sports. Acres and acres of land stood between this mansion and the nearest town, which only informed me that Aria had no intention of ever being found. I glanced up at Kira as she slipped her Borg coat off and dropped it onto the couch, tossing her golden hair over her shoulders, and propping her sunglasses on the top of her head. She was chewing gum as she lifted a brow at me, waiting for a response.

"The plan is to trap the Inner Circle and kill them all at once," I answered, gesturing to the blueprint of the location of our next event. Kira leered over my shoulders, her cerulean eyes scanning what was set on the table before thinning.

"And you plan to do it here?" she questioned, doubtfully. "At the Bay Room?"

I glanced at Xander, who smiled, before he spoke, "Aria initially wanted to storm Enzo's estate but the issue with that is that we don't know when all three remaining members of the Inner Circle will gather under one roof." His fingers brushed the blueprint, tapping on the square in the middle which was where the main hall was located. "We don't want to give the Inner Circle any time to stop and prepare themselves. We want to catch them completely off-guard."

"How are we going to do that?"

Xander pulled out a rough draft of an invite that Sophie had been working on and passed it to Kira, who gingerly inspected the gold and black invitation. "By hosting an event, we can tempt all the members to come to one location and then attack them there."

Kira kissed her teeth. "We'll need something to bait them with, something they desperately want."

"That's the issue we are stuck on," I began, running my fingers through my hair. "We don't know what is enough to bring *all* members of the Inner Circle."

Kira cocked her head to the side and smirked, mischievously. "We might not know, but I know who could."

Viktor Von Dorson had been held captive for over six months. The last time I had seen him was during the event when I first saw Aria again. He was healthy, strong, and held his head up with an embarrassing amount of egotism. Now, he was skinny as a stick, fragile and malnourished, battered and bruised, his head bowing as soon as Kira's overwhelming presence was made known.

Or at least that was what we thought.

"Kira," I whispered, as my eyes widened when I saw the blood that had pooled around Viktor.

She clenched her jaw and knelt, pressing a finger on his forehead to push his head up. Viktor's eyes shot wide open and the thin jagged cut in his neck was still fresh, blooding trickling onto his clothing and staining his body. His face had been mutilated with irregular slashes skimming down the length and width of his face until there was not even an inch left untouched. I heard a sharp intake of air before Kira brushed her hand over Viktor's eyes, closing them. Something caught my eyes when I was scanning his dead body and I knelt beside her, reaching for Viktor's hand where a note was enclosed in his fist.

Unravelling the note, I growled in frustration when I read the message: *Information is lost in the hands of a dead man - C.Z.*

"How did he find us?" I snarled, standing up and pacing around the room. "I thought only you and Aria were aware of this safe house."

Kira remained stooped, her eyes gently caressing Viktor's body as if she was looking for something, murmuring, "Calix was one of Aria's best soldiers. I always knew we wouldn't be able to hide from him forever. He must've been tracking us."

I tugged at my hair, irritation growing with every second. The urge to throttle Calix was becoming increasingly hard to keep at bay. Kira released a long breath of air as she stood up, unperturbed by the blood on her hands and the mangled body of Viktor as if she had seen worse. And perhaps she had.

"What do we do now? Our only source of information is dead," I grunted, crunching the note in my fist. "And now this location is no longer safe."

"The safe house is still safe. For the time being. Calix may have entered undetected this time, but if he were to bring an army, that would be another thing. For now, we will remain here. We'll just need to up our security, have more soldiers on guard. Plus, Antonio has offered us his men. We'll be safe here," Kira dusted off the blood on her hands as if it was grime, but the crimson stains remained on her pale skin. Her cold blue eyes shifted onto me. "As for Calix killing Viktor, they still don't know that we are aware of their 'special guest.' All we need to do is figure out who it is."

"And how do you suppose we do that?" I asked, but Kira didn't respond.

*

In the evening, as the sun began to set over the snowy mountains and the temperature dropped significantly, I found myself drifting towards the small garden outside the mansion. Unlike the Manor, this garden was much smaller and instead of acres of greenery, with arenas to train their combat skills, the ground was planted with beautiful flowers that I never knew could exist in this icy environment. There were granite slabs that ran down the middle until they stopped by a pond. Red, purple, and pink flowers embellished the frost-covered earth as I walked towards the body of water, admiring the blooming colors that surrounded me with my hands tucked into my pockets to keep my fingers shielded from the biting wind. A long black trench coat covered my large frame but as the cold brushed against my cheeks, I shivered with a shaky sigh. Beside me, I felt a presence, but I did not dare look up, watching the pond ripple.

"Seeing me like this means you're going crazy," the person said, voice low and sultry like a purr. "You should get that checked out."

"Amusing," I muttered, and they laughed, yet I still never looked up.

"You know I don't exist."

"Of course, I know that."

I imagined them lifting their brow, as they challenged, "So, why do you still see me?"

"Why do you still come back?"

"Touché, my love," they whispered, cold air brushing against the nape of my neck and I knew they were behind me. "*Touché.*"

"Nero?" I quickly turned to see Kira behind, a frown on her lips. "Are you okay?"

Glimpsing around, I saw that I was alone and slowly ran a hand over my face as my eyes shifted onto Kira, who looked worried. Forcing a smile, I replied, "Yeah, I am. I just have a lot on my mind."

"Want to talk about it?" she murmured, as I turned back to the pond, holding my hands behind my back. I shook my head as a response. She didn't say anything immediately, but I heard her sigh as she walked towards me, before stopping beside me. "Who were you talking to?"

I stiffened. "No one."

"Nero –"

Before she could question me any further, I interrupted her, asking, "How did you meet Calix?"

She pursed her lips, tilting her head and squinting her eyes as she admired whatever she was staring at in the distance. Maybe she could see the memory play out vividly in front of her like a VCR. With her hands by her side, Aria's second-in-command looked more like a soldier ready for war than a girl broken and battered by the merciless hands of the vilest humans in the world.

"Aria and I were visiting Greece, one summer, many years ago, back when it was just me and her. We were planning the demise of the Serpents but that required building an army. We weren't sure where to begin. For the time being, we foiled a lot of auctions hosted by the Serpents which meant we were on their hit list, and thus had to hide under the radar. Aria suggested going to Greece and I agreed, although I suspect to this day there was a deeper reason for why we hid there."

"Aria's grandparents reside in Greece – Athens to be exact," I drew my brows together. "She always said she wanted to look for them."

"Whatever the reason may have been, during a visit to the market,

Aria and I stumbled into Calix. Or at least that's what I thought happened," Kira frowned to herself. "He must've planned it, pretended our meeting was a coincidence."

"What was the story he sold you?"

Kira shivered, but I doubted it was from the cold.

"He was a beggar, running from the Serpents. He had run into me, and at the time I was still weak, so I easily got hurt. Aria being Aria was incredibly protective and nearly lashed out at Calix. But when she saw how broken he was, she stopped. Calix begged for mercy, and she told him to never beg. So, he asked for us to take him in, shelter him until he found his feet. Aria was skeptical but I was the one who convinced her to give him a chance..." Kira paused and then scowled. "Stupid girl."

"It wasn't your fault, Kira. How were you to know?" I reasoned, but it didn't waver her, the anger in her eyes burned as bright as the setting sun, a battle raging within them.

"I let my humanity make a judgement when I should've used my head," she said, coolly, but I heard the crack in her voice, the broken part of her that would forever feel guilty for Aria's death. "Aria and I planned to leave the day after, and when Calix found out, he asked if he could tag along. The arrogant bastard had made a bet with Aria, that if he won against her in a fight, she would have to let him join us. Within a second, she managed to tackle him onto the ground, yet, even then, she allowed him to join, to both mine and Calix's surprise. He never told us what the Serpents had done, only brief, vague memories, but the one thing we knew for sure was that his sister was killed right in front of him. It haunted him. Sometimes, I wonder if that was the only truth he had ever told us, and the rest were all lies."

"How did you know he was held hostage by the Serpents?"

Kira didn't say anything or make any indication that she had heard my question. For a moment, I thought she didn't. Until she pushed her coat to the side, and pulled the hem of her jumper up, revealing a circular branding on the side of her body. It was red, and angry, a reminder of the horrible things that lurk in the darkness. In the middle of the circle was a snake, shaped like an 'S', a mark of the Serpents' victims.

"Because he had one of these too," Kira muttered, indifferent to the scar on her body. I wanted to ask questions, learn more about her tormented past, but as she hid the branding, I knew better than to seek skeletons that needed to remain in the closet.

I inhaled slowly, glancing back into the white landscape past the towering fortress walls which surrounded the safe house. In the sunlight, the mountain peaks were a celebration of greys, from sweet blue-slate to silver-white. Magnificent rocks arose from the ground as if they were reaching for the sky, peaks of the ranges sculpted by the raindrops of eons. They were green at the base, the forests gathered by nature's wand. Then, there were the roads that climbed up, winding this way and that, making tight turns that felt, for all the world, like a fairground rollercoaster ride. The river undulated as the snow fell, melting into the water and disappearing. The sun finally disappeared behind the peaks, and the cloudless sky was dark with colors that merged until it looked like an abstract painting. A butterfly, red and black, beat past me, catching my eyes. In slight astonishment, I watched as it landed on one of the roses. The rose broke apart, but that didn't deter the butterfly as it flew onto the next. How it managed to live in this tundra-like biome was beyond me. The wind gently kissed my cheeks and nipped at my fingers as I bent down and reached for a rose. Coated in snow, I brushed it off and admired the redness of the petals that looked similar to the blood I had on my hands. The blood I thirsted after. The thorns pricked my fingers as I stoically stood up, but I remained impervious to the tingling pain.

"I wasn't aware that roses could grow in the cold," I said. Kira shrugged, shoving her hands into her pockets and turned to me, her nose as red as the rose.

"Aria loved roses; she insisted on growing them in here, claiming that they'd survive through any type of weather," Kira's eyes softened and for a second, I thought she might cry. Instead, her gaze followed the butterfly that winged from one rose to the next, until it left a trail of crimson petals in its path. "She once told me that relationships were like a rose. Beautiful yet deadly. But, if handled with care, it could bloom forever. To her, a life without love and loyalties isn't a life worth living."

I caressed the fragile calyces, remembering all those times that I had given Aria a rose, and the way her eyes would light up, like the fourth of July. I missed her.

"Do you know what day it is?" Kira whispered, her words disappearing with the wind. She swallowed when I looked up and I saw how haunted she was. I saw it all. She missed Aria too.

463

Consumed by my own grief, I failed to see how much thinner Kira had gotten, or the lack of life in her crushing cobalt eyes, her pale complexion, and the way her fingers trembled as if she was trying to hold it back; all the pain and grief in her rested on her shoulders and weighed her down. She was as lost as I, but perhaps two lost people could find their paths again. Or perhaps, we would remain lost forever.

"Yes," was my response, as cold and raptured as the rose petal that swayed side to side to the ground the second my finger touched it. Brittle and broken.

I miss you, Aria.

"It's her birthday."

*

"Aria, come here," I said, to the younger girl with chestnut tendrils that tumbled to her waist in gentle curls.

Hazel eyes that looked golden in the sunlight twinkled as she marched through the snow, closing the distance between us. Her nose was pink, although she wore a scarf, hat and gloves, with the addition of earmuffs, to protect herself from the inclement wind. A large coat over her small frame and boots that were perfect for sledding.

"What?" she huffed, and I pointed to the bottom of the mountain.

"First one down, wins," I announced, grinning at my best friend.

She wrinkled her nose like a bunny and eyed the path uneasily. "Seems like a long way down."

"Don't think you can do it?" I taunted.

Aria laughed. "I was asking for your sake." My face fell as she smirked, raising her brow. "What are the stakes?"

I shouldn't have been surprised but I couldn't stop the flicker of shock as I looked at Aria. She was dead serious. I didn't think she would agree but I was stupid to underestimate her. She was strong and powerful, and I could never amount to her. The way those hazel eyes silently waited for me to place my bet, I found myself unwittingly falling into them.

"Nero?" the twelve-year-old girl called out, breaking the spell I was in. "I don't have all day."

"How about this… The winner can cash in a favor at any time," I suggested.

Aria frowned. "Anytime?" I nodded, and she mulled over the bet before shrugging. "Fine by me."

I said, "On the count of three."

As we readied ourselves at the edge of the mountain, knowing that what we were about to do could put us in grave danger - whether it was being seriously injured or in serious trouble from our parents, I began to count. Aria looked at me and for a moment I expected her to back out but instead, she smirked, sending me a devious wink.

"Three!" she yelled, and shot off down the mountain before I could blink.

I watched as her small frame expertly handled nature's coldest environment and grinned. I guess that was when I knew I loved her. I had loved her for a while. And as I followed her down the mountains, I knew I would love her for the rest of my life.

Whiteface Mountain looked as daunting as it did when we were twelve. After taking a cable car to the summit during the late evening when I found myself unable to sleep, I stood on the peak and inhaled a sharp breath of air as I cherished the landscape. I had enough items of clothing on to keep me warm from the roaring wintry climate, yet I still quaked in my boots, shoving my hands as far I could into my pockets. The mountains had kept safe the souls of this land for a time unmeasured and told of it in words unspoken, along with my secrets. The starry skies greeted me as the moon beamed, brilliantly, my hands curling into a fist when I remembered the first time I had come here, during a holiday with Aria's family. I discovered how deep my feelings were for her, but I hid them well, afraid she that would reject my advances as she had done with several men before. For years, I did not think she would love me back until her coronation for the Italian mafia. It was then that I was sure she harbored feelings for me, but I wondered whether they were as deep as mine.

I wasted too much time, and now…

I sighed, a cloud of smoke forming in front of me before disappearing when the wind whispered by. The snow began to fall heavily and I knew I would have to return back to the safe house or I would find myself stuck in a blizzard. But I couldn't bring myself to move away from the spot I was standing in. Here, everything looked small, everything looked so insignificant. I used to feel like I was on top of the world from this peak, but right now, I felt like the world had moved on and only I remained trapped in the past. At the top of the mountain, in that pristine rarefied air, I felt an expansion of my soul. Into the ice-kissed air came wintry feathers of pure white, a great snowfall that soon gave way to a blizzard as if a sky-dam had burst. I decided then that it was time to return home. Home. That word should have startled me, for I did not know where my home was anymore, but instead, it made me smile because I knew that home was wherever the people I cared the most about were. I stepped back and had one final look around before turning away and returning to the cable car that was waiting to carry me home. And then I stopped.

I frowned, narrowing my eyes.

My ears twitched at the faint sound of someone calling my name. I could barely hear it in this tempest, but I heard it like it was a whisper. My body stiffened and I peered over my shoulder, expecting Calix or one of his men to be standing there, waiting to kill me. But instead, I saw a figure much more slender and slightly smaller than a man. The snow made it difficult to see who it was, but I squinted and began to walk towards them, hearing my name more clearly with every step I took. The figure trekked towards me, dressed in winter attire as the moonlight spilt onto the mountain peak.

Until I could see, crystal clear, who stood before me.

My heart halted. The sound of the howling snow quietened. And the world slowed around me.

It couldn't be. It wasn't possible. This wasn't real.

But it was. It was *oh so* real. And as the slender figure stood in front of me, wearing a smile that was burnt into my memory, that pinched their hazel eyes with golden flecks, I knew I could not deny what I was seeing.

Or was I dreaming again?

I had to confirm my delirious thoughts; I *had* to make sure. I could not bear to live through the pain again if it was not true. So, I reached out to touch them. My trembling fingers caressed their cheek as silent tears rolled down my cheeks and splattered onto my coat. The second my fingers touched their cold skin, flushed with color, I inhaled sharply.

Oh my god.

"Aria," I choked out.

CHAPTER 51

my love

Nero

It was cold in the mountains, especially at night, but I had been to Whiteface several times before. However, this was the first time I had come with someone other than Aria. Kira sat silently as the driver took us through the twists and turns of the mountains until we reached iron gates. After speaking to the guards, the gates opened, and my eyes widened at the sight of a mansion so large that I was surprised it was possible for it to be concealed so well in these regions.

"It's beautiful, isn't it?" Kira finally broke the silence.

"You and Aria built this?" I questioned, and she dipped her head. I looked out of the windows, admiring the aura of antiqueness from the estate. "It is beautiful."

"Aria thought this would be safe enough for us to hide if anything went wrong," Kira's eyes cooled. "She was right."

I didn't respond as we got out of the car. Leaves crunched beneath me as I walked beside Kira to the front door. She didn't shiver from the bitter air, despite wearing a dress that was not suitable for these regions, unyielding to the frosty breeze. The mansion was tranquil, as everyone was asleep, but Kira still gave me a tour, showing me both the east and west wing, which were significantly smaller than their previous Manor. Eventually, we reached a bedroom. Instantly, I recognized it to be Aria's. From the soft pale pink accents that flattered the white walls, to the gold embellishments and ornaments. I saw a few frames hung on the wall – a picture with Kira, a picture with her family, and then, a picture of us. It was taken a while *back, but I was surprised to see it there. Kira leaned against the doorway whilst I stepped inside the room, brushing my fingers against the white oak furniture, delicately reaching out to touch a jug of pearls on the vanity.*

"She loved you, even when she tried not to, for years," Kira said. I peered over my shoulder to find her gazing around the room with a sort of emptiness in her eyes. "But she loved you even when she hated you, even when she was mad. She didn't like to admit it, but she loved you."

"I loved her too," Then, I frowned. "I still love her."

Kira's glacial eyes settled onto me. "I know."

I held her gaze before looking away. "People say, 'there are plenty of fish in the sea, you'll find another.'"

I released a short breathy laugh, shaking my head. Then, I glanced at the frame hanging on the wall, and my smile faded. A picture of us when we were twelve. My heart shattered.

"What they don't understand was that she was my sea."

*

She stood in front of me. Warm, safe, alive.

Her hair was shorter, cut to her shoulders, and a shade or two darker, to the point that it looked almost black in the moonlight. Bangs slightly covered her hazel eyes but they burnt vividly when she stared at me with a spectrum of emotions. She was slimmer, but I noticed that she was slightly more muscular. She did not look like any of the Arias that visited me after her death. I didn't say anything; I couldn't. The words were stuck in my throat, and I didn't even know where to begin to think. She was alive. Alive. Alive. My heart stuttered and I felt my knees tremble, but I remained strong, keeping myself standing whilst the world thundered around us. And she was alive. No. She couldn't be. I saw her die. She died. I saw her heart flatline. This must be my mind playing cruel tricks on me, or perhaps the arctic weather has killed me. That sounded like a more realistic reason why I could see the love of my life in front of me. Suddenly, she took a step forward and instinctively, I took a step back, trying to ignore the way she glanced over at me. I felt sick, my stomach gnawed away in discomfort, and I froze in my spot when her hazel eyes settled on me.

"Nero," the beautiful woman said. A whisper. A merciless lie.

"You're not real," I growled, an overwhelming amount of anger washing over me. I glared at her and shook my head in disbelief.

"You're not real. My mind is playing fucking tricks on me again. You're not real."

"Nero," she took a step forward. This time I did not move back. "*Please.*"

"Stay away from me," I snarled, shaking in my position – maybe the cold was getting to me. "You're not alive. I saw you die!"

"Let me explain," she wanted to touch me, but I didn't let her. I couldn't. Hurt flickered across her face. "I'm real, I promise."

I swallowed, pressing my lips together, and blinking away the tears but even then, a few rolled down my cheeks and splashed onto my boots. This was not right. She was not alive. She could not possibly be. I failed her – I failed to protect her and that was why she had died. This woman was not my Aria. She couldn't be.

My lips quivered. "You're not alive. My baby died and I don't know what I am without her. I don't even know who I am anymore."

The pain in her eyes was evident. I noticed the tears rolling down her cheeks, and I wanted to brush them away. But I was afraid. I was afraid to touch her in case she disappeared; in case she was an illusion, in case she was not real, and it was a malicious hoax that my mind was playing. I was scared. And I knew she was too. I saw the fear in her eyes when she died but it wasn't the fear of death I saw, rather the fear that I would never be happy again. I was tired of seeing illusions of her, spending each day pretending she was there, and I knew it was killing me slowly. The woman in front of me could see the pieces of the man I used to be, the man I was to Aria Moretti – the only woman I would ever love.

So, I wiped the tears away from my cheeks and forced a smile on my lips. "It's okay if you're not real. It's going to be okay. I'm going to be okay, Aria. I promised you, didn't I?"

She didn't say anything. For the longest moment, no one spoke, and I was sure that this was al some kind of wicked deception. Then, she closed the distance between us. One cold hand slipped around my neck and the other on my shoulder as she stood onto her tiptoes to kiss me. My eyes broadened the second her soft lips touched mine, my body stilling under her very real, very conscious, hold.

Aria. My Aria.

Without another thought, I thawed into the kiss, my arms wrapped around her small frame to draw her closer, wanting every inch, muscle, and curve to be pressed against my own body. Until we became one.

The storm around us began to quieten down but the storm within me raged as I kissed her like it would be the last time. Her cold fingers grasped the nape of my hair, tiptoeing to reach my height. Fireworks exploded in the back of my mind, every atom which set me alight and I felt my soul dance with joy. My love. She was alive.

"Aria. My Aria," I murmured, when we tore apart, our breathing heavy and labored. Her hazel eyes glistened as she held back her tears.

Smiling, Aria replied, "I love you too, Nero."

*

"Thank you," Aria said to Kira, who handed her a cup of hot cocoa, a blanket wrapped around her shivering frame.

Despite changing into a fresh set of clothes, Aria quivered, and I fought the urge to wrap my arms around her to share my body heat. I rested against the living room door frame, my arms crossed over my chest, my eyes steadily watching her. Kira sat beside Aria with pure disbelief in her arctic eyes as she waited to hear the answer to her unspoken questions, twiddling her fingers in anticipation. I heard Xander thunder down the stairs before he stopped beside me, his breath hitching when Aria looked up and caught his gaze. It was as if he wanted to fall onto his knees but forced himself to stay upright as he wobbled towards her, his shoulders slugging.

Then, as he stood in front of her, Aria spoke, voice tender, "Xander."

He crumbled onto his knees and cried. Kira and I were both surprised, taken aback by this sudden reaction, but as if she had known, Aria's smile saddened, and she handed her mug to Kira. She reached out and ran her fingers through Xander's hair like a mother soothing their child. The look on Kira's face told me that she had never once seen Xander cry, nor did she think he was capable of doing so. As if it was too painful to watch, she looked away and pursed her lips, a noticeable swallow indicated that she was holding back her own sobs. Xander's shoulders shook as he silently wept, tears splashing onto the oak floor. No one said anything as Aria comforted her soldier, her eyes filled with a warmth that reminded me that she was very much alive. After some time, Xander used the heel of his palms to wipe the tears away. His eyes never left Aria as if he was frightened to blink… as if he was frightened that she wasn't real.

"How?" he asked, a crack in his voice had Aria's eyes soften. She took his hand and directed him to sit beside her, which he did without hesitation.

"That day, when everyone had left me alone in my room for a short while, someone visited me," she began, taking the mug back from Kira and sipped it.

Kira frowned, asking the question we were all thinking, "Who?"

"Me," a voice spoke from behind me.

Aria's lips tugged to her ears as we all turned our attention to the person by the stairs. There stood Violetta in her silk pajamas with incredulity as she looked at Aria. The young girl hopped down the stairs and stood beside me.

"I can't believe it worked; I didn't think..." she muttered to herself.

My eyes narrowed at her in confusion. "I don't understand."

"At first, neither did I," Aria said, reverence lingering in her tone. "I thought she had come to say goodbye again but instead she presented me with a vial, a concoction she had created to reverse the effects of the poison."

Kira's furrowed brows relaxed and Xander's eyes enlarged as we all pieced together what Aria was telling us. Violetta smiled, timidly. "It had no guarantee of working, I didn't even test it out because I knew there wasn't any time. So, Aria took the risk and drank it."

"But you died," I whispered.

Finally, Aria looked at me. *Properly* looked at me. Her gaze swarmed with a multitude of emotions, so many that it was difficult to pinpoint the exact one she was feeling. Her golden irises, with specks of green and silver twinkled as her smile faltered.

"I wasn't sure it was going to work. That's why I didn't tell anyone about the vial. But I didn't die," Aria murmured, her orbs haunted by what had occurred. "It felt like death. The pain was so excruciating that I thought I did die. But I could see the white light, and then, all I saw was blue. All I could see was how blue the world was and suddenly I was holding onto something... I was holding onto this rope, and I tugged, and tugged, and tugged until I found myself waking up in a cold hospital room, alone."

"How... What about your funeral... your family?" Xander stammered, and then paused. His throat bobbed. "Why did you not come back to us?"

"When I woke up, I informed the doctor to tell my family that I

471

was alive and healthy, and that I would contact them soon. I wanted to come to you all, I wanted to tell you guys that I was okay but after several hours of being examined in the hospital… when I was finally discharged, I realized that my death meant that the Serpents would think they had won. That they were two steps ahead of the game. I realized I could change the rules. So, I took a cab to a hotel, called my family, and told them to prepare a funeral. It had to be a closed casket, so no one was aware that my body was missing. I had cash and a new identity hidden in an apartment downtown, in case I was in a situation where I had to become a ghost. I had to resist the urge to come back to the Manor…" she paused, and her eyes found mine again. "To you."

"Therefore, you pretended you were dead," Kira concluded. She wore a conflicted expression as if she couldn't decide whether to be mad or amazed. "And used the opportunity to get ahead of the game."

"I had to. I couldn't let them win. I was lucky to survive, and I don't believe in luck. I knew I had one job and that was why I was still breathing. I hunted them down, small soldiers bidding for the Serpents, and I tore them apart until they gave me the names of the people who were closest to the Inner Circle. That's how I found out about Enzo's masquerade ball."

My heart paused. As if knowing exactly what I was thinking, Aria nodded daintily, and my arms fell to my side.

"It was you. The girl in the black dress," I breathed out.

Aria sighed. "I-I couldn't reveal myself, and it took every ounce of me to turn away from you. I… I knew when the time was right, I would come back. I promised myself."

I didn't realize I wasn't breathing until I exhaled heavily, pressing my back against the door frame. "It was you."

I could feel her eyes but ignored them, trying to wrap my head around the fact that she was there in Toronto… she was there.

"Where did you go afterwards?" Kira questioned.

"After killing a few more of the Serpents' men, I managed to get the name of Enzo's former right-hand man, before Calix climbed the ladder and took over. I tracked him to the Underground's famous subterranean location. It was a place where you could find anything you needed or wanted."

"Wait a second, Calix climbed the ladder?" Xander frowned. "Wasn't he always the boss?"

Aria shook her head. "It seems that Calix was initially a soldier, but he rose through the ranks until he had enough power and influence that Enzo could not control him. To stay alive, Enzo reluctantly handed the reigns to him. The power shift meant a lot of men were either killed because they were too loyal to Enzo, or they pledged their life to Calix, leaving Enzo defenseless."

"That's why Enzo's right-hand man ran," Kira pointed out.

"Yes, but Enzo needed someone on the outside to rely on if anything was to happen to him, which meant his second knew everything about the Serpents' operation. Including what their next plan is," Aria's eyes darkened as they fell onto the girl with striking violet eyes.

Noticing her gaze, the twelve-year-old frowned. "What?"

"They're after Violetta," Aria stated. "The lost Princess of Spain."

Kira sucked in a sharp breath of air, Xander's jaw fell, and I glanced down at the little girl beside me and marveled at how exactly a princess fell right into the lap of Aria Moretti. Violetta looked surprised by what was revealed and shook her head, adamantly.

"That's not true. I'm not a princess, I barely have anything to my name besides what my grandfather had left me," she laughed, but it faded away when she noticed that Aria was not the slightest bit amused. When she realized how her life would change forever. "Right?"

"The King had a mistress, a woman who wasn't Mauve Rossi – your first adoptive mother. The King's mistress became pregnant, and she hid you from him, leaving you with the Rossis," Aria explained, but her words trailed off when she noticed how deathly, pale Violetta had become beside me.

"So… my mother wasn't Mauve? Or that lady in Arizona? It was neither of them?" Violetta whispered. The words pained my heart because they were so lost, because she had grasped that her entire life was a lie.

Kira and I shared a look, as Aria bobbed her head slowly. "When Mauve heard that the Serpents wanted you, she hid you and sent you to live with a close friend of hers in Arizona. I guess, she didn't know that friend was in a terribly bad place, because I know she wouldn't have let you suffer as you did."

Violetta's eyes watered. "How do you know?"

"Whilst I was away, I met with the Rossis," Aria revealed, and my brows shot up in surprise. Kira and Xander both gaped at my wife, who ignored their startled expressions. "Mauve wanted to know if you were well, and when I informed her, she was relieved. She wanted me to tell you that she missed you a lot and wished that she could've spent more time with you, but with a bounty on your head, she couldn't risk it."

Violetta sniffled, wiping her nose with her sleeve. "She-she did?"

"Yeah, Vi. She really does care about you, I promise," Aria assured, with a comforting smile that had Violetta break into a small smile. "The Rossis adored you. You were less than two years old when they received you, but you were loved greatly in their family. Even Adriano Rossi, your grandfather, adored you. Mauve said he was shattered when she had to hide you, and he couldn't know where."

"That explains why he left you all that money," Kira muttered, narrowing her eyes. "Because he knew if he never found you, the Serpents would never have a chance."

"Is it for more money? That's why they were after her?" Xander queried, and Aria's head bobbed.

"What about my brother?" Violetta quivered. "I-I thought he loved me. Isn't Enzo my brother?"

The look on Aria's face saddened. "I think that man died a long time ago, Vi. Maybe once he loved you, but I think his greed got the better of him."

Violetta shook her head in disbelief. "No. He loved me. I remember when I was small, and he used to play with me all the time. I remember…" her words trailed off, as something dawned on her. "Unless that's what I *wanted* to remember."

No one wanted to agree, but I knew we all couldn't help but think that her memories must have distorted to help deal with the trauma. It was not an unusual thing and could happen to people who had suffered a great deal. When I glanced at Kira, I wondered whether it had happened to her before, and the coldness in her eyes gave me my answer.

"Enzo's original plan, before Calix took over, was to hold Violetta ransom and force the King to allow the Serpents to expand their business by controlling the Spanish trading economy. He must've been jealous of Violetta, especially because his own grandfather loathed him. When Calix discovered the plan, he pushed forward with it," Aria continued, running her fingers through her hair, and, beneath the anger, I saw the hurt in her eyes; I saw the pain of Calix's betrayal, I saw through her. Like she was a ghost.

"They want me?" Violetta had said, but it sounded more like a question than a statement. She swallowed thickly and her body trembled. Then, again, she repeated her words, more certain, more shattered, "They want *me*."

Aria didn't say anything whilst Kira and Xander shared a look. This little girl's world was changing every second so I could not blame her for being frightened out of her mind. I inhaled a long breath of air before I knelt to Violetta's height, taking her hands into my own. Her dazzling green eyes, mixed with blue and gold that created a violet illusion, flickered over to me, and they were filled with sadness, confusion and fear. Fear that her life would always be in danger. Fear that she would never be safe.

So, I smiled.

"Do you trust me, Violetta?" I whispered. After a minute, she nodded, slowly. I reached out, brushed her hair behind her ear and placed a hand on her arm, comforting her with a reassurance that she would always be safe. "Then trust me when I say I won't let Calix, or the Serpents hurt you. I will protect you until my last breath, I will give you the future you want."

"Do you promise, Nero?" her voice shook. "Do you promise?"

I squeezed her arm, softly, as I vowed, "With my entire heart."

Violetta studied me, carefully, for so long that I thought she did not believe me. I held my breath, waiting for her response, but, eventually, she did with a short nod. A nod that told me everything – her trust was in my hands. I nodded back to her, receiving her inaudible message. Then she hugged me. My eyes widened and I almost fell onto the floor, but I swiftly regained my balance, unsure of what to do. I glanced at Aria, who did not fight against her smile, as she leisurely drank from her cup, arching her brow, eyes twinkling in admiration. She was safe. They both were. And as I slowly wrapped my arms around Violetta, I vowed they would be safe until the end of my life.

*

I was in one of the guestrooms that Kira had graciously prepared for me when Aria visited. Unbuttoning my shirt in front of the mirror, I watched as she slipped into the room quietly, almost like a phantom, and settled onto the edge of the bed. I didn't say anything, drawing the shirt off my shoulders and discarding it onto the vanity beside me, before grabbing a plain white t-shirt and tugging it over my body. She didn't say anything as she observed me whilst I moved to the wardrobe and hung my clothes, or when I unclipped my watch and placed it on the bedside table. Neither of us said anything until I stood in front of her. Her eyes lazily scanned the length of my body before reaching my eyes, where she gave me the most breath-taking, heart-stopping smile. It caused her eyes to crease into a thin semicircle, her cheeks flushed with color, showcasing her pearly whites.

"Hi, love," she said. Two words I would sacrifice everything for just to hear on repeat.

"Hi, baby," I responded, with a smile that mirrored her own. "How are you feeling?"

"Like I need some kisses," she pouted, playfully, "Want to make it better?"

And, for the first time in weeks, I laughed. A deep, rich laugh that warmed my entire body, that I even felt it in the darkest part of me. Throwing my head back, I kept laughing, and Aria's smile widened. As my laughter turned into chuckles, I smirked at Aria before fulfilling her request. She grasped my shoulders in surprise, steadying herself as my large frame nearly toppled onto her, my hands cradling her face. It was like someone had set me alight, but I didn't mind the burning sensation that overwhelmed me. In fact, I relished in it, basked in it, savored every second of it. Because I knew I didn't want it to ever end. Kissing her felt like I was surrounded by thousands of suns, like everything I needed was right here where they belonged… like I was finally home.

When I broke away from her, my lips gently brushed hers, and I murmured, "How are you feeling?"

She hummed, her eyes closed, but her lips curled into a dreamy smile. "Tired, but I'm much better now."

"By the way," I said, and she slanted her head, doe-like russet eyes squinting innocently at me. The words got trapped in my throat under her heated gaze, and I coughed, awkwardly. "Happy birthday."

Expecting to hear a response, I was caught off guard when she kissed me again, and I allowed her to. I allowed her to consume me. I allowed her because no one could love me the way Aria did. Her love was a burning fire, a reason, a touch, a healing. Her love was mine. And my love was hers. Only hers.

"Thank you," I felt her smile against my lips, triggering a mirroring response of my own.

I pressed myself closer to her until there were only thin layers of clothing between us. I kissed her until she became lightheaded, gripping my arms to support herself. Unlike all the other times I had kissed her, this time felt different, like things had shifted between us. It was hot, heavy and submerged with yearning. It was weeks of being apart that had us pining for each other. It was like standing under the sweltering sun, my feet swallowed by the blistering hot sand, and yet the mirage of an oasis was a blessing. Aria tugged at the hems of my shirt which brought me back to reality, and I pulled away which only had her frowning, her eyes thinned at me in worry.

"What?" she demanded.

"Aria, as much as I'd love to ravish you, and trust me I do," I admitted, lifting a brow, and earning a grin from her. "Can we just stop for a second? Just so I can focus on you properly."

For a moment, I thought she wouldn't understand how deep my grief was, or how lost I was without her presence as my guiding light. For a moment, I thought she wouldn't see the pain in which I drowned. For a moment, I thought she couldn't hear the silent weeps of my soul. But then, her eyes softened, her grin became small, and she took my hands.

"Nero, we can stop whenever you want to," she assured me. "I understand that this is a lot to take in and I can't even express how sorry I am for letting you suffer for so long."

"I understand why you did it, Aria. I just missed you so much, it felt like I wasn't even alive most days," I revealed, quietly.

"I'm so sorry you were alone, but I promise to never let you be alone again," her shaky hand gently caressed my cheek, her lips quivered, and her eyes watered. "I wish that would be enough for you to forgive me."

I shook my head. "It's you and me. Today. Tomorrow and forever. Ride or die. Preferably not die," Aria cracked a small smile, "But that's how committed I am to you. Don't question my love for you, don't ever think you're not enough, because, to me, you'll always be more than enough. You will *always* be more. That's how much I love you. Can you say the same?"

Her golden eyes steadily held mine as she swallowed, bobbing her head. "Yes. *Sempre.* I made a vow to you, for better and for worse... till death do us part."

I took her hand and kissed her knuckles lightly. "Till death do us part."

We held each other's gaze and at that moment, there was nothing more intimate than that. Aria's thumb rubbed my hand absentmindedly, as she looked away, her eyes curiously admiring the room.

"Speaking of vows, I figured out how to draw out the Serpents," Aria suddenly said, and I lifted my brows in surprise. She continued, "We'll hold an engagement party. Our engagement party."

"We're already married, Aria," I chuckled, and she rolled her eyes.

"I know, silly, but we didn't even hold a ceremony for our engagement or wedding. This could be a perfect opportunity to celebrate our marriage properly and get rid of the Serpents. Hit two stones with one bird, I believe the saying is."

"It's actually two birds with one stone, baby, but it's the thought that counts," I cooed, and Aria responded with a scowl as I bit back a smile. As she sulked, I settled beside her on the bed. "How do you propose we do that?"

"Revealing that I am still alive will be enough to stir the Serpents and gain their attention, to grab Calix's attention, but to ensure that we get a reaction, we'll leak that Violetta will be attending. They'll use that opportunity to take her because she'll be exposed with minimal security unlike the Manor or this safe house."

I mulled over the plan, running my fingers through my hair, whilst Aria expectantly waited for a response, her eyes wide with hope. I wanted to tell her the risks, the consequences if it did not go to plan, but I was a hundred per cent sure these were things she had already considered, otherwise she would not have told me her plan. She was asking for me to support her, for me to trust her. And I knew, without a doubt, I would.

"Okay, let's do it," I nodded firmly, and she squealed, wrapping her arms around me. I laughed, breathlessly, as I embraced Aria, holding her tightly as if she would disappear once I let her go, but she didn't.

Instead, she leaned forward and kissed me ever so softly, before murmuring, "Thank you."

Smiling, I tucked a strand of her mahogany hair behind her ear. "Why did you cut your hair?"

"I found myself looking in the mirror and I knew that the girl in the hospital was gone. I wanted a change. So, I grabbed the scissors and the next thing I knew, half my hair was gone."

"I like it," I muttered, curling my fingers around her tresses, lightly. "Makes it easier to pull."

Her eyes widened in mortification. "Nero!"

I smirked. "Shall I demonstrate?"

She scowled at me, which said one thing, but her red cheeks and the naughty gleam in her golden gaze suggested another. Aria rolled her eyes and shoved me away, causing me to break into peals of laughter whilst she cursed me under her breath. Shaking her head at me whilst I laughed, eventually Aria couldn't fight the smile that threatened to expose itself.

"You seriously need to get your mind out of the gutter," she complained, running her fingers through her hair. The sudden motion suddenly reminded me of the lack of a diamond, and I found myself moving towards the vanity where I searched in the drawer for a certain box. "What are you doing?"

I didn't respond, rummaging through my belongings until I found a familiar navy Harry Winston box. My eyes zeroed in on it, and I gingerly took it out, opening the box, which revealed a large engagement ring and its matching wedding band. My mind suddenly took me back to the day when I asked for Aria's hand in marriage.

"Nero?" Aria called out, breaking the spell I was in. Slowly, I glanced over my shoulder and noticed her, wide eyes filled with curiosity, still perched on the bed, and head cocked to the side. "What's that in your hand?"

"Your rings," I revealed.

Surprise masked her face as I lifted the box before her expression morphed into something else, something deeper, something heartbroken. As I strode towards her, I took my time, maintaining her stare as she held mine because I needed to take in all of her beauty. From her sun-kissed skin to her sable hair, to her mesmerizing amber eyes. I wanted to remember how she looked at that exact moment. I could remember it for the rest of my life. Then, there I was, standing in front of her and I knew one thing: I never once doubted that Aria was my forever, not back then, not now, not ever. Perhaps, even from back then, it wasn't even a thought I would consider, or even let cross my mind. She was my equal in all ways. My best friend. My lover. My wife.

And as I got down on one knee, once again… as she inhaled

sharply, gazing down at me... I knew – *with all my heart* – that even in the next life, I would love her because my soul was made for her. Only her.

"Nero, what are you doing?" she questioned, skeptically, but I brushed it off with a smile.

"Aria, I know I already proposed to you before, but the thing is, I'd do it over and over again, because loving you is effortless, easy, peaceful. Loving you is like breathing. Loving you has and will always be the best thing I have ever done," I said instead, watching how her eyes began to water as she cupped her mouth to hold back her sob. "So, I know I'm proposing to you again, and I know you'll say yes, but do me the honor to once again hear you say you'll be mine forever."

She laughed softly, amused, but the tears that managed to escape spoke louder. Warmheartedly, she leaned forward, taking the rings into her grasp before slipping them onto her finger, returning them to their rightful owner.

Her eyes flickered up and she smiled. "Yes, Nero. I'll be yours forever."

Those words would replay in my mind on repeat, like a broken record, as I grinned and leaned up to kiss Aria. "I love you."

Her lips curled against mine. "I love you too."

"Good, because you're stuck with me, and I swear to God, I'm never letting you go," I warned seriously, but Aria only laughed, her eyes glittering with mirth.

"I didn't know you were religious, Nero."

"Oh, I'm not," I shrugged indifferently, but Aria was far too amused, pursing her lips to fight off the teasing smile and most likely holding back whatever she wanted to say.

"Okay, Nero," she finally said, and I tilted my head to the side, inquisitively.

"*Okay, Nero?*" I repeated and she nodded, pressing her lips together but I saw the smile. I narrowed my eyes at my wife. "What is it?"

"Nothing," she responded, far too quickly for it to be true. I was not convinced and she knew it. Nibbling on her lower lip, she looked away and her cheeks darkened. "It's honestly nothing."

I quickly understood that whatever she was thinking was not anything innocent; she would never shy away from the chance to tease me. I smirked, standing up. "Perhaps you need to get your mind out of the gutter?"

"I do not!" she sputtered in protest.

I arched a brow. "So, what's in that pretty mind of yours?"

Twiddling her rings, she glanced up, her hooded lashes shielding her doe eyes. "Nothing... just wondering something," I waited for her to finish her sentence, and she huffed, crinkling her nose in annoyance. "I was just wondering if you'd pray for me."

I studied her for a long minute before coiling my lips, mischievously. "The only time I pray is to thank whoever sent me you."

"Really?" she murmured, as I towered over her, running my fingers down the side of her face, following the contours of her body until I reached the waistband of her jeans, unzipping it. "You pray for me?"

"If praying means I can be with you," I whispered, noticing how her eyes darkened with anticipation and her breathing quickened. I tugged the jeans down her legs, and she obeyed. "Best believe I'll remain on my knees for the rest of my life."

Her eyes were dark and filled with need as she watched me trail my fingers against the curves of her body, over the arches of her breasts before settling my fingers around her neck. Her breath hitched. I excepted her to pull away but the desire drowning her golden kissed eyes had my lips tugging into an impish grin. Ever so softly, I squeezed, feeling her swallow.

Aria gazed at me with the same hunger that wreaked havoc within me. Then, she said, breathlessly, "How about now?"

A challenge. A demand. A request. Whatever it was, my answer would always be the same, "Yes, my Queen."

And then I fell to my knees.

*

Aria

It was past midnight when I slipped out of Nero's room, completely worn out but in dire need of something to drink. I tiptoed downstairs, shivering as I was only wearing Nero's t-shirt, seeing as it was the only piece of clothing I managed to find in the dark room, not wanting to disturb him by turning the lamp on. The cold caressed my legs as I flicked the switch to the kitchen lights and grabbed a bottled water from the fridge. Opening the bottle, I thirstily drank the liquid, relishing the cool sensation which travelled down my throat. After spending hours in his bedroom, he hauled me to the bathroom taking his time to make love to me and then tenderly lather my body in soap, cleaning the grime and sweat off my body. I could remember his body pressed against mine, and how his lips skimmed my legs when he knelt. I could feel his kiss against my navel, my neck, and the way he pulled my wet hair, drawing out moans. I could see the stars when we became one, the tension in my stomach when his hand was wrapped around my throat. I surprised myself by how much I enjoyed that – craved that. But what had me shatter into millions of mind-blowing euphoric pieces, was the smirk on his lips and the adoration simmering in his eyes. I could do it all again, but I was so exhausted that eventually he pulled us into bed and allowed me to be swallowed into his large arms. My entire body ached, and I only had Nero to blame, so I did - under my breath. My muttering stopped when I saw a movement in the hallway and instantly moved into action, ignoring the split second my heart dropped in fear or the anger of someone infiltrating the safe house. Feelings were dangerous, and, if you were not careful, they could get you killed. I moved effortlessly, silently, cautiously, towards the living room where I prepared myself to face Calix but instead was taken off guard when I saw Kira instead.

"Kira?" she jumped at the sound of my voice, spinning around. Her eyes were wide, and I frowned, then I glanced down and noticed the wine bottle in her hand. "What are you doing?"

"I didn't realize you were awake," she whispered, taking a quick peek at the fireplace which she had just lit up.

"Why are you drinking?" I questioned, instead of responding.

Her eyes glimpsed at the bottle before she looked back at me, and answered with a sheepish smile, "Just because?" I stared at her blankly and eventually, she gave in with a sigh, sinking into the couch. "I needed a drink."

"But why?" she didn't respond and for a moment, I was at a complete loss, but then I understood. I was the reason why. "*Oh.*"

She chuckled, seeing that I finally grasped what was flittering in her beautifully complex mind. "I just can't believe you're here, Aria. It doesn't seem real."

I said nothing. I was unsure what to say to the girl for whom I would sacrifice my life. I did not know how to comfort her or how to apologize for disappearing. I didn't know. So, instead, I held my hand out and said, "Pass me the bottle."

She frowned but did as I said, watching me remove the cap of the drink and swallow the red alcoholic beverage. She lifted her brows in surprise as I handed the bottle back to her.

"Did you manage to find Calix?" Kira murmured; her eyes shifted to the mantel in front of her. It was decorated in pretty flowers and golden embellishments. The fire below simmered, the wood churning and crackling, radiating heat into the living room.

"I had his location, but by the time I arrived, he had already gone," Kira didn't say anything, her eyes trained on the dancing flames as if they would give her all the answers. Then I said, in a voice much softer, "I'm sorry."

There was a weighty moment before her shoulders relaxed and she sighed, collapsing onto the couch, and taking a swig from the bottle. "It's okay… It's… okay."

I went and sat beside her, taking another glug from the bottle when she passed it to me. I wiped my lips, ridding the red drink from my skin. "I really am."

"I know," she murmured, drinking the wine. The silence between us was not uncomfortable but I unsure what to say to make it better, to make it up to her. But she spoke first, "Did you know?"

"Know what?"

"That he could betray us."

"Does anyone ever know?"

"I suppose not," there was a pause. "But I would always hope so."

"Why?"

She looked at me. "Because it would hurt less."

Then, she drank again.

My throat felt tight. "I saw it coming."

Kira narrowed her eyes in confusion. "What do you mean?"

"I saw it coming," I admitted. "I think I knew deep within me, all signs pointed to it, but I didn't want to admit it. And now it has cost me."

"Aria…"

"I saw it coming, Kira, but it still hurts. Because you never know when or how it'll happen. You just know it's *going* to," I blew out a breath of air. "You try to prepare for it, but you can't. It still feels like you've been stabbed. Maybe the knife is a little bit sharper, but still. It tears you apart from the inside out…" I paused, trying to keep the sob back, the cries I had been holding for weeks, the tears for someone who betrayed my trust, and this family. "The knowing… And when it finally happens, you're ripped open all over again."

"It's not your fault, Aria. He was the last person we expected," Kira whispered, brokenly.

"That should've made him the first person we thought of," I sighed. She handed me the bottle, but I couldn't bring myself to drink from it, finally feeling the guilt that I had tried to ignore for weeks. "So, what now?"

"Well now, we end the Serpents," Kira answered. "And we kill Calix."

But could we kill him? I think it was a question both Kira and I were asking, yet neither of us said it aloud. We could only hope that when the time came, we would be able to kill the man who was once part of our family. Our family who was now in grave danger. The betrayal of Calix would perpetually torment me but I knew I would risk everything for the family that I spent years building and protecting. I was their savior, and I knew that meant I had to kill Calix. I had to end the Serpents. Only those words were so onerous, deep with gravity, loaded with emotions. Sometimes, some things were better left unspoken. Some plans were better left unprepared. And so, for the rest of the obscure night, Kira and I drank from the bottle and silently savored each other's presence, preparing ourselves for the war we always saw coming, but never expected to see who it would come from.

CHAPTER 52

destruction

Calix

"Get ready," I ordered, as soon I walked into the dark office, making my presence known to the other two men, who I knew would be willing to stab me in the back, and were only waiting for the opportunity to do so. It was a matter of time until they did, but I was prepared for that occasion. If anything, I was ready to kill them before they could even think.

Enzo was lounging on the sofa, lazily inhaling a cigar, whilst Barak, the older yet somewhat less wise man, leaned against my ebony desk with a glass of whiskey in his hand. He frowned, reacting first to my command, whilst Enzo did not flinch or seem bothered. I always wondered who would betray me first, and I knew it would be Barak. The old man killed his brother to save himself and would stop at nothing to find his child, that his seemingly dead ex-wife had hidden. Or at least that was what he thought. Knowing full well where Aria had hidden Barak's child and mistress, I tucked that little morsel of information deep within me so that if a situation arose, I would have the leverage I needed to have Barak completely under my control. But for now…

"Get ready for what?" Barak questioned, drinking the remains from the tumbler glass.

"For war," Enzo drawled, puffs of smoke filling the air. I wrinkled my nose in disgust as I pulled my blazer off and discarded it onto my chair before pouring myself a glass of whiskey. "Boss wants to go to war. I'm assuming you've heard about Nero's engagement party to the very alive Aria Moretti."

"*Allegedly*," I added, but Enzo ignored me.

Barak's face paled. "I thought she was dead." He looked at me in disbelief. *"You said she was dead!"*

I swigged the yellow liquid before exhaling. "And she is dead. I'm pretty sure this is all a ruse to gain our attention, a way to draw us in - a trap."

"Well, our attention has been gained," Enzo slowly sat up, dabbing the butt of his cigar in the ashtray before relighting the end. "The question is: will we be attending?"

"If it's a trap, why would we need to risk it?" Barak urged, pouring himself another glass. "Don't tell me you're thinking of attending? If you say Aria's dead, then she is dead. No?"

I held Barak's distrustful eyes for a long minute before swallowing the whiskey. "She's dead. But that's not why we will be attending."

Enzo's lips coiled into a wicked smirk. "*Ah*. I see."

Barak didn't seem to understand what Enzo had realized, what I truly was seeking, as he looked between Enzo and me like it was a tennis match. "What? What is it?"

"It appears that our little bird will be attending the engagement party," I remarked, with a twinge of amusement that I saw flitter in Enzo's dark eyes.

"Violetta?" Barak said, incredulously. "They're exposing her to the public."

"Which could only mean that Aria is alive, Boss," Enzo mused, his beady eyes trained on me as I walked to my chair, sinking my body against the leather.

I glowered. "I can guarantee otherwise. But, if you would like to settle your doubts, I'm inviting you to attend with me."

"They'll be expecting you. This isn't a good idea," Enzo pointed out, and Barak nodded in agreement. They were irritating me. Aria never irritated me. Aria could never irritate me. And yet, she was dead. Dead. Dead. Dead.

I clenched my jaw. "Regardless, I want to confirm Aria's resurrection myself and ensure that Violetta is safely captured with minimal injuries," I calmly drank the remains of the whiskey, then pushed it across the desk where Barak caught it before it fell. "If this is a trap, I want to make sure I kill all those involved. Especially, Nero Russo."

Enzo and Barak shared a look, one they did not think I would notice, but it spoke more words than our conversation. I knew what they were thinking: the hushed conversations, the doubtful glances, the skepticism shared – they did not trust me, not one bit. A brief memory of my time at the Manor reminded me of a time when people did trust me, with their lives - with others' lives. It was a pity that those were the lives that threatened to destroy years and years of work. I hummed to myself before smirking which caught Enzo's attention, his brow raising with a silent question. A question that would remain unanswered. I had bigger plans, bigger goals, bigger dreams and if that meant killing those who I loved, then so be it. Because nothing, not even Aria, could stop me from taking over what would be rightfully mine. I would have full control of the Underground and I did not care whose blood would be on my hands. I just knew one thing, and one thing for sure. I would kill Nero Russo. For taking what was mine. For forcing me to hurt Kira. For making me kill Aria. I would kill him for loving her and I would make sure that it would be an extremely painful death.

Because he had the one thing I could never have – Aria's heart.

So, I would take everything else.

"Prepare yourself, men, for in a fortnight we will be taking Violetta, and then the rest of the Underground."

CHAPTER 53

hand in his, hand on him

The gown I wore was a deep blue, as dark as Nero's eyes when he strolled into the bedroom and caught me slipping into my silver heels. It cinched around my waist, pooling around my feet in gentle pleats, with an outrageous slit that stopped just before it reached my hip on my left side. The satin material curved over the arches of my breasts like two butterfly wings before plummeting deep in the cleavage where it nearly reached my navel. The dress was scandalous but Kira commented that it was perfect for me, and as soon as I wore it, I instantly fell in love with it. The last time I wore a blue gown was five years ago, on Nero's birthday, and I knew it was time to wear one again. I wanted to mark the beginning of a new chapter in my life, the beginning of a second life that I was extremely lucky to receive, and I was going to ensure that nothing harmed my future with Nero.

Nothing.

His eyes lazily lapped me in as I tightened the straps that wound up my legs, and his hands slid from the cufflinks he was trying to clasp. His suit was the same blue as my dress, sans his shirt and pocket square – both a linen white. His bow tie, a silk sapphire, was slightly crooked so I quickly straightened it, yet he still never spoke, as his eyes trained on my face, intensely, indignantly, intently. My ebony hair, tousled in gentle waves, brushed the exposed skin of my shoulders when Nero's fingers ran through it before he daintily cupped the side of my face. This stopped me in my tracks, my fingers halted at his bow tie, my eyes lazily peeping up, where I caught the wickedness of his blue eyes, mellow like the eye of a storm.

"You look absolutely… magnificent," he whispered, astonished.

I couldn't help but break into a smile, feeling my cheeks ache when they stretched to my ears. "You look pretty good yourself. Although, I really wished you trimmed your beard a little."

He smirked. "I think you'll find yourself disagreeing."

I narrowed my eyes. "You have a dirty mind, Nero Russo. A very dirty mind."

"So do you, Aria Russo. The dirtiest minds belong together," he mused, before kissing the crown of my head. "Did you see the gift Kira gave me?" I began to shake my head but stopped when my eyes caught sight of the silver rose emblem pinned on the lapel of his blazer. "She thought it was befitting for us. A wedding gift she claims."

"Of course, she did," I mumbled, but I couldn't help admiring the beautiful brooch. Although it was small, it twisted out from the main stem where two blue–dipped maple leaves sparkled under the spotlights. "It's gorgeous. I wonder where she got it from."

"It's pretty stunning but I'd like to point out that you are more gorgeous," Nero took a step back, his eyes languidly running down the length of my body, lingering a second longer on my exposed leg, before trailing to the dip between my breasts which caused him to lick his lips. "Can you spare a few minutes for your poor, hungry husband?"

"A few minutes with you means an hour delay," I snorted, moving towards my vanity where I painted my lips a soft nude to compliment the light makeup I was wearing, seeing as my dress was enough of a statement already. On top of that, there was the set of diamonds that Xander gifted me in the morning. He too claimed it was a wedding gift. Teardrops on my ears, and a pendant around my neck. Simple but beautiful.

Nero frowned. "Is that a no?"

Rolling my eyes, I sighed. "Yes, Nero. It's a no." He grumbled under his breath as I closed the distance between us, taking his hands and smiling at the sight of his platinum wedding ring. "Just make it until the end of the evening."

"I doubt I'll be able to. You are just exquisite," he muttered, kissing my neck lightly, my eyes fluttering shut at the warm sensation from the caress of his breath. He did not stop there, moving to my collarbone, then to my arm, returning to my jaw, before finally kissing my lips. "You are mine. From this day until the end."

"*Sempre*," I murmured, meeting his crushing topaz eyes. "From this day until the end."

Nero smiled and I swear the moonlight that streamed into my room brightened at the sight of it.

*

Kira had outdone herself. It should not have been possible to plan an engagement party this big in a matter of a week, but she had managed to do so. I never underestimated her abilities, but even to this day, I was shocked by her capabilities and every time, she reminded me why she was my second-in-command. Situated in New York's Financial District, on the 60th story, the Bay Room was an incredible, scenic venue. It had the most stunning, sweeping views of Lower Manhattan and its adjoining aqueducts, with cars flashing by in a whirl of colorful lights. The venue's vista extended east to the Brooklyn Bridge, which twinkled brilliantly at night. To the north, Midtown could be seen and to the south, the Hudson River. The moonlight poured in through the windows as I approached with Nero on my arm, but it was the location's brilliant spotlights that perfectly illuminated the space. There were at least 500 people in the room, with a thousand eyes on us, nearly trapping the air in my throat. Circular tables were positioned near the glass walls, with candles flickering softly in the center and gorgeous ivy and wisteria vines suspended from the ceiling.

"Kira did all this," Nero uttered. I barely managed to form words, nodding silently in response. "*Holy shit.*"

That caused me to smile. My eyes moved to Nero, and he looked down at me. "Loving you is the best thing to ever happen to me."

He broke into a grin at my sudden declaration. "I love you too."

Holding his gaze, the world around me stopped. It just stopped. Slowly, and surely, we drew closer to each other before glancing back into the crowd, my eyes meeting Kira's, who wore a stunning sage dress that drew out her oceanic eyes. Standing beside her was Xander in a brilliant silver suit, who sent me a cheeky wink, Violetta sat beside him. Everyone from the Manor was in the building, mixed with those from the Italian mafia, including our families. Nero squeezed my hand,

and I took that as a sign to move. One step into the venue and people crowded around us, gushing over how beautiful I looked, and how handsome Nero was, or what a stunning couple we made. The evening ran smoothly but I knew the worst was yet to come. As I made my rounds, Melissa finally saw me and burst into tears. I hadn't ever seen my dear friend cry but seeing her weep as she hugged me brought waterworks to my own eyes. There, we cried silently in each other's embrace. Nero was speaking to Matteo but was seriously concerned when he saw us crying, his eyes flickering over every second or so. When I finally left the comfort and familiarity of my friend's arms, I finally looked at her. It had been five years since I last properly saw her, but she hadn't aged one bit. Her hair was sunlight yellow, and her eyes were the same hazel as her stepbrother's. She looked like a Barbie doll in a soft teal gown that hugged her slim figure and brought attention to how tall she was.

Her pink lips tugged. "You look so fucking gorgeous."

"So do you," I took her hands. "I'm so glad you're here."

"I'm so glad you're alive, *sötnos*. You gave us all a fucking heart attack!" she cried out, her eyes brimming with tears again. "Don't ever do that again."

My throat felt restricted, and I was unable to speak, so I smiled, squeezed her hand, and nodded with resolve. She seemed to be satisfied with my silent response and pulled me into another hug that spoke all the words we could not. Afterwards, we laughed as she yanked me to the bar, snidely remarking to Nero how I was hers for the night. Nero smirked at her before sending me a look that spoke volumes and had my entire body shudder with need. He would be back for me. At some point during the night, Antonio stole my husband away and pulled him over to Claudio, my uncles, and some other men we both knew. Nero grinned as his father proudly patted him on the back, clinking their champagne glasses. I was so distracted by the way Nero lit up with happiness that I didn't hear my aunt call my name until she stood in front of me.

"Aria."

I blinked. Then I smiled sheepishly. "Aunt Gabrielle, it's so nice to see you."

Jade-kissed eyes looked at me with mirth. "Fascinated by your fiancé, I see."

I did not want to correct her, because I knew she would ask

questions that would take forever to answer, so I just shrugged. "I can't help it."

My mother and my other aunt, Chantelle, laughed as they crowded around me. Chantelle rolled her eyes at her cousin, pecking my cheek. "Leave her alone, Gabs. She's in love. Oh, I remember when I first fell in love with Coal!"

While I had visited Gabrielle only a few months ago, it had been years since I saw Chantelle, but she had not aged one bit either. Unlike Gabrielle, who had silky, mahogany hair that cascaded down to her waist, two pearls pinned on the left side of her hair, Chantelle's hair was rich and full, blonde to the point it looked golden, framing her oval face, drawing attention to her rare pink eyes. A genetic mutation, my mother had told me, that both Chantelle and her father had. My aunts both wore different shades of green – Gabrielle's dress was a satin emerald whilst Chantelle's was a light mint. Then there was my mother. Her hair was the same shade as mine before I had dyed it, a dark copper with blonde highlights. Her almond eyes, a gleaming hazel, creased when she saw me. They were warm and tender, reminding me of how much I had missed her presence – how much I needed my mother. Unlike her younger cousins, she wore a soft blue gown that complimented her smooth caramel skin. I mused over how Kira perfectly planned out everyone's attire for the evening so that there was a range of greens, blues and silvers throughout the venue.

My mother drew me into her arms, kissing the side of my head, affectionately. "How are you, dear?"

"I'm good. I'm glad to be back… to be with Nero," I murmured, and they all smiled, tenderly.

"I'm sorry about what happened. Your second informed us about what had occurred," Gabrielle began, her cool, viridescent eyes shifting to the men. "Beau was furious. God, I've never seen him so mad before. He spent hours with Nero trying to track Calix down."

I arched a brow in surprise. "Nero was tracking Calix?"

"For weeks," Chantelle remarked, taking a glass of champagne that a waiter handed her as he walked by. She gave her thanks to him, before continuing, "It was hard to get through to him, but I could only imagine what he was going through. I think we all had our fair share of grief."

My mother shared a sorrowful look with her cousins, squeezing my hand. "As long as you're safe. That's all that matters."

I blinked away my tears, forcing a brave smile. "I'm here." I looked at my mother, and my aunts, taking my time to memorize every inch of them until I knew I could close my eyes and still remember how they looked. "I'm here, and I'm not going anywhere. Not anytime soon. I'm staying for good."

Their smiles broadened but it was Gabrielle who spoke, "I'm so glad to hear that, Aria."

These women had been to hell and back. All individually suffering the cruel fates caused by those who opposed them, but here they were... standing in front of me, more powerful, more strong, more passionate than anyone else I had ever met. I knew I came from a long line of commanding women, women who could take over the world, women who would stop at nothing to protect their loved ones, and that was what drove me to end the Serpents. Men underestimated women. They always had. They would expect submission, obedience, compliance. They would expect dominance over them and that would be their ruin. Because there was nothing stronger than a silent woman, for she would wield the ability to destroy them all. My mother and aunts taught me that. After sharing a few more words with them, they finally let me go when Nero arrived back beside me, stealing me away from watchful eyes. My aunts and mother shared a knowing look as Nero whisked me away, and before I disappeared, all I heard was their laughter. I glimpsed at Nero, who took us into an empty room before closing the door behind us. The only source of light came from the moon as it trickled into the room, irradiating the extra tables and chairs that were not needed.

"Is everything alright?" I asked, when he removed his hand from my back.

"Yes, everything is perfect. I just have a small request," he said, and I lifted a brow. Then his lips curled into a grin. Before I could fathom what he was planning, he raised me onto the table and hooked my leg over his shoulder, leaving me far too exposed that my heart stuttered at the thought of someone catching us in this illicit position.

"Nero..." my words disappeared when he kissed my inner thigh after kneeling. I swallowed. *Hard.* "What are you up to?"

"Fulfilling my request," he murmured, continuing his journey upwards. I gasped, clutching the edge of the table, my eyes rolling back at the sensation. I burned as bright as a wildfire, I melted like ice under the searing hot sun; I could feel the tingling warmth rush throughout my body, and I knew I wanted more.

"Aria..." he purred, and I hummed a reply, dreamily. "Is that a dagger attached to your thigh?"

I froze. My eyes shot open as I peered down at Nero, who looked utterly amused at his discovery. Kira had given it to me when I received my dress. She insisted it was her wedding gift. And I loved it. "Perhaps."

"Should I ask why it's there?"

"No. You should just get back to what you were doing," I ran my fingers through his hair, biting my lip, playfully. "It's far more interesting."

Nero didn't refute, arching his brow, and continued what he was doing. I grabbed the strands of his hair, knowing full well that I would not last the rest of the evening if he stopped right now. I would happily kill him if he stopped right now. It was like being in a desert – hot, thirsty, delirious – and he was the oasis that appeared in my dire state. He gave me water to drink, he gave me shade to sleep, he gave me peace of mind. He gave me life. And I would keep coming back.

"I'm so glad you didn't trim your beard," I blew out. Nero chuckled, the mere sound and feeling were goddamn mind-blowing.

His fingers dug into my thighs as I threw my head back, moving to the dull melody of my thundering heart. All thoughts of someone catching us flew right out of the window, along with all my inhibitions. God, I loved him. I loved him more than I could love myself. I loved him more than anything in this world. I loved him and only him. And when my body became like molten lava, the stars in the night never burnt as brilliantly as they did right then, like the universe approved of mine and Nero's love. My breathing was heavy, labored and short, as he glanced up, looking incredibly ravishing on his knees. The only time he would ever be on his knees was for me. He raised a brow, a smile mischievously playing on his lips, and his radiant cyan eyes twinkled.

"Are you happy?" I managed to say.

"Extremely," he purred, standing up where he captured my lips, kissing me so deeply and passionately that when he tore himself away, I was sure I had no oxygen left within me. "Are you happy?"

I was ecstatic, high on the electrifying sensation, but I neglected to tell him that, narrowing my eyes as I crinkled my nose. "Could you not have waited?"

"Aria, you look delicious and it's taking every ounce of restraint within me to not bend you over this table and take you here. So, unless I was appeased in some way now, I am sure that *everyone* would've heard how loud you can really be."

I gasped, scandalized. "I am not loud."

"Want to bet on it?"

I scowled and he laughed, his hands moving to my waist where he pulled me against him, before dipping down and kissing me again. My complaints disappeared as I curled my arms around his neck and sank deeply against him. In that kiss was the sweetness of passion, a million loving thoughts condensed into one moment. In his kiss, I was home. And I was so glad to be home.

"I love you, Nero, so much that I swear to God, if you leave me, I'll hunt you down," I muttered, and he laughed against my lips. "And I'll kill you. With the dagger on my thigh."

"So violent," he chuckled, before tilting his head to the side, mischief dancing on his lips. "Although, I won't lie, that turned me on a little."

"You're so weird," I stated, feigning disgust, and he smirked.

"I'm not going anywhere, Ariadne," he began softly, weaving our fingers. "I feel you in the air, long for your touch, recall you in a way that sends electricity to spark my mind, body and soul. You are my medicine; you are my light; you are my laughter and hope. I slipped my heart into your pocket some time ago, and there it will stay, safe and sound. So, no. I'm not going anywhere."

I broke into a smile. "Good."

He smiled. "Good."

After some time, Nero and I returned to the main hall where Kira quickly hurried over as soon as she caught sight of us with Sophie hot on her tail. Both of them looked at ease, but I saw the flickering gloom in their eyes and knew immediately something was wrong.

"What is it?" I said softly, smiling at a couple of guests who walked by.

Kira lowered her voice when she spoke, "They're here. I caught sight of Barak and Enzo, including some of their men but I'm not sure where Calix is. He could be anywhere or not here at all."

"No, he's here," I glanced around the room. "He's definitely here."

Nero didn't flinch, his eyes steeled as they took in the room with one glance which was enough for him to see everything. "How can you be sure?"

"I trained him," I answered, looking up at Nero. He held my gaze; it was difficult to see what he was feeling or even thinking, but then he nodded. It was short but it was enough for me to know that he trusted my decision. I turned to Sophie and Kira, who were patiently waiting for my orders. "Where's Violetta?"

"She's been with Xander the entire evening," Sophie informed, her sparkly Sacramento green gown shimmering under the spotlights above.

"Okay, so we know that their main goal is to kidnap Violetta, which means our main goal is to ensure she is protected. Keep Xander by her side and have one other person trail them. Kira, you stay with Violetta also."

Sophie left as soon as I gave my orders, but Kira lingered, hesitation crystal clear across her face. I raised a brow, and she chewed her lip, apprehensively.

"But, what about you?" Kira asked, and I frowned. "Calix came to check whether you're dead or not. He'll come after you again."

"Only if he's stupid enough to."

"And you don't think he is?" Nero's jaw clenched in anger. I smiled, kissing his jaw to ease the tension. It loosened but he was still stiff.

"Oh, I know he is, but I also know that Calix is smarter than that. He won't kill me," My lips coiled into a dark smile as I looked out into the crowd where Calix was hiding. "He *can't* kill me."

Kira rolled her eyes. "I'll be sure to send him your way if I see him. Do us a favor and leave him a souvenir."

I laughed. "Will do, Yakira."

Kira smirked before heading back to the table where Xander was, with Violetta sitting beside him in a pretty sage dress that was poufy and glittery. I wanted to keep an eye on her, I wanted to stand beside her all evening but that was too much of a risk. I had to keep my distance and even though I did not like the idea of it, I had to trust everyone else to protect her. I could not save everyone.

Nero, having seen my internal dilemma, intertwined his fingers with mine. Squeezing my hand gently, he tore my attention away from Violetta. Cobalt eyes softened when he smiled. "Let's try to enjoy the rest of our evening, Aria. She'll be okay."

I exhaled. "I know." I stole one last glance at Violetta. She laughed at something Xander said, her smile reaching ear to ear. "I know."

I was on edge for the rest of the night. I couldn't help it, but Nero was an angel, and he soothed me with silky caresses and light kisses to distract me. I still could not see Calix, but I caught a glimpse of Barak and Enzo before they melted into the crowd. There were far too many people, and while that worked to our advantage, it also left us in a precarious position.

"Why did you marry him?" My uncle, Coal, asked, placing his hand on Nero's shoulder.

I grinned. "Why did you marry Aunt Chantelle?"

He crinkled his nose. "I'm not really sure."

Chantelle laughed, rolling her eyes at her husband's defense. "Please, you were practically begging for my hand in marriage."

Coal smirked as he kissed his wife's cheek, his arms winding around her waist from behind. "I would happily do it again."

"Of course, you would," my father snorted, drinking his champagne. This caused my mother to frown, her eyes thinning at her husband, which had me turning to Nero, noticing the ghost of a smile teasing his lips.

"What's that meant to mean?" she grilled. "You wouldn't do that for me?"

Having noticed his mistake, my father's eyes widened before he shook his head adamantly, kissing my mother but she did not budge. "No, *cara*. I would do anything for you."

"You would?" she questioned, arching her brow. My father nodded naively but I saw the twinkle in my mother's eyes and knew he was far from forgiven. "You can sleep in the guest room tonight."

My father's face fell as she pecked his cheek. Coal and Beau laughed, whilst their wives grinned at my father's misfortune. A hand patted my father's shoulder, my eyes shifting away from my mother. Claudio, Nero's father, shook his head at his best friend's trouble but I saw the amusement in his eyes.

"You never learn," Claudio remarked.

My father glared at him. "Don't push it or I'll give Coco a reason to kick your ass."

Hearing her name, Nero's mother glided towards her husband with blonde hair as shiny as a new penny, as yellow as gold, as straight as straw. Her blue eyes were exactly like Nero's, bright and cool, so sure, so stunning. Although, Nero was spitting image of his father with a straight nose, a sharp and prominent jaw, dark hair and brows, his eyes were the one thing he gained from his mother. His most beautiful feature. Because those eyes told me they loved me more than words could ever.

Coco beamed. "I don't need a reason to kick his ass; I'll do it anyways."

Xena smirked. "So true."

Claudio grumbled at the same time, scowling at his wife, "This is true."

"He must piss you off every day then," my father's mocking response caused the two of them to start bickering like a married couple.

Nero sighed beside me, shaking his head at our fathers, but I could not fight the grin. My aunts and uncles left them to it and went off to speak to the other guests, whilst my mother greeted Coco properly. She had been friends with Coco for as long as I could remember, and even longer still. They were partners in crime. Coco and Xena. Best friends until the end.

I thought of Kira and me. I smiled.

After a few hushed words with her best friend, Coco's eyes finally shifted to me with a friendly smile. I had grown up with Nero, so I always saw Coco as my second mother. But at that moment, it did *not* feel like that. All I could see was Nero's mother, the most important woman in his life, besides me.

"Aria, you look beautiful. I'm sorry I didn't come to see you earlier, there were so many complications with the guests that I had to sort out. Your friend – Yakira – is wonderful. I love her; she reminds me of myself," Coco mused.

"That's exactly what I was thinking!" my mother gasped. "She does remind me of you, Coco."

"I'm glad you guys have come to love her. She's very important to me," I glanced at Nero, who was still watching our fathers bicker, his nose wrinkled like a child who was not allowed to have a piece of candy. "She's important to us."

Coco smiled, a knowing glimmer in her ultramarine eyes. "Can we speak alone?"

Nero's eyes snapped to his mothers, as my heart raced like a wild lion, and my eyes widened. He frowned. "Don't scare her away, mom."

"Scare her away? Son, don't underestimate your wife."

Wife. I bit my lower lip, fighting back a smile, but my mother saw, and she winked at me. Turning to *my husband*, my mother asked, "How about we get a drink, Nero?”

I knew he was reluctant to leave me, shifting his eyes uneasily between me and his mother. So, I kissed him, whispering, “I’ll be okay. Go.”

He was still hesitant but nodded, allowing my mother to hook her arm through his. I watched them walk away, my eyes trained on his retreating back before I remembered who I was with. I glanced at his mother, swallowing, as I forced a smile, trying to hide how nervous I truly was. I didn’t know what to say, or where to begin. I knew she had questions and I knew I should answer them, I just wasn’t sure how. Panic began to overwhelm me, but I stood my ground, trying to not let her piercing arctic eyes get to me.

“Stop freaking out, Aria. I’m not looking for answers,” she suddenly said.

“Sorry?” I managed to choke out.

“I was, at first. I wanted to know what was going on in your mind, and Nero’s mind when you decided to get married in secret. I wanted to understand why my son married the woman, who disappeared for five years. I wanted to know why the girl I saw as my daughter left without a word. I wanted to know the answers…” she paused, inhaling slowly. “But, then one day, Nero called me and said *‘I have found the love of my life, and she makes me so happy. I’m finally happy, mom’.*”

Coco chuckled, to hide the fact that her voice cracked, so I pretended that I did not even hear it. Her blue eyes, so magically pale like a cloudless sky, watered.

“And I knew that those answers weren’t worth knowing because my son was finally happy. He was *finally* happy,” she continued to say, her smile creasing her eyes. “You make him happy. You always have, Aria. I will never know, nor do I want to know, what had occurred all those many years ago but that doesn’t matter anymore. Because right now,” Coco peered at her son, and her smile reminded me of my mother’s. A smile reserved only for their child. “You make him happy. And that is enough.”

I pursed my lips, not wanting to cry, and blinked back the tears threatening to let loose. I mustered a brave smile, ignoring the twinge of pain in my heart, and knew I had to make up for all the time lost. So, I would start here.

“I won’t hurt him. I promise you this,” I murmured, her eyes squinting at me. “He is my air, my water, my lifeline. He is and owns my soul. He is everything I have been looking for, and I promise I will protect him until my very last breath. I love him for all he is. I love him because he saves me from my own chaos. I love him because loving him is easy. He is my everything."

She didn't say anything for a long while, and I almost got worried that she did not believe me. But then, her eyes relaxed and her lips twitched before breaking into a smile that reminded me all too well of Nero. I guess that was another feature he inherited from her. She revealed her pearly white teeth, her nude lips broadened and lifted her rosy cheeks.

"I've never doubted you, Aria. I trust you'll take good care of my son," she drew me into a hug, ignoring how surprised I was, and squeezed me in her arms. "He's in your hands now."

I was tense in her hold, but those words eased me, and my body relaxed as I wrapped my arms around her, smiling as I said, "Thank you."

When we finally pulled away, she didn't bother hiding her teary eyes but still managed to joke, "Go to him. He's looking way too worried and that will only result in wrinkles."

I laughed, fighting back the sobs, but I did what she said after she squeezed my hand one last time before letting me walk to my husband. He waited at the bar, his eyes narrowed in concern and the frown on his lips deepened when he noticed the state I was in.

"What did she say to you? Were you crying? Did she make you cry?" he shot one question after the other but before he could ask one more, I silenced him with a kiss. He instantly yielded, his arms wrapping around my waist whilst mine curled around his neck, my fingers running up the nape of his hair.

"I love you, Nero Russo, more than you'll ever know," I whispered against his lips, brushing my nose against his, feeling his lips lift into a smile that I would always protect.

"Not possible," he argued, and I went to disagree, but he cut me off, "I'll always love you more."

I broke into a smile as I kissed him once more.

"Now, I think Kira wants to talk to you," Nero murmured, my brows drew together as I peered at him, tilting my head in confusion. He bobbed his head, eyes flickering over my shoulder, so I followed his train of sight, noticing Kira's eyes fixated on something or someone in the crowd. I frowned when I saw that she was not with Xander or

Violetta.

"I'll be right back," I muttered. He kissed the crown of my head before letting me go, talking to some guests who greeted him whilst I shot off into the crowd. I began to close the distance between Kira and myself, when someone stood in front of me, blocking my path. My eyes thinned at the culprit. "*Enzo.*"

He greeted, frostily, "I believe congratulations are due."

"For my engagement? Or for being alive?" I questioned, tilting my head to the side.

His creepy smile broadened. I couldn't believe that he was Violetta's brother as he did not resemble her at all. "For both."

"Thank you. I must say, you are either incredibly stupid to appear at *my* engagement party or incredibly pathetic," then I shrugged. "Perhaps you're both. I think it frightens you to know a woman can destroy your operation. This wouldn't be the first. Let me ask you this, Enzo: how many women need to destroy the Petrov's organization before you get it into your thick skull that you'll never win?"

I saw a tick in his cheeks as he clamped his teeth shut, glowering. "Until your family realizes you can never destroy us."

"Never is a big word," I kissed my teeth. "Sounds like a challenge. And do you know what I think about challenges?" I leaned forward, his eyes flickering to my nude lips - the temptation to have what he would never own – but I had his attention. "I love them."

Enzo's face darkened as I moved back, batting my lashes innocently whilst the smirk on my lips said otherwise.

"Don't get too excited, *Mrs. Russo*," he advised, icily. The way he spoke sent shivers down my spine which I did my best to ignore. I could not let him get to me. "The game isn't over yet."

"No. No, it isn't," I arched a brow, mocking him, taunting him, reminding him that I controlled the game. "It's not over until I say so."

"We'll see about that."

His words dripped with sarcasm, and he simpered, scathingly. Before I could say anything else, someone curled their fingers around my wrist, tightly, and hauled me away from Enzo and his unsettling expression. I began to scowl, wanting to fight off the culprit, but instantly stopped when I recognized the familiar dark hair. My heart faltered and I tried to shake the feeling, but I couldn't. The betrayal, the pain, the anger, and the grief overwhelmed me to the point where I only reacted once we were far from curious eyes.

"Get your fucking hands off me," I snarled, jerking my hand back.

He smirked, glimpsing down the hallway. "You don't have to pretend that you hate my touch, Aria. No one is watching."

No one was watching, and that was the problem. I could only hope that Kira noticed my disappearance, or Nero noticed that I had been gone for too long. But until then…

"Why are you here?" I glared at him, but he did not flinch, leaning on the wall, with his arms crossed over his chest.

"I had to be sure. I had to know for sure."

I released a short laugh. "That I wasn't dead?" He didn't respond, his green eyes, which I had recently come to hate, scrutinized me. Those very eyes betrayed me, and this family. Those green eyes with specks of gold. Those green eyes. "I can't believe you tried to kill me."

"I didn't try. I *did* kill you," he corrected, wryly. "Question is: how did you survive?"

"You're not the only one with tricks up your sleeves, Calix," Then I shook my head. "Why?"

He didn't need to ask what I was talking about; he knew *exactly* what I was talking about. Yet, he shrugged in disinterest. "When I first heard of you, you had just taken over the Italian mafia. Aria Moretti, the Don of the Italians, daughter of Xena and Antonio Moretti. You were new, an easy target, so I planned to steal weaponry from you during transport. I wanted to test how strong you were, how easily I could tear the Italians apart, and when I managed to – *three times* – I knew you were a weak opponent."

I didn't flinch at his words, remembering how I was in London when the first attack on the Italians had happened. I resisted the urge to glance behind me, to see if anyone noticed I was down here.

"I thought you were a mere weed for me to root out. But those plans dramatically changed when you stepped away from the Italians and disappeared into thin air," he continued. "Then, I heard one of our favorites had managed to escape." My throat felt blocked, air unable to reach my lungs, but I didn't show how I was feeling. Regardless, Calix saw right through me. "*Yakira.*"

"You bastard," I spat out, venomously.

"You could imagine my surprise when I heard that she escaped and, on top of that, killed two of my finest men," he spoke with a lack of emotions. "I knew she must've had help and eventually, I found out that it was you. That's when I knew you would be dangerous. So, I plotted to infiltrate your little plans, and made sure I knew every single thing you got up to."

"You're sick. You helped me save all those victims and for what? So, that they can return to you. You trained them, fed them, healed them. You became their family, Calix. Does that mean nothing to you?" I hissed.

For a second, I swore his eyes looked tormented with grief, but it disappeared as quick as it had come. His words were bitter, indifferent, detached. "I have no family."

"You had us," I said, before repeating the words again, "*You had us.*"

"I didn't want a family, Aria. I wanted the world," His smile was vindictive. "And you were going to be part of that world. Falling in love with you was not part of the plan."

"And yet, you betrayed me. If that's your type of love, I don't want it."

He shook his head, disappointed. "Oh, Aria. I wished you died in the hospital, so I wouldn't need to kill you by my hand."

"You must be dumber than I thought if you think you can kill me," I laughed, reaching for the dagger on my thigh.

His eyes flickered down the length on my leg, his tongue darting out to wet his lips. "Now, we should at least tell Nero before you sleep with me."

Unsheathing the dagger, I watched the handle glimmer under the spotlights, my thumb brushing against the engraving – *The devil's nightmare*. A smile played on my lips as I cocked my head to the side, studying Calix when he noticed the weapon in my hand. He pushed himself off the wall, narrowing his eyes.

"I'm going to tear your heart out," I swore, words laced in acid.

"You'll die trying," he warned.

"I'm Aria. I'm a ghost. I don't die," then I pounced.

I knew I would have difficulty fighting Calix, seeing as I was the one who trained him, but he would never be better than me. He moved to the side, almost missing the knife impaling his shoulder. He reached out to grab my arm, but I dodged him, my foot colliding into the side of his body as Xander had taught me. Calix grunted, temporarily distracted, but that was enough time for me to lunge for his arm. I managed to nick his arm before he growled, seizing my wrist. He pressed me against the wall. But I spun out of his hold, facing him, and elbowed his stomach. I could only see blood as he staggered back, unable to defend himself when the dagger pierced through his shirt, cutting his torso. He hissed, eyes blazing, and ignored the damage. Calix evaded my next attack, his fist jabbing my ribs, prompting me to cry out in pain. But I held the dagger in my hand, knowing it was my only weapon, forced myself to fight through the pain. Spinning, my dress twirled around me as I lifted my foot and kicked his stomach. Except, Calix was quick. His hand gripped my foot and yanked me towards him, causing me to lose my footing. The second I was immobilized; he took the opportunity to slam me against the wall. My head knocked against the wall, blood dripping from my ear. The dagger slipped from my hold as he moved behind me. He twisted the handle from my grip, the other hand moving to my waist.

"Fuck you, Aria. Fuck you," he snarled, lips grazing my ear lobe.

"I know you want to," I taunted, breathless. "I know that's what you're thinking about. With me pressed against the wall. I bet you're thinking of what you can do with me. Tear this dress off, spread my legs apart, make me scream. I bet that's all you're thinking about."

He shifted behind me, seething under his breath, "*Fuck.*"

"How does it feel, Calix?"

"What?" he grunted, his breath, smelling of cigars, tickled my neck.

I smiled. "To know that Nero had his head between my legs less than an hour ago."

Before he could respond, I snapped my head back, hearing a crunch as my skull collided with his nose. He yelled in pain. His eyes flashed with anger as I kicked him as hard as I possibly could. His back slammed back against the wall, giving me time to grab the dagger from the floor. But I shouldn't have turned my back on him because he lunged for me, fist smashing into my shoulder. I yelped, the dagger dropped on the floor, narrowly missing my foot. Calix clutched the shoulder he hurt, pinching it torturously, but I overlooked the burning sensation and kneed him where the sun didn't shine. He grunted, hunching over, blood spilling from his nose and ruining my beautiful dress.

Damn it.

That pissed me off and I punched him, knocking his head back onto the wall. He landed on the floor, clutching his broken nose, his eyes beginning to swell, his lips bleeding profusely like his torso and head. I thought of all the ways I could snap his bones.

"You bitch," he spat, the spittle of blood flying everywhere, as he glared at me.

"Thank you," I hauled him against the wall before he lurched onto his feet, and I reached for my dagger, holding it to his throat. "I'm going to kill you, Calix. And I'm going to enjoy every second of it."

He laughed, maniacally, blood adorning his face and I wanted to take a picture of it. "Aria, when this is over, I'm going to fuck you until you can't walk, and if I'm in a good mood, maybe I won't fuck you up. Maybe I'll kill you after, or even better, maybe I'll make you watch your family, the Manor, and Nero burn to the ground."

I clenched my jaw, pressing the blade deeper on his throat until I saw blood trickle down his neck, his Adam's apple bobbing in response. "I'd die before you could even touch them."

"You did die, Aria. And yet, I still got them."

"What?" I frowned in confusion. But before I could question him, I heard my name and glanced down the hall to see a distraught look on Kira's face. She was breathing heavily, her lipstick was messy and coated in blood, the side of her face began to bruise like she had been in a fight...

Wait.

My heart sunk.

No.

Calix laughed, an eye turning purple and blue, his lips busted open, blood painted on his face. "I told you. I'll still get them."

I saw blood. I wanted *his* blood. "I'm going to kill you. I'm going to fucking kill you!"

"If you do, Violetta won't live to see tomorrow," My blood went cold, my eyes widened, and I found myself easing away from him. Calix smirked, his shoulders slugging against the wall. "Good girl. You always listened to my orders like a good bitch."

Slowly, my arms dropped to my side, but I didn't lower my guard, my eyes thinning like the dagger in my hands, my body and dress covered in splatters of blood – from his or my own, I didn't care. Then, I inhaled sharply and slowly looked at him, ensuring he didn't look away. I wanted him to see the darkness within me. I wanted him to see the beast that was itching to play. I wanted him to *see* me. For all the chaos and death I was.

I dropped my voice a couple of octaves, asserting I punctured every word with the promise of agonizing death, "I will find Violetta. I will save her. And if I see even an inch of her hair misplaced, I will make your life a living hell. I will gouge your eyes out for every boy and girl you've seen ruin. I will break your fingers for every victim you've touched. I will cut your tongue out for every lie you've told. And I will, Calix Zervas, destroy you until the only name you'll ever know is mine. This, I vow."

He didn't say anything for the longest minute. Then, his blood-dried lips coiled into a malicious grin as he leered. "I look forward to it, Aria *Russo*."

"Good. You've already started."

I pushed myself away from him, walking down the hallway, forcing myself to leave him unharmed, because I couldn't compromise Violetta's safety. I reached Kira; her eyes filled with malice as she continued to glare at Calix. Her fists clenched and unclenched, fighting the urge to pummel him. I placed a hand on her shoulder, her startling topaz eyes stared at me, watching me shake my head. She swallowed. Inhaled sharply. Then released a heavy exhale as her eyes shifted to Calix once again. I straightened my spine, peering over my shoulder, settling my gaze on Calix. He observed us, carefully and cautiously, on edge.

He should be.

I could change my mind.

But for Violetta, I didn't.

Instead, I smiled. Cruelly, coldly, calmly. "Like a good bitch, remember my name."

CHAPTER 54

bloodlust

The gymnasium was still as I leisurely walked in; my eyes trained on the dagger that I spun between my fingers. My soldiers stood in a single line formation, waiting for me to say something, do something, *anything*. Their hands were held behind their backs, their eyes stared straight ahead, but their spines stiffened when I strode by. It was cool for a summer day but that could be from the taut atmosphere or the fact that we were several meters underground in the mountains. Perhaps it was both. Only a few meters from where we were standing was Viktor's dead body. I still had not decided what I wanted to do with it, but I had a feeling I would be inspired soon. Kira and Xander watched from the side, acting as if I didn't know they were sharing apprehensive glances. Finally, I stopped. Then, I turned to face my soldiers. My jaw clenched and I thinned my eyes.

"How did this happen?" I asked. No one spoke, but I saw the looks they gave each other. I inhaled heavily before saying, through gritted teeth, "How did you manage to lose Violetta?"

"Aria —" I cut Kira off with a sharp look that had her thinking twice about speaking. She was reluctant to do so, but she stepped back, pursing her lips.

I knew I should not take my frustrations out on them, but I couldn't help it – I couldn't stop. Violetta was somewhere in the world, scared, alone and in danger. And it was my fault. I couldn't protect her. And that was my fault.

"Violetta was taken from my engagement party when everyone else was distracted with taking down the Serpents. She should've been your first priority!" I roared, my hand snapped back, and I threw the dagger before anyone could blink. It shot through the air before impaling a wall behind them, scarcely missing two of my soldiers. I expected them to flinch, but no one did; no one backed down. "Someone explain to me how we lost her!"

At first, I thought I was going to get silence as a response, but someone stepped forward, my eyes darting in their direction. Mark swallowed as soon as his eyes met mine, but he didn't back away and answered, "She was last with me. Kira got split apart from the group. Barak cornered Xander, Violetta, and me. So, Xander told me to take her away whilst he dealt with Barak. I took Violetta."

"Where were you taking her, Mark?" I questioned, arching my brows. He looked hesitant to reply as if I would bite his head off. Perhaps I would. "Well? Where were you taking her?"

"To you," he replied. My eyes widened in surprise. "I was taking her to you." I didn't know what to say, so I bobbed my head. Mark took that as an indication to continue explaining, "I panicked when I couldn't see you, or Kira. I could hear people following us and I knew I wouldn't be able to take on all the Serpents alone, whilst also protecting Vi. But then, I remembered the safe room Xander showed us during the protocol."

"You took her there?"

"I *tried* to take her there," Mark corrected, his voice laced in guilt. "The furthest we got was the ladies bathroom. Violetta hid in there whilst I tried to fight off the Serpents, who finally caught up. They must've taken her then, whilst I was distracted. I could barely fight them off. Kira finally found me and helped out. But they must've taken her before that."

"Yes, they must have," I murmured, running my fingers through my dark locks. God, I hoped she was okay. "Thank you, Mark."

He nodded stiffly, stepping back into line, his shoulders slugging in relief. I pinched my nose, knowing that the Serpents had separated all of us so that we were all defenseless against a group of them. It was the easiest way to get to Violetta. I glanced at everyone, taking in how tired and bruised they were from fighting off the Serpents and sighed.

"What do we do now?" I rolled my shoulders back, my muscles

aching from the fight I had with Calix. The only thing that tamed the beast within me was that I ensured the next time I saw him, he would be littered in bruises.

"We find Violetta," Xander was the one who answered, my eyes snapped in his direction.

I scoffed. "Thank you for pointing out the obvious."

Xander rolled his eyes, removing the dagger from the wall before walking towards me, undaunted by my wrath. "Let me finish," then he handed me the dagger, "Barak was severely hurt so he'll be resting to heal. We go after him. He'll know where they're taking her."

"How can you be sure he'll be honest?"

"Because you have the one thing he's been searching for his entire life," this grabbed my attention and Xander smiled, "His child. And if that's not good enough, we'll take his kingdom, and his life."

Gradually, my lips curled into a menacing grin.

*

"Are you alright?" Nero asked, closing my office door behind him. I stole a quick glance away from my plans, directing a tight smile at my husband. His eyes skimmed me over, paying more attention to the small scratches across my temples and my bruised lip that still needed to heal. "Have you redressed your wounds?"

"They're minor," I brushed it off as he took his blazer off, dropping it onto the chair and rolling up his sleeves. Temporarily, I got distracted by his arms, veins and muscles that were begging me to touch them, before forcing myself to focus on my plans.

"I wasn't talking about those wounds."

When I didn't respond, he exhaled, exasperated, before striding towards me. Before I could stop him, he propped me onto my desk, silencing me with a short kiss, and then attending to my wound underneath my blouse. A bandage dressing wrapped around my torso, courtesy of Kira, and Nero quickly unwrapped it. I tried not to wince as his fingers brushed the right side of my body, an ugly purple bruise coloring a mass of my skin, but failed miserably, pinching my eyes together. He glimpsed up, lifting a brow.

"These wounds," Nero said. "Did you redress them?"

"Not yet, I haven't had the chance to," I quickly explained but he ignored me, grabbing the spare dressing from my drawer and the first aid kit.

He worked swiftly and skillfully, his fingers moving like this was second nature. When his fingers brushed against my skin, I couldn't help but flinch from both the pain and the cool caress of his skin. Tingles scurried down my back. The sensation rushed throughout my body, my heart thundering at having Nero so close to me. We never discussed properly what had happened during our engagement party; I was not sure where to start. Whereas Kira had updated Nero on everything that had occurred professionally, I had yet to update Nero on everything emotionally. He was giving me space and time, not pressuring me to speak, but I knew he was worried. He should be – I nearly killed the man I saw as family, and I would happily try again. I regretted not slitting Calix's throat that night, but I had to remind myself whose life was on the line. A young girl who got caught up in a world full of greedy and power-hungry men that would kill whoever to get what they wanted, including an innocent girl.

"Xander and Kira are working hard to track down Barak. I think they're really close. Sophie and Mark have been training everyone more often and for longer than normal. We need to be prepared for everything. Dom has been sent to take small groups of the younger ones to another safe house – they aren't safe here," I revealed, but Nero made no indication of hearing me, his attention primarily on my wounds. I frowned but at the pain of the alcoholic wipe cleaning my wound. "We have this safe house in Los Angeles that Kira built recently. It was still under construction but it's habitable. Those who aren't able to fight will be relocated over there. Dom will be overseeing that operation."

He hummed.

I drew my brows together. "Nero, are you listening to me?"

"Yes, I am," – he didn't look at me – "but, what I'm concerned about is how you're feeling since you saw Calix last night?"

"I'm fine," I stated. He bobbed his head, wrapping the bandage around my torso until it covered the wound. He still didn't look up, so I repeated, "I'm fine."

"If that's what you believe."

"Nero, I am fine. Seeing Calix was nothing. I mean, it hurt, and I couldn't shake off that feeling. I didn't even react until we were so far from everyone. If I wasn't so caught up on the feeling, perhaps Calix would've been caught, and perhaps…" I trailed off, and this finally caught Nero's attention. Captivating blue eyes peered up under long dark lashes, fingers grinding to a halt.

"Perhaps what?"

"Perhaps Violetta would still be here," I breathed out the words that had been troubling me the last few hours.

Nero studied me for a long moment, before completing his work, tucking the bandage in place, and drawing my blouse over the dressing. Then, he looked up, his eyes searching for my own. "You didn't know. You don't know everything."

"I knew Calix would be coming. I should've prepared myself for that," Nero didn't respond, his fingers drawing circles on my waist, absentmindedly. There was this long silence between us, before I broke it with a simple, "When you love someone – *like, truly love them* – would you do anything for them?"

"Of course," he responded, without blinking.

"So, what did I do wrong for him to betray me?" I did not intend for the words to sound broken, but I could not stop them from appearing that way, not when inside I was completely shattered by Calix's betrayal. I saw it coming and yet I didn't, and that was what hurt the most.

Nero studied me, carefully. "It's not your fault."

"Maybe not, but it was someone's, and unfortunately, I got in the middle of it and dragged everyone down with me."

"I won't leave your side," he affirmed earnestly, and then leaned down to press his head against mine. "Ride or die, remember?"

My eyes glistened with tears, a crestfallen smile on my lips. "Ride or die."

"And, Aria, no matter how much someone can prepare themselves, the reality of it is far different than the expectation," he brushed my hair away from my face, his fingers weaving through my tendrils as his thumb caressed my cheek tenderly. "You didn't know. But now you do. So, you learn and adapt for the next time, instead of beating yourself up about it. Because you will see him again, and you can't freeze."

"What if I do?" I whispered.

"You won't, Aria, because you know the consequences of it," Nero kissed the crown of my head, and I closed my eyes to savor that feeling. "You'll do your job, and you'll do it well."

"Can I ask you something else?" I murmured, curling my arms

around his neck. Nero arched his brow, and I chewed my lip, nervously. "Do you expect me to return to the Italians once this is over?"

Surprise flickered in his eyes before they softened, and he smiled. "No."

"Why?"

"I don't think you ever wanted the position. Since we were young, you were apprehensive about it. I don't think you'll ever want it back," Nero answered, twirling a strand of my ebony hair around his finger. "Do you want it back? Because I will give it to you."

I shook my head, adamantly. "No. It belongs to you. Always has, always will." My lips quirked up slightly. "But thank you for offering."

"You're the queen, Aria. Even if you've left, you are their queen. You are *my* queen. *Sempre*," he kissed the tip of my nose. "I love you, *cara*."

"I love you too, Nero."

Then, I kissed him, drawing us closer until the only space between us was our clothes. My legs twisted around his waist, my hips rolling against his, the aching and burning need submerged me like a tsunami. I ignored the pain from my wounds and immersed myself completely in the way Nero made me feel. He made my heart beat faster than adrenaline, kissing away the pain, healing me the way medicine could not. I could love Nero always and forever. *I knew I would* love Nero always and forever. Things made sense with him. The sky was bluer, the stars were brighter, the darkness that consumed me shattered into thousands of pieces when he loved me like a bullet to a heart. He was my guardian angel, my knight with the spectacular aquamarine eyes. It was like being at the beach, so peaceful, so calming. It was so easy and at the same time, it was all-consuming. And I loved every second of it.

He pulled away from me, smiling from ear to ear, "Who would've thought we'd be here?"

"I don't know about you, but I've been in love with you since I was ten," I revealed, my cheeks burned, scaldingly.

Nero's grin widened at that revelation. "I've been in love with you since the day you were born, Aria. It's always been you."

The knock on the door broke our spell, my eyes glancing over my shoulder as Kira entered the room, raising her eyes at the sight of Nero and me. "Am I disturbing you?"

"Not at all," I said, before Nero could get a word in. His face fell and I pushed him away from me, hopping off the desk whilst he sulked. "What's up?"

"We've pinpointed Barak's location. It seems you were right; he took off to his private island in Greece, hiding out there until he's needed," Kira handed me a collection of pictures taken of Barak as he boarded his plane, hidden by the shroud of darkness. "Xander hurt him pretty badly. He's in no condition to defend himself."

"All he needs is a gun, and that will be enough," I pointed out. "We will leave for Greece tonight. I'm not wasting any time."

"Do you need me to come with you?" Nero asked, grabbing his blazer.

I shook my head. "I'll call you when we find out Vi's location."

"Okay. Just stay safe," he kissed my cheek tenderly. "I'll catch you later."

"Tell your parents I said hi," I said, as he began to leave.

"I will do," Just before he disappeared out of the room, he stole a glance at Kira. "Look after her. I know she can take care of herself, but that's my future and you must protect her with your entire life."

I rolled my eyes, fighting back a smile, but Kira grinned. "You have my word."

Once Nero left, Kira brought over the file filled with details about Barak's location. We needed to ambush him which meant I needed to know how heavily guarded he was, and how secure his home was. It would tell me how paranoid he was, and I would use that to my advantage. We spent all afternoon preparing so that by the time we arrived at the runway I knew exactly how I wanted to torment Barak Doukas. With twenty of my best soldiers, including Xander and Kira, we set off on our jet under the darkness of night. The journey to his island was long, especially as we had to arrive completely undetected. The night sky melted into broad daylight, cloudless skies, and blistering sun when we finally arrived many hours later. I pushed my sunglasses onto my head as I stepped out of the jet, inhaling the warm, salty air from the sea surrounding the island. It was a good day to kill someone, and I was looking forward to killing Barak. My beast craved blood, and I was sure to satisfy it. Xander, who had left the jet as soon as it landed to ensure no one raised alarms of our presence, strode towards us in pristine condition, despite the blood on his hands. Kira snickered beside me, before throwing Xander a packet of tissues, which he used after sending Kira some colorful words. Sophie and Ciara rolled their eyes whilst Mark and Dom smirked in Xander's direction, ignoring the hateful looks sent their way.

"Are we okay?" I questioned, as he tried to clean the blood, but the faint crimson stains on his fingers would serve as a reminder of what he had done – of what we were going to do. He nodded and so I turned to my soldiers, who patiently waited for my command. "Alright, let's go."

Without another word, they all shot off, heading into the black SUVs Xander managed to procure and, once I knew they were all okay, I got into the last car, with Kira, Xander and Sophie following closely behind. No one spoke, no one wanted to. We saved our energy and knew that soon we would need it. I watched the roads disappear from tarmac and morph into sand as we drove deeper into the island, palm trees sheltering us from the hot streams of sunlight and any eyes that Barak had around the area. I knew he was expecting us – he would be an idiot not to – but I also knew he was not sure when we would be arriving. The element of surprise. It was my favorite tactic and the one that worked the best. Xander drove silently, geared up in a black combat suit and boots, holsters hiding his guns and knives, whereas Kira, who sat in the passenger seat, opted for a lighter set of clothing. She was drenched in black from head to toe, but her attire clung to her body like a second skin. It ensured she could move faster and with an agility that would throw her opponents off guard. Her blonde hair was braided, two chopsticks tucked inside, sharpened and as deadly as a knife. She wore leather thigh-high boots with heels that could slickly impale people. Holsters on her thighs, a belt around her hips, gloves to cover her hands, I knew Kira was heavily armed. In her hands, she twisted a Swiss army knife, her eyes trained on the road ahead with pure concentration.

Beside me was Sophie, and like Kira, she chose to wear skin-tight black tactical gear but switched out heeled boots for combats. Her fawn hair tossed over her shoulders as she sharpened her knives, before sheathing them into their cases attached to her hips. I wore similar clothing to the girls, but instead of black skin–tight trousers I opted for shorts. Ebony dipped thigh-garters were attached to the belt around my waist, where I tucked my dagger and gun. My top stopped above my waist, my bruises faintly exposed, and scooped below my neckline, sleeves coming to my wrist, drawing attention to the rings on my left hand – my wedding rings that sparkled under the sun. I had drawn my dark hair back into a high ponytail, black shades protecting my eyes from the sun's glare as I glanced out the window. Barak's mansion came into view as we turned the corner, the car jolting from the uneven ground. Sophie glanced at me, but I remained impassive to her stare, counting down the seconds until I got to slit Barak's throat. My fingers itched to play with the dagger sheathed on my waist, but I knew all good things required patience. Unfortunately for Barak, I was an incredibly patient woman. Ciara, Dom and Mark were in the SUV in front of us, with the other black cars following closely behind us. It was a risky operation, but we all knew that this was our only option to find Violetta, and that meant we would risk everything to save one of our own. Barak's mansion was similar to Althaia's, with its classical Corinthian pillars that held the roof, white walls, greenery bordering the stairs, flashy lights – all the things that were unconventional for a safe house. He was practically a beacon, and I was the moth attracted to it.

"Get ready," I murmured, as the SUV in front began to slow down, unclipping my belt and tossing my shades onto the seat.

"Are you sure this is a good idea?" Sophie questioned, apprehension in her voice but not on her face. "This is far from an ambush. Barak knows we are here."

"And that's why it's an ambush. Why torture your prey with the unknown, when it's far better to torture them with the known?" I explained, reaching for my phone where I dialed Ciara, who picked up before the second ring. "Is the package ready?"

"Dead and decaying," she responded quirkily, with a thick Egyptian accent. "Shall I bring it in on your command?"

"Yes," Then I hung up. As Xander cut the engine, I glanced at my friends – my family. "Stay safe."

"Yes, Boss," they all responded, simultaneously.

As soon as I stepped out of the car, Barak's men charged from all angles, guns blazing, knives at the ready but they were not fighting to stay alive – they were fighting for money and that would be the reason they would not survive. Xander did not even look in my direction as he swerved the shots and attacked with such precision and ferocity that could plague a man's dreams. Sophie quickly aided Mark; the pair were attached at the hip, back-to-back, moving in sync with one another. Kira grinned at me before charging at the two men who came at us with their knives that did not look as sharp as her movements. Before

I moved, I glimpsed at Dom, noticing he was fighting off three men by himself, preventing them from reaching the SUV where Ciara and our special package was. I turned to help before grinding to a halt when I watched him easily deal with the situation, his fighting had improved dramatically since the last time I saw him in action. I recognized some of the moves and almost smiled, knowing that Kira mentored him without anyone's knowledge. From the corner of my eye, I saw a man quietly approach but before he could pounce, I grasped my dagger and flung it through the air, where it shuttled like a bullet and pierced the man's throat dead in the middle. The man choked, collapsing to his knees, blood spilling onto his hands as he tried to grab the dagger. I marched over, grabbing my gun, shooting two of the men who ran towards me, and withdrew the dagger from his throat. His eyes were wide as the blood did not stop, liquid as dark as the color of my lips stained the marble stairs, and I smiled darkly before slitting his throat. Instantly, he was dead. And then I moved to the next. Within a matter of minutes, we had managed to take down the rest of Barak's men with minimal casualties to us. Sophie and Dom checked on everyone, ensuring they could continue, and once it was okay, I sent them to cover the perimeter. One by one, my soldiers disappeared around or into the house whilst I cleaned the blood on my dagger using the coat of a dead man. Sophie and Mark were the last to leave, fingers entwined before separating when they both set off in different directions.

"Will you be okay?" I asked Dom, who was on high alert.

But even then, he grinned cheekily. "Did you just see me right now?"

"I'm very proud of you," I peeked at Kira, who sheathed her knives back into their holsters. "You had a good mentor."

Dom's honey-colored eyes that accentuated the richness of his ebony skin twinkled as he looked at Kira with a familiar type of emotion. *Ah.* His smile softened. "She's a good teacher."

I shared an amused look with Xander before he spoke, "You're out of her league, dude."

Dom frowned. "I can always dream."

"Dream of what?" Kira asked, suddenly standing beside us. I didn't flinch at her voice, nor did Xander, but Dom's eyes widened in surprise, and I knew he still had much training to go through. Kira arched a brow. "What are you dreaming about?"

"Dreaming about y —" I elbowed Xander in the stomach, "— *Ow!*"

I glared at Xander, who pouted. "Nothing. He was dreaming about nothing."

Kira looked at us weirdly before shrugging. "I think that was all the guards outside."

I ignored the sulking Xander and turned to Dom. "Stay with Ciara and let us know if any more men arrive."

Dom, with red cheeks, nodded and headed back to the SUV. Kira narrowed her eyes at me, but I paid little attention, gesturing to Xander to walk ahead. He stuck his tongue out at me like a child before heading up the stairs, keeping an eye out for any signs of traps.

Kira stood by my side, her icy blue eyes studying the front door. I drew in a breath of air, slowly. "Do you think he knows?"

"Yes," she responded, a moment later. "Why do you think we haven't been killed yet?"

"The lack of guards on arrival suggests that they are all protecting Barak," I mused, my lips twitching in amusement. "*Men.*"

Kira smirked. "Foolish."

"It's clear!" Xander yelled from the top, waving us over.

"Are you sure Barak will know where Vi is?" Kira asked, when we reached the front door; my fingers brushed against the glazed windows on the door and my eyes narrowed at the small camera I noticed hidden in the doorbell.

"We'll have to ask him that ourselves," I replied, before gesturing to Kira and Xander to move to the side. They shifted over and I kicked the door open, breaking the chains attached to the frame. I kissed my teeth in disappointment, and said to no one in particular, "I expected better. You underestimate me."

"Everyone's in position," Xander whispered.

I was the first to enter the mansion, greeted by the lack of life and beautiful ornaments which decorated the floor. The only sounds came from my heels that clinked against the marble floor, my fingers tightening around the dagger attached to my waist. Kira and Xander ranked my sides, guns in hand, eyes scanning our surroundings cautiously, prepared for any surprise attacks thrown in our direction. I heard the gunshot before I saw the gun, the pressure thinning around me, but I moved swiftly, swerving the silver bullet that tunneled through the air, piercing a vase instead of my arm. Kira was faster; her movements were like lightning and another gunshot rang out as soon as I moved, killing the man creeping down the spiraling staircase. The bullet went in and out of his body, straight through his head, one shot and he was dead. He fell down the stairs, wide eyes, blood spilling around him and pooling onto the marble flooring. I arched a brow at Xander, and he shot up the stairs, checking for any others, whilst Kira retrieved the man's gun and extra ammunition. When Xander gave the green light, we proceeded through the eerily silent mansion, passing the empty rooms, and heading towards what looked like the living room. I was a hundred per cent sure Barak had all his men stationed in one place, to protect him, and thus stupidly revealing his own location. I smirked when my theory was correct, finding at least thirty or so men in the living room, crowded in front of another darker mahogany door which I assumed led to his study – if the blueprints Dom found were correct.

Which meant Barak was hidden in there.

I sighed. "Now I'm truly disappointed. This is pathetic."

Kira snickered. "Wanna bet on who has the highest kills?"

"Loser is paying for drinks for the rest of the year," Xander suggested, drawing out his knives, two silver spear points that gleamed when the light reflected off their surface. Kira grinned, spinning her gun, and wiggling her brows as she went into her familiar stance, a move that meant she was out to kill anyone who touched her.

"Better start saving up," I warned, as my lips twitched. "You know I'm the best."

Xander initiated the fight, roaring as he thundered towards the men, who drew their own knives out, which triggered Kira to move within the blink of an eye, her aim being incredibly meticulous, bodies dropping left and right. I laughed, murderously, and instead took my time, unlike my friends. I didn't wear heels to run; they were a statement to the world of the dangerous things I was capable of, especially in six inch stilettoes. I allowed the men to come to *me*, rather than I go to them – an idiotic move that resulted in their death. They charged at me, some with guns, others with knives. But I was quicker and stronger. I was trained by the very best. My mother. I was prepared by the most fearless. My father. And as I sliced open torsos, pierced through hearts and lungs, slit their throats, I couldn't help but muse over how proud they would be of me right now. The air smelt of smoke, bullets and death. There was so much blood that splattered everywhere, some managing to get on my clothes which caused me to wrinkle my nose in annoyance, but it was the most beautiful sight ever like a barbaric ethereal mural. And I was the artist. I had just finished mutilating two men when another cornered me before I reached Barak's study. His eyes were practically undressing me, and a cruel smile played on his lips. I knew I looked forward to satisfying his fantasy… correction, *his nightmare.*

"Aren't you a pretty lady?" he taunted, twirling his large knives in his fingers as if they would intimidate me. Anyone could hold a knife – only the merciless could kill, and that was my best characteristic.

"You should be scared," I cleaned my dagger on the shirt of the dead body lying beside my feet.

"Oh?" he chuckled, and then raised a brow. "I'm more turned on than scared."

"Aren't you a charmer?" My lips curling up into a seductive grin as I stared at him under hooded lashes. His eyes darkened with arousal, cautious and something I recognized to be skepticism. "I am warning you. You should be terrified of what I'll do to you."

"And what's a pretty woman like you going to do?"

His question reminded me of Enzo's second that I met in the Underground fighting rink. It was cocky, daring, and arrogant. They were words laced with underestimation and disdain. Even on a battlefield where half of the men had been killed by me – he *still* underestimated me. It would be the cause of his death.

And so, like in the fighting ring, I purred, "I'm going to rip your heart out."

I struck as soon as the words escaped my lips, tearing my knife down the length of his arm which had him crying out in agony. He roared, eyes blazing with anger, and pushed me with such strength that I lost my footing and staggered back. He clutched his arm, inspecting the wound, before glaring at me.

I cocked a brow.

Then, I smirked.

He barreled towards me, but I broke his knee with my stiletto, impaling his shin, blood emptying out when I removed it from his wound before he could even comprehend what was going on. He fell onto one knee – both an arm and leg bleeding out, profusely. His screams of pain were music to my ears, and I took that moment of distraction to grab his own knife and stab his eye. Crimson liquid gushed out, and I watched it with delight, my sadistic simper stretching ear to ear when I caught the fear that glimmered in his eye.

"I told you," I began, softly. He whimpered. I lost my smile. "You should be scared."

Then, I hauled the knife down from his eye until the blade sliced through his jaw, cleaving his face apart. Using my dagger, I punctured his chest, and twisted the steel in his heart, before removing it. My hands were stained with blood as I savored the life draining from his body, tossing his knife beside his feet.

"I'll always be your worst nightmare," I vowed, and then I kicked the maimed corpse away, striding towards Barak's study. Just before I opened the door, I glimpsed back to check on Kira and Xander, but at the sight of them looking uninjured, I pushed the door open, revealing Barak cowering behind his desk.

With a gun in his hand. Pointed at me.

"Are you going to shoot me?" I questioned, indifferent to the weapon that held in his old, trembling fingers.

"How?" his voice shook.

"How what?" I glanced over my shoulder at the dead men that littered his marble floor. Then, I looked at Barak, clarifying, "How did I manage to kill all your men?" When he didn't respond, I continued with a shrug, admiring the sticky blood on my dagger. "It was easy. I'm the best."

"You were supposed to be dead!" I was pretty sure those words had more meaning to him than to me. "He said you were dead."

"Calix is a liar, a traitor, a two-timing piece of shit," I sighed, slowly inching closer to him. "You shouldn't believe a word he says. I can help you get revenge; you know. If you really want it."

The old man narrowed his eyes. "How can you help? You want to kill me. You're no better than him."

"That's quite an insult," I frowned.

"You'll torture me. I heard what you did to Konstantin. What his own daughter did," Barak spat out, scathingly. "You're inhumane. Monsters."

"Oh sweetheart, I'm flattered with such compliments, but I'm not here to have my ego fed," I tilted my head to the side. "Where is Calix?"

"I'm going to kill you –"

"If you were going to kill me, you should've done it the second I stepped into the room," I interjected. Then, I smiled. Viciously. "Now, you're just too late."

Before he could understand what I had just said, the gun flew from his hand as a shot rang out from behind me. I didn't need to turn around to know that was Kira's handiwork; I could tell from the way Barak screeched as his thumb fell from his hand. He sobbed and I strode towards him, kicking the gun from his reach, and bent over his desk to grasp the collar of his pristine linen shirt. He gagged, cradling his bleeding hand, eyes wide as saucers, as I leaned towards him.

"Where is Calix?" I repeated, darkly. "I'm a patient woman, Mr. Doukas, but not too patient. Either you tell me now, or I'll make you."

"N-No," he choked out.

I held his gaze, watching him flail about. Then I moved back, loosening my grip on his shirt. "Pity."

When I finally released him, Barak gasped for air, swallowing his cries, and staggered back as if the distance between us would save him. He knew he was dead the second I stepped foot on this island. He just wanted to kill me before he took his last breath.

"How about a little housewarming gift?" I suggested, seating myself onto his desk. Barak swallowed but didn't reply, blood soaking his white shirt. But when I looked away, his eyes followed, and we both watched Ciara and Kira drag a large body bag into the study. The girls dropped the bag beside my feet, and I peered at Barak with an arch of my brow. "Open it."

He was hesitant, eyes flickering between us all, but he obeyed, shuffling around the desk, and unzipping the duffel. My smile broadened when he cursed, stumbling back at the sight of Viktor's mangled body – or what was left of it. Arms, legs, fingers, and even a man's most precious possession tucked into a pouch, torn from the body until the only indication that this was a human was its face. Viktor always had such a handsome face.

"Don't you like my gift?" I fluttered my lashes, and Barak scowled at me, stepping back as if he was getting ready to bolt. "Don't bother thinking of running because even if you do, I have this entire perimeter surrounded. You won't be alive by the time you step foot off this land."

"You're sick. You're fucking sick!"

"Don't act so high and mighty, Doukas. I'm not the one who forced girls into marriages, and killed my own brother to save myself," I kissed my teeth, shaking my head in disapproval. "You'll tell me where Calix is, or I promise the next body in this bag will belong to you."

"I don't care if you'll kill me," he snarled. "I'll never tell you where he is."

"Now, who said the body will be yours?" I laughed, delighted. "I said it will belong to you, and from what I recall, you have a beautiful son that will inherit your legacy."

Barak's face paled, and he stilled. Kira and Ciara circled him, as I hopped off the desk, stepping over Viktor's crippled carcass, closing the distance. I had no intention of following through with my threat, but Barak had no idea of knowing whether I would or not. That was what allowed me to hold power over him. Because I was in possession of the one thing he wanted the most – his heir.

"Surprise!" I sang, cheerily.

"You wouldn't dare harm a child," he whispered, his skin so white I couldn't tell whether it was due to the blood loss or horror.

"No, I wouldn't. Not usually, anyway," I crooned, twisting my dagger between my fingers. "But sacrifices must be made sometimes for the good of the world."

"Don't you dare touch my son!" he bellowed, preparing to attack me, but Kira and Ciara held him in place. He thrashed about in their arms, yelling, "Stay the fuck away from my son!"

"I will. I won't let your legacy fade away, or the kingdom that you built crumble to dirt. I won't…" I promised. I looked down at Barak, my pleasure morphing into sobriety. "…If you tell me where Calix is."

"You can't stop him," he cackled, madly. "It's too late."

"That's for me to decide, Barak. What you should decide is whether or not you want to risk your son's life for a man who'll kill you the next time he sees you," I pressed my dagger against his cheek. "What's your decision?"

"I hope you rot in hell," Barak sneered, loathingly.

"And I'll meet you there. I'll show you all the pretty things I can do with this dagger of mine," I nicked his cheek slightly, and he winced but froze when my dagger touched his thigh. "Perhaps, I'll begin with the very thing that makes men believe that they are superior."

"Perhaps, I'll fuck the insanity out of you," he threatened.

I glanced at my girls, and they laughed, surprising Barak as he stared at them, startled by the sudden reaction.

Kira looked at him; her cold, aquamarine eyes were anything but friendly, as she smirked. "Can we just kill him now?"

"I'm getting bored," Ciara pouted.

"Not until I get answers," I hummed, wistfully. "Although, there are other ways you can entertain yourselves."

They grinned at each other at my suggestion, and Barak looked as if he was going to shit himself, quivering in their grasp. I stepped back and crossed my arms over my chest. Kira reacted first, withdrawing the chopstick in her braids, and slicing his arm. Barak screamed, but Ciara didn't wait for him to recover and took her own knife, severing his thigh. The blade was sharp enough to cut flesh as if it posed no resistance. At once a fountain of red came from the wound, the ebb and flow in time with the terrified heart of a shrieking old man. I watched them cut him up, bit by bit, until he was on the floor, weeping whilst the carpet dyed in scarlet liquid. I finally stopped them, kneeling down, and pinching Barak's chin, forcing his swollen eyes to look at me.

"Where is Calix?" I said.

The old man sobbed. "Torr-Torrevieja. He bu-built a man-mansion there. He-he was g-go-going to st-start his op-oper–ration th-there."

"Thank you," I stood up, wiping my hands on a cloth that Kira handed me. I stared down at the severely injured man who had severely ruined the lives of innocent people. "Consider this an act of mercy that you will not die by my hand."

"What?" he managed to gasp, through the pain.

My eyes flickered past him as Xander brought in another woman, dark brown hair, olive skin, dark chocolate almond eyes that were similar to her son's. To the child of the man weeping at my feet. Barak lifted his head to look over, his shoulders sagging at the sight of his mistress. She didn't flinch at how badly mutilated he was, her eyes ran over him as if this was the first time she could truly see him for what he really was.

Salome stepped forward. "Barak."

"Salome," he swallowed. "I thought you were dead. I thought Althaia had killed you. How's Matias?"

"No, you don't get to ask about Matias. You don't get to *care* about him. Not after everything you put us through – put *me* through," Salome shook her head. "You don't deserve an answer."

Barak chuckled weakly, still having the energy to send me looks of aversion. "So, this is your so-called act of mercy. To have my mistress kill me."

"That's the thing you people never understand. If I touched you, I'd spend every second of every day making sure you suffered, except it's not gratifying enough. But if the person you hurt the most touched you, you'd spend the last seconds of your life watching *them* tear *you* apart. The very people who you've harmed. It's like karma," I nodded to Kira, who passed a knife to Salome.

Barak watched the exchange, apprehensively, as Salome inched closer, the softness of her golden eyes contorting to malicious darkness, hungry for blood.

"No," Barak whispered. He shook his head in disbelief, begging me with his eyes, pleading me to stop. I wondered if he ever stopped when the victims he tortured cried to him. I didn't bother asking. *"No. Please. No."*

I stepped around him, sheathing my dagger into its holster; Kira and Ciara followed behind me, as Xander took up a position by the door to oversee Salome. Before I left to head to Spain to save Violetta, I stole one last look at Barak, catching Salome towering over his whimpering frame.

All powerful men fell.

Barak caught my eyes. Fear swarmed within them.

"Remember one thing, Barak; there's no limit to one's pain," then I smiled, callously, "but there's a limit to one's fear."

His screams echoed throughout the house as I walked away, ignoring the dead corpses of the Serpents' fallen soldiers. I quickly dialed the number of the first person on my contacts list, stepping out of the mansion, basking in the warm sunlight.

He picked up on the first ring.

"Are you done, baby?" his deep, gruff voice welcomed me.

My glacial heart thawed, and, for the first time today, I grinned, earnestly, "Meet me in Torrevieja. I know where Violetta is."

CHAPTER 55

speared

"We've surrounded the perimeter," Nero informed me, as I used the binoculars Kira brought to check the location out. "Dom was quick to find where Calix was hiding out."

"Dom is incredibly good at his job," I stated, and handed Nero the binoculars. "He'll probably be the next Xander if he continues with his training."

Nero arched his brow. "You think?"

I smiled. "I know so."

Having arrived in Torrevieja last night, Kira and Xander forced us to rest for the night whilst we waited for Nero to arrive with additional backup. From what I had been told, Dom did not waste a second from when we landed to find Calix's location, and he had spent every waking moment tracking him down. I didn't doubt him for one second, knowing that Dom was one of the most talented people when it came to hunting people, and with Xander as his mentor in this field, I knew he would quickly improve. But despite being told to sleep, I couldn't close my eyes and spent the night staring at the ceiling, counting down the minutes until I had Calix in my grasp. Eventually, my exhaustion caught up with me and I found myself slipping away only to then wake up with Nero sleeping soundly beside me. I found out later that he arrived nearly an hour ago and was waiting for me to wake up but had sent his men to the estate Calix was hiding out at when Dom discovered the location. I was initially irritated that no one woke me up and sulked for most of the morning, whilst filling my mouth with the delicious Spanish breakfast cuisine that Kira had sent to my room. Once I was sure that everyone was prepared for the battle that we were heading into, we finally geared up and set off to the location. Like the attire we wore to Barak's, everyone was dressed, head to toe in black, with knives and guns attached to their bodies, and comms in their ears so that we could discreetly stay in contact with each other. Dom remained at a safe and suitable distance to control the comms and guide us through the mansion with the digital blueprint he managed to obtain. I did not question his methods of attaining said blueprints and praised him before we left. By the time we got to what looked like a pretty rundown villa, it was late afternoon, and the sun was setting, the warm air cooling around us, making it bearable to work in the humidity. Instead of storming into the place, I had us stationed several miles from the location so that I could observe the types of security systems that Calix must have put in place. Although Nero's men had already given me an initial report, I wanted to double-check, because I knew that there was always something that could have been missed.

And with Calix, I did *not* want to take the risk.

"Are we good to go?" Nero asked.

I narrowed my eyes at the ruinous mansion. "Something is missing... we are missing something."

"Dom examined the inside using whatever camera system Calix had installed, and even he has given the green light," Nero sighed. "I know you're worried, but everything will be okay. Right now, a scared little girl is waiting for someone to save her, and we are wasting time by worrying over what Calix may or may not have planned."

It was a tough pill to swallow, and my gut was telling me that something was not right, but Nero was correct and every second I spent obsessing over whatever my gut was telling me, was a second we wasted, when we could have saved Violetta. Thus, with a reluctant nod, I allowed Nero to take me to the SUV. Kira was leaning against the black car, aviators covering her eyes that were as blue as the ocean crashing against the shore. She looked bored, admiring her nails idly, but smiled when she noticed us.

"Are you ready?" she questioned, lifting her brow.

I crinkled my nose. "Not entirely, but we shouldn't waste any more time."

I ignored the look she gave Nero and peered back at the villa. It would only be a matter of time until I saw Calix again, and I knew I was afraid that I would freeze again. I was afraid. Everything I had done in the last five years had come down to this, and I was… afraid. As if he knew, Nero took my hand, directing my attention to him, and smiled. It was warm, reassuring, and safe. It spoke more volumes than words ever could have. I drew in a long breath of air, before exhaling, rolling my shoulders back, and then giving a confident nod to Kira. Her smile broadened as she opened the door, waiting for me to jump into the passenger seat whilst Nero took the driver's. Just before she got into the car, Kira spoke quietly with Xander, her lips moving too quickly for me to even comprehend what was being said. Whatever it was caused Xander's face to tighten, his eyes thinning as he nodded, completely serious. The conversation ended as swiftly as it began and Kira got into the car, whilst Xander got in the car in front of us. I was curious to know what had been said but when I turned to Kira, she avoided my gaze and busied herself with her gun, unclipping the magazine and then clipping it into place again. I frowned, looking at Nero, who shrugged before switching the engine on. Pouting, I slugged into my seat and crossed my arms over my chest like a child who didn't get candy during Halloween. Except, I always got candy during Halloween – even if that meant stealing Nero's. But now that I think of it, I was pretty sure he allowed me to take it. I peeked at Nero, whose attention was on the road ahead, one hand on the steering wheel, the other on the gearstick. My eyes narrowed. He *definitely* allowed me to take his candy.

"Stop staring, Aria. It's distracting," he murmured, quietly enough for me to hear, but not loud enough for Kira to catch.

I pressed my lips together, fighting back a smile, but nodded obediently, nonetheless. I decided to steer my attention elsewhere and began plotting Calix's demise again. I imagined all the different ways I could hurt him, enough that he begged to die but not too much that he would die.

No. I couldn't allow that.

I planned on playing with him for a very long time, or at least until I was bored.

The journey wasn't long, but as I was daydreaming, it felt like only a few short minutes went by until we were far enough that we could sneak in without being caught. Xander's car slowed as we reached the walls that surrounded the mansion. Colossal stone walls with small watchtowers stationed on the four corners of the perimeter. From the guard scheduling table that Xander discovered during his initial surveillance, the shift for the watchtowers changed every two hours, giving us a ten-minute window to slip past without raising alarms. Unfortunately, that ten minutes began as soon as the cars were hidden by the vast trees a few meters back. We didn't waste any time, and as soon as Xander gave us the okay from his position, we all got out of the SUVs and began to trek through the beech forest. Despite wearing boots and the amount of sound-alerting vegetation covering the ground, I managed to get to the walls without a sound. As did everyone else. Safely. With Ciara on the east team and Mark on the west, the plan was to meet in the middle. I mouthed my orders, sending one group to the eastern gates, and the other to the west, whilst Kira, Sophie, Xander, Nero and myself planned on heading into the mansion using the entrance.

Nero looked at me as if I was crazy when I proposed the plan, but Kira didn't complain, nor did Xander. I knew they wanted to kill Calix as much as I did. Even if it meant going into what could be considered a suicide mission. With our backs pressed against the stoned curtain wall, I knew we only had three minutes to get in without raising suspicion. Time was of the essence, so I turned to Xander who began to work on the iron gates that led straight to the villa. He hooked up a device to the electrical box against the wall and worked his magic whilst the rest of us kept an extra vigilant eye out. I silently prayed that everyone would be able to get in safely. With less than a minute to spare, my heart stuttered at the sound of a quiet *beep* which indicated that Xander had successfully infiltrated the security system. He slowly pushed the gate open, only a slight crack, enough for us to slip in, undetected. My heart was racing as we all split up and hid behind the cars parked up front. Guards patrolled the land, sniper guns in hand, dressed in the type of combat uniform that Nero and Xander were wearing. They wore helmets, speaking to one another quietly. Xander, who was on the opposite side of the land with my husband, nodded his head upwards, and I glanced up. The villa had a balcony on the second floor, where two guards walked to their position, overlooking the yard.

Our time was up. Which meant, we were going blind.

I exchanged a look with Kira, who kneeled beside me. I knew she was sharing the same thoughts as myself. Then, I looked over at Sophie, whose back was pressed against a black SUV, and then to Nero and Xander who were hidden from sight due to the large vans. I swallowed thickly, trying to remain calm but I was panicking within. Sophie sensed this, her honey-rich eyes settling onto me where she then arched her brow, as if asking a question. As if she knew what needed to be done, she inhaled and then sent a warm Sophie smile in my direction.

A smile that told me, for the last four years, that everything was going to be okay.

My eyes widened and I shook my head, adamantly.

It was suicidal. She knew it. I knew it.

But that was why she did it.

Before I could jump out to stop her, she weaved through the cars, still hidden, and aimed at the guards. As soon as the first gunshot was heard, the guards were alarmed and all directing their attention to where the shooting was coming from, a distraction that allowed us to head into the estate. I watched in horror as they all cornered Sophie, shaking my head, but Kira hauled me away, stopping me from saving my friend… from saving my sister who sacrificed herself to save our little sister. I nearly tripped over my feet as I tried to keep up with Kira, her hands tightly holding my wrist as if she was afraid to let me go like I would go to save Sophie. And I would have in a heartbeat. When we finally got into the estate and found an empty room, she finally let me go. I breathed heavily, hunched over, my hands on my knees, trying to suppress the panic, and I even took a step back when Nero tried to console me. He didn't seem offended when I didn't let him, but I knew he was worried. They all were. No one said anything. As I tried to recover myself from a near panic attack, I desperately quelled the image of Sophie being surrounded by guards. I couldn't stop seeing her face. And I hated it. I couldn't stop seeing her.

My eyes burned. My heart ached. My body froze.

"Aria, we need to save Violetta," Kira murmured, placing a hand on my arm. The words sounded muffled, but I heard them. I forced myself to look at her. Her topaz eyes glittered, and I knew that was the tears. "She did it to save Violetta."

Violetta. That was why I was here. Why we were all here. Why

Sophie sacrificed herself.

After a few more seconds, I nodded stiffly and brushed the tears that managed to escape. Xander gave me a nod, stiffly, and Nero took my hand, kissing my knuckles, tenderly.

"Okay," I whispered. *I was going to kill Calix.* "Okay." *I was going to kill Calix.*

"Okay," Nero murmured. He glanced at Kira and Xander. "Let's go."

He never left my side as we walked through the villa that looked like it needed serious refurbishment with its wires exposed, lights dangling from the ceilings, walls half-painted, and the flooring not completed at all. It was dusty and seemed to be under reconstruction, ladders here and there, planks of wood piled in one room, and metal poles leaning against the wall in another. We only had Dom's blueprint to work with, and even then, it was difficult to pinpoint what each location was. The villa was huge, and I was sure that we had reached the east wing when I noticed the lack of sunlight. My assumption was correct when I saw Ciara's team flooding the eastern perimeter on the second floor, with additional men that I assumed belonged to Nero. As Kira checked to see if they saw anything, Ciara frowned, eyes flickering everywhere, before settling onto me.

"Aria," she began, and I knew what she was going to ask. "Where's Sophie?"

Kira stopped speaking. Xander's spine stiffened. And Nero looked away.

I held Ciara's gaze, as I spoke, my words were as tense as the atmosphere, "We weren't able to make it into the estate without a distraction because there were too many guards."

Ciara instantly caught on. Her face paled. "No."

"The only way we could get past was if someone drew attention elsewhere."

"No," she shook her head fervently in disbelief, her cheeks already wet with tears. "No. *Please.* Aria, *please* don't say anything else."

I didn't let her words waver me and swallowed hard. "Sophie jumped out before we could stop her."

"*Oh God, no!*" Ciara cried out, stumbling back but Kira caught her, wrapping her arms around our friend. "Please, no!" She sobbed, weeping in Kira's arms, whilst everyone else stilled at the news, shock and sorrow covering their faces. "*Please!*"

"I'm sorry, Ciara, but Sophie was overpowered, and…" my words trailed off because we all knew what that meant. She didn't survive. I looked away from my soldiers, unable to face them because that would mean that I would have to face the truth, and I couldn't do that. I couldn't deny the little hope I was clinging onto. The reality I was desperately trying to avoid. I couldn't. I closed my eyes, whispering, "I'm sorry."

For the longest time, no one spoke, and Ciara's soft sobs eventually morphed into hiccups as Kira soothed her. I knew what we were all thinking. Who was going to tell Mark? At some point, Ciara used the heel of her palms to wipe the tears away, swallowing thickly as she untangled herself from Kira's arms. With reluctance, Kira let her go but stayed at a respectable distance in case Ciara broke down again.

"I'll be the one to tell Mark," she sniffled. "No one else says a word."

Xander looked at me, and I nodded, silently. He answered with a quiet, "Okay."

"We need to move," Nero murmured. "We're risking too much exposure right now."

"Nero's right. We have to find Violetta, and right now we are sitting ducks," Kira bobbed her head. "We still need to meet up with Mark's team, and it seems that we are in the east wing of the villa."

Remembering that Dom was also on comms, I tapped the earpiece, "Dom, can you hear me?"

There was a static sound before a crackling, "Yes."

"How far are we from the west wing?"

"Not that far, but it looks like the middle section is crawling with Calix's men. You should be careful, or you'll risk being caught."

"I think it's too late for that," Kira muttered. "Sophie's presence has already indicated that we are here. He's waiting for us. It will be best if Mark's group meets us in the middle."

I agreed. "Dom, do you have eyes on Violetta?"

"Not yet, but there is one room on the main floor that has no cameras besides the ones in the hallways," he responded, a minute later. "She might be there."

"Send Xander the location, and inform Mark of the plan," I ordered, before turning to everyone else. "I understand that we have lost a soldier, but she sacrificed herself for Violetta, which means we have to do everything in our power to save her. There is no space for

531

mistakes, people. We need to get Violetta without losing anyone else. So, please stay safe."

When I was sure everyone was okay, I took a look at Nero, his eyes softening at my gaze. There were thousands of things we could have said to each other in that moment, but when he bent down and kissed the crown of my head, it was all that needed to be spoken. I smiled up at my husband, and he smiled down at me, crushing blue eyes, as deep as the ocean, twinkled like the stars during a meteor shower. Kira began to take the lead but stopped abruptly, causing me to frown in confusion. Before I could ask, my eyes descended onto the man leaning against the doorway with thirty – give or take – men behind him. Enzo smirked, arching a brow at us.

"Well, isn't this a wonderful surprise," he drawled, eyes lazily skimming over the crowd before settling onto me. "He's waiting for you."

"As always," I replied. "He's an excellent follower. Not so much as a leader, however. "

Enzo shrugged. "I don't disagree. He's too ambitious for my liking. Too... *insane*. But all great leaders are."

"I think you're thinking about the dead ones," I remarked, taking a step forward until I was beside Kira, whose spine was as straight as a stick, her beady eyes never leaving Enzo, always watching, always tracking. "Are you here to stop us?"

"Not entirely," he began to walk towards me, causing Nero and Xander to cock their guns in his direction. Enzo halted, and then his smile broadened as he held his hands up. "I have a proposition."

"I doubt I'll agree but let me entertain you for a moment."

A wicked expression contorted his face. "I'll help you kill Calix if you just leave me and my business alone."

"And why would I ever agree?"

"Because I'll give you Violetta. You already lost one of your loved ones, why lose another?" his rhetorical question lacked all the sympathy that his face showed.

I studied Enzo carefully, pretending to be mulling over the idea when in fact I was nothing but amused, and disgusted all at the same time. I saw the flicker of hope in his eyes – hope that I would show mercy for his life but I was through with mercy, and I intended on killing them all.

"You don't get it," I laughed breathily in disbelief. "It's not about

Calix or his betrayal. I don't put him on a high pedestal. I could hardly give a fuck about him. That's not why I'm doing this. I'm doing this for every innocent person who you've stripped away their freedom for greed and power. I'm the judge because no one else will punish you for your crimes."

Enzo's smile fell. "How unfortunate."

"Not entirely. The best part is that I get to kill sick fuckers like you," I grinned, sinisterly, and then I attacked him, catching him off guard.

As soon as I moved, the rest of my soldiers followed, all of them attacking Enzo's men that rushed into the room. I slammed Enzo against the wall, avoiding his punch to my stomach, and kneed him in the guts. Enzo groaned as I threw him across the wooden floorboards. I didn't give him any time to rest as I unsheathed my dagger, kneeling to press the blade against his cheek.

"Do you want to know what I did to Barak?" I asked. Enzo glared at me. "It's okay; I'll answer the question. I had his mistress kill him." Enzo's eyes widened slightly. "I let her get justice for the years of torment. Don't worry, I also had my fun. I made sure he screamed in pain before handing him bloody to the woman he claimed to love so much."

"So, that's how you found us," Enzo chuckled, blood dripping from his nose.

I pressed the blade deeper against his cheek, enough to create an open wound. I relished in the red liquid that trickled out and smiled, maniacally. "People often say love is a weakness – the reason why loyalty wavers. But I have to disagree. Because betrayal comes from those with little to lose. They are arrogant, think that they are untouchable but what they don't see is that makes them a bigger target."

"Are you saying I have nothing to lose?"

"I'm saying you already lost everything," I arched a brow, "the second Calix took your throne."

Enzo growled and grabbed my wrist, twisting the dagger out of my hand. But when it fell from one hand, it was only captured by the other. He was surprised by the maneuver, completely thrown off so he didn't see the knife impaling his torso. Enzo's cry of pain was music to my ears as I withdrew the dagger, cleaning the blood on his black trousers. Blood spilt from his mouth, nose, and ears, as well as the wound on his stomach. I went to attack again, inflict more pain, because I wasn't entirely satisfied with the damage when I felt someone grip my shoulder and fling me back. I collided with a group of my own soldiers and Serpents' men. I grunted when I met the ground, my elbow skimming the unfinished flooring, and the previous wound on my torso sent a shock of pain throughout my system. My dagger had flown from my grasp, sliding across the ground into the middle of the room. For a short minute, I glanced around the room, taking in the war occurring at this moment. I checked on my soldiers, Xander, Kira and finally, Nero. He killed with passion, leaving no space to breathe before going in for the kill. He opted for a gun instead of a knife. He had always chosen a gun, whilst I preferred knives. He was merciless, tearing limbs from many men, and then maiming some more. I, then searched for the culprit and found a large, burly man helping Enzo escape the room. Annoyance powered me to get back onto my feet, and I ran towards them, grabbing my dagger on the way. I yelled in anger, swerving the men that tried to stop me, injuring them in the process by sliding across the ground, my blade meeting their shins. Jumping back onto my feet, I thundered towards the large man and pierced my dagger into his back. He grunted, recoiling in agony, but loosened the grip on Enzo, who lay crippled on the floor.

"You fool!" Enzo spat out, blood drenching his very expensive suit.

I paid no attention and took the spare knife attached to my thigh, using it to impale the large man's lower back. With two daggers deep in his body, the man snarled as he spun around, trying to grab me but I jumped back and kicked him in the stomach, watching him crash against the wall, breaking the weak plaster. The impact would not normally knock out a man that size but the bleeding within would. Enzo paled as his source of security lay incapacitated on the floor as I towered over the man, withdrawing the knives from his back. Blood poured out, profusely. Instead of enjoying the image, I turned back to Enzo with murder on my mind. He was fearful from the way his body shook, and his eyes were so wide I thought they would fall from their sockets. He shuffled back, trying to create a distance between us, but failed miserably.

"Stop wasting your energy. I hate weak prey," I taunted, maliciously and reached for his arm.

"You're going to die, Aria," he promised, in abhorrence.

"They all say that, and then they end up dead. You aren't different," With my dagger, I pressed against his throat. "Where are Calix and

Violetta?"

"Does it matter if I tell you? You'll find them anyways," Enzo snapped. "I hope he kills her before you get there."

"Do you have no love for your own sister?" I scoffed. "You disgust me."

Enzo blinked at me before cackling, deranged, taking me off guard. "You still don't know."

The smirk on his face was infuriating. I wanted to punch him so badly. "What don't I know?"

Nonchalantly, he looked at me in pure amusement like a chained animal. "Oh, Aria."

"Don't irritate me, Enzo. I'm the one with the dagger in my hand."

"Violetta isn't *my* sister."

I was not sure whether to believe him or not, but my gut told me that he wasn't lying. He wouldn't benefit from lying, not when he was practically dead meat. Enzo laughed at the surprise that must have been visible on my face. I searched for his eyes, wondering if he was telling the truth, wondering why he had pretended she was his sister.

But before I could ask, he mused, "Makes it easier to watch men tear her apart though, like your bitch of a friend that shot all my men."

I saw red. I acted before I could think.

Enzo was stunned as I shot onto my feet and then dragged his body across the room, my grip tightening around the arm. I kept walking with no destination in mind until I saw the balcony. Until I saw a death befitting a man who wanted to climb the ladder. He left a blood trail behind him, thrashing in my hold but I did not let him go; I kept walking. Through the bloodbath. Through the battle. Through the dead bodies of men who chose power for the price of the innocent's lives. I kept walking until I reached the edge of the balcony; a lack of enclosures allowed me to check out how high the fall was. It also brought my attention to the speared garden gates at the bottom.

Then I peered back at Enzo, who had finally pieced together what was occurring in my destructively sadistic mind. He looked at me in horror. "You wouldn't."

"You probably won't die when you reach the ground. But that's fine – you'll die from extensively bleeding. You'll die alone. But you'll die, Enzo," I thinned my eyes. "And so will all your men. But for Violetta? I'll skin those who touch her, I'll break the skulls of those who even thought about harming her. I'll *protect* her. But you, Enzo?" I cocked my head to the side, a slow smirk growing on my face as the man beneath me seethed in hatred. "No one will protect you."

He opened his mouth to speak but I didn't want to hear the words that held no importance to me and, using all my strength, threw him off the balcony. His screams had me grinning as I watched his body fall before it sank onto the gates, a spear impaling him straight through his stomach, ripping his body apart. Enzo's choked gasps told me he survived the fall, but not for long. His death would be long, and agonizing, and he would experience every second of it until the last drop of blood left his unfortunate body.

"Aria, we're good," Kira said, from behind me. "I think we are done here."

I stared at Enzo's blood-soaked corpse. "Actually, we're just getting started."

CHAPTER 56

heavy is the crown

As we moved towards Violetta's location, we joined up with Mark's team, who also suffered a few injuries but nothing too severe. Whilst I double checked that no one was not badly hurt, Ciara took a moment to pull Mark to the side and inform him of the news. I couldn't stop the guilt that hit me like a crushing boulder when Mark's face contorted from confusion to rage. Pure, blinding rage. My feet were frozen in their spot because of the overwhelming feeling of guilt. Because I couldn't save her. I couldn't move, not even when Mark shoved Ciara's arms away from him, or when Kira stood in his path as he tried to leave. I couldn't move, as I watched my friend break down from the loss of the woman he loved most in the world. Xander and Nero had to grasp his arms when Mark spun around intending to head back to Sophie.

Tears streamed down his face as he thrashed his arms, snarling, *"Let me fucking go. Let me fucking go!"*

Kira tried to reason with him, so did Ciara, but he wouldn't listen. Their words flew right over his head. Eyes glared straight ahead, refusing to obey the orders, resisting the people who cared the most about him. I ignored the looks of grief and sorrow everyone shared, as I finally forced myself to walk towards Mark.

One foot in front of the other. One step at a time.

Until I was staring directly at him. Until his dark green eyes found mine. Until his entire body gave in, his arms stopped flailing about, his shoulders slugging in defeat, the anger on his face melting into exhaustion and grief.

Until he allowed himself to accept the reality.

"I'm sorry, Mark. I'm so sorry I couldn't stop her. I'm so sorry I couldn't stop her. I'm so sorry that we lost her… that you lost her," I swallowed my sob, blinking away the tears, "I'm *so* sorry. But there's a little girl in this huge mansion waiting for us to save her. Sophie didn't die for no reason, but if we don't save Violetta and stop Calix – she will have." I placed a hand on his shoulders, his eyes tracking me. "So, can you do this with us or not?"

He studied me for the longest moment, but I didn't look away, patiently waiting for his response. Xander and Nero slowly took their hands off him, and for a short second, I thought he was going to run, but instead, he straightened his spine and nodded stiffly. "Always."

My smile was weak but a smile, nonetheless. "Good. Let's go."

With Kira and Xander leading us, I silently trailed behind everyone else with Nero by my side. The tension was so thick I could slice it with a knife, and I knew everyone was on edge. Everyone was afraid that we would lose another friend. Everyone was afraid that we would lose. And so was I. But I could not show that fear. I had to hold them together, I had to be strong because that was why I was the leader, their boss. I was going to destroy the Serpents and burn down their operation with them. To my surprise, Nero entwined his fingers with mine as we closed the distance between us and Calix. My eyes flickered up just as he looked down. Then the corner of his lips twitched up. I lifted a brow, asking a silent question. He responded by quickly pecking my lips.

"I love you, Aria," he murmured. "I love you more than I can even begin to explain how much I love you."

"I love you too, Nero. Beyond how much you can see," I replied, squeezing his hand. "We're going to be alright."

"Yes, we will."

He kissed me once more. This time longer, stopping me in my tracks. It took my breath away yet at the same time, it gave me the air I didn't recognize I needed. It sent ripples of electricity throughout my body and kept me grounded to the earth all at once. It was like being on the beach and all I could hear was the gentle crashes of the waves against the shoreline. It was toe-curling, mind-consuming, heart-stopping. It was everything. And then, when he pulled away from me, as our eyes fixated on each other, a broad smile on our lips, I knew everything was going to be okay. Because he was here. Right here with me. And I couldn't imagine it any other way.

"Aria!" Kira exclaimed, popping the bubble around me and Nero. I looked over at her, and she pointed at the closed door up ahead. "That must be it."

"Alright," I glanced at Nero, who gave me a confident bob of his head before I looked out at everyone else. "Let's do this."

Kira shot out the orders, and everyone fell into position. One group heading out of the mansion to circle the perimeter, and the other in two single lines behind Kira and Xander. Nero's men blended with mine, and he sent some back on the path we were on to protect us from behind. With sixty soldiers surrounding the room, preventing the Serpents from escaping and protecting us from all angles, I gave Kira a short nod and she moved towards the door, armed, gun in hand. Then she kicked the door down, the oak frame cracking at the force. The doors flung wide open, and I inhaled sharply at the sight of Violetta tied to a chair in the middle of the empty room. She looked barely conscious, and her body was littered in purplish-green bruises. She was still wearing that pretty poufy green dress from my engagement party, but it was no longer pretty and was torn and tattered, grim and dirt clinging to the fabric and her skin. Her wrists looked sore from the ties, as with her ankles, red from rope burn.

"Vi," I whispered, and pushed ahead with only one thing in mind. When I reached her, I bent down, my hands wavering as I was terrified to touch her. She looked so serene, but I knew the exhaustion must have caught up with her. I brushed the strands of hair away from her face and kissed the top of her head, before turning to Mark. "Take her."

Before he could take a step, a gun cocking had us all stilling. I slowly looked past Violetta and met traitorous green eyes belonging to the man that destroyed the lives of so many people. He smirked, lazily walking towards us, gun pointing at Violetta.

"Finally," he began. "I was waiting for you."

Calix, in all his glory, stood in front of me. The white shirt he wore was not buttoned at the top, and his sleeves were pushed to his elbows, revealing the many scars that marked him. I had already seen the scars on his body, but for the first time ever, I was seeing them in a different light. I was seeing them for what they were. Not wounds from the pain he endured with the Serpents, but the wounds he had received whilst working with the Serpents.

Warily, I stood up, and rolled my shoulders back, ignoring the aches from the punches I had taken whilst fighting his men, the adrenaline beginning to wear away. "You're the last man standing."

He tilted his head to the side. "You killed Enzo."

"He's bleeding out, painfully slowly, but I'm sure he'll be dead in a few minutes. The spear didn't pierce his heart; fortunately for us, he will suffer more."

"You're truly amazing, Aria," he chuckled. From the corner of my eye, I saw Nero take a step forward. "It was about time. I knew he'd stab me in the back eventually. I'm assuming Barak must be dead too."

"And Viktor, but you had that taken care of."

His smirk widened. "He was a liability. I'm surprised he wasn't dead sooner."

"I had plans."

"You mean torture," he corrected, with a laugh.

"You already knew of my plans beforehand, but now I intend to carry them out on you," I smiled, wickedly. "I'm going to kill you, Calix."

"No, you won't, because you'll kill everyone else," my smile dropped slightly and Calix caught that, raising a brow. "You didn't think I'd take precautions? You're a sneaky woman, Aria. A man needs precautions."

"What are you on about?" I snarled.

He strode towards me, leisurely, that damn smirk still playing on his lips. "This villa will not be refurbished until it's demolition. Then, I'll build my empire here."

I didn't understand his coded words, but I knew I didn't have time. My eyes flickered away from Calix and moved around the rooms, catching sight of the tools left here and there, along with other equipment used for renovating. And finally, my eyes landed on the small wires in the corner of the room that ran upwards before meeting the ceiling where a small device blinked. I took a step back and glanced to the other side of the room, and then behind me.

Four bombs attached to the ceiling. One in each corner.

"Surprise!" Calix grinned when my wide eyes found his. "Now, you'll do what I say or risking killing your people."

"Aria," Kira breathed, having seen the explosives.

I ignored her, glaring at Calix. "You wouldn't. We were once your family, Calix. You wouldn't harm us."

"Sophie's dead," he said, bluntly. "That should be proof enough. And what did I say to you, Aria? I don't have a family."

I didn't know what to do, stuck in my position, unable to pounce or I would risk killing everyone. Calix closed the distance between us, his hand brushing Violetta's hair, a soft look in his eyes surprised me but it disappeared as soon as he peered up. Sinister eyes that conned me into thinking they were purely green were as icy as the temperature of the room, despite being in a hot country.

"Tell them to leave, Aria. Only you will stay. Or I'll kill them all, even the ones outside the room," he threatened.

I didn't want to listen, stubborn and pissed off at the man I brought into my family, but I couldn't risk everyone's lives. Without looking away from Calix steel eyes, I commanded loudly, "Everyone, get out."

"Aria!" Ciara gasped, at the same time as Xander yelled, "No!"

My eyes snapped over to them, thin and humorless, "Now."

Kira stepped forward but halted as soon as Calix shifted the gun to her. Her eyes sent stabbing glares that promised to put him deeper than six feet and watch him be buried alive. Her jaw clenched in anger. "Aria, this could be a trap."

"I'm not going to ask again," Translation: *I don't want to take the risk.* I held Kira's arctic cobalt eyes, silently praying that she understood my orders. "Go, now."

She didn't look away for a pregnant moment, before backing down, turning to everyone else. "Let's go." Everyone was hesitant to move, even Xander refused to leave, but Kira's gaze was powerfully intense. "*Go.*"

One by one, they all left, throwing looks in my direction, until the only ones left were Kira, Xander, and Nero. Xander's eyes burned with anger, but Kira gently pushed him, and he stormed out. Kira took one look at Calix before glimpsing at me. She stiffly bobbed her head and then disappeared out of the doors.

Finally, Nero remained.

Calix arched a brow. "Staying, lover boy?"

"I'm her husband," Nero responded, gruffly. "Have some respect."

Calix didn't like the tone of his voice, annoyance flickering in his traitorous eyes. "You have some nerve."

Nero took a step towards me. "You're a bastard."

"Nero," I murmured, and he looked at me. I shook my head slowly, hoping he would not push Calix any further. Nero didn't want to obey, but did anyway, tightening his jaw. I peered over at Calix, and then at Violetta. "Can I ask at least why you are doing this?"

"Will it change anything?" Calix asked, after a still moment.

My eyes never left Violetta. A girl so helpless, a girl caught up in the power-hungry world of the Underground. A girl. Then, I turned my focus to Calix. A man so consumed with greed that he threatened the lives of young girls and boys, just like Violetta.

"No, it won't."

Calix held my gaze, his eyes were narrowed, and his lips were pressed together before he said, "When I was a boy, I had everything except my father. But I had my mother and that was enough. She had given me everything, anything I wanted. We were poor, barely surviving, the bottom of the barrel. And she risked her life to keep me safe. I grew up with nothing and when I asked about my father, my mother would turn me away. And then one day, before I turned twelve, my mother came home in tears, and I had never seen her so broken."

I tracked his movement as he strolled to the other side of the room, dropping the arm that was holding the gun to his side.

Calix continued, "It wasn't until nine months later that I finally saw the cause of her pain. Until I was holding a baby girl in my arms whilst my mother died on the bed." Piercing green eyes gazed at Violetta, and I finally pieced the puzzle together.

"She's *your* sister," I breathed out, remembering the first day Violetta allowed a man to be near her – the very man that was holding her hostage.

I could remember the hopeful look on her face when he promised to protect her, and the heartbreak on his when she told him that he reminded her of her brother. It was because they were siblings. And she couldn't remember that.

"My mother died before I could even ask who the father was, and I was left with a baby girl, all alone and trapped in a favela with barely anything to our names. For a short period, I brought her up, gave her everything like my mother gave me, and when I was old enough, I left her on the Rossi's doorstep. They were well known in our town, and I knew they could look after her. I just never knew they were so powerful and rich," Calix smiled, bitterly. "I set off to find our father.

And I found him."

I finally saw the similarities between Calix and Violetta, from their startling green eyes that illuminated exotically in different hues, or their similar facial bone structure with high cheekbones, straight nose, and sharp jaw. I could finally see what had been in front of me for months; what I had been missing this entire time.

And then I saw it again.

From the brief image that I glimpsed in a file Kira gave me when we discovered Spain was a huge factor in the Serpents operation. A figurehead I had seen on television for weeks and weeks now. The man who was Violetta's father.

"The King of Spain."

Calix's dark smile broadened. "My mother was his mistress. I was his firstborn, but my mother had no status or anything to her name, so he rejected me. But he still wanted my mother, and for some twisted reason, she still wanted him, even when he refused to look after us." He shook his head in disbelief and disappointment, an incredulous laugh leaving his lips. "The king refused to look after his people because it could ruin him."

"So, you want revenge," I concluded quietly, but Calix heard me and grinned.

"I do. I was at a loss for years until the Petrovs came into my life. One could call it fate but whatever it was, it led me straight to Dimitri Petrov," Calix's eyes flickered with an unreadable emotion, too quick for me to figure out. "He found a child, homeless and fragile, and brought that child up. He loved me more than his own children. He was my way to revenge."

"Does the King know about Violetta?" Nero questioned, his hand on the gun tucked into his waistband.

"Yes," his response stunned me. "But he only paid attention to her because the Rossis were one of the most influential Spanish families at the time. Violetta was only a toddler, and the King welcomed her because she was now worth something, whilst I was left to rot. He gave her a title I should've gotten." His jaw clenched, as his fists tightened until they were white from the lack of blood circulating, face contorted with fury. "I helped the Petrovs with their entire operation, planning to one day take back the throne, and the Underground with it. I was going to have it all," he paused, and then slowly, too calmly, looked up at me. "Until your family took it away."

Nero shifted closer to me, but I didn't move an inch, not even when the maniacal look on Calix's face sent chilly, alarming shivers down my spine. I didn't move away from Violetta, as I affirmed, "We killed the Petrovs."

"Every single of one of them. Until there was no longer a trace of them on this planet. And I lost everything once more; I had to start from the bottom all over again. I didn't know about the Russian or Italian mafias back then, but when, one by one, your family picked them off, I learnt all about you guys. I learnt your weaknesses and your strengths. Your allies and your enemies. At the time, I wasn't aware that Enzo was Violetta's adopted brother – I had completely forgotten about her and the Rossis. So, whilst Enzo was rebuilding the Serpents, I climbed the ranks until I was powerful enough to take over. Plotting the day that I would finally get revenge on the Italians and Russians for what they did. And when I heard about Enzo's plans with Violetta, the final pieces of my own plan fell into place."

"The Petrovs were traitors. They betrayed us. They stopped at nothing to destroy my family!" I spat out; every word accentuated with rancor. "They killed my mother's unborn child. I could've had a brother, Calix!" Nero seized my arms, holding me back from attacking Calix when the wrath blinded me. "But they wanted more power and look where that has taken them."

"I won't apologize for their actions, not when your family has punished them for it. But I am the only living person that is linked to the Petrovs, and I intend to finish off what they started," he vowed, sinisterly. "And it begins with her."

As his eyes moved back to Violetta, so did my own, and there it was - the final piece to the entire puzzle. I shared a look with Nero, his eyes darkening with concern and rage like he couldn't decide which to feel first. When I turned back to Calix, I saw the smirk on his lips and a diabolical twinkle in his wicked green eyes, and he knew I had figured it out too.

"You're going to hold her for ransom," The plan dawning on me. "That's why you needed her. You're going to threaten the King by revealing Violetta, and your own, true heritage."

Calix's smirk widened until he reminded me of the Joker. "I'm going to do one better," then he pulled something out from his pocket – a remote – and pressed the button. "I'm going to kill her on live television, just as the King hands the throne to his son."

My eyes were wide as they shot from Calix and then to Violetta, where I finally noticed the red lights, small as a pin, blink on her shoulders. Nero jerked back, pulling the gun out to point at Calix, who didn't even flinch as he kept his eyes on me.

Slowly, I gained my composure, hesitant to make any sudden movements, drawing my brows together as I calmly asked, "What will that gain you?"

"Violetta is his only living daughter, and on top of that, she is an heiress with millions to her name. A gold mine. Perfect for political alliances. The King wouldn't want to lose that. So, when I demand he gives the throne to me, the first people I will come after are the Russians…" Calix languidly peered at Nero, tilting his head to the side, still smiling. "…And the Italians."

"You're a monster," I snarled, spitefully, my hands shaking at my sides, itching for my dagger or my gun, anything to kill Calix with.

"And you were a fool," he laughed. "The biggest fool to think you could save them all. I'm going to make you watch as I take over the Underground, and then the world. I'm going to burn everyone you love, and make you watch. And once I'm done, I'll play with you like a doll, ruin you until I hear you beg for me to kill you too."

"I don't beg for anyone," I arched a brow in amusement. "Especially not you."

"I beg to differ," Calix's eyes darkened. "You were quite the beggar in bed."

"You sick fuck!" Nero growled.

I smiled at Calix, crossing my arms over my chest. "Don't get it twisted, Calix. It was always the other way round."

Green eyes blazed in fury as my taunting sneer began to irk him, and before I could blink, his smile dropped and he cocked his gun at Nero, who refused to drop his own gun, glaring at Calix with such an intense hatred that would have sent anyone running. "Always knows what buttons to push but you should be careful, or I'll kill lover boy here."

"No, you won't. You want him to suffer too," I rolled my eyes at the suggestion like it was the dumbest thing I ever heard. "He can't suffer if he's dead."

"Perhaps not," Calix's Cheshire cat smile returned, waving the remote in his hand. "But then, there's always Violetta. So, who are you going to save? Him, or her?"

"Aria," Nero whispered, and I glanced at him. The darkness in his eyes dispelled like the clouds on a stormy day and glowed like the sun in the summer. The depth of his blue irises swam scintillatingly with adoration, admiration, and assurance. "I love you."

I couldn't look away from his hypnotic eyes, as I murmured, "And I love you too. But do you trust me, Nero?"

The corner of his lips lifted until he broke into a heart-shattering smile. "With all my life."

He trusted me. With his entire life. Even if that meant sacrificing him for Violetta. He trusted me. So, I mirrored his smile as I replied, "Good."

And then I shot at a bomb on the ceiling.

CHAPTER 57

and it all falls down

They say when you die your life flashes before your eyes. That didn't happen to me the first time, and it didn't happen the second. Every piece of flesh and every bone of my body ached as I coughed, dusting the rubble off me as I staggered onto my feet. I blinked, my sight was blurry at first but after a few seconds, I could see crystal clear. The ceiling had collapsed as one bomb went off, triggering the other three to explode successively afterwards. Almost instantly, the canopy caved in, and the next thing I saw was Nero jumping in front of me.

Except he didn't shield me.

My eyes moved to the back of the room, settling on the large frame that towered over a significantly smaller body. Neither moved. My heart stopped. The air was caught in my throat. I froze in my spot. And then, I saw it. Nero grunted as he rolled his shoulders back when straightening his spine, arms falling to his side. He peered over his shoulders, eyes finding mine, and I let out a shaky, relieved breath of air when I saw that Violetta was unharmed.

Nero grunted, "You're fucking crazy."

"Is she okay?" I asked, stepping carefully through the chaos until I was by his side. He gave me a quick look over, likely checking for any visible injuries, before answering with a terse nod. Violetta was still unconscious, knocked out by whatever drug Calix had injected into her.

"Take her to Kira; she'll help disable the bomb but be careful. I'm going to find Calix." I searched the room quickly until my eyes settled onto the small remote a few meters from Violetta. As Nero began to untie Violetta, I swooped the remote into my hands. The small device blinked, dusty but still in good condition, and I knew this was connected to the small bombs on Violetta. Carefully, I turned to Nero and passed him the device. "Don't break it. Hand it straight to Xander."

"Okay," His blue eyes simmered.

There was something he wanted to say, I knew it, but there wasn't enough time so after one last smile, I turned to leave. And then his hand shot out, twisting around my wrist and he pulled me into his chest, where he held me in his arms. Stunned, I didn't move as he sighed and tightened his grip.

"Please, *please*, stay safe. I'll come back for you."

I relaxed in his arms. "Okay."

He finally let me go, sparkling blue eyes holding me in a trance before they turned away as he scooped Violetta's limp body into his arms like a knight in shining armor, and slipped out of the villa from the back entrance of the room which led to the backyard. I waited until he disappeared out of sight before forcing myself to look away and hunt down Calix. The destruction of the room left little to salvage which meant Calix must have escaped before the room collapsed. I ducked under the piled pieces of ceiling, pushing through the rubble until I found a barely secure corridor. Discarding my empty magazine to the side, I clipped a fresh one into my gun and moved silently down the hallway, my eyes flickering into any empty rooms I passed until I found a set of marble stairs. They did not look safe to climb up, with no barrier on the sides as they spiraled up to the second floor, leading to the west wing of the villa. Moving away from the central section of the estate, I took my chances and climbed the stairs, making sure I was constantly aware of my surroundings. The west wing, unlike its counterpart, was renovated from top to bottom with fresh new ceilings and flooring, all completely furnished with lavish decor and ornaments. The floor was wider than in the east wing, with fewer rooms that made up in size as opposed to quantity. I assumed they must have been bedrooms. Which meant that further down would have to lead to the master bedroom. The oak doors, with curved embellishments that spiraled up the side like vines, were closed, unlocked but from their golden handles – dust stains – definitely touched. I didn't hesitate to kick the doors open, ignoring the loud *slam* as it met with the bedroom wall when I saw Calix by the balcony door similar to the one I had seen in the eastern wing. The one I had thrown Enzo off.

"Those doors were expensive," he stated, my eyes catching sight of the bandage in one hand and the blood on the other. His right fingers were damaged from the explosion. I smirked. He narrowed his eyes. "This isn't a fair fight."

"I didn't ask for it to be."

Regardless of his injury, I knew he was capable of fighting with his left hand as well as he would have with his right hand. If not, better. He knew it too.

"You know, Aria," he began, settling on the bed as he tended to his wound, ignoring the gun that pointed at him. "I don't know why we are fighting."

"Maybe because you've ruined the lives of so many children, and other innocent people, at their own expense? Or because you tried to kill me, and your own sister? This is just going off a whim here. Need I say more?"

Calix smirked over his shoulder. "You've made your point."

"I don't think I have," I stated, warily moving in front of him, his emerald eyes tracking me with complete calmness.

There was a time when those jade eyes worshipped me and the very ground I walked on. They offered comfort to our fallen soldiers and our broken ones. They held strength, courage, and honor. They were loyal to the core.

And now…

Now, they looked like they belonged to a stranger.

"I don't think you get it, Calix," I paused for emphasis. "I'm *going* to *kill* you," the words were a vow. "*Slowly*. So, by the time I'm done, you'll be *begging* for mercy."

He looked at me as if that was an outrageous claim. "I don't beg for anyone."

Red lips coiled into a wicked smirk.

"Oh, sweetheart, I'm not just anyone," I cocked my gun, hearing the bullet click into place, itching to be released as my beast restlessly waited for the blood. "Watch how you'll beg for me."

No one moved. No one breathed.

And then the sound of a gunshot made the villa shake, birds scattering from the balcony. I twisted to the side, narrowly missing the flying bullet, when Calix jumped onto his feet, both hands on a gun that he didn't think I noticed. I wasn't dumb. He took another shot, and then another, and then another, but I swerved them all, ducking, swirling, spinning out of their paths. The bullets left memorable cavities in the refurbished room, pelting the walls with holes when they failed to pierce me. I grabbed the stool by the vanity, and threw it in his direction, intending it to distract him rather than injure him. That momentary second of distraction gave me time to send a few bullets into him. I didn't expect to hit the target immediately, knowing Calix was well trained to avoid my attacks, but I did grin when a bullet skimmed his arm. Calix grunted loudly, clutching that arm as blood trickled out. The window of distraction disappeared as he tossed the stool to the side and sent a few more bullets my way as he crossed the room. But I was already out the door. I heard his thundering footsteps as he chased after me. But I was quicker, leaping over the banister and landing onto the staircase. I looked up and saw him peering down, his eyes flickering with surprise that made me smile. And then, I was off again. I heard the bullets that followed, ducking when fragments of the plaster blasted off the walls from the impact. I kept running until I was in the center of the villa, where I first entered, and pressed my back against the wall, blending into the shadows, not breathing as he ran past me.

And then he stopped.

His body was unmoving, but I knew his eyes were working.

Cagily and cautiously, I slipped out of the shadows. With his back to me, I brought my gun up, my finger on the trigger. And then I released my hold.

Calix spun around.

Vivid green eyes found mine.

Shocked.

Yet, wickedly amused.

The bullet shot out from my gun. But Calix moved quicker. Whirling his body to the side, the bullet nicked his cheek before piercing the vase behind him. It shattered into hundreds of shards from the impact. Before I could comprehend what had happened, Calix kicked the gun out of my hand, and I snapped back to reality. My weapon flew across the room, so I returned the courtesy by disarming

Calix as well, shoving my foot into his stomach and knocking his gun from his hand with my heeled boot. Calix hissed and threw a punch which I evaded, swerving to the side, before throwing my own blow. But he ducked. And so, I kneed him in the stomach. He groaned and staggered back, a table toppling behind him at contact. I didn't give him a second to breathe. I broke his left rib cage with a single kick. Then, I struck his face with a hammering punch. His face knocked back, blood spilling out from his nose whilst he stumbled, trying to find his footing. I didn't let him. I threw punch after punch, kick after kick, blow after blow, until he was bleeding so much that I could have used the liquid to paint a wall. Calix was hunkered on the floor, laughing coarsely as he looked up at me. I wondered if he saw the bloodlust in my eyes. The anger from his betrayal. The sadness from his lies. I wondered if he cared.

"You lied. And you kept on lying," I suddenly whispered. His laughter came to a sudden halt. "At what point did you start to believe your lies?"

He studied me. His eyes were empty. No remorse. No mercy.

"When I fell in love with you."

I wished I believed him. I wanted to believe him. But I didn't.

"Did you love me?"

"Loving you made me lose my judgement," he revealed, eyes shifting away as if he couldn't face the truth. "Loving you made me… It made me forget why I was doing this."

"It made you human," I murmured, ruefully. I kissed my teeth, staring down at him. "But you'd rather be a monster. You *are* a monster. A heartless monster. You hate and hate, until it consumes you. The world is corrupted, and it's people like you who abuse the power you have and harm innocent bystanders because you fear that you will never feel enough." I soared over him. "Well, know this, Calix, you will never be enough."

"One day you'll understand."

"No, I won't," I shook my head, drawing out the dagger that Kira gifted me. His eyes flickered to it. "Because you lied about loving me. You wouldn't have done that if you knew what love was."

"I do love you, Aria."

"How do I know you aren't lying now?"

"You don't," was his response. It was as cold and aloof as the look in his eyes. There was not a single ounce of emotion. "But you'll die trying to find out."

Suddenly, the doors surrounding us flung open and Serpent men flooded into the room. They circled me; guns pointed at me. From head to toe, drenched in black attire with a serpent embossed on their chests. All Serpent members had a snake tattoo. I saw one on Calix. Or maybe, I wasn't looking closely enough to realize it was ink and not a wound. Distracted by his sinful touch, and loathed-filled kisses, I didn't look beyond the mask he wore. Deep down, I knew I would be scared to find the truth. Deep down, I knew Calix Zervas was lost a long time ago. And deep down, I wanted to be the one to save him. But as his men pulled him onto his feet, handing him a napkin to clean the crispy, dry blood on his face, I knew I would be the one to kill him.

"It seems that you're outnumbered, Aria," Calix grinned, face cleared of the blood, but I saw the stains it left in its place. "Surrender and I'll let you live."

"Did you really think it would be this easy?" I arched a brow.

Calix frowned.

And then the second wave of soldiers rushed in. Except this time, these were my soldiers. I saw, for a fraction of a second, that Calix was surprised as he saw familiar faces surrounding him and his men, gun pointed at them. Kira, Xander, and Nero strode in as soon as everyone was in position. I grinned at my family before turning to Calix. His eyes steeled on the three people behind me.

Afterwards, he gazed at me as I said, "I'll never surrender."

His glacial eyes thinned. "Then you'll never live."

Kira made the first move, shooting the two men who stood beside Calix before anyone could blink. As soon as those bodies dropped to the floor, chaos erupted. Serpent men converged on my soldiers, knives and guns were drawn out, blood and smoke suffocating us. I didn't pay attention to the mayhem around me and zeroed in on Calix, who froze like a deer in headlights. He snapped out of his thoughts as I lunged for him, dagger in hand. He whipped to the side, evading my attacks, before drawing out his own dagger. Dagger to dagger, we fought with the intention to leave neither alive. Except, that was what I wanted him to believe. From the corner of my eye, I saw Kira weave through a large group of men who surrounded her, foolishly ignoring Ciara, who pounced like a cheetah from behind. With Ciara now by her side, Kira ripped through Serpent men more swiftly and easily. Both the girls, back-to-back, tore apart legs and arms, knocking out guns, piercing bodies with silver blades, leaving a trail of blood in their wake. Then, there was Xander, who was violently vicious, taking the time to rid the Serpent men from their limbs also. He was hungry for blood, cleaving apart their bodies. One could see how he enjoyed killing as if he did it for sport. Nero was more precise with his killings, not wasting time to linger on a dying body before moving onto the next man. I saw him glancing my way as he snapped a man's head off his spine.

Calix struck his knife to my unprotected left side, but I grabbed his wrist, fighting against his strength. His jaw clenched as I twisted the dagger out of his hold. And then, his knee met my stomach. The impact had thrown me off guard, my hand slipping from his wrist as I staggered back. Calix attacked again before I could recover. His punch landed on my face. And then another. I reeled back from the pain; my dagger fell onto the floor with a loud *clang*. I heard someone call my name in panic, but my mind was spinning. I was spinning. Slipping. I saw the smirk on Calix's face like he knew he was winning. But I couldn't let him win. But I couldn't fight, feeling his blade slice my thigh. I wanted to scream from the burning agony, but I gritted my teeth and tried to fight him. But he was quick. Like a jaguar, he pounced and lunged, leaving no space for me to breathe. I could *feel* the blood pouring out of me like a leaking faucet. I panted, trying to defend myself. I didn't know how long I could go for. I just needed one second. One second to breathe and then I could fight. But he didn't give me a second. He knew that by giving me a second, he would be finished.

Calix's sadistic smile burned in my mind.

I need a second, I pleaded silently, *someone give me a second*.

And as if my prayers were heard, Calix stopped. His eyes widened as his body stilled. I inhaled sharply, brought my eyes to his and then the knife in the side of his body. Then I looked over his shoulder and saw Nero. Nero, with frightful cool blue eyes that blazed with dancing flames. Nero with blood splattered on his face. Nero, with his handle on the dagger shoved in Calix's body.

One second. It was all I needed.

Nero raised a brow at me, and I breathed slowly with relief, a smile faintly on my lips. He tilted his head to the side, asking a silent question: *shall I kill him, or do you want to?*

A soft shake of my head gave him his answer. Nero withdrew his blade, and Calix keeled over, clutching the wound. Blood spilt from in between his fingers.

I inhaled. Nero didn't move from behind Calix. Calix glanced up. I exhaled.

"You won't die here, Calix," I grabbed my dagger from the floor. "But your men will, and you'll watch your entire operation fall apart once more. I'm going to burn your kingdom to the ground."

"You won't be able to kill me," he snarled, glaring at me.

"Shall we bet on that?" Lazily, I smirked. Nero chuckled deeply from behind, prompting Calix to whip his head back with a scowl. "Take him away, Nero."

"Yes, ma'am," he grinned, reaching to seize Calix.

But he stepped back, avoiding both Nero and I as we circled him like a pair of vultures, and he was a fresh carcass. Calix's bottle-green eyes seethed with a mixture of wrath and malice.

"I'm going to kill you," Calix hissed, at both us and the strain from his leaking wound was clear.

My smile was nasty as it grew until it reached ear-to-ear. "Not if I get there first."

And then I lunged at him.

Calix's eyes enlarged, suddenly taken aback that he didn't realize my grasp on his gun until a second before I knocked him out with the muzzle. He crumpled onto the floor like a bag of bones. At the sight of his unconscious form, I rolled my shoulders back, the adrenaline beginning to fade away and the pain beginning to kick in, but I ignored the sensation as I glanced over my shoulder. I caught sight of Kira slicing apart the final Serpent soldier. Her glacial cyan eyes sparkled as she relaxed from her offensive position; gradually, her arms fell to her side, and her legs straightened from the slightly crouched stance she was in.

I saw her breathe in. *Deeply.*

Before she sighed, her shoulders loosening.

Then, her rich, enchanting blue eyes met mine.

It was over. Finally, over. An understanding passed between us. I stole a look around the room, catching a glimpse at my soldiers. Some had fallen with severe injuries, others with a few scratches, but we lost no one. Everyone was alive. One by one, I met everyone's eyes and then watched as they glanced at each other. I saw Xander, Ciara, and Mark. Whilst the latter two sent me a broad grin, coated in sadness from the loss of our closest friend, the former looked straight at me. His eyes were a shade lighter than my own – they could almost be mistaken for pure liquid gold – but they glistened like a thousand suns. I saw the ghost of a smile on Xander's lips.

And I smiled at the words he mouthed: *Well done, Boss.*

Finally, I took in the carnage left in our presence. Corpses on top of corpses. Mutilated, mangled, and maimed, as if they were left there by a pack of wolves. There was blood everywhere. On the unpainted walls, the incomplete flooring, staining the staircase, and the oak doors. It was everywhere. Blood. So much blood. But wasn't it a pretty sight?

"What do we do with the bodies?" Kira asked, strolling towards me, licking her lips, eyes burning with the same amount of sadistic enthusiasm as myself.

Narrowing my eyes, I took one last look around before turning to my second-in-command. "Burn them, shred them, feed them to the wolves. I don't fucking care."

She raised her brows in surprise before a slow-growing grin appeared on her face. I could only imagine all the atrocious ideas she had in mind. But I didn't care as I pointed at the still body coated in crimson liquid, lying limp on the floor.

"But leave him for me," I smiled, wickedly. "I have the most exciting plans prepared."

CHAPTER 58

assassin's creed

I stood outside the mansion only a couple of miles from the Whiteface mountains. I watched as the construction workers busied themselves, throwing orders at one another, preparing the expansion of our home. After much discussion, Kira and I chose to remain located at the new safe house. With stronger security systems, more security guards, and extra acres of land extending to farther than the eye could see belonging to us, we decided it would be safe to stay here instead of relocating. Especially, as there were too many of us with the additional newer members Xander would be bringing in soon from Serpent camps. It had been over a week since we had shut down the Serpents. For good. After informing my Aunt Gabrielle, we worked together to comb the ends of the Earth until there was nothing left to remember the Petrovs and the Serpents by. With Calix locked several meters under the mansion, the entire operation fell apart within a matter of days. Calix was a tyrant; many feared him, and his capture led to many fallouts as people couldn't decide whether to continue his legacy or run from us.

Many chose to run.

Nonetheless, I stripped apart the Serpents, weeding every last bad rodent out until all that was left were faint memories of what used to be. Whilst I was doing that, Xander, with the help of Nero and his men, hunted down Serpent camps. Because they were ghost camps, it meant they were very nomadic, moving quickly, which meant Xander and Nero had to act fast. With a careful plan devised, the men set off and managed to locate every camp. Along with Serpent men, and any leaders, who were all killed, they also found survivors of the Serpents' cruelty. Many were young children, a few were in their late twenties, and rarely, there were any older than thirty. Most often, they were girls. Xander brought them all back to our home. The new Manor. When I heard about our new arrivals, I immediately set about expanding our home, buying acres of land that hid behind pine trees blanketed in snow. The east side of the mansion would begin to climb up the mountain, whilst the west side met with the banks of the AuSable River, with enough green space for everyone to train and learn how to adapt to the woodland environment, and mountainous regions. These areas were much tougher than the ones we were usually surrounded by, but that only pushed everyone to work harder, become stronger, ensure that they could defend themselves even in the toughest of circumstances. Then, only a few miles from the mansion was a plot of land dedicated to our fallen soldiers.

Sophie was the first person we buried as soon as the area was available, her grave taking over a large part of the land, decorated in all sorts of flowers placed by the younger girls during her funeral. Sophie's family abandoned her many years ago, but her true family stood around her grave, watching her body descend and be concealed in clay. That day was particularly tough. Mark held Ciara as she wept. Kira stood stoically beside me, a black veil covering her face. Xander said the prayers. And I was the last person to leave her grave when the service was over. I think that day we all made a silent vow that she would be the last person we would lose. I knew I would honor that vow until the day I died.

"Watching them again?" Kira purred from behind, breaking my train of thought.

I didn't look back as I shrugged. "Need to make sure that everything is up to the correct standard."

"You mean, *your* standard," she corrected, and that caused me to look back, with an innocent grin. Kira, dressed in camo combat joggers, a ribbed black top, and stiletto boots, was impassive to the brisk, polar wind that blew past. Although I was wearing far more layers, I still shivered when the bitter air nipped against my skin.

She rolled her eyes. "You're a perfectionist. Speaking of which, I checked on the security. There are watchtowers stationed a few miles ahead, both to the east and west of the mansion. There will be a rotation of lookouts every six hours, so there'll be four shift changes in total. Snipers are armed, the main gate leading to the mansion is fully secured with Xander adding extra protection on top of our state-of-the-art locks. Inside, the Manor has been updated with new cameras, even in blind spots, excluding the bedrooms, bathrooms, and your office. These are all monitored from the security room in the western wing, which can only be accessed by key individuals such as you and I. All entrances have automatic locks, and the basement has an extra layer of security before reaching level zero where the gym, and training arenas are. Anything else?"

I blinked.

"Thank you, Kira," I managed to sputter.

"You have added every extra measure possible to keep us safe." "We're going to be okay," she assured, her blonde hair gently swayed with the wind. Then, with more emphasis, she said, "*Violetta* will be okay."

I swallowed and looked away. After bringing her straight home, Violetta was under the intensive care of our doctors until they said otherwise. A few days had gone by where she didn't wake up, but the doctors explained that it was because her body was under such an immense amount of stress that it had shut down to protect itself and recover, and she would wake in her own time. I sat beside her most days, holding her frail hands as I took in the numerous bruises on her body that were beginning to fade away. It wasn't until last night that she stirred whilst I was on the phone with Nero. I immediately hung up and focused my attention to Violetta. Her beautiful lavender eyes watered at the sight of me, and she hugged me so tightly, I almost lost my breath. But I relished in her warmth, knowing she was awake and safe, and embraced her as she cried.

Her recovery was slow, but she was getting there.

"Did you ask what she wants?" Kira murmured to me. I bobbed my head, mutely. "What did she say?"

My eyes followed two builders who began to hammer the frames for the eastern extension. "She doesn't want to see him."

Kira snorted, amused. "She rejected his invitation? The King of Spain's invitation? Can you even do that?"

My lips twitched at that.

During the aftermath, Nero had gotten into contact with the King, having been in business with his heir several years back. After informing the King of Calix's plan, and Violetta's existence, who he believed to be dead after unsuccessfully searching for her, he had extended an invitation to visit him and his family. I left the decision up to Violetta. She did not think twice as she told me no.

"I don't know this man. He claims to be my father, but he never taught me how to ride a bike, or read me bedtime stories, or promised to protect me. The Rossis might not have been my real parents, but they were real, and they were there," Violetta said, her dark green eyes with specks of blue and hazel that morphed together, forming a rare purple hue in the moonlight, stared aimlessly out of her bedroom window. "I can remember them. But I can't remember him because there's nothing to remember. He's not my family. You are."

I didn't push her to think otherwise and held her until her breathing slowed down, and she fell into a deep sleep, dreaming only of sweet things for the rest of the night.

"She's happy here," I stated to Kira.

Kira smiled at me, and then looked at the reconstructed mansion, as the snow fell around us. "I think we all are."

*

The basement was incredibly cold. It was dark with a few arc lights attached to the wall, hazily lighting the corridor. The only sound I could hear was the *tap tap tap* from my stilettos as I walked towards the steel door that looked as if it led to a vault. It had been nearly two weeks which should have given him enough time to recover from the damage inflicted, only for me to then inflict some more. With blood on my mind, I punched in the code to open the door, and with a sharp *beep*, the locks unlatched, and the door opened. The walls were unpainted, revealing the concrete structure of the crypt. There was a single bulb hanging from the ceiling, a mattress on one side and a bucket on the other. Sitting, with his back pressed against the wall, was Calix. His legs were chained, metal shackles extended from the center of the back wall, giving enough length for him to move about. But he rarely did.

He lifted his head up, lazily, looking up. "You finally came? I was wondering when you'd grace me with your presence."

I didn't reply, glancing down the hall to see Xander and Mark bring my exquisite tools. Calix silently watched them set a table against the wall, and roll out a variety of instruments, that he knew of all too well. I wondered if it ever crossed his mind that he would be on the receiving end one day. Mark didn't spare a look at Calix, disappearing down the corridor, whilst Xander faltered when he reached the door. I was admiring the collection in front of me when, from the corner of my eye, I watched Calix and Xander glare at each other. They were brothers, and yet here Calix was, waiting for his impending torture. Perhaps, Calix shared the same thoughts as me for a millisecond, as something shifted in his eyes. I wasn't sure what it was, but it was enough for Xander to turn away, and leave. I lifted a scythe, watching the silver gleam under the light.

"He hates me," Calix stated.

I glanced at him. "We all do."

"I know that. But he *hates* me," Calix frowned, as if he couldn't quite put a finger on what he was feeling.

"Yes. Yes, he does," I glanced down the corridor where Xander once was. "And what you're feeling is guilt. Which is a good thing. I was worried that you were too inhumane to feel anything."

Calix's dark eyes flickered to me like the bulb hanging above us. "So, what are you going to do to me?"

"I have yet to decide."

"Do you think you can hurt me? After all those years we've spent together."

"That went down the drain the second I found out who you truly were," I responded, nonchalantly. My calm demeanor was making him anxious; I saw it in his gaze. He didn't know what I was thinking, he didn't know how to prepare himself. I placed the scythe down on the table. "Plus, that didn't matter to you when you tried to poison me."

"I didn't want to, but you forced my hand," he hissed. Then he composed himself. "I love you, Aria."

"Love? Or loved?" I questioned, studying him.

"Love."

"I find that hard to believe," was my reply.

He narrowed his eyes. "Then, what is love to you?"

I didn't reply immediately, but when I did, I did so with a smile. "Waking every morning beside the only man I'll give my entire self to, knowing that he completely trusts me, and that I trust him too."

"And Nero is that man?" Calix laughed, haughtily. "You must be delirious to think that."

"And if I am?"

"You'll just find yourself with a broken heart…" then he paused, as if to rethink his statement, and then tilted his head to the side. "Or whatever is keeping you alive."

My lips curled, wickedly. "You know me so well."

Calix shook his head in disappointment. "I could've given you everything. I wanted to give you everything."

I wanted to laugh. I *should* have broken into fits of laughter. But instead, I rolled my eyes as my smile broadened in amusement, turning back to my tools of torture.

"What is it with men and thinking that they need to give a woman *everything* to show their love?" I scoffed in disbelief. "I don't want everything. All I wanted was to rescue all those people you held hostage. So, tell me, Calix, could you have given me that?"

When he didn't respond, I glanced over my shoulders. His greenish amber eyes watched me, warily. He didn't know what my next moves would be. For the first time since he had known me, he could not read me. And that meant he was afraid.

Good.

"No, you couldn't," I answered for him, uncovering a dagger. "Which means you couldn't have given me everything. But you know who did? Nero. Xander, Kira, *Sophie* and everyone in that goddamn Manor. They have given me everything. They gave me what you couldn't. Which means, Calix, *they* love me."

There was a thick layer of tension blanketing us as I twirled the knife between my fingers, strolling leisurely towards him. Calix watched me with eagle eyes. Then, I knelt to his eye level.

"So, I'll ask again, love or loved?"

He clenched his jaw.

That was all I needed to know.

"I expected more from you. I expected better but those expectations were for the man I stumbled into in Greece, not the man sitting in front of me," I sighed. "I don't know who this man is."

I let him feel the cold sensation of the blade as I lightly caressed his cheek with the dagger. He didn't wince, unflinching, but that was expected from a soldier of mine. But he was no longer one of mine. I didn't know who he was. All I knew was that I couldn't wait to begin the fun. I couldn't wait to hear his screams. I knew they would be my favorite melody.

"Do you know what my favorite rhyme is?" I crooned. The dagger brushed his arms. "Roses are red, violets are blue," I laughed, bringing the knife above his thigh, teasing the blunt blade against his skin as a reminder of his position. "Fuck with me once, and I'll put a bullet through you."

Then I pressed the knife above his heart and smirked when he winced.

"Answer me this, Aria," Calix breathed. "Can you kill me?"

I held his emerald eyes, dim and imploring, but they would never get their answer. Never again. They would never be able to know my thoughts ever again.

"Now," I cocked my head to the side, smiling wickedly, as I blinked at him, innocently. "Who said anything about killing?"

*

Goddamn. I got blood all over my favorite leather pants. Good thing they were black, but unfortunately my top was not. Now, I have to throw it away. I grumbled angrily to myself as I headed back to my penthouse, tired from the long journey, and an even longer evening. I ignored the curious looks sent my way at the sight of me covered in blood, while, of course, still looking flawless. It was a talent. I wasn't afraid they would say anything, they knew what would happen if they did, so they kept their eyes directed elsewhere when I caught them staring. After spending most of my day below the mansion, I could remember every second of torture inflicted on Calix, like a movie replaying in my mind. I remembered his screams when I broke his fingers, for every victim created under his touch. Whilst, he wept, I moved to his legs, immobilizing his body so that he couldn't escape his punishment. I turned to his prized possession, an execution for all the women he laid a hand on without their consent. I could almost see the blood again when I closed my eyes, the way it poured onto the concrete floor and pooled around him.

I made good on my vow.

I sliced his tongue for all the lies he told, and then I gouged an eye out with the scythe I had been admiring, a sentence for overseeing innocent people's lives become ruined under his reign. I relished in his screams, and cries, and the way he writhed in pain. I savored how he begged me to stop, begged me to kill him. I broke him. And I would continue to break him. But Kira had finally come down. She told me it was getting late. She was dressed in black. And I knew it was her turn to play. I didn't say a word as I left that cell, indifferent to the screams that echoed behind me only a few seconds later.

And now, I wanted my husband.

Entering the living room, I found him watching a movie and dropped my purse by the cabinet, slipping out of my heels and dumping them by the rest of our shoes. He peered over his shoulder and grinned, having changed out of his suit and into loose joggers.

"Well, aren't you looking bloody gorgeous?" he complimented, blithe-filled eyes.

I frowned. "Not even funny."

Chuckling to himself, he shrugged. "I found it funny. How come you're home late?"

"Torture session went on longer than I expected. I didn't realize how much anger I had buried within me," I revealed, honestly, discarding my coat on the table before pulling off my bloody top and tugging my leather pants off my legs.

Nero watched me strip in front of him, his blue eyes studying me, but, unbothered, I gestured for him to hand me his hoodie. He sulked, at first, before reluctantly passing it to me. Afterwards, I gathered my dirty clothes and shoved them into the washing machine. Finally, rid of reminders of what had occurred, I washed my hands before I settled beside him on the couch, drawing my hair back into a ponytail. The mere gesture had his eyes darkening and jaw tightening.

I narrowed my eyes. "No."

Again, he sulked. "You're no fun."

"I just came back from torturing someone and you're thinking about having sex," I stated in disbelief.

"Not sex, necessarily," he grinned wolfishly, his blue eyes twinkling with mischief. "You look pretty hot when you're all mad and bloodthirsty."

"You're a psychopath."

"So are you," he smirked, and leaned forward. "That's what makes us the perfect pair."

Scowling, I shoved his face away from me. Nero laughed, a rich and deep sound which warmed my insides. With a sigh, I sank into the comfort of my couch. "I don't even have the energy to deal with you."

So, he drew me into his arms. After holding me there silently for a few minutes, I heard his slow exhale and knew what he was going to ask as he propped his chin on the top of my head. "Is he dead?"

"Might as well be," I replied, candidly.

He pulled back and studied me with a frown. "Aria, it's okay to mourn over losing a friend. I know you were really close with him; it must be hard to deal with the reality of it being all lies. That's why you're acting this way. You're taking out the anger towards yourself onto him. You're mad you didn't see it sooner."

"If I needed a therapist, Nero, I would pay for one."

"No need. I'll do it for free," he smiled, and I rolled my eyes. "But seriously, stop trying to ignore those feelings."

I didn't say anything for a long moment before exhaling heavily. "It's just easier if I do."

"I know."

"I don't think I can kill him," I admitted, quietly. "I don't know if I can do it."

Nero didn't say anything. Then he kissed the crown of my head. "You know, that's what I'm here for."

Holding his gaze, my heart warmed with love towards this man who was equally as bloodthirsty as I. We were a messy pair with flaws and imperfections, but I knew there was no one else I would want to spend forever with other than my best friend. Smiling at him, I snuggled closer into his warm arms.

"I still can't believe it. I was practically sleeping with the enemy," I murmured, after a short while.

He hissed, "Maybe I should pay him a visit."

I smiled. "It meant nothing."

"Still," he muttered. Then quietly to himself, "I should tear out his eyes since they've seen her body."

Amused, I shook my head and pressed my lips against his jaw, not wanting to tell him that I already did that. "Oh, Nero."

"Or, probably break his fingers. *Hmm*, that sounds like a good idea," he hummed thoughtfully, and I laughed, knowing right here, right now was where I wanted to be for the rest of my life.

CHAPTER 59

salient of saviors

"Do you have to go?" Nero pouted, as he watched me slip into my heels.

"If I could get out of it, I would but since I can't…" I smiled pitifully at him.

Regardless, Nero looked determined to convince me to change my mind as a naughty glint simmered in the blueness of his eyes, a small smirk curling the corner of his lips.

"But I would like to celebrate with you…" His hands found their position on my waist and his lips softly grazed mine when he whispered, "… in our bedroom."

"As tempting as that is. It will have to wait," I pecked his lips, but he frowned in response. "Right now, Kira and Ciara are waiting for me."

Like a stubborn child at Christmas, he huffed while his nose wrinkled. "Fine. If you must."

I grinned at my husband and drew a coat over my frame, covering the beautiful silver satin dress I wore, matching the diamonds on my neck and ears. It was backless with two spaghetti straps holding the weight, forming a cowl neck that left my neck and shoulders very exposed to the cool, summery breeze. It also caught Nero's lustful attention; his eyes quickly directed away from my face to the collarbones that revealed themselves when I pulled the coat on.

"You better come straight back home," he said, grumpily. "Promise you'll come back."

"I'll come back," I rolled my eyes. "Anything else?"

"One last thing. A wedding. A proper wedding. With the whole cake, and white dress, and all that shit. I want it all. At the end of this month."

The demand stunned me so much that I almost thought he was joking but the gravity in his words matched the expression across his face, and something within me melted at the sight. I smiled, tenderly, my eyes softening at my husband. My husband, who wanted a proper wedding. I was content with getting married in city hall; I had achieved my oldest and longest dream. But for my husband, my best friend, the love of my life, I would do it all. The whole wedding. The white dress. The walking down the aisle. The whole thing.

Because he wanted one.

Gently, I caressed his cheek. "Yes. Let's do it."

He broke into a grin and kissed me so deeply that it left my skin tingling all night.

At the club, Kira and Ciara literally bubbled with excitement. There was a bounce in their step as they hauled me to the bar. I nearly tripped over my own feet. Kira wore a beautiful purple silk dress that clung to her like a second skin, the strings twisted around her neck and tied into a pretty bow, enhancing the paleness of her milky skin. Whereas Ciara wore a mauve, satin dress which complemented her rich caramel skin that glistened like it was gold. Whilst the girls ordered our drinks, I glanced around the club, absorbing myself in the flashing, colorful strobe lights, and the sweaty bodies pressed against each other on the lower ground. My lips quirked at the VIP section when I saw Matteo, lounging with a few other men, and some girls. At first, I wasn't entirely sure if I knew what club we were at, but seeing Matteo confirmed my assumption, so I told Kira, and Ciara, to meet me at the VIP section with our drinks. When Kira took a look in that direction, her eyes flared with mischief at the sight of Matteo. She sent me a cheeky grin, before nodding. I bit back a smile, noticing the mayhem gleaming in her cool eyes, and set off to greet my cousin. Almost immediately, Matteo noticed me when I stepped onto the platform reserved for VIPs, sending a charming smile to the security guards who recognized me. I didn't bother wondering how – perhaps Nero informed them of my attendance, especially seeing as this was *his* club. Though, I didn't remember telling him where exactly I was going.

My cousin practically leapt up from his seat, his eyes wide as he shoved the leeching girl away from him, ignoring her squeal, and dusted off the specks on his suit. "Aria."

"Matteo," I looked at his entourage and arched a brow. "Enjoying yourself?"

"I didn't know you'd be here," he looked slightly distracted, worried, if anything. "Nero didn't tell me you'd be here… Does he know you're here?"

"Probably not," I shrugged. "Why? Is it an issue that I'm here?"

"No!" he refuted, too quickly to be believed. My brows shot up in surprise, and Matteo coughed awkwardly, smiling as he ran his fingers through his shaggy mahogany hair. "Not at all."

I frowned. "Are you hiding something from me?"

"No, nothing," he forced a grin. "Who are you with?"

Before I could reply, Kira and Ciara called my name. Matteo looked over my shoulder as I turned to my friends. Kira held two cocktails, whilst Ciara had what looked like tequila, both of them grinning at me.

"There you are," Kira chirped. Then her eyes settled onto my cousin, and a sultry smirk coiled onto her coral lips. She was practically purring as she crooned, "Hi, Matteo."

Ciara and I pursed our lips to fight the smile at Matteo's lovestruck expression, blinking at Kira as he managed to stammer out, "Kira."

Kira, like a predator, fluttered her lashes, pretending she didn't catch him glancing at the exposed skin that her dress left on show. "Will you be joining us?"

"*Er* – If you – *erm* – want me to," Matteo stammered, surprising me when his cheeks began to redden like a lovesick puppy. I almost felt bad for my cousin, shaking my head at Kira's sensual antics.

"Leave him alone, Kira," I chuckled. Ciara's eyes sparkled with mirth as Kira pouted playfully at me, whilst Matteo rubbed the back of his neck in embarrassment. "It's girls' night."

Kira huffed. "Fine." Then she shot a wink to Matteo. "We'll talk later."

Matteo blushed so adorably that you wouldn't think he was Nero's second-in-command. "I'll leave you girls to it. If you need anything, just let me know."

I pecked my cousin's cheek, grinning. "Will do."

Then, someone called his name, and his attention was drawn

elsewhere. Immediately, puppy Matteo morphed into mafia Matteo. His hazel eyes, almost identical to my own, thinned, and his lips flattened. His entire posture stiffened, and he looked far from the sweet, lovable man he was only a mere few seconds ago.

Shifting his attention back to me, Matteo said, "I'll catch you later, Aria."

This sense of pride succumbed to me, and I couldn't help but smile at my cousin, who practically ran the Italians whilst Nero helped me. Those days when we would pick on each other as kids were far gone and a bittersweet feeling was left in its presence.

I went to shoo my cousin away when someone asked, "Wait, you're Aria?"

Matteo's eyes widened, and he stilled at the voice. Frowning at his reaction, I looked past his shoulder to see one of the girls he was hanging out with. Her hair was as fiery as the look in her eyes when she glared at me like I killed her dog. She was barely dressed; a few stray clothes obscured her assets, but I doubt she wore them for that reason.

"I'm sorry," I began, glimpsing briefly at Matteo who looked terrified. "But do I know you?"

The auburn-haired girl stood up, and snarled, "I was meant to marry him, you bitch!"

And then she lunged at me.

*

Great, I huffed silently, whilst trying to open the penthouse door quietly. One of my nails were broken. But the other girl looked far worse than me. I didn't know how I managed to get into a catfight, but I intended on finding out. After Matteo and Kira finally managed to tear the girl away from me, I demanded to know what was going on. Matteo was very reluctant to answer but one look from Kira and he spilt all his secrets; apparently, I had gotten in between the girl's questionable relationship with Nero, and he had sent her to work elsewhere so that I would never find out. I was far from surprised that Nero's past was scattered all over New York but that didn't mean I couldn't have any fun with it. Finally in my own home, I slipped out of my heels, gathering them into my hand before heading into the living room. The lights were on motion sensors; Nero had installed them whilst I was gone. They lit up at my presence. A groan caught my attention, and my eyes shot to the large frame curled up on the couch. As I dropped my heels by the dining table, I sauntered to Nero as he stirred, rubbing his eyes and sitting up when he noticed me.

"You're back so soon," he yawned, groggily. "Is everything okay?"

I tossed my coat and purse onto the tea table and mounted myself onto Nero's lap. The sleepiness in his eyes dispersed instantly as he positioned his hands on my hips, leisurely running his eyes down to my body. But I had other things in mind.

"Are you alright?" Nero questioned, his voice was hoarse, infused with sleep and need.

"I'm good," I murmured, pressing my lips against his throat, where his Adam apple bobbed. "I missed you."

"Is that so?" Nero's hands began to wander to the hems of my dress, hiking it up past my hips. "You should've stayed home."

I hummed. "Maybe." I kissed his jaw, tugging the nape of his hair so that his cerulean eyes found my own. They darkened, dilated with desire. "Then I wouldn't have had the most eventful evening ever."

"I could've made it more exciting," he grunted, breathing heavily as my fingers began to unbutton his shirt.

Amusement rang through me as I kissed him. Deeply, until I knew he would be craving for more. His hands drew me closer to him, and I sank against his body, melting into the warmth that he cocooned me in. Then, I pulled away.

"What?" he groaned, pouting at me.

"Nero," I smiled, absentmindedly drawing circles on his chest. "You love me?"

"Of course, I do," he grinned.

"So," I drawled out, trying to fight away a smile, and he arched a brow. "Who the fuck is Mia?"

Nero's face fell.

*

Meters underground meant it was cold. Incredibly cold. Especially since we were in the mountains. The temperature could have nipped off your fingers and left you toeless. The cold moved in only to meet the warmth of my blood, my defense against such ice. I should have felt it wash over my skin, again and again, only to then be met by the beat of my heart, again and again. But I couldn't feel it. Not a single bit as I watched Xander pummel Calix. He was cruel with his punishments, shattering Calix's bones into smaller fragments if that was even possible. I didn't flinch when I heard a *crack* ricochet throughout the room. I didn't care. The only reaction I offered was the slightest tilt of my head when Calix screamed so loudly that the mansion shuddered.

"Would you like to do the honors?" Nero muttered; his voice as cool as the biting cold.

So much rage. So much hurt.

I studied Calix. His arms were in places they shouldn't have been. I could see the broken bones of his legs as they protruded out. One eye was gone, leaving a swollen mass of skin in its place. The other eye was bleeding varying shades of violet. His throat had burns and his fingers were missing.

"Do you think it's too soon?" I murmured.

"Do you think it's time?"

Yes. Yes, it was time. The words failed to leave my lips, so I nodded, taciturnly.

Nero inhaled beside me. Then, he proposed, "Do you want me to do it?"

My fingers curled into a tight fist, clenching at the sight of Calix bleeding out whilst Xander brutalized his body. When he was done, he stepped back and heaved slowly, eyes blackened with wrath at the body on the floor. Calix spat out the blood, wiping it away from his mouth, and eyed Xander.

"I'm sorry," he croaked, voice hoarse from the screaming, the loss of his tongue making it difficult to understand him, but we all knew what was said.

He was a masterpiece of red, purple, and green. Broken, immobilized, mutilated. It had been a few weeks since he became our prisoner, and I knew it was time to end it all. As the last victims of the Serpents began to arrive at the Manor, I knew that it was now time to kill him so that we could finally move on. It was time for better days. Kira had made sure Calix didn't bleed out by leaving scars all over his body in the same places the Serpents had left innumerable wounds on hers. I had overlooked the Serpent insignia on his hip. It reminded me of the deceptions. Kira, on the other hand, didn't. And she carved it off his body. It was typical of her to act in this manner. She patched him up, healed him just enough, simply so that she could tear him apart again. She was ruthless, unaffected by his cries. And then there was Xander. I could almost see the fury as he pounded the living daylights out of Calix. He was less tolerant and often left Calix to suffer from catastrophic injuries. Nero had his time too. His methods were slow, heart-wrenching, and torturous. He didn't spend that much time with Calix, leaving him to us, knowing that we needed this more. Eventually, it was my turn. Most often, I would draw up a chair in front of his mangled body and sit there. For hours on end. Calix would tentatively watch me as if I was a viper and I would strike at any time. But I didn't. That haunted him more. Psychologically. He was slipping. Going insane. And I watched it. When I was done, I stood up and left him, hearing his weep quieten with every retreating step I took away from his cell.

"You're sorry you got caught," Xander responded, frostily. "If it was up to me, you'd spend forever in this cell."

Calix bowed at the intense glare Xander sent him as he cleaned the blood off his hands with the towel Nero passed him. Xander's golden eyes met mine, and I slowly bobbed my head, an indication for him to leave. He tensed his jaw and held back any urge to tear Calix apart further. Xander was patient, calm and composed. But Calix summoned the monster within Xander, and that creature was *far less* restrained. With all his strength, he shoved himself away from Calix and began to leave. Just as he reached the door, he halted beside me. He didn't look back. He looked straight ahead. His shoulders moved up and down, an indication that he was trying to steady his breathing. And then he spoke.

"I was your brother, Calix. We were your family," The words did not sound broken, but I knew they were. Calix forced himself to look up, his eye burning into Xander's back. "But you were the monster under the bed, and those are the ones we kill."

Xander strode away before anyone could say anything. It was so quiet you could hear a pin drop. The room was still until Nero shifted his body, looking at me. Waiting for me. I moved out of the shadows, feeling Calix track me as I appeared into the light.

He knew I was there, watching and waiting.

Nero held out my gun and my dagger. I chose my dagger.

Sizing up Calix, my body paused. Nero, noticing this, inched closer to me, whispering again, "Do you want me to do this?"

Did I want him to do this? Could I not do it?

I didn't know what to think. I just knew that the tears I had suppressed were finally threatening to appear. I knew the grief was catching up to me. I didn't realize my hand was shaking until Nero wrapped his large one around mine, engulfing it. Calix, still arrogant despite undergoing agonizing torture, cocked his head to the side and raised his brow. With his one good eye, it seethed, lifeless before us. I opened my mouth to speak but Kira's presence stopped me, her frame appearing by the doorway. She sent a menacing glare to Calix, but what surprised me was the light that quickly displaced such a negative emotion when she looked at me. Unlike the last couple of weeks, where it would have taken hours until the anger passed, today was different. It was then that I realized she had finally moved on. To better days.

"What's wrong?" Nero questioned.

She beamed. "The last arrivals. They're here."

The last of the victims. The youngest of them all, Xander had said. Their journey to the Manor was a little more precarious than others. Ciara had to join Xander, a role that once belonged to Sophie, to help transport the guests from their camps to the Manor. A female figurehead often eased their fears, and it was a job Sophie was particularly good at. My heart fractured at the thought of her. She would have been extremely proud.

"We're nearly done here," Nero informed Kira. "We'll be up soon."

Kira bobbed her head, a little hop in her steps as she walked away. She didn't glance back. I didn't expect her to.

"Aria," Nero's fingers brushed against my cheek, my eyes shifting away from where Kira once was. There was this warmness in his eyes, softening when he smiled. "Do you want me to do it?"

He would have if I had said yes. I know he would have. But as I turned to Calix, who was waiting for the verdict, I shook my head.

I faintly heard Nero say, "Good," before he stepped back, giving me the space that I needed.

There was no such thing as a beautiful body when death had claimed the soul. There was no romantic corpse. Death was death. The flesh rotted, the bones to follow, the hair matting into the soil. It was life that was beautiful; life that we cherish; the soul that we nurtured. It was life that continued. Life that would move forward.

We would move forward. And it began here.

I took small steps towards Calix. Crouched down. His green eye scrutinized me.

"What's my name?" I asked, my voice stronger than I thought it would have been.

Calix gurgled, making a noise that sounded like a, "*What?*"

"I told you that I would destroy you until the only name you'll know is mine," I reminded. His eye flashed and I knew he remembered that vow. "So, what's my name?"

He narrowed his eye, pressing his busted lips together, dry blood on his chin, in defiance. I didn't hesitate to shove my dagger in his gut. Calix cried out when I withdrew the blade, blood coating the silver.

"What's my name?"

No reply. So, I moved to his arm. Silent screams.

"What's my name?"

"What's my name?"

When I didn't get a response, I went for his good eye, but he spoke. It was faint, almost incoherent, but I heard it.

"Calix," I slowly brought my dagger down, and ordered, one last time, "*What is my name?*"

"Aria."

I smiled. He stilled.

"Your worst nightmare," and then I slit his throat.

He gagged on his blood as I stood up. I watched the life drain right out of his eye. I never looked away. I wanted to be the last person he saw. Steps scuffed on the ground. I didn't look back to know it was Nero. He placed a hand on my shoulder, and I covered it with mine.

Calix looked up.

My red lips curled into a smirk.

And he took his last breath.

*

As per custom, all the males of the house had to remain in their rooms for the day until I said otherwise, to ensure our guests were not overwhelmed upon arrival. Xander had left Ciara in charge of bringing our guests in whilst he tended to the men and boys upstairs. He didn't ask about Calix, although I knew he wanted to. He didn't ask. But when I left the basement, stoic and silent, Xander took one look at me and smiled. I knew he was going to be okay. Nero had taken my hands and squeezed them. He didn't say anything. He didn't need to. And I loved him for it. I loved him with everything I had within me, and more. I loved him so much, I couldn't breathe. And I knew he felt the same. He gave me a light kiss and then drew me into a tight hug. There he held me until he knew I was going to be okay. Until he knew *we* were going to be okay. Almost instantly, I sunk into the warmth and comfort of his body.

Nero had whispered, "I love you," before he disappeared to our bedroom whilst the girls rushed around the living room, preparing for our guests.

Four girls. All sisters. The youngest was ten. It wasn't unheard of, but it was extremely rare. I prayed that this would be the end. As Kira finished off the preparations, I turned to the group of younger girls waiting by the fireplace. Violetta was amongst them. They laughed whilst they decorated the mantel with beautiful flowers.

"Helping out again?" I said, warmly.

They glanced at each other, smiling, but Violetta was the one who replied, "We wanted to. *I* wanted to."

They shared another look. A look I had seen plenty of times. They were healing, conquering what they once feared, and becoming the powerful women I knew they were destined to become .

"When I arrived, I saw all the girls," Violetta's voice broke but she still smiled. "I didn't feel so alone. So lost. Because I knew that there were others like me and that I was going to be okay. And I would be…"

Amira took her hand and squeezed it with a warm smile, finishing off Violetta's sentence, "…Safe, secure and happy."

I could have cried right there. I knew I could have. Because I was so proud. So proud of how far they had come. How only seven months ago, Violetta was not one of them, and now she was. The girls had formed a sisterhood, a safe space in which they could be completely feminine without the gaze of men. It was their sanctuary in a world that had long sought dominance over prestigious leaders. I opened my arms, and they all fell into my embrace, giggling to one another. My eyes watered when I left them, moving towards Kira who observed us from afar. Her smile was broad as I stood beside her. For a moment, neither of us said anything. We watched the girls in the room, of all ages, and from all countries, become one. It didn't matter who they were or where they were from, in that moment, they were sisters, and something within me finally rested. The unease, and the loss. It disappeared. It just *went away*. The weights on my shoulders lifted, and my body tingled with serenity. I knew – I just knew – that everything was going to be alright.

"We did it, Kira," I said, suddenly. She turned to me as I blinked away my tears. I noticed her eyes were watering too. "We did it."

Something shifted in those artic orbs. There was a change that I did not notice before. Like the scars on her body were just that – scars. There was no meaning to them, no memories, no pain, no suffering. Just scars. They existed and created one of the strongest women I had the pleasure of knowing.

She gasped out a sob, almost in disbelief, "We did it."

"Yeah, we did," I repeated, grinning ear to ear.

Kira nodded, pursing her lips into a smile whilst fighting back the cries of relief. So, I drew her into my arms and hugged her. Silently, she sobbed into my shoulders, and I soothed her with quiet hushes until those sobs turned into hiccups.

"They're here!" one of the girls shouted. Upon hearing those words, we pulled apart from each other, wiping away any loose tears.

"Ready?" Kira said, her blue eyes as clear as daylight.

I echoed, "Ready."

We turned towards the door as it opened. Ciara entered the room with four girls huddling closely together, holding each other's hands as if they were each other's lifeline. They were scared, eyes wide at the girls in the room. When Ciara met my gaze, she bobbed her head slightly, and I stepped forward.

Four sisters.

I didn't want to imagine the horrors they faced, the invisible scars on their bodies, the wounds that would forever remain. I didn't want to think about that. Because I knew, one day, those horrors would be a distant nightmare. Those invisible scars would disappear. And those wounds would provide the strength to remind them that they were stronger than they thought. One of them stepped forward. Like the other three girls, she had dark brown skin, rich in melanin, and eyes that looked like chocolate, stealing a glance around the room. A white cotton hijab concealed her hair, a loose tunic covering her small, malnourished body. She must have been the eldest – probably thirteen or fourteen. On her wrists, there were rope burns, similar to the ones on her ankles. There were a few scratches, some deeper than others, some looked like knife wounds. But she was a fighter. I saw it in her eyes when she peered at me.

"Who are you?" she asked, her voice trembled but her stance did not.

I knelt. "I'm Aria. What's your name?"

She was hesitant to respond but stiffly answered, "Yazia."

Her name made me smile. "Did you know that means warrior?"

She nodded. I looked behind her, my eyes lingered on the youngest who clung to Ciara's leg. She looked terrified, her brown wavy hair shielding her face from watchful eyes. I wanted to hug her and never let her go. I wanted to fight the demons that plagued her dreams. I wanted to be her protector. I wanted to protect them all. But that required trust and patience. I could not risk rushing into things they were not ready for, things they never once received whilst being captive.

First, I had to give them their freedom.

So, I glanced back at Yazia and arched a brow.

"Do you know where you are?" I questioned, and she shook her head. "We create warriors. All these girls here are warriors. And if you let us – *let me* – I'll help you become one too. Would you like that?"

Yazia looked surprised for a moment as if she didn't realize she had a choice, a say in her life. Having been deprived of this, it seemed too good to be true. She blinked at me before the shock morphed into caution, and she peeked back at her sisters, communicating with them silently. Her eyes then fell across the room, studying every individual girl that circled us. Warm faces greeted her. Afterwards, she turned back to me. She didn't say anything for a minute. Then, she rolled her shoulders back, and bobbed her head, fearlessly.

"We would like that."

My smile grew at her answer. "Welcome to the Manor."

I looked at the other three girls.

"You're safe here," I paused, and observed the room.

Everyone was watching, holding their breath. Warriors in their own rights. They smiled when they met my eyes. They held their heads high, a sign that they knew that they could overcome anything. Any fear. Any challenges. Any evil. They knew they could battle the dragons and leave unscathed. I knew they were remembering their own arrivals, the fears they brought with them and the demons that scurried in their shadows. They were remembering how that feeling felt - as if it would last forever. But as I looked in their eyes – colors of blues, grays, greens, and browns – I saw what I had once wished to see in Violetta's.

My gaze landed on her last. Violetta grinned, still healing, but no longer afraid. And I saw it swirl in her magnificent eyes. There it was, within a concoction of colors to create a striking violet hue. *Strength*.

I looked back at Yazia, and I knew one day I would see it in her eyes too, as I said, "You're finally home."

EPILOGUE

"**D**ear friends and family, we are gathered here today," the minister began, his voice thick with an Italian accent. "To witness the union of Ariadne Moretti and Nero Russo in marriage. To celebrate their love and understanding for each other, and their decision to start their lives as husband and wife."

I inhaled sharply as Nero's lips tugged. It amused him to see me this nervous, but I just wanted to smack the living daylights out of him. On top of that, the darkening of his eyes, that were the same hue as the clear summer skies, had only informed me of the terribly unruly thoughts swimming in his mind. I resisted the urge to roll my eyes, knowing that there were hundreds of people watching us right now, including our families who had taken their designated seats in either the bride or groom sections. As if he knew, Nero sent me a wink and I bit back my smile.

"Their decision to marry has not been entered into lightly and today they publicly declare their private devotion to each other," the minister continued. "The essence of this commitment is the acceptance of each other in entirety, as lover, companion, and friend."

*

14 hours earlier

"I'm getting married tomorrow!" I freaked, and Kira shoved a glass of tequila in my hand.

"Which means it's your last day as a free woman," her words slurred, grinning at me.

I frowned. "You do know I'm already legally married, right?"

Ciara snorted, having finished her sixth glass of vodka. "Not in the eyes of God."

Kira nodded in agreement, a stupid smile on her face as she swayed her body to the thundering sound of music. I sulked in my seat, my eyes scouting the club, flashing red and blue lights blinding me. I felt like my eardrums would burst any second as the noise sent vibrations throughout my body. I couldn't remember why I agreed to a bachelorette party, or how Kira had managed to convince me to have one, but the effects of the alcohol were overtaking my inhibitions and seconds later, I found myself on the dance floor. I moved my body in time with the beat, my brown locks dancing as I swayed my hips, running my fingers down the curves of my frame. I became one with the music, adrenaline humming throughout my body. I could feel eyes watching me, but they weren't the eyes I wanted.

I wanted my Nero.

I wondered if he was having fun with the boys. The thought had me stumbling back to my table where my friends were and grabbing my purse. My eyes squinted as I read the time on my phone.

12:48 a.m.

Kira's nose wrinkled. "Where are you going?"

"Back to the hotel," I drank the last shot.

"It's just turned midnight," Ciara whined, and I wanted to correct her, but she reached for my hand, her tight black curls tossing over her shoulders. "You can't leave now."

"I'm getting married," *Again*, I added silently in my head. "I really don't want to wake up with a banging headache."

"Too late!" Kira chirped cheerily as she tipped her head back, swallowing the shot.

"Come on, Aria," Ciara pouted, batting her thick lashes. "Just a few more minutes."

I contemplated, knowing I should really head back, but I couldn't turn away from Ciara's sad puppy-dog eyes, and nodded reluctantly. She squealed, my ears crying at the sound, and shoved a drink into my hand, chanting, "Drink! Drink! Drink!"

Kira smirked and joined Ciara in her chants, so I drank whatever liquor I was given and grinned as my girls screamed my name. They had never looked so carefree, so wild and it left a memory in my heart that had me reaching for another drink. Plus, a few more minutes couldn't hurt.

*

"Love should have no other desire but to fulfil itself. But if your love and needs must have desires, let these be your desires: To melt and be like a running brook that sings its melody to the night. To know the pain of too much tenderness. To be wounded by your own understanding of love and the compassion that love brings. To wake at dawn with a winged heart and give thanks for another day of loving; To rest at the noon hour and meditate love's ecstasy; To return home at eventide with gratitude and a loving embrace; Then to sleep with a vision of the beloved in your heart and a song of love in your dreams."

The minister's words were loud and clear despite being in an open space, the sound of cars and busy city life bustling on the roads several floors down. The rooftop terrace of the William Vale was absolutely stunning. Located in Brooklyn, on the 23rd floor, the venue was a coveted backdrop that I had been dreaming of since I was a little girl. The landscaped terrace was a one-of-a-kind setting that was perched above the city and set against spectacular panoramic views. Beautiful oaken chairs donned each side of the terrace, leaving space for the aisle down the middle which was lined with the finest rayon runner that had been beautifully hand embroidered with our names and the date of our wedding. Exquisite jewels embellished the edges, glistening in enthralling iridescent hues under the serene sky. Fresh greenery, hydrangeas and wisteria adorned the venue, bringing the urban skyline to life, lining up with the horizon.

The sun passed its peak as the minister looked out into the crowd, speaking words that I could barely hear whilst under the lascivious gaze of Nero. He looked quite handsome in a cream wedding tuxedo, a delicate peach rose pinned on the black lapel, a black bow attached to his collar. His hair was drawn back into a quiff, lightly shaved on the sides, and gelled to create a rippling quality. His beard was trimmed, to my despair, but it brought attention to the sharpness of his jaw, and the straightness of his nose, his lips roseate and soft, begging for me to kiss him. I probably would have had I not remembered that my mother and Coco had spent weeks preparing for this wedding, and

Kira's warning for me to not mess things up.

The minister continued, "A good and balanced relationship is one in which neither person is overpowered nor absorbed by the other, one in which neither person is possessive of the other, one in which both give their love freely and without jealousy."

*

11 hours earlier

A few minutes had turned into a few hours within a blink of an eye. I giggled when I stumbled out of the lift, and into the corridor of the hotel. I didn't waste time admiring the lavish interior as I hunted down what I was looking for. Eventually, I found the room at the end of the hall, knocking on the door and grinning to myself. There were no signs of movement within, and I was worried for a moment that Nero hadn't returned yet, but then the white door opened, revealing my half-sleepy husband. Unlike myself, Nero looked completely aware with no signs of having had drinks last night, his hair disheveled, and a pair of cotton pants hanging loosely on his hips. My eyes betrayed me as they skimmed down his body, lingering on the 'V' that appeared by his pelvis and disappeared behind his pants.

"Aria, what are you doing here?" he asked, voice gruff.

"I missed you," I blurted. He blinked at me. My face flushed. "I thought you would still be out."

"Matteo and Dom wanted to go to a strip club," he revealed, and a glimmer of jealousy rang through me. "But I just wanted to head back to the hotel. So did Xander."

My eyes were hopeful. "So... you didn't go?"

"Nope. How comes you're here?" he frowned. "Are you alright?"

"I just... I missed you," I whined, and pushed past him.

Staggering into his room, I noticed it was similar to mine that was just on the floor above. When I complained to Kira why we were in separate rooms, she answered with a glare and said, "Tradition."

I heard the door close behind me, and Nero said, "The bride and groom aren't meant to see each other the day before the wedding. It's bad luck."

I glowered. "We're already married."

Nero shrugged. "The logistics remain the same."

"Do you want me to leave?" I asked, peeling off the thin straps from my shoulders and unzipping the tight dress that I knew Nero was eyeing. He observed me as I lazily slipped out of the dress, smirking. "I *can* leave."

"Screw traditions," he grunted and kissed me hard.

I beamed against his lips, running my fingers through his dark locks and pulling at them. Nero lifted me up, my legs curling around his waist, his fingers running down my spine as he pressed me against the wall. I shivered at the sensation, mewling as his attention went to my neck, and then to the crevice between my chest, before attending to my collarbone. Nero murmured something, but I was too caught up in the euphoria and gasped when he caught my lips with a punishing caress. When he returned me onto my feet, my knees wobbled but with his hands on my hips, he pinned me in place. My skin set alight when I heard the tear of the flimsy material covering my pelvis and I arched towards him, yearning for more. He answered with a dark chuckle and curled his fingers around my throat. My heart thumped loudly, and his name escaped my lips when he tugged my hair back. That triggered something within him, and he spun me around, weaving his fingers through mine and pinning my hands against the wall. With his entire body melting against mine, I was completely consumed by his dominance and all anxious thoughts of the wedding flew right out of the window. It didn't matter how drunk I was. I could remember *every single thing* the morning after. The buzz was even more intoxicating, leaving me needing more. And I was about to spend the rest of my life feeling that.

*

"Marriage is a sharing of responsibilities, hopes, and dreams. It takes a special effort to grow together, survive hard times, and be loving and unselfish," the minister smiled at Nero and me. "So, do you both pledge to share your lives openly with one another, and to speak the truth in love?"

Behind Nero, I caught Xander and Matteo grinning at each other. I was surprised when Nero asked Xander to be one of his groomsmen, and equally surprised when Xander agreed. I had not realized the pair had gotten closer, but Nero explained, one evening, that they found a neutral ground; their dedication to me. I never told Nero how much I appreciated that he asked Xander. I knew Xander was still mourning over the betrayal of his closest friend, and although Nero would never replace the friendship Xander shared with Calix, having someone other than Kira and I was a better start than anything else. Both the groomsmen were in black tuxes, taupe–kissed flowers attached to their lapels, and a white pocket square completing the look. Xander's refined American sweetheart look had caught the eyes of plenty of women when he made his presence known, and though he could feel the eyes and whispers of gossips, he ignored them all. A glimmer of surprise had taken me when I found his attention drawn to Ciara who was greeting all the guests before I walked down the aisle.

My cousin, on the other hand, relished in the attention and adoration thrown in his direction. But when Kira looked at him, the arrogance was tossed right out the window and suddenly he was a teenage boy all over again. Although Kira may never admit it, she loved the affection Matteo would give her, regardless of whether it was snarky comments or stuttering sentences. I had watched from inside as Matteo's cheeks reddened, frustration and desire in his eyes as Kira laughed when they spoke.

My attention jumped back to the minister as he asked, "Do you promise to honor and tenderly care for one another, cherish and encourage each other, stand together, through sorrows and joys, hardships and triumphs for the rest of the days of your lives?"

Nero grinned at me, as we answered, "We do."

*

8 hours earlier

I smiled dreamily as Nero brought me closer to him. I didn't want to wake up although I knew I should have – Kira was going to kill me if I was late – but I lounged in his warmth. I felt him kiss the tip of my nose before slipping out of bed. I frowned, wanting him to bring the heat back as I shivered at the loss of contact. But I also did not want to open my eyes, knowing if I did, I would not be able to go back to sleep, so I just remained under the comfort of the cozy bedsheets. Minutes later, I heard Nero emerge out from the bathroom and shift back into bed. Happiness bubbled within me as his arm curled around my waist and drew me against his chest, my back curving into the arch of his body. His fingers weaved through mine and placed our hands on my thigh.

His lips stroked my ear as he murmured, in his husky morning voice, "It's wedding day."

"I know," I muttered. "But I just want to sleep a while longer. Before Kira hunts me down and drags me away to be poked and prodded."

"Ah, she is your maid of honor," Nero chuckled, shivers running down my spine like a shock of electricity. "Are you sure you want to sleep?"

The suggestive tone in his voice had me open an eye, and peep over my shoulder. There was a devilish smirk across his face, and his cobalt eyes glowered, brightly. My forehead pinched as I narrowed my eyes.

"What do you have in mind?"

Nero's lips stretched as he pulled himself on top of me, a giggle escaping my lips, and then kissed me, starting our morning by getting lost in each other's heated embrace.

*

"Do you have any vows you would like to say to one another?" the minister questioned, and Nero bobbed his head, surprising me as he didn't tell me he had something prepared.

The minister smiled, stepping back as Nero reached for my hands, gently. Under the searing summer sun, I could feel the sweat on my body but couldn't figure out whether that was from the heat or the nervousness bubbling within me. My hands shook in his hold but as his thumb drew light circles against my skin, I felt the anxiety roll off my shoulders and gazed into those opulent azure eyes of his.

His lips twitched, having seen my stunned expression, and he said, "Aria, I always tell you that I loved you since you were born. But I think I loved you even longer before that. I think somewhere, at some other time, our souls met, and we fell in love. I think if I was to meet you in another space and time, I would still love you. Because you were made for me like the stars were made for the moon, or how the sand was made for the ocean. You are strong, fearless, and honorable. You are loyal to the bone. You can protect those around you, but you can also protect yourself. I have never met anyone that was a better match for me than you, and I am honored – *truly and deeply honored* – that you have chosen me as a match for you."

My smile quivered as I blinked away the tears, every ounce of me begging to kiss this man right now. Nero reached out, caressing my cheek lovingly as his eyes softened.

"I love you, Ariadne. *Sempre.*"

*

6 hours earlier

I woke up to the venomous voice of Kira yelling, "Aria, I swear to God, I hope you're not in there!"

I groaned under the blankets as she pounded on the door, subsequently waking Nero up in the process. Unlike me, he offered a lazy grin and a kiss, murmuring, "Should we let her in?"

"She'll break the door down if we don't," I grumbled, tucking my head under his chin.

His arms tightened around me. "I think it's too late for that."

I frowned but before I could respond, the doors flew open and Kira stormed into the room, unbothered by our lack of clothing as she glared. "I can't believe you two. It was one night!"

I mocked her quietly under my breath which earned a smirk from Nero, but a scarier glare from Kira. Smiling innocently at her, I forced myself to sit up whilst she threw me a shirt from the floor. Nero laughed silently, covering his eyes from the sun when Kira tore open the curtains, the light spilling into the room and blinding us. I winced at the intensity and remembered I had way too many drinks last night, which then triggered a headache. Kira, having drunk nearly twice as much as me, looked pristine in her bridesmaid dress, with no signs of a hangover. Made from imported satin, the dress was a soft, matte peach material with a flattering cowl neck that illuminated her pearly skin. It draped elegantly to the floor, pooling around her feet, enhancing her slender frame. Her blonde hair was straightened, parted in the middle, tucked behind her ears to reveal diamante pearl drop earrings.

Her glossy lips frowned at me. "You're going to be late. The stylist is waiting for you in your room, and your mother has been calling you all morning."

"What time did you wake up?" I slipped out of bed, the shirt covering my bare body, and pulled my messy hair into a ponytail.

"Like seven. I had to call the caterers and check on the venue. There was still a lot to get done. Now, let's go," she grabbed my hand and hauled me out the room, shouting over her shoulders, "Get the fuck up, Nero! Don't think you're off the hook!"

I laughed at Nero's groan in response.

In my bedroom, I was shocked to see everyone buzzing about like bumblebees. My mother was yelling orders at the stylists who cowered under her piercing gaze. Similar to Kira, my mother wore a tulle light pink dress which had a lace bodice and lattice sleeves that concealed some of the wounds during her time as an assassin. Her dark brown hair was neatly pinned into a crown braid, and she wore pearls on her neck and ears. Her wedding ring glittered as she pointed to the stylists to set up near the windows.

"I found her," Kira chirped to my mother, pushing me towards the stylists that hounded me, tugging my hair, lifting up my arms, double checking my dress.

My mother's nude lips broadened when she saw me. "There you are! Where have you been hiding all morning?"

"Nowhere," I said, as Kira responded, "In Nero's bedroom."

Shooting my best friend a glare, she smiled saccharinely at me, batting her long dark lashes. My mother rolled her eyes and dragged me to a salon chair, forcing me to sit whilst I was attacked from all angles. I didn't have time to protest whilst men and women I had never met began to paint my face, powdering and brushing understated colors to enhance my features. Kira had disappeared out of the room at some point – something about checking on the boys. Ciara then entered the room wearing the same dress as Kira. Her tight black curls cascaded past her shoulders, and her rich brown eyes beamed at me when she watched as I slipped into my ivory wedding dress. The gown had short sleeves that flew off my shoulders, carefully crafted with beading pearls that followed into the bodice. The corset bodice was appliqued in handmade lace embroidery with detailed floral designs, pearls sown around the hems. It was backless but had a cathedral train which was incredibly long and made from dainty tulle material, pleated in gentle ruffles. Pearls dropped from my ears, and adorned around my neck, laying in between the junction where my collarbones met. My ebony hair was pinned into a low bun, strands of hair lightly curled at the front which framed my oval face.

As they finished my makeup, I stole a look in the mirror and admired how I looked, floored by the beauty and extravagance of the gown. It was simple and minimalistic, yet luxurious and antique. My eyes glittered in soft coral shades, my cheeks rosy and my lips a lustrous cherry. My bronzed skin gleamed as they applied a glimmering lotion on my arms and across the exposed part of my neck and chest. I heard a sob and peered over my shoulder to see Ciara comforting my mother as she wept silently, dabbing her eyes lightly with a tissue to ensure she didn't ruin her makeup.

"You look…" my mother's words trailed off, awe-struck.

"Beautiful," Ciara finished off. "Absolutely beautiful. Nero is beyond lucky."

I blushed and turned back to the mirror, my fingers brushing the pearl choker. It hit me then that I was actually having a wedding. I had always dreamed of one but after marrying Nero in the town hall, it never really crossed my mind again, because it wasn't something I needed anymore. Only, here I stood, all in white, ready to walk down the aisle and proclaim my love forever in front of everyone. To Nero. My stomach had butterflies and I bit my lip, fighting back a smile. I was going to marry Nero, and I knew I would do it over, and over again.

*

"Aria, would you like to say anything?" the minister questioned, quietly.

Eyes enlarging, I stammered, "I-I didn't prepare anything."

"That's fine. We can move on," he reassured, kindly, and Nero nodded, not looking disappointed or angry.

His attention turned back to the minister, who opened his mouth to speak until I blurted out, "Wait."

He raised his thick brows. My cheeks burned.

"I do have something to say," I murmured. Nero's confused expression morphed into shock whilst the minister smiled, knowingly. I could almost hear everyone shift to the edge of their seats, leaning forward to hear what I had to say.

"Very well," the minister nodded, prompting me to speak.

I looked up at Nero, whose head tilted slightly to the side and eyes softly pinching together, waiting for my words.

I didn't know where to begin, or how to start. I didn't plan that far ahead but my mouth ran before my brain switched on and the next thing I said was, "I love my eyes when you look into them. Everything just seems so beautiful. I love my name when you say it. Even when you're angry."

Laughter scattered through the crowd, and Nero's lips quirked. It encouraged me to continue, my voice much firmer and sure than before. Because under his gaze, I forgot the world around us, and it was just me and him.

"I love my heart when you touch it. It reminds me that I'm good, and I deserve to be loved. And I love my life when you're in it. I can't imagine it without you. I've never been scared of losing something in my entire life, but then again nothing in my life has ever meant as much as you do. The happiest I've ever felt was the moment I discovered you loved me too because I have loved you since the beginning," I sniffled, as Nero's eyes watered.

"And when I tell you I love you, it's not out of habit. I say it to remind you that you are truly the best thing that ever happened to me," I weaved our fingers in between each other's like our souls were entwined and smiled at the love of my life. "They say, *'till death do us part,'* but I say, I will love you from this life to the next. And if the next life won't grace me with you, I will still love you until the next one, and the next, and the next. I will love you until death finally gives up on us."

I wiped the tear that ran down his cheek, cradling his face in my hands as I promised with every fiber of my body, "Because my heart belongs to you. Because I love you, Nero Russo. *Sempre.*"

*

1 hour earlier

My body was trembling as I stood in front of the doors that led me straight to Nero. He couldn't see me through the semi-translucent curtains, but I could see him, and my heart faltered at the sight. He was jaw-droppingly gorgeous and I couldn't believe he was mine. I couldn't believe we were here. When, once upon a time we were just children, best friends who secretly loved one another, and now we were to reveal that love to the world. There were so many people outside, seated on either side of the venue. I saw Coco and Claudio, Nero's parents, dressed in soft fawn colors. Claudio spoke to Nero, a broad grin on his face, a hand on his son's shoulder, whilst Coco stood with a motherly smile, her eyes watering with tears. My relatives had taken their seats, welcoming each other as it had been so long since we had gathered together like this. It was not often that my family would be in one location as it could jeopardize our safety. But seeing them all here had me tearing up. My brothers looked dashingly handsome in their light grey suits, shaking the hands of men who greeted them. Nico had a stoic expression whilst Luca was far more friendly, both with their apparent differences and yet startling similarities. Although, I was the oldest out of my cousins, I was incredibly close with all of them and my heart warmed at the sight of them hugging each other.

My aunt Chantelle and my uncle Coal had three children: the twins, Marielle and Mason, and Malina. The twins, both in peach, were a younger version of their parents. At the blooming age of twenty, Marielle had a luminous golden mane and these rose-colored eyes that she had inherited from her mother. It was a genetic trait from her grandfather's lineage that often caught people's attention by how brilliantly pink they were, like a sunset. She was tall, and more on the muscular side from all her training in mixed martial arts, but incredibly skilled in all forms of fighting. Then there was her brother, born several minutes before her, he donned light chocolate hair and his father's dark blue eyes. Unlike his sister, Mason was lean and a few inches taller than her, but he was charming, whilst Marielle was reserved. The twins balanced each other out. From our little chat during a family dinner a few nights ago, Mason had taken over his father's business and planned to expand it to the east. Malina was only twelve, a year younger than Luca, but she was skilled in all sorts of languages. It was a surprise to us all when we discovered she had quite the knack of picking up other languages quickly. Her hair was waves of flaxen and copper, and her eyes were a medley of pink and blue. Similar to Violetta, the color of her eyes changed in the lighting.

My eyes shifted from Chantelle's family to Gabrielle's, who were taking pictures with the scenic skyline behind them. Compared to her cousins, Gabrielle only had two children: Anzhela and Zariyah. Anzhela was the eldest, at fourteen years old, curly chestnut hair with an amalgamation of green and grey eyes. From what I heard, Anzhela was going to be an incredible leader for the Russians as she was strong-hearted and stubborn, but my uncle Beau once said that he was afraid his daughter might be too headstrong, like her mother. Finally, there was Zariyah, the youngest of us all – she was only nine. My lips twitched when I saw her running about, refusing to take any more pictures much to her mother's dismay. Her mahogany hair was pinned into a bun, and when she smiled there was a cheeky twinkle in her grey eyes. Zariyah, although mischievous, was compassionate and patient, like her father. Seeing my cousins touched my heart, my fingers tingling at their happiness. I deeply missed my family and having them here meant the entire world to me. There was a knock on the door which tore me away from my thoughts, I peered over my shoulder to see Kira. Her smile was tender as she walked towards me, holding a box of items.

"I love traditions, and this is one of my favorites," she explained, and I lifted my brows in surprise. Kira gingerly took the first item out – a pearl hair clip. "Something old."

The pearls were similar to the ones on my headband, with a refined ivory shine in the sunlight. I held my breath as she tucked the pin into my bun, securing my locks in place. Then she took out a bracelet, also pearls but I noticed our initials engraved on the gems. I pursed my lips; my brows drew together as I tried to fight the tears.

"Something new," she stated, clasping the jewelry around my wrist. I expected her to take another item out from the box but was stunned to see her discard it onto the table, and then gently pull off a silver band from her fingers. Her mother's ring. I shook my head, wanting to refuse it, but she was adamant and slipped it onto my right hand. "It's something borrowed."

"Kira…" I whispered, overwhelmed with emotions.

But Kira's chin just gestured to outside, and I followed her gaze, settling on Nero who was laughing. "And that's your something blue."

"Does that even count?" I laughed, but it was breathy and stopped an inevitable sob.

Kira shrugged before smiling at me. It was a sad smile, I noticed, but it disclosed more than possible with simple words. Her hands were unsteady, placing a grip on my shoulders when she spoke, her voice so soft, so nostalgic, reminding me of home, "I love you, Aria. I can't even begin to thank you for everything you have given me. For saving me."

"Kira, you saved yourself."

She shook her head. "But you gave me the rope to help pull me out from the ocean. You, Aria, are the best thing to ever happen to me. Because you taught me loyalty, courage, and sisterhood. You taught me how to love and be loved. You are the sister of my heart. And I can't wait for what the future has in store for us."

My heart stopped. "Why does this sound like a goodbye?"

"It's not a goodbye, silly," she rolled her eyes, and I felt my heart race again, but my panic didn't ease. "I'm not going anywhere. But Gabrielle and your father offered me the opportunity to head to Japan... As an emissary for the Italians and Russians... I said yes."

I paused. "Will you be gone for good?"

"Only for a while. I... I thought it was time to head home, to find my mother's family, to find my mother's grave. I need closure, but I'll be back. I promise, I'll come back," she assured.

I had never seen Kira timid, so I couldn't believe I was seeing it now - like she was afraid that I would disapprove. Her blue eyes implored for mine, and she swallowed apprehensively, waiting for my support. I knew she needed this. I knew she would never rest until she found the closure she had been looking for her entire life. So, I smiled and drew my sister into a tight hug, hearing her release a jittery breath of air.

"Go. Find what you're looking for. Just stay in touch and give me a call every now and then to let me know that you're okay. And if you need anything – anything at all – do not be afraid to ask."

I felt her nod against my shoulder. We remained in each other's embrace until there was a knock on the door, and I knew it was time to walk down the aisle. So, with great reluctance, I pulled away from her. There were a few loose tears on her cheeks, but I brushed them away, cerulean arctic orbs sparkling with happiness. In those eyes, I saw the beginning of it all. I saw the ocean and the buoy. I saw the girl that changed my life. As Kira turned to open the door, I stopped her by grasping her wrist, her brows lifting in surprise.

"But, Kira, it should be me that thanks you," I began, and her glacial eyes never looked so warm as they did right then. "Because you gave me a reason when I was lost. You were my rope when I was drowning. And I will always love you, Yakira Adachi – no matter where you are in the world."

*

"May we please have the rings?" the minister asked, and Xander appeared with the two boxes, handing one to me and one to Nero.

Opening the boxes revealed our wedding bands, and I almost snorted when I saw that they were the same rings that Nero gave me in the town hall but stopped when I noticed something different. Already engraved inside on my ring was an *N,* and on Nero's was an *A.* But on the outside, instead of being the simple silver band, it been preened with three small diamonds. And not regular diamonds – diamonds that matched the color of our eyes. On my ring, they were aquamarines and on Nero's, they were yellow topazes. I immediately glanced at Nero who winked at me. The smile on my lips appeared before I could stop it.

"Nero, please repeat after me; I, Nero, promise to love and support you, Aria, and live each day with kindness, understanding, truth, humor, and passion. With this ring I thee wed," the minister said, as Nero took my hand.

He never looked away from me as he repeated those words. When he slid the ring onto my finger, I choked back my sobs, savoring the cold feeling of the metal that was the start of our forever.

The minister looked at me, and my hands tremored, overwhelmed with emotions, as I took his hand. "Aria, please repeat after me; I, Aria, promise to love and support you Nero and live each day with kindness, understanding, truth, humor, and passion. With this ring, I thee wed."

I repeated those words – those promises – slipping the ring into its rightful position, and when I was done, Nero held my hands, tightening his grip as if he never wanted to let me go.

*

20 minutes earlier

I watched as my bridesmaids hurried in front of me, adopting a single line formation, standing beside their partners. At the front were Zariyah and Violetta, holding baskets of rose petals as red as my lips. My cousins followed –Marielle, Maline and Anzhela – dressed in the similar peach tulle dresses as the younger girls. Melissa, in a taupe gown, with her fancy new beau that Matteo had been glaring at, stood behind them. The scene had me choke back a laugh, especially when

Melissa sent me a wink. She wasn't serious about many people, but something told me that this guy was different – especially if she bought him to meet her family. Behind her, Ciara and Xander stood together, and then it was Kira and Matteo. The girls held bouquets of opalescent white roses and lush green leaves. I clutched onto my own set of white roses with dear life, praying I didn't trip when my attention was brought to the man standing beside me. My father's lips pulled as he hooked his arm through mine, dark eyes tenderly gazing down at me.

"You look beautiful, Aria," he spoke, and those words immediately had me breaking into tears.

Drawing me into his arms, he soothed me with gentle hushes until we heard the music hum outside. Despite not wanting to, I parted from my father, and he softly patted the tears away with a tissue, careful not to smudge my makeup. My mouth twitched at his technique, knowing he must have had experience of doing so for my mother.

"Thank you, daddy," I forced a brave smile, but my eyes were streaming again.

He kissed the crown of my head, "You make me the luckiest father in the world because you are the best daughter any man could ask for."

From the corner of my eyes, I saw my bridesmaids push past the silken curtains and glide down the aisle. People stood up, watching in awe as they appeared like angels under the sun. I knew it was my turn soon and glimpsed at my father who waited until I was ready. Bobbing my head, we turned to face the front and with one last comforting squeeze on my arm, my father walked me down the aisle. At first, all I could see were the eyes on me. I saw my aunts, my uncles, and all those from the Manor. I saw business partners, men and women who work closely with the Italians and the Russians, and then I saw my mother up ahead. With her hands to her mouth, tearily, she watched me with so much pride and love in those hazel orbs that I inherited. I gave her a small smile which she mirrored. Finally, I looked straight ahead. The air was lodged in my throat when the intensity of Nero's gaze crashed into me. He looked like he was going to cry, in front of everyone and he wouldn't care. The expression on his face sent tingles throughout my body – awe, astonishment, desire, and devotion.

All I could see was him.

And when we reached the end, my father gave Nero my hand and said in his dark, Don voice, "Look after my little girl."

Nero nodded, his face completely sincere, and so my father,

reluctantly, let me go but kissed my cheek before he went to stand beside my mother. I blinked away my tears as Nero brought me to face him, and we grinned at each other. My happiness was here with him. He was my peace and joy. He owned my heart, and it would be his to keep. *Forever.* And the way he looked at me told me he shared the same thoughts.

Then he mouthed, "I love you."

And I grinned, whispering those words back.

We finally turned to the minister, who was dressed in a clerical robe, and he addressed the crowd on this beautiful summer day, a smile on his face as he said, "Dear friends and family, we are gathered here today to witness the union of Ariadne Moretti and Nero Russo in marriage. To celebrate their love and understanding for each other, and their decision to start their lives as husband and wife."

*

Love was strange thing. It could appear and it could disappear. It was born from the very second you took your first breath into the world, and it continued to grow with every passing day. Sometimes, it was found in the places you'd least expect it. It was a blessing and a lesson. Sometimes you needed to lose someone to find another. Sometimes you needed to lose yourself to find yourself again. The world was dark, scary, and unpredictable. There were shadows and monsters lurking everywhere. They plagued our dreams; they haunted our reality. They diminished the light that guided us. I knew I couldn't save everyone. I knew I couldn't stop all the evil in the cosmos. But, if I could stop as much as I was capable of, that would be close enough for me. With those I loved close to my heart, I knew I could anything.

As I listened to the minister recite words of marriage and faith, I found myself in awe. I never expected to be here. But then again, I never really saw myself getting married if I wasn't marrying Nero. I couldn't see myself with anyone else. He was the other half of my soul. And as we said our words to each other, our vows and our *sempres*, the world looked like it had become more radiant. With my hands in his, Nero looked at me as if I was his entire world – *no* – his entire universe. He stood in front of me, with tears in his eyes, a small crack in his voice when he spoke. He stood in front of me and everyone here vulnerable, and he didn't care. Because I was his entire world and no

594

one else mattered.

"And now, by the power vested in me," the minister's voice boomed. "I hereby pronounce you husband and wife. You may now kiss the bride."

Without wasting a second, Nero met me halfway as everyone cheered around us, cannons of butterfly-shaped confetti exploding into the air. I kissed him earnestly, and he returned the passion, cradling my face and closing the distance between us that had felt too far apart. And just like that, our dark world seemed so much brighter, like all the darkness in the universe couldn't touch us. Not one bit. Not at all. Not when our love was the brightest light of them all.

THE END

RESOURCES

Despite increased worldwide attention from countries and non-governmental organizations, the number of people falling victim to human trafficking continues to rise drastically across the world. The number of victims more than tripled between 2008 and 2019, from 30,961 to 105,787. In 2018, 46% of global trafficking victims were women. Men constituted 20% of the victims. 34% were children. Half of the victims were sexually exploited: 77.5% were female. And a further 38% were forced to work against their will, many who were male.

Such findings concern human rights advocates and investigators as trafficking is an illegal operation that is cloaked in anonymity, making it hard to quantify it in its totality. In 2020, 109,216 victims were identified worldwide.[1]

[1] M Szmigeria, 'Human Trafficking', *Statista*, 2021.

To learn more and see how you can help, visit these organizations working to stop human trafficking.

HUMAN TRAFFICKING FOUNDATION [U . K .]
https://www.humantrafficking.foundation.org

UNICEF [U. S. A.]
https://unicefusa.org/mission/protect/trafficking

UNICEF [INTERNATIONAL]
https://www.unicef.org/

LOVE146
https://www.love146.org.uk/

STOP THE TRAFFIK
https://www.stopthetraffik.org/

GLOSSARY

Agapi mu/ Αγάπη μου [Greek]
My love

Amore [Italian]
Love

Cara [Italian]
Dear

Che bella [Italian]
How beautiful

Figlio [Italian]
Son

Häschen [German]
Bunny

Pakhan [Russian]
Boss / Godfather

Principessa [Italian]
Princess

Sempre [Italian]
Always

Sötnos [Swedish]
Sweetheart

Vasílissa / βασίλισσα [Greek]
Queen

ACKNOWLEDGMENTS

My acknowledgement goes out to all the women in my life. Thank you, for inspiring me every day to be a better version of myself. Thank you, for guiding me and teaching me valuable lessons that I will take with me every step of the way. Thank you, for reminding me that I am capable of doing whatever I put my mind to. Thank you, for showing me that nothing is possible without women.

To my mother, the strongest woman I will ever have the pleasure of knowing. Words cannot describe how much I love you; I can only show you with my actions. I often make mistakes, and I know sometimes I can worry you, but you don't have to be afraid because I'm going to be alright. I know this because you taught me how to love, how to have courage, and how to have faith in God and myself. I will always be your little girl, a bird learning to fly, but I also know that you believe I am capable of everything and more. It's that belief which keeps me soaring above the clouds, your love held close to my heart.

To my sister, whom I love dearly, even though I do not express it or say it nearly enough. Our bond is difficult to find elsewhere, and though we might try, we will always gravitate back to each other. Growing up together, we were each other's best friends and closest confidantes. I like to think it's still like that today. As young, impressionable teenagers, we had grown apart before eventually returning to each other. I suppose we needed that. We may be two completely different people, but we balance each other. I love every part of us. The happiness and the sadness. The loudness and the quietness. The way my stomach aches in the middle of the night because you are making me laugh too much. In the end, I forgot I'm still your little sister, and you are holding a safety net, ready to catch me if I ever fall. But I don't think I will. I know I won't. You taught me to be better. Stronger. Thank you for being my older sister and my first best friend.

To Zaïdi. This book has gone through so much that it's become a part of us. You have shown me, singlehandedly, that you can go through as many hardships life throws at you and still come back stronger than ever. Loving is possible. *Living* is possible. You are *my* possible. You have taught me friendship beyond family, and I want to thank you for that. You taught me to stand up on my feet every time I fall, and that crying is not a sign of weakness but a sign of growth. You've been teaching me since I was ten-years-old. Thank you for reminding me that empathy is the light in the dark. And if we were to meet again in another life, you would still be my most treasured friend because you are *the sister of my heart.*

To my friends, who hold my hand every day, even on my worst nights. Growing up with you is the most magical and beautiful experience I have ever had because you taught me sisterhood. It's perfectly imperfect. It's blissfully dark. It is growth and it is loss. You have loved me for the person I am since the day we met. The world is demanding, but somehow, I am not afraid when I know you are right there with me. I am the most honest version of myself in your presence, and something about that, despite the vulnerability, is comforting. Loving you is like crying in the rain because when you see the darkest parts of me, you never wanted me to change.

To the girls I've loved and lost. I haven't forgotten the memories we once shared and I haven't forgotten you. In this life and the next, I always hope you'll find the happiness that we couldn't find together.

A final message to all the girls reading this: Aria is by far the most astounding woman I have ever written about because she *is* power. When I wrote this book, it was like I became her and it made me feel *powerful.* And when you read this book, I hope you feel the same as I do. Being so sure of yourself is the first step to power, and with Aria, I have never been so sure of a character or book before. Billionaire's Attraction holds a special place in my heart because of this. With Aria, I become the version of myself that is hidden underneath the layers of self-doubt and insecurities. Because Aria represents the most important things I honour in life: loyalty, sisterhood, justice and faith. She is a powerful woman, and to all the girls out there, so are you.

With love,
Fariha.

ABOUT THE AUTHOR

Fariha Rahman introduced herself to the print world when she debuted her first novel in May 2021. Just over a year later, she produced another book, sprinkled with the right amount of femme fatale and domineering alpha males. After joining Wattpad in 2015, she has steadily grown her readership and followings, encouraging her to pursue her dream of publishing. With hopes and ambitions inspiring her work, she continues to produce novel after novel from the endless supply of ideas churning away in her brain 24/7. As a hopeless romantic, and a sucker for an amazing plot, Fariha cannot wait to share more stories because, after boba tea, there is nothing more that she loves than a happily ever after.